A Danger in Dublin

An Elspeth Duff Mystery

Ann Crew

Copyright © 2025 by Ann Crew

A Danger in Dublin is a work of fiction. Names, characters and incidents are the products of the author's imagination. Any resemblance to actual persons, living or dead, is entirely coincidental. Existing locations and persons are used fictionally. The Kennington hotels do not exist.

Front cover photograph of St. Stephen's Green in Dublin © 2012 and back cover of a derelict farm on the coast of Carlingford Lough © 2014 by Ann Crew

Cover design based on earlier books in the series © 2025

Author photograph by Ian Crew

ACE/AC Editions
All rights reserved.
ISBN: 9798264181962

Library of Congress Control Number: 2025919917

Independently published through Kindle Direct Publishing, a division of amazon.com

anncrew.com

elspethduffmysteries.com

Also by Ann Crew

The Elspeth Duff Series:
A Murder in Malta, 2nd Edition
A Scandal in Stresa Revised Edition
A Secret in Singapore
A Secret in Singapore, 2nd Edition
A Crisis in Cyprus
A Gamble in Gozo
A Deception in Denmark
A Blackmailer in Bermuda
A Presumption in Perthshire
An Ultimatum in Udaipur
A Legacy on Lewis
A Betrayal in Belgium
A Challenge in Chelsea
A Victim in Victoria
A Tangle on Loch Tay

The Portia MacRoberts Series:
A Matter of Murder

Praise for *A Murder in Malta:*

"Each main character has a rich backstory with enough skeletons in closets to provide grist for a number of future novels.

"An often compelling . . . excursion through exotic locales featuring unusual, complex characters." — *Kirkus Review*

**To the brave people of Ukraine
and to Wendy, my host in Ireland**

Author's Note

The first draft of this book was written in 2012, when many people regarded Ukraine as being in the power of oligarchs and corrupt businessmen. Now in 2025, since Russia's invasion in 2022, we in the west have a different perception, that of the brave women and men who are fighting for their lives, their property and the life of their country.

Apologies to them that one of the main characters in this book sheds such a bad view on that valiant country.

List of Characters

Elspeth Duff, special security advisor to Lord Kennington of the Kennington hotels, in this book just returned from suspension

Sir Richard Munro, formerly of the Foreign and Commonwealth Office, now retired, Elspeth's second husband

Eric, Lord Kennington, owner of the Kennington hotels

Pamela Crumm, his silent business partner and Elspeth's friend

Harry O'Shea, doorman at the Kennington Dublin hotel

Yuri Koda, Ukrainian oligarch

Moya De Lacey Koda, his Irish wife

Hallam McLaughlin, concierge at the hotel

Sean Clancy, manager of the hotel

Billy Maguire, Moya's bodyguard

Sergi, Yuri Koda's son

Angelika Rostova, Yuri Koda's daughter, a photography student who uses her mother's maiden name

Derek Somerset, Angelika's boyfriend, a theology student

Matt, Billy's son and Angelika's bodyguard

Pierre Savreux, assistant manager at the hotel

Nancy Kendall, Angelika's friend

Zakhar, one of Yuri's employees and a 'goon'

Lars Inversen, a detective from Paris

Donny Cunningham, Lord Kennington's early friend

Patrick Mulligan, limousine driver

Emery Gill, professor of medicine at Trinity College

Irina, his wife, a specialist in Tsarist Russia

Maureen Donahue, a research assistant in the College of Art History at Trinity who specialises in late nineteenth and early twentieth century Russian artefacts

Lorna, Lady Kennington, Eric's wife

Sir Gerald de Lacey, Moya's father

Father Patrick

Mrs Maguire, Billy's mother

Part 1
Moya

Prologue

Headlines in *The Irish Times*, June 2009

BRUTAL MURDER OF UKRAINIAN OLIGARCH
Yuri Koda Found Slain in Dublin Late Saturday Night
Early Exclusive Pictures Inside

KODA ASSASSINATION
Beaten by Unknown Assailant in Dublin
Police Baffled

Dublin, Monday, -- June. A Garda[1] spokesperson has confirmed that the cause of Ukrainian investment banker Yuri Koda's death was massive wounds from probable beating with a blunt instrument. His body was found in the early hours of Sunday morning behind Dublin's National Concert Hall. A full autopsy is to be conducted today by police pathologists and the report will be released within the week. Police have not as yet . . .

KODA KILLING
No Clues As Yet

---

[1] The Irish police force is called the Garda or Gardai and policemen are referred to as guards.

The autopsy expected today . . .

1

Elspeth curled herself out of the car that had been waiting for her at the airport and looked up at the Kennington Dublin hotel. She was full of excitement, and equally feelings of betrayal. She was back at her job.

The doorman, crisp in his navy-blue uniform and grey top hat, stood holding the door of the car and spoke to her by name.

"Welcome to the Kennington Dublin, Ms Duff," he said. "We have been expecting you."

How efficiently things happened at the Kennington Organisation, she thought. Although her posture and carriage were normally excellent, she straightened up, and mounted the stairs which led to the entrance to the hotel with the demeanour of the French countess who had taught her how to walk gracefully. Except for the brass plaque set on the brick wall, one would hardly notice that the Georgian façade hid one of the world's more expensive boutique hotels, a member of the worldwide Kennington chain.

Elspeth smiled. She had learned over her ten years employment with the Kennington Organisation that making friends with the hotel doormen was essential to the tasks that Lord Kennington assigned to her as his special security advisor. Doormen were the eyes and ears at the front of each hotel.

"Good afternoon," she replied. "Is Mr Clancy waiting

for me inside?" Usually hotel managers came out to meet her when she arrived on assignment.

Harry O'Shea, his small name badge declaring his name, put his gloved hand to his mouth and coughed. "A guest has required Mr Clancy's attention and he asked me to convey to you that he will be down shortly."

Elspeth guessed the guest was Moya de Lacey Mulholland Koda, wife of the murdered Ukrainian mogul and the reason Elspeth was in Dublin. She had been warned that Mrs Koda could be demanding.

The doorman rushed up the stairs and held open one of the double doors bearing the Kennington crest and motto 'Comfort and Service'. Elspeth felt the same sensation of richness and good taste she always did when entering a Kennington hotel, although each was different. The hotel decorators had decorated the lobby in the style of an Irish manor house. Wood panels lined the walls; paintings of the Irish countryside and an occasional portrait of a milord or milady from the past were hung and quietly lit and thick oriental carpets were spread across the parquet floors. The concierge's desk was tucked away in one corner. Its occupant came round to greet Elspeth and like the doorman he used her name.

"Mr Clancy sends his regrets that he could not be here to welcome you. Mrs Koda requested immediate attention."

Obviously the concierge knew the reason for Elspeth's visit. Concierges were the watchdogs of the lobby and had a duty to know each guest's name and requirements.

"He asked that you be taken to your suite and he will be with you as soon as possible." From the look on his face

Elspeth assumed that when Moya Koda spoke the staff jumped.

"Thank you, Hallam," Elspeth said, having eyed his name on the badge at the lapel of his uniform, which read 'Hallam McLaughlin'. "Have him call me when he is free."

When Elspeth reached her suite, a small one facing the back street and not St. Stephen's Green in front of the hotel, her two cases had already arrived and a room attendant was unpacking them, according to Elspeth's standing orders with the hotels. The room attendant bobbed a small curtsey to Elspeth, and said she would be finished shortly.

Elspeth went to the window and looked out over the street below. Twelve hours earlier her husband, Richard, had been driving her to the airport outside Perth, Scotland, in order for her to catch Lord Kennington's private plane, which was waiting to fly her to London.

"Are you ready to tell him?" Richard asked.

"Yes, I think so." She blew out her breath.

"He has treated you shabbily, my dearest. You must stand up to him. He can't just dismiss you for six months and then expect you to rush to London because there is a situation he wants you to handle in Dublin. The man has no feelings. You have no option but to resign."

"I've rehearsed the words of my speech and I'll go over it again on the flight," she said.

"And you won't let him bamboozle you the way he has done in the past?"

Elspeth set her jaw. "No, of course I won't." But she knew in her heart that she missed her employment and her forced retirement to Loch Tay had not replaced that emptiness.

Although she had promised Richard she would be resolute and return that evening to Perthshire a free woman, she wanted at least to see if Eric Kennington would apologise for his mistreatment of her after her antics during her last case in British Columbia. After all, she had finally solved the case when the Royal Canadian Mounted Police had failed to do so. But Eric had been punitive about her method of doing so.

Elspeth drew back from the window as she heard the room attendant leave the room. Now she would have to call Richard and tell him she had capitulated. Although he would not understand, he would stay stiffly stoic. Elspeth wished that occasionally he would get angry with her but he never did. If he had, her constant guilt over often going against his wishes might be assuaged.

Elspeth turned into her sitting room and pulled her mobile from her handbag, which she had thrown on the writing desk. But she was saved from the dreaded phone call when the house phone rang. Sean Clancy, manager of the hotel, was on the other end of the line. Sean, like the concierge, apologised.

"Mrs Koda will not be disregarded," he said. "She was just demanding to know if you were here. Lord Kennington told her last night that you would be arriving by early this evening. She wants you in her suite the first instant you can get there."

Last night? Elspeth bristled at Eric Kennington's presumption that she would accept his offer even before he had proposed it to her. She should have suspected his subterfuge when she had seen the newspapers on the plane down from Edinburgh.

The late Sunday edition of the *News of the World* and early morning copies of the *Daily Mail* and the *Sun* had replaced the usual *Times* and *Telegraph* found on his personal jet. The gutter press proclaimed Yuri Koda's death in sixty point type. Elspeth had skimmed through page one which screamed its headlines and the gory details and graphic photographs of the killing inside. She was not one for sensationalism or bloodstains on pavements.

"Give me a few minutes to freshen up. I'll ring you when I am ready," Elspeth said to Sean, hoping she did not sound as torn as she felt.

Elspeth changed from the tweeds she had worn down from Scotland. She chose a black Thai silk suit, suitable for dinner at a Kennington hotel and added a silk scarf resplendent in various shades of grey and deep red that Richard had given her on a trip to Paris the year before. She had brought more jewellery than she usually would take on assignment because Lord Kennington had warned her that Moya Koda dressed in the height of fashion and Elspeth wanted to present herself on equal terms.

Now or never, she thought, as she adjusted the platinum and ruby pendant earrings Richard had given her as a birthday present. She picked up her mobile again, which was laying on her dressing table, and speed dialled Richard's mobile number. Hopefully he would be at dinner with her cousins at Tay Farm and would have left his mobile in their rooms. Before there was an answer a knock came at her door and Sean Clancy was standing behind it when Elspeth opened it. Sean was typical of a Kennington hotel manager, fortyish, straightforward and mannerly.

"Mrs Koda is waiting," he said and rolled his eyes up.

Elspeth had already formed a picture of Moya Koda in her mind–young, opportunistic, not well educated but sexy. Elspeth had seen many of the type during her ten years of employment with the Kennington Organisation and before that in the twenty years she had lived in Hollywood with her first husband. Such women's insecurity often translated into unpleasantness. As the men got older, the wives got younger. Elspeth had been told in London that Moya was Yuri Koda's third wife.

"Lord Kennington has sent me here to . . . calm her," Elspeth said choosing as neutral a word as she could. "I'll go up right away. Keep a quiet table for us at dinner, somewhere I can talk to her without interruption and where we can't be seen by the other diners."

"I'll see to it."

"Sean, have the media picked up yet that Mrs Koda is here?"

"Not that I am aware of."

"Keep them away at all costs."

"Hotel policy," he said with a twinkle in his eye.

"Exactly," Elspeth responded with a smile.

Sean Clancy spoke quickly into his mobile and then he turned to Elspeth. "Madame Koda's in Suite 203 on the floor above here. Her rooms overlook St. Stephen's Green, which is unfortunate because if she looks out her window she could possibly see the National Concert Hall where the murder took place. I asked if she wanted to change rooms but she said she was happy where she was."

Elspeth checked her looks in the mirror by the door before she left her suite. You'll do, she thought, before walking into the hallway and entering the lift. She punched two and knew she now had no longer had a way to back out of the assignment Lord Kennington had foisted on her.

Elspeth knocked at the door of Moya Koda's suite and waited. No one came. She knocked again more loudly. Then she heard footsteps, heavy ones, and a masculine voice said, "Who's there?"

Elspeth had not expected this. She identified herself. An eye appeared in the peephole of the door. Elspeth put up her hand as if in greeting. The door opened on the latch.

"I've come to see Mrs Koda," Elspeth said. "Lord Kennington sent me."

A face that looked like it had been scarred by too many times in the boxing ring looked her up and down. Its owner unlatched the door.

"She's waiting for you," the man behind the craggy face said as he let her in. "We've got to be careful, even here in the hotel," he said his voice giving away his Irish roots. "Sit there. She'll be out in a minute."

Elspeth lowered herself on one of the sofas in the sitting room of the suite and watched the man retreat to the entrance of the suite. He slouched near the door on a chair which had been placed in the alcove usually used for the cleaning staff's trolley when the room attendants did their twice daily rounds.

He was a tall man, nearly two metres in height, Elspeth judged, and had a solid frame. His hair was thinning but what remained was fiery red. The sleeves of his suit jacket stretched in their stitching over what must be muscular arms, Elspeth thought. She tried to ignore the bulge at his waist, which could be a mobile phone but looked more like a pistol in a holster. But the man did not have the face of a thug, despite the crookedness of his features. He ignored Elspeth's scrutiny and turned to a copy of the *Daily Mail*. He carefully turned the first page over so that the headlines of Yuri Koda's murder were not visible.

Elspeth was so focused on the man that she did not hear Moya Koda enter the room.

"Ms Duff,' a voice said in cultured English.

Elspeth jumped and turned. Moya Koda was not what she expected. Elspeth judged Madame Koda was about her own age, perhaps in her mid to late fifties. As Eric Kennington had promised, she was dressed in the height of fashion in a trouser suit of fine wool with embroidery up the sleeves. Her jewellery was minimal but obviously expensive. As a lover of fine clothing, Elspeth noticed these things but her attention riveted on the bruise across her face and a black eye that even beautifully applied makeup could not hide.

Moya Koda spoke again. "Beautiful isn't it?"

Elspeth knew Moya was not referring to any part of her dress, but could not make out what emotion lay behind Moya's words.

"You can see why I have Billy here with me," she said."

Moya turned her eyes towards the man at the door. "Yuri insisted I keep him near me at all times. I've known him since my childhood in County Louth. His father was my father's estate manager."

"Madame Koda, do you want to tell me what happened? It would help me if I know. Like Billy, I'm here to protect you."

"You don't look the type," Moya said.

"My looks have fooled many a wrongdoer," Elspeth said smiling.

"Brains over brawn?"

Elspeth acknowledged the observation with a smile. "I find there are advantages to an intelligent and soft approach to security matters."

As they spoke, Elspeth reassessed her previous ideas as to what the third wife of a well-known international financier would be like. Moya Koda's appearance had shattered all of Elspeth's preconceptions. In front of her was a well-spoken, graceful woman, who looked like she had been in a fistfight. She showed little outward signs of grief, although less that forty-eight hours ago her husband had been brutally murdered less than five hundred metres away.

"Would you like a drink?" Moya asked. "The minibar has a wide selection. Most of it was to Yuri's specifications when staying at a Kennington hotel but I always insist on an excellent dry sherry produced by a small winery in Xerex whose owner is a personal friend of mine. Would it suit you?"

Moya poured out the pale amber liquid into cut crystal sherry glasses from the drinks cupboard. She then took a seat across from Elspeth.

"I ought to tell you that I am responsible for Yuri's killing and I'm terrified at the repercussions. Of course, I can't admit that to the Garda. That's why I asked Eric Kennington to send someone to help."

2

Elspeth nearly spat out her sherry, as good as it was. Taking in her breath she said, "I think you need to start at some sort of a beginning if I'm to make any sense of what has happened."

"It will take me a good long time," Moya said. "I have ordered an early dinner here in the suite. The manager told me your preferences were on file and he had consulted it. I've ordered Dover sole for us both, which he said would suit you. But let's finish our sherry and then I'll call downstairs for room service."

Moya sounded like a person who was not used to having her wishes countermanded. She threw off her four-inch heels and settled into the sofa across from Elspeth.

"Contrary to what you may think, I married Yuri for love. I have money of my own, much more than I need, so his fortune made little difference to me. My first husband made his money in the City of London and we lived handsomely in Belgravia until his death two years ago. I loved Roger, and with his passing was destitute with grief. I wanted to end my own life had it not been a sin against God. I am no longer a practicing Roman Catholic but the concept of mortal sin never leaves a person once the nuns have taught one otherwise. I was educated at a convent school in Dorset.

"My father was Anglo-Irish, although despite stereotyping to the contrary, he has always treated his estate staff humanely, and is sympathetic to many an

Irishman's wish to bring Ulster into the Republic's fold by fair means or foul. During the worst of the Troubles, he ignored certain illegal activity that took place in the part of our estate that borders the lough which lies between County Louth and Ulster. It's better not to question the noises in the night he always used to say."

Over the course of her career Elspeth had learned to listen without interruption. Moya's story was not what she expected. Elspeth's assignment became suddenly more interesting. Now she wished she had paid more attention to the Irish question when she lived in Southern California.

Moya continued. "I met Yuri about a year after my first husband died. At first I found him insufferable. He had the arrogance of a frightfully rich capitalist in the new Ukraine, defying all notions that he had grown up with under communism. He amassed an enormous fortune through investments in oil and gas and, I suspect, illegal arms shipments, although he always denied the last. He pursued me relentlessly and I resisted him with equal force. I told him I didn't respect him and he said he would prove he was at heart respectable. This give and take went on for a year without my relenting. I don't know if it was loneliness or my inability to say no again after so many proposals of marriage. He set siege to my barricades and he won. We were finally married in London in April a year ago."

Elspeth frowned. "You said you loved him."

"In the end I did. But the price was high. Most of my friends told me I was mad and many shunned me afterwards. I got caught up in Yuri's set. There were weeks on end sailing the Med in his grand yacht, skiing in Switzerland at the best resorts in the winter, trips here and there and everywhere around the world, always staying in the best hotels, particularly Kennington ones. My life with Roger had always been staid. Now I was in the thrall of the jet set life. I was uneasy at times but so caught up with Yuri that I didn't ask questions I should have."

"Did Yuri ever discuss business with you?" Elspeth asked.

Moya shook her head. "If I expressed my doubts, he would laugh them off. He was a big man, Ms Duff, in every way. I found him exciting. He touched my wild Irish side, which the nuns had tried so hard to suppress."

"Was he violent towards you?" Elspeth asked, no longer able to stop herself from asking about the black eye and facial wounds."

Moya put her hand to her face. "Oh, this?"

Elspeth sipped her sherry and waited for more. Finally Moya continued.

"It's all a part of what happened Saturday night. Let me tell you in my own way," Moya said. "About a month ago, I could tell that Yuri had changed. He no longer came to me at night. I could hear him pacing in his dressing room. Sometimes he would make phone calls, although he spoke in Ukrainian, which I couldn't understand as Yuri's English was excellent and my Ukrainian nil."

"After that?" Elspeth asked. "How did he change? Was he violent to you?"

Moya shook her head.

"No," she said. "In the morning he would rush from our townhouse without breakfast and not get back until well after dinner. He cancelled our social engagements. About a week ago he asked me to find someone I could trust to be a bodyguard, preferably someone I had known a long time. He said the world was becoming a dangerous place and he didn't want me harmed."

"Thus Billy," Elspeth observed. "Had you had personal protection before?"

"Yuri always had two men with him, his 'goons' I called them, but they always stayed in the background. I never found them intrusive or threatening. Yuri said he needed them because some of his business associates did not always play by the rules. But I always felt free to come and go. I knew nothing about Yuri's business and always thought my distance from it was appropriate. I was the spoiled wife of a tycoon. Perhaps I don't fit the profile of a typical trophy wife but that was what I was, wasn't I? I used to laugh off the concept. Would you like another sherry or shall I call for dinner?"

Elspeth had left Perthshire just as the sun was rising, early as it was almost midsummer, and the rich sherry was beginning to have its effect. She suggested they eat.

As it always was at a Kennington hotel room service arrived quickly. Moya suggested they freshen themselves up while waiting for them. Elspeth wondered if Moya wanted to apply another layer of makeup but when she arrived back in the sitting room, she had only applied a thin layer of powder over her face.

Moya smiled under her battered face.

"I thought you ought to see the extent of the damage. I asked my stepdaughter, an excellent photographer by the way, to document all the injuries. Some of them you can't see. Much of the caked blood has washed off and the bruises are now more colourful. Did I mention my stepdaughter before?"

"Lord Kennington did. He said she was staying here with you."

"Yuri had two children, one by each of his previous marriages. The son, Sergei, will have nothing to do with his father. The last we heard he was in Paris living in squalor and playing a part in an underground theatre. But Angelika, who is now twenty-one, stayed with us in London. She is studying Visual Communication at the Royal College of Art. She's very serious about her studies and also has become very religious, Church of England, not Russian Orthodox or Roman Catholic. Her boyfriend is a divinity student, which may explain her newly found belief. By the way, she prefers not to be associated with her father's surname and uses her mother's—Rostova."

"Lord Kennington told me that as well."

"She has never been to Ireland and had heard me talk about growing up here. Derek Somerset, her boyfriend, was to join us this weekend and we all were going to my family home in County Louth."

Once room service had set up their dinner, served their plates and poured out the wine, Moya Koda asked that they be left alone.

"Should I assume your stepdaughter won't be joining us?" Elspeth said.

"She is spending the evening at an evening prayer service at an Anglican cathedral she has found here, and has an appointment with the dean afterwards. She has her own room down the hallway and won't disturb us, although she may drop in to assure me she is back."

"Are you close?" Elspeth asked.

"Strangely, we instantly hit it off. I treat her like a younger friend rather than a daughter. She often comes to me for advice."

"Was she close to her father?"

"They had a special bond," Moya replied. "I think one of the reasons Angelika and I click is that I always respected her relationship with her father."

"She must be terribly upset about his murder."

"The young are resilient. She said to me after it happened that she always had expected it."

"Did you?"

Moya put her hand to her black eye and nodded. "Good things usually don't last. My marriage to Yuri was too good to be true."

Elspeth took a bite of her sole. During her recent time in Scotland, she had missed the excellence of the chefs at the hotels. She let the fish melt on her tongue. Moya had gone silent. She pushed her food around her plate but did not eat. Once she reached for her wine and sipped it. Elspeth waited. Elspeth knew she was getting tired because of her early rising in Scotland but Moya had so far told her very little of significance regarding Yuri Koda's murder or the reason she had suffered such ugly abuse.

Moya seemed to regain her composure but still fiddled with the stem of her wine glass.

Finally Elspeth said, "Madame Koda, you can trust my discretion. Lord Kennington always has." This was not absolutely true but Elspeth never minded stretching a fact when it suited her needs. Her husband found this trait in her distressing. Elspeth choked slightly on her next bite. She had not called Richard.

"Is something wrong?" Moya asked.

Elspeth smiled her most charming smile. "No, nothing. I just need to remember to call my husband."

"I assumed you were married. I noticed your rings," Moya said. "Your ruby is quite fine."

"Richard and I chose it together just before we were married. Rubies are my birthstone."

The conversation turned to gemstones and veered away from the information Elspeth wanted most to hear from Moya. Moya so far had led their discussion; now Elspeth wanted to take charge.

"May call you Moya?" Elspeth asked. "I have a feeling we will be spending a great deal of time together in the next few days and I think we might be more comfortable on a given name basis."

"I like you, Ms Duff—Elspeth. Yes, given names will do."

"I need to know what you expect from me. The Garda will undoubtedly carry out the primary investigation of your husband's death. I can't be involved in that. The hotel can certainly keep in touch with them and I'm sure they will keep you informed on developments. They must have contacted you."

"I have told them I won't see them. A policewoman did come to give me the news but I already knew what happened and didn't need the Garda's intervention. I told the desk downstairs to send her away. I didn't want them to see me this way. My bruises would only be misinterpreted. I agreed to talk to the inspector over the phone but I told him I was too distraught to see him in person."

"You still haven't told me why the bruises," Elspeth said. She felt Moya needed to be dealt with more directly.

"I was there when my husband died," Moya said. "I don't want the police to know because I fear they will suspect me. I saw nothing that will help their investigation. Do you really have to know all this to protect me?"

Elspeth began to wonder why all the evasiveness. She now sensed that Moya had formulated a story to gain her sympathy but not reveal anything involving Yuri's murder.

"Any information is helpful," Elspeth said. "My job is not to solve Yuri's murder. I have explicit orders from Lord Kennington to protect you while you are here at the hotel. I can do this most competently if I have any information that would reveal a threat to you and to Angelika."

"I have Billy for that. Billy's son Matt is guarding Angelika."

"Then what do you need me for?" Elspeth asked.

"I need you to keep everyone away, including the police."

"Do you think you are in harm's way?" Elspeth asked. "It's important that I know in order to help you. I'll make sure the security staff is aware of the possibility of disturbance in the hotel but it would be helpful to know what you are afraid of."

"For the moment I can't tell you any more than I have just done. If you can protect our privacy, then Angelika and I have Billy and Matt to deal with any chance of physical harm. Elspeth, I can see why Lord Kennington sent you. You have a way of taking command, which I admire. Please allow me to excuse myself. I have a splitting headache. Tomorrow I will tell you more about Yuri but right now all I want to do is go to bed with an icepack on my face."

"Have you seen a doctor? The hotel has one on call."

Moya shook her head. "No doctors. An icepack and some paracetamol will have to do."

Elspeth eyed the strawberry desert on the sideboard, but knew it would be returned to the kitchen uneaten. She rose and took her leave.

When Elspeth returned to her suite at the back of the hotel, she was mystified by the scope her assignment. She knew nothing about the murder except the screaming headlines she had read on the plane that morning. Moya had admitted to being at the scene of the crime. Was she the murderer although she said not? Or was she attacked too and escaped with the injuries on her face and perhaps elsewhere? Most of all, why didn't Moya want to see the police or leave the hotel? Moya's story of her past did little to explain what happened last Saturday night.

More than anyone else in the world, Elspeth wanted to talk to Pamela Crumm. Not only was Pamela a close friend, but also was the part owner of the Kennington hotel chain. She managed the everyday workings of the hotels and left the grand ideas to Eric Kennington. They had been a team for well over thirty years and one could not operate without the other. Although Eric had thrown out the fact that he knew Moya before her marriage to Yuri Koda, Elspeth suspected Pamela would know the whole story. Pamela in her few spare moments was a devotee of the tabloid press.

Even though it was approaching half past seven, Elspeth found Pamela still in her office next to Lord Kennington's in the skyscraper in the City of London.

"I wondered how long it would be before you rang," Pamela said.

"Is Moya Koda mad, Pamela?"

"Why do you ask?"

"I feel she is playing cat and mouse with me. She had terrible bruises on her face but she won't tell me the real cause of them. She says she was at the scene of the crime, but says she won't go to the police because they might suspect she was the murderer. She also says she'll explain more to me about Yuri Koda tomorrow but I strongly suspect she won't be straight with me as to what happened Saturday night. She suggested that I had no need to know. Do you have any idea what was in Eric's mind when he called me and pulled me away from Richard and Scotland?"

Pamela chuckled. "He said you were the only person he knew who could handle Madame Koda."

"Handle her how? Or does he just want her pacified until she decides to leave the hotel?"

"In your job you are always responsible to the hotels first, to see that none of the guests come to any harm and that the workings of the hotels runs seamlessly. I assume in your time away you haven't forgotten that."

"Of course not. But from Moya Koda's condition, I'm afraid my task may be an impossible one. Moya spoke of Yuri's 'goons'. Both she and her daughter have bodyguards. I don't even know if the two of them are registered as guests or if they are staying in Moya and Angelika's rooms. Moya said they were there to prevent any bodily harm. I'll have security beefed up here but I have no idea what to expect."

"That's why Eric sent you, to find out what's happening with Moya."

"I feel Moya is drawing us into something we don't want to be a part of. I don't suppose there is any way to get her to leave the hotel? She seems to have barricaded herself in her room. Have you or Eric talked to her? Eric said he knew her."

"As you know, we have a policy to handle our guests gently. Eric wants to avoid any publicity and a forcible eviction might reach the press. Elspeth, both Eric and I are trusting you to handle this situation."

"Am I on trial to see if I am still fit for my job?"

"Mmm," Pamela said.

"Meaning?"

"Elspeth you're an intelligent woman. I don't need to answer that question."

Elspeth wasn't sure how to react to Pamela's words.

Pamela continued. "I'll see that you are backed up in any way you need. I'll also get you more information of Moya and Yuri Koda and ring you in the morning. By the by, how did Richard take your returning to your job? You looked ready to resign permanently when you came in this morning."

"I was. I even had rehearsed the speech on the trip down from Scotland. I haven't told Richard yet that I am in Dublin. I must as soon as I ring off from you."

"He may not like it, m'friend, but your husband is the truest man I ever met. I expect he'll understand. He has told me that he knew you weren't happy in retirement in Perthshire."

Elspeth no longer had an excuse to delay her phone call to Richard. He had already left three messages on her iPhone and probably as many on the answerphone at their flat in London. She felt she had let him down, which was not a new feeling.

She got his voice mail. The message said, "I am on my way to London and will ring you back as soon as I can. Please leave a message with the time and date you called."

Damn, Elspeth thought. Why did he object to leaving his mobile on during train trips? Or was he flying? How could he react so hastily? She rang their flat and again only got the answerphone. She left a message for him begging him to phone her no matter what the hour, but did not say where she was.

She made her way downstairs and asked for Sean Clancy, the hotel manager.

"He's gone home, Ms Duff," the receptionist told her.

"The director of security will do," Elspeth said although she wasn't sure he would. He might not know what Elspeth's assignment at the hotel was.

The receptionist, an attractive redheaded girl of about twenty, grinned. "He's on paternity leave—twins—a boy and a girl."

"Who's in charge here?" Elspeth asked.

"Pierre Savreux. He's just been transferred from the Kennington Paris."

From the receptionist's smile Elspeth assumed that Monsieur Savreux had taken her fancy.

"Please call him. Tell him I'm coming."

Pierre Savreux was waiting for Elspeth by the bank of security monitors in the back rooms of the hotel. He straightened his long back as she approached.

"Welcome, Madame Duff. You will not remember me but I was at the hotel in Paris when you had your unfortunate accident last autumn. I am glad to see you are fully recovered."

Elspeth grimaced at the remembrance of that day. She had a scar where the bullet entered her shoulder and on wet days she still had an aching pain in the muscles around her collarbone. Luckily the shot had missed her heart.

"Pierre, how long have you been here?" Elspeth said, extending her hand.

"Two months only," he said.

"Were you here when the Kodas arrived?"

"*Oui, madame.*"

"How many did they have in their party?"

"Monsieur and Madame Koda, his daughter and her friend."

"Her friend?"

"Mademoiselle Kendall. Nancy Kendall, a woman about the same age as Mademoiselle Rostova. They are staying in the same room near the Koda's suite."

"And were there other men in the party?"

"No, madame."

"Pierre, please call me Elspeth."

"*Oui*, Elspeth." He struggled with the pronunciation.

"When I just was in Madame Koda's room, a man with a hidden gun was there as well. His name was Billy Maguire. Is he registered at the hotel?"

"I think not."

"Or a Matt Maguire?"

"I can check with the records but I don't think so. I do not recognise the names."

"What about two men who would have been with Yuri Koda most of the time?"

"I have seen them but I do not think they were registered here. I will check right away."

Elspeth deplored this lack of attention on the part of all of the staff. Even the top security officer's absence should not have caused such a breech. Goons, as Moya had called them, were not welcome in Kennington hotels.

"I would like to see the security tapes for Saturday night," Elspeth said. Kennington hotel policy was that the tapes were kept for twenty-four hours and then deleted if there were no disturbances so she hoped they had not been erased.

"You must see the technician," Pierre said, adjusting his rimless glasses. "He will not be in until tomorrow morning. Do you want to speak to the man monitoring the tapes now?"

"How far back do they go?" Elspeth asked.

"Until yesterday evening," Pierre said. Elspeth could tell he was not happy.

Elspeth always treated the hotel staff in a way that would respect their dignity, so thought how best to make the most of a bad situation.

"I would like to see the technician in the morning. Tell the person monitoring the tapes tonight to erase nothing. And tell the technician that I will want to see selected parts of the tapes as far back as they have been saved. Will you check your registers to see about the four men who seem to be bodyguards to the Koda family? I'll be in my suite," she said.

On the way back up on the lift, her mobile vibrated in her pocket.

"Elspeth Duff here," she said, as she did not recognise the number.

"Stay out of things that don't concern you," a husky voice said. Elspeth was not sure of its gender. He/she rang off immediately.

Elspeth leaned back against the mirrored wall. Only a few people in the world knew her mobile number.

Then she remembered that she had given the number to Moya Koda.

3

Unlike his wife, Sir Richard Munro did not act impetuously. He was not heading to London on a whim. He had earned his knighthood after a long career in the diplomatic service as a result of his calmness in crises and careful reserve in debate. He prided himself on his judgement and thoroughness. He considered his one weakness to be his love of his wife and his indulgence of her. When Elspeth did not answer his repeated phone calls to her mobile and to their flat in London, he had rung Pamela Crumm. Richard and Pamela had a bond outside her relationship with Elspeth and he knew he could trust Pamela's discretion.

He had not been surprised by Elspeth's weakening to Eric Kennington's demands. The man seemed to have a hold over her, like a snake charmer over his cobra. As much as he and Elspeth had rehearsed her resignation speech, he knew she would capitulate if Lord Kennington wanted her on an exciting job. Pamela confirmed that this had happened, but asked that he not tell Elspeth that she had done so.

"I don't want to get between the two of you, Richard," she had said. "You will have to work it out. But if you want to go to Dublin, let me know. I can arrange something."

"Is her assignment dangerous?" he asked.

"Not so far but it will require as much ability as Elspeth has."

"Why is that?"

"The guest in question is one of Eric's old friends, which will complicate her job. He is relying on Elspeth's skill to keep Moya happy and the hotel safe."

"You intrigue me, Pamela."

"I haven't heard from Elspeth since she left for the Republic but I expect a call once she has assessed the situation at the hotel."

"I'm coming down to London and will be staying at our flat," Richard said. "Would you have time to meet me for lunch tomorrow?"

"To talk about Elspeth?" she asked.

"That and other things."

"Shall we say half twelve? There's a new restaurant around the corner of our offices I've been meaning to try."

*

Elspeth was normally a tidy person and therefore Richard was amazed at the disorder she had left in their flat. Then he realised that Elspeth no longer kept cases with three sets of working clothes in them, one for each climate zone. She had unpacked them about three months ago when they had come down to London for a week of theatre, opera, ballet and visits to the art galleries. A 'week of culture' they had joked. Richard loved his retirement on Loch Tay, its only drawback being Elspeth's restlessness there.

He knew he would have to resolve the issue of Elspeth's re-employment but also do so without it becoming an issue that would destroy their marriage.

He also knew she had continued doubts about her suitability in their marriage. His first wife, Lady Marjorie, had been the consummate diplomat's wife. Richard had loved her in a companionable sort of way, more like a sister than a wife, but he had loved Elspeth throughout his first marriage. Before his marriage to Lady Marjorie, he had proposed to Elspeth twice but she had turned him down both times, saying she was not a wife fit for him. When they had met in Malta almost five years before, he had been recently widowed and she divorced, which left no obstacles to their marriage or so Richard thought. But Elspeth had put up every barrier possible and only conceded after a painful two-year courtship. Richard knew by then Elspeth did return his passion but her outward façade of sophistication hid a person who still had issues with self-worth. No amount of reassurance on Richard's part could assuage this. They had now been married for three years but their marriage had not been easy. Some days he felt that keeping the marriage together was the hardest job he had ever tackled but he was not about to give up now.

When he got to the flat, the answerphone was blinking insistently. The first three messages were from him to Elspeth and the last from Elspeth begging he ring at whatever time in the evening or night. It was well past ten and Richard knew Elspeth had been up since the early dawn of the Scottish summer. He expected he would wake her, but followed her command.

A sleepy voice answered his call. "Oh, Dickie, I'm in Dublin."

"Yes, I know," he said, without adding anything more.

"Pamela?"

"Yes, my dearest. Who else would I have called?

She told me that Eric got you in his clutches again before you could say a word to the contrary."

"I wanted to," she said.

"Elspeth, you don't need to give excuses. I thought that while you were away, I would stay in London."

He heard nothing on the other end of the call.

"Are you there?" he said.

"Are you angry with me?" She sounded as if she wished he were.

He did not answer her question. "I am having lunch with Pamela tomorrow," he said instead, keeping his voice level.

"I don't think I'll be here that long," she said in a small voice.

"You don't need to rush back," he said and then thought he sounded cruel. Perhaps it was suppressed anger. He added, "I'll be here if you need me."

He did not tell her that Pamela had laid hints that he might join Elspeth in Dublin. In the past he had stayed at the hotels when Elspeth was on assignment. Twice he had saved her from death. He thought it best that he not remind Elspeth of this.

*

Pamela Crumm slept little even at the best of times. A childhood disease had robbed her of any beauty but behind her small, bent frame she had a passionate soul and a brilliant mind. In the moments she allowed herself time away from the pressing routine of handling the precise details of running the Kennington hotels and from the adroitness of handling Lord Kennington in his worse moments, she devoured the purple press. Her promising Elspeth that she would follow up on Yuri Koda and his wife was pure pleasure. When she arrived back in her flat on the South Bank overlooking the River Thames, she took out the supper and wine her housekeeper had left for her and took it and her glass to one of the low sofas she had custom-made to fit her miniscule size. She opened her laptop after she had finished eating.

The first sites she found all referenced the weekend headlines but soon she had probed further, dipping into more obscure websites that she had always found useful before, but would be difficult for a less inquisitive person to discover. Her initial findings did not surprise her but as she dug deeper, she stopped eating and discovered a site detailing Yuri Koda's business dealings. An hour went by without her replenishing her wine. Yuri Koda was more than he seemed and Moya Koda was more involved with his affairs than Pamela thought Moya should wisely have been.

Pamela emailed the notes she had taken to her private email address at the Kennington Organisation, and wondered what she was going to tell Elspeth in the morning.

She went to bed but sleeplessly finally resorted to a classic Regency romance by a favourite author and one Pamela had read many times before.

4

Elspeth rang off from Richard. She knew she had disappointed him once again but never before had his tone been so cool. Why couldn't she just have told Eric Kennington that she no longer was interested in her old job? But she knew when she was on her way to London that she wanted her job back above all things. Despite the beauty of the Highlands she knew she could not settle down there, at least not yet.

She turned her mind to Moya Koda. Her question to Pamela about Moya's sanity was genuine. Elspeth was not a medical professional, but could tell by the way Moya moved that her wounds were more than skin deep. Moya's facial bruises suggested a possible concussion, which might explain her irrationality but her contorted movements suggested more.

Elspeth could employ all the usual devices that she had frequently used during ten years employ at the Kennington Organisation to protect Moya and the other guests but she did not want to get involved in any activity outside the hotel. She had done this on her last assignment with Lord Kennington in Victoria and earned a six-month suspension from her job.

After Richard's phone call, she was wide-awake. She rose and put on her silk dressing gown. She had left her laptop in the sitting room of her suite. She went to the delicate writing desk, put her computer on it and typed in 'Yuri Koda'. The headlines flew in front of her. This time she read the text more thoroughly.

Yuri Koda had been found severely beaten behind the National Concert Hall in Dublin in the late hours of Saturday night. A performer who had stayed late to chat with a stagehand had left by the stage door just before midnight. He had seen the body slumped in a corner and assumed it was a drunkard but then he saw the pool of blood. He had called the Garda on his mobile and fled back into the building. Later editions said that Yuri had been murdered between eleven, when the concert had been over, and half an hour before his body was found.

A zealous reporter had determined that Yuri did not have tickets for the performance, at least not under his own name. He had last been seen having dinner with his wife and two male companions at a well-known Dublin restaurant south of St. Stephen's Green and had left there at half-past nine. No one had determined where he was between the end of his meal and the time he was murdered.

Several gory pictures showing the bloodstained scene of the crime after the body was removed filled the seamier tabloids. All the newspapers carried the same photograph of the Ukrainian oligarch, obviously a formal portrait released by his business organisation.

No mention was made of the Kennington hotel, although Elspeth was sure Pamela was already working with her contacts in the media to suppress this information. One more serious article in the *Irish Times* suggested that Yuri Koda was in Dublin to attend negotiations for a major energy contract. No one mentioned Moya except in passing. The other two members of the dinner party were not identified but Elspeth suspected they were the 'goons'.

Undoubtedly some enterprising employee of the restaurant where Yuri ate his last dinner would produce a photograph for a good price, either from the restaurant's security cameras or a mobile phone, but these pictures had not appeared yet.

None of the press speculated on the cause of the murder. The Garda remained silent on their investigations other than to make a plea to any member of the public who might have seen anything suspicious around the theatre.

None of this information helped Elspeth in the slightest nor did it explain Moya's erratic behaviour.

Elspeth went back to the *Irish Times* website. If Yuri was in Dublin to negotiate a major energy contract, there must be further information about it in the press. Ireland was too small a country to have such a thing overlooked in the financial sections of the capital's major newspaper.

Elspeth's energy flagged as she began reading the business pages and she put away her computer. She kept reminding herself that it was not her task to find the murderer; she was in Dublin to protect the hotel, its guests and its staff. She knew she was good at this job but her curiosity was piqued. How much could she find out here at the hotel that might explain Moya's odd revelation that she was with Yuri when he was killed and exactly who the murderer or murderers were?

Elspeth had ordered breakfast to be served in her suite at eight. Room service's knock woke her from a deep sleep. She cracked her eyes and wondered where she was. Not at the farm on Loch Tay, definitely at a Kennington hotel, but where?

"Leave it on the sideboard," she called out, hoping there was a sideboard. Most Kennington hotel suites had them. Slowly the realisation of her strange circumstances hit her. She grappled for the phone and called down to see if the manager was in yet.

Sean Clancy came on the line almost immediately.

"Can you see me in my suite in forty-five minutes?" she asked, knowing from past experience that she could be ready for business by that time. "And did Pierre Savreux tell you I wanted to see the tapes? Is the technician in yet?"

"He arrived five minutes ago and I have passed the information on," Sean replied. Elspeth had almost forgotten about the efficiency of Kennington hotel managers.

Elspeth rose quickly, now fully alert, and dressed hurriedly but with care. Sean arrived at her suite just as she was finishing her second cup of coffee. He was carrying a slender attaché case with the Kennington coat of arms and the hotels' logo 'Comfort and Service' on it. Once in the suite, he called down to room service to get fresh coffee.

Sean opened the attaché case and took out two copies of a computer-generated list.

"I thought you would like to have an official account of the Kodas' stay. They checked in on Thursday at four in the afternoon. Following the instructions I received from London, I gave the Kodas the best suite on the third floor overlooking St. Stephen's Green. We were not expecting Mr Koda's daughter and her friend but I made a large room available down the hallway, which I was able to give them after shuffling around several of the other guests who had not yet arrived. Mr Koda gave his platinum American

Express card to cover the costs for all of them, and told the girls not to worry about expenses.

"They arrived in a hired limousine and the driver was a local operator well known to us. He helped bring their things in, and told Mr Koda he would be at his service for the following fortnight. Mrs Koda and the girls were scheduled to leave the hotel on Wednesday morning, to go to Mrs Koda's family home in County Louth, I believe. Mr Koda was taking a night flight out of Dublin on Tuesday evening on his private jet."

"Did they have any servants with them? A valet, a ladies maid, a secretary or perhaps a bodyguard?"

"Not when they checked in."

"Later?" Elspeth asked.

"Like all of our hotels, we have personnel to handle any individual needs our guests may have, be it personal or professional. There is no need for bodyguards. Our staff is trained to cope with any situation, as you know."

Elspeth smiled. Lord Kennington had said that having a butler service was getting to be too common. He preferred individualised attention to his guests and the provision of any staff to go along with it. The only thing he forbade in his hotels was an escort service or any hint of prostitution. "They can go elsewhere if that's what they want," he often cried. "I run respectable hotels for respectable guests." He claimed this was one reason for the continued exclusivity of his hotels. Elspeth, however, had never heard Lord Kennington mention bodyguards or goons. He probably never even thought of the possibility.

"I want the security technician to make copies of all the activity around the Kodas' suite and the girls' room from the last time the tapes were erased until the present.

He can cut out all the quiet times. I also want the tapes of the lobby and restaurant areas that show the Kodas and close-ups of any person who made contact with them," Elspeth directed. "Please have the technician send copies to my secure email site so I can view them privately here. I need to talk to Moya Koda and the girls. Do you know if any of them has ordered breakfast yet?"

"Mrs Koda has ordered breakfast for half past nine. The girls ate in the breakfast room and left the hotel about an hour ago."

"Was anyone with them?"

"No, they were alone."

"Did anyone meet them outside?"

"I'll ask the doorman," Sean said.

"Have the doorman come to your office when he is off duty. I want to talk to him personally. Also, please have the doorman who replaces him at my disposal before he goes on duty. Sean, we need to handle the Kodas with a great deal of caution so that they are not responsible for bringing bad elements into the hotel. I fear Mrs Koda is holding a great deal back and I intend to find out what it is. Let me know if there is any unusual activity around her suite."

"Elspeth, it's grand to have you back with us," Sean said. "Your reputation precedes you." He did not explain exactly what he meant.

Elspeth rang Pamela to update her.

"I was about to call you, ducks," Pamela said. "Are you sitting down?"

"I'm ensconced on one of the sofas in my suite. I had

forgotten how comfortable the furniture at the hotels is. I've already talked to Sean Clancy, and have the wheels set in motion to find out what the Kodas have been up to in the hotel. Unfortunately the security tapes were erased for Saturday night."

Pamela chuckled. "Not completely erased," she said. "Recently we have had a backup of all our tapes at the hotels sent to the security offices here in London. They are in deep storage, available only on my instructions. I can have our computer gurus get the recordings out."

"I suppose in the world after nine-eleven, these precautions are necessary."

"They are but we don't want this to be public knowledge. Rather than you fishing for information, I want you to tell me what you are looking for."

"The bodyguards around the Kodas. Sean Clancy seems to have no knowledge of their presence in the hotel but yesterday a man called Billy Maguire was in Moya Koda's suite. I want to see how he got in. The tapes here may show me. What is more Moya mentioned Yuri's 'goons'. I wonder if they were at the hotel, or simply met him outside."

Pamela was silent for a long moment. Finally she said, "Elspeth, I don't need to warn you not to overstep the strictures of your job."

Elspeth muttered. "I know. I'm on probation."

"Let's not call it that," Pamela replied. "But something more serious has cropped up."

"More serious?" Elspeth asked. "Does it affect what I am doing here?"

"It may. I spent a long time on the internet last night, on websites that are hard to find by the general public.

Rather than tracing Yuri's background, I looked into Moya's background. She described herself to you as a dutiful wife. That may be so but I found out a great deal more. Be careful, Elspeth."

"Are you going to leave me in suspense?"

"That would be unfair," Pamela said. "Here's what I learned. Moya, as she admitted to you, is from a distinguished Anglo-Irish family that goes back to Edward the First late in the nineteenth century but the de Laceys, as staunch Roman Catholics, became sympathetic to the Republican cause. They were known to finance Republican organisations, but preferred to work through Parliament rather than illegally. But they secretly gave generously to the Provisional Irish Army who smuggled arms to Northern Ireland. The de Lacey estate borders on Carlingford Lough across from Ulster so smuggling was easy."

"Moya told me that."

"Moya, however, was educated in England. She told you about her earlier life, but not the end of her education. She read art history at Somerville College, Oxford, and then went on to the Courtauld Institute, where she specialised in the art and jewellery of the Russian Court before the Revolution in 1917 and what became of it afterwards. After leaving the Courtauld, she was hired by Northby's, the auction house, where she became one of their assessors of East European jewellery. Shortly after marrying Yuri Koda, however, she was asked to leave Northby's. This morning I called in a favour from the head of the auction house and he told me that she might have been implicated in giving information to the thieves who stole several valuable pieces of jewellery from a family in Paris who claimed to be related to Tsar Nicholas. The family had approached Northby's to put the pieces up for auction. Moya Koda was sent to Paris to do the valuation. A week later thieves broke into the family's Paris flat and took the jewellery before the auction house was able to make arrangements for shipment to London."

"Did you say this was after Moya married Yuri?"

"About two months afterwards."

"But anyone could have taken the jewels. Have they ever been found?"

"Not yet."

"But why did Moya fall under suspicion? Surely she had done hundreds of valuations."

"Nothing, of course, could be proven but Northby's has built its success on its absolute security. They are not as big as the famous auction houses, but are known to serious collectors, who value their integrity and discretion. Many people who have to sell off precious possessions do not want a big splash made about it."

"What has this got to do with Yuri Koda's murder?" Elspeth asked.

"I have no idea but your job is to watch Moya. If she is guilty of collaboration with the people who took the Romanov pieces, she is not the poster child she would make herself out to be. They say there is honour among thieves. I don't believe it."

"And so I not only have to protect the guests from Yuri's murderers but also from international jewel thieves who might or might not be lurking in the shadows."

"Well, ducks, you wanted to come back," Pamela said. "Can't you see now why Eric wanted you on the job?"

"Not just because of my wardrobe, I see," Elspeth said and blew out her breath. An earlier rebuke by Lord Kennington still stung. "I'm off to see Moya once we're off the line. It will be interesting to see what tale she spins today."

"Keep me posted, m'friend," Pamela said. "Eric is particularly interested in this case so stay vigilant."

"What else," said Elspeth. She was sure Pamela did not miss the sarcasm.

Moya was still in her dressing gown, a confection of silk and feathers, when Elspeth entered her suite. Moya wore thick pancake makeup and the bruises were beginning to subside. Her eyes, however, were still heavily bloodshot and she moved as stiffly as she had the night before.

"Have some tea," Moya said.

"I'm awash in coffee," Elspeth said, trying to keep her tone light. "I've come to see what we can do to keep your stay safe. I don't see Billy Maguire this morning.'

"Poor dear. I sent him to his cousin's to get a good night's sleep. Now that you are here, I feel less of a need to have him here all the time."

"Do they know to let him in?" Elspeth asked.

"I have tipped the doorman generously. There should be no trouble."

"And the girls? The manager said they had gone out."

Moya looked at her intently. Elspeth had a feeling that Moya was about to lie but wanted to see if Elspeth would see through it.

"I pity them," Moya said. "Since the murder they have felt so cooped up. I don't think there is any more danger to them now that Yuri is dead. Whatever his murderers wanted, it has nothing to do with the girls."

"I'd like to meet them when they come back," Elspeth said. "The more I know about everyone here, the better I can do my job."

"I'll let you know when they return. They've just gone for a bit of shopping. I've given them some cash, as Yuri's credit cards will probably be frozen by now. Perhaps we all could have lunch together here in my suite."

"You said last night you had more to tell me about Yuri," Elspeth prompted.

"Dear Yuri," Moya said. Elspeth felt Moya's sentiment was somehow genuine.

"Can you tell me about Saturday night?"

"It's all a bit of a blur," Moya said. "We had a late dinner and then went on to a pub for Irish coffee. Yuri was attacked on the way back to the hotel. He pushed me out of the way, causing my bruises."

"Did you see his killer or killers?"

"I may have but I was so terrified, I fled after I saw what they did to him."

"Was anyone with you? You said Yuri had protection with him."

"You mean the goons? No, they had left us by then. It was a beautiful night and had just gone dark when it happened. As a child, I loved the summer nights and the slow fading of the days. Yuri and I were strolling rather romantically. We never expected to be attacked."

"Why won't you go to the police then?"

"I didn't see who did it."

"But you were assaulted too."

"By Yuri pushing me away. Besides I don't think the Garda would believe me. It's best I stay out of it, just as I always stayed out of Yuri's business. Elspeth, he always skated close to the edges of the law and made many enemies along the way. I don't know what deal went wrong but it must have angered someone. Murder is a terrible thing. But I can be of no use to the police."

"Are you afraid the murderer or murderers will come after you?"

"No, not really, but I do want to keep my privacy. I don't want the press digging up things in my family's past. My father, who is still very much alive, has always been a controversial person politically. I don't want anyone to call attention to his connection to Yuri through me."

"Do the Garda know you are here?"

"Didn't I say last night that they had sent someone around to tell me about Yuri?"

"You did. Our hotels have a policy not to disclose who our guests are. I wonder how the police knew?"

"Perhaps they guessed that Yuri would stay in the best hotel in Dublin. Your people turned them away at my request."

Elspeth needed to find out exactly what happened, but thought the hotel staff would be better witnesses than Moya Koda. She decided on a new tack.

"How long do you plan to stay here?" Elspeth asked.

"Until the furore dies down. Then I'll take the girls to County Louth. We had planned to go tomorrow anyway, but may have to delay until we know we can leave anonymously. Father is expecting us but he is old enough that days of the week don't mean a great deal to him anymore. In the meantime I am relying on your help to keep the Garda away."

"Surely a statement from you might help the Garda find Yuri's killers."

Moya brushed away a feather that had come loose from her dressing gown. I think not," she said. "I had nothing to do with what happened except to be with Yuri when he was attacked. If the police saw my injuries, they might assume I was assaulted as well. I wasn't. Yuri was simply protecting me as he always did. The police will have to find his killers by probing into his business affairs. As I told you yesterday, I kept out of them as much as I could, and can't really answer any questions they might ask."

Elspeth began to wonder that if she protected Moya, would she be accused of subverting justice? She wanted to consult Pamela about this before proceeding. Elspeth also had the feeling that she would not be able to change Moya's mind about seeing the police. Had Elspeth not been put under such harsh limits by Lord Kennington and Pamela, she might have considered becoming more proactive but she was treading lightly, still unsure of her continued employment.

"It would be useful," she said, "if I could talk to Yuri's bodyguards. Do you know where they are?"

"Probably back in Ukraine by now. I expect the minute they saw the headlines, they found a way to flee Ireland."

"You said they weren't around when Yuri was attacked."

"No, they left after we left the pub."

"Wasn't Yuri worried to be without them?"

"The centre of Dublin is a well patrolled place, particularly on Saturday night. There was no need for us to be worried. The attack was totally unexpected. I would like to get dressed now. Shall we say lunch here at one?"

Elspeth left Moya's suite and made her way down to the security office. She stopped by the hotel shop and picked up copies of the *Irish Times* and the more sensational tabloids. The latest football scandal had displaced Yuri's murder. Brief articles, mostly on pages four or six, said the Garda had no more clues in the Koda murder but were pursuing several leads. Which, Elspeth thought, meant they were making no progress. She wondered how much Moya's blurry recollection of the murder would help had it been offered. And how much of the truth was Moya telling? Elspeth suspected Moya's narration was laden with half-truths.

She spent the next two hours viewing the tapes that were still extant in Dublin. The Kennington hotel security cameras only worked when there was motion to detect. The hallway around the Koda suite was quiet most of the time. The day before Billy Maguire had gone into Moya's room just after noon and emerged about eleven in the evening. Elspeth went in and out, as did room service. Otherwise the tapes were still.

5

Richard found the restaurant Pamela had suggested and was led to a table in the corner that she had booked. He was early. He sat and watched the City businessmen and women in dark regulation attire come into the restaurant, mobile phones to their ears. He hoped the restaurant had an anti-mobile phone rule but doubted it. Even at the height of his diplomatic career, he had honoured the sanctity of meals, particularly at official functions. The modern world had become too impatient. He suspected business did get done more quickly but he wondered if it got done as thoroughly. Richard had always liked careful consideration of any task and decided he did not like the modern-day urgency. His last diplomatic post was in Malta, where foreign affairs were taken at a somewhat slower and sombre pace. And his last assignment at the European Commission had involved research into international criminal dealings in Europe. He sat back and sighed. He was over sixty years old and he felt he already had the mindset of an old man.

These introspective musings came to an end when Pamela eased herself into the chair opposite him. Pamela, as usual, was expensively dressed with a knack to downplay her bent and small figure. No one confronting Pamela could doubt that she held sway in the world of business.

Richard reached over and put his hand over hers.

"Pamela, thank you for coming."

"No, thank you, Richard. We know each other too well to brush off what must be going on in your mind now. I feel partly responsible but when I talked to Elspeth I felt she wanted to come back to work."

Richard nodded. "When she left for London, I wasn't convinced that she would go through with her resignation, although I urged her in every way I knew how to make her do it. She has made a brave face of it but she has been unhappy ever since Eric Kennington suspended her and we went to Scotland. Even the new house and the old mystery she scraped up didn't compensate for the excitement of her assignment with the Kennington Organisation. I sat here before you came in and looked at the pace of the modern world. Elspeth's a part of that. I'm afraid I no longer am nor really ever was."

Pamela smiled softly. Her eyes behind her large round glasses were filled with concern.

"Are you worried, Richard, about her returning to work?"

"I have no idea what it will do to our marriage. I promised her when we got married that she could carry on at the hotels but after the fiasco in Canada, I was hoping she would want to settle down. I know it was wishful thinking. She never has stayed put, not as long as I have known her."

"Nor have you, Richard. Certainly your life with the Foreign and Commonwealth Office meant constant upheaval."

"One moves from place to place but everything is very much the same in each one. The mode of living varies little although the daily situations may. Once in a long while there is a coup or a riot which added a bit excitement but on the whole the accommodations, rounds of parties, endless and sometimes senseless meetings and the routine of diplomatic life were the same. Marjorie loved it; Elspeth would have hated it."

"Are you worried for your marriage?" Pamela asked.

"Frankly, yes."

"Had you ever thought of joining us?"

"Joining you? Do you mean joining the Kennington Organisation?"

"Of course, I haven't approached Eric about this but you do have skills that would serve the hotels well," Pamela said. "I have a project in mind that would suit you superbly."

"Which is?"

"Assessing the guests in the hotels."

"Isn't that what Elspeth does?"

"In her way but I was thinking of something else. It's an idea that has been rumbling around in my head ever since I knew Eric would probably lure Elspeth back in the fold. I haven't defined my plan fully yet but with all your skills and manner, there is something you can do to help us get out of our current slump."

"Slump?"

"Yes. We aren't immune to the current economic times. Recently the type of guests we are catering to aren't what they used to be. Take Elspeth's current case. Eric knew the woman Elspeth is dealing with but her husband was not top drawer. No, Richard, don't accuse me of being a snob. I already am one. We have built our business as a chain of private hotels on the exclusivity of our guests. At one point, Eric invited each one personally but we now have grown too large for that. What we need is someone who has been associated with the best of people to guide us. Neither Eric nor I are from the gentry. Both you and Elspeth are, despite all her railing against it. We want the old clientele back but they no longer have the money to afford our prices."

"I'm not sure where you are going with this, Pamela. Are you suggesting I join your marketing effort?"

"No. I think you'd hate that. But you could visit our hotels and give an assessment of what you see. I've talked to Eric about downsizing but he will hear nothing of it. Now we are no longer exclusive, just terribly expensive. In the world of all the people around us here at this restaurant, money not breeding counts. It's a changed world from the time Eric established his first hotel. What the guests want these days is quite different from what we provided in the old days."

"I look back with regret that we can't capture something of the best of those times, despite all our advances," Richard said.

"I suspect so do many others. This crowd," she said waving her hand "doesn't care about some of the niceties the Kennington hotels have to offer. They are more interested in bragging about the price of their room than the fineness of the bed linen but they want swimming pools and, yes, access to women or men who will come to their rooms to entertain them. They defy what we have always stood for."

"I'm not sure I can give you any new input."

Pamela grinned conspiratorially. "Why don't you go

to the Kennington Dublin and see if you can come up with any ideas?" she said. "If you like, I'll tell Elspeth you are running a pilot programme for me and Eric. Although she may assume I am up to meddling in your marital affairs, I will assure her I am not."

At that point the food arrived, which gave Richard time to think before answering. "If we say this is only a pilot, then I'll agree."

"Good. Come to our offices later this afternoon. I want to convince Eric first that this is a good idea."

6

Angelika Rostova rose from the kneeler and hurried back to the rear of St. Patrick's Cathedral where her friend Nancy Kendall was waiting. Angelika had been praying for the soul of her father but felt the prayers would do little good. The church was high Anglican and so she looked around for a confessional. It might be best if she admitted to the priest that she had not loved her father. In fact she had loathed him and hated his new wife Moya more. She conceded that Moya tried to be her friend but Angelika distrusted her. Moya took from her father too easily. She might be older but she had all the trappings of a trophy wife.

Angelika recalled her own mother only slightly. Her mother's soft caresses and great blue eyes melded into a sea of remembrance that was only partially complete. Angelika's mother had died when she was four. Angelika suspected that her mother's death was just another convenient thing in her father's life, something to be cast off when it was no longer profitable. Angelika had a photograph of her mother, a blonde haired beauty who stared back at her as if begging to be loved. Angelika loved her and had decided to find out all she could about her untimely death. She would need to travel back to Kyiv, which her father had never allowed her to do on her own. Now he was dead and she was free to go.

Her other prayer was for her half-brother Sergei. He was ten years her senior but she remembered him throwing her in the air when she was small and his kindnesses to her when she was a child.

Finally Angelika rose and crossed herself.

Nancy was waiting for her at the entrance door. "What took you so long?" Nancy asked.

"I was praying for the dead and for those departed from my life," she said.

"Angie, you take this whole church thing too seriously. I know you love Derek but he isn't high church. No incense and chants or that sort of thing."

"I know," Angelika said, grinning at her friend. "I need to get as much from this as I can before we get married."

"Our keeper is waiting outside," Nancy said. "I can't image that we really need him but if it makes your stepmother happy . . ."

"My stepmother is only happy when she is making a fuss," Angelika said.

"Do you think we are in danger?" Nancy asked.

"Because of what happened to my father? No, I don't. I think something must have gone seriously wrong in his business to have caused his death."

"You frighten me," Nancy said.

"Really, Nance, you don't need to worry. Whatever the score was, Papa's death settled it. It has nothing to do with us. My stepmother is making a big thing of staying in the hotel and hiding her bruises. Papa used to hit her, you know. She's good at covering up the consequences, although normally he didn't aim for her face. I hope I'm not shocking you. At least he never hit me."

Nancy took her friends arm. "These things happen even in proper English families," she said. "I had an aunt who 'ran into doors' all the time. I can see why you're attracted to the mild Derek Somerset."

"I know he will never hurt me," Angelika said. "My father had his own ways. He paid for them in the end."

"You don't sound sorry."

"I'm not. But now I think we ought to get back to the hotel and my wicked stepmother. She is expecting us for lunch."

Angelika had not expected another guest in her mother's suite. A beautifully groomed and marvellously dressed middle-aged woman rose from one of the sofas to greet them. She was just the sort of woman her stepmother would cultivate. The woman came forward with a smile and held out her hand.

"I'm Elspeth Duff," she said. "I work for the Kennington Organisation, and am here to see that your stepmother and the two of you are safe and comfortable during your stay. I hope you had a successful morning shopping and sightseeing. I haven't been to Dublin before, but understand it's a fascinating city."

Angelika had been brought up to respond to authority. She had little doubt that Ms Duff was Authority with an upper case A, despite the woman's polished manner.

"Good afternoon, Ms Duff," she said. "Let me introduce my friend Nancy Kendall. She's never been to Ireland before, nor have I for that matter. Dublin is a beautiful city and I hope you get a chance to see some of it."

Having said that, she could think of nothing more to say. Moya stepped in. "Nancy and Angelika, my dears, I have ordered a light buffet for here in the room, which should arrive in a moment and I've invited Ms Duff to stay. She has some questions for you, I'm sure, but I thought we would be civilised and let her ask them over lunch."

Ms Duff was not the only one who had Authority with an upper case A, Angelika thought.

"How thrilling," Nancy said. "I feel like I'm in a detective novel."

"I'm not a detective. My job is to make sure you all enjoy your stay here." But then her eyes glistened, "But I do have a PI's licence in the States, where I used to do real detective work, if you must know." Elspeth grinned as she said this.

"Wow," Nancy said.

Angelika thought her friend a bit naïve. Yuri Koda had hired detectives all the time, many of them to guard Angelika when they were back in Kyiv and when she was younger in England. Most of them were thugs so it was refreshing to meet a detective who appeared to be a lady and spoke cultured English. Once she married Derek, she hoped this would be the type of person she would deal with, not her father's sort.

Room service interrupted the introductions. The light lunch was hardly that, although the food was prepared from fresh ingredients and presented in a beautiful array of lettuces and carved vegetables. Angelika had never stayed at a Kennington hotel before but decided she would again if her father had left her any money. Parsons should occasionally get away from their flock and might need the soft touch of luxury offered at the Kennington hotels. She hoped Derek would not object.

A waiter stood by the sideboard and served the plates to each of the four women. Then he withdrew into the alcove by the door.

"You needn't worry," Ms Duff said. "The members of our staff know never to repeat what they hear at the hotel."

"Is everything so hush-hush?" Nancy asked.

"Of course it is," Moya snapped.

"Here in the hotel, you should feel secure," Elspeth said. "Your stepmother has assured me that what happened on Saturday night has nothing to do with you."

"Except that my father was brutally murdered and she wants to hide here," Angelika said.

"Angelika, I'm hurt. I am doing the best I can in the circumstances to protect you and Nancy. Surely you can try to understand?" Moya said.

How like Moya, Angelika thought, pouring on the guilt.

Ms Duff intervened. "You are all guests here. We don't want you to feel any pressure about leaving the care to the hotel. But do you mind if I do ask some questions?"

Angelika put down her knife and fork.

"I'm OK with that. What do you want to know?"

"Lord Kennington, who owns the hotel, always wants to know if everything is to your satisfaction but after working at his hotels for ten years, I'm sure it is. I'm more concerned about what might happen here because of Angelika's father's death. I want to prevent any unpleasantness to you or the other guests. I understand you arrived on Thursday afternoon. Can you tell me what you did on Friday and Saturday?"

Angelika was amazed at how subtly Ms Duff asked her

questions. Angelika had not been expecting the third degree but Ms Duff had a way of making them relax when asking the questions.

Nancy responded. "Angie wanted to find the cathedral. It's High Anglican, you know, not Roman. Angie's engaged to a divinity student and is into that sort of thing. We found it first thing. It's quite near to here and we walked. While she was inside, I took out my sketchbook and drew some people on the street. I like doing quick sketches. I'm studying fashion and like to get people's poses. Angie was in the cathedral for about an hour. When she came out, we wandered around Dublin and then came back to the hotel for dinner in the dining room. Yuri and Moya were out so we were on our own. Afterwards we went to the bar and joined some young men from Paris. It was great fun. We didn't get to bed until half one."

"Did you see either your father or Moya come in?"

"Angelika shook her head. "I'm afraid we were completely absorbed in trying to speak French. Nancy's better at it than I am, although I'm the one who lives on the continent during summer holidays and Christmas break."

"And Saturday?" Elspeth asked.

"Same thing," Nancy said. "Church in the morning. This time I went too. If my best friend is going to be the wife of an Anglican priest, I need to have some of the church's blessings rub off on me. I'm afraid I was raised by agnostics. Then we went to several museums as it was raining most of the day. The French guys had left the hotel so we had a solitary dinner in the dining room and then came up to watch a DVD. Things are so wonderful here, why would you want to go out?"

"Again did you see Yuri or Moya before they went out for the evening?"

Both girls shook their heads.

"Did you see Moya return to the hotel?"

"No," Angelika said. "We went to bed early."

Elspeth Duff addressed Angelika. "How did you learn of your father's death?"

Angelika answered. "Moya came to our room and told us. She said someone from her father's estate was coming to Dublin to escort us if we left the hotel. He would wait for us outside. She advised us not to leave the hotel before he arrived. We didn't like the idea really. It was so like my father, who never believed I had grown up and could look after myself."

"Did she say what had happened or simply tell you your father was dead?"

"She said he had been murdered by thugs late the night before but that we shouldn't be afraid for ourselves. It was a business deal gone wrong," Angelika said.

"Were those her exact words?"

"Close enough," Nancy said.

"How did you feel?"

"It was hard for me to feel anything," Nancy said. I only met Yuri twice, on the trip in his plane over here and one morning at breakfast. Most of the time he was on his mobile phone speaking in a language I didn't understand."

"Ukrainian," Angelika supplied. "He was here on some sort of a gas pipeline deal."

"Were you surprised when Moya told you the news?"

"Me?" Angelika said. "No, his murder was long overdue. I'm amazed he stayed alive so long."

Elspeth frowned but Angelika could not make out what she was thinking. If only she knew the truth. Nancy had been more upset than she, not because she knew Angelika's father but because of the way he had died. Most well-bred English girls did not brush acquaintanceship with the ilk of her father nor with cold-blooded murder. Later Angelika had gone down to the shop and bought the *News of the World* and the *Sunday Mirror*. The papers did not stint on the gory details, but somehow knowing more of the truth help her cope with the suddenness of her father's demise. But she could not grieve. Instead she had turned her hatred towards Moya. Angelika was convinced that Moya was responsible for Yuri's death. She wished that her stepmother was not in the room. Angelika wanted to speak to Elspeth Duff alone and tell her about the family dynamics and that things were not as they seemed. She had to figure out a way to do so.

The meal dragged on. Angelika found the first excuse she could to flee the room. Nancy came with her.

"Whew," Angelika said once out in the hallway. "I'm glad that's over with."

"I liked Ms Duff," Nancy said.

"You would. You're such a snob, Nance. I can't believe it. Just because she speaks properly and looks like her clothes are worth a million pounds, doesn't mean we can trust her completely. She may be in my stepmother's pocket, you know. But I don't understand why she asked where we were on Friday and Saturday. What's that got to do with the safety of the hotel? Isn't that for the police to ask?"

"Angie, I haven't a clue why all this is happening. I'm sorry about what happened to your dad. It's all rather gruesome. Can we talk about something else? What are we going to do this afternoon?"

*

Elspeth watched the girls go and wished she could follow them and ask more but she was aware during lunch that Moya was watching her. Certainly Moya's telling Elspeth that Angelika was like a younger friend was not accurate. The young woman seethed with hatred for her stepmother. Either Moya was deceiving herself or she needed the myth of a happy family relationship in her new marriage. Elspeth became increasingly wary. The more she was with Moya the more she thought the woman was manipulative. But what was her motive?

Elspeth also noticed that Billy Maguire was nowhere in evidence. What was the meaning of that? She felt trapped by Moya's enigmatic personality and by the limitations Lord Kennington had put on her. She wanted to know more about the murder, particularly Moya's part in it. She had tried twice to question Moya and thought that Moya would not open up further unless she chose to.

Elspeth took her leave soon after the girls left.

"I'll be at the end of my mobile," she said to Moya. "You can pick up the house phone and reach me immediately if you dial seven-seven-nine." The number was a code Elspeth had set up earlier in the security office.

Returning to her rooms, Elspeth tried to phone Pamela but got her voice mail. Richard also did not answer his phone. Frustrated, Elspeth went to her suite and put on shoes she could walk in comfortably. The time had come to see the site of the murder and find out if what Moya had told her made any sense. She prepared for her trip from the hotel.

Strange, she thought, that in all her world travels she never had been to Dublin before. The Kennington Dublin was one of Eric Kennington's earliest hotels and also one of his smaller ones. It still retained the intimacy of the original hotels in the chain. The doorway was quietly marked with a brass sign and the doorman tucked away in a small recess where he could see the street but be hidden from the casual passerby. He appeared out of his hiding place and held the door open for Elspeth as she approached it.

"I hope you are enjoying your stay, Ms Duff," he said. Hotel employees, particularly those out in the public areas, were required to know the names of all the guests soon after they arrived. The doorman was in a typical long coat, blue with black frogs across his chest and a grey top hat covered most of his dark hair. The Kennington coat of arms was stitched on both points of his collar.

"You know who I am, don't you?"

"Yes, of course. Mr Clancy said Lord Kennington had sent you to deal with Mrs Koda."

Elspeth dropped her eyes to his name badge, which said 'Harry O'Shea. "Were you on duty when the Kodas checked in?" she asked.

"I was."

"Can you tell me about them?"

"They arrived in a Mercedes limousine, one from a service that we use here at the hotel all the time. I think Mr Clancy arranged it to meet Mr Koda's plane."

"And who was in the group?"

"Mr and Mrs Koda and the two young women. Two

men were with them but they stayed in the car and didn't come into the hotel."

"Can you describe the two men?" Elspeth assumed that they were Moya's goons.

"They spoke to Mr Koda in a language I didn't recognise. I've learned many phrases in the main languages of the world, but this wasn't one of them. It sounded like Russian but I couldn't make any of the words out. Is that important?"

"At this point I can't be sure. Did you see these men again?"

"I was off my shift at six on Thursday night, but my relief, actually my brother Mick, was a bit late and asked if I could cover until seven. Just before seven the two men came back and stood across the street from the hotel at the edge the Green. They were still waiting when Mick, my brother, came on duty. You have to think the men were waiting for the Kodas."

"Were you here Friday?"

"No, it's one of my days off."

"Saturday?"

"I came on at ten in the morning."

"Did you see two Irishmen, one middle-aged and one young, they are father and son, come in between twelve and one? They may not have been dressed like many of our guests."

"Guests nowadays dress every which way, not like the time when I first came to work here. It's hard to tell who's who. Can you describe them more? I think I know who you mean."

"I can't describe the younger one," Elspeth said, "but

the older one was large, not fat, and was beginning to go bald. His remaining hair was carroty. His face was scarred. He might have worn a cap when you saw him. He was from County Louth if that makes a difference in his accent."

Doormen at the Kennington hotels were trained to identify accents and Harry O'Shea was no exception.

"I know exactly who you mean," he said. "County Louth written all over him. I asked his business, of course. He said that he and his son were from Mrs Koda's father's estate and wanted to see her. He said he had an appointment. I called up to make sure what he said was true. Mrs Koda said she was expecting the two of them."

"Have you seen them since?"

"The younger one was waiting outside this morning when I came on duty. The two girls in the Koda party came out soon after I arrived and he joined them, or rather followed after them."

"Were they aware he was there?"

"Yes, they greeted him and then seemed to ignore him as they went off. He followed behind. He was with them when they came back later. This time he was carrying their shopping bags. I heard them tell him when they got back for lunch that they weren't going out again today. He went off by himself."

"And the older man?"

"He wasn't around today, just the younger one."

"Let me know when your brother comes."

"Of course, Ms Duff. Is there anything else I can do for you?"

"Keep a sharp eye out for the two men who were in the Kodas' limousine Thursday and waiting for them on

Saturday night. If they come anywhere near the hotel, call me."

"I will. This whole murder thing isn't so great, is it?"

"Not great at all," Elspeth said. Now can you direct me to the National Concert Hall?"

"On the trail of the murderer? Your reputation precedes you, Ms Duff. You've been through some exciting events at the hotels. But nothing like this has happened before here in Dublin in all the twenty years I have worked here. Normally the hotel's a sleepy place."

Elspeth followed Harry O'Shea's exacting instructions. She crossed St. Stephen's Green and made her way down Earlsfort Terrace to the concert hall. She saw the police tape by the side of the building and wandered over to it. A young policewoman in a Garda uniform barred her way.

"Move on." The policewoman said politely.

"I used to be in the Metropolitan Police in London when I was your age," Elspeth said. "That was a long time ago. I expect things are quite different now."

The young woman eyed Elspeth up and down. Elspeth knew she hardly looked the part now and so she continued on. "I worked as a private investigator in California for a number of years, although nothing was as exciting as the murder here happened to me in Los Angeles. My first husband was in the film industry so I mainly worked on divorce cases or stalking by obsessed fans. Rather dull considering what the term 'private eye' means to most people. Scotland Yard was more interesting, although I never was involved in a murder there."

Elspeth did not mention the number of murder cases in other places in the world she had been involved in. She felt it would not help the reputations of the Kennington hotels or her family.

"It's a first for me too," the woman said.

"From the papers it sounded as if it was rather gruesome."

"The guards who were called in told me they never had seen so much blood. I'm just here to chase gawkers away."

"A hard job."

"Hard on the feet."

"Yes, I remember."

As she talked, Elspeth tried to see beyond the police tape but all she could see was a drive leading to the back of the building. The young woman had little to add to the already detailed descriptions in the media so Elspeth began to move on. But out of the corner of her eye she could see a white tent jutting out from the side of the building, obviously the scene of the crime but no police seemed to be in evidence.

Elspeth made her way back to the Kennington Dublin, measuring the distance and the time it would have taken Moya to escape from the murderers and get back to the safety of the hotel. The exact time would have depended on Moya's route and the speed with which she ran. Elspeth assumed she must have been wearing high heels and her pace would have been slower than Elspeth's in flat shoes. Elspeth also thought that Moya would have made her way along the streets and not through the green. Elspeth wondered if Moya would ever tell her the truth about what happened after Yuri was killed.

Elspeth knew that she had been told not to investigate the murder, simply to protect Moya and the hotel, but her natural curiosity gnawed at her. Where was the Garda now in its inquiries? Did they know about Yuri's goons? Did they even know that Moya was at the scene of the crime? Would their inspectors be knocking at the hotel doors with a search warrant? Above all, Elspeth wanted to avoid that possibility. She had a decision to make. Should she go to the Garda and tell them her position at the Kennington Organisation? That would be admitting that Moya was at the hotel. Would that be countermanding Eric Kennington's orders?

During her ten-year career with the Kennington Organisation Elspeth had never been in a situation like this one before. She felt her wings were clipped. In the past she had kept an uneasy relationship with the police forces around the world, sometimes cooperating and at others keeping them at bay while she did her own investigations in the hotels. Now she had to stay passive, which was unlike her usual method of operation. But in her last case with the hotel in British Columbia, she had severely overstepped her boundaries and now was fearful to take an aggressive stance.

Harry O'Shea held the door for her when she arrived back at the hotel.

"All's quiet here on the street," he said, "but Mr Clancy wants to see you in his office."

"Thanks, Harry. Let me know about your brother."

7

Sean Clancy was obviously nervous. He held his face rigid. Elspeth wondered if he ever had been in the military because he looked like he was about to execute an order with which he did not agree. Elspeth smiled to put him at his ease.

"Lord Kennington called and seemed anxious to talk to you," Sean said. Elspeth translated this in her mind. Eric was annoyed by her absence from the hotel. He could have called her mobile easily enough but he had apparently not. He had not changed over the six months Elspeth had been away.

"I'll go up to my suite and ring him," she said. "Don't worry if he barked at you. When something is important, he can be impatient."

She hastened upstairs and once in her suite dialled Eric Kennington's private line. She dreaded speaking to him, but tried to keep her voice light.

"Elspeth, where have you been?" he said and added without waiting for her answer. "Pamela has a new idea and I agree. We are sending Richard out to help."

"Richard?" Elspeth asked.

"Your husband."

"I don't need him here. Everything is going smoothly."

"I thought it best I warned you that he was coming. He'll be there by tomorrow mid-morning. He'll tell you more when he gets there."

Eric Kennington rang off without further explanation

for his call. Elspeth scowled. She may have erred in the past but she did not need Richard coming to the rescue. How dare Eric imply that she was incapable of doing her job alone.

She picked up her mobile and paused, not knowing whether to ring Richard or Pamela.

Richard did not answer but Pamela did.

"What in the world is going on? Why is he sending out Richard?" she asked.

"Don't be angry, ducks," her friend said.

"Nothing is going on here, Pamela. In fact I am beginning to wonder why this assignment is so important that I personally was sent here. Moya Koda is a strange one. I'm getting nowhere with her but thankfully the hotel is quiet. The Garda haven't yet stormed the gates but I'm expecting them any minute. The last time they came she wouldn't see them and I've no idea why. I'm not sure how long we can offer her protection or at least keep the police away."

"We're not sending Richard out because of Moya Koda. He is carrying out a special task for Eric. I felt that if you are back with us, we might include him too."

"So it was your idea to send him over here."

"You have a suspicious mind, Elspeth."

"Isn't that why I have succeeded in the past?"

Pamela laughed. "Of course. Now tell me about Moya."

"She's devious. She refuses to see the police, although she says she was at the murder scene and has bruises to show for it. I can't get a straight answer from her, although some of the things she has told me ring false. What is it that Eric wants me to do? I'm floundering without more specific directions, particularly when I'm trying to stay within the bounds of the hotel dicta. I'm itching to talk to the Garda but I'm not certain if this will help keep things calm at the hotel and me out of trouble with Eric."

"Stay close this time, Elspeth. I'll see if I can get more out of Eric. He hasn't told me what his relationship with Moya is but I have an inkling she is more than just a former friend. Normally Eric is boastful about his past acquaintances. This time he is a bit buttoned up but I'll work on him here."

"I'm getting the feeling that this assignment is more complex than it seems on the surface. Please keep me informed. And now tell me about Richard."

"He's such a dear man. He is going to help us at the hotel, nothing to do with your case but he will explain when he gets there."

*

Richard seldom was impetuous but he felt as if he was becoming so in accepting Pamela's assignment. He had been involved many times in Elspeth's work and at the hotels, but always before as a bystander, friend, lover, finally husband and guest but never as an employee of the Kennington Organisation. He had insisted that he be paid only a pound for his first report. With his own pension and investments as well as Elspeth's newly inherited wealth, he had no need for additional money but he could not rightly claim to be a member of the Kennington Organisation team without accepting some compensation. Knowing Pamela's proclivity to promote romance, he suspected that she had devised her scheme more to aid his relationship with Elspeth than to discover how the Kennington Organisation could counter the new culture of the wealthy. Still he had decided to take his task seriously because he too felt that even in the five years he had been reconnected with Elspeth, the hotels were sliding away from Lord Kennington's original mission of small, private hotels for his carefully chosen clientele. The current economic downturn and its effect on the hotels had made a discernible and disturbing difference in the quality of those who chose to stay.

At four he met Pamela in her office in the City to discuss what was expected of him. She took him directly into Eric Kennington's office, a place he had never been before but Elspeth had described it so exactly that he felt he had.

"Well, Sir Richard, Pamela's idea to recruit you on this mission is brilliant. I can think of no person more suited to the job. You have my full authority to snoop around the hotel in Dublin as much as you want and don't let Elspeth drag you into what she is doing. She undoubtedly will try. I have no objection to the two of you admitting your relationship openly. In fact, I think it may help Elspeth to accomplish what I have asked her to do. She is dealing with an old acquaintance of mine who will be impressed by your background."

Richard prided himself on his ability to analyse and synthesise information and to write succinct, accurate and carefully thought out reports. He was not happy with Lord Kennington's implication that his position at the Kennington Dublin was to monitor one of Elspeth's charges. That would be out of character for him. Pamela should know this even if Eric Kennington did not.

Lord Kennington dismissed them shortly afterwards and Pamela took Richard upstairs to the executive dining room for tea.

"Don't pay attention to Eric," she said in a nanny-like voice. "Despite his title, he is impressed by the real aristocracy."

Richard protested. "But my title was earned."

"And your father?" Pamela quizzed.

Richard turned uncomfortably in his chair. "It is of little significance," he responded. Richard was a second son of a noble Scottish father, his brother now carrying the family title. Richard resented the fact that so many people assumed his rise in the Foreign and Commonwealth Office and subsequent knighthood had been predicated on this family connection and his first wife's being the daughter of the Earl of Glenborough, a former Governor General of India. None of this should count in the year 2009. Then he realised that the issue Pamela Crumm and Lord Kennington were addressing was how to get snobbery back into the Kennington hotels. He winced but he had agreed, at least to a pilot run.

How would Elspeth react to all this? She disdained snobbery and firmly believed in meritocracy. Richard sometimes wondered why then she was so taken with her job and was so beholden to her employers. He must ask her when he arrived in Dublin. They could hardly avoid the topic.

8

Elspeth sat back and tapped her fingers on the desk in front of her. She regretted now that she had not given her resignation to Eric Kennington. He and Pamela were playing games with her and she did not like it. As much as she loved Richard, which she did passionately, she was squeamish about having to explain to him why she had caved in to Lord Kennington. She might have felt emboldened to resign if she had not felt a burning need to fulfil successfully her assignment to help protect Moya Koda, although she had to admit to herself that she did not like the woman and only cared that Moya leave the hotel unscathed by her presence there.

Elspeth clenched her jaw, picked up the house phone and dialled Moya Koda's room. Elspeth waited as the phone rang. Finally, following standard Kennington hotel procedure, the receptionist answered.

"May I take a message for Room 203, Ms Duff?"

"Tell Mrs Koda to ring me back when she picks up her messages," Elspeth said.

"She just left the hotel," the receptionist said. "She didn't say when she would be back but she asked for her 'passport case' before she left."

"Passport case?"

"It was more like a small folder. She said her papers were in there. But it felt heavier than just a passport. I got it from the safe deposit box room for her."

"Did she leave by the front door?"

"When she left the desk, she went towards the front door and then seemed to change her mind."

"Did you see where she went?"

"Towards the hotel shop. She was in there for about ten minutes and then came out carrying a small attaché case, a plain black one. I know I shouldn't comment but I would have thought that she'd have bought one of the more elaborate ones. Then she left through the front door."

"How long ago was this?"

"Perhaps ten minutes ago or maybe fifteen. I could have the security tapes checked."

"Don't do that yet. Thank you for telling me. Please put me through to Harry O'Shea."

Harry chuckled when he came on the line. "Good afternoon, Ms Duff. I expect you are calling about Mrs Koda. She looked like the devil was on her tail when she left."

"How so?"

"I've seen people who were frightened before but never as much as our missus now."

"Tell me about it, Harry."

"I saw her coming and opened the door. She stopped halfway through it and took a great gulp of air. She looked around in every direction including back into the hotel. I asked if I could help. She jumped when I spoke. 'Don't tell anyone I've gone,' she said."

"Which direction did she go?"

"She walked up in the direction of Trinity College." He pointed the way. "Then just up the way she hailed a taxi but none came. She turned the corner out of sight."

"Did she have a small black attaché case with her?"

"That she did. She was clutching it to her like her life

depended on it."

"Did you see anyone else about? The Irishmen who came to see her Monday or the two men who were in the limousine?"

"Not a one, Ms Duff. You said to be aware of them."

Elspeth knew she had no way to follow Moya Koda. She wondered if Moya purposely hailed a taxi in a place beyond where the doorman at the hotel could hear her destination. And where was she going? Equally important, what was in the attaché case that made Moya so frightened? Elspeth thought of a number of options, among them a pistol, a large wad of cash and the weapon that had been used to kill Yuri Koda. The newspapers had not reported if any murder weapon had been recovered at the scene of the crime. If Moya was at the scene, she could easily have picked up the object used to beat Yuri, and then hidden it until she could dispose of it later. Now possibly the murderers had demanded it from her unless Moya was the murderer herself.

Elspeth drew in her breath. Was Moya involved in Yuri's killing? If she had been there, perhaps she had arranged for his murder or even done it herself. She had been so adamant about not seeing the police that Elspeth began to think Moya was more involved in planning the murder than she was willing to admit.

Again Elspeth railed against not being allowed to contact the Garda. She could have called her friend, Detective Superintendent Tony Ketcham at the Met in London and she knew he would provide a suitable introduction for her.

Elspeth returned to the reception desk.

"Tell me more about the packet Mrs Koda took out of the safe?" she asked the receptionist. "Can you estimate how much it weighed? Could it have been the weight of a small stack of papers or was it heavier?"

The receptionist tilted her head and frowned. "Heavier," she said. "More like something hard or something in a hard box. I'd guess it was about three or four hundred grams but I'm not very good with weights."

"Give me an example," Elspeth said.

The receptionist looked around the desk in front of her. She picked up several things, each time shaking her head. Finally she drew out a hard cover book from under the desk. Elspeth smiled at the title, which gave away that the contents were rather lurid. Desk jobs could have their boring moments and the book might do well to pass the idle moments for a pretty young woman.

"It was about this heavy," she said, blushing slightly, "and about this size."

Elspeth took the book in her hand and weighed it up and down. If the receptionist was accurate about the weight, Elspeth's earlier assumptions about the contents of Moya Koda's packet might be correct but she had no way to confirm this.

"Are Angelica Rostova and Nancy Kendall in their room this afternoon?"

"I just saw Ms Kendall go towards the spa. I haven't seen Ms Rostova."

"Good," Elspeth said. "Thanks for the help. Keep an eye out for Mrs Koda's return and let me know as soon as she gets back to the hotel."

"Ms Duff, I know this isn't your concern but the Koda's stay was guaranteed by his American Express card.

Is that still valid now that he is dead?"

"Don't worry too much about that. I will have Mr Clancy sort that with London. But the question was an intelligent one. Keep up the good work."

Elspeth left the receptionist beaming.

Elspeth returned to her suite and rang Angelika Rostova, who was in her room and agreed to talk to her in her friend's absence. Elspeth invited Angelika to her suite and ordered tea and coffee to be brought, although only a short time had lapsed since lunch.

Angelika sat stiffly on the sofa and accepted a cup of coffee and a chocolate biscuit from the tray room service had brought.

"I've been wanting to talk to you alone," Angelika said. "You mustn't believe Moya."

Elspeth nodded but said nothing.

"She's the most selfish woman I ever met. She may appear all smiles but behind all that is a grasping bitch. I expect it was she who arranged for Papa's death, to get her hands on his money," Angelika said.

"Does she inherit?" Elspeth asked. "So often in marriages like your father and Moya's, there's a prenuptial agreement. Do you know the contents of your father's will?"

"Papa never told me anything about his financial deals," Angelika said.

"Isn't that just as well?" Elspeth asked.

"Of course you're right," Angelika responded. "Papa's business dealings were, how can I say it simply, very complex. I have no idea how he left his affairs."

"Since we are speaking plainly," Elspeth said, "do you think your stepmother really was involved in your father's murder? Wasn't she hurt too? Surely her injuries were not fabricated? They looked too painful for that."

"I'm not sorry for her."

"You told me you thought your father had struck your stepmother in the past? Did you actually see him do so?"

"Why are you asking these questions, Ms Duff? What do they have to do with hotel security?"

"You have a right to ask. I fear that the people who murdered your father might come to the hotel and try to harm you, your friend or your stepmother. Your stepmother seems terrified that they might."

"She would try to make you think so. She likes to pretend she's hysterical. It's her trademark. Papa loved dramatic women and she definitely is one."

"Do you think your father might have been the one who inflicted her bruises and not the killers?"

Angelika took a long sip of her coffee before responding, and then began to pour out her story.

"Although he was a distant figure in my life, I loved my father when I was a child. My mother died when I was four, sixteen years ago. Papa was the only one I had left. He sent me to school in England because he wanted me to become a lady, as he put it. But money can't buy that, Ms Duff, as you probably know. I did get a good education but I missed my father most of the time. I don't know a great deal about his life, but was shocked when he married Moya Mulholland. I wasn't even invited to the wedding, which took place here in Ireland on her father's estate, although I was in London at the time. Moya had been married before and has no children so she decided to scoop me up into her life. I didn't like her from the start and I still don't. The trip to Ireland this week has been billed as her showing me her family's estates there. Is that supposed to impress me? Through my father I've had money all my life so her mention of the estates doesn't impress me and I don't think I will be dazzled by her family ties here. Am I being too harsh?"

"Mother and daughter relationships are hard enough," Elspeth said with some personal feeling, "but I imagine stepmother-daughter relationships are harder. Has she been difficult?"

"Quite the contrary. She has been sicky sweet. My background makes me a realist. I don't like fakery."

"Your stepmother and father weren't married that long ago. Was your father married to anyone else in the meantime?"

"No. He was married to someone before my mother but she died giving birth to my half-brother several years before I was born."

"Where is your half-brother now?"

Angelika shifted uncomfortable. She started to pick up her cup but it rattled in its saucer.

"I don't know. He disappeared."

"Did he ever meet Moya?"

"Not that I am aware of. He went off to Canada I think when I was thirteen, eight years ago. I haven't seen him since."

"Forgive me for asking but do you correspond?"

"He broke all ties with the family, including me," Angelika said. Sadness crossed her face. "I wish I knew where he was."

"Did he fight with your father?"

"Not physically or verbally. Sergei disagreed with everything my father was. The day before he left he said he couldn't stand what Papa stood for and had to get out from under his clutches. If I had been older, I would have gone with him."

Elspeth was about to ask more about Sergei Koda but her hotel phone rang. She tried to ignore it but it did not stop after five rings. At ten rings, Elspeth excused herself and picked up the handset.

"Ms Duff, I'm monitoring the security cameras. Something very strange is going on at the reception desk. A man has a gun. I think you might want to get down there."

Elspeth grabbed her mobile and pleaded an emergency. Angelika followed her out of the room.

"Don't worry about me," she said and left Elspeth at the lift. Elspeth did not wait for it to arrive, but took the stairs instead.

She felt everything in the lobby was in slow motion. A Slavic-looking man stood, legs wide, and was pointing a pistol at the receptionist. Sean Clancy was standing by the receptionist and was speaking to the man. Elspeth could not hear what he had to say but Sean was obviously asking the man to lower his gun. The man with the gun was shaking his head. Elspeth could hear him say in a guttural voice, "No English, Madam Koda now."

When Elspeth had been at Scotland Yard, she had received training in hostage situations but that had been over thirty years before. She tried to remember what to do. All that came into her mind was 'Keep calm and try to negotiate'.

The man was pointing the gun first at the receptionist and then at Sean Clancy, who was sweating under his breath. As Elspeth approached from the rear, she could hear the man's voice crack.

"Madam Koda now," he said. "No English."

Act slowly, Elspeth thought. She walked towards the man's back and cleared her throat. He swung around and fired. The shot missed Elspeth but broke a light bulb in one of the ornate wall sconces. Elspeth blanched

She tried to guess what he wanted. "Ukraine?" she said in as calm a voice as she could manage.

"Da," he said, but he did not lower his gun. Elspeth assumed this meant assent. She faced the man without backing away. Out of the corner of her eye she could see both the receptionist and Sean Clancy duck behind the desk. She wished she spoke Russian, as it had to be close to Ukrainian and the man might understand.

"Madame Koda has gone out," she said in English, shaking her head and pointing towards the door. "Can I help?" she added. Her heart was still pounding after the shot.

Every Kennington hotel had a telephone at the reception desk that provided a translation service. She pointed to it but noticed that her hand was shaking. She swallowed and tried to steady herself.

"Telephone," she said gesturing picking up the receiver. "Ukrainian, English OK." She hoped he understood.

"Madam Koda," he said again and waved his gun at Elspeth.

She shook her head. "Nyet," she said, using one of the few Russian words she knew, still hoping Ukrainian was close to Russian. Again she pointed to the translation phone. She walked towards it but she didn't get far. He came up to her and put his gun against her ribcage.

She took a deep breath, seriously doubting that her life would last much longer.

Behind her a female voice shouted out. The man turned but did not take his gun away from Elspeth's body. The voice spoke insistently in a language Elspeth did not recognise. She hoped it was Ukrainian. The voice went on. Elspeth twisted her head the best she could and out of the corner of her eye could see Angelika Rostova.

The negotiation between Angelika and the man seemed to go on endlessly, although it could not have been for more than a moment or two. Finally the man lowered the gun from Elspeth's ribs.

Angelika came forward where Elspeth could see her more fully.

"Thank you," Elspeth said and let out her breath, which she must have been holding.

"I can hardly say the pleasure is all mine," Angelika said. "He wants to talk to my stepmother."

"Tell him I will talk to him and that I work for the Kennington Organisation in London. Bring him into the room over there," Elspeth said indicating a door at one side of the lobby. "It's a small meeting room. We can talk privately. Tell him we mean him no harm and will not call the police."

"Do you mean that?" Angelika asked.

"For the moment. We prefer to handle things in-house if at all possible."

Elspeth called out towards the desk, "Five six seven." It was the Kennington hotel security code not to inform anyone outside the hotel what was happening. She hoped someone heard it.

Elspeth, Angelika and the man moved towards the meeting room, the man at the back of her with his gun still jutting out of his jacket pocket.

Elspeth took out her master keycard and unlocked the room's door. Inside there was a table for six and chairs around it. The man motioned with his gun and said something.

"He said we are to sit down and to keep our hands on the table."

Elspeth eyed Angelika sideways. "How did you know what to say to calm him down?" she asked.

"Papa had me trained early about hostage situations. Anyway, I know Zakhar. He worked with my father as a bodyguard."

Zakhar shouted something. Angelika countered with a string of words but quietly.

"He doesn't want us to say anything without my translating," Angelika said.

"What does he want? I assume it has to do with your stepmother."

Angelika translated and listened to a long stream of words.

"To make it short, he blames my stepmother for my father's murder. He thinks Moya had assassins waiting behind the theatre. You can guess what he wants to do to her. I won't translate that."

"Tell him that Moya's not here, that she left earlier this afternoon."

Angelika did so and then turned to Elspeth before Zakhar could speak again. "Do you know where she went?" Then she translated her question.

"No. She took a taxi but the doorman could not hear the destination. Does Zakhar plan to follow her? And does your stepmother speak Ukrainian?"

The man responded through Angelika. "He says he needs to talk to her. He wants to stay here until she returns. And to answer you, Moya speaks simple Ukrainian. She and Yuri used to spent time on the Crimean Sea and he made her learn enough to get around."

The man became impatient and pointed the gun back and forth between the two women.

"Tell him he can put the gun away," Elspeth said.

"He says he wants to stay here until Moya returns."

"Does he plan to hold us here as hostages?" Elspeth asked.

Angelika spoke to the man and obviously said more than a mere translation of Elspeth's question. The two exchanged words, heated ones on his side, calmer ones on hers. He shook his head back and forth. Finally she blew out her breath.

"He is not the smartest man in the world," she said, "but he is probably the most stubborn. He won't let us leave until Moya is back in the hotel and comes into this room."

"Would he allow me to go out to the lobby and make arrangements?" Elspeth asked. She knew this would mean leaving Angelika alone with the man but the last few minutes had shown that Angelika was tougher than Elspeth had previously thought. "Would you feel too uncomfortable if I was gone just for a few minutes?"

Elspeth knew this would leave Angelika as a hostage, but thought Angelika might be able to negotiate further with Zakhar or at least find a way to placate him until Moya returned. Elspeth's mind was racing. What resources did she have at the hotel to contain the damage Zakhar's gunshot had done? She had been so intent on subduing Zakhar that she had not noticed how many guests had witnessed the shooting or his holding up the receptionist and Sean Clancy. She also wondered what Sean had been doing while she and Angelika were in the conference room.

Zakhar said something that sounded like 'no' in Ukrainian. Angelika said something in an exasperated tone. A long dialogue ensued, he shaking his head and she reasoning. Elspeth watched them but could not tell if Angelika was making any headway.

A knock came at the door. Zakhar swung around and pointed the gun at the door. His shot shattered the inside of the door but Zakhar's move allowed Angelika to spring on him. She gave the back of his neck what to Elspeth looked like a rabbit punch. Zakhar fell to the floor.

"Papa would be pleased that my karate has paid off. He won't be up for a while," Angelika said pointing to Zakhar and dusting off her hands. She leaned over and picked up his gun. She blew the end of it, imitating Western films, and grinned. "Not bad for the future wife of a pastor," she said with a grin.

Elspeth stepped over Zakhar's body and opened the shattered door. The lobby beyond was empty. She stepped out through the door and called out. "Sean, are you there? Everything is under control here." But her voice wavered, which she had not expected, and her heart was pounding.

"Elspeth?" a meek voice said from the floor. Elspeth looked down at the prostrate body of Sean Clancy.

"He's been put out of action," Elspeth said. "We have his gun."

Sean rose and straightened his suit jacket. His forehead was glistening.

"What do we do now?" he said through a dry throat.

"Get the hotel doctor and clean up all the mess here in the lobby. I'm afraid the door will have to be replaced. Let's take Zakhar's body into the back. He's not dead and I'm not too sure how long he will be unconscious."

"Shall I call the guards?" Sean asked.

"No, not yet. How many people saw what just happened?"

"I had the front rooms cleared while you were in there," he said. "I explained that an unwanted person came in from the street but that we had the matter in hand. There were only three guests in the lobby and they seemed more frightened than interested. I had them taken into the dining room and we are giving them a cup of tea or a drink if they want one."

"Good. Perhaps you can go in now and tell them all is well."

"Is it?"

"Thanks to Ms Rostova," Elspeth conceded, "but she may be shaken up and I think we need to get Zakhar out of here as soon as possible and the damage cleaned up. I'll take her back to her room."

"Of course. I'll get the staff on it immediately. It may take a short while before we can replace the door, but the light bulb is easy."

"Get two of your strongest men to help with the body and then have maintenance wrap the door as quickly possible in some sort of shroud so that other guests entering the hotel don't see what happened to it. Let's get things back to normal as soon as possible. I want the doctor to sedate Zakhar. I'll go up with Ms Rostova to her room to see that she is all right. Put Zakhar in one of the old servant's rooms. And don't let the staff members leave him alone. Do you have any way to restrain him?"

"I'll find something," Sean said. "There may be straps in the laundry or the storeroom. Leave that to me."

*

From the meeting room Angelika Rostova watched Elspeth take command. Angelika was grateful because now that the crisis had passed, she felt nauseated and wanted to burst into tears. She looked down at the man and was relieved to see that he was breathing. The karate instructor had said the blow she had delivered could be lethal if delivered too hard. Her father had warned her many times that she could be taken hostage. Until now she had not believed him. Now that Papa was dead, would she finally see the end of all this violence? Much would depend on how he had disposed of his affairs. If she had been left a great deal of money, she would always have the threat of kidnapping.

Elspeth came back in the room and put her arm around Angelika's shoulders. Then the tears came. Angelika could feel the sobs shake her whole body. Never before had a woman like Elspeth just held her and let her weep, at least not since her mother had died. As Angelika cried herself out, she thought what Moya would have done. After all, this whole thing came back to Moya. Angelika's tears were soaked with anger.

"That bitch," she mumbled.

"Do you want to come back to my suite and talk about it?" Elspeth said, her voice low and calm.

"I want to go back to my room," Angelika said.

"Let me go with you. Perhaps Nancy will be there."

Angelika had forgotten her friend in the terror of the moment. What could she say to Nancy? And to Derek? How would he feel about someone who had karate chopped a man twice her size to render him senseless? Derek was such a gentle man. How could he understand the threat Angelika had been under all her life and might continue to be so? She wondered if Elspeth Duff would understand and might offer some counsel. Somehow she thought so.

"On second thought, I don't think it's time yet for Nancy to know what just happened. May I come to your suite?"

Elspeth took her arm with the softest of touches. "Of course," she said. "Anything that helps."

As they sat facing each other on the opposing sofas in Elspeth's suite, Angelika began pouring out her fear.

"After the breakup of the Soviet Union, my father became one of the new capitalists in Ukraine. He wanted to make as much money as possible because his great grandparents had been serfs under the old Tsar and his grandparents were driven into the factories. His parents were party hacks but that gave my father an advantage. He was raised in the Soviet system but because of his intelligence and ambition was able to attend engineering classes at the university in Kyiv. When Glasnost came, nothing could stop him. He turned his knowledge of the old state system of energy distribution into a multi-million dollar business, first with the Americans and later with the British. He married my mother, his second wife, when Gorbachev was beginning to free things up. She was much younger than he was, a teenager, and was very pretty I remember. But he quickly outgrew her. I so often wonder if her had her eliminated. He could have done it so simply considering the people he associated with. Sergei and I must have been an inconvenience, but could be shunted off to nannies and schools. Sergei went on to university, but wanted to study dramatic arts. Papa scoffed at him. Poor Sergei. He had to escape."

As Angelika poured this all out, Elspeth sat quietly and listened without interrupting. Her face was filled with kindness. Angelika wished Moya had been like Elspeth Duff. So many times Angelika had prayed to her mother and to the Virgin Mary, a kind woman who would have understood.

"My father sent me to a good boarding school in England when I was thirteen, right after Sergei left. I had some English, but struggled the first year. That's when I met Nancy and we have been fast friends ever since. After we finished school, Papa financed a gap year for both of us in Italy and then we went on to the Royal College of Art together, she to study fashion and me to study graphic design and photography. Papa insisted I do something practical and wanted me to come into his company to manage his advertising. Am I going on a bit, Ms Duff?"

Elspeth smiled. "Please call me Elspeth. No, right now I think you talking will help us both get over what happened downstairs."

"You must be married," Angelika said. "I see your rings."

"Twice," Elspeth said with a crooked smile. "Things don't always go right the first time." Angelika wondered why Elspeth said this.

"I hope everything goes well in my marriage to Derek," Angelika said. "He is so kind and gentle. After all that's gone on in my life, I need someone like that."

Elspeth's face brightened. "Would you like to invite him here? I can arrange a room for him."

"Could you? Oh, that would be super."

"My husband is flying over from London tomorrow morning on the hotel owner's plane. I'll see if I can arrange for Derek a lift with him. Can Derek come at such short notice?"

"Oh yes. I'm sure he can." Elspeth Duff could not have offered a better antidote.

"Do you feel well enough to return to your room now?" Elspeth asked.

"Yes, I think so."

"Then I'll see what arrangements I can make."

Angelika smiled, "And I'll see what story I can cook up for Nancy to make her feel safe here."

Elspeth gave Angelika a long hug before she left. The younger woman put her head on Elspeth's shoulder but did not speak.

*

Elspeth watched Angelika walk alone down the hall. Elspeth now had to deal with London. Eric Kennington's reaction could go either way. Elspeth had saved the day or she should have seen to it that the shootings did not happen. By this time, Sean Clancy would have filed a report with security in London. Had the report reached Eric or Pamela desk yet? And Elspeth was now about to propose that Derek Somerset be given a lift on Lord Kennington's private jet and a room in the hotel. Would they allow this after what just had happened?

Elspeth prided herself on not being faint of heart but she was feeling unsure of how best to broach the incident in the lobby with London. Damage control was in order for the guests who had seen the incident. Elspeth knew she would have no trouble with this. In the post nine-eleven world people, guests at the Kennington hotels expected strange things to happen even at hotels like the Kennington Dublin but the Kennington Organisation also wanted to have these events suppressed firmly and the guests placated. Elspeth hoped she had done the job of subduing Zakhar sufficiently but she could not predict Eric Kennington's reaction to the news.

Elspeth knew she had to deal with Zakhar downstairs but first she rang Pamela Crumm.

"Have you heard?" Elspeth asked.

"Security just called me. Are you all right, ducks?" her friend and employer said.

When Elspeth was done telling her, Pamela asked, "How are you going to handle Zakhar?"

"Will 'play it by ear' do? I haven't decided. We need to get him out of the hotel because he poses a real threat to

Moya Koda. I have had him sedated and put in one of the back rooms. But what worries me is that Moya said there were two 'goons'. Angelika may know who the other one is but he definitely is still at large. He may come in search of his colleague and I want to do everything to prevent that. How is Eric coping with the news?"

"He's away at the moment. Let's hope we can get this solved before he calls in. He's still tentative about your re-employment," Pamela said.

At this point, Elspeth too was wondering why she had agreed to come to the Kennington Dublin. Her wings had been clipped which hampered her proceeding full force to solving the mystery of Yuri's death and why Moya was so frightened, or at least pretending to be. Angelika had said she had seen Yuri strike Moya in the past. Was this reason enough for her apprehension now that Yuri was dead? Elspeth also wished she knew more about Yuri's business dealings and any involvement Moya had in them. Elspeth railed against not being allowed to contact the police. Working with them could be awkward but knowing the results of their investigations could be highly useful.

"Tell Eric that quiet has been restored here. Moya has gone out of the hotel this afternoon, which makes me think she is feeling more confident that any threat to her has lessened. Damn, I do wish she would tell me the truth of what happened on Saturday night."

"Elspeth, m'friend, I must go. Richard will be there tomorrow. Perhaps he can help."

Elspeth wanted to shout that she did not need Richard, but then had to admit that his cool head and loving heart could be an asset. She still had suspicions that Pamela was sending him for reasons other than an assignment from

Lord Kennington.

Elspeth made her way to the back rooms without having a solution for Zakhar's removal from the hotel. She felt her primary task was to see that he would not return but she also realised that he might have helpful information about what happened the evening that Yuri had been murdered.

She found Sean Clancy, who led her to one of the small rooms near the kitchens that were used for the servants of guests upstairs. Few people travelled with maids or valets these days but on occasion foreign dignitaries did have security or personal staff that did not warrant rooms upstairs. Each Kennington hotel had less expensive rooms near the working staff areas. Sean led Elspeth down a hallway near the staff break room. Two large men, one in a chef's hat, were standing outside; they looked rather lost. Obviously playing guard was not one of their usual duties.

Just as they arrived, an older man with the look of authority came out of the guarded room. Sean introduced the doctor who was on call for the hotels.

"Is he conscious?" Elspeth asked pointing to the door to the room.

"I've given him a sedative, which has made him groggy but won't harm him. Right now he seems a bit confused about where he is. I expect in an hour or so, he will regain full consciousness. He had a nasty blow to his neck. Evidence of the bruising has begun. He will be stiff for a long time to come. Whoever hit him knew what he was doing."

Elspeth did not bother to correct the doctor's assumption that the assailant had been a man.

"Has he been restrained?" Elspeth asked Sean. "He may still be dangerous."

"I was afraid to do so. We are open to human rights abuses at every turn. I think we can justify medicating him, saying it was necessary for his injuries, but don't want him making a protest about being treated badly."

"Hasn't the world changed?" Elspeth said with a sigh. "Criminals have more rights these days than normal citizens but I know, Sean, this is always a concern. Let me take care of it."

Sean looked relieved. "Thanks," he said and blew out his breath. "I haven't had anything like this happen in my hotel before. Is this something you deal with all the time?"

Elspeth grinned. "This is my first time too but I'll think of something."

She went into the room cautiously after asking Sean and one of the hardy hotel staff members at the door to come with her. Zakhar was sprawled on the bed. He raised his head slightly at the disturbance and looked at Elspeth uncomprehendingly.

He croaked out some words that Elspeth did not understand but they sounded like some sort of an appeal.

All staff members at Kennington hotels were required to speak English, the language or languages of the country where the hotel was located and one other language. This way guests from all over Europe, Asia, Australia and the Americas could visit a Kennington hotel and be assured that there was someone on the staff at every shift who could translate their needs. French, German, Spanish, Arabic, Dutch, the Scandinavian languages, Russian and

Turkish speaking staff were recruited when possible. Others spoke Chinese, Japanese, Thai, Malay and Korean. Eric Kennington had set up a system for guests from around the world. There also was a 24-hour hotline to London where translators for fifty other languages could be accessed. The only language they were unprepared for three years before had been Mongolian but that error was corrected by the next morning. The Kennington Organisation catered to the affluent from anywhere in the world. But could the help line cater to a Ukrainian speaking thug?

"Sean, can we get the translation service on the phone down here?"

"I can try," he said.

"The doctor said we have as much as an hour. Please set up something so we can talk to Zakhar once he is fully awake. I don't want to involve Angelika Rostova again. She may have been calm when she struck Zakhar but she's shaken. Is there anyone else who can guard the room? I think your chef may need to return to his duties."

"Let me handle that," Sean replied.

As she walked out of the room, Elspeth's mobile buzzed in her pocket. Harry O'Shea was on the line.

"She's back," he said, "and she doesn't look good."

9

When Elspeth finally saw Moya, she indeed did not look well.

After Elspeth took the call in the basement of the hotel, she took the lift to the second floor and knocked at the door to Moya's suite.

"Moya, it's Elspeth," she called through the door. Doors to rooms at the Kennington hotels were heavily padded for sound control but Elspeth hoped she could be heard. She waited. Nothing.

"Moya, may I come in and see you?"

She heard a noise on the other side of the door. Faintly she could hear a voice say, "Go away."

"I want to help," Elspeth called.

Again "Go away."

"I will for now," she called back, "but I do want to help in any way I can."

Elspeth made her way back down to the main entry of the hotel where Harry O'Shea was standing. He was tucked into his alcove outside by the front door. Despite the warmth of the day, a cool wind had come up and rain threatened. Elspeth pulled her suit jacket tightly around herself and ventured out under the portico that sheltered the hotel entrance. Harry came out to greet her.

"Tell me about Mrs Koda," she said.

"She tried to hide it under her sunglasses but her cheek was badly bruised. She held a handkerchief up to it but I could see that she was badly hurt. It looked like someone had struck her with something sharp. I asked if I could call a doctor but she brushed by me and told me to mind my own business. She looked bad."

Elspeth blew out her breath. From Harry's earlier description, Moya had not just gone out earlier for a peaceful stroll. Who had attacked her? One of Yuri's goons was incapacitated downstairs. That left the other. Zakhar had said he was looking for Moya when he came in the hotel. Wouldn't that mean that his partner would think Moya was inside as well? If it was not one of the goons who had accosted Moya, who had?

Elspeth hurried back to Moya's suite. Elspeth knew she could let herself in with the hotel passkey but she hoped she did not have to resort to that. This time she banged on the door as loudly as she could. An eye came to the peephole.

"Moya, you must let me in."

"Go away."

"No, I won't. What just happened to you is too serious for me to ignore it."

After along moment, Elspeth heard the security latch being loosened from its fitting. Moya cracked the door.

"Let me in Moya. I'm here to protect you and I can't unless you talk to me."

Moya said nothing but the door opened. Elspeth made her way in, although Moya had fled to the far end of the sitting room of the suite. Her back was to Elspeth.

"The doorman told me you had injured your face," Elspeth said. "May I ring a doctor? We have one on call. He was here a minute ago on another case."

"No doctors," Moya said without turning around.

"What happened?" Elspeth asked, feeling a direct approach was best but knew Moya's proclivity for lying.

"I fell," Moya said.

"Are you sure?" Elspeth countered. "May I see?"

"No."

"I can't protect you if you won't let me. Eric Kennington told me you two were old friends and particularly sent me here to see you came to no harm. But it seems you have."

"It has nothing to do with the hotel."

"But did it have anything to do with Yuri's murder?"

"If you must know, his two goons set on me. I shouldn't have gone out but I felt so cooped up. I thought they would have left Dublin by now and I wouldn't have to worry if I went out for a walk," Moya said. She still did not turn to face Elspeth.

But, thought Elspeth, one of the goons is downstairs sedated. She was not going tell Moya this.

"May I see what they did?" Elspeth asked instead.

Moya turned around and Elspeth drew in her breath. A bruise was developing across her cheek just below her right eye. The blow must have hurt.

"You must see a doctor," Elspeth said.

"It's just a superficial wound. I stabbed them with my umbrella and was able to get away."

Harry O'Shea had not mentioned that Moya was carrying an umbrella when she left the hotel, only the small attaché case.

"Then let me help you," Elspeth said. "I've studied first aid and there's a kit in every room tucked away in the bathroom. I promise I'll be gentle."

With Moya's consent, Elspeth recovered the first aid kit from the back of the medicine cabinet and took out some clean cotton wool and antiseptic. Carefully she daubed Moya's wound. Moya winced but did not cry out.

Elspeth was able to examine the wound at close range. The bruise was uneven. Elspeth tried to think what could have made such a wound. The only plausible thing was a chain but such a heavy weapon easily could have broken Moya's cheekbone. Elspeth touched it and Moya writhed.

"Moya, they may have broken a cheekbone. Please agree to see a doctor. I assure you he will be discreet."

"Can you assure me he won't contact the Garda? Don't doctors have an obligation to do so?"

"I can ask if he has to," Elspeth said, "and I also can ask him not to. Let me ring down to the front desk and see if he still is here."

Elspeth spoke quietly into her mobile but knowing Moya was listening, she asked Sean to speak to the doctor and get back to her.

When he arrived, the doctor promised that he would invoke doctor-patient privilege and as a result Moya consented to his coming to see her face. Elspeth stood close by as the doctor examined Moya.

The doctor's skilled hands probed Moya's cheek.

"You are lucky to have escaped any injury to your bone," he said. "Did you black out when it happened? You may have suffered a concussion."

"No, I don't think so," Moya said.

"You must be careful how you move your face until the bruise has healed. I don't think a bone is broken but you should have your skull x-rayed. After I've finished, I want to speak to you, Ms Duff. In the meantime, I think time will heal your guest's face most efficiently."

Elspeth followed the doctor into the hallway.

"Ms Duff, I retired from the full time practice of medicine some years ago and appreciate the limited practice I have tending the Kennington Dublin guests but I never have been called here before to attend to acts of violence. Perhaps you can assuage my curiosity. I assure you I will repeat nothing. Did this happen in the hotel?"

"No, it didn't," Elspeth said. "But it was the reason I was sent here. I pray this is the last of the violence."

Her mobile rang and Richard was on the other end of the call. Elspeth thought guiltily that she hadn't called Pamela and made arrangements to have Derek Somerset come to Dublin with Richard the next morning.

"Elspeth, my dearest, I trust all is well in Dublin. My flight is scheduled for nine in the morning so I think I should be at the hotel for an early lunch. Will you join me?"

Elspeth paused. "I hope so. Several things have come up here and therefore I can't commit definitely."

"Why might I have guessed that Eric Kennington called you back to handle a situation where things come up?" he said with a chuckle. "Have you talked to Pamela about my coming?"

"I have," Elspeth said. "I'm looking forward to your being here," she added.

"This time you may be able to help me," Richard said. "Even I must admit that the world has changed, as much as I wish it hadn't. I'm not sure I can give Eric any sound advice but I'll try. You can tell me what is happening there when I arrive."

"Yes, of course," Elspeth said.

"I'm sure you have everything well in hand. I'll see you in the morning."

"I'll have Harry O'Shea ring me when you arrive. Hopefully we can have that early lunch."

Richard's call reminded her that she had business with Pamela that could not be put off any longer. She must arrange for Derek Somerset to join Richard.

10

Richard had not expected to have a fellow passenger, but was delighted that he would have the company of a university student on the short flight from the private airstrip outside London to a similar one outside Dublin. Throughout his later career, Richard had sponsored young men and women in the Foreign and Commonwealth Office but he never before had a chance to talk to someone reading divinity at university.

After Derek Somerset expressed his awe at being in a corporate jet and his initial excitement at take-off, he settled in and turned to Richard.

"Do you fly like this often?" Derek asked.

"My wife does but I less frequently. Towards the end of my career in the diplomatic service, the FCO had become penny pinching and we flew less luxuriously than when I first joined the service. Times change and I've had to change with them."

"You sound regretful."

"In many ways I am. I miss the courtesy and formality of the old days, but tell me about why you chose to study divinity. It is not a common calling these days."

"Like you, I prefer life at is used to be. My parents imagine me to become the Archbishop of Canterbury but honestly I want to be a country parson and live in a village where I can care for a flock. These days the congregation will probably be mainly grey-hairs but tending to the elderly appeals to me and has always been my dream."

"Do you have parsons in your family?" Richard asked.

Derek laughed. "No, my father is a stockbroker and my mother was a fashion model before she married. Now she styles herself as a great hostess. Perhaps that's why I am choosing a simpler way to live, one of service and not greed or pretence. Having been raised where profit and prestige are the sole purpose for living, I want just the opposite. Do you think I'm running away? I see so many people, young, middle-aged and old, being squeezed out by the money mongers, one of whom is my father."

Richard wondered how long Derek's idealism would last. In Richard's day, peace rallies had been the thing, although as a junior member of the FCO he had never participated in one. The hippies of the time were now mundane members of society, weighed down by children, mortgages, car payments for their BMWs and pension schemes. Where Derek would be in thirty years' time? Richard doubted Derek would be occupying Lambeth Palace. Derek struck him as someone who might be happy for the rest of his life in a small and beautiful village in Gloucestershire. Derek's mild manner appealed to Richard, who had spent too many years of his career working with grasping world leaders and self-promoting politicians.

"My wife tells me you are visiting your fiancée at the Kennington Dublin," Richard said.

Derek beamed. "Her name is Angelika Rostova. She's my first convert," Derek said with a grin. "She's had an awfully rough life and now her father's been murdered. Have you read about it? Yuri Koda was her father. She hates everything he stood for, just as I hate my parents' lifestyle."

Richard cleared his throat and tried to look sympathetic.

"Have you stayed at a Kennington hotel before?" he asked.

Derek shook his head and swallowed, which made Richard notice the small but distinct Adam's apple bobbing on Derek's thin neck above the collar of his pullover. Richard tried not to think that this feature and Derek's thinning, short-cut hair and small chin were stereotypical of a young curate. Richard had been raised in the Scottish Episcopal Church and remembered several young men, now probably retired from high position, who could have been clones of Derek Somerset.

"You may find the hotel grand," Richard said. "They cater to the sort of person you seem to disdain."

"Angie only went there because her father and stepmother insisted and I'm only going to support Angie. From what Angie tells me, her stepmother is overbearing and not one to counter. As soon as we are married, I'll make sure Angie is protected from her."

Richard smiled at the young man's protestations.

"I'm employed by the Kennington Organisation to do a survey of the guests. I'll be interested in what you think once you have stayed there. Shall we stay in touch?"

*

Derek drew back into the confines of the limousine that had brought them to the Kennington Dublin. A bright red cordon held back a row of photographers and news cameramen on the other side of the street from the hotel. As the car approached the hotel entrance, multiple flashes went off and Derek was blinded.

"What's this?" he whispered to Sir Richard.

"Take no notice," Richard said. "They must have discovered Angelika's stepmother is staying here. One of my wife's jobs is to subdue the press when they gather outside. I suspect the barrier is her idea. She probably has been out earlier promising them a press conference if they will not converge on the entrance. Unfortunately the media these days are ruthless and often unruly."

How, wondered Derek, could one not take notice? He abhorred aggression of all sorts and never read the lowbrow press. He did not want to think what impact this was having on Angie. She had mentioned press attention before but he had never experienced it first-hand. He must get her away from this.

A doorman in full livery opened the door of the limousine and addressed them.

"Welcome to the Kennington Dublin, Sir Richard and Mr Somerset. I apologise for the commotion across the road. They make a lot of noise but on the whole they are just doing their job. If you must blame someone for the disturbance, blame those that read their papers. They won't harm you because I've threatened them with the Garda if they do. Sir Richard, your wife has them in hand but she said she couldn't come down and meet you just yet. Please step inside."

Derek blanched. Would Angelika come and greet him? He did not want her exposed to this. She was a gentle, kind creature and he wanted to protect her.

"Does this happen often?" he asked Sir Richard.

"When there's a problem, yes. Your fiancée's father's murder is international news so the bloodhounds are after anything they can get. My wife told me last evening that the paparazzi had not yet found Mrs Koda here at the hotel but things must have changed. Ignore them and follow me. Above all keep your face turned away so that they don't associate you with the Kodas."

"How long will this go on?"

"Until there is some other news that catches the attention of their readership or until my wife convinces them that there is no story here. But come along inside. We should find things peaceful there." Sir Richard turned to the doorman. "Will you call ahead and tell Ms Rostova that Mr Somerset is here?"

Derek had travelled on the Continent during his gap year but he could not believe the difference in reception between the Kennington Dublin and the hostels where he had stayed. Here was the excess he so opposed and yet for the moment he was grateful for the hotel's protection. Poor Angelika, to be subjected to this.

*

Nancy Kendall picked up the house phone in their room and shouted out to Angelika. "He's here!" Secretly she thought Derek a bit of a wet blanket but after experiencing a small slice of Angelika's life, she was beginning to understand why the prospect of a life in the English countryside as Derek's wife might appeal to her friend. Nancy would find it dull. She was certain that her career as a fashion designer in London was her destiny, far from the drudgery of a parson's unpaid helpmate.

She did not expect Angelika's reaction. Angelika groaned. "When Ms Duff suggested Derek come, I hadn't thought things out. Now Derek would have to meet Moya and I feel disaster is on the way. *Pauvre* Derek."

"Ms Duff must have gone out of her way to get Derek

here so quickly. You can't be ungrateful now."

Angelika answered, "Can't I? All my life I've been told what's good for me and now Ms Duff has taken up the cause."

"Don't you want to see Derek?"

"Yes, of course, but no, not really. What will he make of all this?"

"His mother and father are well off."

"But not up to Kennington hotel standards. I've never told Derek how wealthy my father was or how wealthy I might be someday soon. He'll be put off."

"Angie, try him."

"I suppose I must. This isn't going to be easy."

*

Elspeth Duff confronted Moya Koda. "Now that the press has found you, I need to work with you, your stepdaughter and her friend to keep you all out of their clutches. From past experience I know several of the more aggressive ones will try to get into the hotel." she said. "I have made provisions for all the entries and exits to have a guard at them and I'm to be called if any disturbance happens."

Moya sighed but nodded her head.

"I'm calling a staff meeting after we have finished talking to make sure none of the staff inadvertently lets one of the reporters in." Elspeth continued. "These days the media will go to great lengths to get a jump on their competitors. In my many cases with the hotel, I am always amazed and sometimes amused at the ruses they dig up to get at their prey."

"Will they come up here?" Moya said.

"It's highly unlikely. The hall staff and the hotel people in the public rooms are on alert. All the room attendants have been given their orders to report anything unusual."

"Do you have this problem often?"

"Often enough to be prepared for it. However, I urge you not to worry."

For the first time Elspeth could see fear, not hostility, in Moya's eyes.

"They want to get me," she said. "Yuri's goons or their ilk."

"I won't let them as long as you stay in the hotel. But I suggest that you begin to make plans to leave Dublin. I can arrange for your exit from the hotel to be secret. We have ways in and out of the hotel that will allow you to get away without notice."

"From the Garda as well as the press?"

"The guards have not returned to the hotel after their initial approach to you, have they?"

"I told them I would call them. I never did."

Elspeth raised a questioning eyebrow.

"Yuri taught me that technique. Don't contact the police for any reason. In any case, I can't see them like this," she said, touching her battered face. The areas surrounding her eyes had changed to amber from purple.

"Moya, I want to help you out of here. Do you have anywhere you can go and take the girls where you cannot be found?"

"I suppose my father and his friends can shelter me."

"Is his estate far from here?"

"About a hundred kilometres. An hour and a half or two hour's drive depending on traffic."

"If we can you get a vehicle to take you out of the hotel, will you go?" Elspeth was praying Moya would consent.

"Vehicle?"

"It might not be a car. We have vans that come into and out of the hotel every day. The transport may be uncomfortable but it will be secure."

"Can you guarantee that?"

Elspeth damped down her frustration. "Reasonably well. Such methods have worked well in the past."

"I feel protected here in the hotel, particularly now that you have set up precautions," Moya said.

Damn, Elspeth thought. Since Eric Kennington had restricted her to the hotel, she hoped that Moya would depart and the Kennington hotels would be absolved of any further responsibility for her safety. Then she remembered that Pamela had told her that Eric's relationship with Moya might be more than friendship. Elspeth resolved that this woman would not defeat her.

"Let me know what you decide," Elspeth said. "I need to get downstairs and make sure my plans are fully in place."

*

Richard watched Elspeth come out of the lift. She was shaking her head and muttering to herself, which Richard knew was a bad sign. But when she looked up and saw him, a broad smile crossed her face but she came across the lobby without hurry to greet him. They had agreed long ago that when they met in the public rooms of any of the hotels their greeting would be subdued but

Richard knew from the way Elspeth squeezed his hand that she was not happy.

Richard introduced Derek Somerset to Elspeth, using her professional name. Elspeth did not use the title which being his wife allowed her to do but Richard had told Derek of their relationship.

Richard watched Elspeth shift into her role as a highly placed Kennington Organisation employee.

"Welcome. Mr Somerset. I'm glad we could arrange for you to be here. Ms Rostova will be pleased by your arrival. Let me ring her room and tell her you have arrived. The porter will take your bag to your room. Please sign in at the reception desk. They will provide you with anything you need."

When Derek moved off, Elspeth spoke softly to Richard. "I have a meeting now, which should take about twenty minutes. Meet me in our suite. I'm so glad you are here."

Elspeth was good to her word. Soon afterwards, she arrived with room service in tow.

"I've ordered our early lunch for us so that we can talk without being overheard," she said.

As they settled over the table the waiter had set up for them and after Elspeth had dismissed the waiter, Richard looked up at his wife. He thought carefully before he spoke.

"Are you glad to be back at work?" he said as blandly as he could.

Elspeth set her jaw. "Things are being difficult but if they weren't, Eric wouldn't have sent me." She paused.

Richard had become accustomed to his wife's

evasions when she did not want to tell him something she thought he did not want to hear. Richard could sense that Elspeth was not totally happy about returning to her job.

Elspeth blew here breath through her pressed lips. "I'm sorry I was so deceptive about all this," she said. "I was so tempted when Eric told me about this assignment and, oh dear, Dickie, I was so bored in Scotland."

"Is your return as good as you thought it would be?"

She averted her eyes and busied herself cutting her chicken. She chewed with consideration before answering.

"The challenge is always exciting. Oh damn. The truth is I don't like the person I've been sent to protect. I haven't seen many of the other guests except from afar but they strike me as being . . . unrefined. Even five years ago guests seemed more mannerly. Perhaps it's that dress conventions have changed but I think it's something more. The Kennington hotels have lost their exclusive quality."

"Exactly, my dear. You aren't the only one to notice. In fact, the real reason I am here is that Eric and Pamela have echoed your concern."

"What's to be done?" Elspeth asked.

"My task is to find out why this is happening and then recommend changes. The Kennington Organisation insisted on paying me to do so but I only would accept one pound in compensation other than my chance to be with you. Did you really find Scotland that dull?"

"Perhaps I hadn't found my place there," she said but he suspected she was not being honest.

"And perhaps you aren't finding this assignment as stimulating as some earlier ones."

She laughed. "No, despite the death of Yuri Koda and

the disagreeable personality of his wife, things here at the hotel are dreadfully routine."

"What you need is a good murder," he said, raising an eyebrow.

"If things go on the way they are," she said, "I may murder Moya Koda."

Later he wondered if she regretted saying this.

11

The ringing of Elspeth's mobile interrupted them just as they were about to sample the strawberries with Irish cream.

"A man is down here and has asked to speak to security. He's just checked in and he says he's not from the press," the concierge said. Elspeth thought he had his hand cupped over his mobile. "Do you want to speak to him? He looks genuine but nowadays one never can tell."

Elspeth wrinkled up her face at Richard. He grinned.

"Yes, I'll talk to him. Put him in the small conference room that has an intact door. I'll be right down," Elspeth said. To Richard she said, "Another pudding to be missed. That seems to be my lot here in Dublin."

"I'll eat both for you," he said with a wink.

When she reached the lobby, the concierge was with a middle-aged woman guest in a tank top that exposed a wrinkled cleavage and, to Elspeth's taste, too much bling. Elspeth turned away in disgust. The concierge twisted his eyes towards the conference room. Elspeth nodded and made her way to the room with the undamaged door. In passing she noted that a workman was already in the process of refitting a door and frame, victim of Zakhar's gunshot.

She had expected a middle-aged man in a business suit but was surprised to find a younger man in khaki chinos, an open necked but crisp white shirt, dark blazer and highly polished brown tassel moccasins. His brown hair was cut in a short, trendy European manner and he wore glasses with almost invisible wire frames. Elspeth guessed his age at about thirty, close to the age of her own son. His briefcase lay open on the table in the room and he looked up from it as Elspeth entered.

The man looked puzzled when he saw Elspeth.

"I am Lars Inversen," he said. "I had hoped to speak to someone in security." His English was practically flawless, but Elspeth, who was highly attuned to the accents of the world, detected a hint of Scandinavian in it.

She held out her hand, "I am Elspeth Duff and work as a security advisor to the Kennington hotel chain. May I be of help?"

The man did not look like a reporter. Elspeth had checked at the reception desk before coming into the conference room and the receptionist had assured her that Mr Inversen's platinum credit card was valid. He had booked in for a four-night stay in a twelve hundred euros a night room, and the tariff was pre-paid. If he were from the press, his editors must think the scoop worth the cost.

Lars reached in his briefcase and brought out a letter with an impressive letterhead.

"I am from a detective agency in Paris and represent a branch of the Russian Romanov family. Here are my credentials. I assure you they are real."

Elspeth took the papers and skimmed over them. Although they appeared to be genuine, she said, "May I have a copy of these to read in more depth?"

"I have a copy here for you. I also have forwarded a duplicate to Lord Kennington in London."

She thanked him, glad that Eric would know.

"We have worked with your organisation before. You

are welcome to verify this with Ms Crumm."

"I will of course," Elspeth said. "Now tell me why you are here."

"Just over a year ago, jewels belonging to our clients were stolen from an auction house, Northby's in London, and my clients are anxious to find their whereabouts and have them returned. We have been working with Scotland Yard and Interpol since the jewels disappeared. My clients always suspected that one of Northby's staff facilitated the theft. Most of the suspicion fell on a woman called Moya Mulholland, who was employed by them, and her new husband Yuri Koda. At the time of the robbery she had just married Mr Koda and was staying with him in his mansion on the Black Sea, far away from London, but my clients always felt that she was behind the theft. On Sunday, when his murder was splashed across the news, my clients asked me to follow up to see if the murder had anything to do with the disappearance of the Romanov's property." He smiled a boyish smile and added, "They said no expenses spared."

If Pamela Crumm had not told Elspeth about the robbery earlier, she might have been more cautious, but between Lars Inversen's impressive credentials and his sincere face, she was inclined to believe him. She was relying on her skill in assessing people on their first meeting.

"I'll have to confirm all this with London," Elspeth hedged. "Normally we don't give out information about our guests. What made you believe Mrs Koda was here?"

"I called all the five star hotels in Dublin. All of them denied Moya Koda was a guest but your receptionist said she would take a message but could not confirm that Mrs Koda was staying here."

Elspeth frowned. Receptionists and telephone operators were instructed to be more evasive. Sean Clancy would have to know about the breach. But the harm was done and Elspeth needed to find a way to heal it. She would not confirm Moya's stay to Lars before she had direct instructions from Pamela to do so. Elspeth had developed a keen sense of people's honesty over the years of her employment. She was inclined to trust Lars Inversen but she had no intentions of overstepping her boundaries whilst on this case.

Elspeth consequently sidestepped Lars's request.

"Have you had lunch, Mr Inversen? If not, I suggest you try the lunch buffet that is served in the dining room off the lobby. I recommend the strawberries with Irish cream for dessert. I'll check with London and get back to you as soon as I can."

Half an hour later, Elspeth found Lars in the dining room with a light smear of cream on his chin and a smile on his lips.

"Were the strawberries good?" Elspeth asked, regretting that her recommendation had not been from first-hand experience.

"The best I ever ate," he said, wiping his face with his napkin.

"London has confirmed your request," Elspeth said, but I would like to talk to you somewhere where we can speak in confidence. I'll give you some time to settle in. I'll meet you in the lobby in an hour."

Elspeth needed time to plan her own strategy in

dealing with Moya. If Moya was indeed involved in the theft, her desire to stay at the hotel may have had implications beyond the murder of her husband and her desire avoid the police. Lars's suspicions might explain Moya's furtive movements since the time of the murder of her husband.

Ever since she had arrived in Dublin, Elspeth had been feeling the need for an ally. Now she had one, someone who could do legwork outside the hotel. Shamelessly she decided she would cultivate Lars.

Once Elspeth and Lars Iversen were settled in the small meeting room, Elspeth said, "Ms Crumm has approved my telling you that Mrs Koda is a guest here but for the moment I want you to agree to keeping that under wraps. I do not want Moya to know you are here and why. You can funnel any questions or concerns through me but above all I do not want you to approach her directly."

"My goal is to find out the truth," he said, "by any means necessary so I agree to your terms."

"Tell me what your plans are and let's see if we can find a way to facilitate them."

"We think Moya Koda may still have the jewels, because we cannot find any record of a sale or transfer, even using all our underworld contacts."

"Do you think that Yuri Koda had them stolen to give as a gift to his wife?"

"That's a possibility. Or he had them stolen and then they were too hot to pass on. Most of the jewellery could be broken down, but some of the gems would lose most of their value if disassembled. The Romanovs think the larger stones at least must be intact but they also hope that the original settings have not been destroyed, as much for family reasons as for their monetary value. The pieces are a reminder of the greatness of the Romanov dynasty. For financial reasons at the time, our clients wanted to sell them last year but my clients have recovered from their difficulties recently and want to get the items back. They have given me authorisation to offer a substantial reward."

"You sound as if you think Moya Koda has them."

"Let's just say there is a good chance she does because once they disappeared from the auction house, they never have surfaced again, intact or otherwise. I think I told you that."

"I'll be honest with you, Mr Inversen. My job here is to protect the guests who stay in the hotel from harm. Mrs Koda had suffered a great deal from the murder of her husband and has gone into seclusion. I have been able to see her but she will see no one else. In any case, if she is responsible for the theft or even in collusion in the crime, I don't think she would tell me or you."

"I have found in my career as a private investigator," Lars Inversen said, 'that it's often productive to stay still and watch your suspect. That is why I have booked in for four days. I plan to stay in the public rooms of the hotel and watch. I hope that is all right with you."

"Guests of course are allowed access to all the public spaces at any time of the day."

"Would you be willing to tell me if Mrs Koda moves from her room?"

"So that you may follow her?"

"Yes. I am good at my job. She won't know."

"Will you let me think about that?"

He nodded. "I know what she looks like, so will have no trouble recognising her, even if you don't warn me," he said with a smile.

Elspeth had to decide rapidly. If she were to get Lars's cooperation, she would need to give him something back. She was here to protect Moya, Angelika and Nancy Kendall as well as the other guests at the hotel. But what harm would Lars do by following them. In fact, Elspeth thought, it might help her ferret out why Moya was acting the way she was. Still she needed to be cautious about giving Lars too much latitude.

"If you could talk to her, what would you ask?" Elspeth said.

"I've found as a young man I have certain advantages with older women. I'd approach her casually and admire some piece of jewellery she was wearing. I would carefully turn the conversation around to famous jewels and then wait to see her reaction. She, of course, is a leading authority on the gems acquired by the late Romanov tsars. I'd try to get her to admit that to me. I might even pose as someone interested in the stolen items. Depending on how the conversation went, I could imply that I might like to buy them if they ever came up for sale. We now live in a world where people my age have a lot of expendable income and not too many morals when it comes to acquiring what we want. I could claim a girlfriend or fiancée who had a taste for old things, particularly fine gems."

"You sound as if you had used this type of persuasion before."

He grinned. "I have."

"Successfully?"

He grinned further but did not respond.

"Lars, I don't think Moya Koda will come out of her suite. She has been holed up there since the murder, and has only gone out of the hotel once since then. She won't let anyone but me, her stepdaughter, her friend and room service see her. I doubt she will venture into the public areas of the hotel."

"Stepdaughter? That must be Angelika Rostova. Is she here?"

Elspeth berated herself for letting slip that Angelika was here. How could she cover her mistake? She decided to take direct action.

"I doubt Angelika knows anything about the Romanov jewels," she said. "But she might help you. I suggest rather than using your charms on Moya, if I can get her to meet you, you try to talk to Angelika. She is in a strange sort of mood. I should warn you that her fiancé is here with her, so flirtation won't work on her. Let me suggest this, however. My husband, who also works for the Kennington Organisation, is here with me. We will be dining at seven in the main dining room. Join us. I can make appropriate introductions and will leave the rest to you. But, Lars, let me tell you. I run a very tight operation when I am on a case at a Kennington hotel. I'll call you on any misdeed I see you committing. Are you willing to follow my direction?"

"Absolutely," he answered. "I seldom get such full cooperation."

Elspeth laughed. "There's a price."

"What's that?"

"First, you must tell me anything you learn. Second, you must in no way harm any guest here, physically or psychologically. I am willing to help you with finding your treasure but not at the cost of danger to anyone one here."

"I assure you I never use methods which will hurt, as you say, physically or psychologically. I don't carry a weapon other than my tongue and my brain."

"I'm trusting you, Lars, largely because Pamela Crumm speaks so highly of your organisation. Please don't let me down."

When Richard heard about Lars, he was less inclined to go along with Elspeth's plan.

"Are you sure of him, Elspeth, other than through intuition?"

"No. I'll admit I'm not but how often does my intuition prove correct?"

He touched her cheek. "Far too often, my witch," he said.

"Dickie, I know you're here for a totally different reason than protecting Moya Koda but I think you can help me with her situation. I'm still on probation."

"And you want to keep your job?" he asked with a raised eyebrow.

She blew out her breath. "You know I do and not just because of Eric Kennington's devious ways of persuading me to come back."

"Because you love the convolutions of a case. The absurdities and mysteries? And you love to use your good brain to outwit any malfeasance?"

"You know me too well. Surely, my dear Dickie, we can find a way to share your retirement and my job? I don't work nine to five. I can arrange with Eric and Pamela to have plenty of time off and be in Scotland."

He knew in his heart that Elspeth loved him but that she would never be happy without the stimulation her job offered. At times he missed his own diplomatic career. He had retired once before, when his first wife died, but could not stay away from returning to it. He had accepted the relatively quiet post of British High Commissioner in Malta and as a result, had reconnected with Elspeth. In the process he had fallen in love with her all over again. He realised he wanted Elspeth to be a different person, one with whom one could be more comfortable, but he also had accepted that he could not change her. Their marriage was the most precious thing in his life and he was not about to jeopardise it because she needed her job for her own personal sustenance.

"Elspeth, so many times I have seen you be right but do you really think Lars is legitimate?"

"Pamela vouches for the agency he works for."

"For him personally?"

"She didn't know him but she checked with the agency before she approved me telling him Moya was here. I'm not going to let him have access to Moya in her suite and I'm sure she won't venture out from there."

"And Angelika and Nancy? You seem to be throwing them at Lars."

"Derek Somerset will protect them both."

"He's not a hearty specimen," Richard said. "Not the sort to defend the two young women if they are threatened. I have this vision of Derek trying to reason with a psychopathic killer and telling him to lay down his arms for the sake of Jesus Christ his saviour and to pray for forgiveness."

"You are not normally so unkind, Dickie. What prompted this?"

"Years of experience with young people. Derek will make an excellent pastor but I suspect he is not a man who knows how to handle violence."

"Meaning you think there will be violence?"

"Hasn't there been already?"

"Outside the hotel and an incident earlier in the lobby," Elspeth said. "Part of me thinks that if Moya can keep to her suite, she will be OK. Another part of me wants her to be out of the hotel as quickly as possible. I've told her I can facilitate her leaving in any way I can."

"Did she accept your offer?"

"She said she would consider it but that she felt safe here. I'll begin to make plans just in case. But I need to go downstairs and see if Zakhar has left. I'll continue to feel uneasy as long as he is in the hotel."

Elspeth decided first to check the lobby to see that all was quiet there and that the repairs to the door and the light had been finished.

A workman was clearing away his tools from the door and the light fixture had been restored. Elspeth was looking up to see if any sign of the gunshot remained in the ceiling, and finding none looked back over the lobby.

As she looked down, a large man was approaching with his finger to his lips. She blinked.

"Eric?" she said in a whisper.

"Eric Smith, Ms Duff. You must remember me. We met in London a while ago."

Elspeth could hardly believe what she was seeing. Eric, Lord Kennington was not a man one easily forgot, particularly if one had worked for him for ten years. Elspeth never had seen him out of a business suit before but even his casual knitted shirt, relaxed corduroys, cotton cardigan and flat cap did not hide his identity.

"Er, ah, yes, of course. Welcome to the Kennington Dublin, Mr Smith," she said loudly enough for anyone nearby to hear. Under her breath she said, "What are you doing here, Eric?"

"I've come to see Dublin," he responded loudly. "I hear it's a lovely city." He added more softly, "We need to talk."

Guilt fled through Elspeth. Had she made some dreadful mistake that had brought Eric from London? But why the 'Eric Smith'? Was she being too fast to judge the reason for his visit? Pamela had said he often visited the hotels incognito. Was this simply one of those times?

"It's so nice to see you again. Mr Smith. Why not come and have tea with me and my husband in our rooms once you are settled in? We can catch up since I last saw you."

"I should like that," he said. "Shall we say in half an hour?"

Elspeth retreated into the security office and first rang Richard to warn him about Eric's arrival and imminent tea and then called Sean Clancy.

Elspeth wanted to see if Eric's visit was expected. "I have just met an old acquaintance in the lobby, Eric Smith. Do you know him?"

"No. He isn't in our registration system. He booked late last night on the internet and arrived fifteen minutes ago by taxi. I've had the booking department put him in one of the smaller rooms. He made no objection."

So Eric Kennington's arrival was not planned until the evening before, or so it seemed.

Elspeth next dialled Pamela Crumm's private line.

"Hello, ducks," Pamela said. "What's up in Dublin?"

"Don't you know?" Elspeth asked.

"Other than what you have told me and the daily log from Sean Clancy, I know nothing."

"Eric?" Elspeth asked.

"He's gone for a short break for a few days."

"Did he say where he was going?"

"Elspeth, m'friend, you know I never talk about Eric's personal life."

"Did you know he was coming here to Dublin?"

A long silence ensued on Pamela's side of the connection. Elspeth could not think what it meant.

Finally Pamela said, "No, I didn't."

"And therefore you have no idea why he is here?"

"None."

"Should I be worried?"

Again a pause.

"No, I think not. If his visit had anything to do with you, I'm sure he would have told me about his reasons ."

"Pamela, you said that Moya Koda was more than a mere friend of Eric. Do you suppose he has come to see her?"

"He told me nothing. When he left, he said he had some personal things to attend to. I assumed he meant either a private golf match or something to do with his family."

"But not a trip to Ireland?"

"Elspeth, if you are worried about your job or Richard's, don't be. Eric would have told me of any displeasure with your performance there. I think you can assume that he is there on what he said was personal."

"Does he often stay at the hotels when he is on personal business?"

"I don't recall that he has ever before," Pamela said.

When Eric Kennington arrived at Elspeth and Richard's suite, he still was in his sporting clothing but without his cap. He rapped twice at the door.

"Wait," Elspeth said to Richard when the first tap came.

The knock came again, this time more insistently. Elspeth nodded and Richard went to let his lordship in.

Elspeth had ordered tea, which had been delivered a few moments before. She had asked room service not to disturb them until she rang to have the tea things removed.

"I suppose you wonder why I am here," Eric Kennington said. He had the look of a small boy who was explaining being in the wrong spot holding on to an item secured by a misdeed. "I sometimes come unannounced to the hotels but this time I have come on a private errand."

Elspeth offered him a seat and handed him a cup of tea. "I was surprised when I saw you downstairs." Elspeth admitted. "Is something wrong?"

"I want to see Moya," he said. "From your report, I assumed she wouldn't see me if I had contacted her ahead of time. I'm relying on you to arrange a meeting now that I am here."

"Moya isn't letting anyone see her right now."

"You have seen her, I know," he said. Obviously he had read Elspeth's reports.

"I have, but only after being carefully screened. She was badly beaten when Yuri Koda was killed, and is consequently admitting very few people into her suite."

"Can you get me in?"

"I'll try to think of some way," Elspeth said. "But it would help if I knew why you want to talk to her."

Elspeth had seldom seen Eric at a loss for words. He seemed to be now. He looked down at his cardigan stretched over his prominent stomach, and then shifted his gaze to the fine porcelain cup he held in his lap.

"I've known her for a very long time," he said. "We first met when I was on a walking tour here in Ireland forty years ago."

Eric was sixty-one, at least according to his internet biography, making him twenty-one when he had first met Moya. If Moya were Elspeth's age, she would have been eighteen and just entering university. Elspeth wanted to presume nothing, but her curiosity was piqued.

"Her father didn't like me," Eric supplied. "He forbad me from seeing her after that summer but Moya and I have been in touch on and off ever since."

Elspeth turned to Richard, hoping he would find a way to clear the tension she was feeling. He seemed to pick up her cue.

"A young romance?" Richard asked, clearing his throat. "I had one once and I twice proposed to her but she turned me down not once but twice. Fortunately I met her later in life and she agreed to be my wife."

Eric Kennington had been at Elspeth and Richard's wedding three years ago and therefore had heard the tale before. Eric had always expressed mixed feelings about the marriage, as he frequently said he valued Elspeth's employ above the dictates of her heart, and saw no reason why her recent marriage should interfere with her work.

"I'm happily married now," Eric said somewhat defensively, "but I always have had a soft spot for Moya and have followed her welfare over the years. When I heard of her distress here, I thought I could offer her help."

Pamela Crumm had always been so protective of Eric's personal life, undoubtedly on his instruction, that Elspeth was wary as to why he was telling her about his past now. She felt she needed to stay circumspect so that he would not accuse her of prying.

"She's in a very bad way and may want some solace from an old friend," Elspeth said, "but please don't hold out too much hope. She seems distraught over her appearance but I also suspect that she is frightened. She's blaming Yuri Koda's bodyguards for her distress but I don't think she is right. Did Pamela tell you about the theft of the jewels?"

"I followed the case when the accusations first came out but I think Northby's accused Moya to divert attention from another member of staff, probably a relative of Jack Northby."

"Why do you think that?" Richard asked.

"Jack is a member of my club. He protects his family, particularly those in the firm. They've done very well in the last two or three decades, and he doesn't want his reputation tarnished. Auctioneers need a reputation for being completely above board if they are to be trusted with people's valuables. Moya was an easy person to accuse. By marrying Yuri, she suddenly had an alliance with someone whose business practices were shady at best if not totally illegal. The press, of course, made the connection without Jack or anyone else having to prompt them. Jack was off the hook if Moya looked guilty."

"Did the police ever question her or formally charge her?" Richard asked.

"Not to my knowledge. The press made the charges but nothing was ever proven."

Elspeth had heard this from Pamela, but suspected that the suspicion of Moya's complicity in the disappearance of the jewels lingered in many people's minds. Unsolved cases could so easily tarnish one for life.

"Now Moya has the added burden of Yuri being killed," Eric said.

"Luckily, at least to date, the media hasn't picked up that Moya was at the scene of the murder," Elspeth said, "Not here in Ireland nor in the UK as far as I can see from reading the news on the internet. The paparazzi appeared briefly outside the hotel today wondering if Moya was staying here. I talked to them and they all seem to have drifted away towards more current stories."

"It sounds as if you haven't lost your knack of chasing the press away, Elspeth. Good for you," Eric said.

Elspeth could feel her face flush. Compliments from Eric Kennington were rare. She felt in an awkward position because she never before had been asked to help Lord Kennington with a private matter.

"After we finish our tea, I'll go up to Moya's suite and see if I can get her to let me in," Elspeth volunteered. "I haven't seen her since this morning but I would have been called if she tried to leave her rooms."

"I'll come with you," Eric said. "I'm sure she'll admit me once she sees me."

Elspeth was not as certain as Eric seemed to be.

"Perhaps I should call ahead, not to warn her that you will be with me, Eric, but to allow her to be fully made up before I arrive. I detect that Moya has a fair share of vanity about her appearance"

"She's always been that way. That's one reason I fell in . . . er, well, rather, I like that sort of thing in women."

Elspeth raised her eyes to his and cocked an eyebrow.

"Don't accuse me of sexism, Elspeth. Pamela does that far too frequently."

Elspeth felt he was diverting attention away from saying he had fallen in love with Moya but from the way he spoke, it was obvious he had when he was young. Elspeth wondered if his emotions carried over to the present day and what this said about his relationship with his wife, whose given name Elspeth still did not know. Elspeth tried to imagine Eric at twenty. Perhaps he had been slender in those days and handsome. His face now was marred by wrinkles beside his eyes and on his forehead and was a developing double chin. His eyebrows had grown out to make him look perpetually fierce and the thinning of his hair was showing despite his skilled haircut. His figure had filled out to the point that his customary Saville Row suits did little to hide his expanding waistline. Even with her bruises, Moya Koda was a handsome woman, rigorously thin and immaculately turned out. She must have been a beauty when young.

Setting these thoughts aside, Elspeth rose and picked up the house phone and asked for Moya's suite.

"There have been some developments here I would like to talk to you about," she said when Moya answered. "May I come up to see you again?"

"What developments?" Moya asked. "Have the goons been arrested?"

Elspeth thought of Zakhar downstairs and hoped he still was sufficiently drugged not to be causing any trouble.

"I've heard nothing on that front," Elspeth said, glad that she wasn't lying. "No, this is something new but I would prefer not to discuss it on the phone. Shall we say in fifteen minutes?"

Elspeth could tell that Moya was not happy but she consented.

Elspeth turned back to Eric Kennington. "How would you like me to handle this? Do you want to go in alone and ask if she will see you or would you like me to come with you?"

She noticed that he had paled. Normally Eric was filled with bravado but the stuff seemed to have drained out of him. His uncharacteristic silence lay like a pall on the room. He swallowed.

Finally he said, "I'd like to see her alone."

"Then I suggest I knock on the door and when she sees me and cracks the door, you can make a plea for your entry. If she asks me to come in too, I think it's best that I do."

"You don't need to act as a safety net."

"Do you think she will want one?" Elspeth asked.

"I have no idea. I'm here because I hope she will want me to be here."

12

Angelika Rostova wished that Derek Somerset's hug had been more passionate. He kissed her dryly on the cheek and had gone on to shake Nancy Kendall's hand. Angelika wondered if Derek did not want to show intense emotion in front of Nancy or if he had become shy in the luxurious environs of the Kennington hotel. Until that moment, Angelika has liked the English coolness that she associated with Derek but she thought that perhaps, since her father had been brutally murdered just three days before, he might have been more demonstrative. Angelika put her arm around Derek's waist and drew him into the room that she and Nancy shared.

"I'll leave you alone and go downstairs. I've seen a book I want in the shop. And I think I'll have a cup of tea in the tearoom. I saw their pastries yesterday and they beg one to break one's diet," Nancy said. "Come down and join me once you have had a chance to say hello."

Good old loyal Nancy. She understood that Angelika might want time alone with her fiancé.

When her friend had gone, Angelika rushed into Derek's embrace and pushed herself against him. He put his arms stiffly around her and Angelika could feel disappointment run through her. Derek's lack of response made her feel that he disapproved of what had happened to her father and that somehow blamed it on her. This couldn't be. Angelika had been disgusted by much of what her father was. Derek knew this. Why now had his ardour seem to have cooled? Or had it? She tried to think back. She realised she had never been needy before in his presence. She had always been the one who had given him support because she felt until now that she did not need any herself. Her life in recent years had been one of shedding her unfortunate background and living in a more normal way in the present. Derek had always been part of the present. She had sheltered him from her past but now no longer could. He continually spoke of the Christian virtue of forgiveness but Angelika did not think at that moment he was forgiving her for her father and what had just happened to him.

"Have you missed me?" she asked but knew the question was weak.

"Of course," he said.

"It's been terrible," she said, "ever since we arrived here—first having to tolerate Moya and then coping with Papa's death. I'm so glad you're here, Derek. I need someone other than Nancy to lean on. She's been a brick but I wanted to be with you, to hear your gentle words and to have you hold me." She slowly began to cry, although she had not wanted to.

"Angie," he said. "You must have hated all that happened." But his voice sounded like a clergyman and not a lover.

"I did. I hate everything that happened since we arrived in Dublin."

"You must try not to hate but forgive," he said.

The floodgates of tears opened and a torrent of bitterness poured out, first at her father's murder and then at Moya and finally at Ireland generally. She turned on Derek. "You can't possibly understand," she shouted.

He drew back as if offended. "God is with us in these moments. He understands."

Angelika did not want God; she wanted Derek. She felt God was the third party in a love triangle. She had never asked much of Derek before except future respectability, she giving more to promote his ambitions and fears than she had needed back at any time before this. But now she wanted more and she did not feel he was providing it.

"I must go and settle in," he said releasing her.

Angelika knew his tidy ways and his dislike of disorder physically or emotionally. She drew back from him and felt he was relieved. She felt more passionately Ukrainian than she had ever done before in her life.

"Do go," she said in the most posh voice she could muster. "Why don't you meet me and Nancy for tea. Shall we say four o'clock in the tearoom?" She hoped she sounded as if she were a vicar's unemotional wife.

After Derek left, she went to the window and stared out on to the green below. She felt devoid of help for all that was churning over in her life. Until that moment she had not realised how intensely her father's death had affected her. The only person she knew who seemed to feel the same way was Moya. Much as she disliked Moya, Angelika had a great urge to talk to her. She went to the house phone and asked for Moya's room.

*

Lars Inversen knew he had a long time to kill before joining Elspeth Duff and her husband for dinner at seven. He had made a reconnaissance of the hotel and realised he could not get to Moya Koda's suite without being seen by the security cameras. Elspeth Duff had said Moya would not leave her suite. If this were true, he wondered, what if he rang her on the house phone and asked to come to her rooms. Lars believed that often when one asked specifically for what one wanted, it was granted.

First he would have to discover which suite she was in. If Elspeth Duff had access to Moya, she would go to Moya's suite at some point. Lars did not want to be seen lurking in the hallways but he could move freely around the public spaces and small lounges on each floor. He had already spotted the security cameras cleverly concealed behind numerous decorations throughout the hotel and he knew his movements would be tracked.

A young woman came into the lobby where he was sitting. In his short observation of the hotel, he had noticed that most of the guests were middle aged or older and to see a bright, young face was refreshing. Elspeth had mentioned that Yuri Koda's daughter and a friend were staying in the hotel and he wondered if this young woman was the friend.

He decided on the direct approach. He followed her into the shop and saw her scanning the rack of paper-backed books. He waited a moment for her to make a selection. Fortunately he had read the book she had picked.

He came up beside her and said, "Do you like psychological thrillers? That one is good but rather gory."

At first he thought she was going to turn away but she looked down at the book and turned to him. "I don't like gory mysteries," she said. "I always flip through the graphic parts and then lose track of the plot. Is there another you can recommend?"

"This one," he said taking down another he had read that was tamer. "I enjoyed it more because the detective is more sympathetic."

"You're not English are you?" she said.

"No, I'm from Denmark. Have you been there?"

"Yes once, on holiday," she said.

Lars knew he had made a conquest. They chatted as she paid for her book. He bought a newspaper, although he had already read it on the plane from Paris.

"My name is Lars," he said. "Lars Inversen. You would know by my name I am Scandinavian."

"Do you live in Copenhagen?"

"No, Paris," he replied.

"Then you speak French as well," she said.

"Few people in Europe speak Danish and so we have to learn English and French from an early age. Are you busy? Would you like to come to the bar and have a cool drink? It's early yet but I am sure they have a cola, ginger beer or lemonade." He purposely used more of a Danish accent than he needed to.

Soon they were chatting easily. He told her about Copenhagen, although he had not been there for ten years. She chatted about Gloucestershire, which apparently was her home. Lars knew by now that Nancy, as she had given her name, must be Angelika's friend that Elspeth Duff had mentioned when she said. "My friend Angie and I have been seeing a bit of Dublin. It's less Irish than I thought it would be. I suppose all capital cities these days have become totally international. Have you seen much of the city?"

"None," he said. "I just arrived from Paris this morning."

"Angie's fiancé, Derek, arrived this morning as well. Perhaps the four of us could go out and play tourists together."

Angie, Angelika, he thought. He had hit pay dirt.

"My friend is a bit upset because her father died suddenly recently. Getting out will do her good."

"I would like that because I do not know anyone in Dublin. I have a bit of business to attend to but would like to get together later. Do you want to call me in my room? It's 209."

"We're in 206."

"Unfortunately I look out over the street and not the green," he said.

"We were very lucky," Nancy said. "We were booked in at the last minute and never expected such a nice room. Angie's father and stepmother were staying down the hallway and her stepmother is still there. Angie's stepmother knows Lord Kennington and he prevailed in making room for us. I understand he's a formidable person."

Lars knew now he was getting close to Moya Koda without Elspeth Duff's help. Finding this out had almost been too easy. He wondered if he could press Nancy to get Moya's exact room number. Then he remembered that his room had an emergency exit plan. The suites as opposed to the rooms would be identified on it. At least he could pare down his options. He might try the same trick he had used when calling around the hotels. He could ask for each suite in succession, each time from a different house phone in the hotel.

Nancy looked at her watch.

"I promised Angie I would meet her and Derek in the tearoom at four. Will you join us? We might go out for a walk before dinner and you could begin to see Dublin. I expect Angie and Derek will want to go to St. Patrick's Cathedral but you and I don't have to. There's a lot of other things to see in the centre of Dublin than churches."

He looked at his watch. It was just after two, which would give him time to track down Moya Koda.

"Where shall we meet?" he asked.

"Join us in the lobby."

"I will," he said hoping his grin seemed boyish.

*

Sean Clancy had recognised Lord Kennington because he had seen him in London several times. Sean had heard of his visits to the various hotels in his empire but not that his lordship tried to hide his identity behind a false name and casual clothes when he arrived. The receptionist had mentioned that Elspeth Duff had recognised 'Eric Smith' but he had quickly warned her not to speak out his real name. Sean trained his staff to be aware of small things around the hotel that were out of the ordinary. Bridey was a sharp young woman and Sean thought she had a small crush on him, and therefore went out of her way to please.

Sean suspected that Elspeth would fill Lord Kennington in on the happenings at the hotel but Sean was still concerned about the Ukrainian in the basement who had let off the gun. Sean had no idea why this had happened, as Elspeth had told him little, but he knew the incident had to be connected to Moya Koda. He also knew that the drugged Ukrainian was still being guarded near the storerooms by the bakery. Being summer, Sean could only spare his kitchen staff so far without their absence from duty affecting the running of the food service. Where was Elspeth Duff? She had promised to take care of the Ukrainian problem but he had not seen her since earlier that morning when she had been down to check on the status of the 'patient' as the doctor called him.

Lord Kennington's arrival had complicated the whole issue. Sean was about to call his security man back from paternity leave, but was well aware of the laws of the European Union and Ireland that paternity leave was a basic human right and not granting it could be an issue. In any case Elspeth Duff was here and surely Lord Kennington must trust her ability to keep things in order. He and many of his fellow managers in the Kennington hotel chain had questioned why she had been 'on sabbatical' for six months but London had never let out the answer.

Sean made his way down to the basement to see if the Ukrainian had left the hotel. He drew in his breath when he saw the muscular pastry chef dozing against the wall of the room where the patient was being kept.

"Heads up," he said as he approached.

The pastry chef jumped to attention.

"Yes, sir," the man said.

"Is he still in there."

"Yes, sir, as far as I know."

Sean took out his passkey to open the door but the door handle turned before he could insert the key.

"Did you know this was unlocked?" he asked the pastry chef.

The man stood rigidly at attention. "No sir, I didn't."

"Did anyone leave the room?"

"Not to my knowledge, sir."

"But you were asleep when I came up to you, so you can't be sure. You may go back to the kitchen. I'll find someone to take your place."

Sean did not need to. No one was in the room. Sean spun around and began to run. He drew out his mobile and punched in Elspeth's security number. No one answered. Rather than waiting for the lift, he bounded up the service staircase and dashed into the security office. The man monitoring the cameras was sitting with his feet up, drinking a cup of tea.

"Did you see any activity in the corridor down by the kitchen in the last hour or so?"

The man put his feet down and straightened up in his chair. "That corridor," he said and lifted an eyebrow. There's always activity down there."

"Replay the last hour for me," Sean cried. His heart was pounding. "And then switch up to the second floor main hallway."

"There definitely has been traffic there," the man said.

"Then replay that first, starting an hour ago. We may need to go back further."

Sean watched the recordings with increasing fear. At the point where the monitor operator stopped the tape of the second floor, someone who resembled Angelika Rostova was coming out of Moya's rooms, although Sean could not see her face. A few minutes later, the young man who had come with Sir Richard Munro, came out of the suite as well. A half hour later the Ukrainian Zakhar appeared and he pushed open the door to Moya's suite, which did not appear to be latched. Shortly afterwards the new guest, Lars Inversen, came into the hallway, looked at the door to the suite, which was now ajar, and went in. He was out again in less than a minute and pulled the door to and disappeared into a side corridor. In ten more minutes, Elspeth Duff and Lord Kennington came into view. Elspeth seemed puzzled when she got to Moya's suite. She knocked at the door and then pushed it open. Lord Kennington spoke to her and followed her in. After that there was nothing. Where was the hall porter? Why hadn't the porter seen what had happened and reported it to Sean?

He rang the front desk and then Hallam McLaughlin, the concierge. "I need everyone you can spare. Send them to the second floor. I'll be up there waiting. And hurry."

13

Considering all the precautions that Moya had taken in the past, Elspeth was amazed that the door to her suite was standing unlatched. She turned to Eric, whom she had instructed to stay out of sight of the peephole.

"Something odd is going on. Moya has never before left her door open when I called to see her."

Elspeth knocked, causing the door to open more fully, but there was no response. She pushed the door completely open and called, "Moya, are you there? It's Elspeth here."

No answer. Now Elspeth was concerned. She gestured for Eric to come with her. If something was wrong, his protection was better than nothing. The sitting room was empty. Elspeth heard a muffled sound from the bedroom. She held her arm back, motioning Eric to stay put. She tiptoed towards the bedroom door, which was cracked open. She drew in her breath as she saw Zakhar.

"Zakhar," she said, as calmly as she could. He turned towards her, his face unbelieving but not malevolent. "Zakhar, I'm coming in."

She saw her hand shaking and she extended it towards the doorframe to steady herself. Fear did odd things to people. Elspeth felt nothing emotionally but obviously her brain was reacting to what she saw before her.

"Zakhar,' she said rounding the door. She saw Moya lying inert on the bed. Elspeth could not tell if Moya was breathing but she was not conscious.

"Dead," he said, although he pronounced the d's like

t's. He was visibly bewildered. "Me no," he said. He must have assumed that Elspeth was blaming him.

"What's going on in there?" Eric Kennington shouted from behind Elspeth.

Elspeth said. "Get help, Eric. Quickly."

"I can't leave you alone with that madman," Eric replied. He was now beside Elspeth at the doorway to the bedroom and must have assumed who Zakhar was.

"I can handle him," Elspeth said, although she was not sure she could. Elspeth was unarmed with anything other than her wits. She wondered if they were enough. She handed her mobile to Eric. "Dial seven-seven-seven for help."

Zakhar lunged at Elspeth, knocking her against the wall and he was shoved by Eric, who went down with a thump and a shocked expression. Zakhar ran across the sitting room and tore open the door to the hallway.

Eric seemed to have regained his composure, although he was still on the floor. He was speaking into Elspeth's phone. "He's just escaped from the suite," he said. "No, I didn't see which way he went. Send the doctor. Now!"

Eric's manner when he was upset was imperious.

Sean Clancy appeared at Moya's suite with seconds. "The doctor will be here in ten minutes. He isn't in the hotel but lives nearby."

"That's not soon enough," Eric said. "My poor, poor Moya."

At this exchange, Elspeth went back into the bedroom to see if Moya was dead. Moya moved on her own and let out a low groan. Elspeth blew out her breath in relief.

"Moya, can you hear me?"

No response came. Elspeth called her name again. She

was aware that Eric and Sean had come into the room but she did not turn to them.

"She may be coming to. She definitely moved. We must get her help, more than the hotel doctor. She may need life support."

Moya groaned again. "No," she said her voice cracking. "No."

Eric fell to his knees by her bedside and took her hand. "It's me, Moya, Eric. I've come to help."

She opened her eyes a slit and slowly closed them. Her voice was the merest of whispers. "Take me home, Eric, "take me to Bish. . ." She drifted off.

"Get me a private ambulance," Eric commanded.

"Yes, milord," Sean said.

"With a doctor you can trust not to blab to the police. Fast."

"Yes, milord." Sean Clancy said again and turned his eyes imploringly to Elspeth.

"Eric, is that wise?" Elspeth asked.

"Be quiet," he said. "I'm in charge. She asked to be taken to Bishop's Head, her childhood home in County Louth, and I'm taking her. If she doesn't want the police, I won't involve them." His face softened. "She recognised me," he said. "She knows she can trust me."

Elspeth doubted Eric's assessment of Moya's intentions but he had overruled her so she stepped back. The responsibility for Moya was his now. But Elspeth agonised. She did not like Moya but no woman deserved the treatment Moya had received over the last few days. Elspeth had seen that Moya had been beaten twice and she appeared to have just sustained another attack just moments before she and Eric had entered her room. Elspeth had delayed contacting the police before in her work but she felt the time had come for the guards to be brought in, despite Moya and Eric's wish to the contrary. Elspeth did not have the means at hand to chase Zakhar or to pursue the person or persons who had hurt Moya. Eric's command had curtailed her.

Eric stayed kneeling beside Moya's bed, whispering sweet words of encouragement for Moya to stay with him until help came. Sean looked up at Elspeth once again and Elspeth knew his thoughts mirrored hers.

"Do what he says," Elspeth said. "And get the best private ambulance you can. How far is County Lough?"

"It's a county north of here," Sean said. "It's not more than a hundred kilometres at the most."

"Find out for me where a place called Bishop's Head is and what hospital facilities there are close by once the ambulance is on the way."

"What about Ms Rostova?" Sean asked. "Shouldn't she be told?"

"Not yet. Let me handle that end. Just concentrate on the ambulance."

Sean fled from the suite, obviously relieved to have a mission that took him out of Lord Kennington's presence. Sean rang Elspeth five minutes later to say an ambulance was on the way and they were being paid generously to be quiet, both when coming to the hotel's service area and revealing their ultimate destination to anyone who asked. Elspeth went into the bedroom and told Eric, who had pulled a chair up beside Moya's bed and was holding her hand in both of his.

"Please live," Elspeth heard him say. "The ambulance

is on the way. Sean says they'll be discreet. There will be hell to pay if they are not," his lordship said.

"Should I call ahead to Bishop's Head? They might want to know Moya's coming and that you will be with her," Elspeth said.

"Get on it," Eric said.

"How do I reach the house? It is a house, I presume."

"It's an estate," he said. "Near Carlingford Lough."

"I presumed it must be," Elspeth said, smarting at his words. "Who shall I ask for there?"

"Her father."

"Who is?"

"Damn your questions, Elspeth."

Elspeth bristled. So much was depending on what he wanted but most of all Elspeth feared for Moya's life. She was in no mood for Eric's attacks on her.

"Tell me her father's name so I can contact him," Elspeth said as quietly as she could muster.

"Sir Gerald de Lacey. Tell him I'm keeping Moya safe. And while I'm gone, clean up the mess here at the hotel. I dislike untidy situations."

Part II
Eric

14

"And top o' the mornin' to you, my posh English friend," Donny Cunningham said. His face dangled upside down in front of Eric Kennington, whose long youthful frame was stretched out awkwardly on the lower bunk. "Did you sleep well?"

The young Eric Kennington had not. His back ached and his feet were cold. The youth hostel had none of the amenities of the Park Garden hotel where Eric had worked for the past four years ever since leaving school at seventeen. Besides he had drunk too many pints of Guinness the night before at a pub Donny said was the best in Dublin.

"You are a devil, Donny, you and your leprechaun ways."

"Now don't be insulting just because I'm short. 'Tis my mother's fault because she was descended from the fairies. Besides I make up for the lack of inches in breadth of my enjoyment of life."

Eric laughed. He had met Donny on his first night at the youth hostel and over the last two days Donny had led a rollicking pace through the front and back streets of the Irish capital. Eric, who considered himself sober and driven by a single desire to succeed, had never succumbed to such merriment in his life. Now Donny had convinced him to walk from Dublin to Carlingford, making way along the Irish Sea to, as Donny put it, 'see the wonders of spring in the most beautiful country on earth'.

A Danger in Dublin

Eric had resisted, giving in only when Donny promised fields of daffodils covering the hillsides. Eric had only seen daffodils in Covent Garden before and Donny's promise enthralled him with a sight that 'only Ireland had to offer'. Eric did not yet know Donny well enough to know that his new friend had the gift of Blarney.

Eric rose from the narrow mattress of the double bunk bed and stretched his back. "At the hotel where I work, they wouldn't allow the beds in the rooms to be used for dogs."

"Do you have separate rooms for dogs in hotels? I thought the English were odd but now you are telling me that what I thought was true."

"The hotel where I work is very exclusive," Eric said. "We don't even allow dogs in the rooms. The kennels are open twenty-four hours a day and individual accommodations for pets can be had—at a price."

"It's beyond belief," Donny said. "I thought the Guinness was talking when you told me about your job."

Eric was proud of his new job. After just four years at the exclusive Park Garden Hotel in Belgravia, he had just been promoted to assistant to the night manager. The management had given him a two-week holiday before he took up his new post and suggested he go overseas to expand his knowledge of the world. Eric had first thought of Paris but decided on Dublin because he had heard recent guests extol the virtues of the Irish capital. The train and ferry fare to Ireland cost less than the plane fare to France. Eric also was not as yet comfortable speaking foreign languages, although it was on his list of things he must study. He had just mastered received pronunciation after listening for years to the presenters on the BBC and to the

English guests who frequented the hotel. In planning his trip he thought of his small savings, most of which he had earmarked for his eventual goal of buying his own hotel. He had a long way to go, and did not want to spend his precious pounds on a frivolous holiday.

"Up you get then," Donny said. "We can take the bus to the outskirts of Dublin, but then we're on our own. Four days of utter bliss."

Eric wondered if this was true. He eyed the new boots and woollen socks he had bought the day before and the used rucksack and anorak, both of which he had purchased at a charity shop.

By the fourth day of walking, Eric had seen no more than a few daffodils by the sides of the road and his heel had a blister the size of a shilling coin. The pubs where they stopped for the night smelled of sour ale and the celebrations of the occupants went on well into the dark hours. He decided Donny's good humour was grating rather than alluring and he longed for the days and nights he had spent at the Park Garden's reception desk studying everything he could find about hotel management and getting snatches of sleep in the staff rooms at the back of the hotel. He vowed he would never travel other than in luxury accommodations again.

The wind had whipped up once again and the passing squall drenched his already saturated clothing. Donny whooped with delight.

"Eric my friend, the luck of the fairies is with us today. I know the cottage down there and it offers all the comforts of home."

Eric's home in a declining middle-class neighbourhood on the south side of London had been modest but it seemed 'sa palace in comparison with the crumbling ruins of the deserted farmhouse in front of them. The walls of the stone structure was perched forlornly on a flat plane above the sea and the exposed rafters stood naked against the backdrop of the rugged mountains beyond. A sign hung crookedly on a single surviving chain at an opening with a collapsed gate and announced that the site 'had poison laid'.

"A smugglers den by night and our shelter during the day," Donny announced. "Across the inlet of Carlingford Lough there, is Ulster and goods flow back and forth without the good offices of the customs."

"Drugs?" Eric asked.

"That and more," Donny said, touching the side of his nose as if Eric should know what the 'more' was.

Donny pushed the rusty gate a bit further open and swept a low bow. "Come into my chamber," he said, "and all will be revealed, or at least we will have a dry place for lunch."

Donny pushed back the tangle of vines at the door opening in the crumbling building. In the semi-gloom of the interior Eric saw that only one part of the main room held any hope of shelter, the roof having remained intact at one corner across from the stone hearth. The remains of the roof structure hung at a precarious angle above the shambles of the room.

Eric eyes took a moment to adjust to the gloom and he drew back when he noticed that he and Donny were not alone in seeking a dry spot. A girl in a riding habit was sitting cross-legged on a pile of ancient straw. She was eating a thick sandwich with apparent gusto.

Eric saw this vision of a woman and for the first time in his life he fell in love.

*

The ambulance drivers had been insistent that Lord Kennington could not be in the back of the ambulance as it sped out of Dublin towards County Louth. He would interfere with the work of the paramedics, who had put Moya on life support. They could not reassure him that Moya would live.

The weather had turned harsh and the wipers hardly kept up with the rain that dashed against the windscreen and despite Eric's dread, he smiled at the thought of Donny Cunningham. Had it not been for him, Eric would never have met Moya de Lacey forty years before.

*

"Donny Cunningham, have you been blown on in the wind or are you merely a ghost of things past?" the girl said. Her blue eyes were laughing.

"Aye, Moya. I've brought Prince Charming to see you."

Eric hardly felt like Prince Charming nor was he in any mood to put up any more with Donny's gaiety. But he did want to meet Moya so he straightened up and bowed a bit stiffly. His rucksack shifted uncomfortably on his shoulders and he twisted his neck in pain.

"And who are you?" Moya asked.

Eric noticed the sweetness of her voice but also that she spoke with a cultured English accent, one that seemed more fitting to the Park Garden Hotel than this derelict hovel.

"Eric Kennington at your service," he said.

"It looks like Donny has dragged you through the wind and rain and every unpleasant place in between. Have you had lunch? I'm afraid my sandwich is almost finished and I can offer you only an apple or some chocolate. I wasn't expecting visitors," she said grandly. A smile spread across her face.

"We were only trying to get out of the rain," Eric said. "We have some sandwiches we brought from the pub where we stayed last night.' He cleared his throat and felt he was sounding pompous.

"Moya, m'love, we won't impose on your hospitality," Donny said.

"I am not your love, Donny. I've told you that a thousand times."

"Hope springs eternal," Donny said. "What brings you home at this time of year?"

"My mother is not well and Daddy thought I should come to Ireland during the spring break." Moya's voice had become serious.

"I'm sorry to hear that about your mother," Donny said. "She has always been poorly."

"She's only poorly when it is to her advantage," Moya said with a slight frown, "but we are being rude to your friend. Come and sit beside me, Eric Kennington, and tell me where you are from." Her voice was silvery.

She pushed around some of the rancid straw and offered Eric a seat near her on the straw.

"From London," he said. "I met Donny in Dublin and he convinced me that a walk to Carlingford would be the experience of a lifetime. It has been but not in the way Donny described it."

"You're not country-born, I can tell. County Lough does offer better than this. Why don't you come with me up to the main house and I will show you some Irish hospitality of the more refined sort."

"I'll be on my way home, Moya. My family is waiting for me and it looks like Eric is in good hands. Goodbye, Eric. The pleasure has been all mine."

Eric secretly disagreed about the pleasure but thanked Donny nonetheless.

After Donny's departure, Moya offered Eric some chocolate. She laid back on the straw and said, "You must find this a strange place. Ireland has many such abandoned farms. This one is part of the de Lacey estate but its tenants left these harsh shores and went to America after the war. Now smugglers and tramps use it mainly. With what appear to be the troubles in the north, those who support Ulster becoming part of Ireland are storing things here to support the Provisional IRA, it seems, to carry over to County Down across the lough. See," she said. She swept away the straw near where they were sitting and pulled up a trap door. Eric peered into the dark hole.

"Hand grenades, twenty four of them," she said. "I counted them."

"Shouldn't you report this to the police?"

"My family's sympathies are with those who want Ireland to be one land free from London's yoke. My father allows this house be used as long as he knows nothing about what is going on here. In any case, I wouldn't turn in people who I've known all my life."

"I see," Eric said although he did not.

"Let's go," she said. "I have my horse here. She's in what is left of the barn. We could ride pillion but you don't look the kind of person who has been on a horse before. It's about a half an hour's walk. Do you mind?"

Despite his sodden condition and blistered heel, Eric could think of nothing more delightful.

Later he remembered little of what they talked about but he could recall her face lit by the occasional streaks of sunshine that broke through the clouds and the wind teasing tendrils of black hair across her cheeks.

Soon after they began to climb out of the plain, Moya pointed out a large Georgian house at the crest of the hill. Its yellow walls stood out among the trees that surrounded it.

"We used to own all of the land around here but since the nineteenth century we have had to sell off bits of it. Many of the farms have been abandoned and the income from the rents has fallen. My grandfather keeps thinking that things will go back to the way they were before but my father is more of a realist. He has various schemes to generate more income, which sometimes succeed and other times don't."

Before they entered the house, Moya took Eric round to the stables and rubbed down her mare. Eric, who knew nothing about horse flesh, was fascinated at the gentle way she treated the horse.

"She's my beauty," Moya explained. "I miss her when I am in England but our groom keeps her well. She was a gift from my father on my sixteenth birthday. I can ride her for hours and she never seems to tire."

"Do you ever come to London?" he asked.

"At weekends sometimes," she said. "I'm studying art history at Somerville College and often come up to take in the galleries."

The words hit Eric hard. This gorgeous girl obviously had brains and was a student at Oxford. How could she ever look at him for more than a few moments diversion in the country?

"If you are up in London, let me give you tea in the hotel where I work." With pride he had told her about his new position there but before he knew that she was at university.

"That would be lovely," she said. He wondered if she meant it. As he would learn, Moya was a hard person to understand.

Eric had five more days before he had to return to London. He spent them all with Moya. She had him up on a horse and laughed at his awkwardness. They walked the paths over the hills and picnicked in the pine forests. She read him poetry by torch under the stars. But she never promised him anything, not even that she would look him up in London.

Eric could see her father watching him.

"Young man, what sort of future do you plan?" Moya's father asked one day at luncheon.

"I plan to run my own hotel. It will be the best one in the world."

"And how do you plan to finance that?"

"I'm not too sure how yet but I will."

"Even with a great deal of luck, posh hotels cost a bit more than hope," Moya's father said.

Eric set his jaw. "I'm determined to do so. It's just a matter of time."

*

How odd, Lord Kennington thought, that he should remember this last conversation. That spring, he had nothing to offer Moya but she had come to tea at the Park Garden Hotel. He always loved her yet knew she was beyond reach but they had remained friends over the years.

Now she was in the back of the ambulance, hanging on to a life that she had almost lost in one of his thirty hotels, all built on determination and hard work.

He thought of her recklessness. Not only had she brushed aside the hand grenades in the old cottage but she also had told him numerous hair-raising adventures across the world that appalled Eric's seriousness. He knew she had been unfaithful to her upright first husband on numerous occasions because she told this to Eric. She had smuggled jewellery of great value from India and Africa into Britain. And she was not afraid to use the 'customs-free' passageway across Carlingford Lough to do so. She laughed about selling these items at a great profit and sending the money back home. She delighted in the prospect of marrying 'the villain Koda', as she called him. While he plodded through his life, she skipped merrily through hers. Was she now paying for her sins?

He thought of the women in his life. His mother, widowed early, had devoted her life to her son and he had eventually been able to provide a comfortable home for her in Tunbridge Wells. Pamela Crumm, who was as ambitious as he, ran things with such smoothness that he never had to worry about the details. And then the redoubtable Elspeth Duff, who annoyed him frequently but who knew how to solve problems that seemed to defy others. Would Elspeth be able to get to the bottom of this case? Damn, he hoped so.

The ambulance slowed. Eric recognised the lane along which he had walked with Moya those many years ago. The yellow Georgian house still stood on the hill but new houses, like mushrooms, had sprouted along the road. The ambulance turned up the drive, still lined with beech trees. As they arrived at the house, he noticed its lack of maintenance and wondered what had happened there since he had last been there forty years before. Once here, would Moya recover just by the fact that she was now home? Eric seldom prayed but he did now.

15

Elspeth sat down on the sofa in her suite at the Kennington Dublin and faced her husband.

"Dickie, I'm completely baffled. But at least Moya is gone. How can I solve this case without the help of the Garda? I need more evidence than what they are reporting in the press. For once I wish I had the cooperation of the reporters who have more reason to snoop out information on Yuri Koda's murder than I do. If I go to the Garda now, they will undoubtedly ask me all sorts of questions, most of which I don't want to answer."

"Do you still think you can solve Yuri's murder?"

"No, I know I can't but I want to find out about Moya, why she refused to see the police and if that has anything to do with her being beaten when she left the hotel after Yuri's murder."

"Haven't you fulfilled your role to protect her while she was here in the hotel?"

"Did I? Dickie, when I last saw her, she was on the brink of death. Several people went into her room before Eric and I arrived, and one of them may have inflicted more injuries on her. Why was she unconscious when we got there?"

"Did you look at the security tapes?"

"Yes, as soon as Eric left."

"And?"

"It seems as if almost everyone associated with Moya had access to her room before Eric and I got there.

Angelika went in and was followed by Derek Somerset. He must have left the door open because even Lars Inversen went in, although only for a split second. That young man is a detective and is probably inclined to snoop."

"Then why didn't he stay longer?"

"I wish I knew. After that Zakhar rushed in. That's when Eric and I found him next to Moya's body."

"Do you think he inflicted the blow to Moya's head?"

"What would you think? His look of bewilderment implies he didn't and that he was as surprised at Moya's condition as we were."

"Are you going to talk to the others—everyone but I suppose Zakhar?"

"I can't think of any other thing to do. I had best get to it soon. Do you think I ought to tell the police about Zakhar?"

"I'd ask Eric that question. Let him be responsible," Richard said.

"He told me not to call him, he'd ring me. My orders were to dig out what really happened here. Do you have things to do right now?"

He laughed. "I intend to sit in the lobby and discover why the wealthy in twenty-first century society have become so unappealing."

"I need to see Angelika and tell her what happened to her stepmother. Afterwards I want to invite Derek, Nancy and Angelika to tea. Can you join us once we go into the tearoom? I'd like it if your arrival appeared unplanned."

"I'm sure by then I should be thoroughly disgusted with the guests in the lobby. What a dreadful thing to say about the indecently rich these days who chose to stay at a

Kennington hotel," he added with a laugh.

As she broke the news Elspeth watched Angelika's face. Her eyes became wary but gave away none of her feelings.

"Are you certain she was close to death? Moya could easily be faking," Angelika said.

"I don't think so. She was unconscious and looked badly beaten. She asked to be taken to County Lough to her family home," Elspeth said. "I have seen people close to death before. I don't think Moya could have been acting."

Angelika said, "It won't be a great loss. Now I can get on with my life without her shadow looming over me."

Elspeth wondered what Derek Somerset would think of this callousness.

"You went along to her suite earlier this afternoon. Can you tell me why?"

Angelika lowered her eyes and raised them again. "In a weak moment, I thought she might offer me some comfort about my father's death."

"Did she?"

"No. She told me that she had suffered the most and waved her hand at the bruises on her face."

"Then she was conscious?" Elspeth asked.

"Very much so. She asked to meet Derek. I called and got him to come to see her. He said afterwards that he thought she was kind. Derek believes the best in all people. He doesn't know Moya very well yet."

In many of her other assignments, Elspeth had liked the guests she had met in the course of her investigations. She wished this were now the case. Still she plugged on.

"Did Derek tell you anything else about their conversation?"

"Moya asked who his family was and what he planned to do with his life. She also asked him how well he knew me. I think that was meant to be an insult even though Derek didn't see it that way. Derek didn't stay long as he said Moya was looking ill. He told her he would come back later."

Having established that Moya was alive and conscious when Derek Somerset left her room, Elspeth went in search of Lars Inversen. She found him in the conservatoire at the back of the hotel. He was napping in one of the lounge chairs under a leafy tree in the corner of the space. He woke as she approached.

"As a detective you would find me remiss if I didn't know you had gone to Moya Koda's room. How did you know which suite it was? We keep this information very close."

He grinned. "I have my methods, just like you, Ms Duff."

"You didn't stay long," she said.

"No one was in the sitting room. I had a quick look around, scoping the place out, but didn't go in the bedroom."

"Did you hear anything when you were in the sitting room?" Elspeth asked.

He shook his head. "Not even a dormouse," he said. "Is that the expression? And don't get incensed that I would suggest such a thing in a Kennington hotel. I'm sure no dormouse would dare to storm the bastions of your hotel."

"They know their place," Elspeth said, caught up by his good humour. "By the way, I have invited Angelika Rostova and her friends to have tea in the tearoom at four. Would you join in?"

"The pleasure would be all mine."

*

Richard was sitting in the lobby reading a copy of the *Irish Times* when Elspeth came into the space. She sat down beside him.

"One can put a paper up and be completely ignored. So far I have nothing to report to Lord Kennington that he does not already know. I wonder how I can write a report that has any positive suggestions other than suggesting he turn back the clock on the modern world."

"During our last few months in Scotland," Elspeth said, "I was aware that most people we rubbed shoulders with there were reasonably polite and helpful. Is it only that they were older and more settled? The only place I saw rudeness was among the rowdies in Perth and Edinburgh, young men who have no jobs and no sense of belonging. What will they have become when they are our age? I remember having such a feeling of security about life when I was young, that I would go on to any shining future I could imagine, even if it didn't turn out that way."

"I've been watching the guests, who one would assume were the people who had achieved the shining future but I don't see any happiness in their faces, only anxiousness. Modern day society has given them no foundation or assurances. Their happiness is based on money, not just personal fulfilment. No wonder they are anxious."

"At least they could show better taste in clothing," Elspeth said, eyeing an ill-clad woman talking to the concierge. Richard often accused Elspeth of being a clothing snob, which she freely admitted. "Dickie, I think your task is hopeless if a woman like that who can afford a room at a Kennington hotel adorns herself with so much lack of taste," she said with a nod towards the woman. "Come have tea with us. I want you to meet the young people."

*

Afterwards Elspeth puzzled over the dynamics among the people at the gathering for tea. She decided to stage her arrival and therefore took Richard's arm as they entered the tearoom. The famous Kennington tea buffet lined one wall of the room and waiters were taking orders for the various types of tea offered in a small menu that they had handed to each guest. At one of the tables overlooking St. Stephen's Green, Angelika flanked by Derek and Nancy sat relaxed. Lars was not yet there. He appeared just as Richard and Elspeth were approaching the table. Angelika looked up at Lars and, almost as if signalling him, quickly dropped her eyes. What did that mean, if anything?

Lars said he had met Nancy earlier in the bookshop, and was glad to meet the others.

Elspeth introduced Richard by his name but not his title, but quickly Derek said, "How nice to see you again, Sir Richard. My room is as comfortable as you promised."

Conversation remained general. The luxury of the hotel, the weather, the various choices of tea and finally the sites of Dublin made their way around the table. Angelika seemed to choose the topics; Nancy chiming in. Derek was polite but added little. Lars joined in enthusiastically and was soon invited to join the other three young people in a tour of central Dublin.

"Will you join us, Richard and Elspeth?" Angelika asked.

Elspeth shook her head. "Why don't the four of you go on? Richard and I have things to do here."

When the four of them had left, Elspeth turned to her husband.

"What did you make of all that?"

He frowned and said, "I had the distinct impression that Lars and Angelika have met before."

"So did I but I didn't want it to seem that I am seeing a conspirator behind every tree."

"Elspeth my dearest one, shall we take the young people's lead and walk out a bit. I think the fresh air will do good for both of us. I am beginning to feel the need to clear my head."

"Now that Eric and Moya are not here, I think that a most marvellous idea," she said and kissed him quickly on the cheek.

16

Eric turned to the driver of the ambulance.

"How much longer now?" he asked. Because his only trip to the de Lacey estate before had been on foot, he had no judge of how soon they would arrive.

"With the rain, it should be about half an hour more."

"Ring your company and see if they have provided the equipment I asked for specifically. I also want your paramedics to stay until Mrs Koda is comfortably settled. Has that been arranged?"

"I'll make sure it has," the driver said and picked up his mobile.

He went to turn on the siren behind a small Nissan driven by a white-haired woman swerving erratically.

"No noise," Eric barked, motioning to the back. "It can only hurt her."

"Sorry, guv." The driver picked up his mobile and tapped in a speed dial number. He mumbled something into the phone that Eric could not hear.

"All set," the driver said. "I've driven this rig for years and never knew a client to demand all the equipment you'd find in a hospital for home use. There's a lorry coming with all the monitors and a drip set up." He raised his shoulders and shook his head.

"It's none of your business why. I'm paying dearly for your services and expect to be catered to."

"Yes, guv," the driver said and lapsed into silence.

Ten minutes later they turned off the motorway. Eric looked through the windscreen wipers and recognised the landscape of the coast along the Irish Sea. Memories flew into his head.

*

The young Moya turned her face to the rain. "I love it here," she said. "My father sent me to the convent in Dorset when I was eight years old and since then I have spent more time in England than Ireland. I learned to speak properly, as the nuns said, and how to be the perfect English lady but my heart has always been here in the wildness of this countryside. I'd happily leave Oxford and come back but my mother has forbidden it. She says that I shouldn't suffer what she has. The whole thing is utterly ridiculous because she has a beautiful home, a dutiful husband and great status in the community. But what she really wanted was to live in London and put on all the pretensions of being Lady de Lacey."

"But she obviously is not well," Eric said as he walked beside her.

"Psychosomatic," Moya said. "If my father won't give her what she wanted, she makes his life miserable. She has never considered that my father has a great force of character and had no intention whatever of being miserable because of her. He only lets her use her illness as an excuse when he wants the same thing—like me coming home for the spring break. How like Daddy."

Eric remembered the conversation in the de Lacey's drawing room the night before and Sir Gerald questioning him. A fire roared in the large fireplace, giving out little warmth but creating the aura of the eighteenth century when it was designed and built. Eric expected servants in wigs to appear at any moment. Sir Gerald was in black tie and Moya had changed into a long frock; Eric made do with his walking clothes but had found a wrinkled tie and clean shirt. He felt awkward.

"Hotels?" Sir Gerald had said. "A risky business with fierce competition."

"I've thought a great deal about this, sir. I want my hotels to be different. I want people who stay there to imagine themselves having the most comfortable and elegant stay of their lives."

"And how will you afford this?"

"I plan to charge outrageously high prices and only invite the best of the best to stay."

Sir Gerald laughed. "You mean the hotels will be private and accessible only if you ask specific people to come."

"That's my idea, at least initially," Eric said. Under Sir Gerald's scrutinising eye, Eric began to lose confidence. "I plan to start small and let the reputation of my first hotel spark enough interest that people will be delighted to come and pay for the privilege of doing so. I'll set my hotels in historic buildings, and hire the world's best decorators, chefs and managers. After I have established myself, I will train my own staff to my own standards."

"And how will you get the guests to begin with?"

"I work at a five-star hotel in London and have been cultivating some of the more influential guests there. Several of them have been encouraging."

"Enough to invest?"

"Initially, yes, but I want to keep control myself. If I borrow money, then I want to pay it back as soon as I can."

"You are a lad with vision," Sir Gerald said. "When you make your first million, let me know." He laughed as he said this.

Moya's mother had been less enthusiastic. In fact she was so unimpressed that later that week, when Eric was leaving County Lough, she told Moya she must not see Eric Kennington again.

*

"The lorry with the equipment is just behind us," the ambulance driver said as they turned off the main road on to a small country road that seemed vaguely familiar to Eric. He remembered an unpopulated road but now large new homes had sprung along the roadside and others were under construction. Being a businessman, Eric wondered who would buy these during the current housing crisis but all the completed houses seemed to be inhabited.

"It's not like the old days," the driver said. "It's the people from the north, who want to take advantage of our cheaper prices here and open border. Most of them are from Belfast. It's only an hour's commute from here. I expect there's some fancy tax dodges surrounding their deals. Ireland needs to be one country not two so the likes of these folks won't prey on our economy and keep most of their money in the north."

Eric had no idea if this were true so he simply grunted in acknowledgement.

The rain had ceased by the time they reached the long drive up to the de Lacey's home. The Georgian house was still painted yellow with white trim, and the beech trees on the drive stood as tall as ever and in June were in full leaf. Eric noticed that the gardens were not as well-tended as he remembered them but he had grown in sophistication over the years and now was a garden aficionado. He smiled to see the sheep grazing in the pastures above the house. Moya loved sheep and had made him admire the young lambs that were just being born the April he first came to Ireland. As an urban person, Eric did not see how one could be so sentimental about animals that would soon end up on people's dinner tables.

Eric could see someone waiting at the front door. A man held up his hand and waved as they turned in the drive. Sir Gerald's stooped figure still sported a full head of hair, although now it was white and not sandy. He raised his cane and twirled it in the air in some sort of affirmation. Whether it was welcoming or directional Eric was not sure.

The ambulance jolted which caused Eric to swear. "Steady on, damn it."

"There was a ramp I didn't see," the driver said. "Probably to slow cars down coming up the drive. Sorry, guv. I'll watch more carefully for the next one."

Eric had by now had his fill of the driver and ordered that he stop carefully so as not to disturb his load. Eric leapt from the driver's cab, and rushed to see the precious cargo in the back.

"How is she?" he yelled to the paramedic as the rear doors opened.

"No better and no worse," the paramedic said. "The trip hasn't hurt her, but she's very weak. She should be taken to the hospital."

"She'll be taken care of here," Eric snapped. "She's better at home."

Moya had told Eric that her mother had insisted she

stay at home as she lingered and died. Eric knew a sickroom had been set up for her in a room looking out over the lough. He imagined Moya recovering there and admonished the paramedics to take her carefully up the stairs.

He was annoyed when one paramedic looked at his colleague and slightly raised an eyebrow. Had the man worked for Eric, he would have been dismissed.

Sir Gerald stepped carefully off the landing at the main door and watched Moya's unconscious body being strapped to the trolley. He turned to Eric, "How bad is she?"

17

"You're thinking of the murder, aren't you?" Richard said to his wife as they finished their meal in the hotel restaurant.

"I can't seem to let it go. I know Eric has taken charge of Moya and my duties are now simply to contain things here at the hotel but nothing adds up. Would you mind if we reconstruct the events of last Sunday evening? Perhaps if we act out what happened between the time Yuri and Moya left the hotel and the time she returned, I could get a better idea of who might have been responsible. If I figure that out, I might be able to grasp why Yuri was murdered."

Richard took the last bite of his sea bass. "Do you want a pudding?" he asked. "If so, we could go out afterwards. It's a long time before it gets dark."

"I'll resist the triple chocolate delight, as alluring as it might be, but a touch of sorbet with raspberries sounds delicious, particularly since I never got the strawberries for lunch."

"They were delectable," he said with a laugh. "I enjoyed your portion as well as mine."

They left the hotel and strolled arm in arm along the edge of St. Stephen's Green as if they had nothing on their minds. Richard squeezed his wife's arm. "It's too bad we are on the track of a murderer. I'm enjoying just walking with you in the summer evening."

Suddenly he felt Elspeth's body tighten. "Stop," she whispered. She pulled him over into a gateway. "That's Zakhar."

"Do you want to follow him?" Richard asked.

Before Elspeth could answer, she pulled Richard into a recess in the bushes. She pointed her finger in the other direction. "And that's Angelika," she said.

"Do you think he's following her?"

"They seem to be going opposite ways. Maybe he hasn't seen her or he wants to conceal that he is following her. Where are the others?"

No sooner had Elspeth asked the questions, when Angelika raised her arm and waved. Beyond her Richard saw Derek Somerset, Lars Inversen and Nancy Kendall. He turned back quickly looking in the other direction but by now Zakhar was out of sight.

"Zakhar must have seen them," Elspeth said. "But why would he be shadowing Angelika?"

"To see if he can get news of Moya? He must be curious to see if she is dead. He may think he will be charged with the murder. If Moya's not dead, he will be in the clear, at least of her demise."

"I don't like this, Dickie. I think Angelika may be in danger although she told me she wasn't afraid of Zakhar."

"I would have thought he would have left Dublin by now."

"I agree. He must have some very good reason for staying and tracking Angelika. I'll warn her when we get back to the hotel."

"Do you still want to track Moya and Yuri's steps?"

"Do you mind if we do it another time? Present events seem to have taken precedence."

Once back in the hotel, they sat in the bar, she sipping a brandy, he a whisky.

"Does this remind you of anything?" he asked.

She frowned momentarily and then a grin spread across her face.

"In Cyprus, the night we first made love?" she said.

"You were as tense that night as you are tonight."

"I didn't want to admit I loved you. Look where my accession led you. I hope you don't have too many regrets."

"I have none, my dearest."

"I've led you on a merry dance."

"It's not the one I expected but I wouldn't change a thing."

"You have always been an artful liar," she said. "But I still love you, Dickie, despite it all. I hope you have forgiven me for coming back to work."

"I haven't seen you so happy for a long time," he said. "I think we can work things out. We somehow always seem to."

"And almost always at your expense," she said.

"I'm not counting, my dearest" he said. He picked up her hand and kissed it gently.

They waited until eleven but the young people had not returned to the hotel.

"I'll leave a message at the desk for the receptionist to call me when they return. In the meantime, let's get some sleep," Elspeth said.

He winked at her and she looked at him sideways.

"The way we did in Cyprus?" he asked.

"As long as you don't leave in the morning the way you did then," she said.

"I had a plane to catch and you were sound asleep," he

replied, "but I plan to stay here in the morning and get on with my task for Lord Kennington."

*

Nancy Kendall linked arms with Lars Inversen, and sensed that he would take the gesture as a casual one, although she did not intend it to be. The Dane intrigued her and had done so since their meeting in the gift shop at the Kennington Dublin. She felt he had something mysterious about him despite his clean good looks. She had known few truly blond men before and found it beguiling.

"I can't imagine why Angie wants to go back to the cathedral again," she said.

"She said she wanted to show it to Derek."

"Don't you think it odd that St. Patrick's Cathedral is Anglican and not Roman Catholic? St Patrick's an RC saint."

"I was raised as a Lutheran," he said, "and don't follow these things. My parents were strict Protestants but I'm afraid I am not much of anything."

"I was C of E but like you am neutral these days. Angie was too until Derek came along."

"How did she meet him?"

"In Trafalgar Square. She had been to the National Gallery and went outside to have lunch. He came up to her and asked if he could share a corner of the wall she was sitting on out of the wind."

"And the rest is history?"

"Exactly."

"She did not know his family?"

"No, they met quite out of the blue."

"They don't seem to suit each other," Lars said.

"I didn't think so at first but she has changed. Now

she goes to church every day, often meeting him there. They have become quite inseparable."

"How long has this been for?" he asked.

"Five months anyway. I find their relationship strange although they seem as thick as thieves. Angie's a strong willed person with a mind of her own. He's a total wimp."

"You don't like him?"

"Not a great deal."

"Have you known Angelika a long time?"

"Forever. Since we were at boarding school together. She had just come from the Ukraine and I was away from home for the first time. My parents were getting a divorce so I was quite miserable. She spoke no English and was equally miserable. We had an instant bond. Anyway we both love art. We've been friends ever since."

"What will you do now that Mrs Koda had left the hotel? Will you go back to London?"

"I suppose so. Angie hasn't said what she wants to do."

"I plan to stay on for a few days. Will you stay too?"

Nancy grimaced. "At the Kennington Dublin? I can't afford even a cheap B&B on my savings."

"I could hire you as my assistant."

"Doing what? I don't think my training in fashion design will do much to help you."

"But you have a talent at sketching people, don't you?"

"How so?"

"I guess I have to come clean. I work for a private detective agency in Paris and I am trying to find some jewellery that was stolen from an auction house in London. I have traced one of the suspects here but I don't want to be seen doing any photographs. As an artist, you can sit and draw and no one will suspect you. I may also need you as a backup since I haven't brought an assistant with me. Normally we travel in pairs but this assignment is too sensitive for me to have brought another detective along. An innocent girl, however, could be a great asset when I am watching someone."

At first Nancy thought Lars was joking but when she looked at his earnest face, she decided to trust him.

"Do you have a prime suspect?"

He grinned. "I do but more of that in the morning. Let's enjoy this evening and get to work tomorrow."

At the end of this conversation, Nancy was not certain as to what she had agreed to do but she intended to do just what he suggested—enjoy the evening.

They caught up with Angelika and Derek as they were coming out of the cathedral. "The concierge said there was a good pub near here," Lars said. "Shall we try it? He said that it has the best Irish music in Dublin."

*

Lars Inversen realised he might have made a mistake inviting Nancy Kendall to stay on in Dublin, that in doing so he had upset his plans to corner Moya. But now that Moya was no longer in the hotel, he needed an overt reason to stay in touch with Angelika, thereby keeping an opening to Moya. Elspeth Duff had told Angelika that Moya had been taken to her family home in County Lough. Could he persuade Angelika and her hanger-on, as he thought of Derek, to accompany him to County Lough and bring Nancy on as well? He would have to think this out carefully. How could he approach Angelika about this?

18

Moya Koda died during the night without regaining consciousness. The nurse whom Eric had hired and who had arrived from Dublin shortly after the ambulance came had tapped on his bedroom door at four in the morning to tell him.

Eric wrapped his dressing gown around himself and followed the nurse to the room where Moya still lay in the bed in which her mother had died. Moya's battered face had been washed clean. The bruises now had turned from purple to orange but to Eric's eyes did not destroy Moya's intrinsic beauty.

"How did she die?" he asked. As yet he felt no pain.

"Ultimately from her wounds, I think," the nurse said, "but only an autopsy will tell us for sure. In my experience I would say it was a haemorrhage, a blood clot that got loose and went to her brain. Someone must have beaten her terribly because I never have seen such devastating bruises from a fall, not even when I had a patient who fell over a cliff in a car."

"I want you to say nothing," Eric said.

"But we will need a death certificate," she protested. "The doctor will have to list some cause of death even if there is no autopsy."

"Let me take care of that," he barked. "Now leave me alone with her."

When the nurse had left, he took Moya's hand. Its coldness seemed unreal, making Moya into a statue frozen in time. He put it to his cheek and said, "Moya, my dear, dear Moya, I'm sorry I haven't shaved." He had said these same words when they had made love the night before he left for London all those years before. She had rubbed her fingers across his chin that night and said 'scratchy', but would not repeat those words now. He wept.

The dawn came slowly over the horizon and spread its rays of light across Moya's body, laid out so expertly by the nurse. Eric watched the growing light but without comprehension that it was not bringing life the silent world of the night but death to a woman he had loved for a long time.

He stirred as the door opened and Sir Gerald came into the room.

"She never wanted to grow old," Gerald said. "But I don't think she would have wanted to die this way. I'm sorry, Eric. I know you tried to keep her alive at the end."

Eric could find nothing to say.

"I'll call the doctor so that we can go through the formalities," Gerald said.

"Yes," Eric croaked.

"You had better go and get dressed."

"Yes. I suppose I should," Eric replied.

For the first time in many years Eric Kennington was glad another person was there to take command.

By the time the funeral directors had left with Moya's body, Eric had found his equilibrium. He picked up his mobile and called Elspeth Duff.

"She's gone," he said, trying to keep the grief out of his voice.

"Gone? Who?"

"Don't be an ass, Elspeth. Moya died in her sleep last

night. And I want you to find out the why."

"Are you giving me full rein, Eric?"

"Of course I am. Now get to it."

*

Elspeth put her mobile on the breakfast table and addressed her husband.

"Moya's dead," she said, "and Eric's terribly upset. He wants me to find out who beat her. Of course, it's all connected with Yuri Koda's death but now Eric wants me to discover exactly what happened."

Richard folded back *The Times* and said, "Is he allowing you go to the police?"

"He's given me carte blanche but I'm not sure I want to contact the Garda right away. I want to talk to Angelika first. She may be able to front for me with the police but I'll need her cooperation."

"Do you trust her?"

"Not in the least. I sense she is her father's daughter despite all the polish she may have gained at a posh boarding school in England and her seeming devotion to Derek Somerset. I also want to go back to the scene of the crime. I suspect the news is old enough now that the press have moved on and the site will no longer be guarded. Will you come with me?"

Richard looked over his newspaper towards the window. "The sun's out and I am feeling restless. Let's go as soon as we finish our breakfast."

On their way out of the hotel, Elspeth stopped to talk to Harry O'Shea, who was ensconced in his alcove near the main door.

"Chilly for June," he said. "Take one of the hotel's umbrellas. You will need it."

Elspeth suddenly had an idea. "Harry, on the day that Mrs Koda walked out on her own, you said all she was carrying was a small attaché case. How big was it?"

"It was like a computer case. Big enough for a laptop."

"Do you think there was a laptop inside?"

"Couldn't tell. Maybe."

"Was the bag filled or did it bend in the middle?"

Harry O'Shea took off his top hat and scratched his head. "It wasn't flat like a laptop, but squarish—maybe something in a box, letter sized."

"Did Mrs Koda have a handbag with her?"

"Mmm. Maybe. No, definitely. A fashionable one, a large leather one, pleated and soft."

"Did she return with it?"

"Let me think. I noticed the attaché case was gone, but I think she still had the handbag."

"Did she take an umbrella?"

"I warned her that it was going to rain but she said she didn't want to be bothered. She was wet when she came back in."

"Was she wearing a scarf or a hat?"

"A scarf—a heavy silk one. It was wet too, just like her mackintosh."

"Do you remember how long she was gone?"

"At least an hour, perhaps a little longer."

A limousine drawing up to the door interrupted the conversation. Harry left his niche with an umbrella in hand, thus giving Elspeth time to formulate her next questions.

"What do you think Moya took from the hotel in the

attaché case?" Richard asked.

"And where did she take it that took an hour? She could have left Dublin, but not gone that far," Elspeth said almost to herself.

"She could have gone and put something in a safe deposit box in a bank."

Certainly that was a possibility or she could have given her bundle to someone else. But to whom? She would have had time to have a meeting with someone rather than just passing the attaché case off.

"As soon as Harry is finished with the new guest, I have another set of questions for him. Will you bear with me, Dickie?"

"I'm at your disposal, my dearest." He said with a slight bow. At moments like this Elspeth wanted to kiss him but knew her business decorum did not allow it.

Harry escorted the new guest into the lobby of the hotel and returned with the umbrella still unfurled.

"Harry, what is the name of the driver of the limousine that brought the Kodas from the airport when they arrived on Thursday? I'd like to speak to him. Was it the driver who just left?"

"It was. Patrick Mulligan. He's off to pick up another guest at the airport but should be back in an hour or so. Shall I have him ring you when he returns?"

"That would be best."

"What was that about?" Richard asked as they moved away from the hotel.

"I'm working on a new theory but have too many loose ends. Moya seemed obsessed with 'the goons' as she called them. I want to track them down. Zakhar is still here in Dublin and the other goon may be too. They were the last people we know to see Yuri alive other than Moya and his killer. Wouldn't it seem probable to you that if they had kept guard in the restaurant near Yuri and Moya, they would have seen Yuri and Moya safely back to the hotel? Because they didn't, I wonder what their real function was? Do you follow me?"

"Not precisely."

"From the few reports we have of Yuri here in Dublin, he was negotiating a contract with some governmental or business entity for a large gas contract. I have no idea what this entailed or why he thought his bodyguards were necessary. Did he feel physically unsafe? Or did he fear competitors from Ukraine or elsewhere? But would these competitors attack him so brutally and so openly? Or was he afraid of old enemies? Moya might have known which one was true. Why was Moya so afraid of the goons? Wouldn't they have protected her as well? Or were they loyal to Yuri but not to Moya? I want to find out."

"Am I assuming correctly that you want to talk to the goons?"

"If they are still here. We saw Zakhar last night. I want to know where he is now and what he's up to."

"Can Angelika help?" he asked.

Elspeth shook her head as if she wanted to clear out her thoughts. Then she responded.

"Angelika says she knew nothing about her father's affairs but I don't know if she is telling the truth or not. She certainly recognised Zakhar when he came to the hotel."

"And knocked him out," Richard said. "Was Angelika as frightened of Zakhar as Moya was, do you suppose?"

"When Angelika talked to him, the exchange didn't strike me as being hostile. It was only when he discharged his gun at the knock at the door that she floored him."

"You were quite fortunate that she came along."

Elspeth took Richard's arm, squeezed it gently and said, "It's wonderful to have you here, Dickie. I think I have an assignment for you that has nothing to do with Eric's directive to you. Do you think you could find out through channels in the FCO what the full extent of Yuri's business was here? Do you know anyone on the Irish desk?"

"Not anymore but I can certainly find out who's there now. I'll get on it when we return to the hotel."

They continued to walk along the edge of St. Stephen's Green towards the pub where Moya had said she, Yuri and the two goons had eaten their last meal together.

"What do you suppose they were discussing on the trip to the pub? Business or pleasure? Were the goons following behind and were they in earshot?" Elspeth speculated. "I wish I knew what was in their minds and what they feared. Everything looks so benign in the morning light. One can hardly conjure up a murder in such a lovely place. How did it seem so to Moya when Yuri dismissed the goons? Did Moya and Yuri feel safe? I wish I knew the answer."

Richard felt happy having Elspeth by his side. His mind was not on the murder but rather on the sunshine and his wife's arm tucked through his. His contentment was interrupted when he felt her jerk.

"Look, Dickie," she cried.

His eyes followed in the direction she was pointing. A

large hand printed poster in front of a shop read:
SUSPECT DETAINED IN KODA MURDER
INVESTIGATION

A rack of tabloid newspapers had a picture of Yuri Koda and beside it another of a younger man.

"That's Zakhar," Elspeth said.

Elspeth grabbed a paper from the rack outside the shop and retreated into the building to pay for it. She was reading the text under the headline when she emerged and almost tripped over the step at the doorway. Richard reached up to steady her.

"It can't be," Elspeth said. "They are saying that Zakhar is Sergei Koda. How can that be? Angelika told me his name was Zakhar. Either she's lying or Zakhar gave the wrong name to the police. Oh no, Dickie. I can only guess that Angelika wasn't telling me the truth."

"Didn't you tell me Angelika floored Zakhar? Why would she do that?"

"I have no idea. I always suspected Angelika of duplicity but now I think I need to assume everything she tells me is wrong or at least evasive. But why?"

"Does it say why they arrested him and why?"

Elspeth folded back the pages of the newspaper and skimmed down the page.

"The Garda must have done a passport check. It says that he entered Ireland ten days ago and was found at five this morning staying at a B&B. I suspect the police had been following him and made the early morning arrest before he could leave his lodgings for the day."

"Do they mention Moya or Angelika?"

'No, nor the Kennington Dublin, thank goodness."

"Do they give a reason for his arrest?"

Elspeth read out the stop press. "The son of Yuri Koda, Sergei Koda, was detained at five this morning at a bed and breakfast where he was staying near the centre of the city. The Garda have not yet given full details of why he was taken into custody but sources close to the police say he was seen near the scene of the crime on Saturday night. He has not been charged with the murder as yet. A Garda spokesperson said he would be questioned this morning. They are due to give a press conference later today and will provide further details."

"Are you sure the picture is of Zakhar? It's not very clear."

"I'm certain it is. The first thing Scotland Yard teaches you is to memorise the details of a face of someone who threatens you. Eyes, nose, ears, chin, hair, bone structure and everything in between. After all these years I haven't forgotten the routine."

"If Sergei is responsible for the murder, why would he come to the Kennington Dublin and brandish a gun?" Richard asked.

"He said he wanted to see Moya."

"Why Moya? I would have thought that Sergei, if Zakhar is Sergei, would have avoided Moya."

"Possibly, if he was at the scene of the murder, he might have wanted to kill Moya, not his father, and then Yuri confronted him to save Moya. Afterwards Zakhar a.k.a. Sergei came to the hotel to finish the task," Elspeth said but she did not look as if she believed her own supposition. "Or Zakhar gave Sergei's name but that's unlikely because the photograph in the newspaper looks like a passport photo. What do you think, Dickie?"

"My dearest, you are the investigator. Don't you think it is now time you spoke to the police?"

Elspeth knew her husband was right. However, she needed to develop a cover story to give them. She doubted a private citizen, particularly a foreigner as she was in Ireland, would be given unlimited access to the information as to why Sergei was detained. She knew she could use her contact in Scotland Yard but would this cut ice with the Garda?

"I'll ring Tony Ketcham at the Yard when we get back to the hotel but I'll need an excuse that doesn't link Sergei to the Kennington Dublin," she said.

"Are you still worried about Eric?" Richard asked.

"A bit. I'm so accustomed to protecting the hotels that it's become normal procedure before Eric came and intervened. I should call Pamela to find out the reason before I call Tony."

"You're still being cautious."

"I suppose I am. While I'm working things out, at least let's go by the scene of the original crime before we return to the hotel."

No member of the Guarda was at the murder site and the police tape had been removed. Richard pulled a pop-up map of Dublin from this pocket and pointed out where the theatre was, as if they were tourists. They walked casually around the theatre as if they wanted to find the stage door.

"Moya never told me where they were attacked. She simply said they were out for a romantic stroll. This hardly seems a place one would come with that in mind." Elspeth said. "But the body must have been found here, as that is where I saw the police investigation tent. I wonder if Yuri was attacked elsewhere and dragged here? Moya described

Yuri as a big man so if he were accosted elsewhere, a strong person would be needed to move the body. Moya also said Yuri pushed her out of the way. I'm not certain that she would have sustained such awful bruises just from being pushed."

Elspeth then remembered another thing Moya had told her. Angelika had taken photographs of Moya's bruises. Why had Elspeth ignored this? When she got to the hotel, she must check with Angelika. Angelika might lie but the picture would not.

19

The doctor leaned up from Moya Koda's body and turned to Eric Kennington and Sir Gerald de Lacey.

"I helped deliver her," the doctor said in a hoarse voice. "I never thought I would help bury her. She was always so full of life that I cannot take in that she has left us."

After swallowing deeply, Eric Kennington spoke quietly. "How did she die?" he asked.

"Ultimately from her wounds, I suspect."

"Can you write accidental death on the death certificate?" Sir Gerald asked.

"I can, but I'm almost certain these wounds were not accidental. She was badly beaten by someone," the doctor said. "I'll leave what I write to your wishes, Gerald. Nothing will bring her back. Shall I write wounds sustained in a fall? That way, there should be no further investigation."

Eric Kennington wanted to agree but he was intelligent enough to know that if the police learned that Moya had died, they might question the death certificate. He remembered Elspeth had said Moya claimed she had been injured when Yuri had pushed her aside but Elspeth had also mentioned that Moya had left the hotel and come back with what appeared to be further injuries. Could they plead that Moya had fallen down a second time because of her first round of wounds? Somehow he felt that this story would seem doubtful.

Eric asked, "Mightn't the police suspect more had happened, particularly in light of her husband's dying several days ago of an attack by an unknown assailant? We need to think of something that will take the police's attention away from Moya. Can you think of a better wording?"

Sir Gerald set his jaw. "I won't have Moya's death broadcast if we can avoid it. Can you simply say 'complications due to head injuries'? Isn't that true but innocuous?"

"I agree," Eric said. "That will take you off the hook, doctor. And hopefully not arouse the suspicions of the Garda. I want to keep Moya's death out of the press. She deserves better than having her death blasted out by the tabloids."

The doctor filled in the required form and left shortly afterwards, giving his condolences once again to Sir Gerald. Sir Gerald showed the death certificate to Eric, as if getting his final seal of approval.

"Come and have some breakfast," he said to Eric.

"I don't have much appetite," Eric said.

"Have some coffee or tea anyway. I'll call the priest. We have our private chapel here where all the family have been buried for as long as anyone can remember. Moya had ceased to be a believer, but for her mother's sake, I want to see Moya buried properly. I can have it done as soon as the body is prepared. I'll ring the undertakers when we have finished our coffee."

"Shouldn't we have the nurse do the final preparations, so as few people as possible see Moya's battered face? She would hate to have anyone see her in the state in which she died."

Sir Gerald laughed for the first time that morning. "She was vain, as you must have known."

Eric smiled. "Until yesterday, I never saw her other than exquisitely made up. Even when she was riding across the fields, when I first met her, she was picture-perfect."

Sir Gerald nodded. "Do you know how much time she spent each day to look so naturally beautiful? Her mother used to chastise her about her vanity. But I loved Moya's care with her appearance. She did it to please, not only others but herself. When she first started taking pride in her appearance, at about aged four, she would come prancing at my feet and flick her black hair like a wild mare. She knew her own beauty. No wonder you were so stricken when you first met her. Did her allure ever fade for you? It never did for most people."

Eric looked down at his teacup and pressed his eyes together to prevent the tears. He had watched Moya age. Sir Gerald was right. Moya's careful attention to her appearance had never diminished but as she grew older, Eric had been aware that she had more and more relied on the skilful application of cosmetics, a talented hairdresser and world-class couturiers. Her love of life had never slackened, despite her lacklustre first marriage. Moya dazzled and she knew it.

Moya came to Eric many times for advice, usually about one affair or another. Eric, being upwardly mobile, marvelled at her audacity. Surely her husband had known about her infidelities. Had he overlooked them simply because he was in her thrall too or because of his position in society?

Once Moya had invited Eric to lunch at the Savoy, before its closure for renovation several years before. Eric preferred the quieter places where they often met. He suspected that Moya was showcasing him as another of her conquests. Eric loved his wife, who had remained quietly by his side through his rise in the hotel business but she was dull beside Moya. Eric often laughed at Moya but he always knew she was a dangerous person. She had the ability to twist people in order to get her way. But in the end she had lost the game, to which the beaten body upstairs gave testament. Was her playing with Yuri's risk-taking the cause of her demise? Eric did not want to consider that she ultimately was the cause of her own downfall.

He thought of Elspeth Duff in Dublin. How much would she want to probe into the cause of Moya's death? How much would he have to tell her about Moya? Would Elspeth assume that Moya's death might be the result of something Moya had done? Moya always lived on the edge, as her marriage to Yuri Koda had proven. Eric had told Moya he did not approve but she had only laughed at him.

"What harm is there in it?" she had said. "Yuri lives life to the full. Few men do."

Eric knew Moya was criticising his strict way of living but he had no choice, he felt, if he were to succeed.

Moya had laughed about this too. She had no understanding of the responsibilities of self-made men.

"Sweet Eric, you have got your hotels. In the end has it been worth all the trouble?"

Eric had smarted at this. Moya had a way of being

cruel. He always had forgiven her because he wanted her to love him the way he loved her.

Sir Gerald broke Eric's reverie. "I'll leave you to your tea," he said. "I need to make the final arrangements for Moya's burial. She will go in the family crypt so there will be no need for gravediggers. I'll ask Father Patrick if he can come and take care of whatever needs to be done to help her soul on to heaven, if there is one."

Eric wondered at this statement, as Moya had always proclaimed her family's deep commitment to the Roman church.

"I would like to stay for the burial but afterwards I need to get back to Dublin and then on to London," he said.

Sir Gerald turned to him. "I need to apologise to you, Eric," he said. "I had no idea you had the power to make your dream come true. We should have let you marry Moya. She would have been better off."

Only Sir Gerald, Eric, the housekeeper, the gardener and the priest were present when Moya was consigned to the crypt. Her body was in a makeshift coffin but Gerald said he would take care of getting a better one in the days to come. The wooden box was laid to rest beside Moya's mother's gilded coffin, one that was in vivid contrast to Moya's simple one.

The housekeeper simpered and the gardener, who had built the box, stood stoically with cap in hand. Sir Gerald sniffed as the priest muttered his often-recited words. Eric kept his face still but inside his heart was twisted in agony. The priest's words meant little to Eric who was a 'social' Anglican, appearing beside his wife when she needed him to be present and at Christmas and Easter. He found religious ceremonies, particularly Roman Catholic ones, uncomfortable.

Eric had hired a simple black saloon car from a mechanic who owned the local garage as driver. The man chatted cheerfully but Eric did not respond with more than a few grunts and nods. The driver grew silent as they arrived at the front door of the Kennington Dublin and the doorman came out with an umbrella. Eric paid the driver generously and accepted the protection from the rain.

"Mr Smith, welcome back," Harry said.

Eric had in the moment forgotten his pseudonym and frowned.

"Is Elspeth Duff here?" he growled.

"Yes, sir. She and Sir Richard came in just before lunch. She asked that she be called when you arrived back."

"Then do so," Eric barked. "Tell her I will be in my room and want to hear from her immediately."

"Yes, m'lord," Harry said.

His mind elsewhere, Eric did not notice that Harry had used his title.

*

"Pamela, have you seen the news?" Elspeth said once her call went through to the Kennington Organisation offices in London.

"Wait a tick," Pamela said.

Elspeth could hear Pamela tapping her computer keys. She did not respond for a long moment.

"It looks like your case is closed," Pamela finally said. "Perhaps now we can rest easily. I can't find any indication that the hotel there was mentioned at all."

"I'm not so certain we are in the clear," Elspeth responded. "How much do you know about what has happened here in the last twenty-four hours?"

"Sean Clancy's report said Moya had left the hotel by ambulance late yesterday. I've heard nothing more."

Eric hasn't connected you?"

"No. Should he have?"

Elspeth blew out her breath. If Eric had not told her of the purpose of his visit to Moya's country home with Pamela, Elspeth needed to decide if it was appropriate for her to do so. She decided to be discreet but honest, fearing Eric's ill temper if she said too much.

"Moya did leave the hotel last night but she died early this morning at her family's home in County Louth," Elspeth said.

"Of her wounds?"

"Probably, which means there was a double murder. The Garda will eventually discover this and Moya's stay in the hotel will undoubtedly come out. I need some firm direction as to where to go from here. Eric isn't here at the moment and I have no idea when he will return. Shall I wait for his return to get instructions?"

Pamela paused before answering.

"Carry on as before and wait for him to advise you," she said. "Most of all protect the hotel and its guests. Is Moya's stepdaughter still there?"

"Yes. I plan to talk to her as soon as I ring off. You must have read Sean's report about the disruption here in the lobby the day before yesterday. I am still uncomfortable with what happened and its effect on the few people who were in the lobby at the time. With your consent, I will offer them an apology and no charge for their rooms."

"Of course, see to that without delay. Sean's report said the gunman was in the employ of Yuri Koda and demanded to see Moya."

"He did. Don't you find it strange that the gunman is the same man the Garda just detained? Angelika was the one who told me that the gunman was called Zakhar and that he was one of Yuri's goons, as Moya called them. Now it appears he was really Angelika Rostova's half-brother. Surely she would have known that when she saw him in the hotel, even if she hadn't seen him for many years. I'll have to confront her about this but I was hoping you or Eric would tell me how far you want me to go with questioning her. If I am to protect the hotel guests, I have to know why Angelika lied and if Sergei will tell the police that Angelika is here. I don't want to stir up trouble with her but I also don't want the police storming the hotel."

Pamela heard Elspeth out without comment.

"Have you talked to Richard?" Pamela asked.

"Non-stop but I can't ask him to answer questions about hotel policy, despite his new employment."

"What did he advise?"

"That I call you."

"You sound as if you are keeping something back," Pamela said. "Does it have to do with Eric?"

"Mmm. I'll let you talk to him. Please contact him and then ring me. In the meantime, I'll talk to Angelika and let you know the outcome."

"I want lunch before I take on Angelika," Elspeth said to her husband as she finished her call and kicked off her shoes. "And I want to enjoy the strawberries without being interrupted. Not even Sergei's arrest can keep me from them."

20

Angelika stared down at the newspaper Nancy Kendall had handed her. Her half-brother stared back silently from the front page. Angelika knew she had a problem.

Elspeth had telephoned and asked to see her. She had put Elspeth off for an hour. At first she had thought to flee from the hotel but once her panic had subsided, she decided she needed time to cook up a good excuse as to why she had said Sergei was called Zakhar. Could she say that Zakhar was a childhood nickname? Or that Sergei had threatened her? She also would have to give an explanation as to why Sergei had come to the hotel with a gun and demanded to see Moya. Angelika did not want to tell the whole truth but perhaps a half-truth would do.

"Nance, could you go down and get the latest papers?" she asked. "I want to know more about the arrest."

"Is he your half-brother really?" Nancy asked.

Angelika paused. "It's hard to tell from the picture in the paper. It might be. I haven't seen him in a long time." That was definitely a half-truth as she had seen him in the lobby of the hotel less than forty-eight hours before. She did not want Nancy to know this—nor Derek for that matter.

Angelika regretted that Elspeth and her husband had seen her shortly before she had left the Green. Angelika had to think quickly.

She also wondered what she could do to help Sergei. He had warned her to lie low if the police found him as he thought they might. But Elspeth Duff was sharp and had seen Sergei leaving her. Would Elspeth go to the police? Others on the hotel staff had seen Sergei as well and would be able to identify him as the gunman in the lobby. Angelika had pleaded with Sergei not to come to the hotel but he seemed determined to confront Moya.

Where was Moya? Angelika's stepmother had not left her alone for such a long time since they had arrived in Dublin. Angelika had left three messages for Moya to ring here. None were answered. Angelika considered going to Moya's suite again but then decided otherwise. For all Angelika knew Moya could be under heavy sedation and not answering her door.

Angelika sat back and waited for Elspeth to knock.

*

The hour's respite gave Elspeth time to formulate her questions. She wished Eric Kennington were back in the hotel to give her some guidance but in his absence she decided to be circumspect. She hoped Angelika would be forthcoming but suspected she would not be.

Once she had arrived, she sat on one of the two chairs in Angelika's room which were positioned around a table decorated with the signature Kennington hotels fresh flowers. She noticed that Angelika had arranged the chairs so that it was difficult to look her directly in the eyes.

"I didn't order coffee as I thought you might have just finished lunch," Angelika said. Elspeth guessed this was another way to cut the interview short.

Elspeth began. "Moya told me that you had taken photographs of her wounds. Would you show them to me?"

"They're only on my phone," Angelika replied.

"Will you email them to me?" Elspeth responded.

"I'll have to ask Moya. She asked me to keep them private."

Elspeth realised that Angelika did not know that Moya was dead. But Angelika would sooner or later. Elspeth chose to tell her now.

"That won't be possible," she said. "Angelika, I know you had mixed feelings about your stepmother but I need to tell you that she died this morning at her family home in County Lough. She slid into unconsciousness before the ambulance came for her here yesterday afternoon but before doing so she asked to be taken to her family home. She never came out of her final coma. I'm so sorry."

Elspeth watched Angelika's face. Even from the side view, Elspeth could tell that Angelika was dealing with a host of emotions. Elspeth wondered what they might be.

"You're right. I didn't like my stepmother but she didn't deserve to die from the wounds she suffered. No person should. Who else knows about this?"

Angelika's words were odd, Elspeth thought. In them Elspeth found a touch of sadness but mainly trepidation mixed with caution.

"Will you show me the photographs now that Moya is no longer here?" Elspeth asked.

"Do the police know about Moya?"

"I don't think so. The death was listed as a result of injuries due to an accident."

"That's a relief anyway," Angelika said sighing. "I suppose I could show you the photographs. Let me get my phone."

Elspeth waited as Angelika rummaged through her

handbag. She was still about her task before the door to the room flew open.

"Here's more," Nancy Kendall shouted, throwing three late editions of the Irish press on one of the two beds. "Oh, Ms Duff, I didn't realise you were here. Have you seen that someone has been arrested on suspicion of murdering Mr Koda?"

Elspeth smiled; Angelika, looking up, did not. Elspeth waited and felt rather like a spider watching a fly.

"All this is quite terrible for Angie, Ms Duff. First her father dying and then her half-brother being accused of murder."

"He's only been detained, at least when I last checked on the internet. They haven't officially charged him with any crime," Elspeth said.

"It may not be Sergei," Angelika said. "The photographs are unclear in the papers."

"But it was clearly Zakhar," Elspeth said, "at least in the paper I saw. Why didn't you mention this, Angelika?"

"I'm not convinced it is Sergei. Zakhar probably used his name. That's it; he must have."

The plea was feeble at best.

"I don't know what to do," Angelika cried out. Her face was filled with confusion and pain.

Elspeth maternal instincts came into play and she softened. "Why don't you let me help you?"

"Why would you do that?"

"My job includes protecting the hotel's guests and I also think you have suffered too many shocks over the last few days. And I would like to help because you remind me in a way of my daughter and I have many years of experience dealing with situations like this. I want you to trust me and tell me the truth."

"I have told you."

"I mean the whole truth. I can't help you unless I know what you do about the circumstances of your father's death and about your brother."

"Sergei had nothing to do with my father's death. That is the truth."

"But not the whole truth. Why did Sergei come here to the hotel to see Moya?"

"He wanted to confront her. He thought she was responsible for my father's death."

Elspeth sensed that Angelika was lying. People acted slightly differently when they lied.

"But your stepmother was beaten too. How could she be implicated in your father's murder?"

"She must have somehow. She must have hired someone to kill him."

"For some reason I don't think so. Your stepmother left the hotel on Monday and apparently was attacked again. I think the killer wanted both your father and stepmother dead."

"But how can that be?"

"Probably the murderer only initially meant to kill your father. In the end, however, the murderer succeeded in killing both."

As Elspeth spoke, she realised she was defending Moya against what seemed an unjust accusation by Angelika.

Nancy Kendall stood frozen by the bedside. "Is Mrs Koda dead?"

"She died early this morning."

"Oh, Angie," her friend said and went to take Angelika in her arms. Angelika leaned on her shoulder and began to sob in great heaves of emotion.

The moment was awkward. Elspeth decided she could not get more information from Angelika, and therefore rose to go. She put her hand on Nancy's arm and said, "Take care of her."

Elspeth quietly closed the door leaving the two young women behind.

When Elspeth returned to her suite, Richard looked up enquiringly.

"Any success?" he asked.

"Yes and no. Angelika didn't say so directly but from what she implied the man the Garda detained is her half-brother."

"It sounds as if she wasn't cooperative. What do you plan to do now?"

"I want to find out where Moya went when she left the hotel the day after Yuri Koda's murder. I think if I knew, I would be further along in understanding what happened to both Yuri and Moya."

"Do you have a plan?" Richard asked.

"The embryo of one. Moya was so determined that no one would see her, particularly the police, that whatever her mission was the afternoon she left the hotel, it must have been urgent. She was away for an hour and in that time shed the attaché case she had bought in the hotel shop and the contents she had put in it. Harry O'Shea's information helps but I need to dig further. First I would like to walk towards Trinity College and see where she might have been headed when she left here. Harry said she disappeared around a corner. What's there? Were there buildings she might have entered or a taxi rank? If a taxi rank, would any of the drivers recognise her? She would be hard to miss with her battered face, no matter how well made up."

"Do you think the taxi drivers will talk?" Richard asked.

"I have my PI licence from California with me. More than one person has opened up to me after they see it. I'll concoct some story."

"What about Eric?"

"He said to do everything I can."

"Don't go too far, my dearest. You know how badly that served you in Victoria."

"I'm staying safely within the law," Elspeth countered. "Eric can have no objection. Dickie, do you mind if I do this on my own?"

"I need to be tending to my task here, so am grateful to leave you to your investigation. But come back to the hotel if you encounter any trouble."

"Yes, my dear avuncular Dickie," she said with a grin and a twinkle in her eyes. "Do you mind if I borrow your mackintosh? It looks more detective-like."

Suitably outfitted in Richard's raincoat and a floppy rain hat, Elspeth set out towards Trinity College. She first asked for Harry to take note as to how far she stayed within his vision. As she walked, she kept turning back to see if Harry was still in sight but soon she reached the end of Dawson Street and had to turn on Nassau Street, out of the view of the hotel. Moya must have done the same thing.

Further down she saw an entrance to Trinity College. She squared her shoulders and made a decision. She crossed the busy street and entered the college grounds.

Elspeth felt at home walking through the quadrangle after passing through the tunnel that led the way into the main area of the campus. Memories of her time at Cambridge came flooding back. For a moment she was lost in reverie, but found herself in one of the courtyards that housed the main library. She came back to reality. What better place to start her enquiry.

Elspeth mounted the stairs and once inside saw a desk with a crinkle-haired woman sitting at it. She was absorbed in her computer and did not look up until Elspeth approached the desk. Obviously the woman was used to the clack of heels across the floor.

Elspeth made up her story as she went along.

"I am a graduate of Girton College, Cambridge and am now involved with the law," she said. "I am here in Dublin on business and need some information I cannot seem to find easily on the internet. Could you help me find someone here at Trinity College who could help me?"

The woman's eyes slid down Elspeth's mackintosh. Elspeth couldn't read the woman's thoughts and wished now she had not wanted to dress up as a gumshoe.

"It's raining on and off so I borrowed my husband's raincoat," Elspeth said in way of explanation but the woman did not seem to care. "Can you direct me to anyone in the department of art history who might be able to answer questions of early twentieth century Russian jewellery?"

"The college is closed today," the woman said and went back to her computer.

Elspeth was not put off. "Is anyone on the faculty here?"

"I have no idea."

Elspeth was beginning to feel annoyed. She abhorred gatekeeper mentality. She was about to turn away when a voice behind her said, "Perhaps I can help you? I am Emery Gill from the college of medicine but my wife is a specialist in late Tsarist Russia and might be able to help you. What is it you want to know?"

Elspeth turned to see a tall man with thick dark hair peppered with grey, old-fashioned round glasses, a rumpled open-necked shirt and battered briefcase.

The woman at the desk did not look up from her computer.

"Professor Gill, thank you. Let me introduce myself." Elspeth paused. How should she represent herself? She did not want to repeat that she was involved with the law. Professor Gill looked a typical academic and Elspeth thought he would want to know the truth.

"I'm looking for information of the disposition of the Tsar's family's possessions after the revolution," she said. "I've hit the problem that many of the pieces are still in private hands and are not listed on the internet. I'm here in Dublin on a case involving the theft of some of the pieces of jewellery believed to be brought out from Russia after the Revolution but their current ownership had never been made public. I'm looking for someone to help me research this. Do you think your wife could help me?"

"She's waiting for me at a café just outside the gates of the college. Why don't you come with me and ask her?"

They found Emery Gill's wife Irina sipping a latte and reading *The Irish Times*.

"This just as well could be last week's paper," Irina said as she put down the paper and smiled up at Elspeth and her husband. "Won't they ever solve the problems of the world?"

Emery Gill introduced Elspeth and told Irina of Elspeth's request. He also mentioned Elspeth's cover story at the library desk. He must have overheard and for the moment Elspeth did not dispute it.

"I'm not an expert on jewellery," Irina said, "but I know a good deal about the tsar's family who left Russia, particularly those who went to France. Such a sad story. So many believed the Revolution would not last. In the end it didn't but the twenty-first century is not a time for hope for the Romanov family. The few successful members of the family are now financiers with seats on the exchanges of Western Europe and America. But tell me more. I may be able to find what you are looking for."

Elspeth still had not decided how much to tell about her position. Instead she told Irina about her problem.

"Do you remember several years ago about the scandal in London about the theft of priceless pieces of Russian jewellery from one of the auction houses in London?"

Irina frowned. "Vaguely. Wasn't one of the employees blamed? I don't remember the follow-up. Did they ever catch the thief?"

"Not yet but we have some suspicion that the pieces have been brought to Dublin recently."

"How exciting. Do the Garda know?"

"I'm acting in confidence," Elspeth said. "My goal is to protect people who might be innocent. If I can establish that the pieces are here, I can save a great deal of unpleasantness to those on the periphery who are not involved."

"Let me make a few phone calls," Irina responded. "I have a friend who is a research assistant in the College of Art History who specialises in late nineteenth and early twentieth century Russian artefacts. She may be able to help. Where can I reach you?"

Elspeth bit her lip. Should she admit her true position?

"I'm staying at the Kennington Dublin," she finally said. "If you reach your friend, would you like to bring her around for tea there?"

Irina grinned. "She won't refuse. Unfortunately we have to decline, as we are leaving on holiday this evening. Her name is Maureen Donahue."

Elspeth hesitated. She did not want to give Irina her business card and so gave her mobile number instead.

"Have her ring me. Tea is from half three until six. I think she will find it delectable."

Elspeth left the café and resumed her search for a taxi rank. If Maureen Donahue did come for tea, Elspeth still had time to question taxi drivers in the area. She saw several taxis in a queue waiting outside a hotel around the corner from the Kennington Dublin and headed for it. She should have known better, as the doorman asked her to hurry on. Elspeth would not be deterred.

"Do you know Harry O'Shea at the Kennington Dublin?" she asked. The doorman was old enough that he might well do so.

"Harry? Of course. All of us old ones know each other

hereabouts."

"Would you mind calling him? Tell him that my name is Elspeth Duff."

After a quick word into his mobile, the doorman smiled. "He says you're to be trusted. What can I do for you?"

"I'm trying to establish if a woman took a taxi from near here on last Tuesday. She was wearing a headscarf and sunglasses, I think, despite the rain, she would have been noticeable because of wounds on her face. I'm trying to find out where she might have gone."

"I don't remember anyone like that and I think I would have noticed. Will you give me some time to ask about?"

"That would be brilliant," Elspeth said. "If you hear of anything, call Harry. He can get the message to me."

Elspeth felt frustrated that she had accomplished so little. Eric Kennington would be back in Dublin soon and she had little to report. She made her way down Dawson Street towards St. Stephen's Green. She stopped by the hotel to speak briefly to Harry O'Shea and then walked on towards the park. She found a bench in an unoccupied gazebo and took a seat facing in the direction of National Concert Hall where all the difficulty had begun. Or had the problem only come to a climax there?

What did she know? Moya de Lacey Mulholland Koda was dead. Her beginnings must have led to her eventual death. Elspeth wanted to know from Eric what Moya had been like when she was young. Moya's own description of her youth and first marriage had been fleeting but were there seeds there of her demise? And Yuri Koda? What was his fascination with Moya? She and Yuri seemed so mismatched but were they really? What about the jewels? Their disappearance kept cropping up and Elspeth was now convinced that a link existed between the murders and the theft. Lars Inversen's arrival at the hotel could be chance but Elspeth didn't believe in this kind of coincidence. What is more, Pamela had vouched for his agency.

Lars was a puzzling addition to the imbroglio. His appearance and manner were certainly respectable. In fact he personified the type of guest Eric Kennington preferred. But was he who he said he was? Appearances could be deceptive and a person who seemed to be above board could be a clever criminal. Elspeth had learned that to her peril on other cases.

Angelika was unreadable but obviously devious. Her engagement to Derek Somerset was incongruous. Elspeth had pegged her as being as hard as nails and a liar but Nancy Kendall, who knew her better, was overly protective, almost more so than a normal friend would be. Had Elspeth read Angelika wrongly? Could she trust any information that Angelika gave her? Angelika would know more about Yuri Koda than anyone still alive, even Sergei, if he was Sergei.

Elspeth put her hand to her forehead, when a voice she knew addressed her.

"You look deep in thought. I hope that means you have solved all the mysteries in the hotel and I can get back to London."

"Eric!"

"I've done all that could be done in County Lough and now must get back to the office." He lowered his bulk down on the bench next to her.

"Eric, we need to talk—about Moya. I can't get on with my enquiries until I know more about her."

"The doctor said she died of her wounds."

"No, not that. I want to know who she was. I think if I do, I could understand why she got those wounds in the first place."

"Didn't she tell you?"

"No. Did she tell you?"

"She never regained consciousness so she didn't."

"Who was she really?"

"Elspeth, what sort of silly question is that?" he snapped.

"Rather too profound a one, I'm afraid. I'm certain Moya died because of who she was. I doubt she was a dutiful wife even though she implied she had been pressed into marrying Yuri by his frontal attack on her affections. Was she a docile person?"

"Moya? Never."

"So I am beginning to understand. What is the real reason she married Yuri?"

"Moya always liked a dare," Eric said. "I would warn her about so much in her life and she would only laugh at me and call me 'Safe Eric'. I didn't have her advantages, you see. My risks had to be calculated. She tended to plunge pell-mell into things, and would say that however they turned out, it would be an adventure."

"Then she wasn't the staid housewife she made out to be?"

"I wish she had been. She would have been alive today." Eric shifted his body as if his physical state was as uncomfortable as this conversation.

"Eric, I never have asked about your private life, because Pamela is so protective of it. I can only assume that you knew Moya . . ." Elspeth cleared her throat, ". . . quite well."

Eric reddened, which Elspeth had never seen him do before.

"When we were young, I wanted to marry her. I'm glad now that I didn't. I'm quite happy with Lorna."

Lorna, thought Elspeth. Now she knew his wife's name.

"I never could have risen in my business with a wife like Moya. She was very demanding of her men and expected them to forgive her all trespasses."

"Yuri as well?"

Eric moved again and looked out over the Green.

"No, I don't think Yuri did. Moya had finally met her match. You see, for all Moya's overlay of gentility, she was an adventurer. So was Yuri. At first I think Yuri felt he had won a great prize in Moya. I expect in the end, he knew she was as unscrupulous as he was."

Elspeth had seen Eric with Moya those last few hours they were in the hotel together. Elspeth suspected that Eric was still in love with Moya, that perhaps Moya represented a life and love he could never have. Elspeth was saddened for him for the first time in her career. Somehow Eric was diminished in her sight, although she could not have said why. The great hotel mogul was after all only a man.

"But who would have wanted to kill the two of them?" Elspeth asked almost to herself.

Elspeth thought of Moya's battered face. "Her wounds weren't the right kind to have been caused by a shove or a fall. I certain the person or people who killed Yuri beat her. I wish I knew if they left Moya for dead. The most confusing part, however, is the second beating."

"What about the second beating?"

"She left the hotel for about an hour on Tuesday. When she returned her face was in worse condition than when she left, according to the doorman. I saw her before and after and can confirm what she looked like in the end. When she left the hotel the day after Yuri's murder, she was carrying something that she didn't have with her when she returned. I need to know what that was and why she was beaten a second time."

Elspeth glanced at her watch. "I'm meeting someone for tea who can help me. When do you leave?"

"Pamela is sending over the company jet. I'll leave as soon as it arrives."

"Eric, eventually I am going to need to talk to the Garda and find out what they have discovered. Do you mind?"

"Can you leave the hotel out of it?"

"I'll try but I can guarantee nothing. Trust me to be discreet."

"I'll have to. Do you have any ideas, Elspeth?"

Elspeth had never heard him use this pleading tone before.

"I'm working on one. You may not like it, Eric. It may involve some culpability on Moya's part."

Eric lowered his eyes and swallowed visibly. "I'm afraid that might be true. I want you to report to me directly from now on, not to Pamela. She doesn't need to know all this."

Maureen Donahue was punctual, which pleased Elspeth. Eric Kennington would have approved of Maureen as a guest because of her sober dress but Elspeth knew the clothes were inexpensive despite the care with which they had been put together. Elspeth doubted Maureen could afford even a cup of tea at the Kennington Dublin.

The American woman of middle age had greying hair that to Elspeth's eye could do with a bit of dye and a lot of styling. She had a friendly smile but a wrinkled brow. Elspeth felt she could trust Maureen who was probably the sort students would flock to.

"Ms Donahue," Elspeth said as they were seated in a quiet corner of Elspeth's choosing, "do you remember the case of the Russian jewellery that was stolen from an auction house, Northby's in London, several years ago?"

"The minor Romanov collection that had been brought out of Russia to Paris after the Revolution? Yes, I do remember. Moya Mulholland was accused by the press although the police never arrested her."

"Do you know the collection?"

"I do as a matter of fact. After the robbery, I was asked to verify the pieces that had been stolen. Since they had been held in private, there was no official catalogue of them. I knew Moya, you see. We had worked together on several occasions. I wanted her to be innocent, although that didn't affect my work."

"You wanted her to be innocent?" Elspeth said. "But were you sure she was?"

"One can never know, I suppose."

"Did you know Moya well?"

"Only professionally, not personally."

"How would you describe her professionally?"

"She was brilliant. In the many emails we exchanged, she was always quick to provide information. I assumed she had everything packed away in her head.

"She had information that was different from that I could access otherwise. I'm an academic so I always like a new source of information. I wondered at the time why she didn't get further credentials and join the faculty of some prestigious university. She had the brains for it. When I asked her, she sent me back an email with a smiley face saying she enjoyed life too much to be involved in professorial politics. They are fierce," Maureen said with a wry smile.

Elspeth wondered if Maureen had been passed over for a professorship as Irina had described her as a research assistant.

"Tell me about the jewellery," Elspeth said.

"As you would suspect, most of the pieces were small, easy to hide in one's clothing if you were on the run from the revolutionaries. Much of their value is historical and they would lose some of their worth if taken apart but there were two rubies and an emerald of some size as well as some sizeable real pearls, which even if taken out of their settings, would fetch a good price."

"Do you have any idea of the full value of the collection?"

"If auctioned on the open market, probably nine or ten million euros or more. Since the recession, the price of some historical collectibles has gone up considerably. They're considered a good hedging bet against the falling economy."

"Are there any collectors here in Ireland who might be interested if the thieves contacted them?"

"That's not my field," Maureen said, this time with a full grin. "I suspect Moya would know. That's the kind of information she would delight in. Have you thought of asking her? I can give you a contact email."

Elspeth decided not to tell Maureen of Moya's death.

"Can you give me the name of any dealers here who might give me further information about selling historical gems?"

"Legally?"

"Yes. Do you know any ones that might be interested in buying the collection?"

Maureen shook her head. "I try to stay out of the commercial side of things. I'm sure someone here in the hotel might be able to help you. Don't concierges know this sort of thing? On television shows they seem to be a font of all knowledge."

It was Elspeth's turn to grin. "Don't believe everything you see on the television."

The conversation turned away from the Romanov collection and on to the history of the movement of precious objects out of Russia. Finally Maureen rose.

"As much as I would like to extend our conversation," she said, "I have a child at home waiting for her supper. I don't think I will need anything more to eat today but she will be hungry."

"I'll have the kitchen box up some things for you and your daughter," Elspeth said. "Thank you for your information."

"Thank you. I have never before had such a sumptuous tea."

**Part Three
Angelika**

21

Richard Munro sat deep in thought in the lobby of the Kennington Dublin. He had been watching the habits of the guests in order to report back to Lord Kennington but the afternoon was quiet and soon his thoughts wandered. He worried about his wife. When he had first come to Dublin, she had seemed excited about returning to work. She had her usual tension when working and although she remained puzzled by her assignment, Richard recognised a familiar pattern in her feelings. He had been on enough cases with her that he knew the signs of her mind working through a problem.

Something had changed as soon as Eric Kennington had arrived. During the six months they were in Scotland together, Elspeth had fidgeted during the day but she had slept quietly at night. The freshness of the Scottish air and their long walks by the loch, through the forest and on the braes, however, might account for this. Here they were cooped up in the hotel for the most part but that was common when Elspeth was on assignment.

When Eric arrived, however, Elspeth had tightened, not visibly, but when she lay by Richard during the night. She did not relax into his body in her customary way. She mumbled to herself at night but in her sleep pushed him away when he tried to comfort her. Her normal wry take on things had disappeared. He did not think this was because she was baffled by the case. Her good brain would figure things out in the end, he was certain. He had thought in the past that Elspeth relished her work. When she had finally accepted his proposal of marriage, she had made him promise that she could continue her work. Elspeth had hated the hiatus in Scotland but Richard wondered if her return to work was not living up to her anticipation.

When he was leaving the hotel, Eric Kennington had come over to Richard.

"See that Elspeth doesn't get distracted," he had said. "She knows how important this case is to me. I regret that I have to return to London. I'd have preferred to stay here and see that she resolves everything quickly."

He seemed absorbed in his own thoughts and had not said anything about Richard's assignment, which Richard knew had no immediacy.

*

Elspeth returned to the lobby shortly afterwards. At first she did not see Richard, which gave him a chance to watch her. Her handsomeness, her elegant bearing and her magnificent clothing had beguiled his colleagues when she appeared at Foreign and Commonwealth Office functions and he imagined it affected the hotel guests in the same way. Richard had known Elspeth for over forty years and saw beyond her outward appearance. Elspeth exuded confidence that was often a front. Watching her, Richard suspected that at that moment Elspeth had fallen into her habit of authority softened by good manners and a canny sense of manipulating people when her job required it. He could see her straight back and also her tightness.

Elspeth turned and saw him. She gave him an affectionate smile and came to join him.

"Eric has left," he said.

"I'm relieved," Elspeth replied, and let out a long breath. "I just talked to him. He asked me not to tell Pamela anything about this case, which is extremely odd. I have never been on a case where Pamela wasn't eventually in charge of the details. I feel I have lost my main prop at the Kennington Organisation because she has always helped me gauge Eric's moods. No one else can read them."

"Do you have any idea why he would do that? Pamela is so reliable and also discreet."

Elspeth bit the corner of her lower lip. "I think because he doesn't want anyone of us to know he is human underneath his bluffness. He is obviously profoundly disturbed by Moya's death. I suspect he won't be satisfied with my work until he knows her murderer is safely in prison for life. I wish I knew all the dimensions of his relationship with Moya. Then I would know where not to tread. Pamela could have helped me with this."

"Can't you consult her as a friend?"

"I promised Eric I wouldn't. Now I'm sorry I did that. I never realised before how much I rely on Pamela."

"I can talk to her," Richard said. "I'm here on my own assignment and can consult her on that. She could at least tell me his general mood."

"That would help, of course. Keep in touch with her, Dickie. But now I must go. I have another person to consult who may help me. Let's meet in the suite before dinner."

*

Harry O'Shea had promised to get her in touch with the chauffeur who had driven the Koda's to the hotel. What was his name? Patrick Mulligan, that was it. Elspeth wanted to know more about Yuri Koda's 'goons' and perhaps the chauffeur could help.

Harry had done as bidden and told him Patrick was waiting in the car park below the hotel. Patrick's Mercedes limousine stretched in front of a row of upmarket cars. Patrick sat at the wheel.

Elspeth climbed into the front seat. Patrick removed his hat and smoothed his dark hair.

"Harry says you want to talk to me about one of my rides. My employer doesn't like me saying anything about our clients or what goes on in the car when I'm driving. If he finds out about this, I'm in trouble."

"If you do have a problem," Elspeth said, "let me talk to him. I'm sure future Kennington hotel custom is valuable to him."

She added a sweet smile to this threat. He squirmed at her words.

"There are reasons I need to know more about the Kodas. Like you, I am instructed not to discuss our clients with others. But I'm hoping in this case you will bend the rules. I won't report you and no one will see us down here in the corner. Anyway I've asked the attendant to direct cars to the other side of the car park where the lift is and not to disturb us. What is more, Harry will have an envelope for you the next time you bring someone to the hotel."

Elspeth would judge the amount to put in the tip once she had received information from Patrick. She suspected that he would guess this.

"What do you want to know?"

"I'm curious about the two men who were Yuri Koda's

bodyguards. Didn't they come from the airport with you? Can you describe them to me?"

"They sat at the front with me, so I saw them from the side mainly," Patrick said. "The Kodas and the two girls sat in the back, Mr and Mrs Koda on the back seat and the girls on the tilt-up seats. I always put up the window between the front seat and the back seats so my passengers can feel private. Mr Koda asked that the two men sit in front, although normally I don't like that. But Mr Koda made it worth my while. I saw them, of course, when they left the car but they had their faces turned away most of the time."

"Tell me what you can about them."

"They were tough although they wore suits. I grew up in a rough area of Dublin and can recognise that sort. Thugs they were. The one next to me was carrying a gun. It rubbed against my arm. You wonder how he got it through security, but probably on these private corporate jets the border authorities have a way of not seeing things. If I was someone like Yuri Koda, from what I see in the papers, I'd want my own security and I'd want them to be like the two men who sat beside me."

"What did they look like?"

"Slavic. High cheekbones, broad faces. Both had shaved heads; one had a scar from the corner of his eye to his neck."

"Were they big?"

"You bet they were. Not tall but muscular. I don't want to use the word apes but you know what I mean."

"Harry said they were waiting on the street when you picked the Kodas up to go to dinner on Saturday."

"Yeah. But this time they sat in the back on the tilt-ups since the girls weren't with us. I did notice that one of them, not the one with the scar, had brownish scar tissue on his neck; you know the kind that forms when someone is in a fire."

"It seems so both of them were fairly easy to recognise," Elspeth said.

"I'd know them anywhere," Patrick replied, "but I hope I never see them again."

Elspeth opened her handbag and drew out the photograph of Sergei Koda that she had clipped from the paper. "Do you recognise this man?"

"That's the one they just arrested. They say he's Koda's son."

"The man isn't one of the two men with the Kodas, was he?"

"No way."

"Thank you Patrick. I'll let Harry know if I need anything else. I'll see he has the envelope for you next time you come round the hotel."

"Thank you, madam," Patrick said. Elspeth noticed he had slipped into a more formal manner. "I'll look forward to that."

"I think I have definitely proved that Sergei Koda a.k.a. Zakhar was not one of the goons, as Moya called them," Elspeth said to Richard.

He handed her a glass of her preferred sherry. "I suspect the two of them have long since found a small boat out of Ireland and I don't really need to worry about their whereabouts," she said. "But I still don't know why Moya was so afraid of them. From what Eric said, Moya liked danger. I can't grasp what Moya's relationship with them was or how she treated them. Now I'll probably never know."

"Do you think Angelika was right that the goons thought Moya was responsible for Yuri's death?" Richard said over the top of his whisky glass.

"We never will know," Elspeth said. "The only person who is able to tell us more is Angelika but I don't trust she would tell the truth."

"Elspeth, you always have been able to read people well but I think you may be misjudging Angelika. She is obviously protecting her brother. She must be desperate to prove his innocence. Perhaps if you approached Angelika with an offer to help her, she would be more cooperative. Use your Scottish sensibilities," he said with a smile. The joke was an old one between them. "I suggest that we go down for dinner. Angelika and her party will hardly want to leave the hotel tonight but none of them have a room big enough for room service. Undoubtedly they will be downstairs. I suggest that we watch them."

"You mean the interactions between them?"

"Precisely. If afterwards you can persuade Angelika and possibly Nancy Kendall to come and join me without Derek Somerset or Lars Inversen and I can talk to them woman-to-woman."

"I can make myself scarce. I might even ask them to the bar and see if I can engage Derek and Lars in conversation. I won't ask direct questions but I will steer the topics towards the happenings of the last few days. I would be interested in their take on these times and I suspect they won't open up to you as easily as they will to me. I'll offer to pay for the drinks. Derek probably will have juice but I think Lars will have more. He intrigues me. His presence here seems worth questioning."

"Won't they think you are probing?" Elspeth asked.

"Elspeth, my dearest, don't you trust my diplomatic tact? They very well may give me some insight into how to attract better guests to the hotel, or shall I say guests more to Eric Kennington's taste. I must admit that I haven't come up with many good ideas to date. They may be able to help."

*

Elspeth called down to the dining room and requested that she and Richard be seated in plain view of the table reserved for Angelika's party. They found the four young people in the dining room when they entered. All were consulting the menu, which was printed on parchment in a leather cover. Elspeth had never been sure how this would appeal to vegans. According to Kennington standards, local food was featured first, followed by traditional British food and then continental food. Starters were plentiful often causing guests who were slimming to order two of them to make a meal. Desserts ranged from simple fresh fruit with cream to extravagant gateaux, parfaits and tarts. The menu was changed frequently but the standard of food never varied.

Richard always read the menu with delight, calling out some of the more delectable choices and reading their flamboyant descriptions. She had asparagus and prosciutto for a starter. He had mussels in a garlic sauce, which he had ordered before but said he wanted to try again. He decided on a steak with rosti potatoes and vegetables à la Kennington and she grilled chicken with fresh greens.

"Elspeth, you really should really try something new."

"Do you want a pudgy wife? No, I don't think so."

"Do you ever give in to temptation?"

"Only in moments of great personal stress," she said with a chuckle. "Our young people seem to be delighted with the selections."

She watched the banter occurring at the table where Angelika, Nancy, Lars and Derek were sitting. Even Derek seemed relaxed.

Elspeth nodded to the *maître d*, who came over to her table.

"See that the table with the young people over there have as much wine and drink as they want. Tell them it is compliments of the hotel and put it on my expense sheet."

"Of course, Ms Duff. Will the two of you be having wine as well?"

Richard, it seemed, had already made his selection of merlot that would go with both their mains and promised Elspeth she would like it.

They sat in comfortable silence sipping the wine as they waited for the food. Elspeth saw Richard turn towards the young people's table and she followed his eyes.

"You watch Angelika and I will watch the others," he suggested.

"I'm interested mainly in how the appear when speaking to each other so let's watch them all and compare notes," Elspeth said. "Ostensibly they are two couples, Angelika and Derek and then Nancy and Lars but I think the more interesting grouping is going to be Angelika and Lars. I still think they knew each other in the past."

"I would agree," he said

"I also wonder why Angelika chose Derek to spend the rest of her life with. And Lars? Is he really attracted to Nancy or is he trying to establish a link to Angelika that will appear natural and therefore explainable later on?"

The sommelier made his way to their table and first handed Lars the wine menu. Kennington hotel wine stewards were trained to spot the most likely guest at a table who would direct the choice of wines. He handed out menus to the others with equal grace.

Derek waved him away and put his hand over his wine glass. Angelika laughed and Elspeth could almost hear Angelika say 'more for the rest of us'. Lars took charge, Angelika agreed with his choice and Nancy demurred. Elspeth was perpetually amazed at how people's actions almost spoke more loudly than their words. The sommelier bowed, smiled at Lars and then nodded slightly to the rest of the party.

"Lars is in command," Richard said, "Angelika agreeing and the rest following."

"One would almost pair Lars and Angelika, although Nancy and Derek would make an odd pair. I sense Nancy is not pleased with her friend's choice of a fiancé."

"He's a bit limp," Richard said. "Not Archbishop of Canterbury material."

"I think Angelika is hiding behind him but I seriously wonder if she will go through with it and marry him."

"He must present calm in a storm. Angelika's life up to now and particularly in the last week has not been easy," Richard said. Their starters arrived at this point and Richard showed his approval.

"Somehow I think Derek is not the answer. Angelika

has too much fire in her. It may eventually burn out but right now I feel it is smouldering," he continued.

"I agree," Elspeth said. "See how she keeps glancing at Lars."

"Do you think they might make an item?"

"Maybe, maybe not. I'd say more of a partnership for their mutual benefit." Elspeth said this without much thought but knew it probably was true. Her concern, however, was that if Angelika were lying, then undoubtedly Lars was too.

"How do you suppose this all connects with Sergei?" Elspeth said as she raised a spear of asparagus to her lips.

"I'll leave you to figure that out," Richard said. He attacked his mussels with relish. "I wonder what the chef has done with the mussels to make them so good? Would you like one? They have enough garlic that you should taste one if you are going to sleep with me tonight."

Elspeth looked over again at the couples. Angelika and Lars had ordered escargot. Derek had ordered plain shrimp with cocktail sauce and Nancy a plate of pâté, greens and crisp breads twisted in an ornate shape.

"OK, I'll have one," Elspeth said, "but I hope Angelika won't notice the garlic when I talk to her later."

Lars seemed to be leading a merry conversation. The wine gasses at the table were filled twice as was Derek's glass of water. Lars reached over and touched Nancy's hand. She reddened slightly and then looked up at him with a trace of a smile. Angelika put her arm over the back of Derek's chair, which seemed to displease him. Angelika did not remove her arm as she addressed a comment to Lars. He smiled broadly at her. Nancy followed the smile and looked hurt. Derek laughed timidly. Elspeth wondered if Lars's comment had been a bit bawdy.

The meal progressed but the dynamics among the four guests changed little, except that Derek became more reticent and Lars more buoyant. Angelika played to Lars's pitch and Nancy glared.

Elspeth called the waiter over to the table where she and Richard were seated, and requested that their meals be served at the same pace as the table they were watching. When dessert and coffee at both tables were finished, Richard and Elspeth rose. At Elspeth's bidding, the two of them approached the four young people.

Elspeth had thought hard of how to convince Angelika to come with her after dinner so she decided to be straightforward. Angelika looked displeased when she saw Elspeth and Richard coming towards her. Elspeth pretended not to notice.

"Shall we be a bit old-fashioned," Elspeth said. "I thought the ladies might withdraw and leave the men to their port, so to speak, although I suspect none of you smoke cigars. Angelika, why don't you and Nancy join me in one of the small lounges whilst Richard, Lars, and Derek repair to the bar."

Angelika glowered.

"Seriously," Elspeth continued, "I'd like to talk to you, Angelika, about today. I felt you would feel easier if Nancy were along."

"And I want to catch up with Derek and get to know Lars," Richard said. Elspeth cocked an invisible eyebrow. Richard was a convincing liar. Was it his diplomatic training or had some of Elspeth's penchant for stretching the truth, when needed, rubbed off on him?

Nancy nodded. "Come on, Angie. You said we needed some advice. I think Ms Duff is just the person to give it to us."

Elspeth had made arrangements to have a spot in one of the small lounges set aside for her use. One of the staff was waiting near the door, and was ushering people who wanted to be in the same lounge to the other side of the room. He showed Angelika, Nancy and Elspeth to the quiet corner. Elspeth had made sure that both regular and decaf coffee were there to greet them. She asked the girls if they wished an after dinner drink.

"The service here is incredible," Nancy said. "No sooner do you want something than it is provided."

"'Comfort and Service' is Lord Kennington's motto. He's spent years building up a reputation for just that. Angelika, I hope you will forgive my waylaying you, for that's exactly what I have done. I think I can help you with the whole situation around Sergei. I once worked for Scotland Yard in London, and also for many years was a private investigator in Hollywood. It sounds glamorous but neither job really was. Along the way, however, I learned how to ferret out information. I'm not trying to scare you but I think my skills may help you."

"How?" Angelika asked. Her voice was truculent.

"Sergei will only be freed if we can prove he was nowhere near where your father was murdered. We need to establish why Sergei is in Dublin. Do you know why and why he came to the hotel and used the name Zakhar? It would be a starting point."

"Why do you want to help?" Angelika asked.

"Frankly, because I've been charged by my employer to do so. He knew Moya a long time ago and wants to find out who her murderer was. I have been investigating for many years and my gut feelings are that your father's death had nothing to do with Sergei. I'd like to verify that but I can't be successful without your cooperation. Perhaps I'm wrong in my assumptions but I think you know why Sergei is here and why he came into the hotel to demand to see Moya. Think about it. The longer the Garda held Sergei, the more likely they are to charge him with the murder. In the meantime will you have some more coffee? Please order any drink you would like."

Elspeth dispensed the cups and offered some delicate after-dinner biscuits to go with them. Angelika ordered a Cointreau and Nancy a brandy. Elspeth stuck to coffee.

"He didn't do it," Angelika said after the after dinner drinks were brought.

For once Elspeth thought that Angelika was speaking the truth. "I don't think he did either but as yet I have no basis to back up my opinion other than instinct. Can you give me any concrete facts, or at least a lead to go on?"

"I think you should trust Ms Duff," Nancy said.

Angelika blew over her coffee, which was always served hot at the hotels. "I don't know much that will help," she said.

"Anything could," Elspeth urged. "You may think it insignificant but it might help us find a line of questioning that will open up doors we don't yet know are closed." Elspeth had used this line many times before.

"I promised Sergei," Angelika said.

Finally a chink in the armour, Elspeth thought.

"If you could talk to him, won't he want someone on

the outside, other than you, to try to get him free? I'm not exactly sure how much I can do but I think together we could do more than you can alone. Do you have any idea where Sergei was on Saturday night when your father was attacked? The press indicated that he was already in Dublin. Did you know that he was?" Elspeth said.

Elspeth prayed that Angelika would not say Sergei had been with her. She had told Elspeth that she and Nancy had stayed in the hotel all that evening and been in the bar with some French guests. The security tapes backed that up.

Elspeth let silence fall.

Finally Angelika said, "I thought he might be." An equivocating answer.

"Then you must have been in contact with him before you came to Dublin. Did he contact you and say he was coming?'

Angelika skewed up her lips and looked down.

"I only can help if you will tell me why you thought he was here. Did he contact you or did you contact him?" Elspeth asked.

"He contacted me."

"Did he give a reason?"

"He said he wanted to see our father again. He had read about my father coming to Ireland. He asked me if I knew where Papa was staying."

"I presume you told him."

Angelika nodded.

Elspeth sensed that Angelika was not being completely forthcoming, but wanted to tread lightly.

"Did you tell him you were also coming?"

"I hadn't decided yet. Nancy's and my coming was a

last minute thing."

Elspeth looked up and Nancy who, with a nod, confirmed this.

"Mrs Koda called Angie about three days before we came. Mrs Koda said she wanted Angie to see the de Lacey family home, assuring us it would be lovely at this time of year. Angie and I were at loose ends over the summer holidays. London was hot and a few days at a posh hotel and then a trip to the Irish countryside seemed a wonderful break for us, especially when paid for by Moya. We were sharing a flat for the summer and were talking about getting out of London."

"Did Sergei contact you once you were here?"

"I never saw him," Nancy said.

"But you did, didn't you, Angelika? In St Patrick's Cathedral."

Angelika sat up. "How did you know?"

Elspeth tried to smile softly. "I'm fairly good at my job. As far as I can tell the only times you and Nancy were apart was when you went to the Cathedral and she didn't want to go in. Two and two adds up."

Angelika looked down, avoiding eye contact.

"Was your meeting pre-arranged? Did you see him before your father was killed? Please, Angelika. If I can figure out what happened, the Garda may be able to as well."

"I saw him Saturday morning for the first time, and then again on Monday."

"By Monday he would have known about your father's death."

"What did the two of you talk about?" Elspeth asked, trying to keep her patience.

"On Saturday he wanted me to tell him where Papa and Moya were. On Monday he asked me to forget he was in Dublin."

Elspeth found this answer odd. From Angelika's answer, it appeared that Sergei wanted to disappear but the next day he had come into the hotel brandishing a gun and demanding to see Moya. Once again Elspeth was irritated that Angelika was such a difficult person to be helped.

"Did he tell you he was coming to the hotel on Tuesday to see Moya if he could?" Elspeth continued.

"You mean the gun," Angelika said.

"Precisely. Did you know he would come to the hotel and bring a gun?"

"Sergei always could be a bit hot headed."

"I don't understand why you called him Zakhar and said he was one of your father's bodyguards."

"I argued with him in Ukrainian when we were alone with you. I knew you couldn't understand when we were speaking. I told him to go away from the hotel and not do anything more to see Moya. He wouldn't listen but our relationship always was like that when we were children. He hadn't changed. And he said he was using the name Zakhar."

Elspeth suspected that Angelika was answering with painful half-truths.

"Do you have any idea why Sergei wanted to see your father and stepmother after all the years of separation? Was it for emotional reasons or did your brother want something?"

"I don't know," Angelika said.

Elspeth was certain she was lying and therefore

changed her tactics. "You know Lars, don't you? He seems to know you." She purposely asked this question to put Angelika off her guard.

Angelika paled. Elspeth would not have noticed if she had not been looking for a physical reaction.

"No," Angelika said a little too loudly. "Can we go now and join the others? I don't think I have anything else to say to you," Angelika said. "Come on, Nance. Let's get out of this Gestapo inquisition."

Once again Elspeth felt Angelika had outmanoeuvred her. What an obstinate person she was. Or was she hiding something critical to the case that would implicate her or Sergei in Yuri's murder?

*

Richard had always enjoyed mentoring young men. Although over the years styles and attitudes had changed, what went on inside the young men's heads was identical. Most of them, at least the ones Richard knew, wanted to succeed in one way or another. As he talked to Derek and Lars, different as they were, Richard saw that each had a vision of his future and his ability to achieve a dream. Derek may have seemed sad to some but Richard found Derek's desire to help the old and needy in an old-fashioned but honourable way.

Richard detected a warm heart and saw that Derek was taking on the greater task of defying his parents' way of life for something more satisfactory to him.

Lars, on the other hand, was more of a mystery. He was obviously a man about town, spoke at least three languages probably fluently, and indicated that he lived the bachelor life in Paris. Richard wondered how much of this was Lars's cover. Lars had told Elspeth that he worked for a large Parisian detective agency, not a notably high paying job, but at the same time he appeared to be completely comfortable in the surroundings of a Kennington hotel. Richard could not make out if the sophistication or the life of detecting had come first. He decided to try to find out.

He ordered drinks for the three of them. Once again Derek ordered water but Lars opted for a fine brandy. Richard followed suit, hoping that his or Elspeth's expense account would cover it.

"I never served in Paris," Richard said, "but I have had many colleagues in the Foreign and Commonwealth Office who had served at the embassy there. Most of them enjoyed the lifestyle offered. They considered it an ideal posting. They could relish the culture and the urbanity of the French capital, but could get home to the UK at weekends. Personally I preferred postings further away, although I am retired now. Do you get a chance to be away from Paris often, Lars? In your line of work, I would think you would go all over the place."

Lars sipped his brandy and grinned. "I go where I am told. Because my firm is Paris-based, most of our work is in France but sometimes like now spreads across most of Europe."

The answer was ingenuously evasive, Richard thought. He pushed further. "My wife said you are here on the track of the thieves of the Romanov collection of jewellery. Have you dealt with jewellery theft before?"

Lars shifted in his chair. "We handle many kinds of theft, of course, but more often spend time on divorce cases, which are very tedious, but the pay is good so I don't complain. A man has to support himself and I like the flexible hours."

"How did you train for the job?" Richard asked. He hoped his question seemed innocent although it was not. "It's not the sort of thing one studies in school."

Lars frowned and paused before answering. "We team up with the older people in the firm, an apprenticeship really."

"Do you have to study criminal psychology?"

"We—er—don't necessarily. Many of our cases aren't criminal, you see."

Richard thought Lars was searching hard to find plausible answers.

"This case appears to be criminal, however. Do you often work with the police? Aren't both Scotland Yard and the Sûreté interested in the Romanov jewellery and what happened to it?"

"Most of our clients require that we keep things from the police. They would prefer that things be settled away from the authorities, although we sometimes step in when the police have failed."

Richard assumed what Elspeth would call his most avuncular manner. "But aren't you sometimes just a step ahead of the police? Isn't that nerve-wracking?"

"Our business is at times nerve-wracking but I like the excitement," Lars answered.

"Surely you would be working with the police on this?"

"Sir Richard, neither the Metropolitan Police in London nor the Sûreté achieved anything in the case. That's why my firm was called in."

Derek sat sipping his water and listening. Finally he said, "Is Angelika mixed up in this at all? I hope not."

Richard found Derek's question his most pertinent of the evening. Was Angelika involved? And was that why she and Lars kept exchanging glances of familiarity whenever Richard and Elspeth had seen them together?

Richard felt he could get nothing more out of Lars, but felt that what he had learned would help Elspeth. He turned to telling stories of his diplomatic career, which seemed to keep the two young men entertained until Elspeth, Angelika and Nancy joined them a short time afterwards.

Elspeth and Richard excused themselves from the young people as soon as was feasibly polite.

"Let's walk," Elspeth suggested. "It seems to have stopped raining and the evening is still light. In any case, I'd like to talk to you out of hearing of anyone else."

The doorman who had replaced Harry tipped his hat to them and remarked on the fine evening. Elspeth smiled and said, "If any of the younger guests go out this evening, try to find out where they are going."

"Yes, Ms Duff, will do."

Richard and Elspeth strolled arm and arm without speaking, and wandered into St. Stephen's Green.

They watched the ducks swimming leisurely in one of the lakes whilst Richard told Elspeth what had transpired at the bar.

"It strikes me that there is a conspiracy here between Lars and Angelika," Elspeth said.

"I agree. Do you think Sergei is involved too?"

"More than likely but how? Lars seems interested in the theft of the jewels not the murders. Sergei probably was interested in finding his father but for what reason? To murder him or reconcile with him? Reconciliation seems more likely because he came later to the hotel to find Moya. He had a gun. Does that mean he thought Moya was involved in Yuri's death and wanted to take justice in his own hands? Angelika thinks so," Elspeth said, tumbling out her thoughts. "There are too many wheels within wheels in this case. I want things to be tidier. Usually they are."

Richard laughed. "My dearest, you are forgetting a number of your cases, particularly the one in Chelsea."

"That, Dickie, was an oddity."

"And mightn't this one be too?"

Elspeth shook her head. "No, I don't think so. It's too tight and all centred around the young people."

"Do you think that the things Moya had in her attaché case were the jewels?"

"Increasingly yes. I also feel that the theft of the jewels and Yuri and Moya's murders are connected. And what connects them has to be Angelika."

"She couldn't have been involved in the murders," Richard said. "She was at the hotel."

Elspeth blew out her breath in bewilderment.

"Angelika saw Sergei on Saturday."

"Why is that important?" he asked.

"You and I both agree that she also seems to know Lars, who arrived at the hotel on Wednesday. Did Sergei ask Angelika to communicate with Lars, perhaps signalling him to come to Dublin? If so, Sergei might be involved with the jewellery theft as well as the murders. They have to be connected. I wish I could figure out how. The Garda don't know about the jewels but we do. It gives us an advantage they don't have."

"But how much do you actually know about the jewels, my dearest?"

"As yet not a lot, but I intend to find out more."

22

"We have a message for you, Sir Richard," the concierge said as Elspeth and Richard returned to the hotel. "It was hand delivered. You'll find the note in your room."

The heavy white envelope was propped up on the writing desk and was addressed to 'Richard Munro', without his title. Richard took it up and said to Elspeth, 'No return address. I wonder whom it's from. Not many people know I am here."

He found the letter opener on the desk and slit the envelope along the top. The note was handwritten and brief:

British Embassy
Dublin

Dear Richard,
The FCO has passed on your request and I hasten to reply. I remember you well from Singapore. I was but a lowly consul at the time and hope you remember me as well. I'm now Deputy Chief of Mission here at the embassy. Considering the nature of your request, I think it best we speak in person. Ring me at home at my private number -----. I usually am up until midnight.

Sincerely yours,
Keith Roberts

Richard handed her the note, which she read quickly.

"Request, Dickie? What request?" she asked.

"You mentioned my asking if anyone at the FCO could help regarding Yuri Koda's reason to be in Dublin. I wonder why Keith, whom I do remember vaguely, wants to see me in person rather than by email."

"I suspect he wants everything off record. Why not invite him for breakfast. We can meet here in the suite. Let's say half eight in case he has to get back to the embassy later in the morning."

Elspeth put her arms around Richard. "Dickie, I'm so glad you are here."

He grinned with pleasure and returned the embrace.

Keith Roberts arrived at the hotel at precisely half-past eight. At Elspeth's request, he was escorted to their suite. Richard would not have recognised him as the same person who had served under him in Singapore fifteen years before. Keith's waistline and chin had filled out but most of his hair had disappeared. He had disguised this by having his head shaved but a hint of grey hair was visible. He was dressed in a pinstriped dark grey suit and turquoise checked tie, which matched a light turquoise shirt. Richard did not like the combination, but tried to curb his old-fashioned idea of proper dress when one worked at Her Majesty's official offices in foreign countries. Richard was reminded that times had changed, but did not think the Deputy Chief of Mission at the British Embassy should look so much like a peacock.

Keith, as his girth suggested he might, dived heartily into the breakfast.

Wiping his mouth, Keith said, "I'm assuming I can talk

in front of Lady Munro."

Richard nodded.

"What I say will be off the record and I will deny it if necessary. I hope you don't mind. Yuri Koda has been a thorn in the FCO's side for quite some time. He has dual British and Ukrainian citizenship and uses his British passport whenever he travels outside Ukraine. The trade section in London has continually monitored his progress because we think his dealings shady if not illegal. I had London send me the summary of his dossier. What is it that you want to know?"

Richard considered his words. "My wife works for the Kennington hotels in security. Do you mind if she asks the questions? Yuri Koda was staying here when he was killed and the hotel is anxious that this remains unknown to the wider public. I can assure you that Elspeth has been involved in cases involving the FCO before. You can trust her discretion."

Keith turned to Elspeth. "I must say you are well known in FCO circles. Everyone was delighted when we heard Richard had married again." He made no comparison between Elspeth and Richard's first wife Lady Marjorie. "But I didn't know you worked for the Kennington Organisation. I've never been able to afford any of the hotels so it is a real pleasure to be sharing breakfast with you here today. Certainly the food is as delicious as it is touted to be. What is it that you want to know?"

Richard wondered how straightforward Elspeth would be and he intended to follow her lead. Elspeth paused before speaking.

"Just as you wish to be able to deny that this conversation ever took place, so do I." she said.

He seemed pleased.

"I need to know some things about Yuri Koda in order to protect his daughter who is staying here as a guest. Angelika Rostova, Yuri's daughter that is, and Moya's stepdaughter, is staying on at the hotel. It is my responsibility to see that she is safe until the Koda murder case is resolved or other arrangements are made for her. You may not have heard but Mrs Koda died yesterday at her family home in County Lough, probably as a result of the wounds she received when she was attacked along with Yuri."

Richard noted that Elspeth did not mention the second attack on Moya.

"The police have arrested her stepson," Keith said.

"They have detained him for questioning," Elspeth said gently, correcting him, "but none of us know if the Garda have enough information to remand him to prison. I'm not familiar with the legal system here in Ireland but I assume it is similar to that of England. I suspect the police have the right to question him for a certain length of time and then must let him go if their case against him is not good enough to arrest him. I have no access to the Guarda or to Sergei Koda, but for Angelika Koda's sake, I would like to learn as much as I can about the family. You just said that Yuri Koda was a UK citizen. Is Sergei one as well?"

"I don't know but I can check," Keith said. He rubbed the side of his nose, a gesture of his that Richard remembered Keith using when he was unhappy in his early career in Singapore. "I'll have to ask my assistant to research the matter."

"I recall that in the past when a UK citizen was arrested in a foreign country, a member of the FCO staff was sent to see if they could help. Is that still true?" Richard asked.

Elspeth looked up as he spoke and he suspected he had used the same tone he used for his juniors when he was high commissioner. She cocked an eyebrow at him.

"Are you suggesting I have someone go to the jail to see Sergei Koda?" Keith asked.

"Could you?" said Elspeth with a pleading smile.

Clearing his throat he said, "I'm very busy and rather short staffed at the moment."

"Then perhaps you could let me go with one of your consuls," Richard said.

Keith twisted uncomfortably.

"Keith, I always admired your ability to arrange difficult things. It's one of the main reasons I recommended you for promotion," Richard said although he did not remember if this was true. "Surely the Irish are not as sticklers for strict rules as the Singaporean Chinese. In any event my past authority should lend credence to your representative."

"I, er, suppose I could arrange something. At least I could make inquiries. I'll have to see when I get back to the embassy. But I thought you wanted to know more about Yuri Koda. That's what I came prepared for."

Elspeth turned to Keith. "Yuri Koda, his wife, his daughter and her friend have been or are our guests and therefore I am trying to help undo the puzzle of why both Yuri and his wife were attacked last Saturday night. My intention isn't to solve the crime but rather to understand how it came about and how we here at the Kennington hotel can prevent future harm to our guests. I know the crime was not committed on the premises but Mrs Koda returned to the hotel after the incident and stayed here until shortly before her death."

Keith looked up at her as if puzzled.

"My employer, Lord Kennington, was a friend of Mrs Koda, and has asked that I follow the developments in the case closely. It will help me a great deal if I understand what brought the Kodas here," she said.

Keith seemed to relax at this request and asked for more coffee. He poured an ample amount of cream into it and added three teaspoons of sugar.

"The dossier we received on Mr Koda, when we heard he was coming to Dublin, showed that he was offering favourable terms to Energy Ireland to purchase a large quantity of natural gas from Ukraine," he said. "We were somewhat surprised by this as our records indicate that Koda Enterprises had been in financial difficulties in the last year or two. Our analysts went back through their records and found he had severe losses in his businesses in 2008. It was estimated that he would need six or seven million pounds to satisfy his creditors. Flags were instantly raised when Yuri said suddenly he had enough capital to buy and supply the Irish with the amount of gas under discussion. We were doubtful at the time," he said blandly.

He continued after taking a sip of coffee. "We understand from undisclosed sources that he assured Energy Ireland that he had a ready source of cash. He said that when he arrived here he would provide balance sheets that showed he was solvent and statements from his suppliers that they were willing to ship the gas upon receipt of the guarantees from his bank. He certified that his creditors had been paid off and that he had sufficient money in his accounts to place a sizeable deposit on gas to be shipped. We have an inside source who reported that Yuri was prepared to present all of this at a meeting set for Monday morning. Of course this never happened."

Keith looked at Richard, as if he were hoping Richard would rescind his earlier request to go and see Sergei Koda. Richard knew that speaking in confidence was one thing; acting on his suggestion about the Garda and Sergei was quite another. Richard wondered how Keith could have achieved his success in the FCO with so little mental flexibility. Or was the ability to act with expedience rather than rigidity, something that had crept into Richard's psyche over the years that he had been involved in Elspeth's cases? He did not remember that he was a stickler for rules when he was in the FCO but he might have been.

"Of course we will honour your wishes but I'm interested in Yuri Koda's financial situation. I understand that Yuri always played close to the edge. Has the FCO any information on how Yuri was to get this sudden influx of cash?" Elspeth asked.

"I can check but his dossier has nothing on this. It may be awkward if not impossible to follow up on that."

Richard thought his supposed promotion of Keith many years ago was perhaps a mistake. At this point, Richard did not want to go higher up than Keith in the embassy or FCO, but would if necessary.

"When you get back to the embassy," Richard said, "find out when you can arrange that visit to the Garda. If both Lady Munro and I can be present at the interview with Sergei Koda, that would be excellent."

Richard was certain that when Keith left the suite he was a less happy man than he had been when he arrived, despite the quality of the food. Richard hoped that the general quality of the younger staff of the Foreign and Commonwealth staff was better than this.

"Dickie, you're both brilliant and becoming increasingly devious. What made you think of going to see Sergei?" Elspeth asked.

"We always used to do this sort of thing when a British citizen got in trouble overseas. I thought you might like to question Sergei."

"At this point, I'm not sure what I would ask him. I fear that, like his sister, he would not tell the truth."

23

Angelika had been uncomfortable since the evening before when Elspeth Duff had confronted her. Not wanting to wake Nancy up, she had rung Lars on her mobile from their bathroom soon after she was up. Lars answered sleepily.

"I need to talk to you immediately. May I come there?"

"Give me ten minutes," he said.

Once in his room Angelika faced Lars. He was unshaven and robed in a dark blue Kennington hotel dressing gown over his pyjamas.

"Why the early conference?" he said. Angelika could not tell if he was annoyed or amused.

"I think Elspeth Duff is on to us," she said.

"Oh, I know she is but she can prove nothing. We've covered all our tracks far too carefully to have a hotel security advisor trip us up. She's a bit of an odd one, isn't she? She looks like the lady of the manor rather than an investigator. I didn't know the Kennington hotels were so exclusive that they hired titled ladies to carry out their dirty work, even if she doesn't use her husband's title. I googled him. He is quite distinguished. Google has nothing on her but that she is married to Sir Richard. But why is he here with her?"

"The only thing that matters is that she is now suspicious of us. How can we carry on as if we weren't working together with Sergei? If she makes the connection, she definitely will think we were involved in the murder."

"We have to carry on," he said. "

"I wish I never had agreed to come to Dublin. Now I have my best friend involved too and I don't want to harm her."

"What about Derek?" he said with a smirk.

"Leave Derek out of this."

"Why? You'll never be happy with him."

"I will," she said. She stuck out her jaw.

"Angelika, you have lived far too long in your father's world to settle into life as a parson's wife."

"It will be a relief after this. When will it all end? Sergei didn't commit the murders. You know that as well as I do."

"Do I?"

"You don't suspect him?"

"There's no definite proof he is innocent."

Angelika felt the blood rise in her face. She swung her hand to strike Lars's face but he caught her arm and gripped it. "Now's not the time to fight. We'll get nowhere if we do."

"Then what do you propose? We're no closer to our goal and Sergei is mouldering in jail. If I try to protect him, the police might suspect me of having something to do with the murders. I can't risk that because then we never will accomplish what we set out to do. I wish Sergei hadn't got me into this."

"You agreed to help," Lars said. "Are you backing out now?"

"How can I?"

"You can't, not without consequences."

"What do you think we should do?"

"If Ms Duff offers you help . . ."

"She did."

"Then let's use her to our own ends."

"How?"

"Give me a little time to think about this. In the meantime, stay as cool as you possibly can. Why don't you and Nancy go out and sightsee or shop or do whatever friends do in a foreign city? I have some plans of my own to make. Let's meet for lunch. After we've finished eating, find a way to get rid of Nancy for a few minutes and I'll let you know what I've come up with."

24

Eric Kennington rang at ten. From his tone of voice Elspeth could tell he was not happy.

"You haven't called me," he barked. "Does that mean you haven't done anything? Do you think Sergei Koda murdered Moya?"

"No, I don't think he did," Elspeth said, annoyed by his tone, "But I've found a way to talk to him in jail. I don't expect him to tell the truth but I'm working on questions that might lead me to the truth."

"When are you seeing him?"

"Hopefully today. It hasn't been confirmed."

"Damn it, Elspeth, how are you always able to arrange these things?" Elspeth could hear praise in his voice.

Elspeth blushed and was glad Eric could not see her but she was not about to admit that it had been with Richard's help.

"Eric, before I see him, I want to know a bit more about Moya. Do you know if she usually carried a gun?"

"What's that got to do with anything? She was beaten to death."

"I am trying to find out if she had any self-protection."

"She laughed at self-protection. Rather like you, Elspeth, she thought her wits could get her out of anything."

"Was she into anything troubling frequently?"

"Often. I wished she hadn't been quite so open to the general public about her skill in getting out of uncomfortable situations."

"Eric, I must pry. Everyone seems to be assuming that Moya was killed as a result of the consequences of the attack on Yuri but she went out of the hotel the next day and came back with her face in a worse condition than when she left."

"Are you sure of that?" he asked.

"Yes. I have verbal proof. One can only assume that she met someone when she was away from the hotel who wished her further harm. I have been trying to track down where she went, but still have had no luck although I have feelers out. Still I have nothing concrete yet. I have also been asking about the Romanov jewellery theft. Did you ever discuss it with Moya?"

Silence filled the connection from London.

Finally he said, "She said she was innocent."

"Did she say anything else about the theft? Did she think that Yuri Koda might be involved? I have just found out that Yuri was in financial trouble. The value of the jewels, even if they were fenced, was close to the amount he was in debt."

"How did you find that out?"

"A source I promised confidentiality. I can't tell even you who."

"Are you suggesting that Yuri had the jewels stolen in order to get himself out of a business difficulty?"

"Yuri Koda was not the most honest of men. I'm only considering that it might be a possibility."

"And you think that had something to do with his murder? And Moya's?"

"I'm not limiting my options at this point. I wish I knew what happened to the jewels. They keep looming too large in this case. I'm expecting a call. Do you mind if I ring off now?"

"Have you spoken to Pamela?"

"No, you told me not to."

"If you need her help, call her. Just don't mention my relationship with Moya."

"Thank you, Eric. I tend to rely on her."

Elspeth had not thought of contacting Pamela but once she disconnected from Eric, she dialled Pamela's private number. As always, Pamela answered immediately.

'Have you talked to him since he came back?" Pamela said without introduction.

"Just now," Elspeth replied.

"Whatever happened there has upset him terribly. I have never seen him before unable to carry on working. He just stares out the window."

"He's asked me not to talk about his time here. It was terribly difficult for him. But you can help me with something. According to one of Richard's friends, Yuri Koda was in financial trouble recently. Can you find out more about that? The person who told me was a bit cagey so I don't know the full extent of what happened. Yuri came here to negotiate with Energy Ireland. He planned to sell them large quantities of natural gas from Ukraine and assured his potential buyers that he was fully liquid financially. Can you find out how this happened?"

"I'll try through my friends in the City," Pamela said. "It may not be today. These people still tend to head for the country on long summer weekends, although they probably are at their laptops all the time."

"I told Eric that I might be able to see Sergei Koda in

jail. I'm not certain what I'll ask him but I want to tie his visit here in with Angelika."

"Any ideas?"

"She's thick as thieves with the man from the detective agency in Paris and I increasingly feel they are up to something regarding Sergei."

"Does Eric approve?"

"They're both guests at the hotel so I don't think I'm overstepping my boundaries in following up on their activities," Elspeth said ambiguously.

"You sound as if you are still worried about what you call your probation. Stop fretting, Elspeth ducks. Eric seems to be in a mood to think you are his best employee. He keeps saying how well you are handling things there."

"Does he? I don't think I have done anything extraordinary but I'm pleased to be off the hook. Tell him to call me if he needs anything, either through you or directly. I know he's concerned about this whole mess being cleaned up. Everything here is still in a tangle."

"Do you have any ideas on how to work things out?"

"I wish I could say yes but I can't. Every time I think I'm making progress, a barrier is thrown up. Something needs to break soon."

Something did break. Sean Clancy called shortly after Elspeth had spoken with Pamela with startling news.

"Nancy Kendall was just down here," he said. "She said Angelika wasn't in their room this morning ."

Elspeth arrived in Sean's office within moments. Nancy Kendall was there and it was apparent that she was scared.

"Angie would have told me if she was going out,"

Nancy said.

"When were you aware she was last in your room?" Elspeth asked.

"About midnight. We stayed up watching a film on the telly after returning from the bar. I fell asleep. Angelika must have turned off the box as the room was quiet this morning and the shades were drawn."

"Were there any signs that she dressed this morning?"

"Her pyjamas were hung up on the bathroom door so she must have had her clothes on when she left."

"Was her handbag missing?"

"No. She had thrown it on her bedside table last night. It still was there, with everything in it even her mobile and passport."

"Was her room key card in it?"

Nancy shook her head. "I don't know. She always tucked it in her wallet. I didn't open the wallet."

"Let's go up to your room," Elspeth said, "and let me take a look around. Sean, check all the public rooms. Have security look at the tapes."

"Tapes?" Nancy said.

Elspeth regretted she had mentioned them in front of Nancy but explained. "We have cameras in the hallways for your safety," Elspeth reassured her. She went on to clarify.

"They are erased if nothing happens but if Angelika did leave your room, we should be able to see where she went. I'm sure she is somewhere in the hotel but we'll be able to find out quickly. Mr Clancy will call us as soon as he finds out where Angelika is. Don't worry, Nancy. We keep the hotels secure."

Nancy looked as if she didn't believe it. She followed Elspeth reluctantly out of the manager's office and on to the lift.

As they rode up to the second floor, Nancy said, "Angie's been so fidgety ever since we left London. She jumps at the slightest thing."

"How did she react when her brother was arrested?"

"She said he didn't 'do it'. I think she meant he didn't attack her father."

"Did she tell you why Sergei was in Dublin?"

"She just said she didn't want to talk about it. That's so unlike Angie, you know. She's always, you know, talked to me about everything. No secrets."

"Did she tell you that she knew Lars before he came here?"

"What? No way. She would have told me that."

Elspeth wondered.

"How else did Angelika change when she came here?

"I've no idea why Angie decided to come. It was a last minute thing. It was hot in London and I told her I'd never stayed in a Kennington hotel before. Angie said how posh they were, you know, far better than our flat in Bayswater. We jumped at the chance, although Angie said we would have to put up with her stepmother. She hated her stepmother. I'd met Moya once or twice before. She was a bit insufferably sweet but I told Angie we could bear up for the chance to come to Dublin. I wish now we hadn't. No amount of luxury is worth what Angie's been through. Now she's disappeared. Do you think she went out to go see the police? She said she didn't want to but I know she was worried about her brother. But surely she would have told me."

"I doubt she went to the police without identification," Elspeth said. She felt Angelika not taking her passport or other document to establish her identity was worrisome.

Angelika and Nancy's room was chaotic. Elspeth knew the hotel staff hated messy guests because it made housekeeping a nightmare. The room attendants were instructed not to move personal items but the sofa pillows, furniture arrangement and the bedrooms had to be tidied, the carpets hoovered, the beds made, flowers changed, bathrooms scrubbed and towels changed. An array of the guests' items spread around made this difficult and often the housekeeping staff complained about guests who caused havoc in the rooms. Management always responded that the staff should do as well as they could. Above all nothing should be perceived as missing.

Elspeth took a quick survey of the room and spotted Angelika's handbag on one of the bedside tables.

"May I search inside?" she asked Nancy.

"Do please. Maybe you'll find something I missed."

Elspeth emptied the bag on Angelika's unmade bed and began to sort out the contents.

She found a comb, lipstick, a small makeup case, a packet of tissues, two biros, a chequebook, wallet and Angelika's passport. The room keycard was not in the wallet. Elspeth unzipped an interior pocket and out fell what looked like a fat fountain pen. She started to unscrew the top but then her previous police training stopped her.

She turned to Nancy, "Do you know what this is?" Elspeth asked.

Nancy averted her eyes.

"Then you do'" Elspeth said.

Nancy bit her upper lip. "She said it was protection. It's made of some sort of plastic that doesn't show up in metal detectors."

"Mace?"

"Something like that," Nancy admitted. "I always told her it was dangerous to carry around. She wouldn't listen. Angie was afraid most of the time."

"Afraid of what?"

"She said that her father had enemies and that they might kidnap her. She wanted to be prepared." Nancy's face paled. "They couldn't have kidnapped her, could they?"

"It's impossible for kidnappers to find a way into the hotel. You heard us talking about the tapes. All the entrances and exits are monitored continuously. It's something we have had to do since nine-eleven, although before that we still had cameras about the hotels for security reasons. Many prominent people stay here and don't want their adversaries or stalkers to interrupt the comfort of their stay."

"Then what happened to Angie? She always took her mobile with her. Why did she leave it behind?"

"I don't know," Elspeth admitted "but I intend to find out. Nancy, stay here in the room. Order anything you want from room service. The hotel will cover the cost but above all don't let anyone in the room except the room service waiter and me."

"Isn't Lars OK?"

"Particularly not Lars."

Nancy frowned and pushed her lips together. She's soft on him, Elspeth thought.

"I'll be back later this morning; I'm not sure when," she said. "Please sit tight."

Elspeth hoped she had conveyed a confidence that she was not feeling.

She hurried back to Sean Clancy's office.

"What's on the tapes?" she asked.

"I've got them here on my computer," Sean said. "Angelika left her room and went across the hall into Lars Inversen's room. She came out ten minutes later and took the back stairs down to the staff area. Daily household supplies, linens, and uniforms were coming in from a local laundry. She must have slipped out of the hotel behind one of the delivery vans because we lost her from any of the cameras."

Elspeth ran through the tapes and silently cursed. Where could Angelika gone without her handbag and everything in it? What was she trying to achieve? Elspeth was convinced that Lars was involved.

"Has Lars Inversen left the hotel?" she asked.

"I checked that too," Sean said. "He's in the breakfast room eating a meal from the international buffet."

Elspeth was torn. Should she chase Angelika out of the hotel or go confront Lars? Since Lars was closer at hand, Elspeth chose him.

Elspeth calmed herself mentally and walked with as much grace as she could muster into the breakfast room. Lars was sitting at a small table by the window. He was in the midst of attacking a plate brimming with food. As if surprised, Elspeth looked over at him and he waved at her. She approached his table as casually as possible.

"I trust you are enjoying your breakfast," she said. "I was looking for Angelika. Have you seen her?"

Elspeth watched Lars face but it didn't change expression. "Haven't seen her this morning," he said. It was a lie of course. Elspeth had seen the tapes.

"Nancy said she had gone out. I hoped you knew ,where she might have gone."

"I'm not her keeper as much as I would like to be" Lars said taking another bite.

Elspeth changed tack. "Are you having any luck on your investigation?" she asked.

"Not a lot. I'm beginning to think I have been sent here under a false premise." Which, Elspeth thought, must mean he is making progress and doesn't want me to know.

"I talked to someone yesterday afternoon who knew about the objects of your search. She knew Moya." Elspeth let the lure float in the air. She hoped Lars would take the bait.

"Then you know more than I," he said.

Damn his cool.

"I need to talk to Angelika," she said. "Perhaps we can talk later and I can help you with your investigation."

For the first time she sensed in him a flicker of interest.

"Perhaps," he said and returned to his meal. She left him eyeing the poached egg à la Kennington on his plate. That small spark in his eyes gave her some hope she might be able to make him cooperate with her.

Elspeth left the hotel by the front entrance. She asked the doorman if he had seen Angelika and got a negative answer. She hurried towards the narrow alleyway at the back of the hotel where Angelika had disappeared. The deliveries continued but Angelika was nowhere in sight. A young, carrot-headed hotel staff member was standing at the delivery door.

"Good morning, Ms Duff," he said.

His name badge said he was called Gordon.

"Gordon, have you seen Angelika Rostova? The cameras recorded her leaving by this door half an hour ago."

Gordon nodded. "I tried to tell her that for their own safety guests were not allowed in the service area. She smiled at me and sent me a kiss with her fingers. Then she ran out." He blushed. "She's a cheeky one."

"Did you see where she was going?"

"She took the alley towards the Green. I saw her running across the street. She dodged in front of a car but luckily the driver avoided her. He slammed on his brakes and she continued running."

"Towards the green. Is there an entrance to the park in that direction?"

"A little bit down. She must have gone there."

"But you didn't see her enter the green?"

"No, you can't see the entrance from here."

"Thanks for being so vigilant," Elspeth said. "I'll let Mr Clancy know her leaving here was not your fault."

He blushed further and thanked her.

Elspeth followed Angelika's route, cutting across the street as Angelika had. Traffic was light and she did not have to avoid oncoming traffic. Once in the Green, Elspeth stopped. Where would Angelika most likely go? Elspeth surveyed the open space in front of her. She almost missed the figure huddled on a bench by the side of the path. Elspeth could see that Angelika had her face in her hands. Her body was shaking. Elspeth stopped herself from sprinting and walked calmly to where Angelika sat.

Elspeth lowered herself next to Angelika and put her arms around the young woman's shoulders.

Angelika turned into Elspeth's shoulder and sobbed. Elspeth said nothing and let Angelika cry herself out. Finally Elspeth reached into the pocket of her jacket and pulled out a handkerchief, a delicate one made out of Maltese lace that Richard had given her on a day when they wandered around Valletta soon after their marriage. Angelika blew her nose loudly into it. Elspeth hoped Richard would not notice any damage to his gift.

"Angelika, tell me what's wrong. I have a daughter a bit older than you and she finds it comforting to talk things out."

Elspeth was not speaking the truth as her daughter Lizzie had spent her life avoiding Elspeth's comfort thus creating a sad place in Elspeth's heart. But Angelika seemed to relax as Elspeth spoke.

"May I trust you, Ms Duff?"

"Of course."

"You won't tell the police?"

"Not if you don't want me to," Elspeth said, again not quite truthfully. Elspeth's loyalty was to Eric Kennington and the Kennington hotels not to Moya Koda's stepdaughter and her friends.

"You see it's all Sergei's fault. He put me in this bind. And now he's in jail and I have no way to talk to him. I wish I never had given in to his scheme."

"Tell me what scheme. I may be able to see Sergei but I can't help you unless I know what's bothering you. It's part of my job to protect our guests against any discomfort they may experience at the hotels."

Elspeth felt manipulative but she was on the verge of discovering what was happening in the hotel with Lars and Angelika which was more important than her tactics. She also was aware that Angelika was calculating too and might be using Elspeth for her own ends.

"Lars asked Sergei to help him find the jewels," Angelika said. Which probably is true, Elspeth thought. "That's why Sergei came to London and begged me to help. Sergei had no way to approach Moya. Lars is convinced that Moya still had the jewels when we came to Dublin."

Elspeth was not completely sure Moya had. Perhaps the attaché case Moya had taken from the hotel did contain the jewels since they were not found among Moya's effects in the hotel.

Angelika continued, "Lars and Sergei wanted me to find a way for either one of them to approach Moya. That's why I accepted my father's invitation to come to Dublin. Lars was to follow me to the hotel and Sergei came too separately. He couldn't afford to stay at the Kennington Dublin but Lars said his client would pay for him to stay at the Kennington Dublin."

"How did Lars and Sergei meet?" Elspeth asked.

"Sergei said Lars approached him in Paris. Sergei had just returned to Europe from Canada, where he had gone after he left Ukraine, and was acting at a small playhouse on the Left Bank in Paris. Lars must have been there and seen his name. Sergei had made no attempt to hide it."

"What did Lars want?"

"He promised Sergei to help with his acting career if Sergei would find a way to get Lars in touch with my father or Moya. Lars gave him some money too, I think.

"Do you think Sergei had anything to do with your father's death?"

"No! No, it's impossible."

"Why? The police must have some reason for holding Sergei."

"Papa was always in the news. Lars says the police generally need to find a suspect quickly when a well-known person like Papa is murdered."

Elspeth said, "I see." What she did see was that Lars seemed to be controlling Angelika and that he wanted Angelika to stay out of the limelight, but why?

"Angelika, do you have any proof that your brother was not involved in your father's death?"

Angelika began to cry again, but this time quietly. She blew once more into Richard's gift. Elspeth hoped the hotel laundry could restore it to its original pristine condition.

"Sergei has always been gentle."

Hardly proof that he was innocent. His attack at the hotel showed differently.

"Do you know if Sergei and your father met before his death?"

"When Sergei came to the hotel to find Moya, he told me that the reason my father and Moya let his bodyguards go on Saturday night was that Sergei had asked to see my father alone."

Which puts him at or near the scene of the crime, Elspeth thought. No wonder the police had detained him. The police must have picked him up on the CCTV cameras around the theatre. She was curious if there had been any other eyewitnesses.

"Angelika, does your brother have a lawyer? I think he needs one."

"Won't that be expensive?"

"Yes but I think I may have a way of getting him one without you or he being able to pay for one." She was aware she was being cautious of overstepping her boundaries by committing the Kennington Organisation to an expensive defence lawyer. But Eric had said to pursue all leads. Sergei at the moment seemed the best one. If he had seen Moya and Yuri after they let the goons go, he might actually be responsible for attacking Yuri who then pushed Moya away to protect her.

"Angelika, come back to the hotel."

"No, I'm afraid."

"I don't understand. You'll be safe there and we can talk further. If you want, you can come to my suite. No one will disturb us. My husband may be there, if necessary, I'll chase him out."

Angelika laughed. "Do you always push your husband around? He seems so self-assured."

"He is. That's why he puts up with me. Sometimes I'm not a very good wife."

Why was Elspeth telling Angelika this? Shouldn't she present a professional front? Was she slipping into the sloppy ways she had used in British Columbia, which had caused her to be put on suspension by Eric Kennington and having to spend six months in Scotland? But Elspeth thought Angelika might relax if Elspeth seemed more human.

Soon they rose. Elspeth steered them back towards the hotel. Elspeth kept her arm draped around Angelika's shoulder.

"Let's go through the back door," Elspeth said. "I have a keycard that opens it." Back doors at Kennington hotels had no handles on the outside so that no one without a keycard could enter them. They took the service lift up to the second floor, also controlled by Elspeth's master passkey card. They reached Elspeth's suite without meeting anyone, not even a member of the cleaning staff. Fortunately Richard was out. Elspeth blew out her breath in relief. Elspeth sent Angelika to the bathroom to freshen up.

When Angela had left the room, Elspeth picked up her mobile and dialled Eric Kennington's personal number. Unlike Pamela, he took five rings to answer.

"Have you found out anything?" he asked.

"Not yet, but I have just learned that Sergei Koda saw his father just before Yuri was killed. Undoubtedly the police know too and that's why they have retained him. He'll need a lawyer. Will you pay for it?"

"For the person who may be responsible for Moya's death? Elspeth, have you gone completely off your head! I have no intention of paying for Sergei's defence. Don't bother me again unless you come up with a solution."

Elspeth swallowed. "A solution to what, Eric? Finding Yuri's murderer? I thought my job was to protect the guests and the reputation of the hotel and not get involved outside of the hotel."

"I want Moya's name cleared and I don't care what means you have to go to in order to do so. If that involves you affirming that Sergei is Yuri's murderer then use your excellent brain to do so." With these words he rang off, leaving Elspeth frustrated with his unclear mandate.

All right, if that's what you want, she said to herself. She held a trump card and she was just about to play it.

*

Angelika looked at her tear-stained eyes and pale cheeks in the mirror of the bathroom. And you call yourself Yuri Koda's daughter, she said to herself angrily. Her father, and Sergei too, had backbone. She felt spineless and deflated. She also considered that she was letting the two of them down. Lars and the jewels didn't matter.

Up to this moment finding her father's murderer and getting Sergei out of jail did. Why had she given in to Ms Duff's soft and persuasive tones? Other than Nancy, the last person to show her such compassion was her mother or was that just a distant wishful memory?

Her feelings were a morass of confusion. Yuri had been a stern and distant father, more concerned with Angelika's safety because he feared she might be used as a pawn in disrupting the building of his financial empire. Sergei had selfishly run off and left her to her own devices when she was thirteen. And yet now she was filled with the need to exonerate them both. Why? What had they ever done for her as a person with feelings and needs of her own? She thought of Derek. Why wasn't he here for her? He was always so unctuously full of the dispensing of human kindness in words but he had offered little real love to her. And Lars? He wanted the jewels and would use whatever means he could to get them. Now she was going out on a limb to help and forgive them all. What a coward she was to keep giving in.

When Angelika had repaired her face and bucked up her courage, she went back into the sitting room of Elspeth's suite. Elspeth was sitting on one of the sofas and she looked provoked. Angelika had no idea why. Was it something she had done?

Elspeth looked up with a jerk.

"Sorry," she said. "I just had a call but no matter. Now let's see what we can do to help you."

To help me, Angelika thought. Not Sergei, not my father, not Moya, not Lars, not Derek, but me. As much as she had mistrusted Elspeth Duff before, she now felt she had an ally.

Angelika sat down across from Elspeth and looked her straight in the eye.

"I want to leave here and take Nancy with me."

From Elspeth's reaction, she had not expected this request but she seemed to rally.

"Where would you like to go?" she asked.

"Somewhere where no one will find us. Somewhere where we can be alone. I need time to think without being pressured by the others."

"What about the others?"

"For once they can fend for themselves," Angelika said more bravely than she was feeling. "Do you know where I might go?"

Elspeth sat back and frowned. She appeared to be puzzled and therefore did not respond immediately.

"There is at least one place where you can go temporarily," Elspeth said at last, "but first I need you to tell me all you know about your father and stepmother's deaths. From your request, I'm assuming you no longer have any wish to defend your brother."

Angelika pressed her two lips between her front teeth. "That's right."

"What changed your mind?"

"It's time I stood up to them all. I've been a puppet all my life. I don't want to be anymore. If I do get any money from my father's estate, I shall emigrate—to the States or Canada or Australia, anywhere that will have me. I just want to get away where they can no longer find me."

Elspeth drew in her breath. "It's not quite that easy in the modern world."

Angelika smiled. "My father had contacts I can use," she said. "That's one of the few advantages I have over people who have led ordinary lives. I just need to get away to think for a while, to decide what I really want to do with my life."

"And Derek?"

"He's as bad as the rest of them," Angelika said with more vehemence than she knew she was feeling.

Elspeth looked surprised.

"He's using me just as the others are. He preaches humbleness but I'm not convinced he really cares. I think he wants adoration, and a country parish is the way he has chosen to get it. He's shown me no compassion since we've been here. He's become a rabbit in the face of the wolf."

"Wolf?"

"Then there's Lars. He thinks he can charm everyone. He's got Nancy twisted around his little finger and he's convinced Sergei that succeeding in an acting career can happen only under his—Lars's—influence. Under his suave exterior Lars is out for his own gain. I doubt he cares about anything but the jewels. Don't you see, Ms Duff, that the pack of them don't care a fig who I am nor who Nancy is for that matter?"

Elspeth Duff at first did not seem to hear Angelika's concern.

"Do you have any idea, Angelika, how Lars is planning to find the jewels?" Elspeth asked, not addressing Angelika's latest plea.

"He told me earlier this morning that he had a plan and would talk to me about it later in the day."

"Would you be willing to pretend to cooperate with him for the moment? That would help me and also give me some time to arrange for your and Nancy's departure. I need to know as much about Lars as I can for my own purposes as well as yours. From what you say, Lars may not be the genuine article. The Kennington Organisation doesn't want the likes of him to use our hotels for any illegal activity. I hope you understand. You see I have my job to do as well as wanting to help you."

Angelika liked Elspeth Duff for her honesty. She also was relieved that genuine help might be at hand for Nancy and for her.

"Can you explain more?" Angelika asked.

"Here's what I have in mind," Elspeth said.

When Angelika left the suite, she was smiling. Elspeth Duff had briefed her well. Elspeth's methods might be devious but Angelika knew they would be effective. And Elspeth had offered her an escape from the current chaos of her life.

25

Richard sat in the breakfast room and watched people serve themselves at the buffet. He could have predicted the size of the servings as they correlated directly with the size of the guest. It seemed that the larger the person was the more unkempt their clothing, with disastrous visual effect. Should he tell Lord Kennington that in order to raise the level of respectability of his clientele that he should only allow thin guests? He smiled at the absurdity of his thought. The world was getting to be supersized but manners and pride in one's appearance did not seem to follow their abundance. He thought of his early days at the Foreign and Commonwealth Office, and wondered if the standards of those days would ever return, standards that were based on pride in oneself and how one presented that pride to the world. People did not now care for other than their own gratification, as the servings from the buffet reflected. He wondered if he could find any way to help Lord Kennington return to bygone days but feared people's insatiable urge to feed their appetites boded ill for Eric's quest.

He was interrupted from his musings by the approach of Lars Inversen.

"May I join you, Sir Richard? I was hoping you would help me with something."

Richard knew that Elspeth was leery of this young man's intentions but Richard was willing to hear him out.

"Have another cup of coffee," Richard suggested, "and

tell me what you have in mind."

"I don't know how much your wife has told you about my reason for being here."

"She said you worked for a private investigatory firm and were looking for the Romanov jewels that were stolen a year or so ago."

"You see," Lars said, "we are almost sure that either Yuri Koda or his wife was responsible for their theft. We have followed every lead in the European underworld and finally came to the conclusion that neither Yuri nor his wife hired anyone to help them and that they must have been personally responsible for removing the items from Northby's. Moya Koda is the most likely suspect. In fact, we are almost certain that she brought the jewels to Ireland but I haven't been able to trace them any further than the hotel. And now she's disappeared."

So, thought Richard, Angelika has not told Lars about Moya's death.

"Do you think she took the jewels with her when she left?" Richard asked although he knew Moya was in no condition to do so.

"No, I think they are still here."

Richard was startled. No one had suggested this before.

"Can your wife find out if they are?" Lars asked.

"Elspeth's job is to protect the privacy of the guests," Richard said, and hoped he sounded non-committal.

"Would you ask her for me? The jewels are stolen property and I'm sure the police would like to know if they are here."

Richard sensed a threat but he had been put in difficult situations many times before in his life. In fact, he was beginning to enjoy being able to use the tact he had used so many times before in his career. But the young man had a point. If the hotel was protecting the jewels from their rightful owner, then the Kennington Organisation might be accused of abetment. Richard wondered if Elspeth had ever dealt with this sort of problem before.

"I'm not a lawyer nor do I know the ins and outs of the liability of the hotels in this situation but I will approach my wife and tell her your concern. But why do you think the jewels are here?"

Lars settled back and took the cup of coffee the waiter offered him.

"We have been tracking the jewels ever since they were reported missing. Our agency has contacts throughout the criminal world in Europe and we normally would expect to hear if the jewels were circulating among the normal receivers of stolen goods or unscrupulous collectors who are willing to cut corners to obtain items they particularly desire. But we have only been met with silence. At first we thought the jewels were taken to be sold to a private collector, most probably negotiated though Yuri Koda's connections. But we have traced his bank accounts, please don't ask how, and found that he received no large amount of untraceable cash that might be associated with the sale of the jewellery. We also checked Mrs Koda's accounts with the same results."

"You seem to have access to a great deal of confidential information," Richard said.

"We have to in our profession. The internet has made it much easier."

"You mean hacking? Isn't that illegal?"

Lars did not answer directly. "We are dealing with items of great value here, in the millions."

"What makes you so sure that the jewels have not been sold privately and the cash put in a safe deposit box in Switzerland?"

"The Swiss authorities have been helpful," he said. "I believe they no longer can conceal money obtained by criminal means."

"But what would be the purpose of the Kodas keeping the jewels?"

"Things of their value have a fascinating effect on people."

"Are you saying that Moya Koda kept the jewels because she was mesmerised by them?"

"Mrs Koda has a large fortune in her own right according to our records. In my experience, she would be more likely to keep them for personal reasons than financial ones."

"And Yuri Koda?"

"Judging from his many ups and downs in his business dealings, I think he would be more likely to sell them, or put them up as collateral on his next deal."

"Are you saying that Moya took the jewels for herself and has hidden them away?"

Lars nodded slowly. "Which is why I think they may be here in the hotel. Don't be upset, Sir Richard. I already know they were not in her room."

Richard did not want to pursue this possibility. Therefore he said, "I'm not certain I can help you. Elspeth doesn't like me meddling in her work."

Lars looked askance which made Richard explain.

"I'm employed separately by the Kennington

Organisation on a task that does not involve the Kodas. Are you married, Lars? You must appreciate that when a couple work for the same firm, they sometimes can't discuss with each other the intricacies of their respective jobs. But I will ask Elspeth. She may want to talk to you on her own."

"I would appreciate that, Sir Richard. Now I must go. I have an appointment."

Richard watched Lars leave. He suspected that Lars was not an honest man. The activities he spoke of—underworld contacts, computer hacking and even surreptitiously searching Moya Koda's room—made Richard wonder how much Lars had said was true. He knew Elspeth did not trust Lars and now Richard agreed with her. But he was left with the suggestion that Lars had planted in his mind, that the jewels were still in the hotel.

Richard put down his napkin, rose and hurried from the breakfast room without finishing his meal.

*

Lars ducked behind one of the Kennington Dublin's large planters filled with an abundance of fresh flowers and smiled as he watched Richard head for the lift.

Mission accomplished, he thought. Now his plans were beginning to form. Angelika was the key but after their earlier interview that morning, he knew he would have to approach her carefully. He had a feeling she was about to bolt and was prepared to stop her. He needed her. He also needed to find a way to get Sergei out of jail. Sergei knew too much and might eventually break.

He took the stairs two by two to the second floor. He was startled as he came out through the fire door to meet

Angelika head on. She appeared to be coming from Elspeth Duff and Sir Richard's suite. She looked up at him with eyes that held his. Something had changed in her.

"Angie, come to my room before anyone sees us," he said catching his breath. "I have a plan."

She continued to stare straight at him and at last said, "Be quick about it. Nancy doesn't know where I've gone and she may be worried."

He let her enter his room first and directed her to sit on one of the chairs.

"Have you asked Ms Duff to help with Sergei?" he asked.

"She said she might be able to see him."

"Good," Lars said and meant it. "We need to get him out of jail as quickly as possible. I don't want him telling the police about the jewellery."

"Why would he?" Angelika said. Lars detected a hint of defiance. "As far as I know they don't use torture here in Ireland and besides the jewellery is irrelevant to my father's murder."

Torture? He wondered how much such brutality Angelika had seen in her life.

"We have to find evidence that will prove that Sergei was not near the scene of the crime," he said.

"But he was. That's what the police have on him, I think. They must have caught him on the CCTV cameras. Ms Duff told me that they only are questioning him and have not technically arrested him."

"They must not have a record of the murder itself then," Lars said. "If the crime had been on the CCTVs, it would be an open and shut case. Sergei would either be guilty or cleared. I'm afraid the police may wear him down and try to get a confession. My dear Angelika, your brother can be weak. It's all a part of his personality and his need to be an actor, I think."

"Don't underestimate my brother," Angelika replied. "He had the courage to defy my father and flee from the family, which I never had."

Lars wanted to reply, 'but you are a woman', but somehow he felt this would not resonate with Angelika in her current mood.

"Does Ms Duff think she can get him off?" Lars asked.

"She didn't say. She asked what I thought she should ask him."

"And what did you say?"

Angelika smiled, a bit slyly Lars thought. She had a certain Slavic charm, with her high cheek bones and thick, blonde hair. He liked the new spark in her.

"I said I would have to think about it and that I would ask you as well?"

Lars was horrified. "Me?"

"I told her that you had approached me about helping find the whereabouts of the jewels. She seemed to know that already. She also said she hoped to put the case to rest. She seemed anxious for us to leave the hotel as quickly as possible. She said her responsibility would end there."

"Did you believe her?"

"She was straightforward about it. Her job is with the hotel, not the police."

"We need her assistance," Lars said. "I approached her husband this morning and he said he would speak to her about helping us. In the meantime, I want us to concentrate on finding out what your stepmother may have done with the jewellery. When you talk to Ms Duff again, I want you to say that in Moya's absence, you want to take everything left belonging to your father back to London to have the lawyers sort things out as to who owns what. If the jewels are here still, you may have a good excuse to get hold of them."

"And if she says no?"

"It's your job to convince her. In the meantime, I want to get Sergei away from the police. Do you have any suggestions?"

He waited, as Angelika's ideas might be better than his own. She said nothing. Earlier she would have demurred to him, as she had all during their plotting with Sergei. He had always considered her a bit of a passive milksop and an easy entrée to Moya.

"There is nothing to link Sergei to the jewels," he said.

"Isn't that the reason he was here?" Angelika replied. A small smile twisted on her lips.

"The police do not need to know that."

"Don't you think they will ask?"

Lars could not fathom this new attitude on her part but her new fire fascinated him. He thought it reflected her father and not her mother, who, he had speculated, was a typical trophy wife, beautiful but submissive.

Angelika's new persona puzzled him. He felt he had lost some of his control over her. "Angie, we are too far committed to our assignment here to give up now. Even if Sergei remains in jail, we can't give up."

Lars discovered something he had not considered before. Angelika Rostova had more backbone than her brother. How odd, he thought, I think I'm falling for her. He shook his head, which provoked a smile from Angelika.

"Lars, why does this mean so much to you? Isn't finding the jewels only a job, just the way Ms Duff says her job is to protect the hotel's guests? Do you always take your assignments so personally?"

He tried to gather his thoughts before answering. He had not told Angelika or Sergei why he was so intent on recovering the Romanov's property. He decided that for the moment he would keep that to himself but he needed a way to get Angelika's full support back.

She kept looking at him. "Do you?"

"Not all of them," he admitted. "This one has got under my skin. Angie, I, damn it, I need to find them and you're my mainstay."

"I haven't done much."

"Maybe not so far but I want you to become more involved, not just because of your brother but for me personally." He startled himself with the intensity of his statement. Was he losing perspective? "I've been racking my brain about where Moya might be hiding the jewels."

"Moya's dead," Angelika said.

He blanched. "Dead? When did she die?"

"Early yesterday morning."

"Here at the hotel?"

"No, in County Louth, where she grew up. I'm told that she knew she was dying and therefore asked to be taken home. The hotel hired an ambulance."

"She must have taken the jewels with her. I can see no other way they might have disappeared."

"I don't think she did. Ms Duff told me she was unconscious when she left the hotel. In the end she never came out of her final coma."

"Who went with her? Someone must have been."

"I don't know."

"Dear Angie, are you able to you find out?" he asked and then felt himself blushing. Why had he called her that? This was no time to get romantically involved. He felt he was so close to his goal and he did not want to be distracted. But he felt her magnetism. She was a fool to get engaged to the pathetic Derek Somerset.

She looked puzzled and he wondered if she could read his thoughts. "I can ask Ms Duff but I suspect that she might not tell me. Lars, honestly I'm feeling uncomfortable about continuing. Everything has gone wrong since Sergei asked me to help you. My father's been killed, my stepmother has died and Sergei has been arrested. I feel totally powerless."

Lars had been so absorbed in his own quest that he had not seen what had happened through her eyes. He knew he had used her and her brother as well. Lars's urgency had been so strong that he had forgotten about the others and that they might have feelings of their own.

"You aren't powerless," he said. "In fact, the two of us—and Sergei if we can get him out of jail—have a great deal of power. The hotel seems to want us out of the way and we have no reason to be here now."

"Why?"

"Now that your father and stepmother are dead, we no longer need to be near them. By the way, can you find out where your stepmother's home was?"

"I don't need to find out. Nancy and I were scheduled to go with Moya to visit her father before all this happened."

"Can you still go now? You could say you wanted to pay your respects to the family."

"Lars, I don't want to be a part of this anymore. There's nothing in it for me, or for Sergei or for Nancy. I just want to go back to London and forget about all of this. But first I want to make sure Sergei is freed."

"I do too. Let's put our heads together and see if we can get Ms Duff to help us with that. Are you OK with that?"

"Yes," she said. The corners of her lips turned up, her eyes brightened. She seemed to relax.

*

Elspeth felt depleted. She was getting nowhere but, even worse, she was not sure exactly where she should be going. She felt she was swimming in a morass of unanswered questions. But most of all what did Eric Kennington expect of her? He was being exasperatingly unclear. Had his emotional commitment to Moya left him so bereft that he was deflecting his anger over Moya's death on to Elspeth? Or did he think she could come up with a magic formula that would ease his pain?

Her phone call with Eric and her interview with Angelika had left her without a plan. What outcome would solidify her position with the Kennington Organisation and also help Eric deal with his grief? She was in the process of thinking this out when Richard came in from breakfast.

"Elspeth, my dearest, you're in a dark place I can tell. Do you want to talk?"

Relief filled her but she choked back her need. He must have seen her do so.

"Dickie, I'm feeling rudderless. How can I find out what's happened here? The police have arrested Sergei but I am convinced he is innocent. Eric Kennington has forbidden me to hire a lawyer for him. Angelika is ready to bolt. Lars seems more grounded. Derek Somerset and Nancy Kendall seem as if they are paddling aimlessly about feeling unloved. I should try to hook the two of them up, although they would be mismatched. And Eric is in London fuming away at the world and, according to Pamela, not minding the store."

Richard laughed at her description.

Elspeth frowned at him.

"It's not funny. Why did I ever agree to come here in the first place?" she said.

"That's the first time I've seen you wavering at your need to return to your job."

"I'm not wavering. If I get Angelika and Nancy to leave and Lars to go away of his own accord, I should be over and done with the affair but it's not as simple as that. I've no clear idea who killed Yuri Koda or Moya or why." She paused. "But I think the answer to that question may be here in the hotel. I just don't know how to get at it. Do you think that's what Eric wants me to do, to ferret out the truth about Yuri's murder and its consequences? I'm afraid I am letting this whole thing about the Romanov jewels distract me."

"You always tell me that sort of thing when you think you're reaching a dead end. You should reverse your mind and see at what point you had lost your way. Do you want to try that approach? I'll listen."

Elspeth twisted up her face. "Ever since Pamela told me about the jewellery, I have assumed that the theft and the murder were connected, particularly after Lars showed up at the hotel. The link, however, may have taken me on a wild goose chase. I need to get back to Moya, who she was, not if she stole the jewels."

"Why do you say that?"

"In my early interviews with Moya, she kept telling me the reason she didn't contact the police was that she thought they might accuse her of arranging the attack on Yuri. At the time I thought she was being hysterical. One only needed to look at her face to see that she had been badly beaten. She blamed her husband trying to protect her, but at the time, and even now, I think that was a diversionary tactic on her part. And then I got caught up in her relationship with Eric. I don't know why I always allow myself to be badgered by him. Dare I call them his tantrums? They have a way of setting me off, particularly on this case when I'm trying so hard to play by the rules."

"If he hadn't come to Dublin or if you didn't get to know about his relationship with Moya, what then?" Richard asked.

Elspeth raised her head and looked up at the ceiling. "I would have tried to find out more about what happened on the night of the murder, and would have followed up Moya's leaving the hotel on Tuesday and coming back further beaten."

"That sounds sensible," he said.

"I'd discount the jewellery theft, at least for the moment," she said. "After all, there is no proof Moya took the jewels. Northby's accused her but Eric thought that that might have been as a cover-up to protect one of the Northby family relatives. I also want to know more about

Moya. She's the centre of this whole thing. Eric told me some disturbing things about her but I haven't looked into on them yet."

"And Yuri Koda?"

"I don't think Eric cares about him, only that he might have been the reason Moya was injured in the first place. Moya said she received her wounds as a result of Yuri pushing her out of the way. Technically I suppose that meant he was partly responsible for her death."

"Why do you say partly?"

"Because of her foray from the hotel later. Moya told me she loved Yuri. It's possible she may have gone out to confront his attackers."

"And the attaché case?"

"Possibly a ruse and not a packet of jewels. She may even have had a weapon in the case because she feared she would be attacked. Or her attackers may have seized the case from her, thinking she had a weapon in it."

"Giving you far too many possibilities."

"Not if I don't let them distract me. I need to concentrate on how Moya got involved in Yuri's murder and if she was really shoved aside by him. I'm not a pathologist but after looking at her face, I would speculate that her battering was the result of more than Yuri pushing her away. She was beaten severely, Dickie. I saw her."

"Didn't you tell me that she was covered with heavy makeup when you went to her suite?"

"She was. But wait. Angelika has pictures of her taken soon after the beating. I must get them. She said she'd give them to me but she never did. Why is it that every time I turn around in this case I meet stonewalling—first Moya and then Angelika. Angelika said she'd get back to meet after she met Lars. I'll have to pressure her to give me the electronic photo files when I see her next. Now how can I find out more about Moya? Eric's not going to tell me anything negative but Pamela might be able to dig up some dirt. Even Eric hinted that there is a great deal of it."

"Didn't Eric say to keep Pamela out of this?"

"He just told me I could talk to Pamela. I'm not allowed to tell her his feelings for Moya. Knowing Pamela, she probably has already guessed. Dickie, you're an angel to listen to my plight." She rose and kissed him.

"The pleasure has been all mine," he said making a funny face. "Now I have to get back to my impossible task of finding a way of telling Eric that nowadays it's impossible to tell a lord from a dustman by the way they dress or act. I'm off. Say hello to Pamela for me."

Elspeth remembered that she had asked Pamela to help her discover more about Yuri's business dealings but suddenly Moya's past activities seemed more important.

Pamela was not at her desk and so Elspeth left a message. Taking advantage of this lull, Elspeth reviewed the case notes she always kept on her secure internet site. She tried to look at her observations from every angle possible. Slowly an idea formed in her head. She picked up her mobile and telephoned Sean Clancy.

"I want to make a thorough search of the Koda's suite. I'm sure no one has been in there since Moya Koda left. Please alert the security team of this."

26

The suite stood undisturbed in front of her. Eric Kennington must have told Sean to leave everything untouched. The bed where Moya had last lain was in disarray. The chair where Elspeth had last seen Eric Kennington sitting when he had begged Moya to live was still there but probably pushed aside by the paramedics. The whole traumatic scene crossed through Elspeth's thoughts. In the disorder of the room she could feel the calm procedures of the medical staff and see the agony on Eric Kennington's face. Now everything was silent.

Elspeth had her smartphone with her and decided to make an inventory of the two rooms and the bathroom. She began in the sitting room, the least disturbed of the spaces. Elspeth recognised the precision of the Kennington hotel room attendant service. Little of the Koda's presence could be seen in the room. The only things out of order were the television remote, which had been thrown on the coffee table, and two of the cushions of the sofa. The small rug at the door to the bedroom was askew, perhaps by the trolley that transported Moya to the ambulance. Otherwise order reigned.

The bedroom was quite different. Elspeth wanted to make sure she had everything recorded and so took extensive photographs with her phone. Then she began taking notes.

As she progressed, what amazed her was that an unknowing observer would have assumed that Yuri Koda had recently been an inhabitant of the suite.

The table at the side of the bed where Yuri had slept had a book and two magazines written in Cyrillic script, all tidily stacked. One of the magazines had suggestive photographs; the other seemed to be a business publication with graphs and stern looking men, but no women, shaking hands. The book was thick but had no pictures or charts. Moya's side of the bed, however, was more chaotic, as if she had just been there and had been interrupted while skimming through several fashion magazines, some in French and some in English. A copy of the American edition of Vogue was on top. A page had been ripped out and had fallen to the floor. Elspeth picked this up and thought the style of the dress on the cover would suit Moya. Had she planned to have it copied, the way Elspeth did with her clothes? The house phone had been knocked over and the headset lay as if pushed aside by the ambulance staff.

Elspeth examined the bedding and the pillows. She found streaks of pancake makeup on the pillowslips and several patches that might have been the thin blood-like serum that oozed out of wounds that had not quite healed. These traces were grizzly reminders of the state of Moya's face. The sheets were in disarray, although Elspeth noted that the duvet was still neatly folded and lay at the foot of the bed. An ivory-coloured throw from one of the room's chairs had been used as a makeshift blanket and was twisted around the top sheet.

She noted that the curtains were half-drawn and let in light. The summer sun made patterns across the floor and up into the crumbled bed linen.

Any traces of the wheels of the trolley that had taken Moya's body from the room had long since been absorbed into the heavy weave of the woollen carpet. Otherwise the room showed the signs of the cleanliness that Lord Kennington insisted upon.

Elspeth next examined the wardrobe in the passageway into the bathroom. Yuri Koda's clothing was carefully hung on one side. Elspeth went through his suits and a blazer. The pockets were empty save for a handkerchief she found in one of the inner pockets. His laundered shirts and ties showed the attention of the Kennington Dublin's laundry's careful care. The drawers to the side of the clothes bar held his underwear and socks, all from a well-known Bond Street haberdasher. Somehow Elspeth found the items impersonal, as if they had been bought for the trip but never worn. In the top drawer she found his cufflinks and other jewellery, all of which were on the verge of gaudy without being completely vulgar.

Elspeth turned her attention to Moya's half of the wardrobe. Eric Kennington had touted Moya's sense of style and he had not spoken out of hand. With appreciation, Elspeth went through Moya's clothes, shoes and undergarments, which were numerous. Elspeth should have expected this.

All the garments were originals and sported the best names in modern fashion for the well-dressed woman of a certain age. Envious, Elspeth lingered and then sighed. She took careful photographs of a dress she particularly liked for her own future reference. Unlike Yuri, however, Moya had no baubles in the drawers provided, which made Elspeth assume they must be in the small safe at the bottom of the cupboard. She tried the lock but it would not give way.

The Kodas' cases were neatly stacked in ascending order of size above their clothing. Yuri had three pieces of luggage, Moya seven, including a makeup case. Elspeth took this latter piece down and saw that it was empty save for a discarded tissue.

Then Elspeth went into the bathroom, which seemed to be the large repository of Moya's cosmetics and a small shaving kit, which had been zipped and pushed to one corner. In it Elspeth found an electric razor, aftershave from Yves St Laurent, an electric toothbrush and toothpaste, a nail set and a tortoiseshell comb and brush set. In the bottom she found a George V half-crown piece, perhaps a lucky token because it was well-rubbed.

Elspeth photographed Moya's cosmetics but did not attempt to catalogue them. She did notice that several jars of pancake makeup were lidless and were almost empty.

The hotel amenities were intact. Obviously the Kodas were not the sort to take hotel samples with them, although the Kennington hotels offered the highest quality of these.

Before she left the suite, she made one more round of the rooms to see if she had missed anything. Nothing caught her eye until she was ready to let herself out.

The alcove meant for the room attendant's equipment where Billy Maguire had sat when Elspeth first came in the suite was slightly out of order. No one would have noticed any disruption had they not been on the staff of Kennington hotels. Elspeth closed the folding doors that normally covered the space. She did this automatically but in doing so her mind kicked into gear. What happened to Billy Maguire, who had sat in the space with a gun in his jacket? Billy Maguire whom Moya had trusted since childhood. Where was he now?

Elspeth made her way to Sean Clancy's office.

"I want to get into the safe box room and want you to come with me. And also bring up the entry log for the space."

Although smaller safes were provided each suite, every Kennington hotel had a safety deposit room. This room could only be opened with two electronic keycards, one held in a secure drawer at the reception desk and one in Sean's office. This second one could only be activated by a password that was only known to the manager, the night manager and the head of security. The numbers of both keys were changed daily.

Elspeth had no love of tight spaces after being shut in one on an earlier case but Sean insisted that the door to the safety deposit room be shut when they were in there.

"There's a ventilation system and an automatic release on the door," he explained.

The wire shelving had tags identifying room numbers, although Elspeth noted that these tags could be slid along the edge of the shelving to accommodate larger or smaller individual drawers and items. She followed the numbers with her fingers and reached the spot of the Kodas' suite number. She judged that a metre's length had been allowed for the Kodas' goods. At one side was a leather jewellery box with the letters 'MdeLK' stamped in gold on its front. Elspeth removed it from the shelf and opened it. She did a quick survey of its contents. The items were mainly gold and platinum and a few had gems and semi-precious stones but to Elspeth's trained eye, these were the adornments of a wealthy woman who was travelling and certainly not nineteenth or early twentieth century treasures of the Russian court.

She put the box back on the shelf, but as she did so, one of the small drawers fell out and with it an ornate brooch of miniscule proportions with a fine ruby in the centre. Elspeth picked it up and examined it. Could it be one of the Romanov jewellery collection?

"The lawyers will have to sort out who owns these. In the meantime, let's leave then here. Sean, were you here when the Kodas initially left their things here? What was in the empty space?"

Sean looked perturbed. "I try not to look when guests use the safety deposit room but I came in later with another guest. Where you now see a space there was a large brief case, Yuri's I would guess."

"Check the log. When was this removed and who signed it out?"

Sean flicked through the pages on his smartphone. "Yuri signed something out on Friday morning and then brought it back that afternoon. Moya removed something on Tuesday afternoon. I think both times they took a small briefcase." He pointed to the empty shelf.

Elspeth assessed the length of the empty space.

"By my estimate that's about the size of a standard folder for an A4 sheet. Now I just have to figure out why Moya didn't return it here and where she might have taken it."

Elspeth was beginning to feel comfortable with the idea that the briefcase probably had to do with Yuri Koda's business in Ireland and its contents had been the thing Moya had taken from the safety deposit room on Tuesday.

The small brooch puzzled her. Was it part of a larger haul or was it a single item that Moya had kept as a family heirloom? Elspeth wanted to find out.

Elspeth found Richard sitting in a comfortable chair in the lobby and sipping a cup of tea.

"I've spent many years learning to drink multiple cups of tea without having to use the loo but this assignment is taxing my limit," he said with a smile. "In any case I've read every magazine here twice and three of today's papers front to back including all the adverts."

"Have you come up with any dazzling ideas for your report to Eric?" Elspeth asked, holding back a grin.

"No, but I think we should consider heated flooring for the barn renovation on Loch Tay. I'm not at all certain doing so would be 'green' but it would be nice to get up during the night and not face a cold floor. It's quite the thing according to the Irish press."

"I wonder if it would be allowed under Scottish environmental policies. Have you see adverts for it in *The Scotsman* or *The Courier*?"

"I have never looked. But how doeth my favourite lady sleuth get on?"

"How do you fancy a trip to County Lough?"

"To Moya's home? Would Eric approve it?"

"He might if I catch him in a good mood. I think a key to the mystery of the Kodas' deaths lies there."

"Lead on, Lady MacDuff."

Elspeth smiled at his use of his long-time nickname for her. He had also called his boat by the same name and had asked Elspeth to christen it in Malta shortly after they were married. She had been seasick on its maiden voyage and refused to go on it after that, much to his regret. Elspeth wondered why Richard had chosen to marry someone who had such an aversion to the motion of the waves, even the tame ones on Loch Tay.

"I'll make arrangements through Pamela. I'll have the concierge get us a hired car. I understand it's only about ninety kilometres. If you drive, we should be there quickly."

Seeing that no one else was in the lobby, she kissed the top of his head and headed back to their suite.

*

Without Elspeth Duff's help, Lars could think of no way to communicate with Sergei much less get him out of jail. His discovery of Sergei's name in Paris had been coincidental. By then he was already working on the theory that Yuri and/or Moya Koda had stolen the Romanov jewellery. After he had attended the play on the Left Bank in which Sergei was part of the cast, he had gone on the internet and found the connection. Sergei was not central to Lars's search but he was a useful conduit to his father and stepmother through his half-sister Angelika Rostova. Lars was convinced that the Kodas did have the Romanov items but he was equally sure that Yuri's murder and Moya's death had nothing to do with their theft. Had Lars not feared that Sergei might give his surname to the Garda, he thought he might have left Sergei to his own fate or convinced Angelika that she needed to stay out of the police investigation. Lars's main purpose was to retrieve the jewellery without the police being involved and to restore it to its rightful owners. If the police had seized the stolen items, it might be years before the Romanovs repossessed them. He decided that he would leave Sergei's lot in Angelika's hands. Her new bravery and her obvious desire to help her long-lost brother made Lars feel he could put this task on the sidelines of his concerns. But he needed to convince Angelika to help him get an invitation to Moya's family in County Lough.

*

Angelika checked her phone and pulled up the original email from Moya inviting her and Nancy to the de Lacy home. Moya's gushing praise of her birthplace had initially put Angelika off but Nancy had read the email over her shoulders and had said that a week in the Irish countryside sounded divine.

"Can you put up with my stepmother for that long?" Angelika had asked.

"Can you? Isn't that more of the question? Just imagine how lovely it will be. We can go climbing and bathe in the sea and all for free. Why do you hate your stepmother so much, Angie? She's a bit over the top but she means well."

"Does she?"

"Angie, can't you put up with her just this once?"

"It would be lovely to go to County Lough if we could go without her."

Angelika remembered this conversation vividly. The day had been overcast, hot and humid in London and the prospect of country air seemed glorious. Before Angelika had replied to her stepmother's invitation, she had received the first email from Sergei. Initially she did not believe it was genuine but he had asked to meet her in London, in Hyde Park near the Serpentine. Although she cautiously had agreed to the meeting, Angelika had almost not gone to it at all. She had not seen Sergei in so many years that she was not sure she would recognise him.

She planned to be early and to sit within eyeshot of their agreed meeting place. But he was there before she was. She had no doubt about his identity and memories of her childhood with her big half-brother had flooded over her.

But who was Sergei now? He had led her into the plot with Lars. When they were young he always had been able to convince her that his schemes would reap vast rewards. Usually things had failed but she had loved being included and usually got off lightly because of her age and childish charm. Sergei's departure from her small family had devastated her.

Sergei's lack of communication had cut her deeply but now he was back. How easily she was drawn into his relationship with Lars Inversen.

But now where was she being led—and did she want to be involved any longer? Half of her wanted to flee back to London with Nancy; the other half felt Lars's magnetism and what seemed to be his genuine belief that Moya had taken the jewellery. Angelika hoped that Moya had been responsible for the theft and that even in death her name would be discredited. But all this thinking did not help her long-held feelings towards Sergei—or her new conflicted ones towards Lars.

Nancy was waiting in their room and flew up and hugged Angelika when she came through the door.

"I thought you had been kidnapped," Nancy cried out. "I told Ms Duff you had vanished but she convinced me that you probably were OK and that I shouldn't worry but I have. Oh, Angie, I'm so glad you're back. Where have you been?"

Angelika did not want to lie to her friend. "I needed to think," she said, "so I went and sat in the park for a long time. Ms Duff found me there and convinced me that she could help me. I've taken her up on the offer. She says she may be able to get access to Sergei. What should I do about him, Nancy? If he was near the scene of my father's murder, how do I know that he wasn't the murderer?"

A rapping came at the door and Nancy rose to answer it. Derek Somerset stood in the doorway and asked if he could come in. Angelika looked up at him but he avoided her eyes.

'I have been at prayer for you both," he said. The words came out as if they were memorised. Angelika suddenly wondered why she had been so attracted to Derek. The word 'wimp' came to her mind. Rather than him praying, she wished he would either help her solve the problem of Sergei's incarceration or at least offer some physical token of love.

"Your prayers aren't helping," she said.

"Prayers are often answered in mysterious ways."

Angelika wondered if these words had been part of the curriculum at his theological college.

"I wish they weren't so mysterious. Did your prayers reveal any concrete suggestion?" She used sarcasm purposely.

He recoiled as if being hit by her. "Trust God," he said.

"Right now I need to trust something more than God. I need help getting Sergei out of jail and getting us all back to London without any more fuss."

"Shall I leave you to it?" he said meekly.

"You and God may leave now," she said.

He turned on his heel and quietly closed the door behind him.

"Good riddance!" Angelika called after he had left.

"Angie, that was cruel," Nancy said.

"No, Nance, he was being cruel."

"Isn't ineffectual a better word?"

"You're right. I have to tell you what has happened and perhaps you can be of more help."

Angelika skirted around her interviews with Lars, merely mentioning that he suggested they all go to County Louth after all. She did explain to Nancy more of Elspeth Duff's offer to help with Sergei.

"When are you going to come clean about all this, Angie? I'm your friend and I can offer you more help than prayers."

"Now who's being ineffectual?" Angelika said.

Nancy burst out laughing. "Mates again?" she asked and smacked Angelika's palm.

"Mates."

Angelika flopped back on her bed and began to tell her friend the intricate ins and outs of her last few weeks. At the end she said, "And now, you know, no one is any closer to the truth than they were at the beginning."

27

Under Richard's skilled hands the BMW that Elspeth had hired slid along the Irish roads through the green countryside on the way north to the de Lacey home in County Louth near the Northern Ireland border.

"How did you get Eric to relent and arrange for our trip?" he asked. He had not been in the room when Elspeth had made the call back to London.

Elspeth laid her head back on the headrest and blew out her breath. "Dealing with Eric is always a trial when he's in one of his moods. He's such a brilliant man but as he gets older he gets more irrational. Now that I have a 'secret' with him, however, I seem to have more ability to twist him around to my way of thinking. I persuaded him that Sir Gerald de Lacey might be able to give me more insight into what Moya was doing before she came to Ireland. I'm becoming more convinced that it was for no good. Eric told me that he often was worried by Moya's recklessness. He said that he had been so distressed by Moya's death that he had not thought to ask Sir Gerald anything about Moya's last days."

"Do you manipulate me as easily as you do him?" Richard asked.

"No, you're much harder because you're more level headed."

He laughed out loud and put his hand on her knee. "Lady MacDuff, you are incorrigible."

As they neared the de Lacey home, Elspeth rang Sir Gerald.

"I'm expecting you for dinner. I'm old fashioned and like to dress. Will that be an inconvenience?"

Elspeth told Richard that she had foreseen this and insisted that they both bring something along that would pass for country evening chic. He admired her when she appeared in a long cotton frock, ruby red with a miniscule pattern and a short grey jacket cut stylishly. He had not seen it before and admired it openly.

"I don't get much chance to show my finery in Scotland," she said. "Perhaps when we move into our barn, we can have dinners that are a bit more formal than those at the kitchen table at Tay Farm."

Richard cocked his head. "Perhaps I can lure you back to Perthshire if we set up a fashionable retreat for our friends who like more style than just country air," he said half-seriously. She simply smiled in response. He was not sure what the smile meant. Elspeth's underlying feelings often eluded him.

"What role would you like me to play tonight?" he asked.

"I'm not certain what will happen. I want to get Sir Gerald to talk about Moya. Anything about her may prove helpful. You might pretend that you met her at one time when you were serving abroad. You'll have to be vague about the time as I have no idea where she might have been when."

"Better yet," he said, "I can say I met her in London. I might even say I have entrusted her when she was at Northby's with some of Marjorie's jewellery after she died. Marjorie did have a few good pieces she had inherited from her grandmother, the Edwardian Countess of Glenborough. That would get us on the subject of Northby's and Moya's role there."

"Brilliant, my dearest Dickie," she said and leaned over and kissed him.

Sir Gerald met them at the door. Elspeth noticed that his evening jacket had a small moth hole in the shoulder and his tie was badly tied. His effusiveness at their arrival made up for his carelessness, the obvious signs of grief in the circles under his eyes and sallow complexion.

"Come in, come in. I no longer can offer the hospitality shown in this house when my wife was alive but my housekeeper, Mrs Maguire, and I keep up pretences and welcome visitors from the outside world whenever they take pity on a bygone like me."

"You are kind to see us considering all you have been through," Elspeth said. Richard nodded in agreement.

Sir Gerald looked saddened. "I have heard nothing from Eric Kennington since he left here after Moya died other than a brief phone call asking me to see you. At least he's sent someone who might help me come to terms with Moya's death. Old men like me still haven't morphed into the modern world where electronic communication has replaced human contact. Eric said you had seen Moya the day Eric Kennington brought her here."

Elspeth took his hand warmly and was glad she could speak truthfully. "I hope you will forgive us that our visit is at the behest of Lord Kennington and not merely a social call. He, like you, is trying to understand Moya's death and has asked me to help. Let me introduce my husband, who is travelling with me."

"Richard Munro," Richard said.

"You have no need to introduce yourself, Sir Richard. Eric spoke of you when he rang and said you would be coming with Lady Munro."

Elspeth bristled internally. How dare Eric use her title, which she abhorred although she loved Richard. She suspected Eric had done it to impress Sir Gerald.

The interior of the house was cool and Elspeth was glad she had brought a shawl. She wrapped it around her shoulders and wondered why women through time had never been allowed the warmth of men's dinner jackets. They settled in front of a fireplace in a big, draughty room. The coal fire produced only token heat. Sir Gerald offered sherry and Irish whiskey[2]. Elspeth accepted the former and Richard the latter.

"May I talk about Moya?" Sir Gerald asked.

"Of course. Eric said you might want to," Elspeth replied, glad that she did not have to lead into the subject.

"I loved her but she was always a mystery to me. Her mother was a quiet person, Moya quite the opposite. Moya loved being outrageous, probably because her mother and I would have allowed her anything she wanted when she was growing up. Sometimes I regret we were not more disciplinary but Moya's spirit and energy was a joy to both of us. She kept us amused and we indulged her during her childhood. But then we decided to rein her in and sent her

---

[2] In Scotland it is Scotch whisky and in Ireland Irish whiskey.

off to the nuns in Devon. We got many despairing accounts from the mother superior at the convent school. The damage to Moya's personality had already been done. She was genuinely a free spirit. We never thought that this quality would bring her to so much harm in the end."

Elspeth gave a brief and hopefully undetected hand signal to Richard to let Sir Gerald talk. He nodded almost imperceptibly back.

Sir Gerald went on. "After the convent, we were glad that Moya decided to go on to Oxford. She was a brilliant girl and we thought the rigorous requirements of university would tame her. Unfortunately in the end they did not. She would go up to London on the weekends and meet with an unsavoury crowd. The head of college finally asked that we withdraw her for a term to allow her to consider that her behaviour was unacceptable despite her apparently solid scholarship. We brought her back here and kept what we thought was tight control of her. Her main pleasure seemed to be her mare but later we learned that she was having a liaison with the married son of one of the other landowners near here. Luckily nothing ever came of it. Even my wife, who was a strong member of the RC Church here, said she hoped Moya had taken the necessary precautions not to become pregnant. There was many a time when my wife and I said we should have encouraged her romance with Eric Kennington, who seemed the steadiest of her many flings. Are you a mother, Lady Munro? If so, you must understand the difficulties of raising a girl."

"I am. I have a daughter of my own." Elspeth said. Her sympathy was real.

"The years after Moya came down from Oxford were ones of great worry for Moya's mother and me. She took up with numerous unsuitable men. When she was twenty-four, she came back here and announced she was pregnant. She won't tell us who the father was, only saying that they could not marry, and that she intended to have the child. I suppose one shouldn't be happy when a child dies before it is born but it was a blessing for us that the foetus did not reach maturity for natural reasons. The sad part was that the doctor said Moya could no longer have children. Both my wife and I agreed that it was time for Moya to get married. Roger Mulholland was a neighbour of ours who had gone to London and was doing well in the City. He was a widower with definite prospects. I spoke to him about Moya and was very frank about her barren condition. He had two children of his own and, although he wished to remarry, he did not want to start a new family. Mulholland and I came to an agreement and he and Moya were married that October here. I gave him some needed capital for a project and he said he would see that Moya behaved herself in London."

"How well did it work?" Elspeth asked.

"For the first few years I think reasonably well. Roger's children were away at boarding school and spent the summer holidays here in County Lough with their grandparents. Roger continued to do well in the City and could support Moya in a lavish style. She worked hard to complement him and seemed to enjoy being a London hostess. She acted and dressed exquisitely, entertained beautifully and used her Oxford education to advantage with the best of the London's business establishment. But then things began to fall apart.

"Finally Roger came here about six years after the marriage and begged my help. Moya had begun to mix with a less reputable group of people. He felt it was because she was bored. Moya's mother and I put our heads together and suggested to Roger that Moya might find a job in the art industry. To make a long story short, Roger arranged for Moya to be taken in by Northby's."

"Yes, I met her there once," Richard said. "My first wife had some old family pieces that no one in the family wanted and so she considered selling them. Your daughter helped me price them for auction."

"Was she helpful?" Sir Gerald asked pitifully, as if he doubted his own daughter's abilities.

"Extremely," Richard said. "My wife's family has never gone to another auction house since."

Elspeth doubted that the Earl or Countess of Glenborough, Lady Marjorie's brother and his wife, had ever gone to an auction house but then again she did not like them and never turned generous thoughts in their direction. But Elspeth tipped her hat to Richard, who seemed to be learning to lie with impunity.

"I have heard from other sources," Sir Gerald said, "that she was good at her job. I directed several clients her way and they were pleased with the valuation that Moya put on their goods. But, over time, I began hearing other rumours, that some of the items she accepted for auction had less than sterling provenances. I confronted Moya about this, since the de Laceys are an ancient and respected family here in County Lough.

Elspeth recalled Moya telling her that her father had

turned a blind eye to some of the activities by the Irish Republican Army smuggling contraband across Carlingford Lough to County Down during The Troubles, but did not bring this up.

"I didn't tell my wife. She had been poorly for a long time and the earlier problems with Moya had always exacerbated her illness. She died content that Moya had finally changed her ways. I agreed that Moya should take an extended leave from Northby's and travel around the world with Roger, who by now was wealthy enough that he could allow others to run his business. By internet he could stay in touch with the City and make final decisions when they were necessary. Moya sent myriad post cards from the States, Canada, Japan, China, Singapore, Indonesia, and Australia. But then one day I had a hysterical phone call from her from New Delhi saying Roger was ill and that they were rushing back to London. He died shortly after they returned. That was two years ago."

"How very sad," Elspeth said, meaning it.

"The worst was that Moya seemed delighted with what she called her 'release'. She went back to Northby's four weeks after Roger died. She called me often from her mobile, bragging about this acquisition or that. She sold Roger's home over the objection of his children and bought a flat in Chelsea on the Embankment. By her own reckoning, she was 'flying high' and loving it. And then one day she rang and said she had married Yuri Koda. What would you think, Lady Munro, if your daughter called to say she had married one of the most notorious of the new Eastern European oligarchs."

Elspeth thought of Lizzie, her daughter, who was ensconced in the life of a suburban wife in Tunbridge Wells, mother of twins and part-time internet graphic artist. Lizzie thought her mother reckless, not the other way around.

"Did she tell you why she had married him?" Elspeth asked.

"She said for adventure. Look how her recklessness has ended."

In the past Elspeth had been called upon to give sympathy to relatives of murder victims. She had never found an easy way to do so. Sir Gerald, like others to whom she had spoken, seemed depleted. Elspeth wondered if Moya was the end of the proud de Lacey line.

Elspeth was spared replying by the arrival of Mrs Maguire, Sir Gerald's housekeeper and cook. Elspeth had envisioned her as an old woman of Sir Gerald's age, the two of them inhabiting the house as relics of a bygone age. To Elspeth's surprise Mrs Maguire was a middle-aged woman with a modern haircut and she wore jeans and a cheerful green pinafore adorned with shamrocks and the words 'Luck o' the Irish' on it in Celtic lettering. Mrs Maguire announced that dinner was served and Sir Gerald led Elspeth and Richard into a formal dining room with a long table. Three places were set at one end with heavy silver cutlery and crystal goblets. Elspeth felt she had stepped back in time.

"We eat simply here," Sir Gerald explained. "Mrs Maguire bought some fresh salmon this morning and I asked her to make it in the traditional way with Irish butter, watercress and colcannon, a typical cabbage and potato dish. She has also made some French onion soup."

The soup was served over conversation about the weather and the pests in Sir Gerald's garden. Only after Mrs Maguire had served the fish and withdrawn did Elspeth feel comfortable about returning to the subject of Moya. She did so cautiously.

"Did Moya ever talk to you about the accusations against her in the disappearance of the Romanov jewellery?" she asked. "Eric is convinced of her innocence but there are many lingering suspicions. In fact, several people have suggested that the attack on Yuri was motivated by the theft and the current whereabouts of the items taken from Northby's after Moya had visited the Romanovs in Paris and acquired some of their jewellery 'for the auction house'.

"She came here shortly after the charges were levelled at her and Yuri Koda. I won't call him my son-in-law as I never accepted him. She came alone because she said she needed time to gather her thoughts and defend herself. I never was absolutely sure from whom she thought she needed protection—him or the authorities."

"Then it was your impression that Yuri was involved?"

"If either one of them were involved it would have been him and not her. Moya may not have had the most orthodox of characters but I never knew her to be dishonest. Of course he was quite a different story. I doubt he ever did a fully honest thing in his life."

"Could he have coerced her into helping him with the theft?" Elspeth asked. "I understand he was in financial trouble and probably could have done with the money obtained by fencing the jewels."

Sir Gerald busied himself with his dinner before

answering. His voice quavered. "I think their relationship was abusive. Moya didn't say so but when she came here, she had bruises on her arm. She never explained them other than saying they were the result of an accident. I couldn't fathom what kind of accident would cause bruises that looked like the ones on both of Moya's arms. At first she attempted to hide them, but one night I went to her bedroom to say goodnight and they showed below the sleeves of her nightgown. I said nothing to indicate that I didn't believe her. Now I wish I had. When she came back here for the last time, the sight of the bruises she got in Dublin reminded me of that night."

"Sir Gerald, may I be blunt? Do you think Yuri Koda killed your daughter?"

His eyes filled with tears. "Yes, at least indirectly. Moya was frightened of him. She didn't say so but I could feel she was. Moya wouldn't admit she had made a mistake but having known her for all her life, I could sense she felt she had."

"Could Yuri have taken the jewellery or even forced her to do so?"

Sir Gerald drew his bushy eyebrows together in a scowl.

"If Moya was an accessory to the crime, she only acted out of fear. You see, my intrepid daughter was by now way over her head. Yuri Koda was a gangster, even if he always seemed to appear to stay inside the law."

Elspeth cautiously considered her next question. "Did Moya ask you to keep anything for her? A box perhaps."

"Are you implying that she might have passed the items of jewellery to me? Lady Munro, I must protest."

Elspeth looked imploringly at Richard, who said, "Forgive my wife. Eric Kennington has charged her with getting to the bottom of the matters around Moya's death. I think she is merely suggesting the possibility that, if Moya were forced to by Yuri Koda, she might have brought the jewellery to Ireland."

"I'm sorry, Sir Gerald. I didn't think before I spoke," she said.

Elspeth had thought carefully about her accusation and Sir Gerald had not denied Moya's action. Elspeth discreetly decided to let the topic die.

They finished the meal in uncomfortable silence. Richard made attempts at small talk but Sir Gerald did not seem in the mood to reply.

"I retire early," he said as the rose from the table. Mrs Maguire will have breakfast for you at half past eight."

"Let's walk out and see the garden," Richard suggested after their host's departure. "I could do with a breath of fresh air and it's a long time until dark.

The clouds to the west were gold rimmed in the evening sun. A slight wind had come up and Elspeth wrapped her shawl more securely around her.

"It's amazing how different Ireland is from Scotland," he said, "and yet we both share a Celtic tradition. I wonder what happened along the way, both geologically and historically that the differences are now so pronounced. Looking out across to the hills, one instinctively knows we are in Ireland. I find a curious unfinished quality here."

Elspeth linked her arm through his. "Dickie, I feel we are close to discovering what happened in Dublin the night

Yuri Koda was killed. I tend to believe Sir Gerald that Moya was in over her head. I think Moya's plea to me to protect her was more than histrionics on her part. I also think that in all her rantings about her fears, she told me something which will help me get to the bottom of all this. Do you think I can question Sir Gerald more in the morning?"

"If he appears at all," Richard said.

"I must think of some way to get him back on our side. Let's enjoy this lovely evening. Maybe something will come to me in the night."

"Meaning you will toss and turn all night long," he said with a loving sigh. "But, yes, let's do enjoy this evening."

Elspeth was too tired to toss and turn or even to spend time thinking about what Gerald de Lacey might reveal to her. She woke early and put on comfortable clothes that she had brought with her, ones suitable for a day in the country. Before Richard was fully awake, she slipped out of their room and made her way to the kitchen. She found Mrs Maguire there making the final preparations for breakfast.

"Could you spare me an early cup of coffee?" Elspeth asked. "My husband will be down soon but I would love something to wake me up before he arrives."

Mrs Maguire wordlessly poured the requested drink and handed it to Elspeth.

"You're Billy Maguire's mother, aren't you?" Elspeth asked. "I met him briefly in Dublin last week."

"He's a damned fool helping the likes of her," Mrs Maguire said. The 'her' was obvious.

"She always was trouble but she could lead any man on. Look where it got her." Mrs Maguire obviously was not accepting of Moya Koda. Elspeth wondered if Moya had at some point seduced Billy.

Elspeth asked her next question carefully.

"Did Billy get back here with no trouble?"

"Trouble. Moya was always trouble. Billy shouldn't have gone to Dublin in the first place but any time she beckoned, he would be there. It's a wonder he wasn't murdered himself."

"Do you think she was murdered?"

"Don't you? Isn't that why you're here?"

"I'm here because Lord Kennington, my employer, asked me to come. He was very fond of Moya and . . . "

"And like all other men, he was in love with her. Did you ever meet her?"

"Yes, in Dublin. She was a guest at the Kennington hotel, where I work."

"You said you met Billy with her. What was that like?"

Elspeth was not sure what Mrs Maguire meant about 'that' but Elspeth decided to answer directly.

"Billy seemed determined to protect her. He met me at her hotel room door and held me off with a gun until I told him who I was."

"Leave it to Billy. I told him not to take the gun when he left. Guns cause crimes because men with guns can't control themselves when they are acting the protecting angel."

"As well I know from experience," Elspeth said with a smile. "But tell me, when did Billy get back to County Lough?"

"It was Tuesday night."

"Did he have anything belonging to Moya with him?"

Mrs Maguire's face contorted and she said 'Duck!'" Instinctively Elspeth did so. A shot rang out and hit one of the copper pots hanging near the cooker.

"Get over there," Billy Maguire said pointing his pistol towards the kitchen table where Mrs Maguire had been slicing the bread for breakfast. "You too, Mother. Put your hands up, both of you."

"Oh, for heaven's sake, Billy. Put the gun down. Lady Munro means no harm. She's trying to help Sir Gerald out. He's in a sad way."

"You've no right to question my mother," Billy said. He clenched his heavy jaw and did not lower his weapon.

Elspeth tried to regain her composure. She had never liked being threatened with a deadly weapon, but knew from past experience that coolness usually helped defuse similar situations.

"If you wish, Billy, I'll stop. Now will you let us put down our hands. I mean no harm to you or your mother."

"Oh, shit, Billy don't be an ass," his mother said less graciously.

A great roar came from the doorway. "Billy Maguire, if you do one more thing like this, you're out of a job."

Elspeth had no idea the frail Sir Gerald de Lacey had such a commanding voice. "I'm dreadfully sorry, Lady Munro. Billy has a hot head. Why don't you go into the dining room? Sir Richard is just coming down. Billy, give me your gun and get your snivelling body out to the garden, which is in much more need of your help than your mother."

Elspeth did not realise she was shaking until she left the kitchen. Sir Gerald put his arm around her shoulders and said, "We Irish are quick to blow up but equally quick to calm down. Billy's been jumpy ever since he got back from Dublin. I'll see that he doesn't cause you trouble again. Now, come have some breakfast. It should calm you down."

Elspeth's usually good appetite failed her. Martha Maguire did not appear in the dining room. Instead Sir Gerald brought in the tray from the kitchen.

"Billy was devoted to Moya all her life," he explained. "They grew up together but she was the daughter of the head of the house and he the son of the groom. He'd follow her around like a puppy and she would treat him less well than she treated the dogs or her mare. That only seemed to make his ardour more passionate. I asked Moya not to lead him on but she only laughed. My wife and I ignored this cruel streak in her, I'm afraid, only admonishing Moya to be a lady when dealing with the servants. I don't have horses or a groom anymore. Billy acts as undergardener and general man of all jobs outside; Martha rules the inside of the house. All the others have gone now." Sadness filled this last statement. "I won't be needing them much longer. My health isn't good and Moya's gone."

He swallowed. "I suppose my wife's cousin will take the house. He doesn't appreciate the old, so I'm afraid that before they put the last nail in my coffin this old house will be torn down and the land will be dotted with new houses for the rich of Belfast. How odd that after all this time, the de Laceys should fade into oblivion. We've been here in the Cooley Mountains since the twelfth century." He set his mouth. "But at least Yuri Koda will not inherit all this."

Elspeth wondered once again what Moya had done about making a will. It might be a long time before it was probated. And how much money did Moya have? And to whom had she left it if Yuri Koda were to predecease her? The condition of the house seemed to indicate Sir Gerald himself had little interest in maintaining the house the way in had been in the past. Elspeth assumed he would now be Moya's next of kin.

Elspeth took a piece of toast from the toast rack and buttered it without much relish for her task.

Sir Gerald said, "Mrs Maguire makes the bread from Irish oats. I've never tasted anything like it in England."

Elspeth took a bite. "We do have oat breads in Scotland, where Richard and I are from, but not this good. I must get the recipe." Elspeth took a few more bites but finally she put down the bread. "Forgive me, Sir Gerald. I still need to defuse a bit after what happened in the kitchen."

"Damn Billy," Sir Gerald said with some feeling. "I wonder why he reacted the way he did. What were you asking Mrs Maguire that set him off?"

"I asked if Billy brought anything of Moya's back from Dublin."

Sir Gerald looked up at Elspeth and held her eyes. "What would he have brought back?"

"Something she had on Tuesday but that wasn't in her suite at the hotel or in the hotel safety deposit room afterwards. Most of her things are still at the hotel. Eric Kennington instructed the management of the hotel to keep everything as it was when Moya was last there, at least until we understand better what actually happened to

Moya."

"Are you going to call in the police?" Sir Gerald asked.

"Not if we don't have to. Eric dislikes the police coming into his hotels. If there is any police business, we try to have it conducted outside of the hotels, not only on this occasion but also in all cases. Police in the hotels make the guests nervous. They pay enough money that they don't need to think something has gone wrong."

"Good," Sir Gerald said. "Keep the Garda out of this."

Elspeth wondered why Sir Gerald was so adamant. What did he think the guards would stir up? She pushed onward, hoping that Sir Gerald would not cut the conversation short the way he had the night before.

"Did you see Billy with anything when he returned the from Dublin?" she asked.

"I wasn't here," he snapped.

Elspeth noted the evasion.

They finished their breakfast, Richard, who had joined them, eating heartily and Sir Gerald lightly. Elspeth drank two more cups of coffee, hoping they would soothe her.

As they rose from the table, she said, "I think I'll go out onto the garden."

"Let me come with you, Elspeth," Richard said.

"No. I think I'd rather have a few minutes alone."

Richard looked at her with a frown. She wondered if he had picked up that she intended to see Billy Maguire but alone. Now that he had been disarmed, she was no longer afraid.

The morning was cool but humid. Elspeth drew her jacket on and was glad for her stout walking shoes. The grass in the garden still was wet from the rain the night before and sparkled in the morning sunshine. If only all had been well in the world but it was not and Elspeth was determined to get to root of it.

Elspeth saw Billy down in the corner of the flowerbeds. He was weeding with vengeance. From a distance Elspeth was not certain if the plants he was pulling from the ground were really unwanted in the beds. She walked towards him. He was sufficiently occupied with his task that he must not have heard her approach. She watched his massive hands grab at the weeds and fling them into a pile. Elspeth guessed that he had still not forgotten Sir Gerald's admonitions.

"Billy," Elspeth said.

He straightened up in astonishment. "What do you want?" he growled.

"Billy," she said again. "I want to know what happened after I saw you at the hotel in Dublin."

"Why?"

"Because I'm trying to figure out what happened to Moya between the time I saw her with you and the time the ambulance came to bring her here. I know on Tuesday she went out of the hotel carrying an attaché case. I wonder if you met her and at her request brought the case back here. I think she would have wanted it that way." Elspeth carefully did not mention the bruises that Moya had when she came back to the hotel.

"What's it to you?" he said.

"Billy, I more than anyone want the reason for Moya's death to come to light. If she did give you the case, it might contain something that will explain what happened when her husband was murdered and she was injured."

"He weren't her husband. He were a thug. She didn't

love him."

Elspeth remembered her conversation where Moya had professed her love for Yuri. Was Billy's angry response a way for him to continue thinking that Moya loved and trusted him above Yuri?

"Did she hand over something to you, knowing she could trust you?"

"What of it?"

"If she did, it could solve everything. I think the attaché case had something in it that will lead us to Yuri Koda's real murderer or murderers. And I also think that Moya knew this and gave the case to you because she knew you would guard it with your life."

"What of it?" he said again.

"Nothing can be settled until we know what happened the night Yuri was killed and Moya injured."

"Why do you think the case had anything in it that had to do with that slug Yuri Koda?"

"Because Moya knew it did and she gave it to the person she thought she could trust most in the world."

Elspeth waited. She could see Billy trying to make up his mind.

"Give me time to think this out," he said finally.

"All the time you need," she said. "I'll go back to the house and wait for you there." She turned from him and made her way up the path to the terrace outside the drawing room. But before she reached her destination, she heard a rush behind her, a great thud and then a clatter. She swung around and saw Billy lying on the ground at her feet. He seemed to have dropped a pitchfork, which was lying at his side. Lars Inversen was standing behind him holding a small shovel held like a baseball bat.

"It's the only weapon I could find," he said. Then his face broke into a smile. "He was about to attack you with the pitchfork."

"Lars, you are my saviour. What in the world are you doing here lurking in the garden?"

"Rescuing you from a grisly death it seems," he said, lowering the shovel to the ground.

Billy groaned.

"I guess he isn't dead," Lars said. "I'm not certain whether that is a good thing or not. But better him than you, Ms Duff."

Elspeth blew out her breath. "I suppose so. Tell me what just happened. I didn't suspect Billy would try to attack me."

"I saw you talking to him and heard what you said. You and I are on the same wavelength I think. Like you, I'm certain Moya arranged to have the attaché case you were talking about brought here. And I suspect that the Romanov jewellery is inside."

"But how did you know to come here?"

"Angie, Angelika, suggested it. She said that Mrs Koda had invited her and Nancy to come here for a summer holiday. I put two and two together and came up with the idea that Moya Koda was planning to bring her loot here and hide it until she could find a way to sell it. From your conversation with this fellow, it looks like I was right."

"Is Angelika with you now?"

She and Nancy are at the B&B where we stayed last night in Carlingford. I couldn't convince Angie to call Moya's family and ask to stay here. Angelika said she would feel better about dropping in today and asking in person. I decided to come up early this morning to do a recce. Lucky for you that I did."

Elspeth was annoyed by Lars's self-assurance, but silently admitted that he being in the garden when she spoke to Billy had benefits. She preferred that her body not be perforated by a pitchfork, which might have happened had Lars not been there.

"We need to get Billy inside," she said. "I don't think he poses a further threat. I'll go get help. Stay here, Lars and watch Billy. As you may have worked out, I don't trust him."

Elspeth rushed to the French doors that lined the drawing room on the south and pounded on them. It seemed a long time before Sir Gerald and Richard came to see what the fuss was about.

"Elspeth, my dearest, what has happened? You look ghastly," Richard cried.

Elspeth straightened herself up, trying to regain her dignity.

"Billy decided to attack me with a pitchfork," she said as evenly as possible. "Luckily someone was there to stop him."

28

Richard led his wife into the drawing room and made her sit down on a large leather sofa. He tried to ignore Sir Gerald's roaring behind him.

"That damned fool," Sir Gerald yelled. He flung the French doors open and peered out. "Who's that holding the shovel? By the mercy of the Lord, Billy's cold out and by the looks of it that young fellow isn't going to help him up. How'd he get here?"

'I think Billy is coming around and will need some attention. From the sound of it, he was hit hard," Richard said.

"His head is like a block of wood, both physically and mentally. Are you all right, Lady Munro?"

"I'm fine," Elspeth said but Richard could tell from the way she held her head that she was rattled. "I tried to reason with Billy. He must have taken offence. I'm glad Lars was there to stop Billy. I didn't hear him come up behind me."

"Lars? Who's Lars?" Sir Gerald roared.

"The man with the shovel," Richard said. "His name is Lars Inversen. He was a guest at the hotel in Dublin and is a friend of Angelika Rostova, Yuri Koda's daughter."

"And what's he doing here on a bright Irish morning?"

His accent slipping into a strong brogue, which Richard suspected was put on for effect as he had not been aware of it before.

"He's here," Elspeth said, "because he's trying to find

the Romanov jewellery. He's convinced Moya had the jewels and gave them to Billy Maguire before she died."

Sir Gerald turned on her. "Is he now? And what would give him that idea?"

"He works for a detective agency in Paris. The Romanov family has hired him to find the jewels. They still believe that Moya or perhaps Yuri Koda stole them."

"Do you believe that, Lady Munro?"

Elspeth slowly shook her head and bit her lower lip. "I don't but I'm glad Lars was here when Billy was about to attack me. Oughtn't we get Billy inside? I think he may be coming to consciousness and I wouldn't want him attacking Lars. I also want to introduce you to Lars. He's well-meaning if perhaps misinformed."

Sir Gerald strode out of the French doors. Richard stayed inside with Elspeth and begged her to lie down. They only had a few minutes to exchange words.

"Dickie," she whispered, "I wasn't hurt—thanks to Lars."

"What did you say to Billy? Why did he attack you?"

"I asked him if he had brought the attaché case from Dublin to here and he fell into my trap. As Sir Gerald said, Billy's not the sharpest tack in the box. Billy implied he had brought something here for Moya, although he didn't actually say what. I thought it must be the missing Romanov jewels."

"Is that why Lars is here?"

"Lars must have been hiding in the shrubbery and must have heard my conversation with Billy so he knows what Billy said to me. I don't want Lars running off and trying to find the attaché case on his own. It's to my advantage to go with him. If the case does contain the jewellery, they belong by rights to Lars's clients and perhaps they can be returned without any fuss. Eric would prefer that I think."

"And if something else is in the case?"

"I expect we're going to be surprised," Elspeth said in one of those cryptic statements that Richard hated.

They were interrupted by Lars and Sir Gerald dragging Billy's half-conscious body into the drawing room.

"Don't worry about the dirt," Sir Gerald said. "I bring it in all the time. Mrs Maguire fusses at me but this is the country. One can't expect town ways here."

The two men hoisted Billy on to a chaise longue in the middle of the room. Billy groaned and opened his eyes.

"Holy Mary Mother of God, that hurt," he said. He put his hand to the back of his head.

"It should have, you scoundrel," Sir Gerald said. "You deserved worse."

"Who hit me?" Billy asked.

"Let me introduce Lars Inversen," Elspeth said raising her eyebrows. "Luckily he is faster with a shovel than you are with a pitchfork."

Richard eyed his wife, who was grinning, and wondered how she could resort to humour at this point. When in danger she often assumed quirky qualities that he often did not understand.

"Damn you, Billy," Sir Gerald said. "You can't go stabbing pitchforks into my guests and get away with it. What made you so bird-brained?"

"She attacked Moya's reputation," he said. "She said Moya was a thief."

"No, Billy, that's not what I said or meant," Elspeth said correcting him. "I think we all here want to get to the bottom of what happened in Dublin last Saturday. None of us want the police to come here and ask questions."

"Bloody guards," Billy said.

"I merely wanted to know what Moya asked you to bring here. If I can confirm what I think now is in there, the mystery may be solved. Where is the case, Billy?" Elspeth asked.

Billy clenched his jaw.

"Billy, damn you, tell us," Sir Gerald added. "We don't want any trouble here, and if you keep your mouth shut, all of us are going to be responsible to the Garda."

Richard couldn't follow Sir Gerald's logic but it sounded threatening enough that Billy's lips wobbled.

"OK, I'll tell." he said. Richard saw the beginning of tears in Billy's eyes.

"You will indeed," Sir Gerald thundered. "What did you do with the thing Moya gave you?"

"I hid it, like she said. I weren't supposed to tell anyone where and only give it back to her."

"How can you give it to her if she is dead?" Sir Gerald asked, his voice choking with rage. "Billy, you're a blockhead. Now tell us what Moya wanted you to do with the case?"

Richard wondered if Sir Gerald was in the habit of raining such abuse on Billy's head.

"I hid it in a place no one can find it but me and Moya. I said I wouldn't tell."

"He's hopeless," Sir Gerald said.

"I have had many years of talking to people who want to keep secrets. Would you like me to try to make Billy see some sense?" Richard asked.

"I don't seem to be able to. Give it a try."

"Billy, my name is Sir Richard Munro and I am high up in the Foreign and Commonwealth Office in London." His statement was no longer true but it seemed to catch Billy's attention. "Moya was helping us and we had asked her to care for the attaché case even if she were to risk her life. She did just that. All we have left now to avert a terrible international situation is to find the case and recover what's in it. Ireland and the United Kingdom do not always see eye to eye on many issues but in this case both countries will be seriously endangered if we do not recover the contents of the case. Moya wanted to hide the case so that some very ugly Ukrainian gangsters wouldn't get what was inside. We think that was why Yuri Koda was killed and Moya so badly injured that she died as a result of her wounds. You have to help us, Billy. Moya would have wanted it."

Billy's eyes got rounder and rounder as Richard spoke. Richard thought he might perhaps be laying it on a bit thickly but he seemed to have sparked something in Billy that Sir Gerald's remonstration had not.

"I didn't know," Billy said. "She said it was important, that's all."

Richard was pleased with the success of his fabrication and continued. "We need to recover the case as quickly as possible because we think the gangsters are on to us. They could be here at any moment. Time is of the essence," Richard said dramatically.

He looked up at Elspeth and saw the laughter at his story in her eyes although she held her face without expression.

"You're the only one who can help us, Billy," Elspeth said. "Moya would have wanted you to."

Billy closed his eyes. Finally he said, "It's in the old place where we used to hide the shipments."

Elspeth frowned and looked at Sir Gerald. Elspeth had shared with Richard that Sir Gerald had turned a blind eye to Republican activities across Carlingford Lough during the Troubles. Richard was curious if Sir Gerald knew of the location of Billy's 'old place'. Sir Gerald drew in his lips and said nothing.

"Can you take us there, Billy?" Elspeth asked.

Billy reached around and touched the back of his head again. "I don't think I can stand up," he said.

"Someone get some whiskey." This from Sir Gerald.

Sir Gerald had served Richard the night before and so Richard knew where to go. Richard found a crystal decanter half full. He poured out a healthy portion for Billy and offered Sir Gerald a glass as well. He looked grateful and accepted.

"Anyone else," Richard asked but both Elspeth and Lars declined.

Billy downed the whiskey in one go, which pained Richard because it was the best Irish whiskey he ever had tasted. Sir Gerald did the same with his. Alas, thought Richard, all for a good cause.

"Now, Billy," Richard said, "I want you to help us. If Moya were here she would tell you that it's all right to do so. Tell us where the 'old place' is."

Billy's eyes travelled around the room, looking at each person in turn, but he didn't speak. Richard was puzzled by his reticence.

Richard turned to Sir Gerald and asked, "Do you know?"

Gerald shook his head. "I expect it's somewhere down by Carlingford Lough. There are several derelict buildings there. Moya used to ride down there on her mare and take with her a hamper that my then housekeeper would prepare for her. I didn't like Moya going because the Provisional IRA used the ruins to store guns and ammunition for shipment across the lough to Ulster. I warned Moya but she simply laughed and said I would know the men who used the old barn if I met them."

"Is that true, Billy?" Richard said.

"She told me not to tell anyone."

In Richard's experience, the less intelligent were the most difficult to move. "What do you think Moya would do if she were here?" he asked.

Billy stared dully at Richard.

"Think, Billy. Now that she's gone, what would she like you to do," he said trying to use his skills of persuasion. The Foreign and Commonwealth Office had cited him many times for this particular talent.

Richard could see the others in the room watching him. He knew from experience that silence at this point usually got results. He let the silence hang, motioning to the others to stay silent.

Billy said, "May I have more whiskey?"

Sir Gerald began to speak and Richard stopped him.

"I'll get you some," Richard said, hoping the drink would loosen Billy's tongue.

Billy took the glass Richard had refilled for him but this time drank it more slowly. Richard wondered what was going on in Billy's head.

Finally Billy said, "I could show you where it is, but only you, sir. I don't want the others to know."

Richard nodded his head. "Why don't we get your mother to have a look at your head and, if you need it, dress the wound and put a plaster on it. Have something to eat; then come back here. I'll be ready. The others will stay behind, I promise."

Elspeth helped Billy to his feet and led him away.

"I'd like to come too," Lars said.

Richard shook his head. "I think Billy trusts me now, but he won't trust anyone else. At any minute Billy might change his mind. I had this happen once in Zimbabwe, with disastrous results. Let me go alone with Billy."

Lars frowned. "He might try to hurt you the way he tried to hurt Ms Duff."

"He might but I think not. Lars, you must not try to follow us. If he sees you, he could clam up once again and all this will be for nothing. You too, Sir Gerald."

"Are you sure you'll be safe?" Lars asked.

"Not entirely sure but it's worth the risk. I don't think there is any other way to recover the case."

Billy came round to the front door. He was driving a muddy four-by-four that looked like it had seen hard use. Richard had put on the heavy shoes that Elspeth insisted he bring and a hunting jacket he favoured in Scotland.

"I wish you had a pistol." Elspeth said as he dressed.

"Billy's probably a far better shot than I ever will be. As you know, I never liked shooting even when I was a child, although my father despaired that I didn't take up what he called a gentleman's sport. I've never needed a gun, even during a coup in Africa. Just as you do, I find using my wits is usually more effective than force of arms."

"Should we follow you, Dickie?" she asked.

"Above all things, don't. I think that would be disastrous."

Richard mounted the four-by-four in a backward facing seat behind Billy. The machine was not muffled and hurt his ears. He shook off the smell of the exhaust. Billy took a dirt track down through the rough hillside, causing Richard to hang on so tightly to the sidebars by his seat that his knuckles hurt. Richard knew Billy was testing him and did not rise to the bait. The track was narrow and the brush tore at Richard's clothing. They splashed through puddles that cast mud over them and flew over rocks that took the four-by-four off two if its wheels. Richard was glad Billy could not see the terror that must have been on his face.

To Richard it seemed forever for them to reach the main street that led into Carlingford and cross over on to a one-track road. He glanced at his watch and saw only ten minutes had passed. At least he was still alive.

They sped on, Billy driving like someone possessed but at least the road had levelled off. They rounded a bend and Richard could see Carlingford Lough spreading out by their side. The hills of Northern Ireland in the distance flanked the lough. Because of the rain the night before, the potholes in the road held water, which sprayed over them.

Richard suspected that Billy was purposely trying to drench him.

Billy slowed the four-by-four and pulled into a weed-lined path. A five-bar metal gate held with a chain and large padlock hung crookedly by a yellow sign with red letters that read "Poison Laid". He dismounted and bade Richard to do the same.

"Don't worry about the sign," Billy said. "We put it there to discourage people from climbing in the ruins."

Billy scaled the gate and watched Richard to see if he would do the same. After spending the last six months in Scotland, Richard was more fit than he had been in many years, and climbed over the gate without faltering.

"This way," Billy said. They walked down a narrow dirt track, which once must have been the drive into the crumbling stone buildings in front of them. Richard was careful to avoid the nettles, as he was highly sensitive to them. Billy led them round what must have been the cottage because of its derelict chimneys and towards a larger building that had the remains of a hayloft.

Billy went through a doorway without a door and wiped away a cobweb in doing so. Richard followed docilely. In one corner, which was partially covered by a slate roof half-capsized over a pile of rotting hay, stood an old table covered with bird droppings. Several broken wooden items, which at times must have served as chairs, stood around it.

"Sit here," Billy said and pointed to one of the boxes. Richard did as he was told. Billy disappeared through a doorway. Richard listened intently and only detected the call of a gull from outside. Then he heard a squeal like the movement of rusty hinges through the door where Billy has disappeared. Richard held his breath, although afterwards, when he was describing his adventure to Elspeth, he couldn't tell her why.

Richard waited. He could hear scrapings and then another protest from the hinges.

Billy reappeared shortly afterwards. In his arms he was hugging a black attaché case as if he would never let it go short of surrendering his own life. With his head, Billy indicated that they should leave the crumbling barn. Richard nodded without saying anything and followed Billy back the way they had come.

When they got to the gate, Richard said, "Let me take the case, Billy, while you scale the bars and then I can give it to you when I make my way over."

Billy paused. He must not have contemplated the dilemma. He shoved the case at Richard and with two steps was over the gate. He held out both hands for the case. Richard's climbing over the gate was less agile. They made their way back to the four-by-four, Billy still clutching the briefcase to his chest.

"I'll carry it carefully," Richard said. "I won't drop it on our way back, I assure you."

Frowning, Billy looked at Richard. Billy slowly seemed to grasp that he could not drive the four-by-four and guard the case as well. Reluctantly he handed it to Richard.

For Richard the trip back was not as difficult as the one down the hill. He put the case under his legs and gripped the bars by his seat as tightly as he could. He thought later that by his having to concentrate on not losing the case, he forgot how frightening Billy's handling of the four-by-four was.

*

Elspeth could see the four-by-four making its way up the track coming through the fields of Sir Gerald's estate. The vehicle careened along, tipping often at a precarious angle, Richard at the rear sitting on a briefcase. The roar of the four-by-four was deafening as it approached the house.

Lars and Sir Gerald stood behind her. They both had crossed their arms over their chests. Elspeth could feel her heart pounding. Suppose she had been wrong about the briefcase?

Billy ground the vehicle to a halt by a path leading to the garden. He jumped from the driving seat and faced Richard. Without any coercion, Richard handed the case to Billy and from a distance nodded a confirmation of the success of his journey. Elspeth noted the dirt on his clothes, a testament that his ride with Billy had not been a gentle one.

Billy stalked up to where they were standing. He loosened his grip on the case and held it out to Elspeth.

"He says I can trust you," Billy said.

"Why don't you bring it inside, Billy?" Elspeth said.

Billy lowered the case to his side. Sir Gerald held the door for him. Elspeth, Lars and Richard followed Billy into the drawing room. Billy marched in and finally put the case on a large coffee table near the fireplace.

Richard was the first to arise to the occasion. "Billy, I think you should be here when we open this as you were the one who so carefully protected it."

Elspeth could see once again why Richard had been so successful in his diplomatic career.

Billy beamed. "Right, guv," he said.

"Moya would have been proud of you for keeping her secret until you could give it over to us," Richard continued.

"I'd never give it to no thugs," he said.

Elspeth did not mind that Billy got Richard's imaginary thugs confused with Yuri Koda's bodyguards. Richard's story of international intrigue had deceived Billy into recovering the case Moya had given to him days before.

They all gathered around the coffee table.

"You open it, Elspeth," Richard said. "You seem to have the best idea of what might be inside."

Elspeth leaned over to the case. It was locked and the numbers on the locks were turned to nine-seven-zero-nine and zero-eight-five-three. The wheels on the combination locks were obviously well oiled and spun without effort.

"Do you have a screwdriver, Sir Gerald? I think we are going to have to destroy these the locks."

Inside Elspeth found what she was looking for.

29

"I'm torn as to whether to go to the Garda right now or not," Elspeth said to her husband as they sipped their pre-dinner drinks in the sitting room of their suite at the Kennington Dublin. "I believe that the blood on the blackjack we found in the case will be Yuri Koda's and it will be sufficient proof to prove Sergei's innocence."

"Then you are certain that Moya killed Yuri," he said.

"Undoubtedly. Moya told me from the very beginning that she was afraid the police would accuse her of the murder. Her expressed fear was tantamount to admitting that she actually had. I should have listened to her."

"But what about the beating she received on Tuesday, when she went out?"

"She deceived us. Angelika eventually showed me the photographs she had taken of Moya right after Yuri was murdered. Except for some yellowing, the bruises and cuts were no different from the ones Moya had when she returned to the hotel the day after Yuri's murder. Remember my telling you that Moya was always heavily made up when I saw her? When she left the hotel on Tuesday, Harry O'Shea said her face was partly hidden but when she returned her terrible bruises were apparent. Moya wanted to put us off the scent, so after she gave the attaché case to Billy, she must have gone into the loo somewhere and wiped off her pancake makeup, exposing her original wounds. No one had seen them except Angelika, who luckily for us had recorded them."

"Why do you think Moya allowed that?"

"She wanted proof that she had been attacked, in case the police did come for her."

"But she obviously was attacked," he said. "Her beating must have killed her."

"It did in the end."

"Do you mean that she killed Yuri with the blackjack but was eventually killed by someone else?"

"Not by someone else, by Yuri. He must have put up a terrible fight when she attacked him. She always contended that he had hit her, although she said he did it in the act of pushing her away."

"I'm afraid, my dearest, that you will have to be clearer. Are you saying she killed him but he killed her?"

"Exactly. He was pushing her away, but in all likelihood, she attacked him first. What a fitting end for them both," she said.

"Aren't you being a bit cruel?"

"No, I think not. They both were rather despicable characters."

She leaned over and kissed his cheek. "Now I just have to figure out how to tell Eric. He won't want to hear the truth."

"Elspeth, you may have concluded that they jointly killed each other but you have failed to explain all the loose ends. What about the bearer bonds we found in the briefcase?"

"Moya must have had a reason to attack Yuri. I can only guess on this but probably the reason was the amount of the bonds. Before I asked Sir Gerald to lock them away in his safe, I counted them. The sum total was ten million euros. Remember Pamela told me that Yuri needed to convince the Irish gas and oil folks that he was solvent."

"I don't follow," Richard said.

He took the bonds from the hotel safety deposit room on Friday, when he met Irish Gas and Oil to prove that he no longer was in debt. After I talked to Pamela, I asked myself how Yuri could show proof that he was financially able to carry out the deal he was proposing. Eric had already told me that Moya became well off after her first husband died. I think that the bonds were part of her inheritance from him. Remember Roger Mulholland was a banker and could easily have converted some of his wealth into bonds for Moya to use quickly in case anything happened to him."

"So the bonds were Moya's to begin with," Richard said.

"I suspect that Yuri convinced Moya to put them up as collateral for his gas deal, but in the end argued with Moya about them. Of course, I can't prove this. Bearer bonds are as good as cash, but have the advantage of being in larger denominations and therefore take less space. When I thought the contents of the attache case were bank notes, I forgot to calculate how much space even ten million in hundred euro notes would take—far more space than a briefcase."

"But what about the Romanov jewels?"

"A classic red herring."

"Didn't you find a piece of jewellery in Moya's case?"

Elspeth could feel herself blushing. "I did and I'm glad I took it. I showed it to Lars. He couldn't identify it. Then I showed it to Sir Gerald, who said that it had belonged to his wife. Moya must have put it in her jewellery bag at some point and forgotten that it was there."

"Case solved," Richard said. "Shall we drink to it?"

"Not exactly solved," she said. "There still is the matter of going to the Garda with the evidence and keeping the hotel out of it, not to mention our forthcoming interview when we get back to London."

"Our interview?" he said.

She arched an eyebrow. "Don't you have to report your findings to Lord Kennington?"

He coughed. "In all the excitement, I forgot about that. It's only Saturday evening. I've got Sunday yet to write a report for him. We can easily get the last plane out on Sunday evening for London. That'll give me a little more time to watch guests and work something out."

*

Pamela Crumm waited for Elspeth and Richard on the twentieth floor of the building that housed the Kennington Organisation offices in the City of London. She spoke quietly to the receptionist in the foyer, asking her to step out and go to the executive dining room upstairs to check on the coffee and tea Lord Kennington had ordered. The receptionist looked puzzled as this was not part of her usual duties but in the moment it was the best Pamela could think of to get rid of the young woman, who had been Eric's choice and not hers.

The doors of the lift opened and Richard and Elspeth stepped out. Both had long faces. Elspeth raised her chin and Richard looked down.

"Cheer up, ducks," Pamela said. "He's glad you solved the mystery of Moya Koda's death and wants to hear all the details. He's asked me to come along too. Coffee and tea are on their way. He's asked that your favourite scones be served, Elspeth, which means he must have forgiven you for all past sins."

Her eyes glistened under her large black round glasses. "He's in a good enough frame of mind that he doesn't seem to mind that I hear the outcome as well."

When Pamela had rung Eric Kennington on Sunday to say that Elspeth had worked everything out in Dublin, he had not grumbled that she had disturbed his weekend. Instead he had said, "I knew she was the one for the job. No one else could have got to the bottom of it."

But Pamela was curious. Elspeth had only explained briefly that Sergei Koda had been freed from jail and that the Garda would drop the case against him without involving the hotel at all.

Eric Kennington was at his Chippendale desk and hastened to rise as Pamela showed Richard and Elspeth in. He came around his desk and extended his hand to Richard. Then, most unexpectedly he threw his arms around Elspeth and said, "Well done. Now come sit down and tell me what happened."

As she began to talk, Elspeth, whose posture was exquisite, straightened her back even more severely.

Elspeth cleared her throat. "Moya Koda was a clever woman but she had a flaw and that is why she died. She attracted men all her life and had the power to transfix them. In some cases, the feeling was real, particularly when she was younger. Later seduction became a game for her."

Pamela turned her attention to Eric Kennington and saw his face twist up and his eyes drop.

"Surely Eric, you knew this because she was such a friend to you over the years," Elspeth said. "You told me that she told you about her 'adventures'. But then she met Yuri Koda and I think she truly fell deeply in love for the first time in her life. That proved to be a fatal mistake. Yuri offered life on the edge; Moya was entranced. The unfortunate part was that Yuri married Moya not for love but for her fortune. Pamela, you confirmed that Yuri had numerous bad debts but that in order for him to procure the contract he wanted in Ireland, he had to prove his solvency. Moya must have become his way to do that. At first she must have gone along with him, but probably, being as intelligent as she was, she insisted that the money be returned to her as soon as his credibility was established with the Energy Ireland board."

Eric Kennington had become mute but he waved his hand at Elspeth to continue.

"Yuri always had his goons, as Moya called them, with him. She must have been frightened of them. I wondered from the first why she didn't have protection of her own, but later discovered that she did, which I will get back to. I think Yuri and Moya argued about what would happen to her money once Yuri had shown it to his prospective clients. The money was in bearer bonds and therefore had no owner listed. As much as Moya loved Yuri, she did not want to give him ten million euros outright. I can imagine that the argument was a pitched one. Moya must have been terrified that she would lose the entire amount. I have no idea how much of her fortune this amount represented but in any case the total of the bonds was vast. Up until this point, Moya must have thought she had full control but Yuri must have made it clear that might makes right and that by using force he could use the bearer bonds in any way he liked."

Eric Kennington sat back and put his arms across his vast stomach. His attention was rapt but he said nothing. He watched Elspeth. Pamela shifted her eyes to Elspeth, who had looked up at Eric for some response, Pamela thought. He offered none. Pamela knew Elspeth well enough to know that her presentation to this point had been thoroughly thought out but Elspeth seemed to falter.

Pamela broke in. "Don't keep us in suspense, Elspeth." This request seemed to relax Elspeth.

"I've thought again and again what I might do in this situation," Elspeth said. "Moya needed to get Yuri alone without his goons and try to persuade him that the bonds in the safety deposit box room in the hotel were hers alone. I think by this time she had contacted Billy Maguire to have him help her get the bonds out of Dublin and safely hidden in County Lough."

Eric started to laugh. "Moya, my beloved witch," he said. "She was going to bury them in the hole in the ruins by Carlingford Lough where the Provisional IRA hid their arms. No one would know to look for them there."

Elspeth looked relieved. "That's where Billy did take them. It took Richard's best diplomatic skills to get Billy to unearth them. He can tell you how he did it when I finish. But let's get back to the night of Yuri's murder. Moya must have suggested that she and Yuri go for a late stroll after dinner. Being the beginning of summer, the sky was still light. I suspect that it was Moya who convinced Yuri to leave his goons behind."

Lord Kennington said, "Moya had a way of getting men to do what she wanted." He did not explain what he meant.

"When Moya got Yuri alone, she must have told him that she was not going to let him have the bonds. I know for sure that their battle became physical because I found a witness."

Pamela looked around the room at this statement. Even Richard looked shocked. "You didn't tell me that," he said.

Elspeth grinned. I wanted to keep the secret until I could explain everything to Eric."

"Quite so," Lord Kennington said.

Elspeth went on. "Sergei Koda was being held by the Garda. They must have had a reason to question him. What could it have been? Dublin, like London, is covered by CCTV cameras, particularly in the centre of the city. I learned from Angelika that Sergei was following his father on Saturday evening. Sergei probably was caught on one of the cameras. I went back to the location where the murder took place but I couldn't find any cameras at the back of the concert hall that would have shown Yuri's attacking Moya. But Sergei, I learned for certain later, was in the area and did see the murder. Richard had met with an official in the British Embassy in Dublin and through that contact I was able to go to the Garda and get into the jail to see Sergei. Once I confronted him, he confirmed that he had seen his father and Moya fighting. He also said that no one else was near them. Moya put up a gallant fight in order to protect herself and finally downed Yuri in self-defence." Elspeth smiled. "You see in the end I didn't have to involve the hotel at all."

Eric Kennington rose from his chair and began to clap slowly. "Well done, Elspeth. Well done. Poor Moya. She never should have become involved with the scoundrel."

"I tip my hat to Moya," Elspeth said. "She was a gutsy woman, although she died for being one."

"May God rest her soul," Pamela said.

*

On their way back to their Kensington flat, Richard eyed his wife. "Didn't you give Eric and Pamela a rather skewed version of what happened in Dublin? You never mentioned the blackjack. You told me that Moya had purposely attacked Yuri and not the other way around."

"That's undoubtedly true but Eric didn't need to know. Had I admitted to the Garda that we had a blackjack with Yuri's blood on it, how could I have avoided telling them the full extent of the tale and the hotel's involvement? But, Dickie, my dear, I did get you off the hook. Eric never once asked about your report."

"That's a blessing anyway because I really hadn't a clue what I was going to tell him. But I have one final question for you. Do you intend to keep your job or was this case your final one?"

"Don't you have to finish your report for Eric and Pamela?" she asked. "I will definitely have you come to the hotel on my next assignment."

"And I suppose," Richard said, "you'll find a suitable murder to solve there."

Epilogue

Pamela caught Elspeth just as she was walking out of the Kensington flat.

"The office received a call from Angelika Rostova and the switchboard forwarded the message to me. Do you remember her from the Dublin case six months ago?"

"Yuri Koda's daughter. I remember her well and often wondered what happened once Richard and I left the hotel there," Elspeth replied.

"She asked if she could speak to you. Would you be willing to see her? You could come here and lunch in the executive dining room. I told her I would ring you and see if you would be willing to talk to her."

"Did she say what it was about?"

"She said that she wanted to tell you some things that you might be curious to know. She also asked if she could bring two others with her. I suggested Wednesday at one."

Elspeth smiled at Pamela's gentle command. "Wednesday at one it is," Elspeth said. "Did she say anything more?"

"No, she said she wanted to see you and, if you wanted, Richard as well. "Did she say who the others were?"

"She simply said you would recognise them."

Elspeth, with Richard in tow, arrived at the dining room fifteen minutes before schedule. A table for five, looking out over the City and the River Thames, was waiting for them. Elspeth spoke to the headwaiter, who nodded at her request.

"What was all that about?" Richard said.

"I asked that Angelika be seated directly opposite me so that I could watch her face. I still don't trust her completely. I wonder whom she is bringing with her? I'll let them sort out their seating. Dickie, sit on one side of me so I can see the others clearly as well."

Angelika and her two guests were punctual. Elspeth smiled as the three of them walked in.

Elspeth whispered to Richard. "Angelika, Lars and Sergei. Should I be amazed that Derek Somerset is not among them?"

"He never was a good fit, was he?" Richard whispered back. "Rather a wet blanket."

The headwaiter accompanied the newest arrivals across the dining room. Elspeth saw them all looking out of the windows as they approached the table.

"This is totally awesome," Angelika said.

"I always find it so," Elspeth said. "Come and sit down, the three of you." The headwaiter held the seat for Angelika. Sergei sat to her left, next to Elspeth, and Lars to her right.

"Before we begin," Angelika said, "I think I need to make formal introductions. Ms Duff, you have met my brother Sergei on several occasions, although he did not always use his real name. You have met my other companion as well, but never by his right name. Therefore, may I introduce Alexander Romanov, who refuses to let me use his title of prince? He says it has been almost a hundred years since the Russian Revolution and the use of

Romanov titles no longer has much credence except among his older relatives in Paris and their toddies. His parents raised him to be a commoner."

Elspeth laughed. "Lars, or Alexander, I always thought there was something suspicious about you. You never acted like an investigator, not by what you did, but by your manner. But how did you deceive the Kennington Organisation as to your identity?

He bowed from his seat. "Lars Inversen exists and he is an employee of the detective agency my family hired to find our stolen jewellery. The agency was so sure that Moya Koda had stolen the items that my family wanted someone related to us to recover the jewels. Lars worked with us for several years and was willing for me to take on his identity. I didn't want to tell anyone who I really was for fear that Mrs Koda might hear."

Angelika reached over and took Alexander's hand. "I only discovered that he might not be Lars when he bumped his leg at the B&B in Carlingford and swore in Russian. I responded quickly in my mother's native language and he knew he had been caught out. He promised me to keep his secret until he discovered the truth about the theft."

"Have you?" Elspeth asked turning to Alexander.

"You helped us realise that Moya Koda was not guilty. Now I'm following other leads. I think that the real thief was within the Northby family. I haven't proved it yet but I'm getting close."

Elspeth remembered that Eric Kennington had raised this possibility. She wondered how Alexander had found out.

"But there is more," Angelika said. "Alexander and I have decided to get married. Aren't you pleased for us?"

Elspeth refrained from saying, "But what about Derek?"

Sergei smiled. "Alex and Angie's match was made in heaven. She has the cash and he the panache."

Angelika glowered at her brother. "Perhaps you ought to tell me and Elspeth the whole story," Richard said.

"In the end," Angelika said, "we discovered that my father had a great deal of money squirreled away in the Bahamas and Switzerland but he did not want to admit it to anyone not even to Moya. If he had told her, perhaps they both would be alive today. But Angie and I were sure that all of his assets were gained by illegal dealings. We are still turning up more and more accounts, and may never find them all. My father did leave a will. He left nothing to Moya, although the will was executed after their marriage. He must have thought her wealthy enough. Instead Angie and I were joint heirs of everything. So far we have turned up fifty-five million euros."

Elspeth raised her eyebrows. "Then you both are very well off indeed."

Angelika grinned. "Not because of that. Sergei and I decided our father had caused enough evil in the world through his greed. We have given his entire fortune to the United Nations Children's Fund with the proviso that they tell us how the money is to be spent. We both feel very righteous about this. But that's not the end of the story."

"Didn't I say Angie had the cash?" Sergei said. "Tell Sir Richard and Ms Duff the startling end to your relationship with our stepmother."

The brother and sister looked at each other. "Moya made a new will just before she died, in fact the day before. She left most of her money to me, except a few bequests including ten thousand euros to Billy Maguire for his good service to her and five hundred thousand euros to her father. The total of her wealth was not fifty-five million euros but it was substantial. She said that I was her closest relative other than her father, and that she loved me. I may be duplicitous in accepting the money but after all that I suffered from her hands, I haven't refused the bequest. Alexander and I will put it to good use. We plan to live in Paris and help endow a fund for victims of crime."

"And Nancy?" Elspeth asked. "What has happened to her?"

"She took my engagement to Alexander with good grace. She was rather keen on him, you know, but when we came back to London, she met someone else."

"There is one thing that always has bothered me," Elspeth said. "Why, Sergei, did you come to the hotel posing as Zakhar?"

"I wanted to tell Moya I had seen her kill my father," he said.

"To what end?"

"I'm not entirely sure. I wanted to make amends with him and she had denied me the chance. I also thought she was a wicked woman and needed to know she couldn't get away with murder. Looking back, I don't think I would do it again. Ms Duff, I've never expressed my appreciation for rescuing me from the Garda."

"I think," said Elspeth, "I was rescuing us both."

"And so all is well that ends well," said Richard. He raised his glass. "Here's to the three of you. You made my wife's task difficult. She always likes that kind of case."

Elspeth looked at him from under her eyebrows and burst out laughing.

Author's Notes and Appreciation

A Danger in Dublin was written before Russia invaded Ukraine in 2022. News buffs will remember that before that time Ukraine was mainly noted for its corrupt businessmen and politicians but since then for its brave people and leadership. I am an ardent follower of the news to this day and follow the destruction in Ukraine with horror and compassion. Since the first draft of this was written before 2022, I have portrayed the current thinking at the time. My apologies to the Ukrainian people.

I have visited Dublin and County Lough many times and enjoyed taking Elspeth and Richard there. Many thanks go to Wendy Hanratty of Grove House who frequently was my host in Carlingford. She often made Irish soda bread especially for me.

As always, I appreciate the brilliant skills of my editor, Alice Roberts and excellent proofreading by Bev Mar. I could not do without them.

And love to Ian and Gim Crew, whose encouragement leads me forward.

Ann Crew is a former architect and now full-time mystery writer who has travelled the world gathering material for the Elspeth Duff mysteries.

Visit <u>elspethduffmysteries.com</u> or <u>anncrew.com</u> for more.

Made in United States
North Haven, CT
20 September 2025

73104654R00202

ハンズ・オンとこれからの博物館

ハンズ・オンと
これからの博物館

インタラクティブ系博物館・科学館に学ぶ理念と経営

ティム・コールトン 著
染川 香澄　芦谷 美奈子　井島 真知　竹内 有理　德永 喜昭 訳

東海大学出版会

Hands-on exhibitions:
managing interactive museums and science centres

Copyright © 1998 by Tim Caulton
Japanese translation rights arranged with Routledge, London
through Tuttle-Mori Agency, Inc., Tokyo.
Copyrighted in Japan by Tokai University Press.

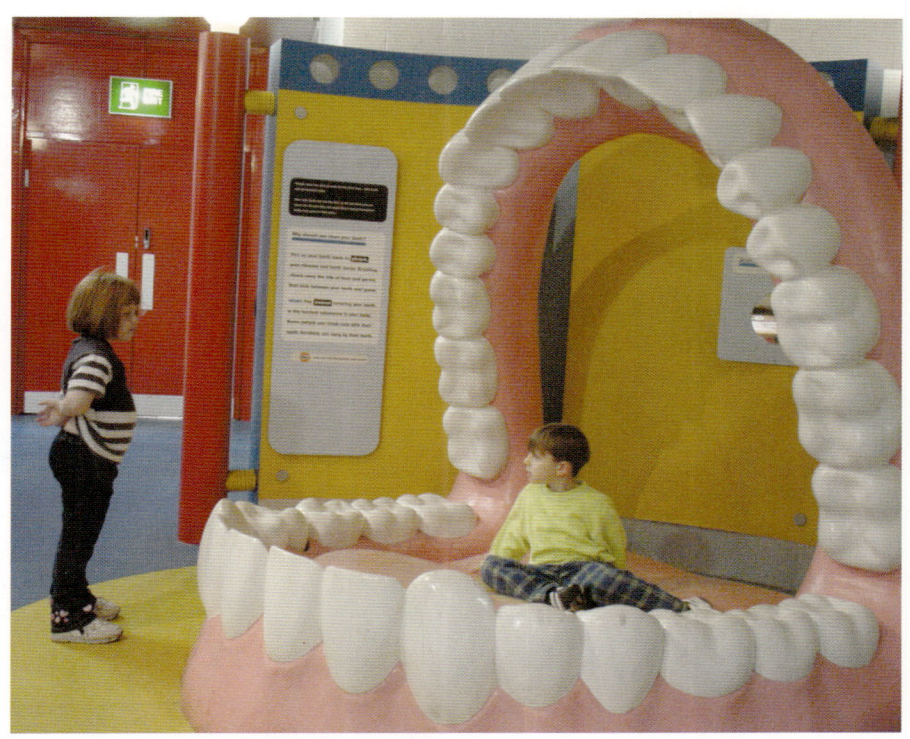

▲ユーリイカ！こどものための博物館（ハリファクス市）
"わたしとからだ"の展示室で，大きな口の模型を独占してすっかりくつろぐ男の子。抗議をするように後ろ手を組む女の子は，場所をかわってほしいのかな？
（撮影：稲庭彩和子）

▲テクニクエスト
1986年にカーディフ市（ウェールズ）につくられたテクニクエストは2度の移転を重ね、95年に現在の場所に新しくオープンした。イギリスの科学館のさきがけともいえる新しいタイプの同施設は、いつも家族連れや学校団体などでにぎわっている。ウェールズの国旗に使われている赤、緑、白の3色をベースにしたカラフルなデザインとガラス張りの建物が明るく楽しい雰囲気をかもしだしている。

◀ユーリイカ！こどものための博物館
"わたしとからだ"展示室のオリエンテーションエリアでは、動くロボットのスクートが、ビデオ映像も交えて展示室内でどのようなことができるかの概要を教えてくれる。この部屋の入り口には、スタートまでのカウントダウンの数字が表示されるようになっており、学校団体の子どもたちに声を合わせてカウントダウンをして入るようイネイブラーと呼ばれるスタッフがもちかける。期待を十分にふくらませた後入室して概要を聞き、グループに分かれて体についてのプログラムを試す。
（撮影：稲庭彩和子）

▼ユーリイカ！こどものための博物館
"わたしとからだ"展示室内。垂直跳びは「どのぐらい上まで跳べる？」体を使って実際に試しながら，自分の体の特徴や力，不思議について発見していく。このような展示物がたくさんあり，パスポートなどに書き込みながら遊び進める。

▲タリーハウス博物館（カーライル市）
タリーハウス博物館の歴史ギャラリーには多くのハンズ・オン展示があるが，新しいリーフレットに7世紀の石造物（レプリカ）に書かれた文様を写し取っている子どもの写真を載せたところ，入場者数が増えたという。これらの展示を通して従来の博物館とは違うことをアピールしている。　　　　　　　　　　　　（同館のリーフレットより）
© Tullie House Museum & Art Gallery, Carlisle

◀ユーリイカ！こどものための博物館
エントランスホールにある果物の木のオブジェ。協賛企業の名前の入った洋ナシやリンゴがずらりと並ぶが，デザインがよくて威圧感を感じさせない。

◀エクスプロラトリアム（サンフランシスコ）
子どもを連れてきた家族を見ていると、親のほうが展示に夢中になり、子どもの存在を忘れてしまうほどに次々試して歩く姿を見かけることもある。

◀ロンドン国立科学博物館
3〜6歳向けの展示室"にわ"（The Garden）の水ゾーン。特大バケツから流れ出る水がさまざまな形の水溜まりやタンクに流れ込む様子を観察したり、ダムやポンプで流れを変えて実験することができる。

日本の読者のみなさまへ

　本書『ハンズ・オンとこれからの博物館』を1998年に刊行して以来，ここで分析し論述した時代傾向はイギリス国内において加速しつつあります。そのほとんどは国営宝くじ基金がもたらした成果であるといえます。芸術，科学，文化遺産・産業遺産の各分野が，大義名分に与えられる国営宝くじ基金からの恩恵に浴したのです。とりわけ，国営宝くじの一機関である二千年紀記念委員会は，28件の主要なプロジェクトに対して資金を交付しましたが，その多くがインタラクティブ系集客施設でした。1999年中にオープンしたものもあり，以降2000年，2001年のオープンをめざしています。

　そんななかで，イギリス国内の展示で最大の話題を呼んでいるのは，なんといっても西暦2000年1年間の会期で開催されるロンドンのミレニアムドームでしょう。7億5000万ポンドを超える資金が宝くじの収益金から投ぜられ，国家の存立を祝祭した1851年の第1回万国博覧会や1951年の英国祭の再来とみなされているほどです。ドーム内に設置された展示は多岐にわたる調査を経て開発されたもので，楽しみながら学習できるように考え抜かれています。それらはほとんどがインタラクティブな展示で，たとえば"プレイゾーン"は世界中から集められた電子工学の先端技術をもとに構成されており，そのうちの少なくとも1つは日本人の電子工学技術者の業績によるものです。"プレイゾーン"はイギリスのインタラクティブな展示デザインのなかでも最高のものといえます。この展示が会期中に予想される1200万人，しかもピーク時には1時間あたり4500人と見積もられている入場者を迎えて，いかに1年間維持されていくかは見ものです。大勢が参加できるプログラムも1つありますが，残りの18種類ある電子工学系の展示装置は同時に1人か2人でしか利用できないので，短時間の利用のために長い列ができてしまうのは避けられません。

ミレニアムドームを始めとした28件のミレニアムプロジェクトがイギリス国内の他の集客施設に対してどのような影響を及ぼすかはわかりませんが，余暇市場はすでに飽和状態にあることは確かで，利用対象とする市場を獲得できず，財政的に行き詰まっている科学館もあるくらいです。ミレニアムプロジェクトの多くは地域の活性化の足がかりとなるように，意図的に失業者の多い地区を対象としています。実際，筆者も本書がイギリスで刊行されてほどなくシェフィールド大学講師を辞めて，現在はそうしたプロジェクトの1つであるロザラム市のマグナにおいて開発部長の職にあります。マグナは，1993年に閉鎖された世界有数の製鉄工場だった大きなシェル状の建物内に計画中のインタラクティブ系展示施設です。マグナに隣接する一帯は再開発を待たれているのですが，1マイル圏内に年間延べ3000万人規模のショッピングセンターと南北縦貫高速道路があるという大変有利な市場性をはらんでいます。これより先，マグナやイギリス国内のほかの地で，新たなインタラクティブ系展示施設の命運に立ち会うのは興味深いにちがいありません。

　最後に，本書の日本語版の出版を大変うれしく思います。そして，ある意味でイギリスに特有な考え方を翻訳するという困難な仕事をされた翻訳チームのみなさんに感謝したいと思います。また，日本の読者にとって本書が有益で興味深いものとなればさいわいです。

1999年12月29日
ティム・コールトン

まえがき（原著序文）

　博物館や科学館の展示にハンズ・オンという手法を採り入れたところが増えてきました。ここ10年ほどの余暇産業の推移を見たとき，このことは最も際だった特徴の1つといえるでしょう。新しい展示施設の計画案も，ほとんどがインタラクティブな要素を備えています。1980年代に，私（筆者）はある労働産業博物館の教育担当を務めていましたが，当時ずっと心を砕いていたのは，館内の学習室で多くの児童・生徒が取り組む製鉄を扱ったプログラムについてでした。子どもたちにとても人気があったとはいえ，単純に手足を動かすだけのこのプログラムをどうすればインタラクティブな博物館体験に転換できるか，それもすべての利用者が安全な環境のもとで毎日参加できるものにしたい，という問題でした。博物館のプログラムには，どんなものであれ訪れた人が単に参観するのではなく参加できるための方策が用意されているべきだ，と考えたのです。

　84年にロンドン国立科学博物館に登場した“テストベッド（航空機エンジンの試験台）への旅”という展示が，さらにこの考えに拍車をかけることになりました。博物館内の学習室での一方的なレクチャーを事実上やめにしてハンズ・オン方式を採用したところ，プログラムは秀逸なできばえとなったのです。展示評価の方法に関する知識などないに等しい当時の私には，館内の案内係を今日ではエクスプレイナーと呼ぶ展示解説スタッフに転換するなどということは，そのための予算獲得とあわせて実現不可能なものに思えました。88年，私は“ディスカバリードーム”という国内巡回展示を南ヨークシャーの州都，シェフィールド市に誘致する事業に携わりました。そして翌年，同市で開催された英国学術協会の年次総会の終了後，科学普及推進委員会（COPUS）から市の博物館にハンズ・オン系の特別展を開催するための助成金を得たのです。地方自治体からの予算削減という状況下にもかかわらず博物館の理事会は前向

きで，ハンズ・オン系常設展示施設をケラム島に開設する計画が現実味を帯びたものとなったのです。

　1990年，さいわいなことに私は西ヨークシャー州ハリファクス市に計画中だったユーリイカ！こどものための博物館の教育普及部長に任命され，初めてハンズ・オンという考え方を普及する運動の最前線に押し出されることになったのです。3年の間，ユーリイカ！は常に積極的な取り組みの場を提供してくれました。その間，すべての展示装置の企画開発，展示解説スタッフの採用，研修，配置ほかの管理責任を負ったのです。入場者が50万人を突破した93年の夏は，さらに高い地歩を目指して前に踏み出す時でした。ユーリイカ！における経験が私に極めて多くの門戸を開き，全英さらには海外のハンズ・オン系博物館の新規開発事業を手助けする機会をつくってくれました。この10年の間に公立から民間の公益法人立，あるいは地方レベルから全国レベルと，多種多様な博物館においてハンズ・オンの考えを広める運動にかかわってきましたが，端的にいえば，これは自分に許された特権とすら感じています。

　現在，私はいくつかの新しい博物館での仕事を続ける傍ら，大学の講師としてハンズ・オン運動の研究ができるようになりました。本書はイギリスのハンズ・オン系博物館や科学館の発展について，アメリカやヨーロッパで同時並行的に発生した動向も視野に入れて論じてみたものです。博物館はもちろん他の集客施設でインタラクティブ展示の開発をしようとしている人を読者に想定しましたが，同時に博物館や，文化遺産・産業遺産施設，余暇施設，観光施設などの経営を研究している人にも読んでいただきたいと思います。本書は，経営管理の基礎理論について教えるというのではなく，ハンズ・オン系展示施設の経営の実際について，特定の館のケーススタディーを通して得られる情報を提供しようと意図しました。

　イギリスのハンズ・オン系博物館や科学館といってもいろいろです。執筆にあたっては，当然ながら私自身が獲得してきた知識や経験，また英米の二次資料はもちろんのこと，独自に行った調査結果や公開されている一次資料に多くを頼っています。

　この小論の考察における主要な成果は，ハンズ・オン運動にはそれぞれ目的こそ違っていても集客施設という名のもとに相当数の施設が含まれると認めら

れること，またハンズ・オン系博物館づくりやその運営には唯一の"正しい"方法などない，という点でしょう。にもかかわらず，どのハンズ・オン系博物館や科学館も同じような課題に直面しているのは確かです。特に，タイプの異なる他の余暇施設との境界があいまいになるにつれ，将来，博物館・科学館としての個々のアイデンティティーを維持していくのは難しくなるかもしれません。ハンズ・オン系博物館・科学館が公的財源の削減にもかかわらずなお生き延びていけるとしたら，また余暇施設が大量に増加する時代にあってある程度の水準で入場者を確保できるとしたら，そして最新技術を擁した他の集客施設から仕掛けられる企画開発競争に耐えていけるのなら，これらの施設は近いうちに財政，マーケティング，人材配置，現場運営をうまくこなす最良の経営手法を手中におさめるに違いありません。さらに，これらの施設の活動がハンズ・オンによる学習という教育目標に合致するとしたら，インタラクティブな環境で人はどのように行動し学ぶかについて一定の認識を形成していくことに貢献するでしょう。

　つまるところ本書は，ハンズ・オン学習を通して事物や現象の本質にふれるために，頭も手足も使って利用してもらう展示法の改良に腐心する施設が増加する状況下において，ハンズ・オン系博物館の開発とその経営に関して，運営管理上の論点を提示することを目的に著したものです。

もくじ

日本の読者のみなさまへ
まえがき（原著序文）
翻訳にあたって

1章　ハンズ・オン系施設 ──────── 1

はじめに　3
ハンズ・オン展示とは？　4
ハンズ・オン系展示施設の起源　6
　草創期の自然科学博物館　6
　こどもの博物館　9
　事例紹介：テクニクエスト　11
　ハンズ・オン系施設の支援団体　15
現在のハンズ・オン系施設と利用者層　17
ハンズ・オン系展示施設のライフサイクル　21
　事例紹介：グリーンズミル科学館　22
　事例紹介：考古学リソースセンター　24
　事例紹介：エクスプロラトリー　24
まとめ　25

2章　教育的側面 ──────── 29

はじめに　31
学習の個人的側面　33
　学習理論　33
　インタラクティブ展示を用いた学習の実際　36

学習の社会的側面　39
　　学習の物的側面　44
　　　大人と子どもがともに学ぶために　45
　　　インタラクティブ展示のデザイン　47
　　　文章の役割　50
　　　グラフィックの役割　52
　　　事例紹介：ユーリイカ！のコミュニケーション戦略　53
　　博物館資料とハンズ・オン展示の混在　57
　　構成主義理論に基づく博物館と学習　60

3章　展示開発 ─── 65

　　はじめに　67
　　イギリスにおける展示開発　71
　　　事例紹介：ユーリイカ！における展示開発　73
　　展示評価　75
　　　利用者の属性調査　76
　　　企画段階評価　77
　　　制作途中評価　78
　　　総括評価　78
　　　事例紹介：ユーリイカ！における展示評価　79
　　　事例紹介：ロンドン国立科学博物館における展示評価　88
　　まとめ　89

4章　財政 ─── 93

　　はじめに　95
　　アメリカのハンズ・オン系施設の財政　95
　　　インディアナポリスこどもの博物館／シカゴこどもの博物館／プリーズタッチ博物館（フィラデルフィア）／マンハッタンこどもの博物館
　　イギリスのハンズ・オン系施設の財政　97
　　　ユーリイカ！こどものための博物館　99

テクニクエスト　　101
　　エクスプロラトリー　　103
損益評価指標別に見る実績　　104
　　入場者1人あたり事業収入／収入金額に占める事業収入の割合／収入金額に占める企業協賛金と補助金の割合／入場者1人あたり経常費／職員1人あたり人件費／経常費総額に占める人件費の割合／入場者1人あたり広報・宣伝費／経常費総額に占める広報・宣伝費の割合
営業指標別に見る実績　　107
　　展示床面積1㎡あたり入場者数／1㎡あたり経常費／1展示装置あたり入場者数／1展示装置あたり経常費／入場者1人あたり経常費
建設資本の財源　　109
建設にかかわる費用　　114
　　用地取得費　　114
　　建築費　　115
　　展示制作費　　116
まとめ　　117

5章　マーケティング　　121

マーケティング計画　　123
ハンズ・オン系施設の需要　　125
　　人口統計的傾向　　126
　　余暇時間　　128
　　事例紹介：ユーリイカ！の利用者　　132
主要な市場　　133
　　基本市場　　133
　　教育市場　　134
　　二次市場　　135
　　旅行者市場　　135
　　市場の重複　　136
料金設定　　138
広報・宣伝　　140
まとめ　　144

6章　現場の運営 ──────────────── 149

はじめに　*151*
収容力について　*151*
　定員の設定　*152*
　時間制限の設定　*153*
　待ち行列の管理　*155*
団体の予約　*158*
　予約システム　*162*
昼食時間の問題点　*163*
展示装置の故障　*164*
苦情の対応　*168*
まとめ　*169*

7章　組織・人材管理 ─────────────── 173

はじめに　*175*
ハンズ・オン系施設における"人"の重要性　*175*
博物館の組織構造　*177*
フロア解説スタッフの役割　*178*
　事例紹介：エクスプロラトリアム（サンフランシスコ）のエクスプレイナー　*179*
　事例紹介：ボストンこどもの博物館のインタープリター　*180*
　事例紹介：ニューヨーク・ホールオブサイエンスの理科教育キャリアラダー　*181*
　アメリカのハンズ・オン系博物館とボランティア　*182*
　ヨーロッパのハンズ・オン系博物館　*183*
　イネイブラーの「燃え尽き現象」　*187*
　考古学リソースセンターのボランティア活用事例　*189*
ハンズ・オン系施設における人材管理の実践例　*190*

8章　教育プログラムと特別イベントの運営 ─────── 197

はじめに　*199*
アメリカの博物館教育　*201*
　アメリカの事例　*204*
　イギリスの事例　*207*
学校でのハンズ・オン展示　*210*
イギリスの博物館教育　*213*
英米の博物館教育の比較　*215*
イギリスの博物館教育のこれから　*217*

9章　これからのハンズ・オン展示 ─────────── 223

原著 参考文献　*235*
関連施設・機関一覧　*239*
訳者あとがき　*249*
索　引　*253*

コラム目次
　歩みよる科学館と博物館
　アメリカのこどもの博物館
　「キュレーター」と「学芸員」
　インディアナポリスこどもの博物館
　入場者数の制限
　全員が教育担当!?
　宝くじが文化を支える？

翻訳にあたって

日本語版の訳出にあたっては，つぎのとおりの方針でのぞんだ。

1. 本書は博物館学のいわゆる研究書というよりは，現在博物館にかかわっておいでの人々，博物館を学ぼうとする学生，展示・企画開発や建築・デザインなどの分野，各種集客施設の関係者はもちろんのこと，広く博物館や教育などに関心を寄せる一般読者をも対象においた。
2. 訳文はつとめて平明をこころがけ，常体ではなく敬体を採用した。
3. 原著にあげられた原注のほとんどは各種論文などの典拠を示すもので，日本の一般読者が原著の記述を理解するために不可欠のものでは必ずしもなく，煩雑にわたるとの判断から，ほぼ割愛した。
4. 原注にかわって，訳者による注を脚注として掲載し，読者の理解を図った。
5. 原著に掲載された参考文献一覧を巻末にそのまま収録したが，そこにあがっていない著作についてはその都度本文中に明示した。
6. 口絵や本文中の写真は原著にはなく日本語版独自の編集になるもので，日本の読者の理解を図るために訳者らが撮影したものやその他の資料から選んで掲載した。また章扉の裏ページに訳者によるコラムを載せたのも同様の趣旨に基づく。
7. 本文中に言及される各館の展示名は" "で示し，各種機関名および団体名などとあわせて，英文表記を巻末の一覧に掲載した。

なお，本文中に頻出する施設名・団体名等の略語については下記のとおりである。

AAM	米国博物館協会
ARC	考古学リソースセンター
ASTC	科学館技術館協会
AYM	青少年博物館協会
BIG	英国インタラクティブグループ
COPUS	科学普及推進委員会
EC	欧州共同体
ECSITE	欧州科学系展示施設協力機関

1章
ハンズ・オン系施設

エクスプロラトリアム
1969年にフランク・オッペンハイマーが科学と芸術の融合を思い描き、開設したサンフランシスコにある科学博物館。同時期に東海岸ではボストンこどもの博物館でマイケル・スポック館長が活躍し、現在のハンズ・オンの流れが生まれる。

歩みよる科学館と博物館

「科学館も文化の一部である」と科学館界が博物館の仲間入りを求めている。日本やアメリカでは，制度上，科学館は博物館の1つとして位置づけられているが，イギリスでは，科学館と博物館はそれぞれ独自の道を歩んできた。前者は教育，後者は有形の文化遺産の継承を重視している。けれども最近，その境界がだんだんぼやけてきているようだ。博物館は以前にもまして教育機能の重要性を高らかにうたうようになり，最近新しく改定された博物館の定義でも博物館は人々のためにあるということをコレクションの保管より前にうたっている。そしてハンズ・オンは従来の博物館の展示に大きな変化を与え，科学館と博物館を結びつける新しい共通言語となっている。

(竹内有理)

1章 ハンズ・オン系施設

　最初の章ですから，まずイギリスやアメリカ，ヨーロッパでハンズ・オン系施設がどのように発展してきたかをざっと見ることにしましょう。博物館，文化遺産・産業遺産，余暇産業などの各分野における施設内容の変遷としてたどってみます。

はじめに

　博物館のガラスケースに収められた資料を，それがいかに価値があるからとはいえ，ただ眺めるだけの展示にはもう誰も満足しなくなっています。展示そのものに夢中になりたい，気ままに学びたい，とにかく楽しみたいという期待があってのことです。博物館は一方で政府予算の削減に対処を迫られながら，同時に目の肥えた利用者の要求を察知しこれにこたえる必要にも迫られています。しかもそのうえ，余暇時間とそこで使われるお金をめぐって，テーマパークやショッピングセンター，家族向け娯楽施設など，余暇産業の各種施設との競争も余儀なくされているのです。要するに，増収の道を見いだすと同時に公的助成の現状維持を図るための理由づけをするにも，利用者市場の拡大をめざし，社会における自らの役割をとらえ直さなければならない必要性に博物館はようやく気づいたというわけです。

　もっと多くの人に楽しんでもらうには，どのように展示の利用手段を改善したらいいのか，世界中の博物館がその方法を模索している最中で，それにはいろいろな手段が考えられます。たとえば最新技術を使う，見える収蔵にする，肉声で展示解説をする。博物館の難しさをぬぐい去り，収蔵品の理解を助けるには，どれも素晴らしい試みです。そうはいうものの，20世紀も終わりに近づくにつれ，新しく生まれる多くの展示施設のデザインはハンズ・オン展示でのみ構成されるようになりました。それと同時に，従来型の展示施設もこれ

まで以上にハンズ・オン展示を採り入れたり，解説のしかたも混合的な手法を使うところが増えてきました。イギリスでは，ハンズ・オンという手法は，最初，科学館で採用されましたが，いまでは博物館はもちろん，史跡などの施設や農村地域の展示施設にまで採り入れられています。ハンズ・オン系展示施設の開発や管理，運営の手法は従来型の展示施設のそれとは大きく違うので，以前とは異なる専門技能が必要になります。本書はそうしたことへの助言を意図したもので，インタラクティブな展示施設発展の経緯をイギリスやアメリカ，ヨーロッパでの経験をもとに考察していきます。

ハンズ・オン展示とは？

博物館の伝統的展示形態といえば，動かないものか（ガラスケース），動くものか（模型，機械）で，展示の手法としてはどちらも「ハンズ・オフ[1]」といえるでしょう。展示室内では見たり考えたり聞いたり，場合によればにおいをかぐようにすすめられますが，触ってよいことにはなっていません。これと逆にハンズ・オン展示，つまりインタラクティブな展示では，じかに展示装置にふれて利用してもらおうとしています。「ハンズ・オン」と「インタラクティブ」は似たような意味のことばで，大体において置き換えて使っても問題にはなりません。「ハンズ・オン」ということばには，単にボタンを押したりコンピューターのキーボードをたたくだけにせよ，あるいは働きかけに応じてもう少し込み入ったプログラムに参加させられる仕組みになっているにせよ，利用者が展示装置を相手にして直接的に獲得した相互作用という響きがあります。もっとも，ただボタンを押すだけでは本当の意味でインタラクティブとはいえないので，反応的というのが妥当でしょう。つまり，そのような展示装置の場合，前もって設定された結論をただなぞっているにすぎないのです。

「ハンズ・オン」という用語が正しい意味で使われる場合，ハンズ・オン活動では当然のこととして相互作用がなされ，教育的な付加価値があると考えられます。さらには，元のことば自体にそのような意味はないのですが，行き着

---

[1] 「ハンズ・オン」に対して，従来型の博物館施設に多く見られるような，ケースなどで展示物が保護されていて利用者が触ったり物理的にかかわることができない展示形態。

く先は「マインズ・オン[2]」であるとの暗黙の了解があるのです。もう1つのインタラクティブ系展示装置のほうには頭を使う相互作用という響きがありますが，こちらは身体的な相互作用が全くなくてもかまいません。「インタラクティブ」ということばはパソコンゲームでよく用いられますが，その場合はキーボードやジョイスティック，バーチャルリアリティーのヘッドギアを通して身体を使った遊びをするだけですし，娯楽と教育は必ずしも目的において結びつくものではありません。ゲームとは違って，この用語の定義ははるかに複雑です。

　まとめると，「ハンズ・オン」と「インタラクティブ」は一般用語としても専門用語としても大体において互換性のあることばとして使えるようになりましたが，どちらにしても必然的に身体的な相互作用を伴うもので，学習目標が明確で，利用者のかかわり方次第で結果に多様性の見られる展示のことを十分に定義することばとはいえません。ほかに適切な用語が見当たらないので，本書では「ハンズ・オン」と「インタラクティブ」を同義語として扱っていますが，どちらを用いる場合でも，当然，以下のような幅広い意味があるものとします。

　　　　博物館のハンズ・オン系展示装置あるいはインタラクティブな展示装置
　　　には明確な教育目標がある。その目標とは，個人もしくはグループで学習
　　　する人々が，事物の本質あるいは現象の本質を理解するために，個々の選
　　　択にもとづいて自ら探求してみようとする利用行動を助けることにある。

　すぐれてインタラクティブな展示装置とは，年齢も能力もばらばらな利用者相手に幅広く対応して機能するものです。インタラクティブたらんとしてハンズ・オン系展示装置をハイテクにする必要はないし，また，じかに博物館資料にふれずとも事物や現象の本質を探求できるようにデザインされます。このようにハンズ・オン展示装置というのは博物館資料やレプリカを手で直接操作す

---

[2] 単にボタンを押して展示が動くのを受動的に見るような「触るだけ」のハンズ・オン展示と区別するために，手（ハンズ）だけでなく心（マインズ）も動かす展示の意味でマインズ・オンということばを用いる。利用者が試して考え，発見するという能動的な心の動きを誘発するものを指す。

るものもあれば，展示装置と一緒に陳列された原資料の理解を助けるものもあり，あるいは全く資料を置かない施設（科学現象の理解向上を重視する科学館など）にも置かれうるのです。

ハンズ・オン系展示施設の起源

　今日のハンズ・オン系博物館や科学館の起源は，並行して発展してきた2つの流れのなかにあります。すなわち，19世紀後期のアメリカに生まれたこどもの博物館，および20世紀初頭の欧米における伝統ある主要自然科学博物館です。

草創期の自然科学博物館

　科学館の源流は，通常，1925年，ドイツ博物館（ミュンヘン）が始めた工業用エンジンの運転装置や，37年，発見博物館（パリ）が実演した化学実験などの先駆的な試みとされています。同様の試みはアメリカにもあり，33年にはシカゴ科学産業博物館に実際に人が下りていける規模の模擬炭坑が作られ，35年にはフランクリンインスティテュート（フィラデルフィア）に二層で内部を通り抜けられる鼓動する心臓模型が展示されました。これら草創期の自然科学博物館は展示施設としての素晴らしい伝統があるのはもちろんですが，同時に卓越した展示表現や解説手法にも長い歴史があるので，最近の趨勢であるハンズ・オン系展示は明らかにこの伝統の延長線上にあるものといえます。実は，古くからの自然科学系博物館と今日の科学館との違いは，使命に関してのことよりも，設立後の年数に関してのほうが大きいかもしれません。

　ロンドン国立科学博物館付設の"こどものギャラリー"は31年オープンで，やはり最も古い科学館の1つです。ボタンを押したり取っ手を回したりするような従来型の博物館展示と比べると，もっと「科学技術のゲームセンター」に似た趣で，後年，科学技術に関して生涯忘れられない興味を抱いたきっかけは幼少期にここを訪れたところにあると述懐する何世代もの子どもたちのよりどころになっています。当初，この展示室は国立科学博物館のオリエンテーションエリアとしてあらゆる年齢層を対象にデザインされたのですが，機械の運転模型やジオラマが若年層に大変な人気になったため，"こどものギャラリー"として名前が通るようになったのです。ここも，今日のハンズ・オン系科学館

につながるさきがけ的存在といえるでしょう。実は，その当時ですら，「ミュージアムズジャーナル」誌（31年4月号）の批評は遠慮のないものでした。「これらのどれも行きすぎかもしれず，正しい方向を向いているとはちょっといえないという懸念を禁じ得ない」。そればかりか，展示装置の開発をめぐる問題では，ちょうど今日，ハンズ・オン系施設で見受けられるのと同じような問題も経験しています。

　　　機械の運転模型は……公開後間もなく利用者の酷使に耐えられないことが明らかになるだろう……ひっきりなしに運転され続けるという尋常でない条件下での動作を要求される新しい部類の展示装置は……いかなる運転模型であれ満足のいく形で登場するには，よほど工夫されてからでなくてはならない。（同誌）

　エクスプロラトリアムの創始者のオッペンハイマーはその構想を"こどものギャラリー"とドイツ博物館から啓示を受けたといいますが，実際に全く新しいタイプの施設がサンフランシスコにできたのは69年になってからでした。エクスプロラトリアムこそ本当の意味でハンズ・オンの手法を採り入れた世界初の施設となり，アメリカに科学館の成功の波が広がったのです。エクスプロラトリアムは新設の施設のために触媒となるものを用意しています。インタラクティブな展示装置を作る「レシピ」を200種以上も載せた『クックブック』[3]を出版することで，新設の科学館でも信頼性の高い検証済みの展示装置が備えられる条件を整えたわけです。そのことはまた，全世界の科学館でエクスプロラトリアムの展示装置が転用できることの保証でもありました。

　エクスプロラトリアム設立の年には，カナダのトロントにオンタリオ州からの2300万ドルの助成でオンタリオ科学館が開館しています。同館の移動展示部門である"オンタリオ・サイエンスサーカス"が81年の夏にイギリスのバ

---

[3] エクスプロラトリアムの展示装置について，他の施設の展示制作者が同じレベルの展示を制作できるように，装置のサイズ，配線，材質，グラフィックにいたるまで細かく図解したレシピ集。実際に世界中の科学館で展示制作に使われている。1976年に初めて出版され，その後何回かの改訂を重ね，新しい展示も追加して現在は3巻ある。姉妹編として，学校や家庭で簡単に楽しめる実験を収めた『スナックブック』も出ている。

ーミンガム市と，ロンドン国立科学博物館で巡回展示を行いました。科学工学研究会議が後援した国立科学博物館での巡回展示は11日間の会期で最大級の成功を収め，イギリスの博物館界に刺激を与えています。

　　利用者は徹底して体験を楽しんでいる。大半の展示が参加型なので喜びが増しているのは疑いのないところだ……評価をした結果は，イギリスの科学館構想を発展させるうえで心強い味方になっている。次に進むべきは，"サイエンスサーカス"の経験に基づいて同様の方式の展示装置をいくつか試作してみることであろう。（同館教育部発行の報告書より）

　国立科学博物館では81年と82年の夏に，ささやかながら自前の"ディスカバリールーム"を実験台にしました。そうして，84年には，その1つである"テストベッド"（飛行機エンジンの試験台の意）に2万人を超える人々を迎える結果になったのです。このことを，当時，同館教育部の責任者は「参加型博物館という考え方におけるフォワード陣の大飛躍」と表現しています。研究開発から得た貴重な教訓に学び，この実験はやがて86年の"ラウンチパッド"の設置へと直結していくのです。総費用100万ポンド超というこの展示室は圧倒的な成功を収め，初日だけで2万人以上の人が訪れました。

　"ラウンチパッド"がイギリスで博物館（資料は全くもたない展示施設ではありますが）のなかに併設された初めてのハンズ・オン系科学館とすれば，独立館として最初の科学館は86年にカーディフ市にできたテクニクエストと，87年にブリストル市に生まれたエクスプロラトリーの2館です。このころにはもう，イギリス国内でインタラクティブな博物館を目指す運動は，セインズベリー財団，リバーヒューム信託，ナフィールド財団，貿易産業省の助成を受けて具体化しつつありました。この運動はヨーロッパ中でも同じように急速に進んでおり，86年の開館当時フランス政府による多大な投資が話題となったインベントリアムがパリのラヴィレットで公開されたのを皮切りに，新しい科学館が誕生しています。89年の年初までに，巡回展形式の"ディスカバリードーム"も含めると，イギリス国内には12館のハンズ・オン系展示専門の科学館が開館していました。サイエンスプロジェクト社（"ディスカバリードーム"の設置母体である公益法人）の理事，ピジーは，イギリスのすべての都市

に科学館をという夢を提唱していた人物です。

こどもの博物館

　1987年のこと，科学館技術館協会（ASTC）は会員を対象に調査を行い，結果をいくつかのレポートにまとめています。科学館は多様性が特徴の施設ではありますが，共通した重要な傾向がいくつか明らかにされました。その1つは，60年代に創設された科学館の多くが生命科学や自然科学に努力を傾注していたのが，70年代には生命科学を除く自然科学が優勢になり，80年代には子どもと青少年を対象とした博物館が最も人気があるものとして出現した，ということです。実は，こどもの博物館というのは，世界の博物館界でも最速の成長分野なのです。とはいっても，その考えは新しいものではありません。それに，こどもの博物館の多くは科学館よりもはるかに古い歴史があります。ブルックリンこどもの博物館は1899年まで遡ることができますし，ボストンこどもの博物館もそのすぐ後に開館しています。これらの老舗館は，当初は，従来からの収蔵品で子どもが興味をもちそうだと考えられるものをもとに展開していました。ハンズ・オンの手法は，当時ボストンこどもの博物館の館長だったスポック（育児書で有名な小児科医の子息）が64年に試みてうまくいくことがわかって採用されるようになったものです。スポックはガラスの陳列ケースは処分してしまい，子どもが学べる環境をつくるために展示プログラムを組み直しました。この結果，ボストンこどもの博物館は，博物館はなによりもまず人のために存在するもので，もののためではないという考え方のさきがけとなったわけです。それ以来，この考えは，世界中のこどもの博物館で通用するようになりました。

　ここでブルックリンこどもの博物館も同様の方針を打ち出しました。もともと，この館は利用者が収蔵品にふれてもいいという立場をとってはいました。とはいえ，77年に建物も新たにしての新装開館は劇的でした。インディアナポリスこどもの博物館も同じような歴史をたどっています。ここは世界で4番目に古く，しかもいちばん大きな施設であるうえに，14万点以上の資料が素晴らしい状態で保存されているこどもの博物館です。この館で発行している『こどもの博物館のコンセプト』（1991年）には，こどもの博物館と従来型の

博物館との本質的な違いが，以下の4点にまとめられています。

1. どんな資料，プログラム，特別イベントであっても教育こそが基本となる。個々の展示物の背後には目的があり，展示装置には合わせて語られるべきストーリーがあり，展示室には包みを解かれるのを待つ概念がある。
2. 注意を向けさせるために，明るく鮮やかな色彩と劇場のような照明効果を利用する。解説パネルはわかりやすく，現代の子どものことば遣いで記す。
3. 展示装置は最年少の子どもでも見えるよう，細心の注意を払って配置する。また資料は特定しうる順序で提示する。可能なかぎり，展示装置は「ハンズ・オン」つまり参加型とする。
4. 展示装置がどんなに洗練されていても，最も重要な学習のよりどころは人と人とのふれあいである。

こどもの博物館は70年代には8館程度でしたが，運動が急速に広がったために，80年代の終わりには，アメリカに本部のある青少年博物館協会（AYM）が把握している数は400館を超えました（アメリカだけで350館）。70年代と80年代にアメリカでこどもの博物館が驚くべき勢いで増えたのは，60年代後半に伝統的な考えのなかで教育の改革をしようという試みが失敗に終わり，その直後に教育に新しい形態を求めようとする強い衝動が働いたところに原因があるとされています。これらの新しい博物館の多くは小規模で，目標においては素朴，運営においてはアマチュアの域を出ません。そうはいっても，世界中でこどもの博物館が急速に生まれ出ているのは，文化の違いを超えて意義があると思える施設に向けての意気込みが反映しているためといえるでしょう。

こどもの博物館には，ブルックリン，ボストン，インディアナポリスのように，従来の収蔵品に確固とした基盤を置き，インタラクティブなものと博物館資料をうまく統合しているところがあると同時に，デンバーのように，博物館界の慣例を無視して資料は一切置かないという新しいタイプの施設もあります。この行き方には批判が向けられ，収蔵品のないこどもの博物館は博物館ではないとの論争を巻き起こしていますが，米国博物館協会（AAM）では，こ

どもの博物館を会員として100％受け入れており，登録目的のためにこどもの博物館を次のように定義づけています。

> 子どもの好奇心を刺激し学習の動機づけを図る展示や教育プログラムを提供して，子どもの要求や興味関心にこたえることに専心する施設。こどもの博物館は組織化された常設の非営利団体で，目的は本質的には教育にあり，資料を有意義に利用する専門職員がいて，定期的な日程に従って一般に開放される。

この定義は92年にAAMが作成した討議資料にあるのですが，ここで子どもの要求や興味関心に関する記述が収蔵品よりも先に置かれているのは重要です。これに対して，イギリスで一般に受け入れられている博物館の定義では，「公衆の利益のために物理的資料と関連情報の収集，記録，保存，展示，解説を行う施設」とあるように人よりも資料に力点が置かれています[4]。こどもの博物館は博物館界の伝統的な線引きによる境界線に疑問をつきつけ，定義のし直しを進めていることになります。いいかえれば，保存，研究，ガラスケースでの陳列中心の従来型の博物館観に対して，利用者本位でインタラクティブな展示戦略によって博物館の教育的役割を強調しているのです。資料というのはまずなによりも学習の動機づけを図るための道具として役立つものであり，子どもの発達のうえで必要な何かを提供するものです。したがって，資料それ自体の価値のために収集される必要は必ずしもないのです。

事例紹介：テクニクエスト

テクニクエストは小さな建物に込められた大きな夢からスタートしました。1986年のことです。その後10年間に3度の移転をし，有機的な展開を図ってイギリス最大のインタラクティブ系科学館になりました。86年7月，公益法

---

[4] イギリスの民間（非営利）部門の博物館専門組織である博物館協会（1889年創立）によって採択された博物館の定義。「博物館とは，公共の利益のために，物質的な証拠とその関連情報の収集，記録，保存，展示，解説を行う施設である」。88年より博物館・美術館委員会によって実施されている博物館登録制度ではこの定義を満たすことを登録博物館の条件としており，資料をもたない科学館やプラネタリウム，および個人コレクションは「登録資格のない施設」とされている（博物館の定義は98年に改訂されているが，本書が書かれた時点では84年に採択された定義が用いられている）。

人として設立。設立にあたってはウェールズ大学（カーディフ市）の科学教育学教授ビートルストーンの指導を受けました。同年11月，ウェールズの首都カーディフの都心に開館。建物は以前はブリティッシュガス・ウエールズというガス会社がショールームに使っていたところで，無償でその一画を借りたのでした。当初の運営資金8万3000ポンドはギャツビー財団からの助成。この財団はセインズベリー家の信託財団です。テクニクエストは開館から6カ月の間に4万5000人もの利用者を迎えたので，この仮設の施設は利用者は無論のこと，これから先スポンサーや後援者になってもらえそうな団体や企業などに対してもまさにショールームの役割を果たしました。87年に第2期の展開を進めるときにはギャツビー財団が60万ポンドの助成を認めてくれたし，新たにカーディフ港湾開発公社も資金を提供してくれ，これでカーディフ湾のウォーターフロントに新築された工場の建物を5年間借り受けることができたのです。最初の仮設展示場は87年8月に閉鎖し，翌年9月に第3期テクニクエストがオープンしました。この総工費は約100万ポンドで，1000㎡の床面積に80種の展示装置が用意されたのです。

　図1.1でわかるように，第2期テクニクエストは初年度に約10万人の利用者がありました。これに対し，隣接するウェールズ産業海事博物館の90年の利用者数は3万9000人にとどまっています。この博物館はかなり新しいところですが資料中心の従来型展示施設です。こことの数字の比較で，ハンズ・オン系施設がいかに魅力があるかが説明できるでしょう。カーディフ市の中心から離れた荒廃した地域で成功した原因は，多くをビートルストーンの教育思想と運営陣に負っているといえます。教授は自分のことを「科学のお店の店主」，すなわち来てくれた人に楽しんでもらう素晴らしい体験をプロデュースする座長と考えていました。その関心はファラデーの『ロウソクの科学』で有名な王立研究所のクリスマス講演会の伝統を手本に，より幅広い層の観客を相手に科学を消費するところにあります。王立研究所の講演では科学を演劇的に実演してみせていました（第3期テクニクエストの科学劇場が実際に王立研究所の講堂を基にして造られているのは興味深い）。テクニクエストでは子どもを通して大人にも手をさしのべようと努力していて，彼らに「クリスマスパーティーで3杯ウイスキーをひっかけた後のように」ふるまってほしいといっているほ

どです。このことは，おそらくテクニクエストの魅力のわかりやすい例証でしょう。教授が観察したところでは，「テーマパークでは人間からではなくて展示装置から騒音が発せられるが，ディスカバリーセンター（発見施設の意。教授は科学館という用語よりもこちらを好んで使う）では展示装置ではなく人間から騒音が発せられる」といいます。

テクニクエストではディズニー流の哲学，つまり展示室はまるで昨日オープンしたばかりのようにぴかぴかで，全体の雰囲気や快適さに格別の注意を払うことを運営の指針に採り入れています。ここが成功している理由の1つは展示装置のデザインのよさで，素晴らしいうえに頑丈で，鮮やかな原色で特徴づけられていることでしょう。そのほとんどは館内制作で，新機軸の展示装置のデザインを担当する複数のアーティストや，その図面を問題なく機能する装置に仕上げる製品デザイナーたちを擁しています。教育効果の高いディスカバリーセンターの開設には大きな資本を要しました。さらに，それを清潔に維持し，

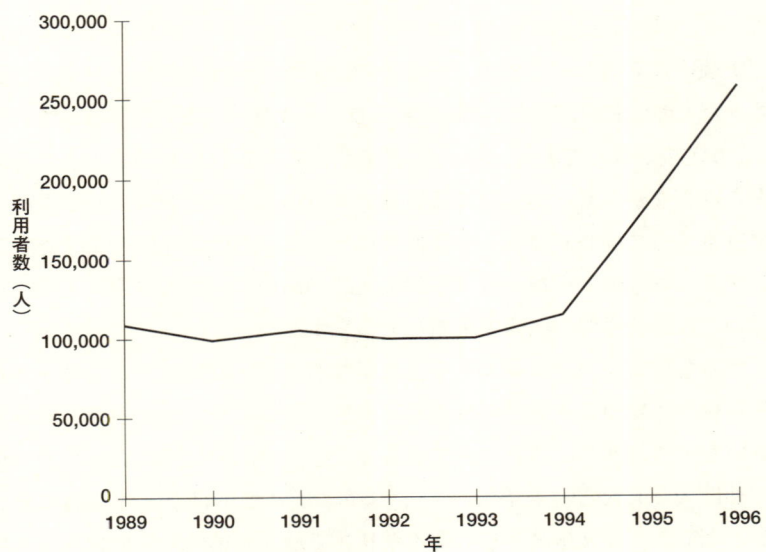

図1.1：テクニクエストの利用者の推移

出典：テクニクエスト提供の資料による
注記：1）95年5月，第3期テクニクエスト開館
　　　2）96年の数字は9月末の時点で見積もったもの

いつでも利用可能な状態にしておくにはそれなりの財源が必要となります。この施設には教育施設と娯楽産業としての両面があるとビートルストーンは見ていて，財源の多くは教育界では従来から普通になっているお金の出所よりも事業収入から得ています。そうはいっても，もしインタラクティブな科学館がいくらかでも利益を生むものなら，はるか以前にディズニーかほかの営利的な余暇施設の経営者が手を染めないわけはなかったでしょう。

　第2期テクニクエストは，7年の間に70万人以上を動員しました。91年11月，家賃の提供をしてくれているカーディフ港湾開発公社はテクニクエストを開発プロジェクトのいわば主役に抜擢しました。こうして第3期に着手し，95年5月に開館するのです。同開発公社による基金のほかウェールズ局，ヨーロッパ地域開発基金，ウェールズ開発庁，ウェールズ観光局の分担も加え，この最新施設の総工費は700万ポンドにものぼりました。いまではテクニクエストは，19世紀に工房として使われていた鉄骨組みの建物のまわりに設計された新しい建物のオーナーです。おかげで展示の数を倍の160に増やすことができました。そのうえに，科学劇場，プラネタリウム，"ディスカバリールーム"，ラボ（実験室）も備わっています。ここでは来た人が個々独自のお楽しみ計画をつくりだすのに意味があると考え，展示をテーマ分けしないことにしました。「綿密に考え抜かれたでたらめさ」で構成されているのです。確立した運営哲学を引き継ぎながらも，第3期には設備の水準の高さが加わり，利用者層を広げるアウトリーチプログラム[5]も教育プログラムも高度に発展しました。この新しいテクニクエストは最初の1年間で23万6000人もの人を迎え入れ，うち約3分の1は学校単位の団体で来館しています。

　まとめるならば，テクニクエストは大胆な夢のような構想からスタートして有機的な統一体につくりあげられたことを示しています。しっかりした事業計画とあいまって（さらにささやかではあったものの，先見性のあったカーディフ市が仲間入りしたことも手伝って），テクニクエストは夢を連続的に発展させることができ，独立施設としてはイギリスで最大規模の科学体験施設になれ

---

[5] 通常博物館を利用しない（できない）人々を対象に，利用者の枠を広げることを目的に行う活動。博物館という建物の枠を超えて行われる移動展示や資料の貸し出し，他施設での出前授業，ホームページの利用などがある。8章で詳述。

たのです。

ハンズ・オン系施設の支援団体

　アメリカ，イギリス，ヨーロッパでこどもの博物館や科学館が発展した陰には学会や協会など多くの団体の支えがあります。これらの団体ではハンズ・オン学習について組織的なキャンペーンを展開したり，できて間もない施設には惜しみなく援助の手をさしのべてきました。アメリカでは青少年博物館協会が，こどもの博物館に代わって専門家機関としての役割をしています。その一方で73年には，一般人の科学技術に対する理解を深めることを目的とした科学館技術館協会（ASTC）が設立されました。これは博物館で構成する非営利団体として組織された協会でお金には換算できないような貴重な情報源を提供し，ヨーロッパのインタラクティブ系展示施設とも連絡をとっています。それで88年にはヨーロッパにも同じような意義のある共同機関を設立するという決定がなされました。こうしてECSITE，すなわち欧州科学系展示施設協力機関が組織されました。創設会員はヨーロッパ7カ国の代表です。ECSITEのニューズレター（90年2月号，3月号）から，創設目的を書き抜いておきましょう。

　　　一般の科学，工業，技術に対する理解の促進，とりわけ……インタラクティブな科学館，博物館，展示施設に関して……非営利団体の実効性ある協同の促進。

　ECSITEは展示施設の創作，交流，保守などにまつわる経験や情報を全員のものとするための素晴らしいネットワークを整備しました。また，そうすることで，ハンズ・オンの博物館や科学館の発展を推進するのを助けるうえで計り知れない役割を果たしています。この共同機関は欧州共同体（EC）からの資金提供も一部受けていますが，ナフィールド財団の基金によって計画が始まり，当初は本部も財団内においてありました。この財団はイギリスでは重要な存在で，学校における科学教育の援助活動に長い歴史があります。ほかの施設のモデルになるような斬新な試みがないか常に目を光らせていて見つかれば資金援助するのですが，86年のエクスプロラトリー（ブリストル市）の第1次拡張改良工事はこの財団の基金によりました。また，88年には巡回展である"デ

ィスカバリードーム"，このほか同様のプロジェクトの数々，たとえば"ライトワークス"と呼ぶ学校に持ち込めるような規模の小さなインタラクティブ展示装置やテクニクエストの学校向けキットなども同財団の資金援助によるものです。そうこうするうちに，イギリスの技術館振興を目的に，インタラクティブ技術館開発基金がセインズベリー財団により設立され，その運営に先述のピジーが携わるようになりました。彼が"ディスカバリードーム"の開発にかかわる以前の話です。

87年，ナフィールド財団は，貿易産業省と共同して，インタラクティブ科学技術プロジェクトを設置しました。目的は科学館の発展を促進し，認識や専門的意見を共有できる拠点を用意するところにあります。エクスプロラトリーのグレゴリー教授を議長に，このプロジェクトは初期のイギリスの科学館の発展のうえで有用な討論の場を提供して，90年に役目を終えました。実は，最初のころのニュースレターの送付先は50人にも満たないものでしたが，89年12月には400部を超える数にまで発行数が伸びたとのことです。

ナフィールド財団，インタラクティブ科学技術プロジェクト，ECSITEの活動の足りないところは科学普及推進委員会（COPUS）が補いました。これは一般の人の科学に対する理解の促進を目的とする合同委員会で，王立協会，王立研究所，英国科学振興協会をメンバーとして86年に創設され，科学技術に対する一般の意識を高めるための拠点の役割を担っています。多彩なプロジェクトに助成し，たとえば科学館に対する少額の助成や，イギリスのハンズ・オン教育の発展初期に関する報告や記事を収集した貴重な出版物の刊行（ナフィールド財団と共同事業）などがあります。

こういった振興団体の影響を過小評価してはいけません。実は，80年代の終わりに，インタラクティブ科学技術プロジェクトが解散になるとき，その代表でECSITEの事務局長であるクイン女史が，注目すべき洞察的発言を残しています。

> 私はスティーブ・ピジーの夢を共有しようと思うものです。ちょうど今日，ほとんどの町に図書館，美術ギャラリー，劇場，スポーツ施設があるように，いつの日か，おそらく，どの町にもインタラクティブな科学技術館があるという夢です。けれども，私ははっきりと予言します。「ハン

ズ・オン」が『科学技術を超えて広がるでしょう』と。コミュニケーションの手段として，それには大きな可能性があります——利用者が参加することで史料や絵画などに対する評価には新たな次元が付け加わることでしょう。——また，それは付加価値のある余暇活動から教室での豊かな授業の間に確かな虹の橋を渡すことになるでしょう。

現在のハンズ・オン系施設と利用者層

イギリスのハンズ・オン博物館と科学館の数は，1986年以降，着実な伸びを示しています。図1.2でわかるように，86年から95年の間に毎年3.5館の割合で新しい施設がオープンしています。その中には，ユーリイカ！こどものための博物館のようにめざましい成功を収めたところもあります。ユーリイカ！では，92年に開館して以来，2年ちょっとで100万人に及ぶ利用者を迎えました。この初期の，もっぱらハンズ・オン手法にこだわった博物館の成功が，従来型の博物館の既存の陳列品にインタラクティブの手法を徐々に組み込んでいくという結果を招いたのは避けえないことだったでしょう。実際，ヨークシャーとハンバーサイドにある科学，デザイン，技術関連の収蔵品を有する博物館85館のうち25館が，94年にはインタラクティブ展示装置があると公言しているほどです。

いまではもうイギリスのハンズ・オン系施設の完全な一覧を作るのは簡単な仕事ではなくなりました。というのも，95年以降に開館したところで，複合メディア系施設にインタラクティブな要素を組み込んだ新しい展示施設は非常に多いからです。イギリスでは国営宝くじ[6]を財源とする資金が新施設の建設促進の役割を果たしており，特に二千年紀記念用に計画されているインタラクティブな展示施設に対する活動が目立ちます。確信をもっていえるのは，新しいハンズ・オン展示施設の開館の割合は95年を境に劇的に増加していること，また，ハンズ・オンの考え方が科学や技術の域をはるかに超えて，歴史，考古学，スポーツ，美術，ポピュラー音楽の博物館までをも包含するまでに広がっ

---

[6] 1993年に制定されたイギリスの国営宝くじ法によって，宝くじの収益金が芸術，文化，スポーツ，二千年紀記念事業等に充当されることになった。主に施設・設備の建設や改修工事に対して助成を行っている。

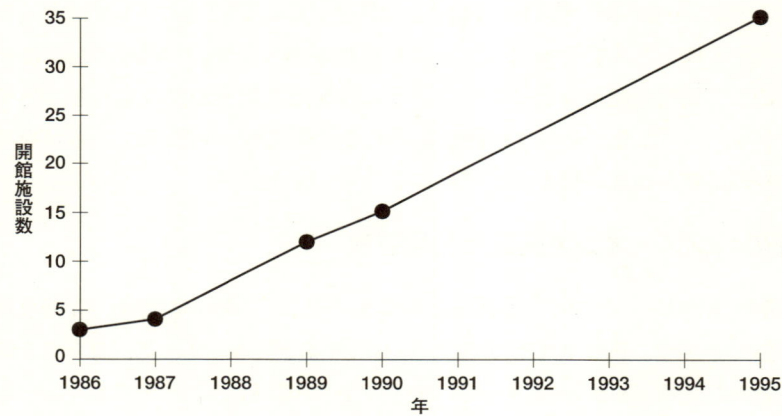

図1.2：イギリスにおけるハンズ・オン系博物館・科学館の伸び
出典：『英国インタラクティブグループハンドブック』および筆者の推定

たことでしょう。さらにそのうえ，博物館ではないところ，たとえば史跡展示施設や農村地域展示施設などでもハンズ・オン展示装置を導入するようになってきているのです。

　需要面からみると，インタラクティブ系施設は利用者に好評です。というのも，イギリスで博物館の市場可能性を分析した最近のレポートでは，来館を決めた理由の二大要素として，展示装置を使ってインタラクティブな体験ができることと，関連した子ども用のプログラムが用意されていることが示されていました。利用者の3分の1は子どもに占められており，最も重要な利用者層は子ども連れの家族（学校団体ではない）なのです。第2次ベビーブームの続く20世紀末までは，こういった成長市場に目を向けた家族型集客施設は顧客の増加を期待し続けられることでしょう。

　ハンズ・オン系博物館や科学館は近年，世界のいたるところで，主要な集客施設として目を見張るような成功を謳歌しているようです。86年に行われたASTCの調査では，130館からの回答を集計した総利用者数は5000万人を超えており，しかも圧倒的大多数の館では収入から経費を引いた残りのお金で運営がなされているとのことでした。ある積算では，今日，科学館は全世界で年間1億人の人の心をひきつけているといいます。

イギリスでは，この20年間の博物館全体の利用者数の伸び率は24％で，89年から95年の間の伸びは9ポイントです。最新の見積もりでは，さまざまな情報をもとにすると約1億人の人々が毎年どこかの博物館を訪れているとみています（この数字は世界中の科学館の利用者数に等しい）。ところが博物館は約2500館もあるので，供給の増加が需要の増加を上回ってしまいました。実は，国営宝くじが生まれてから施設の増え方に加速がかかったのですが，需要のほうは92年からわずかに減っているのです。イギリスではいま供給過剰にある博物館が少ないお客を追い求める状況になっています。また，超過密状態の余暇市場のなかで，テーマパークや家族向けの娯楽施設，郊外ショッピングセンターなどの営利的な集客施設の横で負けまいと奮闘している博物館の姿があります（特に日曜日。従来から博物館に行くのに好まれる曜日）。97年には何館かの博物館が厳しい決算を経験しました。また，よく知られていたいくつかの博物館の閉鎖とか，従来型の博物館や新しいタイプといえる施設の中で失望させられるような事態もありました。ハンズ・オン系博物館がもつ訴求力は，この過密市場での競争の中で強力な位置を占めているはずですが，ではハンズ・オン系博物館は現在どのように機能しているのでしょうか。

　イギリスにおけるハンズ・オン系博物館と科学館全体の市場規模を概算するのは非常に難しい作業です。というのも，何がハンズ・オン系展示施設で何が違うかの定義以前に，困難な理由がたくさんあるからです。そういう状況ではあるのですが，95年版『英国インタラクティブグループ名鑑』に英国インタラクティブグループ（BIG）[7]がインタラクティブ系施設と認めた35館のリストがあるので，これを分析すれば市場規模の積算は可能になるでしょう。観光施設を訪れる人の数は，英国政府観光庁／観光局リサーチサービスが年刊の『イギリスの観光』で毎年公表しています。ただし，この数字は最初に思ったほどには資料価値がありませんでした。なぜなら，まず年間3万人以上の利用者がある施設のデータしか載せていないうえに，第二に大きな施設に併設されているインタラクティブ系施設，たとえばロンドン国立科学博物館の"ラウン

---

[7] ハンズ・オンによる学習に興味を持つ個人のメンバーによって構成されている組織。原著者はこのグループの会計を担当している（99年現在）。例会を開催するほか，ニュースレターを発行しており，本書でも数多く引用されている。

チパッド"やマンチェスター科学産業博物館内の"エクスペリメント！"などの個々の施設別の利用者数がないからです。もう一点，入場料無料の施設の利用者数は，いくら好意的にいったとしても当て推量でしかありません。

　このデータを用いると，前述の BIG のインタラクティブ系施設のリストにある 13 館の独立館[8] の年間利用者数は，95 年には約 165 万人になります。別に，インタラクティブ系施設を併設する博物館 5 館[9] では，全館をひっくるめると 415 万人を迎えています。この人たちがもれなくインタラクティブ系展示施設を利用したとはもちろんいえないのですが，国立科学博物館では 50 万人，つまり 144 万人の利用者の 35% が"ラウンチパッド"を訪れたといっています。そこで仮に，残りの 4 館の博物館にあるインタラクティブ系施設の利用者数を控え目に全体の 10% として積算してみると，27 万人がこれらの施設に行ったことになります。このようにしてみると，95 年には少なくとも 242 万人が BIG 認定のハンズ・オン系施設 35 館のうちの 18 館を訪れたと概算できます。この数字には主だったハンズ・オン系博物館と科学館はすべて含まれているので（そのうち 11 館は 95 年に 10 万人以上の利用者を迎えている），インタラクティブ系施設 35 館全体の市場規模は，推計年間 300 万人から 400 万人の間と見込めるでしょう（この数字はインタラクティブ系施設の世界市場の 3～4% で，同時に博物館のイギリス国内市場の 3～4% である。科学館の利用者が多数いるのであるが，イギリスでは科学館は博物館と見ていないため，博物館利用者市場には含めていない）。

　年間 300 万人から 400 万人というハンズ・オン系博物館・科学館利用者の数は，入手しうるデータをもとにした概算数字ですが，新しいハンズ・オン系施設がオープンしたり，従来型の博物館にハンズ・オン手法が採り入れられるようになるにつれ，この市場の規模は拡大しているように思えます（新しいハンズ・オン系施設の成功が新しい需要の創出や従来型の博物館からお客様をいた

---

[8] 原注によると，これら 13 館はヨーク考古学リソースセンター，アーマープラネタリウム，カタリスト，ユーリイカ！，エクスプロラトリー，エクスプロアイット，グリーンズミル科学館，サトロスフィア，ジョドレルバンク科学館，ニューキャッスル・ディスカバリー，セラフィールド・ビジターセンター，スニブストン・ディスカバリーパーク，テクニクエスト。

[9] 原注によると，これら 5 館はロンドン国立科学博物館，国立自然史博物館，国立海事博物館，バーミンガム科学産業博物館，ノースウエスト科学産業博物館。

だくものであって，既存のハンズ・オン系施設を犠牲にするものではないという前提で)。アメリカでの例ですが，最近オープンしたいくつかの科学館では来館者数が目標に達しないで，既存の施設の数字が成熟期に入ったという証言があります（実際には，93〜94年に全体で10％の減少)。したがって，ここでハンズ・オン系博物館と科学館個々の成功をある周期にわたって検証してみて，その商品としてのライフサイクルを追跡してみる必要があります。

ハンズ・オン系展示施設のライフサイクル

　商品のライフサイクルという考え方は，相対的にしか測れないハンズ・オン系博物館の成功を判定するのに役立ちます。この概念はすべての商品には市場に出てから不要になるまでの過程があるととらえるもので，成長期，成熟期を経過して市場が飽和状態の時点で売り上げはピークに達し，そのあとは下り坂になると考えるものです。異なったタイプの商品には明らかに異なったライフサイクルがあります。たとえば，スケートボードパークは非常に短命でしたが，従来型の博物館の場合は未来世代のために建物や収蔵品を大事にする責任もあって非常に長いライフサイクルが求められています。新しいタイプの博物館は，概してライフサイクルが短い過当競争ぎみの余暇市場で運営されています。新しい集客施設がオープンするとき，2つのシナリオが考えられるでしょう。安定した運営を目指して建築途上の状態でオープンするか（テクニクエストのケースのように)，もしくは完全に一人前になって臨むかのどちらかです。後者の場合，余暇産業での先例によると，大規模な都市型集客施設の利用者のピークは開館早々に達する傾向にあるといわれています。つまり2年目か3年目に最高の数字に到達し，4年目で安定するわけです。それ以降は，展示装置を新しくしたり追加投資をしないかぎり，この数は一気に減少しうるといいます。

　『イギリスの観光』は年刊なので，各年度版を見れば開館後5年以上たったハンズ・オン系博物館・科学館のライフサイクルを追跡することができます。すべての結果を重ね合わせれば，ハンズ・オン系博物館・科学館の典型的なライフサイクル曲線が描けるはずです。実際，ハンズ・オン系施設のライフサイクルは，図 1.3 でわかるように，余暇産業の先例から外れていないように見えます。

　図 1.3 でデータに使った7館[10]のハンズ・オン系施設はいわば一人前の施

図 1.3：新しいハンズ・オン系施設が示す典型的なライフサイクル曲線
出典：『イギリスの観光』各年度版をもとに作成
注記：ハンズ・オン系施設 7 館のデータをグラフ化した

設としてオープンしたところで，開館後 5 年以内には大きな追加投資はされていません。この標本が示すところをもとに考えれば，新しいハンズ・オン系施設のライフサイクルがまさに余暇産業の先例に従うという結論を導き出せます。つまり，ライフサイクルは短く，開館（この時期は紹介記事がよくメディアに取り上げられる）後，2 年目か 3 年目で利用者はピーク数字を達成します。そして 4 年目には 5 年間の平均利用者数となり，そのときその施設は安定期に達したと考えられます。実効を伴う追加投資を行わなければ，その後利用者数は着実に衰退期に突入します。このため，多くのハンズ・オン系博物館・科学館では，3 年から 5 年サイクルでの展示装置の入れ替えを計画しており，たとえば，ユーリイカ！では 92 年の開館から 4 年目に"リサイクル施設"という展示をロンドン国立科学博物館の"もの"の展示の複製に入れ替えました。

事例紹介：グリーンズミル科学館

ノッティンガム市にあるグリーンズミル科学館はイギリスにおける草創期のハ

---

[10] 原注によると，これら 7 館はヨーク考古学リソースセンター，アーマープラネタリウム，グリーンズミル科学館，ジョドレルバンク科学館，サトロスフィア，セラフィールド・ビジターセンター，テクニクエスト。

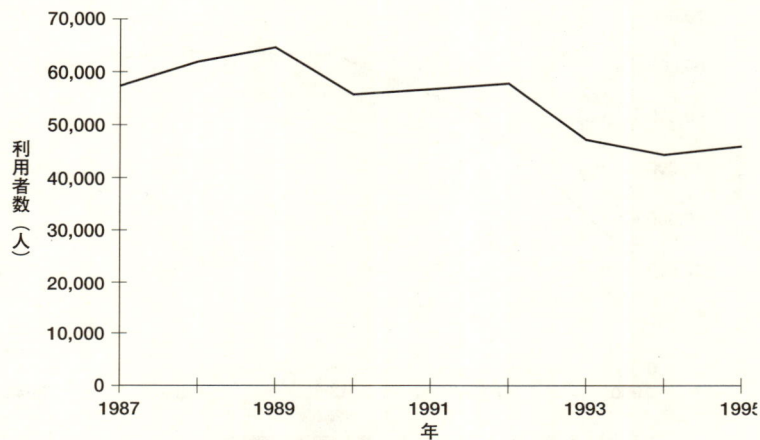

図 1.4：グリーンズミルの利用者の推移
出典：『イギリスの観光』各年度版をもとに作成
注記：入館料無料のため利用者数は概算である

ンズ・オン系科学館の1つであるために，**図 1.4** でわかるように，長期にわたるケーススタディーができる例として興味深いものがあります（グリーンズミルは風車の意。科学館はその付属施設なので，以下，グリーンズミルと略す）。

　グリーンズミルでは利用者のピークを開館して3年目，イギリス初の科学館の1つとして当時でも非常に斬新な施設であったときに迎えました。**図 1.3** で示した典型例のように，グリーンズミルの利用者は4年目に安定期に入っています。この年の利用者数（5万4973人）は，開館後9年間にわたる平均値（5万3928人）とほぼ同じでした。ほかにも博物館が生まれ，家族向け集客施設が増加したためにグリーンズミルはかつてのような斬新な施設ではなくなり，ライフサイクルでいう衰退期に入りました（91〜92年にかけてと95年に微増したものの，長期的傾向は下降）。バクストン市のマイクラリアムでも同様のパターンが見られ，87〜89年に年間3万5000の入館者で，90年には3万2675人，91年には3万3612人と減少していっています。それ以降，『イギリスの観光』にはデータが載っていません。なぜならマイクラリアムは衰退期に入り，利用者数が3万人を割ってしまったためです。示唆的なことにマイクラリアムは閉鎖され，95年の冬にはユーリイカ！こどものための博物館と

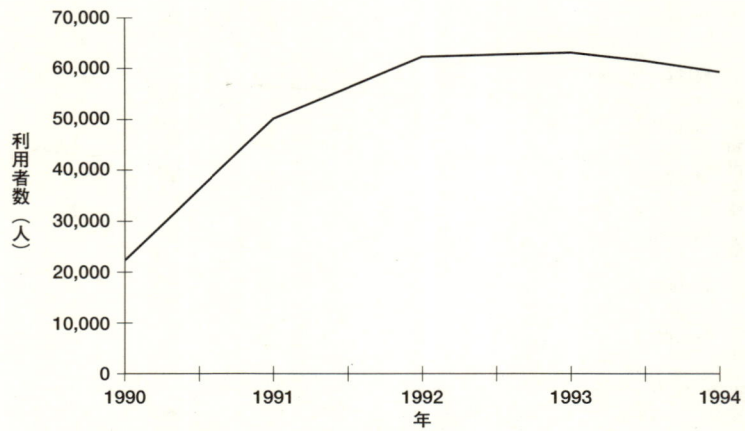
図1.5：ヨーク考古学リソースセンターの利用者の推移
出典：『イギリスの観光』各年度版をもとに作成

の統合が検討されているとの発表がありました。

事例紹介：考古学リソースセンター

　ヨーク市にある考古学リソースセンターのライフサイクルを図示すると、**図1.5**のように典型的な曲線を描いています。この館は90年の年度途中に開館したので初年度の数字を除いて計算すると、年平均5万8112人の利用者を迎えたことになりました。**図1.3**や**図1.4**で見たように、この平均数字は4年目の数字（94年の5万8420人）とほとんど同じです。

事例紹介：エクスプロラトリー

　段階を経て発展させていくタイプの施設の例はエクスプロラトリー（ブリストル市）とテクニクエスト（カーディフ市）で見ることができます。後者の例はすでに図1.1に示しました。エクスプロラトリーは87年に開館し、90年に新しい場所に移転、その結果来館者数は2倍になりました。テクニクエストのように、さらに次の移転が日程にのぼっています。二千年紀記念委員会賞を受賞して4100万ポンドの賞金を得、「ブリストル2000」計画の一環として西暦2000年にサイエンスワールドへの移転が決まっています[11]。ちなみにサイエン

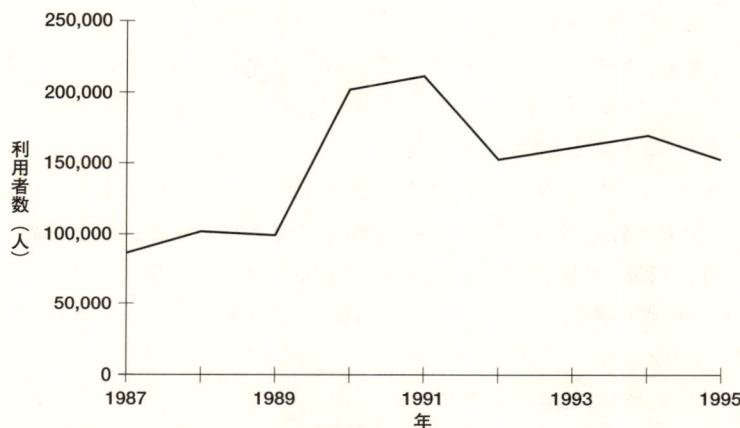

図1.6：エクスプロラトリーの利用者数の推移
出典：『イギリスの観光』各年度版をもとに作成

スワールドは 2500 万ポンドを投じた新しいハンズ・オン系科学館です。

　図 1.6 の曲線は，90 年からの第 2 期展開で利用者が 2 倍になったことと，3 年目の 92 年に減少したことをはっきり示しています。90 年からの 6 年間の平均利用者数は 17 万 3089 人で，移転後 4 年目の 94 年には 16 万 8000 人でした。けれどもエクスプロラトリーの利用者数が固定化したとはいい切れず，この先かなり長期間にわたってこの状態が続くでしょう。というのもサイエンスワールドは，国営宝くじの収益を利用した二千年紀記念委員会の記念碑的な画期的プロジェクトだからです。

まとめ

　イギリス，アメリカ，ヨーロッパのハンズ・オン系博物館・科学館の増加は，ここ数年目覚しいものがあります。これらの施設は科学博物館やこどもの博物

---

[11] 二千年紀記念委員会の助成を受けたミレニアム記念事業としてブリストル市が進めている「ブリストル 2000」計画は，アットブリストル（@Bristol）という名称で 2000 年春にオープン予定となっている。自然をテーマにしたワイルドスクリーンと科学をテーマにしたエクスプロアという 2 つの施設から成っているが，現在閉鎖中のエクスプロラトリーはエクスプロアに移転することになっている。なお，二千年紀記念委員会については 4 章 97 ページ脚注 3 を参照。

館，特にアメリカで長い伝統がある革新的なコミュニケーション手法に基礎を置いています。西欧社会では教育と娯楽を結合した質の高い集客施設を求める声は顕著でしたが，**図1.2**からはイギリスではいまもなおハンズ・オン系施設が成長段階にあることがわかります。

　ところが，イギリスの博物館全体の状況を見ると飽和状態にあり，ハンズ・オン系博物館・科学館は，ほかの2500館もの博物館やさまざまな商業的余暇施設との間で利用者の争奪戦を繰り広げているのです。余暇施設の経営者がアメリカやその他の地域で成功している非営利のこどもの博物館の活動を見過ごすわけがありません。ディスカバリーゾーンやプラネットファンというような子ども向けの冒険的遊戯施設が，アメリカやイギリスで急速に建設されつつあります。

　ライフサイクル分析によると，新しくできたハンズ・オン系博物館・科学館は，特に中心的施設に再投資をしないと，開館後4年目以降も高い数字で利用者を維持するのは難しいのがわかります。現在のところ，テクニクエストやエクスプロラトリーのように長期的展望をもとに発展中の大規模施設に比べ，小規模な施設が利用者数の維持に苦労しているようです。全体として見ると，新しい施設での増加数のほうが，利用者の減少を抱えているこれらの施設での減少数をはるかにしのいでいます。ハンズ・オン系施設5館の実績を，データのある1989年から95年で比較してみると，この7年間に49％増加しました。92年から95年のデータがある9館のハンズ・オン系施設の実績は，4年の間に28％の増加です。

　このように，ハンズ・オン系博物館・科学館の全体的傾向は好ましいものです。イギリスでは，新しい施設がオープンするにつれ，ハンズ・オン系博物館を訪れる人の総数は増加しています。ところが，古い施設は新しい展示施設に再投資しないかぎり，利用者争奪戦で競争相手に水をあけられかねません。個々のハンズ・オン系博物館・科学館は，高水準の経営手法を採り入れ，運営目標と対象とする利用者像を綿密に定義し，各施設が成熟期からさらなる発展を遂げて，超競合市場での存続を確実にする必要があるでしょう。

"ラウンチパッド"

ロンドン国立科学博物館にある"ラウンチパッド"という展示室はインタラクティブな展示が50種以上あり，子どもから大人まで，展示で遊ぶ人の姿がいつも絶えない。来館者の多いときには整理券が発行され，入場規制されるほど。写真はどの形の車輪が曲がっているレールにも適合するかを試す展示。車輪の素材はウレタン製でものものしくなく，扱いやすい。

インディアナポリスこどもの博物館

インディアナポリス市では一般向けの博物館施設などが貧弱なこともあり，科学館，歴史博物館などの教育機能も兼ね備えたこの館は，周辺地域一帯の代表的な博物館施設として多くの人々の利用を得ている。1925年に小さな車庫で開館された同館は移転を繰り返し，現在ではボランティア職員だけでも1000人近くを数える世界最大のこどもの博物館となっている。

2章

教育的側面

ユーリイカ！こどものための博物館外観
敷地に入ると建物の入り口までイラストパネルやカラフルで独創的な遊具が続き，博物館がこどものための楽しい場所だということを強く印象づけている。
（撮影：稲庭彩和子）

アメリカのこどもの博物館

こどもの博物館発祥の地アメリカでは，ほとんどの場合において博物館の設置主体は非営利民間組織（NPO）となっている。ワシントンDCなどの博物館群を擁するスミソニアン協会や日本からの訪問者も多いメトロポリタン美術館もいわゆる公立ではない。こどもの博物館も例外ではなく，本書に取り上げられているインディアナポリスやボストンなどのこどもの博物館はすべてNPO。私企業などのように経済的な利潤追求が目的でもなければ，行政の一機関でもない。NPOはその存在理由に公益性の実現という使命をもつ。使命達成をアピールし認めてもらうことが大口寄付などの資金獲得につながる重要なポイントになるために，活動内容の質をさらに高める努力を重ねるというNPOならではのあり方が，アメリカの博物館の水準の高さを生んでいるといえる。　　　　　　（染川香澄）

2章 教育的側面

　この章では，インタラクティブ展示の手法を裏付ける学習理論を検証します。そのうえで博物館において利用者が楽しみながら学ぶということが本当に可能かどうか，考えていきます。

はじめに

　インタラクティブ展示を根底で支えているのは，ハンズ・オン展示のほうが，従来型の博物館の展示よりも利用者にとって興味深く，楽しいものだ，という考え方です。ハンズ・オン系の博物館を訪れる人の数や，そこでの人々の反応を見れば，この考えは正しいといえるでしょう。利用者が楽しんでいるかどうかで成否を測ってよいのであれば，インタラクティブ系の博物館や科学館がその目的を達成しているのは誰もが認めるところです。しかし，ことはそれほど単純ではありません。博物館や科学館には教育[1]という目的があるからです。エクスプロラトリーの創設者であるグレゴリーが「最近の科学館の人気ぶりを見ると，年齢を問わず，かなり多くのイギリス国民が科学原理の探求を楽しく興味深いと感じていることがわかる」と述べていますが，この見解にほぼ異論はないでしょう。もっともその一方で，科学者でもあるグレゴリーは「ハンズ・オンは，具体物を見て学ぶには効果的で欠くことのできない手法であるが，科学的理解を目的とする場合には適切な方法とはいいきれない」との懸念も示しています。

　科学離れの風潮に対策を講じようとする人にとって，科学館で科学の大衆化が図られることは喜ばしいことです。しかし同時に，科学館では単に科学の原

---

[1] 米国博物館協会は，博物館教育を，探求，調査，観察，批判的思考，熟考，対話を含むものであると述べている（*Excellence and Equity*, 1992）。本書の「教育」という言葉も同様に広義の意味で用いられている。

理の表面をなぞっているにすぎないのではないか，さらに科学館は科学に対する誤解を生み出しているのではないか，との論争が何年にもわたって続いており，「科学館の利用者は本当に学んでいるのか。単に遊んでいるだけではないのか」という疑問が繰り返し発せられています。グレゴリーたちも，実際の科学研究は時間がかかって退屈で，決して華々しいものではないのに，科学館では科学を単純化してしまい，科学研究によって何でもすぐに解答が出るという印象を与えてしまうとの懸念を表明しています。これに対して，インタラクティブ展示を支持する立場では，利用者が楽しんでいるとすれば，それは同時に学んでいるといえる，少なくとも科学的研究に対する熱意を感じて帰ることになる，との主張があります。つまり，「科学館の利用者は本当に遊んでいるのか。単に学んでいるだけではないのか」と，先の疑問に問い返しているのです。

　この章では，人間は楽しんでいるときに多く学ぶものであるという仮説を検証し，実際にハンズ・オン展示から利用者はどれほど学んでいるのか，その根拠を探ります。インタラクティブ展示を利用した結果，利用者は理解や知識の点で何か変化（認知的学習）をして帰っているのか，それとも，展示の役割は主に利用者の気持ちを変えること（感情的学習）にあるのか。インタラクティブ展示は作り手の意図を伝えると同時に，誤ったメッセージを伝えてしまう可能性もあるのか。同じインタラクティブ系の展示でも，科学館と博物館では学習に何か違いがあるのか。利用者の積極的な学習を誘発する要因は何か，つまり，グレゴリーのことばを借りるならば，ハンズ・オンをマインズ・オン[2]にする要因はどのようなものか。こうした疑問に答えるために，個々の利用者の博物館での行動や学習について（個人的側面），集団での行動や学習について（社会的側面），さらにデザインが学習環境に与える影響について（物的側面），順に検証していくことにします[3]。

---

[2] 1章5ページの脚注2参照。
[3] フォークとダイアキングが，*The Museum Experience*（1992，邦題『博物館体験』雄山閣出版）のなかで，博物館体験を個人的，社会的，物的の3側面から検証している。

学習の個人的側面

学習理論

インタラクティブ展示がその根拠をおく教育理論の多くは，ピアジェをはじめフレーベルやヴィゴツキーなどの発達心理学者の研究に端を発しています。ピアジェは，学習は環境との直接的な相互作用の結果であると述べて，子どもの誕生から成熟に至るまでを，連続的な発達段階に分けました。その研究によれば，誕生後の数年間，子どもは主に自分の運動・感覚能力を探求し，2歳から4歳には身近な世界の探求を始めます。4歳から7歳には他者とより多く接点をもって自己中心性から脱し始め，7歳になると，世の中の仕組みを理解するようになり，思春期を迎える頃には，論理的・抽象的な原理を理解できるようになります。

ピアジェの考え方は，教育に多くの示唆を与えています。子どもは大人とは違ったふうに考え，違った観点から世界を見ているという考えに従えば，大人の学習に適切なことが必ずしも子どもにもあてはまるとは限りません。ピアジェによれば，子どもはただ静かに観察するよりも活動することから学び自分で知識を構成するので，教師の役割とは自分の知識を分け与えることではありません。つまり，最も効果的に知識を構成する環境をつくりだすことが大切であって，子どもが何の疑問も抱かずに情報を受け入れるのを奨励するのではないのです。子どもが質問を発するように助けるのが教師の役割です。学ぶペースを決めるのは子ども自身であって，教師は子どもが発見をしていく過程のガイド役にすぎません。

ピアジェは心理学という学問が誕生して間もない1920年代に研究を始めていましたが，その理論が広く知られるようになったのは50年代，60年代になってからです。小学校の教師たちは机といすが堅苦しく並んだ教室での一斉授業をやめて，実験や少人数での授業を行うようになりました。教師が子どもの学習を支え強固にするガイド役を果たすようになったのです。同じ頃，博物館もその教育的役割を見直し始めていました。イギリスでもアメリカでも，以前から博物館の資料を手にとって見ることの価値は認められており，館内の教育プログラムに組み込まれたり，学校に資料を貸し出す際に実践されていました。

アメリカでは，子どもが手にとって探求するのに向く資料を中心に，ボストンやブルックリン，インディアナポリスなどで，こどもの博物館が設立されていました。そうはいうものの，ガラスケースの中から資料を取り出し，子どもが自由に探求できるような展示手法が採用されたのは，64年にスポックがボストンこどもの博物館の館長に就任してからのことです。1章で触れたように，この実験的手法は，その後ブルックリンこどもの博物館やオッペンハイマーによるサンフランシスコのエクスプロラトリアム（真の意味ですべてがインタラクティブ展示による初の科学館）でも採り入れられていきました。

　学校の教室ではカリキュラムが決まっていて，時間や資料不足などの制約があるので，子どもは自分のまわりの環境を十分に探求することができないのが実情です。反対に，インタラクティブ展示では豊富な資料や展示装置を使って探求や実験ができるうえ，時間にしばられることなく，集中力の続く限り自分の興味を追求できます。ハンズ・オン系の博物館が提供するインフォーマルな学習環境[4]は時間的な枠ではなく，空間的な枠を設定しているからです。インタラクティブな展示室（特にこどもの博物館）では，普段から見なれた空間が設定されていることが多く，ありふれた場面を新しい観点から見ることができるようになっています。逆に，来館者の感情をゆさぶったり既成概念や誤った認識を問い直す目的で，刺激的な環境を提供する展示も多くあります。

　1970年代になると，ピアジェの理論は疑問視されるようになりました。研究の方法論的な問題や子どもがある課題を遂行できるようになる年齢の食い違いが指摘され，特に能力が現れてくる年齢が子どもによって異なることや，各発達段階の間の推移は急激なものでないことなどが論難されたのです。このような批判はあるものの，子どもの年齢によってニーズが異なること，そして学習とは人が環境との相互作用を通じて継続的に問題を解決していくことなどを明らかにした点で，ピアジェは重要な存在です。子どもは段階を追って成長し，その発達は環境との相互作用の直接的結果であるという本質は今にもあてはまるのです。

　ピアジェの発達心理学的な学習理論はハンズ・オン運動の広がりに大いに貢

---

[4] 決まったカリキュラムのない自発的な学習。いつでも，どこでも，生涯を通じてできる学習。学校教育などのフォーマルな教育と対比して用いられる。

献しました。またインタラクティブ展示は，ブルームが「学習分類」として示した3つの学習領域を満たす方法としても注目されるようになりました。つまり，インタラクティブ展示は，認識的学習（知識と理解），感情的学習（考え方や関心，動機），心理―動作的発達（操作と供応の身体的技術）を促進すると考えられています。

人にはそれぞれ異なった学習スタイルがあることを示す学習理論もあります。たとえば，マッカーシーの4 MATシステムは学習者を4つのタイプに分類しています。他の人の意見を聞いたり他者と意見を分かち合いながら学ぶ想像的学習タイプ，順を追って考え抜いて学ぶ分析的学習タイプ，各種の理論を検証することで学ぶ常識的学習タイプ，試行錯誤を繰り返しながら学ぶ実験的・動的学習タイプです。コルブとグレゴークも似たような枠組みで，いくつかの学習スタイルを示しましたが，ここで重要なのはフォーマルな学習環境[5]では上述したような学習スタイルのすべてに対応できないことです。ところが，インフォーマルな学習環境，つまりインタラクティブ展示がつくりだす環境のもとでは異なる学習スタイルそれぞれに対して効果的な学習機会を与えることができると考えられています。

インタラクティブ展示の重要性に注目している著名な心理学者がガードナーで，こどもの博物館を「心の遊び場」になぞらえました。そこは，子どもが興味のおもむくままに自分のペースで探求し，自分で理解することができる場です。ガードナーは人間の脳には少なくとも7つの能力つまり知性が存在すると考え，それぞれの知性が発達する度合いは人によって異なるとの説を唱えています。

ガードナーのいう7つの知性とは次のとおりです[6]。
1. 言語的知性：人の感情を揺さぶり，喜ばせ，確信させ，刺激したり，情報を伝える言語を使う能力。
2. 論理的・数学的知性：物事に共通するパターンを見つけ分類し，相互関

---

[5] 学校教育のようにカリキュラムが定められた学習環境。カリキュラムの内容は学習者自身でなく，国や学校，教師など，学習者以外によって定められる。
[6] ガードナーは最新の著書 *Intelligence Reframed: Multiple Intelligences for the 21st Century*, 1999 のなかで，ここにあげた7つの知性に加えて，自然的（Naturalist），実存的（Existential），精神的（Spiritual）の3つの知性を提示している。

係を探求し，秩序立った実験をする能力。
3．音楽的知性：音楽を楽しみ，演奏し，つくる能力。
4．空間的知性：形や物体を知覚して頭の中で操作し，視覚的・空間的な表現を構成する能力。
5．身体的・運動感覚的知性：スポーツや芸術・工芸などにおいて体全体もしくは体の一部を使う能力。
6．人間関係的知性：他人を理解し，意思伝達ができ，他人とうまくやっていける能力。
7．内面的知性：自分自身の考えや感情を理解し，人に頼らず，自らの力で行動する能力。

　ガードナーは，どの知性が優位となるかは人によって違うと述べる一方で，学校というフォーマルな学習環境では，時間や教材，カリキュラムなどの制約があるので，各人の秘められた知性が可能性いっぱいまでに発達しないのではないかとの見解を示しています。そのうえで，多彩な学習方法によって知性の多様性を刺激するインタラクティブな博物館は重要な学習環境であると注目しているのです。
　以上見てきたように，発達心理学の研究はハンズ・オン運動の発展に力を貸してきました。ピアジェらは，人は自分のまわりの環境との相互作用を通じて学ぶこと，子どもは大人とは違ったふうに，しかも年齢によって違ったふうに学ぶことを示しました。ガードナーやマッカーシーなどは，人はみな違ったスタイルで学ぶことを示し，ガードナーは学校教育というフォーマルな環境では，多様な学習スタイルが十分に発達し得ないと指摘しました。このように理論のうえでは，インタラクティブ展示は豊富な資源を使って年齢や学習能力の異なる人々に適した多様な学習環境を提供できることは明らかです。では，実践の場ではどうなのでしょうか。

インタラクティブ展示を用いた学習の実際
　利用者が理解しやすいように改善する目的で，ある特定のインタラクティブ展示の効果を検証することは数多く行われてきましたが，博物館利用者の学習

に関する系統立った研究は今までほとんどありませんでした。いいかえると，個々の博物館の環境を改善する目的の実用的な研究は多く行われてきたのですが，人はどのように，また，なぜ学ぶのか，という一般論を扱った研究はほとんど行われていません。これまでの研究はほとんどが応用研究なのです。一般的には利用者の属性や利用目的を調査し，デザインの有効性（たとえば展示装置や解説パネルの配置）を検証します。そして館内での行動や来館者同士のやりとりを観察し，博物館体験に影響を与える要因（たとえば利用者の予備知識）を考察します。このような応用研究は，研究を行った博物館に即実用的な成果をもたらしてくれるため実施例も多いのですが，科学館やこどもの博物館での学習行動や認知に踏み込んだ基礎研究は，それほど多くはありません。

　ロンドン国立科学博物館は，展示室の開発と運営に関して大規模な調査を実施した好例で，館内の独立した2つのインタラクティブ系展示室である"ラウンチパッド"と"フライトラボ"，そして就学前の幼児から中高生までの子ども向けの新しい教育展示室で調査を行いました。現在，国立科学博物館では，"ラウンチパッド"でスティーブンソンが行った来館者調査をもとに，科学館における学習についての基礎研究にも着手しています。

　スティーブンソンは一連の調査を組み合わせて行いました。まず"ラウンチパッド"で家族連れの後について行動を観察し，出口で1人ひとりに質問をしました。数週間後には郵送でアンケート調査を行い，6カ月後には面接調査を行っています。その結果，子どもたちは目的なく展示室を走り回っているわけではないこと，また，利用者は展示室で過ごす時間の81％を家族や他の利用者とのやりとりにあてていることがわかりました。出口調査では家族のだれもが展示について生き生きと話を聞かせてくれ，6カ月後の調査でも展示をどう利用したかはもちろん，展示を見て感じたことも思い出せました。つまり，この調査は利用者が展示をどう理解し解釈したかについてではなく，展示が利用者に与えた影響に焦点を当てていました。科学教育をほとんど受けたことのない利用者が，"ラウンチパッド"を前にしても圧倒されることなく，科学知識がなくても気おくれしなかったと述べています。子どもは展示から刺激を受け，博物館へ行くことは楽しくためになる（単なる大きな遊園地でなく）と感じていました。総じていえば，この調査はインタラクティブ展示を利用した人の記

憶や感情が持続することを示しています。けれども博物館での経験がもとで科学に積極的な姿勢をもつようになったと述べる利用者が多い半面，そこに科学に対する態度や理解の変化を読み取ることは困難です。つまり，この調査は"ラウンチパッド"が来館者の感情面に長期的な影響を与えたことを明らかにしましたが，認知面にどのような変化をもたらしたかは示していないのです。

インタラクティブ展示の効果は何なのか，そして一般の人々は科学をどのように理解するのか。こうした問題について理解を深めていくために，理論だった幅広い議論を行っていく必要があると，スティーブンソンは提言しています。たとえば，ハンズ・オン展示を従来型の展示や実物資料の隣に設置したほうが効果的なのか，それとも研修を重ねた解説スタッフのいる独立したインタラクティブ系展示室に設置したほうが効果的なのか。スティーブンソンは国立科学博物館の教育部長でしたが，彼の後任のジャクソンは，スティーブンソンの研究を早急に継承していく必要があると述べています。博物館で楽しく過ごし，その体験を覚えているのと同時に，人は本当に何か学んでいるのか。いったい何を，どのように学んでいるのか。利用者の行動を観察することは，比較的簡単です。しかし目下のところ，利用者の行動の変化が利用者の思考や態度の長期的な変化と関連があるといえる根拠はほとんどないのです。

ほかの基礎研究も，こうした問いに答えを出すよりはさらに多くの問いを投げかける結果となっています。アメリカのフィーハーは学習手段としてのインタラクティブ展示について研究し，展示を利用した科学の学習は，経験的・探求的・説明的という3つの過程をたどると述べています。第1段階は参加することで，次に自分の体験に自分なりの解釈や説明を加え意味を与えるのが第2段階です。そして，ほかの関連した展示を使いながら，先の自分の解釈を再確認したり自問自答するのが第3段階です。つまり博物館という環境は利用者の既成概念に疑念を抱かせ，さらに深い理解へとつなぐ突破口となる可能性をもっているのです。ところでフィーハーの研究によって，今後研究が必要な分野も明らかになりました。たとえば，人は目の前の事実がそれまでの自分の認識と矛盾することがあっても，どうして自分の誤認識にこだわるのでしょうか。

このような研究を通じて，インタラクティブ展示の利用者がそこでの体験を十分に楽しんでいること，そうした体験が科学やその他の分野に対する態度を

変える可能性があること，さらにそこでの体験を長期にわたって覚えていることが明らかになりました。しかし，利用者が本当に何かを学んでいるのか，また，展示が利用者の誤った認識を補強する結果になっていないかどうかについては明らかにされていません。インタラクティブ展示を支持する教育理論には説得力がありますが，現時点ではそれを証明できる証拠はまだ不十分で逸話の域を出ておらず，インタラクティブ展示がつくりだすインフォーマルな環境での学習に関する系統的な研究は，まだ十分に行われていないのです。

学習の社会的側面

前述したスティーブンソンの研究はインタラクティブ系の博物館を訪れた家族連れを対象としていますが，その理論や研究は学習の個人的側面に関するものでした。現実には1人で博物館に来る人は少ないうえ，たとえ1人で来た場合でも博物館職員と会話をしたり展示の解説ラベルを通して間接的に対話をしています。ヴィゴツキーは，言語を共有することによって，そして，両親，家族，友人やその他の媒介物との接触によって，学習が文化的仲介を受けることが多いと考え，学習理論において社会的側面を重視しました。子どもは，直接的・間接的な経験を通じて知的発達を遂げます。そして，より多くの概念を理解するにつれて思考はより洗練される，つまりより多くの概念を理解すればするほど最大限の知性を使うようになる，とヴィゴツキーは述べています。

子どもの知的発達を助けるうえで大人の役割は重要です。博物館での学習における解説スタッフの役割は第7章で詳述するので，ここでは博物館を訪れる家族連れの学習について社会的側面を考えてみようと思います。ハンズ・オン展示の利用者で最も多いのは家族連れで，教育的で楽しい体験を求めて来館します。84年と91年のアメリカの調査では，外出先として博物館をあげる人が急激に増えており，最も人気のあるものとなっています。もし入館者数で施設の成否が測れるとすれば，インタラクティブ系の博物館は家族連れのニーズに応えているといえます。しかし，入館者数だけでは博物館での体験の質や内容，あるいは家族同士の交流や学習の全体像は見えてきません。博物館で家族連れがどのように学びふるまうのか，小規模な研究の積み重ねによってその全体像を推計しようとの試みはありますが，館種の異なる博物館やインタラクティブ

系施設を対象に体系的に行われた研究はありません。最近，フランクリンインスティテュートのボーランが科学館4館で家族連れの行動を調査しており，展示を利用した家族連れの学習を行動指標を用いて定義する方法を開発しようとしています[7]。この節では，欧米の博物館（その多くはインタラクティブな展示がある）における家族連れの学習に関する研究を概観しようと思います。

　ウッドは，博物館の将来を長期的な視点から考えて，家族で博物館を訪れることの重要性を強調しました。というのも，人が余暇に何をして過ごすかは，教育活動としての体験よりも子どものときの家族での余暇体験と深い関連があるからです。アメリカの調査によれば，よく博物館を利用する人の60％が，子どもの頃に家族と一緒に行った経験がもとで博物館に興味をもつようになったと述べています。これに対して，学校行事で博物館を利用した経験がきっかけだと述べた人は3％にすぎません。家族での博物館利用には，その他の場合とは異なる特徴があります。もちろん，各家族にそれぞれの目的や予定があるわけですが，欧米の来館者調査によれば，家族連れは博物館においてある一定の行動パターンを示します。家族連れの来館目的は教育と娯楽の2つですが，最大の楽しみは，展示そのものよりも公共の場で家族という親密な単位で過ごすことであるといいます。余暇利用の選択肢や費やせるお金が増えたおかげで，家族は時間を共有することに価値を置くようになっており，一緒に外出して家族の絆を強めています。家族で博物館へ行く計画が前もって立てられることはほとんどありませんが，博物館は安全で，安心していろいろなことに挑戦できる環境として家族連れに人気があります。博物館利用が家族の慣例行事となっていること，それが家族の絆を強める性質があることに言及した研究もあり，たとえばマクメイナスはこう述べています。

　　親は博物館は資料や現象を通じた直接体験ができる場であると考えており，それが家族全員で博物館へ行く動機になっています。さらに，それが家族1人ひとりの興味関心に合った内容であれば，……博物館へ行く計画は家を出る前から成功が保証されることでしょう。

---

[7] この研究の成果が1998年に出版されている。'Family Learning in Museums', *The PISEC Perspective*（PISEC刊）

これまでの調査研究は，博物館での家族連れの行動（たとえば家族同士の交流，時間配分や来館目的）や学習の特質に焦点を当ててきました。調査の結果，館種にかかわらず家族連れはある一定の行動パターンを示し，家族連れ以外のグループの行動パターンと異なることがわかりました。以前の調査ではある特定の展示装置を利用している家族連れの行動を記述するのが主でしたが，最近の調査では博物館全体での家族連れの行動を検証しています。たとえばダイヤモンドは科学館で家族連れの学習行動を調査し，1家族あたり平均62種類の展示装置を利用し，2時間以上を過ごしていると報告しました。また展示装置を利用する前には解説ラベルを読まないのが普通ですが，うまく使えなかったときや利用後にも関心が残る場合には読むといいます。さらに子どものほうが展示装置を利用する傾向がある一方で大人のほうがラベルや解説を読む傾向にあること，館内で過ごす時間の80～90％を展示の見学に費やし，残りの時間を，カフェやショップ，トイレに行ったり他のメンバーを待つことに使っていることもわかりました。

　イギリスのクリーソープスに，そこから見える河口についての展示をもつ小規模のディスカバリーセンターがあります。そこで最近行われた調査によれば，利用者が1つの展示装置に費やす時間は平均44秒で，施設全体の利用時間は平均21分（5～50分のばらつき）でした。この施設は29種類のインタラクティブ展示装置しかない小さなものですが，この調査結果は利用者の学習の質について大きな疑問を投げかけています。つまり，娯楽面でも教育面でも展示に大変満足していると利用者はいうものの，これほどに短い利用時間で，いったい何を学んでいるのでしょうか。調査の結果によれば，利用者は展示を見ていくにつれて利用する展示を選ぶようになり，選んだものを時間をかけて見るようになるといいます。

　もちろん，博物館や科学館で費やす時間は展示の規模によるので，小さな施設で2時間過ごしてもらおうというのは無理な話です。フォークは自然史博物館2館において調査した結果，家族連れの時間配分を4段階に区分しました。
　第1段階：オリエンテーション。博物館の環境に慣れ親しむ。3～10分。
　第2段階：熱心に展示を見る。集中して展示を見学，利用する。25～30分。
　第3段階：ぶらぶらと展示を見学。展示をざっと見る。30～40分。

第4段階：帰る準備。ショップに行ったり，クロークやトイレに行く。5～
　　　　　　10分。

　マクメイナスは，博物館を利用する家族連れを，「興味をもったトピックや資料に関して，また博物館の職員が収集・研究しているトピックや資料について，自分たちの好奇心を満たそうと，協力して博物館の中を探しまわる狩猟・採集者集団」にたとえています。マクメイナスによれば，主に親が見学する展示室を決定しますが，その後の探求や情報収集は家族の全員が行います。つまり，見るべき展示室が決まると意識的にお互いから少し距離を置いて展示室を見ていきますが，その際，一般的には子どもが家族をリードします。また何かおもしろいものを見つけると，それぞれが家族にその情報を伝えます。子どもが親に知らせた場合，親はたいてい説明を加えますが，子どもは親が伝えた情報についてはあまりコメントしません。全員がリラックスし家族単位でまとまって行動していると，博物館での探求作業はおおむね成功するようです。

　マクメイナスは，ほかの研究者による研究をもとに，家族連れの行動を人類学的に分析しました。欧米の研究の多くが認めるところでは，博物館の種類には関係なく，家族連れの行動には非常に共通したパターンがあります。ただし，行動に見られる男女差についての見解には共通性が見られません。フォークとダイアキングは，母親は家族の中でどの展示を見るかを決定することが少なく，また母子間の交流は娘とよりも息子との間のほうが高いレベルにあると推察しています。これに対して，マクメイナスは根拠が希薄だと反論しており，理由として，母親，父親，息子，娘の全員が一緒にいる場合の研究がないこと，子どもの年齢差が考慮に入れられていないことをあげています。

　これまでの研究から，家族連れの行動について次のことがいえます。
　1．家族連れで博物館へ行くのは，かしこまらない，普段の生活の延長である。行くことが決まるのは前日であることが多い。博物館行きは，家族の絆を強めるよい機会になっている。
　2．来館目的や行動計画には個々の家族独自のものがあるが，共通しているのは，娯楽と教育を兼ねたインフォーマルな環境での学習である。
　3．欧米では，博物館の種類に関係なく，家族連れは共通した行動パターン

を示す。
  4．家族連れの行動はウインドーショッピングのようで，何かおもしろい展示が見つかるまではぶらぶらと見てまわる。
  5．親がどの展示室を見るかを決めることが多いが，展示室の中で利用する展示装置を選ぶのはたいてい子どもである。
  6．大部分の家族連れはハンズ・オン展示を利用する前に解説ラベルを読まない。
  7．子どものほうが実際に展示装置を利用する。逆に，大人のほうが解説ラベルを読む。
  8．展示の種類や来館してからの経過時間によって家族連れの行動や学習の仕方は変わる。

　こうした家族連れの行動パターンは，欧米で行われたいくつかの小規模な調査の結果をまとめたものです。調査対象の多くはアメリカの科学館や動物園，水族館など，インタラクティブな要素の強い施設で，結果から家族連れの行動には確かに共通したパターンがあることがわかりました。しかし，男女の行動の違いなどに相違もあり，国や時代による文化的な違いが反映しているのかもしれません。各種の施設を包括するような，より系統だった大規模調査が待たれます。現在のところ，同じインタラクティブ系施設でも歴史博物館や美術館での家族連れの行動はどうなのか，あるいは欧米以外ではどうなのかなどはっきりわかっていないのが実情です。
　台湾の故宮博物院で（インタラクティブ展示ではない）で，家族連れの行動に関する小規模な調査が行われたことがあります。その結果，中国人の家族も欧米の家族と似たような行動をすることがわかりました。しかし，この調査では，中国人の家族は解説ラベルを読み，「親が教える役割を果たすだけでなく，子どもも教える役割を果たしている」と結論づけています。そして，このような行動の違いは，中国で教育が重視されていること，また子どもに対する両親の期待が高いことが原因であると説明しています。

学習の物的側面

　インタラクティブ展示を開発している人たちは，展示室での学習が進むように，親しみやすくて魅力的で形式ばらず，快適で理解しやすい環境の実現を目指しています。家族連れが娯楽と教育の2つの来館目的をもつとすれば，博物館は家族が交流しながら楽しく学ぶことのできる環境である必要があります。つまり，親しみやすく人を引きつけ，生き生きとしていてわくわくさせ，ダイナミックで温かく，刺激的で考えさせるような，さらには動きと楽しさに満ちていないといけません。それに加えて人間の基本的な快適条件に気を配れば，博物館での体験の質はより高いものになるはずです。博物館において，学習にふさわしい環境を提供するために留意すべき項目は多岐にわたります。

- 入り口で博物館の目的が明示されているか。
- その日のイベントや活動がわかりやすく示されているか。
- わかりやすい館内地図が用意されているか。
- かばんやコートを預けるクロークやロッカーはあるか。
- 乳母車を預ける場所はあるか。
- 赤ん坊を背負うためのバックパックを借りることはできるか。
- トイレは子どもが利用しやすいようにつくられているか。
- 赤ん坊のオムツを替えたり，授乳のための場所が別に設けてあるか。
- 子ども向けの水飲み場があるか。
- カフェの食べ物や飲み物の値段は家族連れにとって適切か。
- お弁当を食べる場所があるか。
- 休憩用のいすは十分にあるか。
- 展示は幅広い年齢の子どもや大人が利用できるか。
- 展示は家族がみんなで交流しながら利用できるようにつくられているか。
- 展示は車いすや，そのほかの障害のある人々が使えるようにつくられているか。
- 展示はすべて，子どもの目の高さから見えるようになっているか。
- 解説ラベルは子どもが読めるように書かれているか。
- 興味をもった子どもや大人に対して，さらに詳しい情報の用意があるか。

このチェックリストは決して十分ではありませんが、利用者にとって心地よい物的環境をつくりだすために注意すべき項目です。博物館が利用者に提示するものはすべて、つまりハンズ・オン展示や博物館資料、構造物、ラベルや解説パネルなど、あらゆるものが利用者にメッセージを発信しています。効果的な展示にするには、効果的なコミュニケーション戦略が必要です。つまり、博物館のデザインのすべてに気を配り、利用者が博物館の環境を理解しやすいように、また効果的に展示を利用できるようにする必要があるのです。

オリエンテーション（導入）はコミュニケーション戦略のなかでも非常に重要な部分です。オリエンテーションには4つの要素があります。空間的オリエンテーション、これは館内の案内となるもので、利用者に博物館の構造を知らせます。次に心理的オリエンテーション、これは利用者を博物館利用に適した気持ちにさせることです。さらに知的オリエンテーションは内容の理解を促すもの、概念的オリエンテーションは関連した概念を発展させるためのものです。利用者は、空間的・心理的な導入を受ければ、知的・概念的学習も促進されます。説明文の役割については後述しますが、言語も（ラベルに書かれたものであれ解説スタッフのことばであれ）、博物館資料やグラフィック、模型やオーディオ機器やコンピューターと並んでコミュニケーション戦略において重要な役割を果たします。

大人と子どもがともに学ぶために

通常、インタラクティブ系の博物館を訪れる人の半数は大人で、展示装置の教育意図を達成するうえで重要な役割を担っています。子どもに説明したり、教えるという難しい作業を手助けしてくれるからです。つまり、大人は博物館と子どもの仲介者となるので、大人が快適に過ごせるように環境を整え必要があります（たとえば、いすを十分な数そろえたり、清潔なトイレ、カフェテリア、赤ん坊のための施設を用意するなど）。もし大人が博物館で不快な思いをすれば、子どもを他の施設へ連れていってしまうでしょう。家族内で決定権をもつ大人が博物館を楽しむことができなければ、その家族は2度とその博物館を訪れることはないかもしれません。

展示が子ども向けにつくられていると感じた親は、それを好意的に受け止め

るようです。博物館で何ができるのかを利用者に明確に示すためには，広告に載せる展示の写真から入館時のオリエンテーション，展示室全体のデザイン，レイアウトにまで気を配る必要があります。展示の大きさや構造，材料や色の選択，仕上げの質，床や照明の種類などすべてが，誰を対象に展示がつくられているのか，また，そこでどんな学習ができるのかを示すことになります。

　なかでも心理的なオリエンテーションは非常に重要です。というのも，ハンズ・オン展示という概念はまだ多くの利用者にとってなじみのないものだからです。来館者の多くは博物館で展示物に触ってはいけないと教え込まれており，大人がハンズ・オン展示を使いこなせないがために学習機会を十分に生かせない家族連れも見られます。子どもが展示を使っているのを後ろから見ているだけで，子どもの学びに手を貸したり一緒に学ぼうとしない大人が多いのはその例証です。実際，ユーリイカ！が92年にオープンした当時，こどもの博物館はイギリスではまだ新しい概念だったため，大人は子どものコートをもって展示を探求している子どもをただ眺めているだけでした。大人が子どもと一緒に体験して楽しむことができるようにするためのオリエンテーションが必要なのです。

　幼児用施設の提供も難しい問題です。幼児に適した物理的条件や学習に関するニーズは年齢が上の子どもの場合と異なるので，幅広い年齢層の人に都合がよく，同時に幼児にも適した展示をつくるのは大変難しいことです。そこで，5歳以下の子どものために専用の展示スペースをつくってはどうか，という考えがあります。大きな子どもたちを締め出して幼児のニーズを満たす場所を用意するのはよい方法のように思われますが，両方の年齢の子どもがいる家族にとっては不都合です。そこで現実的には，幼児用であるとはっきりわかるものを博物館の至るところに配置するのがよいでしょう。展示が幼児に安心して使わせることができるものであれば，親は同じ展示室内でほかの展示装置を体験している上の子どもの相手をすることもできるのです。

　子ども連れの親は，当然ながら子どもの安全に注意を払っています。費用的には5歳以下の子ども用のスペースに専任のスタッフを配置するのが効率的かもしれませんが，幼児向けの展示装置が一般の展示室に混在する場合には，それぞれの展示装置に専任スタッフを配置するのは不可能です。親は監視のない

ところに子どもを置いてはいかないので，5歳以下の子ども用の展示装置は展示室にいる親やスタッフの目が届く場所につくる必要があります。

インタラクティブ展示のデザイン

　本章の前半で触れた学習理論を考慮しながら，望ましい展示デザインを考えてみましょう。
　1．直接的，そして明確な動作や反応を伴う。
　2．目的が明確である。たとえば，身体的能力を発達させる，知識や理解が増す，感情や意見を洗練させるなど（心理—動作的学習，認識的学習，感情的学習）。
　3．使い方が直感的にわかり，解説ラベルを読む必要が最小限ですむ。
　4．広範囲の知的レベルを満足させる。つまり幅広い年齢や能力に適している。
　5．友達同士や，家族間の交流を促す。
　6．決まった正解がない。多様な成果が得られる。
　7．対象とする利用者の既得知識や理解度に関する調査に基づいてつくられている。混乱をもたらすような情報を与えない。
　8．五感に働きかけたり，多様な手法を用いて，関心や学習スタイルの異なる利用者にアピールする。
　9．利用者に疑問をもたせたり考えさせたり，課題を提供する。一方で，難解すぎて利用者を圧倒しないように，利用者が自信をもてるようにする。
　10．楽しめるうえ，以前より何かを理解したと感じさせる。
　11．デザインがすぐれていて，安全。丈夫でメンテナンスが簡単。

　ハンズ・オン展示のデザインは非常に難しい仕事です。実際，経験豊富なデザイナーでも，うまくやろうと思うよりは，あまりみっともなくない程度の失敗ですむように心がけるべきだ，と述べるほどです。もちろんこれは冗談だと思いますが，完璧なハンズ・オン展示をつくろうと必死になっている者にとっては自らの苦い経験をほうふつさせるものかもしれません。ハンズ・オン展示でうまくいったといえるのは，ウィンターボータムのいうように利用者を「何事にも受け身のボーッとしたカウチポテト族から，鋭敏な心をもった体操選手」

へと変えたときです。逆に，失敗に終わったハンズ・オン展示は，利用者に「だから，何なの？」という態度をとられてしまいます。このような失敗は，単純でハイテク技術を使わないインタラクティブ展示のみならず，往々にして（むしろ，より多くの場合）多額の資金を投じて最新技術を駆使した展示に見られます。実際問題として，シンプルなものがよい場合が多いのです！　あらゆる展示ストーリーにインタラクティブ展示を採用しようとするのも間違いです。ハンズ・オン展示は人気があるのでとても魅力的な手法ですが，ハンズ・オン展示が適さない展示ストーリーも多数存在するのです。

　効果的なハンズ・オン展示をつくるうえでの留意点は多々あります。ユーリイカ！の開館準備にあたってはデンバーこどもの博物館の経験豊富な展示開発者の協力を得ることができました。重要な助言は2点ありました。1つは軍隊並みの高い安全基準に沿うようにデザインし，利用者の予期せぬ行動に備えておくこと。その展示を使って起こりうることはどんなことであれ誰かが実行してくれるものなので，展示をつくる側は起こり得るすべての行動をを予側し，あらゆる危険から利用者と展示を守らなければならないのです。展示は最高の安全基準に従う，たとえば可動部分にはガードを付けたり，けがのもとになるようなとがった部品は使わないなどの配慮も必要です。

　利用者の予期せぬ行動に備えることが展示開発に関する第1のルールであるならば，もう1つのルールは，もし展示が壊れる場合があってもそれは博物館の責任であって利用者の責任ではない，ということです。身体的な安全も大切ですが，展示をうまく使えなかったがために利用者がイライラしたり，まごついたり，誤解することがあれば，その責任は利用者ではなく，そのような展示をつくった制作者にあります。もちろん最初から完璧な展示が完成するわけにはいきません。完成までの過程で何度も修正が加えられることがふつうです（展示室に展示する前に安価な素材でつくった試行模型でテストすることが望ましい）。展示をつくるにあたって知っておくべきことはたくさんあります。たとえば，利用者は順序に従って展示を見るわけではありません。したがって，概念上，相互に関連している展示も，ほかの展示と切り離されても独立して機能しなくてはなりません。現に，隣り同士の展示は利用者の関心を引き留めておくという点で競争関係にあります。人気展示の影になってしまったために，

ほとんど利用されない展示がよくあるのです。

　利用者は1人で来ていたり，家族連れや学校団体だったり，人数もまちまちであるうえ，なかには障害をもった人もいます。また個々人の文化的な背景や関心，理解の度合いもさまざまです。したがって，展示デザインの物的側面には大いに気を配る必要があります。展示の外観や構造，図表や色など，すべての要素が利用者の反応に影響を及ぼします。展示を動かす制御装置を何にするか，障害の種類や程度の異なる人々にどう配慮するか，人間工学，見やすさ，隣接展示との音声の競合など，すべてが細心の注意を要します。展示を動かす制御装置を選ぶだけでも大変で，滑車にするかレバーかハンドルかという選択肢があります。電気のスイッチにも多くの種類があります。コンピューターの入力装置にしてもトラックボール，マウス，タッチスクリーンなどがあります。もちろん，どんな場合にも適する理想の解答はありません。たとえば，滑車にハンドルをつけると大きな力が出せるので，大きな動力を要する展示には適していますが，ほかの展示には力が強すぎてしまうので，くぼみに指を入れて動かす装置のほうが壊れなくていいでしょう（しかし，運動障害がある人には使いにくい）。つまり，決定を下す際には，いくつもの要素を考慮しなければなりません。理想をいえば，展示の制御装置が展示で伝えたいコンセプトを強調するとよいでしょう。たとえば，てこの原理についての展示であれば，その制御装置はてこがぴったりといえるでしょう。

　展示装置は，頑丈でメンテナンス不要であることが重要です。地元で調達できる丈夫な部品を用い，理想をいえば，コンピューターやスイッチ，水の汲み上げに使うポンプなどの基本部分は多くの展示装置で共有できるように博物館内で規格化するといいでしょう。また展示装置が故障したときに修理工房への移動が簡単であれば，壊れた展示を利用者の目にふれさせずにすみます。もし動かすのが困難であれば，その場で修理ができるように容易に装置の中を触れるようにしておく必要があります。熟練した技能をもち，しかも親しみやすいキャラクターの技術者がいれば，修理の過程を見てもらうこともすばらしい教育の機会になり得ます。

文章の役割

　よくできたハンズ・オン展示とは直感的に使い方がわかるもので，難解で膨大な説明を読む必要がないものです。そうはいっても，文章やそれに伴うイラストは利用者の手助けをする点で重要な役割を果たし得ます。子どもは，何の説明も読まずに展示を利用することが多く，大人は子どもの後ろに立って説明を読んでいます。展示の使い方が直感的にわからない場合は，解説パネルなどによって，展示の使い方を明確にしなければなりません。さもないと利用者の頭を混乱させるだけの「うまくいかない」展示になってしまいます。理想をいえば，その展示装置の教育的価値と子どもの学びを手助けするために大人が手助けすべきことが説明されているべきです。そうでないとただ楽しいだけで，教育的価値の限られた展示になってしまいます。つまり説明文は，子どもが理解できる魅力ある内容であると同時に大人にとっても興味深く，大人と子どもの間で展示を介した会話が弾むようなものでなければなりません。このように説明文にはいくつもの役割があるのです。

　来館者はインタラクティブ展示の説明を読まない，という通説があります。しかし，調査の結果，そのような断定は早計にすぎることが明らかになってきました。つまり，多くの家族連れ（特に子ども）が説明を読まないで展示を体験するのは事実ですが，後から説明を読んでいるのです。特に展示を使ってみてうまくいかなかったときには説明文に頼っています。また博物館の環境に慣れてから疲れが出るまでの間は，より説明を読む傾向にあります。

　家族連れは家族行事として博物館に来ており，説明文の一部を会話に取り入れています。このように説明文を断片的に用いていることを考えると，構成が明確で，家族の会話が弾むようなシンプルな会話体の説明文が必要だとわかります。説明文の構成要素として，展示全体のメインメッセージ，つまり博物館が来館者にいちばん伝えたい概念があります。展示室にあるものすべてが，このメインメッセージと一貫性を保ち，そのメッセージを補強する働きをもたなければなりません。メインメッセージは時には来館者の常識をくつがえすものであるかもしれませんが，その場合は質問形式を用いて来館者に問いかけをするのも効果的でしょう。

　説明文の構成は重要性に応じて3段階に分けられます。まず博物館が最も重

点を置くメッセージ，次に伝えたらよいと思うメッセージ，最後に，できれば伝えたいメッセージです（段階が下がるにつれて受け取る側の数も少なくなくなると考えられます）。インタラクティブな学習環境では，最初の2段階のメッセージを伝えるくらいがわかりやすいでしょう。

　子どもが理解しやすい説明文とは，短く，専門用語を使わず，要点が厳選され，大きくてシンプルな書体を使ったものです。視覚障害のある子どもが読みやすいように，白地に黒の文字を配すのがいいでしょう。わかりやすい説明文をつくるためには，以下の4方向からチェックすることが大切です。

1. 対象とする利用者を明確に設定する。
2. 説明文を文法，難易度の点から分析する。
3. 説明文を，対象年齢の言語発達に詳しい教師に評価してもらう。
4. 最後にこれが最も重要で，実際に子どもに読んでもらって評価を受ける（できれば，展示模型や図表も一緒にテストするのがよい）。

　文章は，目的に応じてさまざまな種類が必要です。展示室の入り口で方向を示す案内板や導入に使う説明文は，先に述べた空間的・心理的オリエンテーションを促します。各展示装置に大きなタイトルを付ければ，展示のコンセプトを理解するのに役立つでしょう。また展示の内容を理解してもらうためには，展示の操作方法の説明も不可欠です。その際に用語が不適切だったり展示内容が簡潔に説明されていないと，その展示装置はつまらない，退屈，はては壊れていると思われてしまうかもしれません。展示内容に関する予備知識を提供することによって，利用者の知的理解はさらに進みます。こうした情報はレベルを変えて（たとえば展示の操作方法を説明する文より小さい文字にする，主な対象である大人の目線に配置するなど）示すことができるでしょう。この方法は教師や親に補足的な情報，たとえば学習過程を補うために展示室で実践できる子ども向けの活動や，家や学校に帰ってからのフォローアップ活動などを提案する際にも使うことができます。展示を使って子どもが何を学んでいるのかを大人に知らせることによって，退屈している親も，子どものやっていることを興味をもって観察するようになるかもしれません。

グラフィック[8] の役割

イラストも文章と同様に利用者の理解を助長したり，オリエンテーションに役立つもので，コミュニケーション戦略の重要な部分です。文字が読めない人や外国人も理解できるので，イラストはあらゆる来館者にメッセージを伝えることができます。イラストにはいろいろな活用の仕方があります。

1. 場所やテーマを示す。
2. 雰囲気をつくりだす。
3. 展示の伝えるメッセージを強調する。
4. 展示について，またはその他のサービスについて説明する。

グラフィック戦略の枠組みを決めるのにコーポレートアイデンティティー（CI）の考え方を応用するとよいでしょう。その枠組みで視覚的な統一性を保つと同時に展示のメインメッセージを強調することができ，利用者の博物館への導入もうまくいきます。だからといって，グラフィックをすべて1つのスタイルや方法に統一しなければならないわけではありません。むしろ，グラフィック作成時に全体の枠組みを決めることが重要なのです。いいかえれば，この枠組みから外れたものをつくる場合はねらいを明確にし，よく考えたうえで決定すべきなのです。反対に，行き当たりばったりでグラフィックをつくっていると見る人を混乱させてしまいます。

子ども向けにデザインされたイラストで空間的オリエンテーションや展示解説をすると親の評判もよく，つまりは心理的オリエンテーションにも一役買うことになります。グラフィックによって学習環境を演出すると概念的オリエンテーションに役立ちますし，イラストは展示装置の操作説明を簡単にできるので知的オリエンテーションを促します。まさに「百聞は一見にしかず」です。しかし，それもイラストが明確，簡潔で子どもになじみがあり，魅力があって，わかりやすいものである場面に限ります。複雑なイラストは利用者を混乱させるばかりです。

イラストが，本来意図していないメッセージを伝えてしまう恐れがあること

---

[8] 解説パネルなど，展示物以外の視覚媒体をいう。写真やイラスト，図表や図解のほか，解説文の書体や絵画的処理などを指す。

は，気に留めておく必要があります。たとえば差別的表現や公平さを欠く危険がありえます。文章の場合なら民族や性差に関して不適切な用語を使っていないかどうか，比較的簡単にチェックできますが，イラストに関しては問題はもっと複雑です。展示ストーリーの中でキャラクターを使うときはなおさらです。ある特定のキャラクターを選ぶのが難しいので，民族や性別が特定できない動物や宇宙人を使うことがしばしばありますが，こうした場合でも，そのキャラクターがある含みをもっているとみなされることがあり，理想的とはいえません（たとえば，ユーリイカ！で用いられている性別のはっきりしないロボットのスクートは男と見られることが多い）。ユーリイカ！ではキャラクターの決定の際に調査をしましたが，描き方をちょっと変えるだけで見る側の理解が大幅に変わることがわかりました。

　要するに，グラフィックは利用者を安心させたり理解を助けるという重要な役割を果たしています。展示装置とそれに伴うイラストや実物資料，模型，視聴覚教材，コンピューター装置が一貫したコミュニケーション戦略のもとに展開するためには，文章の場合と同じように，グラフィックもまた展示と同様に制作過程でテストされること（制作途中評価[9]）が望ましいでしょう。

事例紹介：ユーリイカ！のコミュニケーション戦略

　92年にオープンしたユーリイカ！は12歳までの子どもとその引率の大人が対象です。その意図のもと，展示室，教材，宣伝材料のすべてに鮮やかな原色と強烈なロゴを使用し，グラフィックや文字，展示を一貫したデザイン戦略のもとに統一しています。絵本作家のきたむらさとし[10]による「子どもに親しみやすい」巨大な子どもの像が博物館の外に置かれ，館内外の表示において重要な役割を果たしています。この戦略はベネズエラのカラカスにあるロスニーニョス（スペイン語で子どもの意）博物館に学んだもので，子どもも大人も歓迎されているような雰囲気をつくること，つまり心理的オリエンテーションを

---

[9] 展示評価調査の手法については3章で詳述。
[10] ロンドン在住の日本人絵本作家。1956年東京生まれ。71年に初めて渡英し，その数年後からイギリスで絵本づくりを始める。82年，*Angry Arthur*（邦題：『ぼくはおこった』）の絵で新人イラストレーターに贈られるマザーグース賞を受賞。

目的としています。空間的オリエンテーションを目的として，やはり，きたむらのイラストによる吊りパネルがあり，主な展示室や設備を詳しく説明しています。なかでも男の子用と女の子用のトイレのパネルは特にユーモラスで，子どもにも大人にも評判です。

　このように案内標識に関して統一した戦略がある一方で，各々の展示ではその方法に少々変更を加えています。最大の展示室である"わたしとからだ"は，なかでも最も統一されたデザイン戦略を用いています。この展示には導入部門（オリエンテーションエリア）があるほか（導入部門のある展示は館内でここだけ），タイプの異なる展示装置がいくつもありますが，展示装置やグラフィック，説明文にはどれも統一した方法が用いられています。中心的キャラクターのロボット・スクートは2次元のイラストや3次元の造形物に形を変えて現れては子どもたちに子どもたち自身についての質問をします。つまり，子どもたちを「自分自身と自分の体についての専門家」として扱います。展示室には，短時間でできる簡単な活動がいくつも用意されています。それは子どもにわかりやすい内容で，大人が見ればそこでどんな学習ができるのか，はっきりわかるようになっています。

　どの展示装置にも大きなタイトルがついていて，ほとんどが問いかけのスタイルになっており，その後に簡単な説明パネルがあります（オレンジで強調されたDo！というパネルがある）。イラストには男の子と女の子がそれぞれ同じ数使われており，民族的背景や体の大きさなど特徴の異なる子どもたちが，愛嬌のある漫画タッチのイラストで描かれています。この展示室の成功の秘密は，各展示装置で何を学べるのかがわかりやすいこと，また，それぞれの展示装置が独立して機能しながらも個々の展示装置で学んだことが展示全体として累積した効果を生むことです。ユーリイカ！の開発チームは，子どもたちが自分自身について何を知っているのかについて既存の調査結果を大いに利用し，健康教育の分野で効果が認められている方法も採用しました。展示で採り上げた質問項目は，ふだん子どもたちが自分について感じている疑問です。大人の視線の高さには，各展示に関する情報が掲げてあります。また，もっと知りたいという大人や子どものために補足的情報が展示室内の静かな場所にファイルされています。入り口に置いてあるパスポートをもって展示を見ながら書き込

んでいくこともでき，これは来館者の関心を持続させるのに役立っています。

"わたしとからだ"は視覚デザイン的に一貫した方法でつくられていますが，"ともに生きること，はたらくこと"と"発明と創造"（後に"発明・創造・通信"と改題）はそれほどではありません。"ともに生きること，はたらくこと"では，子どもたちがごっこ遊びをしたり簡単な技術について学ぶことができるように，街で見られるさまざまな場面（家，店，銀行，自動車修理工場，郵便局，工場，リサイクル施設）を再現しています。この展示は"わたしとからだ"を開発したチームより小さなチームによってつくられましたが，各場面はお互いに似てはいるものの，グラフィックや使用する言語などはそれぞれ少しずつ異なった方法を採っています。各場面には短い導入パネルがあって（きたむらのイラストによる），そこで何ができるかの説明はありますが，何を学習するかはそれほどわかりやすくありません。

この展示では，説明文とグラフィックの役割は主に3つあります。展示の使い方の説明，情報の提供，ごっこ遊びをしようとの提案です。とはいうものの，ごっこ遊びは文字による呼びかけよりも，解説スタッフとの会話から始まるほうがふつうです。ところが解説スタッフは展示がどう機能するかの説明に夢中になってしまうことが多く，たとえばお店の場面でごっこ遊びの手伝いをするよりも，レジがうまく使えているかを監視していたりします。

"ともに生きること，はたらくこと"の内容の多彩さは長所であると同時に短所でもあります。すぐそこに何か特別なものがあるのではないかという期待感と小さな親密な空間が，すばらしい学習の機会を提供しています。けれども，なじみのあるありふれた場面のなかで一貫した視覚デザイン戦略を用いて，珍しく興味を引くものを展示するのは難事で，この展示室での試みは部分的に成功しているとしかいえないでしょう。

"発明・創造・通信"は，旧来からよくあるインタラクティブな科学展示で，"ともに生きること，はたらくこと"のような親しみのわく学習環境もなければ，"わたしとからだ"のような簡潔で一貫性のあるデザイン戦略もありません。この展示では，子どもたちが通信技術を使う機会がもてるような場面が設定されています（たとえば原始的な方式を使うために無人島，遭難の信号を送るためにヨットなど）。また，それぞれの通信技術の長所と短所がわかるよう

に工夫された簡単なゲームが用意されてます。オウムのスクオークというキャラクターが説明役で登場しますが，その役割は"わたしとからだ"のロボット・スクートほど明確でもなければ目立つものでもありません。

　この展示はそれほど成功しているとはいえません。理由の1つにファクスやテレビ電話などの現実の通信機器を使ったために，非常に細かい操作説明が必要になってしまったことがあげられます（博物館での使用を考慮して機器は一応単純化されている）。また通信機器を使うために2人の人物が必要なうえ，2人がお互いに離れている必要があることも理由にあげられます。通信し合う機器同士は色付けされたケーブルやパイプによって頭上でつながってはいますが，これだけではこの展示を利用するために2人の人物が必要であることはわかりません。"ともに生きること，はたらくこと"のお店の場合と同じように，ここでもフロア解説スタッフは個々の機器の説明に精一杯で，ごっこ遊びを手助けするには至っていません。

　要するに，ユーリイカ！の成功の理由は，5歳から12歳の子どもと付き添いの大人に焦点をはっきりと合わせた学習環境をつくりだしていることにあります。館の統合的な戦略によって，ここは子どもが発見をしながら学べる特別な場所ですよ，というメッセージを大人にも子どもにも伝えています。しかし，そうしたなかでも，うまくいっている部分とそうでもない部分があります。2年以内という短い期間で展示が開発されたため，基本的なコンセプトに関する調査以外は開発の段階でしっかりとした評価を行う機会がありませんでした。"わたしとからだ"では子どもが自分自身について知っていることについて既存の調査結果を利用できたことが成功につながりましたが，"ともに生きること，はたらくこと"や"発明・創造・通信"の展示は実験的なものでした。開館後に行った調査によると，大人たちは博物館での学習環境を一応理解はしているものの，自分が果たす役割や，個々の展示内容についてもっと情報が欲しいと感じていました。また各展示の対象年齢を示す手引きが必要だと感じていることもわかりました。この調査結果は，博物館のオリエンテーション，特に空間的オリエンテーションはまだ改善の余地があることを示しています。

博物館資料とハンズ・オン展示の混在

　1章で触れたように，従来型の博物館でも次第にハンズ・オン展示が増えつつあります。元来こうした博物館の教育部の職員は，来館者が資料を手にとって学ぶ手助けをする点では経験豊富です。これまでは主に人の監視下で手にとることが許されていたのですが，最近では，どんな資料でも自由に手にとって見ることができるディスカバリールームを導入する博物館が多くなっています。最初の実験的なディスカバリールームがカナダのロイヤルオンタリオ博物館にオープンしたのは1977年のことで，一般の利用者もその展示の評価をした人も，このハンズ・オン施設は大成功であると認めました。この施設は83年に260㎡の"ディスカバリーギャラリー"として再オープンし，大人も子どもも標本や展示装置に直接触ることができるようにさまざまな手法を使うようになりました。たとえば，戸棚やディスカバリーボックス[11]，または引き出しに資料が入っていたり，「発見の道」や「触る壁」があったり，資料を詳しく調べるための実験器具が使えます。この施設では来館者が順を追って発見をするように順路を定めていましたが，調査の結果，来館者は順番通りに展示を利用するのではなく，自分の関心やレベルに応じて行き当たりばったりに展示装置や資料を選択していることがわかりました。さらに，誰かの手引きを受けて発見するのではなく，仲間と一緒に問題解決することによって多くを学んでいる様子もわかりました。こうした調査に基づいて，この展示室は86年にリニューアルオープンしました。89年にロイヤルオンタリオ博物館は"ディスカバリーギャラリー"に関する経験をまとめたマニュアルを出版し，子どもから大人までを対象にディスカバリールームを計画中，あるいは運営中の博物館に，その経験を公開しています。

　博物館にとっての課題は，博物館資料とインタラクティブ展示にふさわしい場所を，つまり両方を最高の状態で利用してもらうための配置を決めることです。従来型の博物館の展示室にハンズ・オン展示を取り入れること（あるいは

---

[11] 館により考え方や運営方法は異なるが，一般的に両手で運べる程度の大きさの箱で，触ったり間近に観察できる素材や解説をテーマごとに入れたもの。ハンズ・オン活動の基本的なアイテム。

独立したハンズ・オン展示専用の展示室を博物館のなかにつくること）は，その博物館の他の機能と必ずしも矛盾しませんが，矛盾を生む可能性があることも否定できません。たとえばインタラクティブギャラリーが資料の保存や記録のための財源を使ってしまう，ハンズ・オンという手法が実物資料を傷めてしまう，インタラクティブ展示に隣接する従来型の展示室で利用者の不適切な行動が見られる，ということが考えられます。

　ハンズ・オンという手法はどんなテーマにも適するわけではありません。単なる参加体験に解釈の方法が限られてしまうと，非常に表面的な筋書きになってしまい，歴史的・科学的事実をねじ曲げてしまいかねません。たとえば物理学はインタラクティブ展示で解説するのに格好のテーマといえますが，他の科学現象で，逆反応や繰り返しが不能なもの，反応があまりにも遅すぎたり速すぎるもの，規模が大きすぎたり小さすぎるものは，インタラクティブ展示での説明には適しません。また，科学の研究はなかなか進展せず，つまらなく退屈であることが多いのに，インタラクティブ展示が「科学は楽しい」というメッセージを伝えることで科学に対する誤解を招く危険もあります。同じように，ハンズ・オン展示を通じて歴史について考えることは楽しい半面，いつの時代でもどんな立場の人にとっても「歴史は愉快だった」ということを伝えてしまう危険もあります。バウルズがいうように「楽しげなデザインのグラフィックに囲まれて，家族がポチと呼びかけるなか，奴隷の首かせをつけて人間の極限状態を体験してみるのは，好ましいとはいえません」。つまり，ハンズ・オン展示は非常に魅力的な方法であるけれども，それだけですべてを語ることはできないのです。

　重要なのは博物館資料とインタラクティブ展示が共存できるかという問題ではなく，博物館の強みを生かして，来館者が博物館資料に対する理解を深めるようなインタラクティブ展示がつくられているかどうかです。ブルックリンこどもの博物館には，博物館にある資料の謎を説くことを目的にした"ものの不思議"という展示があります。やはり"もの[12]"という名前のロンドン国立科

---

[12] 同館地下の子ども向け展示フロアにある展示コーナー。「もの」の素材や使われる用途，文化的な違い，形と機能など，「もの」についてのさまざまなハンズ・オン展示物がある。同じ内容の展示コーナーが，後にユーリイカ！にもつくられた。

学博物館の新しい展示室もハンズ・オンの手法を用いて低学年の子どもが博物館の資料に興味をもつように意図されており，この年齢の子どもにとっての博物館入門になっています。国立海事博物館の"オールハンズ（船の乗組員の意）"展示室では解説プログラムのなかで博物館資料とインタラクティブ展示を併用し，その効果について包括的な評価も行っています。このように利用者の反応を調査して初めて，博物館は博物館資料とインタラクティブ展示の併用について，あるいはフロア解説スタッフなどのその他の手法について適切な判断を下すことができるのです。異なった手法の効果的な組み合わせが博物館資料に対する利用者の理解を助け，限られたハンズ・オン展示を利用した利用者も，博物館やその収蔵品に対して「マインズ・オン」な理解をして帰ることができるわけです。

　明確な目的をもち，その目的達成のために多様な手法を統合した展示室と，ハンズ・オン展示を後からいくつか追加しただけの従来型展示室では大きな違いがあります。しかし，博物館資料とハンズ・オン展示を併用することは，どの博物館にも関連するさまざまな問題を提起しています。

1．博物館がハンズ・オン展示を導入する理由は何か。解釈・説明の効果的手法として明確な教育的理由があるのか，それとも利用者数の減少に呼応してインタラクティブ展示の時流に乗っただけなのか。
2．ハンズ・オン展示を加えたことで利用者数は増えるのか。それとも博物館はそのライフサイクルの頂上期を越してしまったのか。
3．従来型の博物館は新設のハンズ・オン系の集客施設と競い合えるのか。
4．博物館は本来の強みを生かして博物館資料にもっと重点を置くべきなのか。
5．ハンズ・オン展示を導入した館ではハンズ・オン展示について次のことを考慮しているか。ハンズ・オン展示が館内の限られた展示面積を占めてしまう，定期的なメンテナンスを要する，寿命（ライフサイクル）はよくても5年，資料の保存や記録に必要な貴重な財源を費やしてしまう，専任の解説スタッフを要する。
6．博物館は博物館資料をハンズ・オン展示に利用するという危険を冒してもよいのか。
7．ハンズ・オン展示を加えたことで展示室の性格を変えてしまわないか。

ほかの展示室で,利用者の不適切な行動を助長していないか。
8.ハンズ・オン展示という手法がどんなテーマにも適するとは限らない。ハンズ・オン展示が歴史や科学に対する偏った表面的な理解を引き起こす危険はないか。
9.ハンズ・オン展示の利用者が博物館資料に対するマインズ・オンな理解をしたという証拠は何か。ハンズ・オン展示と博物館資料が展示室に混在する場合,どうしたら博物館資料に対する理解を深めるようなハンズ・オン展示がつくることができるのか。

構成主義理論[13]に基づく博物館と学習

　この章では,インタラクティブな要素をもつ博物館で個人や家族連れがどのように学んでいるのかを理論と実践面から簡単に見てきました。そして,博物館での体験が利用者の個人的,社会的,物的側面から成ることを示しました。従来型の博物館では,学習とは講義を受けることに等しいと考えられています。つまり,キュレーター[14]が知識がだんだんと増すように順を追ってストーリーを展開し,その専門的知識を伝えるのです。ハンズ・オン展示の場合も展示の作り手が伝えたいメッセージを明確に定めていますが,利用者が展示との相互作用を通じて,つまり誰かに教えられるのではなく自分で教育目的を発見する造りになっています。こどもの博物館の展示は子どもの生活と関連の深いなじみのある環境に設定されていたり,科学館では物理的現象の種類別に展示を

---

[13] 構成主義(constructivism)とは,哲学的な立場の1つで学習論としても展開されている。この立場では,学習は専門家の思考方法や内容をただ受け入れる受動的なものではなく,学習者自らが積極的に対象とかかわって既得概念や誤認識をつくりかえていくものであるとする。博物館においても,知識や経験の度合いの異なる利用者がそれぞれ資料や展示と能動的にかかわることで,その人なりの発見や経験ができるよう望まれる。こうした学習過程を理論づけるものとして,博物館においても構成主義の考えにもとづく学習観が採用されるようになってきた。

[14] 日本では博物館の専門職を総じて学芸員と呼び,研究,教育活動,展示開発などの多くの役割を兼務することが一般的であるが,欧米の博物館では分業体制をとるところも多く,職務に応じた呼び名がある。館によって呼び方や職務内容は若干異なるが,一般的にキュレーターとは博物館資料の研究を主とする専門職を指す。他の博物館職員として,資料の登録を主とするレジストラー,保存を主とするコンサバター,教育を主とするエデュケーターなどがいる。

配置していたりしますが、いずれにしても順序は決まっておらず、個々に独立して使うことができます。もちろんフィーハーの研究が示したように、利用者が誤った認識を得ることがあり得ます。ハンズ・オン系の科学館で利用者を観察調査した科学者の多くが悩むのはそこです。利用者が展示からどのようなメッセージを得ているのかに関してたくさんの研究が集中している理由もここにあります。しかし、利用者は経験を通じて徐々に学ぶといわれています。つまり、自分の既得知識に基づきつつも、同時に既成概念に疑問を抱かせるような展示と相互作用することによって、誤った認識が正しい認識に置き換わっていくのです。

　伝統的な学習法も発見的な学習法も、正しい知識というものが存在することを前提にしている点では同じです。これら2つの学習法は、利用者が専門家のものの見方に到達するまでの方法が違うだけのことです。つまり、来館者が誰かに教えてもらうのか、それとも自分で試行錯誤のうえで発見するかの違いです。ところが、このように学ぶべき知識自体を重視するよりも学ぶプロセス、特に利用者の関心やニーズを重視する方法があります。構成主義の考え方では、学習とは単に自分が知っていることに事実を付け加えていくのではなく、まわりの世界との相互作用を通じて自分のもつ情報や世界観を再構成していくことである、といっています。いいかえれば、人は世界と相互に作用するなかで自分で知識を構成していくのです。

　構成主義の考えに基づく博物館は、個々の利用者が、それぞれの個人的、社会的、物的な文脈のなかで、自分で知識を構成すると考えています。したがって資料を展示する際には来館者への教育的配慮が優先され、ストーリーの内容や資料のもつ社会的・政治的・文化的・歴史的背景や性質だけが重要視されるのではありません。つまり、提示された資料の解釈の方法は1つではないのです。来館者は展示室のどこから入っても出てもかまいません。各展示はそれぞれ独立して機能するようにつくられているからです。ガードナーのいう多様な知性を刺激するために、さまざまな解釈の方法が導入されています。また来館者にとってなじみの深い概念やものとの関連性も重視します。というのも、提示されたものと自分がよく知っていることを関連づけることによって、来館者は自分の知っていることを再確認したり疑問をもち、その経験に意味を見出し

ていくからです。

　つまり，構成主義の考えに立つ博物館は，展示という物的な環境のなかで利用者の1人ひとりが個人的，社会的な相互作用を通じて知識を構成することを助けします。展示がその人にとってどんな意味をもつのかは，それぞれの利用者の結論にゆだねられているのです。こどもの博物館の多くがピアジェらの学習理論をもとに，こうした構成主義の考え方を採り入れて成功を収めています。ところで構成主義の考えによる博物館とは，ハンズ・オン展示や実物資料，その他のメディア等さまざまな手法を用いて，関心や年齢の異なる多様な人の学習ニーズに対応した物理的環境をつくりだすもので，子どものみならず，より幅広い層の人々に対して意味のある博物館体験を提供できる可能性を秘めています。イギリスで最近発行された博物館教育に関する報告書『コモンウェルス』[15]には，アンダーソンの次のような指摘があります。

　「自由に探求しながら学べるような，そして疑問をもって挑戦するよう促してくれるような環境の展示室を，子どもだけでなく大人も求めているのです」。

---

[15] 1997年発行。報告の詳細については8章214ページ参照。

2章 教育的側面   63

ユーリイカ！こどものための博物館
女子トイレの案内用吊りパネル
ほかにも，男の子用，赤ちゃん用などがあり，字の読めないこどもにも一目でわかるように楽しく施設の案内をしている。
　　　　　　　　　　　　　　　　（撮影：稲庭彩和子）

ユーリイカ！こどものための博物館
展示室"わたしとからだ"2次元のロボット・スクート
スクートとともに，多様な人種のこどもたちのイラストが展示室の至るところに現れて，利用者に質問を投げかける。　　（撮影：稲庭彩和子）

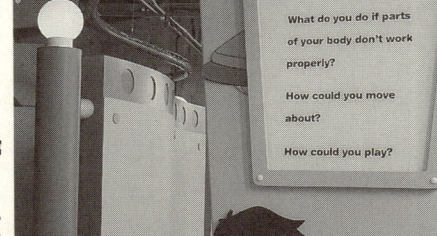

ユーリイカ！こどものための博物館
Do!の解説ラベル
実行してみて，観察して，考える，というプロセスを重視したラベル。「やってごらん！」と呼びかけたうえで，その活動の目的も明確に示されている。

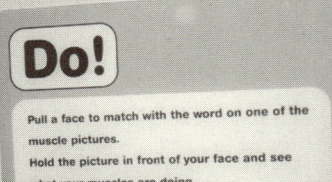

$3_章$

展示開発

ロンドン国立科学博物館
科学博物館で出している『日本語版ガイドブック』（1996）では，館内に展示室が43室あり，子どもに特に適した展示室として10室に好適マークがつけられている。扱っているテーマが産業・工業・医学など，難易度の高い展示になりがちなところを，全館において子どもたちの興味や関心に配慮しているため，家族連れの利用者があとを絶たない。

キュレーターと学芸員

欧米のキュレーターは，日本の学芸員と同義とされるが，実はそれほど単純ではない。キュレーターは主に収蔵資料に関係した専門職で，ほかにはたとえばエデュケーター（教育担当），リサーチャー（研究担当）などが，それぞれ博物館に関する仕事を分業する。日本の学芸員は上記の3つを兼ねたような仕事で，これが「雑芸員」と呼ばれる所以だが，この呼称ではまるで仕事が雑なようである。琵琶湖博物館では，学芸員資格のない職員を学芸技師と呼ぶ。で，「学」と「芸」しかない「学芸員」より，さらに「技」を持っている「学芸技師」のほうが偉そうだ，というつぶやきも。たかが職名されど職名といったところか。カッコよさそうなキュレーターという呼称は，日本では美術系のフリーの方が好んで使うようだが，普通の博物館や美術館ではあまりなじみがない。「キュレーター」を冠した本の取材を受けた際「私はキュレーターではない」と答えたら「"学芸員"より"キュレーター"のほうが本が売れる」と出版社から申し入れがあったとのこと。思惑はさまざまである。

（芦谷美奈子）

3章 展示開発

　この章では，ハンズ・オン展示の開発の方法を検証し，特に展示の企画段階，制作途中，制作後に，評価[1]という工程を加えることの重要性を明らかにします。

はじめに

　展示開発者とは，展示の構想・展示ストーリーを組みたて，解説パネルを書き，インタラクティブ展示をデザイン，制作し，展示の利用説明やグラフィックをつくり，展示で使用する実物資料や照明，色遣い，材料などを選択し配置するなど，要するに，展示の物的側面をつくりだす人です。2章で示したように，博物館の物的環境（ハンズ・オン系であれ従来型の展示であれ）は，利用者の体験に影響を与える重要な要素ですが，そのほかにも利用者の既得知識や博物館に対する期待，一緒に館に来た人の影響が考えられ，結局のところ，利用者の体験は，個人的，社会的，物的の3つの側面が相互に影響しあうことで成り立っています。したがって，展示を開発する際も，この3つの要素を考慮しながら，利用者の体験の質を高める工夫が必要です。展示を利用した人が，そこに自分なりの意味を見出すことができるような物的環境を提供することが，展示開発者の役割です。

　ハンズ・オン展示のデザインと開発で最も重要なのは，利用者層にとって適切な展示目的を設定することです。展示開発の過程は，展示のおおまかなコンセプトを決定し，それを伝えるためにどんな展示装置が考えられるのか，その展示装置を使ってどのような活動が可能なのかを考えることから始まりますが，各展示装置の案を煮つめていくに従って，想定される利用者層に見合った

---

[1] 展示やプログラムなど，博物館が行う活動の効果を，利用者の意見を採り入れながら検証すること。博物館が自らの実践を振りかえり，自己点検を行う活動。

展示目的を設定することが必要になります。しかもそれは達成したかどうかの測定が可能な目的でなければなりません。たとえば，身体的活動や楽しさ，行動や感情，考え方や理解などに関連した目的が考えられるでしょう。明確な目的がなければ，展示の効果を測ることは不可能です。目指すべき結果が定められていてこそ，それに照らし合わせて利用者の感情的，認知的，身体的反応（つまり，利用者がどう感じたか，何を学んだか，どう動いたか）を評価することができるのです。

　展示開発の過程で特に重要なのは，展示がどのように利用されるかを常に考えておくことです。伝統的な博物館の展示開発では，展示そのものが重要視されるため，展示開発の責任を負うのはキュレーターで，デザイナーと相談することはあっても，通常教育担当の職員は展示開発の過程から除外されます。この場合の展示の目的は（もし，あればの話ですが）主に資料の安全性や博物館学的な重要性で，展示がどう利用されるか，そこで利用者がどんな経験をするかには注意が払われません。こうして，伝統的な博物館の典型といえる，学術的で展示物重視の展示が生まれるのです。『コモンウェルス』[2] によれば，1996年現在，展示やイベントを開発する際に教育的な配慮をしているのは，イギリスの博物館の33％にすぎません。

　最近できた博物館，特にインタラクティブ系のディスカバリーセンターでは，もっと利用者のことを考慮して展示が開発されています。開発の過程ではさまざまな技術や知識を必要としますが，なかでも核となるのは，展示がどのように利用され，どんなメッセージを伝えるべきかについて明確な教育目的をもった人です。展示開発者は，展示で扱う情報の正確を期すために，学術専門家や，特に実物資料を伴うときはキュレーターと相談する必要がありますが，同時に，想定される利用者の意見を聞くことが重要です。たとえば，展示内容の企画段階には，利用者が展示を楽しく利用できるか，そして，展示が伝えようとしているコンセプトを理解できるかどうかを調べたり，その後も展示の制作や設置など，開発の各段階で利用者の声を聞いていきます。また，資金提供者をはじめ，展示の内容やデザインに関心をもつ関係者たちの意見を聞くことも必要です。

---

[2] 2章62ページ脚注15参照。

3章 展示開発 69

　展示開発の過程をメッセージの伝達にたとえるならば，展示開発者はメッセージの発信者です。発信者は各分野の専門家と相談しながら，発信するメッセージを学術的に正確なものにするとともに，そのほかの関係者の要求も満たすように工夫します。ところが，メッセージの伝達には障害がつきもので，伝達の過程で情報が混乱する恐れがあります。たとえば，利用者は展示が伝えようとするメッセージを理解できないかもしれません。そこで，受け手がメッセージを読み解く際にできるだけ妨害が入らないように工夫しながら展示にメッセージを込めることが，展示開発におけるデザイナーの役割です。つまり，展示を利用した人が，そこに自分なりの意味を見出せるように，しかも，その意味が展示開発者の意図にできるだけ近いものになるように展示をデザインするのです。展示利用者の経験は，デザインという物的側面だけでなく，社会的，個人的側面の影響も大いに受けるので，展示開発チームは利用者の経験をすべてコントロールできるわけではありません。つまり，メッセージの伝達は科学的な正確さで行うわけにはいかないのです。しかし，来館した個人やグループの社会的，個人的側面がどうであれ，利用者が自信をもって探求できるような環境をつくりだすことが，デザイナーには求められています。

　草創期の科学館でつくられたハンズ・オン展示の多くは科学研究者が開発したもので，科学の探求の楽しさを共有し，一般の人が科学に対する理解を深めることを目的にしていました。エバンスはイギリスの多くの科学館に影響を与えた人物ですが，自分自身やテクニクエストのビートルストーン，エクスプロラトリーのグレゴリーを称して「ワンダースミス（驚きの製造人）」といっています。こうした草創期の科学館は，オッペンハイマーのエクスプロラトリアムでの成功と，その展示案を掲載した『クックブック』という本の影響を強く受けたもので，利用者の経験を重視するというよりは，主に展示装置そのもの，つまり科学現象の探求自体を重視していました。事実，オッペンハイマーは，展示の対象者を設定する考えには否定的な態度を示していました。エクスプロラトリアムの展示装置は多様なレベルの人に適するようにできているうえ，来館者が2～3時間を過ごすのに十分な展示装置（400種類以上）があるので，対象を設定する必要はないというのです。

　エクスプロラトリアムでは，展示装置のデザインは館内で行い，そこで「た

くさんの遊び，学び，議論，実験，そして修正」を行いながら試行錯誤が繰り返されます。展示予算のおよそ80％が開発のための研究や企画にあてられ，実際の制作費は20％にすぎません。展示は共同で開発されるため，たくさんの人々が提案をしたり，アイデアを提供したりしますが，皆での議論を経た後は，1人の担当者が展示を考え，制作するのがふつうです。展示開発の過程でアーティストが重要な役割を果たすのも特徴で，オッペンハイマーによれば，それは「単に美しいものをつくる目的ではなく（もちろんそうした効果もありますが），ものの性質についてアーティストは物理学者や生物学者とは違った発見をするからです」。展示装置のコンセプトが決まると，次に廃品などを利用して試行模型をつくり，展示室内で評価を行います。展示の機能や開発者の好みによって展示のデザインが決定されるので，各展示装置の間で大きさや色，形の標準化はしていません。展示室内での評価と，その結果を受けての修正を経ながら，だんだんと展示装置ができあがっていきます。こうした試行期間を経ずに，館内の制作工房から完成した展示が一気にできあがってくることはほとんどありません。

　こうして開発した展示装置は非常に人気があり，エクスプロラトリアムのような草創期の科学館は成功を収めました。ところが，最近のイギリスのハンズ・オン系博物館では正反対の方法で展示の開発をしています。というのも，イギリスの施設では，うまく動いて，見た目が美しく，解釈や維持のためにできるだけ人手のかからないインタラクティブ展示が求められているからです。一方，ハンズ・オン展示を試みるうちに，インタラクティブな環境で利用者がどのように学び，行動するのかについて，本格的な研究が急速に発展してきました。現在，アメリカの先行事例に多くを学びながら，イギリスでも新たな研究成果が生まれています。イギリスでハンズ・オン展示が発展してきたここ10年ほどの間に，新たな技術をもった専門家たち（展示開発者，デザイナー，制作者，エバリュエーター[3]など）が誕生しています。

---

[3] 評価研究の専門家。大規模な博物館では，館内にエバリュエーターを雇っているところもあるが，大学の教員（教育心理学や社会学，心理学などの分野が多い）やコンサルタントとして活躍する個人や企業が，プロジェクトごとに参加して評価を行うことも多い。

イギリスにおける展示開発

　イギリスの展示開発の方法は次の3種類に大別されます。
　1．展示の企画，デザイン，制作のすべてを博物館内部職員が行う。
　2．展示の企画は博物館内部の職員が行い，デザインと制作を外注する。
　3．展示の企画，デザイン，制作のすべてを外注する。
　展示のデザインや開発，制作，そして評価の一連の過程を内部の職員がすべて行い，独自の展示装置を開発しているハンズ・オン系施設もあり，テクニクエストはその1例です。テクニクエストの展示開発過程は，エクスプロラトリアムのものと似ていますが，テクニクエストでは見た目を重視し，展示の外観がすべて統一されている点がエクスプロラトリアムと異なります。テクニクエストでは，展示開発の技術を何年もかけて培ってきましたが，今では開発した展示を，展示開発の専門技術をもたない他の機関に販売するまでになっています（この収入は，館で展示開発の専門家を雇うためにあてられている）。同様に，サイエンスプロジェクト社もイギリス国内で多くの科学館（巡回展である"ディスカバリードーム"など）を運営するとともに，ほかの科学館への販売用の展示を制作しています。
　テクニクエストやサイエンスプロジェクト社のように，ハンズ・オン系の博物館が展示開発にかかわる一連の技術を保有することはまれです。むしろ，館内に小さな展示開発チームをつくり，必要に応じて外部の専門家を雇うほうが，イギリスでは一般的です。たとえば，ロンドン国立科学博物館は，当初はすべての展示を館内の職員が開発していましたが，現在では，展示の開発と制作の多くを，1社，もしくは複数の展示制作会社に外注しています。国立科学博物館によれば，インタラクティブ展示の制作を業者に委託する際は，博物館が展示開発の目的と手法を明確にもつこと，そして，期日通りに予算内で効果的な展示をつくるために，業者と対話を密にすることが重要とのことです。
　ハンズ・オン展示を用いた学習の場を提供したいと願ってはいても，独自に展示を開発するだけの専門知識と財源をもたない小規模な博物館や科学館では，展示業者から展示を購入しています。たとえば，エルスカー・ヘリテイジセンターにある"パワーハウス"（発電所の意）は，外注のストーリーライタ

ー，デザイナー，展示制作者の3者によって開発されました。このように，展示開発に関するさまざまな技術を有する専門職が発達してきており，個人や企業で，または科学館や博物館，大学で活躍しています。

　新たにハンズ・オン系施設を計画中の組織で，内部に独自の展示開発チームをつくる技術や経験，財源があるところはほとんどありません。すると，多くの職員が十分な経験のないままハンズ・オン展示の開発にかかわることになり，その結果，同じ失敗が何度も繰り返されてしまいます。こうしたハンズ・オン系の博物館には，展示開発に関するリスクをいかに減らし，伝えたいコンセプトを効果的なインタラクティブ展示に結実させるかという課題があるのです。たとえば，デザイナーと制作者の間で確執が生じることがあります。というのも，デザイナーは，全体の演出を考えるものの，個々の展示装置の制作は外注することが多く，制作者は案を出しデザインを起こし，効果的な展示装置を制作しますが，デザイナーに比べると全体への配慮が足りません。デザイナーが実現不可能な案をつくったために，制作の際に制作者が一からやりなおさなければならない，ということもあるのです。

　展示デザインだけでなく，展示ストーリーの作成や展示品の入手，展示品の配置までを業者に任せる博物館も多くあります。こうした展示デザイン会社ではデザイナー以外にもさまざまな分野の専門家を抱えており，必要に応じてさらに外部の専門家を使うこともあります（これは建設工事など下請け業者を活用するのに似ています）。つまり，たくさんの人から成るチームが，デザインや解説に関する企画書をインタラクティブ展示に形づくっていくわけです。博物館が業者にすべてを任せてしまう利点として博物館側のリスクが軽減されること，さらに開発過程のすべてを1業者に委託し，必要に応じてその業者が制作業者を探すことになれば，効率が非常によくなることがあげられます。

　しかし，この方法には多くの問題も潜んでいます。第1に，館内に職員を新たに採用しないですむかわりに，費用は高くつきます。デザイン業者は開発や制作のあらゆる段階で多額の料金を請求し，下請け業者分の手数料もとるからです。第2に，博物館が用意した展示目的があいまいだったり，館が開発の主導権をもっていないと，博物館が最初に意図した展示メッセージが途中でゆがんでしまう恐れがあります。第3に，展示デザイナーは専門職ではありますが，

教育者でもエバリュエーターでもありません。展示業者のなかには，教育や評価の分野の専門知識をもっていたり，専門家を雇うところもあるものの，博物館が注意を怠ると教育的観点が抜け落ちたり，評価の工程が省かれる懸念もあります。たとえば，展示デザイナーの多くは評価の必要性を認めず，プロとしての自分の経験に頼る傾向が強いので，博物館が別に教育や評価の専門家を雇ってデザイナーの主観を取り除くようにしたほうが効果的な展示が生まれます。

　これまでの施設の経験を集約すると，博物館が展示の企画書をつくった後で入札を行い，1社に展示ストーリーの作成からデザイン，展示品の調達，展示の設置までを任せるのは簡単なやり方ではあるけれども，その方法では必ずしも展示の成功は保証できません。展示デザイン過程のあらゆる局面において，教育面，学術面，安全面がきちんと考慮されているか，博物館が業者を監督することが必要です。そのためには，展示の開発・制作の監理専任のプロジェクトマネジャーを置くか外部のアドバイザーに委託する必要があるでしょう。すべてを業者1社に任せるより効率は悪いかもしれませんが，博物館が展示開発の過程で主導権を保ち，完成した展示に責任をもつには重要なことです。こうした方法は，最近のイギリスの大型展示開発では広く採用されています。

事例紹介：ユーリイカ！における展示開発

　1992年7月に開館したユーリイカ！こどものための博物館では，展示の開発にあたって多様な方法を採用しました。まず，館長とデザイン部長に教育普及部長である私（筆者）の3名が核となる展示開発チームを編成し，1990年末の3カ月間で前任の館長がつくった展示の企画書（この企画書は，前館長が世界中の科学館やこどもの博物館を見学して作成した）を検証し，さらに独自の案やコンセプトを加えました。次の作業は，詳細な展示開発データベースをつくり，すべての展示のねらいと目的，対象とする利用者層，展示を使って行う活動についての情報を入力することでした。後に，このデータベースは，利用者が各展示でどれくらいの時間を費やしているのか，1人でもしくは何人かで展示を体験しているのかを調べるほか，技術面の詳細をまとめるのに役立ちました。

　展示開発が進むにつれて，次に採用されたのが，デザイン部にグラフィックデザイナー1人と教育部に2人の職員でした。また，デンバーこどもの博物館

の副館長が，91年に3カ月間支援にきました。教育部が子どもたちに展示企画の評価をしてもらったり，教師や研究者への聞き取りを行う一方で，デザイン部は展示のデザイン会社と制作会社を決める準備を進め，全体の企画書ができあがったところで，まずデザイン会社を，次いで制作会社を指名しました。こうして，92年7月の開館時に設置した展示はすべて，館外で制作されたのです。博物館に技術系の職員を置いたのは開館直前で，その役割は展示の制作ではなく，維持管理でした。

開館後の観察による調査から，展示によって利用者の体験の質に明らかな差があり，教育目的が明白なものとそうでないものがあることがわかりました。展示開発チームの1人が指摘するように，これは各展示室の開発手法が異なるためと考えられます。たとえば，健康教育を扱った"わたしとからだ"展示室は，イマジネーション社というデザイン会社1社が開発しましたが，ここのデザイナーには，子どもが自分自身について何を感じ何を知っているのか，既存の研究に基づいた情報が与えられ教育目的が明確に示されていました。すぐれた健康教育を実践しようと願ったユーリイカ！の教育部が，その分野の専門家から広く助言を求めていたのです。また，完成した展示が開発チームの意図に近づくように，イマジネーション社の作業の進行を丹念に監理しました。この展示は，博物館とイマジネーション社との密な協力関係が実を結んだものといえます。

"ともに生きること，はたらくこと"の場合は事情が異なりました。この展示は，街の広場周辺に，家，店，銀行，自動車修理工場，工場，リサイクル施設，郵便局が並ぶという設定でした。館側では，各構成場面を教育部の担当者が分担して学習目的を設定し，業者については，各場面ごとに別々の若いデザイナーを採用したのです。これは"わたしとからだ"でイマジネーション社がすべてのデザインを一貫して行ったのとは違って，各場面にバラエティーをもたらそうとの意図で，実際，それは達成されたといえるでしょう。しかし，それぞれの構成場面の内容，デザインを館側が監理したにもかかわらず，かなり短い工期で完成させなければならないという圧力もあって，成功している部分とそうともいえない部分ができてしまったのです。

ユーリイカ！のデザイン部は小世帯ながら，展示デザインの全体を監理し，

発注先のデザイナーの企画を調整したり，館内の共用設備やオリエンテーションエリアのデザインを担当したほか，技術面についてロンドン国立科学博物館に助言を求めながら，"発明と創造"展示室のデザインを手がけました（後に"発明・創造・通信"と改題）。つまり，この展示に関していうと，外部デザイナーの監理が主な仕事であったほかの展示と異なり，ユーリイカ！のデザイン部が直接開発に携わったのです。このようにユーリイカ！では展示開発にさまざまな方法を採用しましたが，展示開発チームの主な役割は，外部スタッフが理解できるようにデザインや教育目的をまとめた企画書をつくることと，それに照らして作業の進行を監理をすることでした。

展示評価

利用者がとまどうことなく読み解けるように，博物館が伝えたいメッセージを展示にうめこむことが展示デザイナーの役割であるならば，展示評価という工程は，デザイナーが利用者からフィードバックを得る唯一の方法です。コミュニケーションは双方向で成り立つものなので，利用者による評価を行ってその声に耳を傾けなければ，展示の成果を検証することはできません。博物館での利用者調査[4]が，さまざまな状況下で，利用者の体験の質や博物館が利用者に与える影響を幅広く研究するのに対して，展示評価はもっと限定的で，特定の展示がその目的を達成しているかどうかを検証するものです。利用者争奪戦が激しくなっている昨今，評価を行いながら，利用者の要望や期待に見合う展示をつくることが求められます。また，博物館の説明責任（アカウンタビリティー）が問われるなか，展示評価の結果を示すことによって，資金提供者である財団やその他の関係者に，博物館がその目的を果たしていることを説明することもできるでしょう。

最近アメリカやイギリスで展示評価が増えているのは展示業界が急速に専門化した結果で，博物館が情報を効率よく利用して，対象を設定した効果的な展

---

[4] 利用者調査と展示評価調査は，観察や面接など手法の点では類似するが，研究の目的や焦点が異なる。前者が比較的大規模な調査によって利用者の行動や学習を研究し一般的な原則を導きだそうとするのに対して，後者は小規模な調査によってある特定の課題を解決しようとするものである。

示をつくる助けとなっています。利用者の体験に焦点を当てた展示評価は，博物館職員が利用者の期待やニーズに目を向け，館内部の事情や展示物至上主義から脱却するきっかけになります。ほかの博物館がみなやっているから，すでにわかっていることを確認したいから，または，すでに決定したことの裏付けのために評価研究を始めるのでは，お金をつぎこむに値しません。評価の成功の秘訣は信頼できる質の高い情報を集め，たとえ結果が期待通りでなかったり，受け入れがたいものであっても，その成果を実践に生かすことです。結果が有効（正確）で，信頼できる（繰り返し行われた調査結果と一致する）ものならば，その情報は展示開発にとって有益なものになりますが，集めたデータが不正確で信頼性が低いと，展示開発チームは安心してその結果を生かすことができず，間違った方向に向かってしまうかもしれません。つまり，評価を成功させるためには，まず時と場所にあった最も適切な調査方法を用いることが大切です。そして，その結果は利用者の考え方や行動を反映しているとの確信のもと，自信をもって結果を実践に生かさなければなりません。

利用者の属性調査

　展示評価の成功例の多くは1回限りのものではなく，展示の開発過程に組み込まれて行われています。つまり，評価の工程の第1段階は，人材，予算，時間の制約のなかで何を評価するのかを明確にし，計画を立てることにあります。たとえば，すでに開館している施設では，現在の利用者の職業や収入，また，性別，年齢，家族構成，人種，などの特徴や，嗜好などを明らかにする大規模な調査を行うことがまず重要です。現在の利用者層の特徴を把握できれば，次に対象を絞って小規模な調査を行えるからです。この場合，無作為抽出法による量的質問紙調査[5]をするのが一般的ですが，そこからさらに対象を絞りこんだ小集団（サブサンプル）について正確な情報を得ようとすれば，サンプル数を大きくする必要があります。つまり，無作為抽出法の正当性はサンプルの数によるのであって，母集団に対するサンプルの割合によるのではありません。

---

[5] 質問と答えの選択肢から成る質問表を用いて調査する方法。回答をカテゴリー別に分けるのに便利である。

しかし，サンプルの数が大きくなるほど精度が高くなる一方で，調査の正当性はそれと同じ割合で高くなるわけではありません。そこで現実には，調査にどの程度の正確さを求めるのか，また，どの程度の回答の回収が可能なのかに基づいて，ある程度のところで妥協する必要があります。イギリスで行われた利用者調査の85％は無作為抽出された350人以下（平均279人）のサンプル数で行われていますが，信頼性のある相関を見るには，500人のサンプル数が望ましいといわれています。

博物館に来る人の特徴や考え方，行動を調査するのは比較的簡単ですが，来ない人の理由を調べるのは困難です。アメリカの研究者で500人以上を対象に大規模な電話調査をして，来館頻度別（よく来る人，たまに来る人，来ない人）に美術館に対する評価や態度を測定しようとした例がありますが，非来館者の考えを調査する際には，フォーカスグループ[6]という調査手法を用いるのが一般的です。これは，特に博物館の非利用者を対象に新しい展示を開発する際に利用されています。

利用傾向がある人と，そうでない人の特徴を明らかにしておくと，後で調査対象を絞って詳細な展示評価を行うことができます。もちろん調査のタイミングもとても重要で，展示開発の早い段階に実施すれば潜在する問題点を早期に知ることができ，訂正が可能になります。

企画段階評価

企画段階評価とは，これから開発する展示の利用対象者が，どう考え，何を理解し，どのように誤解しているかを明らかにする調査です。フォーカスグループの手法で行うのが一般的で（前述の非利用者調査と同じ），ストーリーボードやイラストを使って被験者の反応を引き出し，少ないサンプルから詳細な情報を得ることを目的とします。ユーリイカ！でも主としてこの方法を取り入れて評価を行いました。企画中の展示の内容がある程度決まっている場合なら，

---

[6] ある共通点をもつ人々を数人（10人前後が一般的）集めて行う調査。年齢や民族，興味・関心などの共通事項で集めることが多い。集団で面接を行ったり，お互いに意見を交換し合うのを観察することによって調査を行う。

従来のマーケティングの手法を利用して大規模な調査をすることも可能です。たとえば，私は，シェフィールド市にあるポピュラー音楽センターの展示に関して430件の回答規模の調査を行い，関心の度合いを調べたことがあります。

制作途中評価

制作途中評価とは，企画中の展示装置の試行模型をつくった段階で，それに対して利用者がどのように反応するかを調査するもので，既存の展示室で，もしくは展示室以外の場所で実施します。展示開発の初期の段階でこうした評価を行うことで，展示のねらいや目的を利用者が理解するか，説明文はわかりやすいか，照明は適切か，人間工学の要求する条件にかなっているか，展示の制御装置は対象とする利用者に適しているか，また利用者がその展示に好意的かどうかを明らかにできます。繰り返しになりますが，展示の開発段階で評価を行って問題点を見つけ修正できれば，展示装置が完成してから修正するよりもはるかに経済的です。展示の利用対象者層を明らかにし，対象となる各層から無作為に25～30人のサンプルを抽出すれば，この種の評価に十分な情報が得られます。もちろん，調査の後に展示装置の修正が生じたならば，そのたびに，繰り返し制作途中評価を行う必要があります。

総括評価

総括評価は展示の設置が終了した後で利用者が実際にどのように展示を利用しているかを調べるもので，もし問題が明らかになれば展示の改善へと発展します。実施するには最も簡単な方法ではありますが，完成品のやりなおしとなるので費用はいちばんかかります。質問紙法，自由回答方式の面接法，構造化手法による面接法，観察法，追跡法など，さまざまな調査方法がありますが，特に観察法と追跡法[7]は，利用者のたどる順路や展示への導入の成否，展示の吸引力と持続力[8]を知るのに効果的です。評価の専門家には，数種類の方法を併用することで，より厳密で信頼性の高いデータを得ることができると述べる

---

[7] 展示室内で利用者のあとをついて回り，その行動（順路，費やした時間，行ったこと，会話など）を観察する方法。

人もいます。たとえばマクメイナスは，いろいろな評価手法を併用し，それぞれの調査結果の相関を見て信頼性の高い結果を導き出しています。バーミンガム市博物館の民族学ギャラリーにおいて，マクメイナスは少なくとも9種の手法（出口調査，観察法，追跡法，利用者の書いたコメントの分析，展示の長期的記憶についての調査など）を用いて利用者の属性，利用頻度と利用パターン，展示が利用者に与える感情的，知的な影響，そしてインタラクティブなビデオ展示の利用法について調査しました。クリーソープス・ディスカバリーセンターでの利用者の行動研究もこれに類似したもので，観察法，追跡法，面接法，利用者の会話記録など，一連の手法を用いています。

このように展示の評価は開発に必要な情報を提供してくれるもので，その方法も多様です。現在の利用者，あるいは対象となりうる利用者の属性分析をしておくと，後に利用者を各層に細分化した小規模なサンプルでの調査が可能になります。多くの場合，開発の早い段階で展示の評価をすれば，変更にかかる費用は少なくてすみます。しかし，展示評価は，1回こっきりのものではなく，展示の開発工程に組み込まれたものでなければなりません。当然ながら，何回も評価を繰り返すほど正しい結果が得られるし，多様な手法を併用すれば，いっそう信頼性は高くなります。

事例紹介：ユーリイカ！における展示評価

ユーリイカ！で行った展示評価は大部分略式のものでした。開発のプロセスが断片的なうえ，展示開発チームの規模が小さく，しかもチームの結成から開館までの間がとても短かった（22カ月）ためです。しかし，ユーリイカ！には地元の小学校の支援があり，展示開発期間中に教師が1週間に1度博物館に派遣されていたので，何か展示案が生まれると，すぐに教室に持ち帰って子どもに評価してもらい，結果をフィードバックしてもらえました。地元の教育委

---

[8] 展示装置の利用者の注意を引きつける力と，いったん引きつけた注意を持続させる力のこと。吸引力は強いが持続力の弱い展示装置が多いと，利用者は展示の間を行ったり来たりするだけで，展示をじっくりと利用することがない（ピンボール効果）。

員会も協力的で，コールダーデール地域の学校をいくつか研究校に指定してくれました。都心校，郊外校，裕福な階層の多い地域の学校，低所得層の多い地域の学校，マイノリティーの子弟が多い学校，養護学校などが選ばれていました。

ユーリイカ！での展示評価は，パリのインベントリアムでの経験をもつトーマスの指揮で行われました。インベントリアムは4年にわたってさまざまな手法で評価をした結果を反映させたため，ラヴィレット科学産業都市のなかで最も成功をおさめた展示施設です。そのインベントリアムと同じように，ユーリイカ！でも，時間と予算の制約のなか，評価が断片的になることは避けられなかったので，企画段階評価に焦点を絞り，開発中の展示テーマに対する子どもの考え方を確かめることにしました。最初に行ったのは既存の研究成果の収集です。"わたしとからだ"関連は，サザンプトン大学教授のウェットンによる「くらしと健康」という研究がありました。これは健康教育公社の小学校研究プロジェクトで，子どもたちが自分自身や自分の体に対して抱いている考えを年齢別に調べていました。"ともに生きること，はたらくこと"は，現代社会を構成するさまざまな役割や職業をテーマにした展示ですが，これには貿易産業省が実施した労働に対する子どもの概念に関する研究が有益でした。しかし，この研究は包括的なものとはいえず，「くらしと健康」ほど展示テーマと直接的な関係もありませんでした。ただ，この2つの研究成果から，開発中の展示テーマに対する子ども認識（誤った認識も含めて）について知ることができました。たとえば，労働に関する研究では，店頭で繰り広げられるやりとりにまつわる子どもの理解を調査しており，市場で仕入れた果物を青果商の店主はいくらにして店で売るべきかと尋ねています。すると，経費と利益を上乗せした値段で売ることに反対の子どももいて，特に小さな子どもは，果物は再度売られることになるし，新鮮でなくなるので，仕入れの値段より安く売るべきだと考えていました。ここで重要な点は，大人は自分たちにとって当たり前なことは子どもにとっても明らかだと考えがちなことです。実際には，子どもは必ずしも大人と同じよう考えるわけではありません。ユーリイカ！では，子どもの興味や理解に関する既存の研究を活用したので，限られた時間や予算のなかで効果的に展示を開発することができたのです。

「くらしと健康」の研究でも，子どもの思考の発達に関して似たような特徴

が明らかになっています。ところで、子どもの考え方を調査するうえでの問題の1つは、子どもは大人ほど読解力や作文力が発達していないため、大人にとって有効な手法が子どもにも適用できるとは限らないことです。そこで「くらしと健康」の調査では、絵と文章を用いた手法を採りました（ドロー・アンド・ライト法）。つまり、子どもに質問を与えて、それに対する答えや関心をもったことを絵に描いてもらい、その後でその絵の主要な要素について説明してもらうという方法です。調査の途中で子どもが答えを描くのにとまどうことがあれば教師が手助けし、自分の考えで描くように促します。また、文字を書けない場合も教師が手助けをするので、文章の書けない子どもでも調査に参加できます。教師の役割は調査の仲介役として重要で、子どもが自分の視点で絵を描いたり、ことばを書く手助けをし、子どもに不適切な質問をしないように配慮しなければなりません。

「くらしと健康」が子どもが自分自身をどう理解しているのか、詳細な情報を提供していたので、ユーリイカ！ではこの研究結果に基づいて展示をつくりました。子どもが自分自身や自分の体について感じている疑問と同じ質問を、ユーリイカ！の各展示装置のいちばん上に掲げたのです。たとえば、「くらしと健康」では子どもが自分の骨をどのように理解しているかを調査しており、小学校低学年の子どもは、皮膚の下に「犬」の骨をばらばらに描くのが一般的であるという結論を導いています。この結果は文化の違いを超えて一般化できるものではありませんが、インベントリアムで行った人体の骨に関する調査も同様で、この展示では調査結果を反映させました。つまり、子どもの誤った認識や感じている疑問、子どもがよく使うことばをそのまま展示の呼びかけの文に利用したのです。

「くらしと健康」では、大人になることや思春期の体の変化に対する子どもの知識や感情は調査していませんでした。これはとてもデリケートなテーマですが、ユーリイカ！ではこれを展示に取り上げたいと考え、さらに調査を進めることにしました。そこで「くらしと健康」の研究を指導したウェットンを顧問として迎えて適切なドロー・アンド・ライト法を考案し、調査の実施にあたっては学校の十分な協力が得られるように配慮しました。調査の手順は次の通りです。まず子どもに、ティーンエイジャーがはじめて1人で外出するところ

を絵に描いてもらい，自分はどんなふうに大人になっていくのか，大人になることについてどのように考えているのか，また外出するときに何をもっていくのかを話しながら，絵の解説をしてもらいます。次に，ティーンエイジャーがお風呂かシャワーから出てきたところを描いてもらい，そのティーンエイジャーがどんなふうに大人になるのか，大人になることについてどう感じていると思うか，また，回答者である子ども自身が大人になることをどのように感じているかを教えてもらいながら，絵の説明を受けます。子どもに直接的な質問をすると仲間同士でプレッシャーを感じたり恥ずかしがってしまいますが，このような手法を用いることで，それを避けることができました。また，環境の異なる学校で調査を行ったため，文化的な背景の違いによる微妙な差を確かめることができ，その結果は展示に反映されました。

"ともに生きること，はたらくこと"については，ドロー・アンド・ライト法，子どもとの討議，スーパーマーケットその他の実地見学など，多様な手法を用いて企画段階評価を行いました。ドロー・アンド・ライト法による調査では，子どもに自動車修理工場や店，銀行，工場で行われていることを絵にしてもらい，そこで大人たちが何をしているのか，自分ならそこでどんなことをしたいかを説明してもらいました。次に，小集団で討議をさせ，「働くとはどういうことか？」「なぜ働きにいかなければならないのか」について尋ねました。次に示すのは10歳児によく見られる回答です。

質　問	働くっていうのはどういうこと？
アスマ	おもしろくないけどやること。
ロバート	パパとママが家以外の場所ですること。したくないのに新聞配達をする子もいるね。
ジェームス	努力をしなければいけないもの。お金をもらえるときもあるし，もらえないときもある。ふつうは，疲れるもの。
ジョン	難しいって感じること。
ヘレン	生計を立てること，つまり仕事。掃除みたいに家ですることもあるね。
質　問	どうして働きにいかなければならないの？

ジュリア	生きていくためにお金をもらうため。仲間をつくるため。ほかの人を助けるため。
ロバート	お金持ちになるため。人に会って話をするため。
ヘレン	退屈しないようにほかの人と一緒にいるため。子どもにお小遣いをあげるためのお金をかせぐ。ローンの支払いをするため。
ジョン	楽しいことをして，それでお金をもらうため。

　働くことに関する子どもたちの回答は，大人びたものから素朴なものまでさまざまでした。開発中のそのほかの展示場面についても同様に多様な回答が得られましたが，一方であるパターンも見えてきました。たとえば，大人社会の職業や社会的役割を描かせると例外なく自動車修理工場を男性の職場として示すなど，類型的な男らしさ女らしさのとらえ方が多く見られました。この調査結果は展示のグラフィックのデザインに示唆を与え，伝統的に男の職場とされる環境の展示に女の子のキャラクターを置いて，子どもの既成概念に挑戦してみることにしました。ドロー・アンド・ライト法による調査からは，年齢による興味の差も明らかになりました。つまり，幼い子どもは車の下に入りこんだり車を洗ったりタイヤを交換することに興味を示しますが，年齢が上がると，車を運転したり，車がどうやって動くかに興味をもつようです。ユーリイカ！の展示装置で行う活動は，こうした調査結果から生まれており，洗車の活動は小さな子どもの多くが洗車に興味があるという報告に基づいたものなのです。
　銀行の場面でも，子どもは予期しなかったことに興味を示しました。多額のお金に囲まれたいというのです。本物のお金を展示に用いるわけにはいかないので，ユーリイカ！内でのみ通用する「お金」をつくることにしました。また，多くの子どもが「壁の穴」からお金を取り出したいというので，展示に自動支払機をつくるほか，ごっこ遊びを通じて，お金を引き出す前にお金を預ける必要があることを学べるようにしました。調査中にこんなできごともありました。銀行業務についての子どもの認識を調べるため，銀行の支店長の仕事は何かと尋ねたところ，10歳児の集団は，なんと一斉に机に足を投げ出してみせたのです。調査の早い段階で多くの子どもが銀行強盗をしたいと思っていることも明らかになりましたが，これは展示のスポンサーには問題です。そこで，展示

に保安設備付きの金庫をつくり，アラーム装置を外さなければ金庫の内部にたどりつけないようにしました。子どもの考えを展示開発に利用すると，スポンサーの意向とかみ合わない恐れはあるものの，子どもの思考を研究すれば，子どもが興味をもつ分野や知識の程度，認識の誤りがわかるので，展示の適切さや利用法についてスポンサーを説得することもできます。銀行はユーリイカ！のなかで最も成功している展示の1つですが，それは銀行の場面で行う活動には，企画段階評価の結果が生かされているからです。

こうした調査から，子どもによって驚くほど理解に差があることも明らかになりました。スーパーマーケットの店長に，職員の白人とアジア人の構成比率を聞いたり，職員や客から訴えられたことがあるかとたずねる幼い子どももいれば，逆に，8歳でも工場が何をするところなのか知らない子どももいるのです。また，多くの子どもが，工場といえばチョコレートを連想していましたが，これは地元ではチョコレート工場が主な雇用主であるためでした。知識の差は年齢によるだけでなく，同年代の子ども同士でも著しいことから，「工場では何をしているの？」など展示の導入をわかりやすくすると同時に，ものごとをよく知っている子どものための活動も用意する必要があることが認識されました。

評価のために同様の調査を"発明と創造"でも行った結果，子どもは特に今日の大人が使う通信技術に興味をもっていることがわかりました。また一般的に，過去の技術や未来の技術（テレビ電話など）には無関心でも，はじめてファクスを使うことはとても楽しんでいるようでした。この結果は，"ともに生きること，はたらくこと"で行った調査結果とも一致しています。子どもは銀行の場面で自動支払機などの技術を使いながらするごっこ遊びに非常に興味を示していたのです。つまり，ふだん見慣れてはいるものの，子どもには手が届かない大人の世界にふれる機会を提供するのがこどもの博物館の成功の秘訣です。子どもに全くなじみのないもの，たとえば工場やテレビ電話などにふれる機会を与えてもあまり人気がないうえ，概念的にも理解が困難なようでした。

このように企画段階評価は子どもの興味や誤認識を明らかにし，展示開発に有効な情報を提供してくれますが，展示が目的を達成したかどうかを判断するには展示装置自体を評価する必要があります。開発途中で問題点を発見して修正できれば，完成後にやりなおすよりはるかに経済的なので，制作途中の段階

で評価を行います。ユーリイカ！でも，子どもの反応を評価するために，英国電気通信（BT）の協力を得て学校に通信機器をいくつか設置して使ってもらいました。もともとファクスは操作が複雑なものですが，制作途中評価でわかったことから，2台のファクスを使って相互にやりとりができるような簡潔な操作解説をまとめることができました。ただ残念なことに，開館前のユーリイカ！では展示装置制作を外部の業者に委託していたので，試作品を用いたテストはほとんどできませんでした。展示装置をすべて内部で制作する施設ならば，展示の試作品を用意して利用対象者に使ってもらうことができます。現に開館後のユーリイカ！では新しい展示装置をつくる際には試作品でテストをしており，来館者のオリエンテーション用の新しい展示では，開発途中の93年夏に制作途中評価を行いました。

　制作途中評価に代わる方法として，展示が完成し解説パネルもできあがってから改善する方法があります。すべてができあがってから評価を行い，その結果に基づいて修正を加える方法は，開発の途中で変更を加えるのに比べ，はるかにお金がかかります。しかしユーリイカ！の展示開発チームは"わたしとからだ"にある5つの展示装置について当初の目的が生かされていないと考えていたので，設置が終わってから一般公開される直前に外部コンサルタントに依頼して総括評価を行いました。すると，消化活動を説明する目的で作った展示装置の開発意図を，多くの子どもが誤解していることがわかりました。奇抜なデザインは子どもに人気がありましたが，展示が複雑なため，小さな子どもはそこで何が起きているのかを推測し，大きな子どもも少ない手がかりをもとに展示の意味を考えていました。端的にいうなら，展示のデザインが，伝えたいメッセージの簡潔さと逆行していたのです。このため，展示は人間の消化機能について伝えようとしていたのに，奇抜なデザインを見た子どもの多くは，この展示装置を魚かサメ，ロボットや機械であると考えていました。かじる，かむ，飲みこむなどの一連の動作も同様に誤解を招いており，たとえば，肺を意図したオレンジ色の収縮する袋を，9歳の子どもは，息を吹き込むと膨らむ吹き流しだと考えていました。

　92年7月のユーリイカ！開館後，展示開発チームと外部コンサルタントが

共同して以下の点について公式な総括評価を行いました。
 1．展示が教育目的を達成しているかどうか明らかにする。
 2．改善を目的として，人気のない展示を再評価する。
 3．成功している展示の要因を明らかにする。

　まず，利用者の属性を知るために調査をしました。これは，後でより細分化した層のサンプルを抽出して個々の展示の評価をしたり，マーケティングや展示開発のための意見を集めるときに役立つ基本データになるものです。コンサルタントが共同で600人の来館者に対する質問紙をつくり，93年夏に，600人を対象に学生を使って調査を実施しました。その結果，いくつかの驚くべき事実が明らかになりました。たとえば，利用者の25％が5歳未満であるのに，ユーリイカ！にはその年齢層を対象にした展示がほとんどなかったのです。

　次に行ったのは，個々の展示，教育プログラム，そして博物館へのオリエンテーション，特に心理的，地理的オリエンテーションについての評価でした。博物館で何をしたらよいのかわからないがために，ユーリイカ！での学習機会を十分に生かしきれない子どもがいることを展示開発チームは強く感じていました。今までこどもの博物館を訪れたことがないために，子どもの学習を手助けするどころか，子どもを過剰に興奮させてしまう親が多く，他人に迷惑をかけたり，時には展示を壊すことさえあったのです。そこでこうした問題を解決するためには，オリエンテーションを心理的見地，地理的見地から改善する必要があると考え，評価のための調査を行うことにしました。

　この評価の結果，118組の利用者のうち，少なくとも70％が入館してすぐ左に曲がり，"発明と創造"展示室に向かうことが明らかにされましたが，この展示は小さな子ども連れにとっては適切とはいえないものでした。続いて，今までにユーリイカ！に来たことのない人々に対して小規模な面接調査を行ったところ，決められた順路はいらないという一方で，展示の対象年齢や展示内容の説明が必要と考えている人が多いことがわかりました。大部分の人はタイトルを見て展示の流れを把握してはいるものの，内容に関してはほとんど理解していないことも判明しました。また，多くの人はユーリイカ！の利用が子どものためになると考える一方で，大人のためになるかどうかは半信半疑でした。ユーリイカ！は楽しさ，活動，光と色の場であると理解されてはいたものの，

こどものための博物館という概念はまだなじみが薄く，大人と子どもが一緒に学ぶことができると考える人は多くても，子どもに積極的に接していくことが博物館での大人の役割だと感じている人は，その半分にすぎませんでした。

このような総括評価の結果は，博物館へのオリエンテーションの改善に利用されました。駐車場に着いてから入場券売り場に着くまでの間，なかでも行列して待っている間に，博物館からのメッセージを伝えるような工夫をしたのです。つまり，こどもの博物館という考え方を強く押し出し，温かいフレンドリーな雰囲気で来館者を迎えます。そして博物館の空間について説明し，そこでの大人と子どもの適切な役割と行動を示し，さらに博物館が非営利団体であることを強調しました（利用者研究の結果，博物館が非営利団体なのか営利団体なのか，それとも地方自治体運営なのか，理解されていないことがわかったからです）。オリエンテーションの計画のなかで特に難しかったのは，命令的にならないように配慮することでした。発見学習の考えに基づき，ユーリイカ！では，意図的な方向づけや順路，行動規制は避けたいと考えていたので，オリエンテーションで使用することば遣いについては，開発チームから案が出るたびに利用者の評価を調べました。

ユーリイカ！で行った展示の評価が目的の調査は，限られた時間と人材のなかで開発を進めるための実践的なものでした。したがって，学術調査としての厳密性は満たしていません。調査結果は包括的というよりも，示唆を与えるという程度です。職員数や時間に余裕があれば，もっと正確な結果を出せたかもしれません。しかし，企画段階評価は，子どもの興味や理解の度合いについて貴重なデータを提供し，その結果，展示開発チームは自信をもって展示づくりにあたることができました。厳しいスケジュールのなか，しかもユーリイカ！のあるハリファクスから離れたところで展示装置の制作が行われたため，制作途中評価ができなかったのは不利な要素でしたが，利用者の属性調査から得た信頼できるデータをもとに将来の調査の方向性が明確になり，92年には総括評価を実施することができました。これはそれまでの問題点を解決し，将来の展示開発に役立つ情報を得るためには当然の論理の帰結といえる試みでした。

事例紹介：ロンドン国立科学博物館における展示評価

　ロンドン国立科学博物館の地下展示室（95年オープン）の開発に際しても，同様の評価が行われています。"もの"という展示室は，7歳から11歳までの子どもがものをよく観察し，それがどのようにつくられ，機能するのかを考えるように促すもので，子どもがそのほかの博物館資料に親しむためのオリエンテーション的役割をもっています。この展示の開発にあたって企画段階評価を行い，子どもが博物館資料のどんなところに興味を示すのかを調べた結果，博物館の役割に対する子どもの認識が明らかになり，展示室で取り上げる資料を選択する助けとなりました。また，"ラウンチパッド"を訪れた団体の協力を得て開発の途中で試作品を使ってテストも行いました。この調査は行動観察と面接法で行われ，結果はその後の開発に利用されています。また，展示室が一般公開された直後の95年の10月から96年の1月にかけては総括評価を実施しました。学校団体と家族連れを対象に60件に及ぶ追跡調査をした結果，展示を利用する時間の中央値は15分で，最高が59分，最低が1分でした。この調査では，いつ，どれくらいの時間をかけて展示を利用するかを観察し，個々の展示がどの程度利用者の関心を引き留めておけるかを明らかにしています。また，展示室のデッドスペースも特定できました。たとえば，利用者の目につかないところや行き止まり，人気のある展示の「影」になっている展示は，ほとんど利用されていないのです。

　観察に加えて，学校団体と家族連れを対象に80件に及ぶ出口調査を行い，"もの"展示室での人気を調べました。子どもの好みは体を使う機械仕掛けのインタラクティブ装置に集中していましたが，それは自分で制御できたり，友だちや家族にやって見せることができるからでした。当然ながら，動かすのが難しいものや動かないもの，説明が多すぎたり難解な展示は好まれていない様子でした。この調査では，展示室内を同行した調査員が14組の利用者集団を詳細に観察し，反応，行動，見学の順路，個々の展示に対する好みを調べていますが，その結果欠けていた安全対策も明らかになりました。

　このように，国立科学博物館では，"もの"展示室のあらゆる段階で小規模な調査を行って対象とする利用者の評価を確かめ，少ないサンプル数ながらもいくつかの研究方法を併用して信頼性の高い結果を得ています。ユーリイカ！

と同様に，さまざまな手法を用いて調査をした結果，利用者の関心や理解の度合いの全体像が把握でき，将来の展示開発への指針を得ました。ただユーリイカ！と違うのは，国立科学博物館には科学の普及推進部に評価を専門とするチームをつくった点です。このため，初期のユーリイカ！の調査と方法的には似ていますが，国立科学博物館のほうが徹底的，系統的な研究といえるでしょう。それでも，信頼性の高い学術的研究と呼ぶには調査規模が小さくて，その結果をよそのハンズ・オン系施設や外国の事例にあてはめるのは困難です。しかし，こうした研究が展示開発過程に大変有用な情報を提供してくれるのは確かです。得られたデータを論理的・客観的に解析して利用するかぎり，展示関係者の体験や主観的・本能的な感覚だけに基づいたこれまでの展示評価方法に比べ，非常に大きな前進が図れたといえるのです。

まとめ

インタラクティブ展示の開発を成功させるのに決まった方法はありません。大規模な博物館や科学館では，いろいろなデザインや制作，評価を館の職員が経験し，失敗と成功を繰り返しながら時間をかけて専門性を培うことができますが，小規模，または新設の施設では財源が乏しく，館内に展示開発チームをつくるのが難しいことが多く，かりに財源があったとしても経験豊富な展示開発者を採用しないかぎり，他館と同じ失敗を繰り返してしまいます。そこで新設館では，他館で経験を積んだ専門家を採用することがありますが，その際にも，展示デザイナーに頼むか，インタラクティブ展示装置を専門に開発している業者に委託するか，難しい判断に迫られます。実際，どちらにもよい点，悪い点があり，いずれにしても博物館が企画書のなかで目的を明確にし，その後も主導権をもって，当初設定した目的に見合った展示が完成するように，さらに決められた納期と予算内で仕上げるように監理することが重要です。そこで多くのハンズ・オン系博物館や科学館では，展示のデザインや制作を外注した場合も，開発プロジェクトの監理機能を内部にもつ（または専任のプロジェクトマネジャーを置く）ようにしています。

インタラクティブ展示を成功させるには，対象とする利用者層に展示を評価してもらうことが必須です。デザイン会社や展示開発会社は自分の経験にたよ

る傾向があるので，博物館や科学館が展示開発を外注する場合も評価の工程を開発過程の一部に組み込む必要があります。評価は展示開発の重要な要素なので，その全体を指揮する技術を博物館がもつこと，または最低でもエバリュエーターに評価を依頼することが望まれます。

　ロンドン国立科学博物館のように，エバリュエーターの特別チームを編成できる博物館は多くありません。大部分の博物館では限られた財源のなかで効果的な展示を開発する必要から，現実的な対策として評価をしています。ユーリイカ！が成功したのも，企画書を用意する段階で子どもの評価を確かめたからでした。しかし，展示装置の多くがユーリイカ！から離れた場所で制作されていため，試作品を使って制作途中評価を行うことは不可能で，特にテストもしないまま展示を完成させてしまいました。そこで，設置した後にしっかりした総括評価を行うことにし，外部のエバリュエーターに博物館職員の教育，評価のための調査手続きの計画・指導を依頼し，職員とボランティアの学生による調査を実施しました。いろいろな制約があるなかで，ユーリイカ！ではこれが最も経済的な方法だったのです。

3章 展示開発 91

**ユーリイカ！こどものための博物館
"ともに生きること，はたらくこと"展示室の銀行**
ユーリイカ！専用のキャッシュカードや小切手，紙幣があり，こどもたちがお金の出し入れなど銀行での用事と仕事を考え出しては遊んでいる。奥には金庫があり，むやみに近づくと警報装置が作動する。　　（撮影：稲庭彩和子）

**ユーリイカ！こどものための博物館
消化不良をおこした消化の展示**
食べ物の消化活動を扱ったこの展示は子どもたちに人気は高かったが，評価の結果はさんざんであった。ロボットのようなデザインが勝ちすぎたため，展示の意図するところを子どもたちはほとんど理解していなかったことが判明したのである。（撮影：稲庭彩和子）

**ユーリイカ！こどものための博物館
"発明・創造・通信"の展示室**
子どもたちが通信機器にどのような興味を示すかを事前に何度も試し，その結果から展示の構成アイテムが決められていった。

4章

財　政

テクニクエスト外観
ウェールズの首都カーディフ市にあるテクニクエスト。19世紀の建造物を改築してオープンしたハンズ・オン展示を主体とする科学展示施設。

インディアナポリスこどもの博物館

インディアナポリスこどもの博物館は常勤非常勤の職員約400人、ボランティア約1000名近くを抱え、室内展示面積だけで3万㎡を有する世界最大のこどもの博物館。一般的なこどもの博物館活動と合わせて、長期療養中の子どもたちへの出張サービス、重度の障害をもつボランティアのために専用の送迎車を所有して働く機会を提供し、世界中からの視察者を手厚く迎え入れ、大学生のインターン制度なども有する。世界で最初に設立されたブルックリンこどもの博物館を見た女性が地元インディアナポリス市内での設立を切望し、有志を募って1925年に小さな馬車の車庫を改造して開館したのがそもそもの始まりだそうだ。地元の人々を巻き込み、物心両面からさまざまな形の協力を得て、このNPOも長い年月をかけながら古ぼけた車庫から世界最大のこどもの博物館へと発展を遂げたのである。

(染川香澄)

4章 財　　政

　この章では，インタラクティブ系施設の資金づくりや収益のあげ方について考察し，あわせて損益評価指標・営業指標を通じてその経営実績を検証します。

はじめに

　ユーリイカ！こどものための博物館が多くの賞を受賞したり，1章で概観したようにハンズ・オン展示が近年急激に増えていますが，これはハンズ・オン展示が大きな成功をおさめていることの表れでしょう。利用者に人気があることが成功を意味しているのなら，確かに成功しているといえるでしょう。一方で，遊びに力点を置いた収益本位の集客施設が私企業によっていくつかつくられ成功してはいますが，それらの余暇産業はハンズ・オン系博物館と競合しようとはしてきませんでした。この点は重要です。ハンズ・オン系博物館はつくるにせよ運営するにせよ莫大な費用がかかります。この章では財政面からその存立の条件を検証していきます。

アメリカのハンズ・オン系施設の財政

　アメリカの科学館・科学博物館の財政事情は，1986年に科学館技術館協会（ASTC）が81館を対象に行った調査で詳しくわかります。これらの館のうち86％では過年度3期とも収入が費用を上回っており，しかも64％ではその期中に黒字幅を増やしています。ほぼすべての館が損益分岐点のあたりで運営されており，47％では収入金額の5％以内の黒字または赤字でした（4分の3以上では10％以内）。

　総じていうと収入の35％は事業活動からで，65％が寄付や助成によるものです（小規模館と大規模館では中規模館より助成金割合が高い傾向はあるが）。事業収入の29％は入場料収入で，大規模館ほど入場料に頼る割合は低くなり

ます。小規模館の事業収入のうち，飲食物は大したことはないのですが，ショップの売り上げが9〜15％を占めます。補助金の出所は約半分が行政機関からで，最も大きいのはどの規模の施設においても地方自治体による助成です。次に大きいのは，小規模館の場合は国で，大規模館の場合は州政府になっています。寄付の内訳は，個人6〜22％（小規模館には最重要の財源），企業6〜9％，財団6〜11％でした。

　つまり，全体的には，事業収入，行政補助，個人・企業からの寄付がおよそ3分の1ずつということになります。けれども，79年以降に開館した施設では収入の約3分の2を事業活動から得ており，86年以降開館の施設となると，その比率はさらに高くなっています。事業収入に依存する割合が行政補助や企業や個人からの寄付によるよりも高くなる傾向が広がってきており，最近開館した施設の中には事業収入だけで生き抜いていこうとしているところもあるほどですが，そこがうまく運営できているかどうかはまだ立証できません。

　こどもの博物館4館を例に90年の収入明細を比較してみましょう。なかなか興味深い事実が浮き彫りになります。

インディアナポリスこどもの博物館
　事業収入42％（入場料17％，ショップ売り上げ・レストラン賃貸料25％），個人・企業からの寄付金19％，資産運用益40％（90年度年次報告書より）。

シカゴこどもの博物館
　事業収入51％，寄付金42％（財団・企業28％，個人14％），行政補助金4％，その他2％（90年度年次報告書より）。

プリーズタッチ博物館（フィラデルフィア）
　事業収入60％（入場料・友の会会費・特別イベント参加費48％，ショップ売り上げ12％），補助金・寄付金37％，受取利息その他4％（90年度年次報告書より）。

マンハッタンこどもの博物館
　事業収入62％（入場料・友の会会費・特別イベント・プログラムの参加費55％，ショップ売り上げ7％），行政補助16％，寄付金17％（個人，企業・財団），その他5％（90年度年次報告書より）。

最も規模の大きいインディアナポリスこどもの博物館の事業収入が4館中最も少なく，40％を資産運用による収益に頼っているというのは興味深いことです。それに比べマンハッタンこどもの博物館では収入のほぼ3分の2は事業収入で，残りの半分ずつは行政補助と民間からの寄付によっています。プリーズタッチ博物館では似たような割合で事業収入に頼っており，残りの収入（37％）の大部分は助成金や寄付によるものです。シカゴこどもの博物館は財団や支援企業，個人からの寄付の割合が4館中最も高く（42％）なっています。4つの博物館を比べてみると，似たタイプの博物館ではあっても，その財源は実にいろいろなところから得ていることがわかります。ただ，マンハッタンこどもの博物館だけは公的補助の割合が高く（16％）なっています。

イギリスのハンズ・オン系施設の財政

　イギリスのハンズ・オン系施設の多くは政府機関か非営利の公益法人によって運営されており，私企業による経営はあまりありません。実はイギリスでは私企業の施設は博物館に該当しないので，公的助成を受ける資格がないのです[1]。けれどもいくつかのハンズ・オン系プロジェクトが国営宝くじ収益金[2]の交付機関である二千年紀記念委員会[3]から主要な賞を受賞しています。そのような助成を受けるには，プロジェクトの財政が健全であることを証明しなければなりません。では，ハンズ・オン系施設は財政的にみてうまくいっているのでしょうか。また，その評価はどのように行われるのでしょうか。

　行政が設置主体の場合，その施設の会計だけを，その施設が含まれる余暇サービス部門全体の会計から切り離すのは困難です。しかも国立科学博物館などのように，ハンズ・オン系の体験施設が大きな施設の一要素になっている場合にはなおさらでしょう。ロンドン国立科学博物館の"ラウンチパッド"や"フ

---

[1] 1章11ページ脚注4参照。
[2] 1章17ページ脚注6参照。
[3] 国営宝くじの収益金を交付する12の機関の1つで，二千年紀記念事業にかかわるものに対する助成申請の受理・審査を担当する。この委員会が助成している科学系施設の建設プロジェクトにはアットブリストル（助成金額4130万ポンド），バーミンガム・ディスカバリーセンター（同施設が設置される複合施設全体に対して5000万ポンド），グラスゴー科学館（3500万ポンド），エジンバラのダイナミックアース（1500万ポンド），アースセンター（5000万ポンド）などがある。

ライトラボ"，また新しく地下にオープンした展示室など，建設費は正確に算出できるとしても運営費は無理でしょう。なぜなら中心的なサービスの大部分は博物館のほかの部分と共有しているからです。それに大きな施設の場合，収入に占めるハンズ・オン系展示の利用比率を割り出すことも非常に難しいでしょう。というのも，入場料は博物館内部の全施設の利用をカバーしていて，ハンズ・オン系の展示だけを目的に来る人もまずいないからです。しかし，かりにこれらの国・自治体の施設が併設のハンズ・オン系施設の会計を独立させてあったとしても，その数字を自由に見ることはできません。

これに対して，公益法人のハンズ・オン系施設では会計の分析が可能です。これらの機関はカンパニーズハウス[4]に年度ごとに会計報告の提出を義務づけられており，その記録は一般の監査請求に応じられるようになっているからです。公表されているユーリイカ！こどもの博物館，テクニクエスト，エクスプロラトリーの会計報告を見ると，各館の財政状態を診断することができます。

表4.1に3施設の1995年度の損益計算書を示します。

この数字の単純比較は，施設ごとの状況や会計手法が異なるので，当然のことながら厳密な方法とはいえません。3施設とも収入金額の3％以内ながら欠

表4.1 1995—96年度経営成績の比較（イギリスのインタラクティブ系施設）　単位：英ポンド

	ユーリイカ！	テクニクエスト	エクスプロラトリー
事業収入	1,176,099	624,760	441,697
補助金・寄付金・企業協賛金	1,014,686	747,943	85,330
受取利息	−7,278	38,297	3,815
経常費	−1,433,577	−976,913	−541,925
減価償却	−795,114	−442,825	−6,034
経常損益	−45,184	−8,738	−17,117

出典：カンパニーズハウス提出の会計報告をもとにまとめた。テクニクエストは館提供の情報を加味してある
注記：1）ユーリイカ！の会計年度は95年1月～12月
　　　2）テクニクエストの会計年度は95年8月～96年7月
　　　3）テクニクエストの数字から第3期建設費用は除いた
　　　4）96年1月決算のエクスプロラトリーの数字は16カ月間の実績なので，比較のため12カ月のデータに調整した

---

[4] 貿易産業省の外局機関で，法人登記業務やイギリス国内の法人に関する情報の提供を行う。

損を示しており（ユーリイカ！2％，テクニクエスト1％以下，エクスプロラトリー3％），財務実績は大きく異なることがわかります。この実績の評価尺度は，前述した86年のASTC調査で見たアメリカのハンズ・オン系施設の場合と極めて似たものになります。

3施設を比較すると，エクスプロラトリーは事業収入が最少で補助金・企業協賛金・寄付金への依存度も最小，また，テクニクエストは収入金額に占める事業収入の割合が最小で補助金等の割合が最多となっています。ユーリイカ！はテクニクエストと比べて事業収入がかなり多いにもかかわらず，経常損失は多くなっています。これは多分に500万ポンドと評価される有形固定資産の減価償却が，テクニクエストの240万ポンド，エクスプロラトリーの2万ポンドという資産に対しての償却費と比べかなり高くしてあるためでしょう（展示設備の耐用年数つまり償却の対象となる期間をユーリイカ！とテクニクエストについてはエクスプロラトリーより短くみている。たとえばコンピューター化されていない設備については10年に対し5年，コンピューター化された設備については3年に対し5年）。

表4.1は3施設の経営実績について95年度単年度の状態を示すだけで，これはある断面を切り取ったにすぎません。これからもう少し長期にわたって数字を見てみることにしましょう。そこで経営成績を診断するのに損益評価指標を用いることにします。以下のような項目です。

・入場者1人あたり事業収入
・収入金額に占める事業収入の割合
・収入金額に占める企業協賛金・補助金収入の割合
・入場者1人あたり運営費
・職員1人あたり人件費
・経常費総額に占める人件費の割合
・入場者1人あたり広報・宣伝費
・経常費総額に占める広報・宣伝費の割合

ユーリイカ！こどものための博物館

ユーリイカ！は92年7月に開館したので，初年度の会計は1年間の経営実

績を反映したものではありません。けれども，図4.1 でわかるように，93～95 年の会計報告がより長期の財政状態を診断してくれています。

　ユーリイカ！では 93 年から 94 年にかけて入場者数が 2％伸びたため，事業収入（入場料収入およびショップやカフェテリアでの副次的収入）が 1 人あたり 2.89 ポンドから 3.03 ポンドに増えました。同時に経常費は 8.6％下がり，

単位：英ポンド

年度	1993	1994	1995
入場者数（人）	407,000	414,000	358,000
〈収入〉			
事業収入	1,178,061	1,255,792	1,176,099
入場者 1 人あたり	2.89	3.03	3.28
企業協賛金・補助金	722,189	528,945	1,014,686
総収入	1,908,038	1,790,924	2,199,722
総収入に占める事業収入の割合（％）	62	70	53
総収入に占める企業協賛金・補助金の割合（％）	38	30	46
〈経常費〉			
経常費総額	1,488,211	1,360,631	1,433,577
入場者 1 人あたり	3.66	3.29	4.00
人件費	706,512	634,631	659,678
職員数（人）	58	52	70
職員 1 人あたり人件費	12,181	12,204	9,424
経常費総額に占める人件費の割合（％）	48	47	46
広報・宣伝費	102,719	124,012	158,656
入場者 1 人あたり広報・宣伝費	0.25	0.30	0.44
経常費総額に占める広報・宣伝費の割合（％）	7	9	11
〈損益〉			
税引き前経常損益	−375,635	−384,110	−45,184

図4.1　ユーリイカ！の損益計算書（93—95年度）

出典：カンパニーズハウス提出の会計報告の財務諸表をもとに作成。入場者数は法定会計報告（1995）と『イギリスの観光』による

注記：1）会計年度は 1～12 月
　　　2）減価償却は経常費から除いた

入場者1人あたりの経常費も3.66ポンドから3.29ポンドに減少しました。94年から95年にかけて見てみると，入場者が16％減少したにもかかわらず，1人あたり事業収入は3.28ポンドに増えました。また同期中に経常費は5％増えています。

この損益計算書には経常費の全内訳は示されていませんが，広報・宣伝費が1人あたり93年の0.25ポンドから95年の0.44ポンド（対経常費7〜11％）に増えており，ユーリイカ！では この費目にますます大きな予算を割かねばならない状況にあることが如実にわかります。つまるところ，入場者数減と広報・宣伝予算増がユーリイカ！の現状です。これはライフサイクルの成熟期に入ろうしている開館3年目の施設に共通して見られる傾向で，それゆえにもう最初のときのようにマスメディアに取り上げられることもなくなってきているのです。

職員1人あたりの給与額と経常費に占める人件費の割合は93年から94年を通じてほとんど変わりありませんが，この間に58人から52人に減員したので総人件費は減りました。95年になって70人に増えましたが，人件費割合は変わっていません（実際，94年に比べて平均給与は23％低いのですが，職員の数は多くなっています）。

ユーリイカ！の財政は企業協賛金と補助金にかなり頼っており，事実，95年には全収入の46％を占めるほどです（93年は38％，94年は30％）。この費目の収入は94年対比で実質92％増になりますが，このおかげで入場者減による事業収入減と経常費増を相殺することができたのです。全体的にみて，ユーリイカ！は94年から95年の間に税引き前の経常損失を実質的に減らしはしましたが，入場者数の減少と運営費の増加があいまって，事業収入よりも補助金や企業協賛金に依存する体質がますます強くなりつつあります。

テクニクエスト

図4.2は，拡張して新しい展開をするにつれ（第3期テクニクエストのオープンは95年5月），根本からの変革を経験してきた施設の例を示しています。なんといっても示唆的なのは，新しい施設の入場者が実質倍増し，事業収入の割合が増えたことです（96年の事業収入のうち79％は入場料収入。94年は

68％，95年は67％。ただし，この実績はユーリイカ！のそれと比較できない。というのはユーリイカ！の公表データでは入場料収入を特に区別していないため）。95年から96年にかけてテクニクエストの事業収入は増えているにもかかわらず，依然として補助金や企業協賛金への依存度はユーリイカ！より大き

単位：英ポンド

年度	1994	1995	1996
入場者数（人）	107,277	125,414	250,433
〈収入〉			
事業収入	204,278	299,465	624,760
入場者1人あたり事業収入	1.90	2.39	2.49
企業協賛金・補助金	379,540	392,564	747,943
総収入	602,621	693,288	1,411,000
総収入に占める事業収入の割合（％）	34	43	44
総収入に占める企業協賛金・補助金の割合（％）	63	57	53
〈経常費〉			
経常費総額	529,834	691,342	976,913
入場者1人あたり経常費	4.94	5.51	3.90
人件費	304,036	416,271	681,117
職員数（人）	48	60	104
職員1人あたり人件費	6,334	6,938	6,549
経常費総額に占める人件費の割合（％）	57	60	70
広報・宣伝費	35,074	48,400	60,977
入場者1人あたり広報・宣伝費	0.33	0.39	0.24
経常費総額に占める広報・宣伝費の割合（％）	7	7	6
〈損益〉			
税引き前経常損益	54,731	-14,450	-8,738

図4.2 テクニクエストの損益計算書（94—96年度）
出典：カンパニーズハウス提出の会計報告およびテクニクエスト提供の情報をもとに作成
注記：
　1）94年度の会計年度末は3月。95年度と96年度は7月
　2）95年7月決算の会計報告は16カ月分の数字を含むので，比較のために12カ月のデータに調整した
　3）減価償却は経常費から除いた
　4）第3期の建設費用は除いた

いようです。

　支出面を見ると経常費総額の 6 ～ 7 ％を広報・宣伝費にあてていますが，これはこの施設がライフサイクルの成長期にあることを示しています。ユーリイカ！では入場者数を維持するために広報・宣伝費を増やさなければならない状況にあるのですが，96 年時点のテクニクエストの場合は，まだ第 3 期の立ち上げに関連した宣伝・広報の恩恵にあずかっているのです。

　職員 1 人あたりの人件費はユーリイカ！に比べて低いのですが増員を続けており，96 年の人件費は経常費総額の 70 ％を占めています。これは 95 年度の 46 ％というユーリイカ！の数字よりかなり高く，しかもアメリカよりも高いのです。アメリカの場合，人件費は 51 ～ 53 ％が普通です。

エクスプロラトリー

　図 4.3 が示しているように，エクスプロラトリーでは収入の主要部分は事業活動からのものです（95 年は収入金額の 83 ％）。その大部分は入場料収入ですが（94 年には事業収入の 85 ％），94 年から 95 年の間に 8 ％減り，必然的に事業収入も 8 ％減りました。この施設は補助金や企業協賛金への依存度はほかの 2 館に比べて低いのですが，94 年から 95 年にかけて 6 ％減らしています。

　経常費を見ると，94 ～ 95 年に 1 ％以下の支出増がありました。入場者 1 人あたりの費用はユーリイカ！の場合と非常によく似ています。全般的にいうならエクスプロラトリーは，支出に関してはまあまあ安定していますが入場者の減少に悩んでいるといえましょう。95 年の数字は記載されていませんが，93 年から 94 年にかけて広報・宣伝費が 6 ％から 11 ％に増えているのは興味深いことです。これはエクスプロラトリーが恐らくライフサイクルの衰退期に入ったことを示すもので，広報・宣伝に多くを割かなければならない状態になったというのに 95 年には入場者も補助金も減って赤字決算となりました。ちなみに 93 年と 94 年は利益を計上しています。ユーリイカ！も同様の特徴を示していますが，こちらでは 95 年に補助金の増収がありました。エクスプロラトリーではライフサイクルの衰退期対策を講じました。つまり，2000 年までに 2500 万ポンドを投じて新設するハンズ・オン施設サイエンスワールドに移転するのです（第 1 章を参照）。

単位：英ポンド

年度	1993	1994	1995
入場者数（人）	157,408	165,969	153,194
〈収入〉			
事業収入	401,523	477,865	441,697
入場者1人あたり事業収入	2.55	2.88	2.88
企業協賛金・補助金	170,633	90,986	85,330
総収入	572,896	571,275	530,841
総収入に占める事業収入の割合（％）	70	84	83
総収入に占める企業協賛金・補助金の割合（％）	30	16	16
〈経常費〉			
経常費総額	510,339	538,593	541,925
入場者1人あたり経常費	3.24	3.25	3.54
人件費	219,773	303,940	310,601
職員数（人）	39	43	40
職員1人あたり人件費	5,558	7,068	7,765
経常費総額に占める人件費の割合（％）	43	56	57
広報・宣伝費	32,638	59,690	N/A
入場者1人あたり広報・宣伝費	0.21	0.36	N/A
経常費総額に占める広報・宣伝費の割合（％）	6	11	N/A
〈損益〉			
税引き前経常損益	256,970	25,054	−17,117

図4.3 エクスプロラトリーの損益計算書（93—95年度）

出典：カンパニーズハウス提出の会計報告をもとに作成，入場者数は『イギリスの観光』による
注記：
1）93年度と94年度の会計年度末は9月。95年度は96年1月末まで
2）96年1月決算の会計報告は16カ月分の数字を含むので，比較のため12カ月のデータに調整した
3）減価償却は経常費から除いた

損益評価指標別に見る実績

入場者1人あたり事業収入

　1人あたり事業収入の実績は，3施設とも3期連続増収傾向を示しました。テクニクエスト＝1.90ポンドから2.49ポンド，ユーリイカ！＝2.89ポンドか

ら 3.28 ポンド，エクスプロラトリー ＝ 2.55 ポンドから 2.88 ポンド。事業収入の内訳は入場料，物品販売，飲食サービスで，3 施設の平均は 2.70 ポンドです。

事業収入に占める入場料収入の割合は，テクニクエスト 79％（95 年），エクスプロラトリー 85％（94 年）で，ユーリイカ！のデータはありません。

収入金額に占める事業収入の割合

収入金額に占める事業収入の割合に関しては施設間でかなり大きなばらつきがあります。テクニクエスト ＝ 34～44％，ユーリイカ！ ＝ 53～70％，エクスプロラトリー ＝ 70～84％。3 施設の平均は 60％です。

収入金額に占める企業協賛金と補助金の割合

収入金額に占める企業協賛金と補助金収入の割合も施設間でかなり大きなばらつきがあり，テクニクエスト ＝ 53～63％，ユーリイカ！ ＝ 38～46％，エクスプロラトリー ＝ 16～30％です。3 施設の平均は 39％になります。

入場者1人あたり経常費

入場者1人あたりの3年間の費用を見ると，ユーリイカ！とエクスプロラトリーの平均は似ています（エクスプロラトリー ＝ 3.24～3.54 ポンド，ユーリイカ！ 3.29～4 ポンド）。テクニクエストでは移転前の 95 年の 5.51 ポンドに比べ，移転後の 96 年には 3.90 ポンドに減りました。3 施設の平均は1人あたり 3.90 ポンドです。

職員1人あたり人件費

職員1人あたりの人件費は，ユーリイカ！ ＝ 9424～1万 2204 ポンド，テクニクエスト ＝ 6334～6938 ポンド，エクスプロラトリー ＝ 5558～7765 ポンドです。これらの数字は気をつけて見る必要があります。法定会計報告によると，たとえば 94 年のエクスプロラトリーで 43 人と記載されている職員数の内訳が，実際には常勤（給与制）16 人と非常勤（時間給制のパートタイマー）27 人の職員からなっているのです。この数字は 93/94 年版，96 年版『英国インタラクティブグループ名鑑』記載の情報とも矛盾しており，2 冊とも 10 人の

常勤と25人の非常勤職員で構成されていて16人の常勤体制に匹敵するレベルだと記しています。会計報告にある人件費の総額は正確な数字ですが，職員の数は必ずしも常勤のポストの数とは限りません。したがって，この情報から平均人件費を推計するのは危険かもしれませんが，あえて出すとすれば，3施設平均，年間8225ポンドとなります。

経常費総額に占める人件費の割合

この数字は1人あたり人件費より確かで，ユーリイカ！＝46〜48％，テクニクエスト＝57〜70％，エクスプロラトリー＝43〜57％です。95年のテクニクエストの数字は38％なのですが，これは第3期施設オープンに伴い建設費を含めた費用総体が大きく膨んだためのゆがみです。3施設の平均は54％。これは86年のASTCの調査結果に見られるアメリカの科学館の場合よりもわずかに高いだけです。

入場者1人あたり広報・宣伝費

エクスプロラトリー，ユーリイカ！ともに，この期中，1人あたり広報・宣伝費は増えています。ユーリイカ！＝0.25ポンドから0.44ポンド（93〜95年），エクスプロラトリー＝0.21ポンドから0.36ポンド（93〜94年）。テクニクエストは第3期施設オープンの95年には0.39ポンドですが，翌年，0.24ポンドに減らしました。まだメディアに取り上げてもらう恩恵があったのです。総じていえば，ユーリイカ！とエクスプロラトリーに見られる広報・宣伝費の増加は，いよいよ激化するイギリスの余暇市場での競争の反映といえます。入場者1人あたり広報・宣伝費の3施設平均は年間0.32ポンドです。

経常費総額に占める広報・宣伝費の割合

ユーリイカ！＝7％〜11％（93〜95年），エクスプロラトリー＝6％〜11％（93〜94年）といずれも増加しています。96年のテクニクエストは6％でした（ちなみに94年度の旧施設では7％）。これらの数字は，余暇施設の促進費・PR費は経常費総額の10％前後が一般的という普遍性の高い「経験則」に合致します。ユーリイカ！とエクスプロラトリーに見られる広報・宣

伝費の増加は，激化する競争に直面して古い施設が促進活動に力を入れる必要があることを物語っています。経常費総額に占める広報・宣伝費の3施設平均の割合は8％です。

営業指標別に見る実績

前節で見た指標別の実績は各施設が提出している法定会計報告と，同報告もしくは『イギリスの観光』から引いた入場者数をもとにしています。これに展示の面積や展示装置の数を加味すれば，さらに別の面から実績を分析することが可能になるでしょう。ただし，その取り扱いにはいくつか気をつけなければならない点があります。具体的には，ユーリイカ！とテクニクエストの展示面積は，延べ床面積の3分の2という，施設提供の概算数字です。エクスプロラトリーの展示の面積（延べ床面積の52％）は，『英国インタラクティブグループ名鑑』の情報に基づいています。各施設内の展示装置の数は『英国インタラクティブグループハンドブック』と各施設の発行資料所載の情報に基づいています。また，明らかに，インタラクティブ展示の定義が施設によって異なる場合もあるかもしれません。**表4.2**，**表4.3**，**表4.4**に経営実績をまとめました。

展示床面積1㎡あたり入場者数

床面積あたりの年間入場者は3施設ともほぼ同じで，最少最多ともエクスプロラトリーで108人（95年）から146人（94年）の範囲です。ほかの2つの施設のいずれの年の数字もこの範囲内に分布しています。1㎡あたり入場者数の3施設平均は129人です。

86年のASTC調査によると，アメリカの科学館では44％の館で1ft^2あたりの入場者が4～10人（1㎡あたり換算では37～92人），23％で101～186人となっています。つまり，イギリスの3施設の1㎡あたりの入場者数はアメリカの平均に比べて少し高く，ASTCの調査では2番目に多いカテゴリーに入ります。

1㎡あたり経常費

年間の1㎡あたり経常費は382ポンド（95年，エクスプロラトリー）から

662ポンド(94年,テクニクエスト)の範囲で,3施設平均は480ポンドとなります。

1 展示装置あたり入場者数

1展示装置あたりの入場者数も3施設でほぼ共通しており,ばらつきの範囲は957人(95年,エクスプロラトリー)から1565人(96年,テクニクエスト)までとなっています。3施設平均は年間1173人です。

表4.2 ユーリイカ!の経営実績(93―95年度)　　　　　　　　　　　単位:英ポンド

	1993	1994	1995
入場者数(人)	407,000	414,000	358,000
経常費総額	1,488,211	1,360,631	1,433,577
展示室延床面積(㎡)	3,000	3,000	3,000
床面積(1㎡)あたり入場者数(人)	136	138	119
1㎡あたり経常費	496	454	478
展示装置総数(点)	350	350	350
1展示装置あたり入場者数(人)	1,163	1,183	1,023
1展示装置あたり経常費	4,252	3,888	4,096
入場者1人あたり経常費	3.66	3.29	4.00

出典:カンパニーズハウス提出の会計報告,『イギリスの観光』,同館発行資料,『英国インタラクティブグループハンドブック』をもとに作成

表4.3 テクニクエストの経営実績(94年度と96年度)　　　　　　　　単位:英ポンド

	1994	1996
入場者数	107,277	250,433
経常費総額	529,834	976,913
展示室延床面積(㎡)	800	2,200
床面積(1㎡)あたり入場者数(人)	131	114
1㎡あたり経常費	662	444
展示装置総数(点)	80	160
1展示装置あたり入場者数(人)	1341	1,565
1展示装置あたり経常費	6,623	6,105
入場者1人あたり経常費	4.94	3.90

出典:カンパニーズハウス提出の会計報告,『イギリスの観光』,テクニクエスト提供の資料,『英国インタラクティブグループハンドブック』をもとに作成
注記:95年度は同館が移転したため除外

1 展示装置あたり経常費

1展示装置あたりの経常費は3387ポンド（95年,エクスプロラトリー）から6623ポンド（94年,テクニクエスト）の範囲で,3施設平均は年間4418ポンドとなります。

入場者1人あたり経常費

入場者1人あたり経常費は3.24ポンド（93年,エクスプロラトリー）から4.94ポンド（94年,テクニクエスト）までの範囲で,3施設平均は年間3.73ポンドとなります。86年のASTC調査によると,アメリカの科学館では入場者1人あたりの経常費は平均7ドル（97年の為替レートで4.40ポンドに相当）となっています。この数字にはインフレの進行や為替レートの変動などは考慮に入れていないとすれば,明らかに程度は似ているといえ,英米の入場者1人あたりの経常費の有意な比較は難しいといえます。

建設資本の財源

1章で,イギリスの草創期の科学館が,セインズベリー財団やナフィールド財団などの財団からどのようにして相当額の財政援助を受けたかを詳しく紹介しました。1980年代の終わりに,ナフィールド財団は故ナフィールド伯爵遺

表4.4 エクスプロラトリーの経営実績（93—95年度）　　　　　単位：英ポンド

	1993	1994	1995
入場者数（人）	157,408	165,969	153,194
経常費総額	510,339	538,593	541,925
展示室延床面積（㎡）	1,140	1,140	1,140
床面積（1㎡）あたり入場者数（人）	138	146	108
1㎡あたり経常費	448	472	382
展示装置総数（点）	150	150	160
1展示装置あたり入場者数（人）	1049	1,106	957
1展示装置あたり経常費	3,402	3,591	3,387
入場者1人あたり経常費	3.24	3.25	3.54

出典：カンパニーズハウス提出の会計報告,『イギリスの観光』,同館発行資料,『英国インタラクティブグループ名鑑』をもとに作成

贈の基本財産から，年間にして125万ポンドを教育のために提供しました。初期段階のエクスプロラトリーも86年にはこの財団から資金提供を受け，88年からは"ディスカバリードーム"という巡回展示も多額の援助を受けています。ナフィールド財団はほかにもこの分野のパイオニア的な活動に対して援助をしており，"ライトワークス"と呼ばれるワゴン車で小学校を訪れる移動科学館や，テクニクエストの学校貸出用の学習キットなどがその資金で開発されました。

87年には，ナフィールド財団と貿易産業省の協力でインタラクティブ科学技術プロジェクトが設立されています。科学館の建設を促進し，情報やアイデア交流の拠点となるものです。財団は3年にわたり毎年2万ポンドを提供し，貿易産業省は同じ期間に1万ポンドを交付しました。90年にはECSITE（欧州科学系展示施設協力機関）の発足資金として3万3000ポンドを助成しています。ECSITEはヨーロッパにある非営利の科学館と博物館からなり，会員館の間で情報や活動を交流する場所として存在するものです。

イギリス国内にはCOPUS（科学普及推進委員会）という機関があります。王立研究所，王立協会，英国学術協会が共同出資して86年に設立した合同委員会で，一般の人の科学技術に対する意識の向上を目的に組織されました。89年にはナフィールド財団との共同事業で，イギリスにおけるハンズ・オン手法を採り入れた教育の現状についての報告書を出版しており，また活動の一環として科学の啓蒙活動に対して少額の助成もしています。90年には平均2000ポンド，総計4万8000ポンド超の助成が行われました。実は，筆者も89年から93年の間に4件について助成を受けています。シェフィールド産業博物館のグレートシェフィールド・エクスプロラトリー建設計画（89年），ユーリイカ！，およびエルスカー・ヘリテイジセンターにつくった"パワーハウス"というインタラクティブ展示の準備作業にその助成金を使いました。95年にCOPUSは上限3000ポンドの従来からあったシード基金に加えて，それを補うものとして，新しく年間2万ポンドを上限とする開発基金を設けました[5]。

ナフィールド財団，COPUS，ECSITE，貿易産業省は，イギリスにおける科学館の初期の発展段階において，資金援助はもちろん，支援体制，アイデア交

---

[5] 種まきを意味するシード基金は地域レベルの活動を対象にした助成制度で3000ポンドが上限。開発基金は大規模な事業を助成する制度で2万ポンドまで枠がある。

換のための拠点を用意したことで重要な役割を演じたといえるでしょう。けれども，草創期のハンズ・オン運動の発展に大きく貢献したものがほかにもあるのです。

　ユーリイカ！こどものための博物館は，元をたどれば，こどものためのディスカバリーセンターへの貿易産業省の補助金5万ポンドから始まっています。ディスカバリーセンターは，ロンドンにこどものための博物館を設立する目的で79年にボストンから帰国したゴールドスミス女史が創設したものでした。この資金によって採算性などをみる予備調査が行われ，また80年代の半ばには，財政支援をとりつけるための冊子も作成されました。これがちょうど子どもと一緒のボストン訪問を終えて帰国したばかりのダフィールド女史のもとにも送られたのです。ダフィールドは，テイトギャラリーのターナーコレクション展示室の増築に資金を提供したクロア財団の創設者，故クロア卿の娘にあたります。クロア財団とビビアン・ダフィールド財団は，こどものための博物館の建設プロジェクトにまず500万ポンド提供し，そのプロジェクトがその後，87年になってハリファクスの地に居を構えることになったのです。影響力のあるダフィールドを理事長として迎えたことによって，92年にユーリイカ！が一般公開されるまでに，クロア財団とビビアン・ダフィールド財団からの700万ポンドに加え，さらに企業や個人の後援で200万ポンドの資金導入が可能になったのです。実際，**図4.1**に示したように，ユーリイカ！は95年にも引き続き館の財政を左右するほどの補助金・寄付金収入を得ています。

　ダフィールドは97年現在もユーリイカ！の理事長職にある一方で，クロア財団とヴィヴィアン・ダフィールド財団は他のハンズ・オン系施設にも支援を続けています。たとえば，国立自然史博物館の"移動ディスカバリーセンター"，国立科学博物館の展示，"もの"，国立海事博物館に95年オープンしたインタラクティブ展示施設，"オールハンズ"の建設などの主要な財源がそうです（"オールハンズ"は総工費200万ポンドで同博物館内のレオポルド・ミューラー教育センターにつくられた施設。レオポルド・ミューラー・エステイトが130万ポンドを負担）。イギリスでは名門一族の名を冠した民間の財団が多くのハンズ・オン系博物館・科学館の発展に重要な役割を果たしてきています。たとえば，ギャツビー財団（セインズベリー家の信託財団）は，第1期テクニ

クエストの立ち上げ資金に当初8万3000ポンドを提供し，第2期には90年までに合計68万ポンドを補助しています。民間の財団が，いわば種まきの資金を供給することは，新しい博物館建設に他の機関や組織を説得して財政援助を引き出すのにしばしば役立ちました。例を示すと，93年には50以上の機関がテクニクエストに対し1000ポンドから25万ポンドまで大小さまざまの補助金や寄付金を提供し，第2期には合計が100万ポンドを超えたほどです。同様に，エクスプロラトリーも92年までに1000ポンド以上の7機関を始め，80以上に及ぶ組織や企業から資金提供を受けています。
　草創期の科学館やハンズ・オン系博物館は，概して自治体や中央政府からの補助金よりも公益団体や企業スポンサーに多くを依存していました。けれども700万ポンドかけてつくられたスニブストン・ディスカバリーパークは例外で，ここでは展示の開発にレスターシャー（州）から450万ポンドの補助を受けており，さらにほかの公的機関からの助成や民間からの企業協賛金や寄付金も投下されました。既存の博物館内に設置されるハンズ・オン系施設の場合，国・公立でさえ，新しい建設事業を興すときには企業の後援や個人の寄付金に大きく依存してきました。たとえば，"ラウンチパッド"の初期開発費用の100万ポンドは国立科学博物館予算と政府補助金のほかに，リバーヒューム信託からの援助によってまかなわれています。
　これからのハンズ・オン系施設の発展にとって企業スポンサーや公益団体の支援は依然として重要ですが，一方で，ますます大規模化する開発事業では新しい公的資金への依存度が高まっています。"パワーハウス"というインタラクティブ施設があるエルスカー・ヘリテイジセンターでは，ヨーロッパの基金と，炭坑の跡地利用に対して与えられる助成金が大きな財源です。同様に，カーディフ港湾開発公社の目玉プロジェクトとして，テクニクエストの第3期に要した700万ポンドの大部分は，ウェールズ開発庁，ウェールズ観光局，ヨーロッパの基金によりまかなわれました。このディスカバリーパークとテクニクエストの敷地が都市再開発地域であるので，このように実のある財政援助を受ける機会に恵まれたのです。ある批評家は次のように記しています。「科学館の将来は政治家と開発業者の手の中にあり，夢を追う人が圧力団体の役になるのを妨げているようだ」。

イギリスでは，今後，ハンズ・オン系博物館や科学館の建設資金は国営宝くじの収益金による助成に非常に多くを頼ることになっていくでしょう。特にその配当機関の1つである二千年紀記念委員会は，数々の大規模な新規建設や既存施設の改修に対して資金提供を行っています。96年5月，この委員会は「ブリストル2000」計画にかかわる8200万ポンドの費用の半分を援助すると発表しました。その中には2つの新しいインタラクティブ施設があり，その1つが前述したサイエンスワールドという名のエクスプロラトリーの新しい本拠地です。このプロジェクトのエクスプロラトリーにかかわる部分は250万ポンドで，プラネタリウム，バーチャルシアター，ハイテク利用の「解説者」（インタラクティブなコンピューター技術を使って来館者の興味や要求に応じて情報を提供する設備）など，全部で400もの展示装置がつくられます。計画全体に対して4100万ポンドのパートナーシップの助成金[6]がブリストル市，イングリッシュパートナーシップス[7]，ハーバーサイドスポンサーグループ（近隣の商業地開発や住宅地開発からの税収があてられる），ワシントンのスミソニアン協会，その他民間の基金から提供されることになっています。

　また，バーミンガム市博物館にある"ディスカバリーセンター"では"科学に光をあてて"という名の新施設をディグベスにできる複合施設ミレニアムポイント内に設置する計画で，二千年紀記念委員会から5000万ポンドの助成を受けます。そこには，科学，産業，自然史，郷土史関連の博物館資料と，ハイテク，ローテク利用の展示を組み合わせた複数のハンズ・オン展示室が置かれることになっています。この事業には，ヨーロッパ地域開発基金[8]，バーミンガム市，民間部門からのパートナーシップ助成資金もあてられます。

　サイエンスワールドもバーミンガム市博物館"ディスカバリーセンター"も，二千年紀記念委員会が助成するインタラクティブ系施設の数多くのプロジェクトのうちのほんの一例にすぎません。これらのプロジェクトは，既存施設に対

---

[6] 二千年紀記念委員会など国営宝くじの助成を受けるには，申請者は助成金と同額の資金を自らまかなわければならない。共同で資金を獲得することからこのシステムをパートナーシップ助成と呼んでいる。
[7] 住環境の改善や雇用創出など生活環境改善のために国内の地域再開発を推進している政府機関。99年4月に新しくできた地域開発局と共同で，イギリス国内におけるさまざまな再開発事業を行っている。

して競争をあおることになるでしょう。本書の執筆時点では，どのプロジェクトが必要とするパートナーシップ資金を実際に調達するか定かではありませんが，はっきりしているのは，大規模かつ革新的な新規事業を支援する二千年紀記念委員会以外に，ハンズ・オン系博物館やとりわけ科学館が宝くじの収益金に財源を求められる道はないということです。国営宝くじの収益金交付機関にはほかに文化遺産宝くじ基金[9]がありますが，ここは文化遺産の管理に重点を置いているため文化遺産に利益がもたらされるような大きな計画の一部でないかぎりインタラクティブ系施設に助成することはありません（国立科学博物館のウエルカムウイングは，文化遺産宝くじ基金が初めて理工系科学分野に助成した資金2300万ポンドで新築された。この翼棟の展示は現代科学，医学，科学技術を扱っている）。英国学術協会や王立協会は，科学系の施設がもっと直接的な方法で宝くじの収益金を利用できるよう運動しています。一方，芸術宝くじ基金[10]のほうはシェフィールド市にできるポピュラー音楽センターに対して助成を行っており，この施設には展示室全体を通してインタラクティブの要素が大きく取り入れられることになっています。"作曲してみよう"という展示室ではそれが顕著に表れています。

建設にかかわる費用

　新しくインタラクティブ系施設を建設する際に必要となる費用は，いうまでもなく用地の取得費・造成費，建物の建設費，展示の制作費を合わせたものです。

用地取得費

　用地の取得にかかる金額はどんな場所を選ぶかで全く異なります。後にユーリイカ！となるこどものための博物館の立地として当初はロンドン地区が考え

---

[8] EU（欧州連合）がその加盟国に提供している助成基金の1つで，経済的な地域格差をなくすためにインフラの整備や地域の再開発事業などに資金を提供している。94〜99年に約700件，イギリス国内では99年5月までに84件のプロジェクトが助成を受けた。
[9] 国営宝くじの収益金を交付する12の機関の1つで，文化遺産にかかわる事業に対する助成申請の受理・審査を担当する。
[10] この基金も国営宝くじの収益金を交付する12の機関の1つで，芸術活動にかかわる事業に対する助成申請の受理・審査を担当する。

られていました。最終的にハリファクス市となった理由はいくつかあって，その1つはユーリイカ！のパトロンであるチャールズ皇太子が会長を務める地域ビジネスという組織がコールダーデールを再開発事業のパイロット地区として選んでいたからです。そのおかげで，280万ポンドに相当する12.5エーカーの空き地（旧国鉄所有地）を35万ポンド125年リースという条件で取得できたのです。先に述べたエルスカー・ヘリテイジセンターやテクニクエストなども，放置されていた跡地利用に対して与えられる助成金を活用しました。このように用地の選定には，たとえば開発助成を受けられるかどうかなど，市場価値以外にも大きく左右される要因があります。

建築費

　草創期の施設の多くは既存の建物を改装して転用するという安上がりの方法で造られていました。テクニクエストは，最初，カーディフ市中心部の商店街でガス会社がショールームとして展示に使っていたスペースを利用するところから始まり，その後，現代的な工場ビルに移り，さらに現在の質の高い施設に移ったのです。この建物も工房として使われていた鉄骨構造の19世紀の建築のまわりに建てられたものです。エクスプロラトリーはブリストル市のビクトリアルームでの仮住まいから始まり，その後現在の建物に移りましたが，ここは元はテンプルミーズの駅舎でした。エルスカー・ヘリテイジセンターの"パワーハウス"も旧国鉄施設（機関車修理工場）を使っています。他方，ユーリイカ！は，当初，現在の敷地にあるグレートノーザンシェドという巨大な鉄道車両庫内に設置される計画でした。

　実際には，ユーリイカ！は費用的な理由でグレートノーザンシェドの隣に建物を新築することになりました。公共の利用のためには，古い車両庫の改造よりも新しく建物をつくったほうが安くすむのです（新しい建物は駅にも繁華街にも近いし，ランニングコスト面でもビクトリア時代の工業建築を改造利用するよりはるかに安い）。ユーリイカ！の建物にはだまし絵のような巧妙さがあります。その設備はきわめて高い基準に合わせて設計されていますが，正面のガラスが巧妙に隠している建物の本質は工業建築です。石の壁がガラス壁を切り裂いているデザインは建物を切り開こうとしている「ナイフ」をシンボライ

ズしたもので，その建物の中には多くの構造物や設備がガラスケースの中ではなくむきだしのまま展示されているのです。この建物は王立建築家協会の優秀建築賞を受賞しました。一般建築の1㎡単価は500ポンドぐらいですが，ユーリイカ！の場合はわずかに高く総工費約240万ポンド，つまり1㎡あたり約533ポンドでした（92年）。

　いま建築にかかわっているデザイナーや建築家はもっと野心的な試みが可能になっています。国営宝くじが巨額の公的資金を提供してくれるのはもちろん，助成対象の建物に対して特徴的であることや，できるかぎり高い基準を満たすことをも要求するようになっているからです。筆者は宝くじ基金の申請をいくつも行ってきました。その場合，質が高く，特徴のある建物を新築するのに，1㎡あたり1000ポンドかそれ以上の予算を申請するのが普通です。現在，シェフィールド市に建設中のインタラクティブ系施設，ポピュラー音楽センターは芸術宝くじ基金から多額の助成を受けています。この施設の「革新的でランドマークとなる建築」は総工費840万ポンド，1㎡あたり1853ポンドです（96年）。これはユーリイカ！（92年）の単価の3.5倍も高い数字です。

展示制作費

　上述の建築費には，通常，基本的な設備工事費と，床・壁・天井の仕上げ工事費は含まれていますが，展示関連の費用は別途予算になります。ユーリイカ！の場合，質の高い建物を比較的低い予算でつくることができたのと同様に，展示関連の費用もあまり高くならずにすみました。これは，内部の管理がうまく行われたのと，展示装置の多くがローテク利用のものだったためだといえます。展示関連の費用は，現在のところ，ローテクの展示装置で1㎡あたり1500ポンド前後，ローテクとハイテクを合わせたもので同2000ポンド，ハイテクのもので同2500ポンドほどです。この費用には，展示装置の開発・制作・設置，展示にかかわる一切，グラフィック制作，照明の費用，さらにデザイナーその他専門家への報酬（通常，展示関連総費用の15％前後を計上する）が含まれます。ショップやカフェテリア，収蔵庫，事務所，作業場など，展示以外の空間については上述の数字よりはるかに低くなります。ただカフェテリアやショップなど展示室でなくても公共の空間は，収蔵庫や事務所などの公共

空間ではない部分の工費より高いのが一般的です。

　展示装置個々の制作費は，通常，5000ポンドから2万ポンドぐらいまでの幅があり，展示の複雑さの程度によって違ってきます。概していえば，新しい技術を使ったもの，特に新しくコンピューターソフトを開発しなければならないものは，ローテクのものよりお金がかかります。一般に，1つの展示装置は10㎡前後の空間を占めますが，これも展示装置のタイプによってかなり大きな差があります。

まとめ

　この章では，イギリスとアメリカにおけるハンズ・オン系の科学館・博物館の経営実績を詳しく見てきました。そのなかで3つの規模の大きな施設を例に法定会計報告書を精査することで，ハンズ・オン系施設の経営実績を診る尺度をつくってみました（ただし，これらの指標は非営利団体である大規模館に通用するだけで，規模や設置主体の異なる施設には当てはまらないかもしれません。現に，アメリカのASTCの調査には，アメリカの科学館の特徴は多様なことであるとの指摘があります）。イギリスの場合でもアメリカの場合でも，ハンズ・オン系施設の財政がいくつもの収入源に依存しているのは明らかです。財源，特に建設資本として企業協賛金・補助金・寄付金収入は依然として重要ですが，日常の財源として事業活動からの収入がますます重さを増してきています。

　アメリカでは，最近開館したハンズ・オン系施設ほど老舗の施設に比べて事業収入に多くを頼っています。財源の限られたこうした若い施設は生き残るために苦闘を強いられることになるでしょう。一方，新しい施設との競争で古い博物館や科学館では入場者数が減少するかもしれません。イギリスでは，すでに過密状態にある余暇市場で宝くじ収益金の導入が集客施設どうしの競争をあおっており，ユーリイカ！やエクスプロラトリーなどは，財政報告書が示すように広報・宣伝にお金をかける必要に迫られ実行したにもかかわらず入場者数減に悩まされています。両施設とも開館後まだ数年しかたっていないのですが，すでにライフサイクルの減衰期に入ったという兆しが見られるので，核となるプロジェクトで興味を一新しようと大規模な改革を計画しているのは意味があ

ります。ハンズ・オン系施設とほかの集客施設との間でこのように激しい競争が繰り広げられる状況にあっては，すぐれたマーケティング管理が不可欠です。この部分については，章を改めて考察することにしましょう。

シカゴこどもの博物館
1982年にシカゴ市立図書館内で開館した同館は，95年にミシガン湖畔のネイビーピアと呼ばれるシカゴでも最大級のショッピングモールに移転した。ネイビーピアは呼び名のとおり湖に突き出た埠頭。年間400万人の市民や観光客が訪れるため，そのなかの主要施設である同館の入場者が飛躍的に伸びたのはいうまでもない。

テクニクエスト
カーディフ市にあるテクニクエストには科学や人体に関する160にのぼる展示があり，どれも参加体験型になっている。心臓や肺，腸など体のいろいろな器官をパズルのように順番にはめ込んでいくことによって体の内部がどのような構造になっているか知ることができる。

5章

マーケティング

5章 マーケティング

　この章では，ハンズ・オン系博物館や科学館に対してどのような需要があるのか，そして，より多くの人々の要求を把握し，それに応え，満足させるためには，どのようなマーケティング計画が必要なのかを考えていきます。

マーケティング計画

　マーケティング研究所はマーケティングを次のように定義しています。
　「（マーケティングとは）効果的に，そして，利益が上がるように，顧客の要求を理解し，予測し，満足させる経営のプロセスのことである」
　マーケティング計画の考え方は簡単です。まず，その組織の財政その他諸々の目標を設定し，組織の強み（**strength**）と弱み（**weakness**），機会（**opportunity**）と脅威（**threat**）について把握するSWOT分析を行います。次に，サービスを提供する現在の市場と潜在的な市場について分析し，それぞれの市場でサービスを向上させるための市場目標を設定します。それらの目標は，組織全体の目標やSWOT分析の結果（の主要な部分）と一致していなくてはなりません。最後に，マーケティングの目標に合致した長期的・短期的戦略を立て，継続的にその業務を評価し，市場の条件の変化に応じて戦略を修正します。
　ハンズ・オン系博物館や科学館は，市場志向型の施設といえます。展示と利用者の相互作用を通して学ぶプロセスは，利用者のニーズを把握し，満足させることによって成り立ちます。成功しているハンズ・オン系博物館では，展示開発にあたって，企画段階評価，制作途中評価，総括評価などの評価をあらゆる段階で行っています。これらの展示評価調査は利用者の要求を把握し，展示がそれらの要求に合致しているかどうか試すことを目的としています。さらに，利用者によりよい体験を味わってもらうために，研修を受けたスタッフを配置することもあります。そのとき提供されるサービスの質は，クオリティーコン

トロール（QC）によって維持されなくてはなりません。また，利用者調査によって，利用者の属性や体験が実際に期待にそっているかどうかがわかり，コミュニケーション戦略の効果を測ることができます。マーケティングは，ハンズ・オン系博物館のまさに核でもあるといえます。マーケティングを成功させるには，予算の範囲内で利用者志向のサービスの提供を効果的に行うことが必要です。たいていどの組織にもマーケティング担当者がいて，マーケティング予算が組まれていますが，ハンズ・オン系博物館がその教育目的を達成するためには，利用者志向の考え方が組織全体に浸透していなくてはなりません。

　本書ではマーケティングの手法をハンズ・オン系博物館の経営にあてはめて書いています。つまりマーケティングと，計画立案，人事・組織，現場の運営，教育プログラムや特別イベントの運営などはそれぞれ密接に関連しているためマーケティングの観点から書いているのです。余暇関連市場全体のなかでのハンズ・オン系博物館の役割については1章と9章で論じています。2章ではインタラクティブな手法を用いた教育目標の土台となるものについて説明し，利用者の側に立った展示の開発については3章で見てきました。4章（財政），6章（現場の運営），7章（組織・人材管理），8章（教育プログラムと特別イベントの運営）では，効果的な経営という視点から組織全体の目標を達成するための望ましい経営のあり方について考察しています。このように，マーケティングというのは経営の補足的な側面ではなく，この章を独立して設けていることからもわかるようにハンズ・オン系博物館の成功にとってまさに核部分であり，本書の土台となっているものでもあるのです。

　マーケティングの教科書でマーケティングミックス[1]として知られる手法（商品 product，場所 place，宣伝 promotion，価格 price，人 people，有形物 physical evidence，プロセス process の7つのP）は，ハンズ・オン系博物館の開発と経営にもそのまま当てはめることができます。以下にあげたのは，ハンズ・オン系博物館を効果的に経営するための条件です。

　1．対象とする利用者の学習その他の要望を把握し，それに応える商品を開発する（商品 product）。

---

[1] 標的市場の状態に合わせ，そのニーズを満たすために最適なマーケティング手段を組み合わせることをいう。

2．対象とする多くの利用者が利用しやすい立地に施設を建設する（場所 place）。
3．潜在的利用者と企業などの支援者にその組織のすぐれた点を伝える（宣伝 promotion，広報 public relations）。
4．対象となる利用者が支払い可能な範囲の金額で，なおかつ組織の財務目標に則った料金を設定する（料金 price）。
5．利用者がよりよい体験を味わえるようにすぐれた人材による人とのかかわりあいを大切にする（人 people）。
6．はじめての利用者や潜在的利用者にハンズ・オン体験の考え方を理解してもらう（有形物 physical evidence）。
7．質の高い商品を継続的に提供し続ける（プロセス process）。

　本書全体を通してマーケティングミックスのほとんどの要素に見られるような望ましい経営のあり方についてふれていますが，そのなかで特に重要な2つの要素（料金と宣伝・広報）について詳しく見ていきます。その前に，マーケティングを成功させるにはある特定の利用者層を対象とした手法を採る必要があるので，1章で紹介した市場の分析に従って，ハンズ・オン系施設の潜在需要がどのようなものか見ていくことにします。

ハンズ・オン系施設の需要

　1章でハンズ・オン系博物館や科学館がどれくらい人気があるかということを紹介しましたが，デービズがイギリスの博物館利用の潜在的需要について分析した94年の報告によれば，博物館に人を引き寄せるための重要な要素は2つあり，展示を操作できることと，子どもを引きつけるさまざまな活動が用意されていることをあげています。あわせて，博物館を訪れる人の3分の1は子どもで，家族（学校団体ではない）で訪れる子どもが最も重要な利用者層であると述べられており，95年のデータでもイギリスで博物館を訪れた人の31％は子どもであることが明らかにされています。ただし，地域によって大きな隔たりはありますが（スコットランドでは24％で，北アイルランドでは53％）。『イギリスの観光　1996』によれば，イギリスの集客施設全体でも利用者の

32％は子どもです。このように，博物館を訪れる子どもの割合は，業界全体の平均とほぼ同じであるといえます。ここでいう博物館の入場者数は，すべてのタイプの博物館を含んでいるので，家族連れに人気のあるインタラクティブ系の博物館の場合には，もっと子どもの割合は高くなるでしょう。

2章で社会的な側面から博物館の利用について考えることが重要であるということと，家族連れで訪れた来館者にとって安全で教育的な環境とは何か，彼らが本当に必要としているものは何かを紹介しました。博物館，特にハンズ・オン系博物館や科学館では，家族で体験できる魅力的な環境づくりがなされています。そこで体験する内容が，来館者数を左右する主要な要因となりますが，そのほかにも社会的，文化的，経済的，政治的，人口統計的な要因によって博物館の利用は左右されます。

人口統計的傾向[2]

前述したようなハンズ・オン系博物館に対する需要の増加の理由は，人口統計に現れた傾向からもうかがうことができます（表5.1）。

91年時点のイギリスにおける子どもの数は過去30年間で最も低く，16歳以下が1170万人でした。子どもの人口動態には周期があり，現在は上昇傾向にあることがわかります。16歳以下の人口は，年齢構成にばらつきはありますが，2001年には1991年比の5％の増加が予想されます。2001年までに5～

表5.1 イギリスにおける16歳未満の子どもの数（1961-2001年） 単位：千人

	0～4歳	5～10歳	11～15歳	0～15歳合計
1961年	4,274	4,585	4,289	13,148
1971年	4,553	5,580	4,124	14,257
1981年	3,455	4,553	4,533	12,541
1991年	3,885	4,409	3,444	11,739
2001年	3,844	4,680	3,873	12,398

出典：人口統計局国勢調査（OPCS）をもとに作成
注記：2001年の数字は1992年時点の予測による

---

[2] 人口現象に関する統計によって得られた傾向。人口増加，人口構造，人口分布，出生率，死亡率，結婚率，人口移動などを統計的にとらえたもの。

10歳の子どもの数は増加し，その後減少します。11〜15歳の子どもの数は，2001年以降増加します。

　子どもの人口は過去の出生率の変化を部分的に反映しているといえるでしょう。つまり，現在の上昇傾向は60年代のベビーブーム世代が子どもをもつようになり，出生率が上がった結果ということができます(第2次ベビーブーム)。71年は10歳以下の子どもの数が多かったことが，92年の人口構成に表れています。表5.2を見ると，25〜34歳の人口（現在赤ちゃんや小さな子どもがいる58〜67年生まれの人々）が最も多いことがわかります。

　しかしながら現在の人口統計の傾向だけでは，子ども向け施設の需要の増加を説明することはできません。なぜなら，今日のイギリスの人口に占める子どもの割合は今世紀の初めに比べてずっと低いからです。1911年には，イングランドとウェールズで子どもは全人口の約30％を占めていましたが，91年になると約20％に落ち込みます。イギリスの人口は産児制限によって出生率が下がり，医療技術の向上によって寿命が延びたため高齢化しています。子どもの数は今世紀の初めの頃にくらべて相対的な意味で重要ではなくなりましたが，60年代のベビーブームに生まれた子どもが現在自分自身の子どもをもつようになり，子どもの数がわずかに増加しています。表5.1が示しているように，最近のブームのピークに生まれた子どもが年をとるにつれて現在の子ど

表5.2　イギリスの人口構成（1992年）

年齢	人口（単位：千人）	％
0〜4	3,781	6.7
5〜14	7,026	12.5
15〜24	7,713	13.7
25〜34	8,954	15.9
35〜44	7,616	13.5
45〜54	6,720	11.9
55〜64	5,646	10.0
65以上	8,933	15.8
合計	56,388	100.0

出典：CACI社『人口統計ポケットブック』(1994) をもとに作成

人口自体が高齢化しますが、この上昇傾向は21世紀の初めまで続くことが予想されます。このように、人口統計上の傾向が重要な要素であるとしたら、2000年までに家族向けの集客施設を計画している組織は、重要なターゲットとして、必然的に幼児よりもティーンエイジャーを考える必要があります。

　これらの人口統計から、90年代の初めに子どもや家族向けの施設の需要が増加した理由を部分的に説明することができます。これは、今後数年間にわたって、ティーンエイジャーを対象とした施設の需要が伸びることを示唆しているといえるでしょう。また、子ども向け施設の需要は、以上見てきた人口統計上の傾向以外に、確保できる余暇時間、家族の余暇活動にあてられる所得など、さまざまな要因によっても影響を受けます。

余暇時間

　94年にミンテルが1678人の成人を対象に行った余暇時間に関する調査によると、独身者と所帯をもった人では余暇時間の長さに大きな隔たりがあることがわかりました。成人の余暇時間の平均は1週間あたり42時間ですが、男女によって違いが見られます。女性は男性に比べて余暇時間が短く、子どものいる女性では1週間あたり平均27時間であるのに対し、子どものいない女性では、48時間となっています。余暇時間が最も少ないのは35〜44歳までの働いている女性で、15歳以下の子どもがいる人たち（多くのインタラクティブ系施設がまさに対象としている層の親にあたる人たち）です。91年にアメリカで行われた調査によると、平均的なアメリカ人家族の自由時間は1週間あたり19時間で、家庭の外で働いている女性ではたった12時間であるという結果が出ています（回答者の21％は全く余暇時間がないと回答）。これら2つの調査で用いられた方法は異なるため、単純に比較できませんが、イギリスでもアメリカでも家族の余暇時間が急激に少なくなっていることは明らかです。それはひとり親家庭の増加や働く女性の増加とも関係しています。

　図5.1は、時間とお金をどれだけもっているかを簡単なマトリックスで表したものです。低所得者層の家族の場合、余暇時間が少ないだけでなく、お金もないことがわかります。これが集客施設の需要にも影響を与えているのです。ひとり親家庭の場合は余暇時間と可処分所得両方の不足に影響される傾向があ

	余暇時間が豊富にある	余暇時間が少ない
お金をもっている	裕福な早期退職者 専門職でない就労男性 専門職でない／子育てをしていない就労女性	フルタイムの専門職就労者 仕事をもつ母親
お金がない	パートタイムの就労者 失業者 公的手当を受けている退職者	低所得者層の仕事をもつ母親 単親家庭

図5.1 余暇活動ができるのは誰？
出典：レジャーコンサルタント『余暇活動の動向 1996-2000』をもとに作成

ります。一般的に，博物館の利用者は社会経済的地位が高く，職業的にもエリートといわれる層が多いといわれています。実際，社会経済的階層A，B，C1[3]はイギリスの博物館利用者の大半を占めていますが，すべての社会経済的階層が博物館を訪れており，その構成は全体的な人口構成と似ています。また，博物館の需要に影響を与えるもっと大きな要因が学歴であることを示す証拠もあります。つまり，学校教育を受けた期間が長いほど，博物館利用者になりやすいということです。

先にも引いたデービズの調査によると，人口の40％が少なくとも1年に1回博物館か美術館を訪れ，40％がたまに訪れ，残りの20％がほとんど訪れないという結果が出ています。また国民遺産省は，人口の32％が毎年博物館を訪れ，21％が美術館を訪れていると報告しています（両者は明らかに重複している部分がある）。入館料の負担能力や自由時間の不足が利用を抑制する要因になってはいますが，すべての社会経済的階層で明らかに需要があることがわかります。つまり，ハンズ・オン系博物館や科学館の需要は児童数の増加が原因であるともいえますが，実際には，そのような人口統計的な変化よりも，収入や余暇時間に影響を与える社会全体の変化のほうが重要なのです。

イギリスの博物館利用者の大部分は施設から1時間以内の距離に住んでいま

---

[3] 職業的地位によってA，B，C1，C2，D，Eの6つに区分した社会的階層。イギリスでは市場調査などでこの階層区分がしばしば用いられる。A＝上級の経営管理職またはそれに相当する専門職，B＝中間の経営管理職またはそれに相当する専門職，C1＝監督または事務・下級管理職，またはそれに相当する専門職，C2＝熟練労働者，D＝半熟練・非熟練労働者，E＝年金受給者または寡婦・日雇い労働者・長期失業者（*Social Trends 29*, 1999 より）

すが，これは家族で過ごす余暇時間が少ないことの反映ともいえます。91年，92年に行われた調査によると博物館を訪れる人の48％は30マイル以内に住まいがあり，13％が30～50マイルの範囲内，39％が50マイル以上のところに住んでいることが明らかにされています。

　どの社会経済的階層でも家族の余暇時間は限られていますが，それにもかかわらず，これらの家族連れが博物館の主要な利用者となっているのです。したがって，2章で述べたように，家族連れが安全で楽しい環境の中で過ごせるようにすることは，すべての社会経済的階層に対していえることなのです。家族連れが積極的に利用するのは，子どもが十代に達するまでの間だけです。けれどもこの層は新しい家族が子どもの大きくなった家族と入れ替わることによって常に新しくなっているという点で，施設にとって大きな利点となります。ハンズ・オン系博物館が家族連れであれ，学校団体であれ，13歳未満の子どもを対象にしているのはこのような理由によるのです。

　表5.3は，89～94年までのテクニクエストの来館者数を示していますが，

表5.3　テクニクエストの月別入館者（1989-94年の平均）

	入館者数（人）	月別構成比（％）	全英の博物館入館者の月別構成比（％）
1月	4,543	4.3	3
2月	10,014	9.6	7
3月	9,112	8.7	7
4月	11,427	10.9	10
5月	8,898	8.5	13
6月	7,323	7.0	15
7月	10,501	10.0	11
8月	14,424	13.8	10
9月	5,614	5.4	7
10月	10,903	10.4	6
11月	7,377	7.0	7
12月	4,583	4.4	4
合計		100.0	100

出典：テクニクエスト提供資料および人口統計局『英国の日帰り旅行　1988～89』にある博物館関連データをもとに作成

家族と学校という市場がともに重要であることがわかります。博物館全体の平均では，利用者の50％が5～8月の4カ月間に訪れており，夏季にピークとなる利用傾向が見られます。テクニクエストの利用者は1年を通して平均的に散らばっており，5～8月の間に訪れる人は39％にすぎません。テクニクエストは，博物館全体の傾向と比べると夏季の利用者数は少ないのですが，利用者数がピークに達した月はすべて休暇の期間を含んでいます。つまり，8月（夏季）と4月（復活祭）と10月（秋期休暇）です。次に多いのが7月（通常学期中にあたる）と2月（春期休暇を含む）です。このように，年間を通して学校の休暇期間に利用する家族が多いことがわかります。また7月は学校団体の利用がいちばん多い月ですが，テクニクエストに来る人は，学期中よりも休暇期間のほうが多くなっています。

　マーケティングの成功の秘訣は，対象とする実際の利用者層と潜在的な利用者層の要求を把握し，それに応えることです。マーケティング理論では，市場に浸透させることが最も有効な戦略だといわれています。ハンズ・オン系博物館にとって重要なターゲットとなるのは家族や学校団体ですが，それ以外にも考慮に入れるべき層が2つあります。それは50歳以上の中高年とティーンエイジャーです。これらの層の博物館利用率は低いため，これらの層をハンズ・オン博物館の潜在的市場ととらえることができます。たとえば，早期退職者は経済的余裕も時間的余裕も十分にあり，交通手段ももっており，孫もいることが予想されます。これらの人々が1人であれ孫を連れてであれ，博物館を訪れたら，重要な利用者層となるでしょう。ティーンエイジャーも興味深い市場といえます。なぜなら，収入は少ないですが，暇は十分にあるにもかかわらず，これらの層を対象にした娯楽施設は少ないからです。お金もなく交通弱者でもあるため，地域という市場の境界を越えることはできないかもしれませんが，入念な計画をすれば，インタラクティブ系施設はこれらの層の要求を満たすことができるかもしれません。現にイギリスでは，ロンドン国立科学博物館が最近，ティーンエイジャーをターゲットにしたインタラクティブ展示をつくりました。また，アメリカでも多くのすぐれた事例があります（これらについては8章でふれます）。

事例紹介：ユーリイカ！の利用者

　ユーリイカ！では93年夏，来館者のなかから596人の成人を任意に選び，6週間以上にわたって利用者調査を行いました。最も多かったグループは4～5人連れの白人のヨーロッパ系家族でした。子どもの男女比はほぼ同じでしたが，成人では女性が男性の2倍以上も多くなっています。72％の子どもは，ユーリイカ！が対象にしている5～12歳ですが，25％が5歳未満でした（この年代の子どもに合わせたコーナーは1カ所しかないので，これは予想外の結果でした）。ユーリイカ！は5～12歳の子どもを対象にしていますが，11～12歳の子どもはたった11％だったことからも，ユーリイカ！が比較的幼い年齢層を対象にした施設と見られていることがわかります。実際，13～15歳の子どもは来館者全体のたった3％にすぎず，ティーンエイジャーを重点対象としていないユーリイカ！の方針が功を奏しているといえます。成人については49％が35～44歳で，27％が25～34歳となっています（2つの年齢層を合わせると76％となるが，これはイギリスの博物館全体で利用者の年齢構成を見た場合の平均値である44％よりはるかに高い）。さらに面接調査をした人のうち66歳以上の人はわずか5％でした。

　調査対象の半数以上は社会経済的階層A，B，C1に該当する人々で，その構成比はイギリスの博物館全体の平均より高くなっています。非白人は2％以下，障害者を連れた人は6％でした。自宅から来た人は86％，休暇で滞在している人は7％，友達や家族と一緒に来ている人は6％でした。西ヨークシャー，もしくはランカシャーとグレーターマンチェスターの周辺地域に住んでいる人が半分以上で，イギリス以外のところから来ている人が4％でした。また，車で来た人は80％，鉄道12％，長距離バス・路線バスが6％でした。

　ユーリイカ！について友達や家族から聞いたと答えたのは回答者の半分以上を占め，23％の人が，個人的にすすめられたと答えています。来館を決めたのは女性だと答えたのが62％，子どもが決めたという答えが22％でした。また，前の週に来館することを決めた人が45％，1週間以上前に決めていた人が33％でした。初めて訪れた人は75％，以前にも来たことがある人が25％でした（調査の時点では，博物館はまだ開館して1年もたっていないのに10回目だという人が2人いました）。博物館での滞在時間は最も短い人で50分，

主要な市場

インタラクティブ系施設のカギとなる利用者層は，重要な順に並べると以下のようになります。
（1）車で1時間以内のところから来ている日帰り客（基本市場）
（2）学校団体，学校以外の団体（教育市場）
（3）車で1〜2時間のところから来ている日帰り客（二次市場）
（4）イギリス人および外国人旅行者（旅行者市場）

この節では，上記4つの利用者層についてそれぞれ詳しく見ていきます。そして，ユーリイカ！の利用者の傾向を，93年の利用者調査と一般に公表されている市場情報から予測してみましょう。

基本市場

ハンズ・オン系博物館や科学館の第1の市場としてまずあげられるのが，車で1時間以内のところに住む13歳未満の子どものいる家族です。そのほかに博物館が引きつけることのできる潜在的な層として，余暇時間が豊富にあり交通手段ももっているお金のある早期退職者，それから余暇時間は豊富にあるけれども，交通弱者で，お金はもっていないティーンエイジャーがいます。

あるコンピューターソフトを使ってこの市場に相当するエリア，つまりユーリイカ！まで車で1時間以内の範囲を抽出してみました。その範囲は，イングランド西海岸のリバプールと東のハルの郊外を結ぶ楕円の形をしており，高速道路M62に沿って東西に延びています。また南北はハロゲイトからシェフィールドに広がっています。つまり，リーズ，ブラッドフォード，マンチェスター，リバプール，シェフィールドなどの大きな都市が，すべてユーリイカ！から車で1時間以内のところにあるということになります（5章扉の地図参照）。ユーリイカ！が建てられたハリファクスは，立地としてふさわしくないという声が計画段階からありましたが，人口が多い都市の中心部に位置していれば，既存の観光客市場がない場所でも大規模な観光施設をつくることができるということを，現在の成功が証明しています。

車で 1 時間以内の地域の比較調査と 91 年の国勢調査によると，ユーリイカ！の基本市場にあたる地域の人口は 790 万人になります。主要なインタラクティブ系施設の利用者は通常，基本市場となる地域の人口の 2〜3％ にあたる人々であるといわれています。大々的に宣伝している新しい施設では，小規模の平均的な施設より利用者の人口比も高くなっています。ユーリイカ！の 93〜95 年の来館者数は年間平均 40 万人です。93 年に行った来館者調査と『英国の日帰り旅行』の調査データでは利用者の約 60％ が日帰りで，50 マイル以内の基本市場にあたる地域に住んでいることがわかりました。この調査では学校団体や学校以外の団体客（約 10 万人）は含まれていません。年間利用者数 40 万人から団体客（約 10 万人）を引いた残り 30 万人のうち，13％ の人々（3 万 9000 人）はその地域に滞在している人々であることがわかりました。そして，約 15 万 6600 人（26 万 1000 人の 60％）が，基本市場の地域から来ている個人の来館者であることが推測できます。これは，基本市場地域の人口 790 万人の 2％ にあたり，業界全体の傾向とも一致しています。

教育市場

　2 番目に大きな利用者層は学校団体とボーイスカウトやガールスカウトなど学校以外の団体客で，その多くは基本市場の地域から来ています。この層の利用を左右する要因として，ナショナルカリキュラム[4]との関連性，競争の度合い，費用（教育的効果に照らし合わせて）などが考えられます。たとえば，マンチェスター科学産業博物館では，小学校，中学・高校，高等教育機関の団体利用者が多く，来館者全体の 40％ 近くを占めています。複数の教科とさまざまな学年に対応した内容は，ナショナルカリキュラムとも関連しているため，博物館で 1 日過ごすなど，学校関係の団体に人気があるのです。一方，ユーリイカ！は，基本市場を主要な対象としていますが，高学年の生徒の利用には消極的です。ユーリイカ！で教育的効果が得られることははっきりしているので

---

[4] イギリスの教育改革の一環として 1989 年に導入された初等・中等課程の全国統一学習カリキュラム。それまでカリキュラムの編成は各学校に任されていた。この改革を受け，博物館においてもナショナルカリキュラムに対応したサービスが積極的に行われるようになった。

すが，対象年齢が科学産業博物館より低いため，学校団体の利用は来館者全体の約25％にすぎません。

　国勢調査によれば，ユーリイカ！の基本市場圏内で学校に通っている児童の数は115万人だそうです。そのなかで，ユーリイカ！が対象としている5～12歳の子どもの数は84万8000人です。学校団体や学校以外の団体でユーリイカ！を訪れる子どもは約10万人です。これらの子どもがすべて基本市場圏内から来ているとすると，この地域に住む5～12歳の子どもの約12％がユーリイカ！を訪れていることになります。けれども，実際には基本市場の地域以外からの団体利用も多いので，この割合はもっと低くなるでしょう。

二次市場

　3番目に大きな利用者層は，ユーリイカ！から1～2時間の範囲内に住んでいる家族連れです。二次市場はその施設の新しさや他の施設との競合の程度，さらには宣伝の仕方などによって左右されることが多く，基本市場に比べてかなり利用率が低くなるでしょう。ユーリイカ！から，車で1時間～2時間の範囲内には1140万人の人が住んでいます。93年に行った来館者調査と『英国の日帰り旅行』の調査によれば，来館者の約40％は基本市場の圏外に住んでいます。団体利用者や旅行客以外に10万4000人（26万1000人の40％）が，この二次市場地域から日帰りで来ていることがわかります。これは1114万人の人口の0.9％にあたり，業界全体の傾向と一致しています。

旅行者市場

　イギリスでは，毎年5億5000万人の人が日帰り旅行をしていますが，そのほとんどは1時間以内の旅行です。ここでいう旅行者とは，自宅以外の土地に宿泊する人のことをいいます。イギリス観光局が出している93年の年次報告書によると，92年の国内のイギリス人旅行者は7700万人，海外から訪れた外国人旅行者は1600万人となっています。ハンズ・オン系博物館を訪れる旅行者の数は，その地域の観光地としての規模や中身，宣伝のされ方によって左右されます。一般に旅行者は，博物館やテーマパークより名所旧跡を訪れることが多いようです（『イギリスの観光』によれば95年にイギリスの博物館を訪れ

表5.4 細分市場別にみたユーリイカ！の利用者属性

	人口	入館者数(推計)	構成比(％)	市場浸透率(％推計)
基本市場（車で1時間以内）	7,900,000	156,600	39	2
団体（基本市場域に住む5〜12歳の子ども）	850,000	100,000	25	12
二次市場（車で1〜2時間）	11,400,000	104,400	26	0.9
イギリス人旅行者（西ヨークシャーへの一泊旅行者）	9,200,000	27,000	7	0.3
外国人旅行者（西ヨークシャーへの一泊旅行者）	3,400,000	12,000	3	0.4
合計		400,000	100	

出典：自動車による交通時間分析，国勢調査，ユーリイカ！の来館者調査，ヨークシャー観光局発行資料，『イギリスの観光』，『イギリスの日帰り旅行』をもとに筆者が推定
注記：団体の市場浸透率は全団体客が基本市場から来ていると想定して算出した。実際にはそうではないため，もっと低くなることが予想される

た人の21％が外国人旅行者であるのに対し，名所旧跡を訪れた外国人旅行者の割合は34％となっています。）。

　ヨークシャー・ハンバーサイド地域では博物館を訪れた人の8％が外国人旅行者でしたが，93年に行ったユーリイカ！の調査では，利用者に占める外国人旅行者の割合はたった4％，イギリス人旅行者は9％でした。ヨークシャー観光局によれば，95年に西ヨークシャーに滞在したイギリス人旅行者920万人のうち0.3％，外国人旅行者340万人のうち0.4％にあたる人がユーリイカ！を訪れたと報告しています。この数字は業界全体の傾向とも一致しています。これを表したのが表5.4です。

市場の重複

　いくつかの主要な科学館の間で，基本市場と二次市場の重複が見られます。図5.2は，利用者数が年間10万人以上の科学館とハンズ・オン系博物館でどのように市場が重なっているのかを示したものです。

　イギリスの主要なインタラクティブ系の施設，特に二次市場の利用者の獲得

	エクスプロラトリー(ブリストル)	テクニクエスト(カーディフ)	国立科学博物館(ロンドン)	ユーリイカ!(ハリファクス)	スニブストン(レスターシャー)	ニューキャッスル・ディスカバリー	科学に光をあてて(バーミンガム)	エクスペリメント!(マンチェスター)	ジョドレルバンク(チェシャー)
エクスプロラトリー(ブリストル)	■	P	S		S		S		
テクニクエスト(カーディフ)	P	■					S		
国立科学博物館(ロンドン)	S		■		S		S		
ユーリイカ!(ハリファクス)				■	S		S	P	P
スニブストン(レスターシャー)	S		S	S	■		P		S
ニューキャッスル・ディスカバリー						■			
科学に光をあてて(バーミンガム)	S	S	S	S	P		■	S	S
エクスペリメント!(マンチェスター)				P			S	■	P
ジョドレルバンク(チェシャー)				P	S		S	P	■

図5.2 イギリスの主要なハンズオン系施設の重複市場
P：重複している基本市場
S：重複している二次市場

をめぐって競争が行われていることがわかります。この図は年間入場者数が10万人以下のハンズ・オン系施設やその他の競合施設にはふれていませんが，この市場のなかで明らかに競争があることを示しています。カーディフ市のテクニクエストとブリストル市のエクスプロラトリーは，お互いの基本市場の地域にあります。96年の7～10月までに，テクニクエストを訪れた1万620人の郵便番号を調べたところ，カーディフ市の番号が半分で，ブリストル市の番

号はわずか2％でした。ウェールズのセバーン川対岸にあるブリストル地域の人々はテクニクエストの入館者に占める割合としてはそれほど大きくありませんが、両施設が近接しているということは基本市場への浸透力が弱くなることを意味しています。この問題は国営宝くじの収益によって新しくインタラクティブ系施設が建設されたり、既存施設の拡張や改修が増えることにより、ますます複雑になっていくでしょう。実際、競争を余儀なくされる同じ基本市場の地域内に、いくつか新しい施設の建設が計画されています。

ハンズ・オン系施設同士やほかの集客施設とのこのような厳しい競争に対処するには、入念なマーケティング計画が必要となります。次節では、マーケティングミックス（価格と宣伝）の2つの手法を、どのようにして戦略的かつ有利に使うことができるかを考えてみます。

料金設定

集客施設の料金設定にはさまざまな要因が考慮されますが、それらがすべて経済的に理に適っているとは限りません。料金を設定する際には、過去の料金設定がいくらだったか、競合相手が設定している料金はいくらか、市場で一般的に受け入れられている料金はどれくらいか、といったことが1つの目安となります。民間部門、公共部門、民間非営利部門ではそれぞれ経営上の目的や社会的使命が違うため、料金設定も一様ではありません。入場料を取っている施設の割合が博物館では全体の51％であるのに対し、博物館以外の一般の集客施設では60％と高くなっています。入場料を取っている博物館でも公的補助を受けている場合が多く、国または公立の博物館に限っていえば、入場料収入だけで経営を維持しているところはほとんどありません。さまざまな種類の入場券を作ったり、割引料金を設けたり、また特別イベントや特別展は追加料金にするなど、入場料によって収入を増やすことも可能です。料金設定はマーケティング上の判断であるといえるでしょう。なぜなら、料金設定は潜在的利用者に、ある種の強いメッセージを植え付けることになるからです。

博物館では大人の入場料金の平均は1.82ポンドであるのに対し、他の集客施設では2.42ポンドとなっているように、博物館の料金設定は一般の集客施設よりも低くなっています。子ども料金の平均は博物館で1.02ポンドである

のに対し集客施設では1.40ポンドとなっており，それぞれ大人料金の56％と58％に相当します。ユーリイカ！では子ども料金が大人料金（97年現在4.95ポンド）の80％で，13歳以上は大人料金になるので異例といえるかもしれません。この料金設定は潜在的利用者に次のような印象を与えています。第1に，料金が高いため質への期待が大きくなること（95年時点で4ポンド以上の大人料金を取っているイギリスの博物館は全体の7％にすぎない），第2に，13歳で大人料金となるため，ターゲットとしている5〜12歳より年齢の高い子どもの利用を意図的に抑えていること，第3に，大人料金に対する子ども料金の比率が他の博物館や集客施設の平均よりかなり高いことです。

子ども向け施設の大人と子ども料金の関係には興味深いものがあります。子ども料金が高いのは搾取であると考える親もいれば，その施設の設備がある特定の年齢を対象につくられているとしたら，その年齢の子どもをもつ親は高い料金でも妥当だと感じるのです。実際，ユーリイカ！は，一般的に大人料金が子ども料金より低いアメリカの子どものための博物館の方針に従って入場料金を検討したのです（たとえばデンバーこどもの博物館では大人の入場料は子ども料金よりも低く，クリーブランドのこどもの博物館では同一料金となっている）。こどもの博物館では大人と子どもが一緒に学べることを目指しているため，より多くの大人に来てもらえるよう料金を低く設定しているのです（大人が多ければ展示物が壊れることも少なくなる）。アメリカでは，民間の遊戯施設の多くが大人の入場料を無料にしています。ユーリイカ！では，多くのイギリスの集客施設に見られるように，団体利用での大人の参加を多くするために学校などの団体の場合には無料の場所や大人の割引料金を設けています（学校団体は，家族連れに比べて大人の占める割合がかなり低い）。けれどもイギリスの習慣ではデンバーの例とは異なり，家族連れの大人に割引料金を導入することはあまりありませんでした。たとえば，テクニクエストでは大人料金4.50ポンドの56％に当たる額を子ども料金にしていますが，これはイギリス全体の傾向に従ったものです。

ユーリイカ！は，92年以来，子どものための博物館市場の中心的な立場に立ちながら，入場料金の維持や引き上げを行ってきました。93年の来館者調査によれば，博物館に来る前は高いと感じたけれども博物館を去るときには金

額に見合っていると感じた，というコメントに表れているように，来館者の80％は入場料金に満足していることがわかりました。92〜97年の間に行った入場料金の引き上げ率は大人41％，子ども58％，学校団体等50％，家族連れ58％でした（家族チケットの利用可能な人数は92年に5人から4人に変更）。けれども，ユーリイカ！はびくともしませんでした。つまり，値上げに対して利用者の数は減らなかったのです。一方，学校団体等の引き上げ率はほかより低くしたにもかかわらず，この層が家族連れよりも金額に敏感であることがわかりました。料金の引き上げはすべての利用者層に影響を与えることになりましたが，一方でピーク時以外の時間帯の利用を多くするため，特に学期中の午後3時以降（その時間帯の利用が極端に少ない）の入場料を半額にするなど，抜本的な割引制度を導入しました。アメリカでは多くのこどものための博物館で，夕方やピーク時以外の時間帯に無料または低額の料金設定をしています。たとえばフィラデルフィアのプリーズタッチ博物館では，日曜日入館は自発的な寄付を募ることにしています。

以上見てきたように，料金設定は利用者からの収入を最大限に増やすためだけでなく，ピーク時の利用を減らし，閑散期の利用を促すこともできる，マーケティングの重要な道具であるといえます。また，（割引料金の設定を通じて）社会的な目的を満たし，（家族チケットや大人料金の割引などによって）大人と子どもが家族で参加することを促し，間接的には（無料または割引チケットによって大人の利用を促すことで）展示に対する損傷を減らすこともできるのです。

広報・宣伝

この章では，マーケティングというのが単に効果的な販売促進にすぎないという考えを打ち砕くことを目的としています。もし，ハンズ・オン系博物館がより大きな教育目標を達成しようとするなら，利用者志向のアプローチがあらゆる経営の側面に浸透していなくてはなりません。そうはいっても，宣伝・広報はマーケティングの重要な手段の1つであり，博物館では多くの場合，広告や宣伝・広報費のことをマーケティング予算といっています。

マーケティング予算の規模は余暇産業によってもさまざまで，特に公共部門

と民間部門では異なっています。自治体のマーケティングへの取り組みについて，ある調査から次のことが明らかになりました。92年の時点で自治体の余暇サービス部局でマーケティング予算が年間5000ポンドに満たないところが半分もあったこと，マーケティングの戦略や計画がなく，担当者もいないところが半数以上もあったことがわかりました。一方，国・公立の3施設（国立自然史博物館，国立科学博物館，ビーミッシュ野外博物館）の広報・宣伝費（95年時点）が10万ポンド以上だったのに対し，民間の2施設では100万ポンド以上を費やしていました。4章で述べたように，ユーリイカ！の95年の宣伝費は15万9000ポンドでした。ハンズ・オン系博物館がほかの博物館や集客施設との競争に勝つために宣伝にかなりの額を投じる必要があることを示しているといえるでしょう。

　支出の規模は個々の組織によって異なり，またライフサイクルのどの時期にあるかによっても異なりますが，経常費の10％を宣伝活動にあてるというのが一般的に受け入れられている数字です。実際，4章で見てきたように，ユーリイカ！，テクニクエスト，エクスプロラトリーでは平均して宣伝費に経常費総額の8％を費やしていますが，ユーリイカ！とエクスプロラトリーは最近になって宣伝費を11％に増やしました。それにもかかわらず両施設とも利用者数が減っています。これらの費用の増加はイギリスの余暇市場における競争の厳しさを反映しているといえるでしょう。ユーリイカ！では，93〜95年の間に1人当たり0.25ポンドから0.44ポンドへ，エクスプロラトリーでは93〜94年の間に0.21ポンドから0.36ポンドへ増加したことになります。

　宣伝広報戦略は施設のライフサイクルによって否応なしに決定づけられる部分があります。たとえば新しい施設の場合には，対象とする利用者層にその存在を知ってもらう必要があるため，広報に重点を置く傾向があります。一方，歴史の古い施設の場合には，利用者にその存在を思い出してもらうための広告をはじめ，その他の形態の宣伝活動に力点を置く必要があるでしょう。いずれにしても成功へのカギはさまざまな宣伝広報手段を通じて伝達されるメッセージが明確で一定しており，現実的であることを示すことです。ユーリイカ！の利用者調査によると，利用者の半分が友人や家族から聞いて博物館について知ったと答え，ほぼ4分の1が以前に訪れたことのある人からすすめられたと答

えています。このように，口コミは常に宣伝の最も優れた手段であるということを覚えておかなくてはなりません。別の言い方をすれば，悪い評判は早く広まるので，できないサービスについて約束するようなメッセージは決して伝達しないことです。

広報（PR）とは，新聞やラジオ，テレビにできるだけ多くさらされるよう，地元，地域，全国メディアとの関係をつくっていくことでもあります。広報活動が成功したかどうかによって掲載スペースや放送時間が決まってきますが，ただでそれが実現するわけではありません。プレスリリースやプレスパックなど，マスコミ向けの広報資料を通してメディアに専門的なイメージを訴えるには，多くの時間とお金を要します。博物館の広報はまだ稚拙で素人くさかったり無計画で行われていたりなど，あまり成功していないことが多いようです。一方で，マスコミの効果を理解している博物館は，すぐれていて，しかも費用効率のいい広報手段によって，潜在的な博物館利用者やスポンサー，その他の受益者にうまくメッセージを伝えています。

地元や地域レベルではマスコミは博物館に非常に好意的です。子どものための博物館やハンズ・オン系施設では，記者が求めているような人間味あふれた話題や非日常的な話題を提供することができます。全国メディアに取り上げられるのは不可能ではありませんが，かなり難しくなります。ユーリイカ！は開館前の数カ月間，広報にかなり力を入れたため，すべての主要全国紙やイギリス全土の地方ラジオ局，数多くの子ども向けテレビ番組に取り上げられました。たとえば開館前に企画段階評価というユニークな試み（仕事の世界について子どもに意見を聞いたもの）について宣伝し，ラジオやテレビがそれを取り上げ，ごくわずかな費用で全国に放送されました。テレビでの放送は大変重要です。テレビに宣伝費をかけられるイギリスの博物館はほとんどありませんが（95年には3館がテレビの宣伝費に4万ポンドをかけている），ユーリイカ！は子ども向けテレビ番組と教育番組の両方によく取り上げられます。つまり，マスコミの効果を知り，専門的な方法を取ることが，広報を成功させるカギとなるのです。

既存のハンズ・オン系博物館にとって，新しい展示やイベントなどは魅力的なニュース素材ですが，広報を通じてメディアの関心を引くのは容易ではあり

ません。イベントが終わってからではなく，開催される前に取り上げてもらうようなタイミングが重要です。とはいうものの，歴史の古い博物館では，今後ますます広告やポスター，リーフレットの配布など，伝統的な手法の宣伝に時間とお金をかけなければならなくなると思われます。これらの分野で成功するカギは，博物館が対象とする層を把握し，宣伝活動を通してそれらの層に効果的に働きかけることです。つまり，リーフレットをほかの博物館や観光情報センター，ホテルに置いて，基本市場の地域に効果的に配るのです。博物館に来たことがない人々に来るように促すよりも，博物館に来そうな人々にまとめて宣伝するほうがより効果的です（ただし博物館が地域へのアウトリーチ活動[5]を目的としている場合は別ですが）。将来，対象を絞って宣伝活動を行うには，どこで来館者が博物館について知ったのか調べることが必要不可欠となります。

　印刷物の役割も重要です。カーライルにあるタリーハウス博物館の歴史ギャラリーには多くのローテクのハンズ・オン展示がありますが，この博物館の宣伝用の印刷物からは，それがよくわかりませんでした。ところが，96年に，7世紀のレプリカの石造物に刻まれた文様を擦って写し取っている子どもの写真を新しいリーフレットの最初のページに載せたところ，入場料収入が46％も上昇したのです（口絵参照）。ハンズ・オン系博物館では，マーケティングミックスの6番目のPである有形物が重要であることを物語っているといえるでしょう。別のいい方をすれば，提供しているサービスが潜在的利用者に目に見えるようにすることが必要なのです。リーフレットの子どもの写真が，ハンズ・オン系博物館は従来の博物館とは違っているのだということを伝えているのです。

　教育市場については特別な注意を払わなければなりません。対象地域にあるすべての学校を網羅したコンピューター化された住所録や学校の種類別（養護学校，小学校，中学・高校など）のリストを購入することもできますが，ほとんどの自治体の教育委員会は郵便物の配布システムをもっていて非営利団体に教育関係の資料を配布しているので，それを利用することもできるでしょう。このサービスを有料にしている自治体もありますが，ダイレクトメール（DM）

---

[5] 1章14ページ脚注5参照。

より費用効率がいいと思われます。資料を配布する場合は目立つもので，なおかつそのサービスが教育効果のあることを強調しなくてはなりません。さもないと，毎週配達される郵便物の山に埋もれてしまったり，きちんと配達されなかったときには，ごみ箱に捨てられているかもしれません。学校団体客を継続的に誘致したいのであればイベントや新しい展示について定期的に案内を送り，学校向けのニューズレターに載せてもらうことが重要です。

博物館に来たすべての人にDMを送るのはあまりに数が多いため，費用的に見てあまり効果的ではありません。それよりも学校や以前来たことのある団体に送るほうが現実的です。また，コンピューターの予約システムに収録されている情報を使って，教師あてに的を絞って送ることも可能でしょう。友の会の会員，誕生日会の申込者などもDMを送ることによってリピーターになる可能性があります。

このように，マーケティング担当者が博物館の宣伝のために利用できる手段はたくさんあります。最近は，多くのハンズ・オン系博物館でインターネットを使っていますが，これは今後ますます重要になっていくでしょう。バーチャルな世界でよその博物館より目立つようにするには，画面構成にインタラクティブな要素を取り入れることが必要です。どのような手段を使うにしても，宣伝広報を効果的に行うには時間とお金が必要であるだけでなく，豊かな経験と管理能力も必要となってきます。新聞紙上に広告を載せたりラジオで宣伝するのは簡単にできますが，費用は高く，必ずしも効率がいいとはいえません。競争の激化する余暇市場でハンズ・オン系博物館が勝ち抜くためには，革新的なマーケティング経営を行うことが必要です。成功のカギは，博物館に来てもらえる可能性のある十分な数の潜在的利用者層に対して明確な訴求目標をもちマスコミの効果や利用するタイミングを理解することと，信頼性の高い市場調査を通して宣伝広告と広報手段について1つひとつじっくり検討することです。

まとめ

マーケティングは，ハンズ・オン系博物館のまさに中核となるものです。マーケティングと，計画立案，人事・組織，現場の運営，教育プログラムや特別イベントの運営などさまざまな館の業務は密接な関係があります。したがって，

マーケティングにかかわる意思決定は，あらゆる経営上の意思決定において重要なものとなり，マーケティングを効果的に行うことによって館の教育目標を達成することができます。マーケティングを成功させるには，対象となる利用者層の要求を把握し，予算の範囲内で利用者志向のサービスを効果的に提供する必要があります。料金設定や広報・宣伝など，マーケティングミックスの手法をうまく使うことによって，潜在的利用者にハンズ・オン系博物館や科学館の特性を伝達することができます。とはいっても，多くの人は友達や家族にすすめられて博物館に来るため，マーケティング計画を効果的に行うには，来館した人が実際に期待どおりの体験を味わえるように利用者志向の考え方が館の組織全体にわたって行き届いている必要があります。現在のような過密状態の余暇市場でハンズ・オン系施設がこれからも長く成功していくには，あらゆる段階で利用者に質の高いサービスを提供することが必要であり，そのためには現場の運営と人材管理を効果的に行う必要があるのです。

ユーリイカ！こどものための博物館のパンフレットなど
きたむらさとし氏のイラストで，パンフレットなどがデザイン統一されている。同館のほとんどの印刷物や看板などにも使用されており，デザインを統一することでアピール力も増している例。

5章 マーケティング　147

タリーハウス博物館歴史ギャラリーの展示
カーライル市にあるタリーハウス博物館の歴史ギャラリーにはいろいろな体験型のハンズ・オン展示がある。ビクトリア時代のファーストクラスの客車に座って当時の上流階級の列車の旅を疑似体験できる。
© Tullie House Museum & Art Gallery, Carlisle

6章
現場の運営

ロンドン国立自然史博物館　絵はがきのイラスト
自然史博物館のショップで売られているオリジナルの絵はがき。歴史的価値の高い荘厳な建物のなか，楽しげな恐竜たちの様子が，広く親しまれたいと願う同館の思いを表している。恐竜たちがサンタクロースの指揮でクリスマスキャロルを演奏しているクリスマスカードバージョンもある。

入場者数の制限

博物館などの学習環境の質の確保には，やはり入場者数の調整が必要だが，日本の施設の場合，そのための独自のマニュアルをもつことは少なく，管理の委託を受けている会社が作成したり，経験的に取り組むことが多いようだ。たとえば大阪の海遊館では，ゴールデンウイークや夏休みに館外にできる列を運営する際に係員が無線で連絡し合って調整したり，待ち時間の札を立てたりしているが，特にマニュアルはないとのこと。琵琶湖博物館のディスカバリールームでは当初から定員を決め，入場制限をするために上下別開閉の出入り口をつけた。混雑する時間帯には下の扉を閉めて入場制限をするなど，室内外の利用者に配慮したマニュアルをつくっている。海外では，たとえばアメリカのデンバー自然史博物館の"プレヒストリックジャーニー"という展示室で，ボランティアが入り口で入場制限を行い，さらに最初のシアターで入場する人数を管理している。この「パルスエントリー方式（時間をおいて人を送り出す）」は実際には当初考えたほどうまく機能しなかったそうである。

（芦谷美奈子）

6章 現場の運営

　この章では，利用者が主役であるインタラクティブ系の施設において，展示室その他の利用者に関係した現場を効果的に運営するのに必要なことがらにふれます[1]。

はじめに

　個人の博物館体験の質が個人的，社会的，物的な要素のからみあいによって決まると，第2章で述べました。博物館の側がこれらの要素すべてをコントロールするのは不可能ですが，利用者の博物館体験をできるだけ期待どおりにするには，質の高いサービスがつねに同じレベルで提供されなければなりません。博物館に行くのを決めるとき，家族や友人からの口コミの宣伝が大きな役割を果たします。しかし，1日，1週間，1年間のうち，人が常に平均して博物館を訪れるわけではありません。したがって，提供するサービスの質を常に一定に保つような態勢や事業を展開するのは困難です。たとえば，職員が多すぎて効率が悪く，資源の無駄遣いになったり，逆に職員の不足から本来の教育目的が果たせず，展示が壊されやすくなったりします。このように，現場の運営は財政活動，マーケティング，人材および教育プログラムと複雑にからみあっています。

収容力について

　ハンズ・オン系の博物館や科学館について，他の余暇産業との競争がかなり激しいことについては本書で何度かふれており，第1章，第4章では，ハン

---

[1] 本章で取り上げているユーリイカ！の事例は，原著者がユーリイカ！に在籍していた1992～93年に実際に行われていた内容に基づいている。

ズ・オンに対する全体的な需要が高まっているにもかかわらず，近年いくつかの施設で利用者が減っていると述べました。効果的なマーケティングを行って，ピーク時以外の利用者数を増やすことは，どの施設にとっても大きな課題です。施設を運営する側は，1日中ないしは1年中常に一定数の利用者が訪れるよう望んでいます。しかし現実はそうではなく，時間帯や時期によって利用者数は変動します。実際に，イギリスでハンズ・オンに取り組む多くの施設は成功を収めており，1995年には少なくともハンズ・オン系の博物館や科学館3館で年間20日以上定員に達しています。全体でも，全施設の5％が少なくとも20日は，23％が少なくとも1日は定員に達しました。定員に達したことのない大半の施設では，そのような問題なら大歓迎だと考えるでしょう。しかし，次のような理由によって，利用者の数は適正に管理される必要があります。

1. 火災その他安全管理のため
2. 適度に心地よく過ごしてもらうため
3. 家族連れ，団体を問わず，博物館体験の質を一定にするため
4. 行列ができているのを見てガッカリさせないため

映画館や劇場のように開催時間や収容人数が限られている場合，その経営者は時間帯と込み具合によって料金を上げたり下げたりすることで需要をコントロールできます。こういった料金の上下は，同様の料金システムを導入していない博物館のような施設や，長期間一定料金であることを広報したい集客施設では，あまり現実的ではありません。これらの施設では，たとえ定員に達するのが年に1日から数日で，それ以外はそれほど利用されないとしても，せっかくのピーク時にただ値上げをして利用者を減らすのは，需要に対して逆効果になりかねません。

定員の設定

どのような展示施設でも，自治体の消防条例によって，非常時の避難を考慮した人数が最終的な定員数として決められます。これ以外では，たとえば床の強度が規制条件となります。さらに，利用者の快適さ（列をつくらずに展示にアクセスできるかなど），展示空間そのものの収容可能人数もあります。多く

の場合，建物自体の定員よりも展示室の収容可能人数のほうが少なくなりますが，一般的な通例はありません。それぞれの展示空間は，たとえば非常口や建築資材，展示の内容や展示装置の数などによって，大きく異なってきます。私（筆者）の経験では，展示空間 2 ㎡あたりに利用者 1 人というのがハンズ・オン展示室の利用人数としては適切でした。

消防条例によるユーリイカ！の定員は 1750 人でしたが，経験から利用者の快適さを考えると，その数はもっと少なくなりました。93 年のユーリイカ！の 1 日あたりの来館者は 1118 人でしたが，平均の数字からは曜日や季節による違いがわかりません（たとえば，一般的に集客施設では週末に向かって利用者が増えます）。週末には，1 日を通して 1500 人の利用者が館内に散らばって混雑することなく，展示室では興奮や発見が満ちあふれ，入館時でも展示室でもカフェで食事をするときも，長い列をつくる必要がありませんでした。消防の安全基準では，ユーリイカ！は 1 日あたり 4000 人の利用者を受け入れられますが，この人数をフルに入館させると運営上の問題が数多く生じ，結果として体験の質が低下することは避けられません。

まず考えるべきことは，一時的に館内にいる人数を施設側が把握できるようにすることで，これを正確に行うには，館に入る人数だけではなく，館から出ていく人数も数える必要があります。出口がいくつかある場合，人数を把握する作業は大変複雑になりますが，このために回転式計測装置[2] を複数設置するのは高くつきます。しかし，現場運営責任者が展示室内の利用者数をいつでも把握できる正確な（つまり機械的な）計測システムは，強く望まれています。

時間制限の設定

来館者が定員に達したとき，次の 2 つの対応策が考えられます。
1. 館内の利用者を管理する
2. 館外の待ち行列を管理する

---

[2] バーを体で押すことで 1 人だけが通れる仕組みのゲート型人数計測装置。逆戻りはできない構造になっており，スタッフが無人状態になりがちな出口に設置されることが多い。

運営責任者は，入館料を払って館内に入った利用者が，展示室で可能なかぎり高いレベルのサービスを受けられるようにし，同時に展示室の中を人がスムーズに流れて外の入館待ちの列が減るように配慮しなくてはなりません。展示室が定員に達すると，中にいる利用者が帰らないかぎり次の人は入れません。利用者を確実に流すことができるのは，入場者全員が着席できるアトラクションです。たとえば，ヨービック・バイキングセンター[3]にあるようなテーマライド[4]では人の流れはカートの定員とその進み方によって決まり，劇場形式のものでは座席数と番組の長さによって決まります。ハンズ・オン系の施設ではこういった方法で人を流せないため，施設によってはピーク時に利用時間の制限を行っています。

　さまざまな集客施設の例から，一般的に1日の20〜25％の利用者がピーク時に施設を訪れることがわかっています。ロンドン国立科学博物館の"ラウンチパッド"では，混雑する日には整理券（入館料は支払いずみなので，これ自体は無料）を発行するようにしました。利用者は先着順に整理券を受け取り，番号で指定された時間帯（同日中）にならないと展示室に入れません。この方法で，ピーク時の入場を1日全体に分散できました（入場時間になるまでほかの展示室を探検するようすすめられます）。ただ，入場はコントロールできるようになりましたが，"ラウンチパッド"の利用時間まで制限できませんでした。パリのラヴィレットに以前あったインベントリアムでは，利用者は1日のうち決められた2時間の時間帯のみ入場でき，その合間には展示室を整頓する時間がとられていました。ここでは，上で述べたような整理券が前もって配られました（ただしインベントリアムへの入館料は，ラヴィレット内の他施設とは別料金）。

　ユーリイカ！では，混雑する日には展示室の利用を3時間に制限しています。入館時に手に動物の形のスタンプが押され，30分ごとに動物が変わる仕組みになっていました。3時間たつと，たとえば「ウサギか恐竜のスタンプを押さ

---

[3] ヨークの考古学リソースセンターに併設してある歴史テーマパーク。実際の考古学の発掘成果に基づいて1000年ほど前のバイキング時代のヨークの町並みを再現している。

[4] カートに乗って，展示の中を進むアトラクション。ディズニーランドの"スモールワールド"や"カリブの海賊"のような方法。

れたお客様は，カフェ，ショップまたは出口へお進みください」といった館内放送をしました。これは，スイミングプールで利用者に色の付いたアームバンドを付けてもらうのと同じ方法です。

　このような時間制限を設定したのには，いくつか理由があります。入館料分の価値を提供するためであるのはもちろんでしたが，明らかに施設の教育的な目的が重要だったからです。半面，これらの制限は，経営に必要な一定の入場者数を確保するという考えには必ずしも添うものではありませんでした。疲れると展示装置を壊す利用者が出てくるという経験則とともに，集中して学習する環境下では子どもが学習疲れを起こすのも大きな理由です。しかし，イギリスではこのような時間制限を設けている施設がほかにないため，ユーリイカ！に来る人も多くは館で丸1日を過ごすつもりで訪れます。館の印象を悪くしないためにも，来館者には込み合う日の時間制限について十分に説明しなくてはなりません。そのためユーリイカ！では，混雑する日の利用を3時間に制限することを，広報資料や入館前のお知らせで念入りに呼びかけています。

待ち行列の管理

　列に並んで待つのを好まない人が多いため，現場運営責任者は列をできるだけ効率よく管理し，入館料に見合った範囲で博物館体験を最大にしてあげる努力をしなくてはなりません。待ち行列の管理の研究についてはコスト計算面や心理学的アプローチなどもあって，たとえば券売窓口を増やしたらどうなるかとか，並んでいる人に優先順位を付けて列の秩序を変えた場合にはどうかなどが検討されています。実際，経費と列の長さは，つねに反比例の関係にあるのです。新しくできたテクニクエストでは，建物の外に列ができると券売窓口を増やすので，どんなに混雑した日でも30分以上待たされることはありません。このように対応する人員を増やせば列は短くできるのですが，人件費が高くつくことになります。しかも中が満員になってしまうと入館スピードを上げる利点はなくなるわけで，一転，全くの不都合と化します。

　ユーリイカ！でも，建物が人でいっぱいになり，外の列がなかなか縮まらないことがあります。建物の保安上の定員を超えることは不可能なので，安全性は最も重要な問題です。ピーク日には来館者は1時間あたり800〜1000人

（1日の合計4000人のうちの20〜25％）にもなり，開館して2時間もすると満員状態になります。ほとんどが最低でも3時間を館で過ごしていくため（93年の来館者調査では，カフェやショップも含めて平均滞在時間は3時間40分），建物が満杯になってから少なくとも1時間はたたないと出ていきません。この時点では，入館待ちの列はほとんど動きません。しかし，遠路はるばる訪れた来館者を入館前に失望させないことより，まずはすでに料金を支払って館内にいる利用者に配慮すべきです。また，もし入館待ち行列がうまく管理されていないと，他の集客施設にお客を取られてしまいます（特に天候が悪い場合）。

　通常，列は先着順に受け付けをしますが，特定の人を優先することもあります。ユーリイカ！では，障害者のいる家族連れは優先的に入館できますが，これに対して時に他の家族連れから不満が出ます。いつ入館できるかという不安感を減らす方法として，予約システムの導入があります。これは，列に並ぶという行為を予約をした時点から来館までの時間で肩代わりし，必ず入館できるという信頼感を与えるものです（ただし入館がうまくいかない場合は不満のもとになる）。しかし，予約システムは少人数の団体にはあまり適しておらず，込んだ日にあらかじめ予約した団体が列の前に優先されると，並んで待っている家族連れを大変不愉快にします。このような理由から，ユーリイカ！では混雑が予想された日には予約を受け付けず，休みの日や週末には予約件数の制限を行いました。

　結局のところ，待ち行列（待っている利用者）を管理する場合，待ち時間の長さよりも待つ側の感じ方のほうがより重要です。たとえば，テーマパークでは列を曲げたり，上下させたり，くぼみを通らせたりして，列の長さよりも進み具合に意識が行くようにうまく工夫しています。

　サービス全般において利用者が列で待つことをどう感じ，それがどのような経験となり，列がどう管理されるかについては，2つの論点があげられます。まず1つめは，サービスが期待を上回れば客は満足しますが，反対に下回れば不満を覚えるということです。何を感じて，それをどう受け取るかは心理的な現象であり，待つ間の感じ方や期待感をうまくコントロールするとそれが列に影響します。

　2つめは，最初にいやな経験をしてしまうと，あとで修正が利きにくいとい

うことです。一般に，訪問して最初のサービスとの出合い方が，その博物館体験の成功を左右するといわれています。もし来館者が最初に気持ちよく迎えられれば，押しつけがましく無愛想な迎えられ方をした場合より，よい印象をもつでしょう。これは接客の基本ですが，その最初のサービスとの出会いが入館を待つ列であるため，これをうまく管理するのに予算や時間を費やして十分に配慮するのは当然といえます。

　つまり，現場運営責任者は列で待つ人の心理をよく理解するべきで，これにはさまざまな側面があります。何もしていないと時間がより長く感じられるため，待っている客に「何かすること」を提供したり，飲み物を販売するなどして気をそらすことが重要です。ユーリイカ！では，込んでいる日には待っている子どもたちに対して，列から外れてボール遊びやお手玉遊び，パラシュートゲーム[5]に参加するよう呼びかけています。大道芸人や道化師などが手配され，飲み物などが売られます。同じく，列で待つ環境を安全に心地よく，雨などに濡れず，トイレに行きやすくするのも重要です。ユーリイカ！では列に並んでいる人が濡れないように，冬の間だけ臨時に屋根を設置しました。2章と3章でオリエンテーション，つまり利用者への導入説明の大切さについて強調しましたが，列で待っている時間は，たとえば施設の目的や中での大人の役割の説明などを始める格好の機会です。このようにして入館料を払う前に利用者の期待を正しいレベルに調整しておくと，あとで生じうる失望感を少しでも減らせます。

　イライラと不信感があると，待ち時間が実際より長く感じられるため，多くの集客施設では待ち時間を表示しています。ユーリイカ！では，かつては担当責任者が列に沿って歩きながら並ぶ人々に状況を説明し，入館を約束して安心させていました。放置された状態で待たされると無気力感がつのり，結果としてイライラが目に見えるようになります。ユーリイカ！では，建物が定員に達したときになぜ券売窓口が減らされるのか，当初多くの人が理解できずに待ち続けていました。現実に建物が満杯状態になると，券売のスピードを落とさざ

---

[5] イギリスの子どもたちに一般的なゲームで，大きなナイロン製のパラシュートのまわりを子どもたちがもって遊ぶ。

るを得ませんが，それを説明なしに行うと待っている人にははなはだ効率悪く見えます。

つまり，現場をあずかる責任者が行列する人の感情をよく理解することにより，客の満足度に大きく影響を与えることができます。賢明な解決法として，並んでいる時間が可能なかぎり楽しく時間の浪費と思わずに過ごせるように，あらゆる手段を考えておくべきでしょう。

団体の予約

少人数の団体にはあまり適していない予約システムですが，効果的に使えば大きな団体を扱うときには欠かせない手段となります。ねらいは，目に見える列を短くし，高いサービスを維持保証することです。予約をすることで，予約から来館するまでの時間が列の代わりになります。これによって，人が集中する時間を外して来館してもらうよう働きかけられるので，施設の受け入れ能力が高くなります。つまり，予約システムは現場の運営ばかりでなく，同時にマーケティングの手段にもなります（人気のない時間帯の利用団体に割引料金を適用することも可能なので）。

現実には，予約システムの導入によって，次のような運用の問題が生じます。
1．予約することで施設への期待が高まりすぎる
2．団体が到着しない場合，施設が十分に利用されずに入館料収入が減る
3．予約が集中すると，1日中混雑が生じる可能性がある

つまり，実用的な予約システムを導入すると，収容力を高める，入場を保証する，混雑を防止する，不測の事態への柔軟性をもたせるといった需要を相互にコントロールできるようになります。予約システムに基本的に求められることは，団体の到着時間の管理と，それによる施設全体の入場者の流れの管理です。予約システムは，学校団体やその他の団体の引率者に対して，あらかじめ決められた時間に入館できることを保証します。現場の管理責任者は，入館する人数を可能なかぎり増やし，同時にその利用の教育的な価値を保証することで，これらの団体に何度も繰り返して来館してもらうよう努力する必要があります。どのようなハンズ・オン系施設でも，それを超えると学習的な環境が大

きく劣化し始める利用者数の臨界点があり，この人数は消防条例による施設の定員数を大きく下回る傾向にあります。これは，ハンズ・オン系施設の教育環境が，ある部分大人と子どもの人数の比率に依存しているためで，家族連れに比べて団体の大人の数が少なくなるのは，利用者側の予算上の事情にもよるため避けることができません。したがって予約システムでは，混雑を予想してそれを防ぎ，団体の引率者に対して日にちや時間帯の選択肢を素早く効率よく示す必要があります。

　学校団体の場合，到着時間と出発時間を教師が自ら決めたがるため，利用時間帯が午前10時から午後2時30分までに集中しがちです。よくある例として，小学校の団体（たいていバス1台に2クラス）は午前9時に学校を出発し，10時に館に到着，2時間を自由に館内で過ごし，弁当を食べ（できれば室内が好ましいとされる），午後の指導付き見学の前に外で子どもたちに自由時間を与えて遊ばせます。そして帰りに少しだけショップに立ち寄り，午後3時30分の終業ベルが鳴るまでに学校に戻ろうとします。この標準プランでいけない場合，教師は博物館で過ごす時間の前後を埋める計画（これには別の予算措置が必要となる）を別途準備しなければなりません（このような団体を丸1日受け入れられないハンズ・オン系施設では，マーケティングの方策として，無料で立ち寄れる近くの場所を提案できるのが望ましい）。

　学校団体が到着する時間はもちろんのこと，1日の後半の混雑を防ぐために，団体利用者が館から立ち去る時間をも管理する必要があります。さらに，室内の昼食場所の設備の利用についても当然考えなければなりません。団体の受け入れ方には，次の3通りの方法があります。

1．館内の利用者が流れやすいように，到着時間をずらす。

　帰りの時間を同じようにずらせるかどうかは，場合によります。この方法では，入り口に列ができることを防ぐ半面，学校側が午前10時に来館したいと考えても希望がかなわないこともあるため，受け入れてもらえないかもしれません。帰りの時間が決められていない場合，1日の後半に混雑が生じて博物館での学習体験の質が損なわれるでしょう。

2．滞在時間を制限する。

　ユーリイカ！では，学校団体が来館する日を，2時間ごとの3つの時間帯

(午前10時から正午，正午から午後2時，午後2時から4時）に分けました。さらに，その2時間の利用のうち，最初の1時間はあらかじめ予約した展示室を借り切ることを決められ，残りの1時間で自由に他の展示室を見学できるようになっていました。昼食と買い物の時間は2時間の見学時間以外に認められましたが，2時間を過ぎると再び展示室に戻れません。この方法で，ユーリイカ！では学校団体を管理できるようになり，人気のない時間帯の利用には料金の割り引きも行われました（夏の午後は半額にすることも試された）。しかし，この予約方式は，当初，学校から歓迎されませんでした。理由の1つめは，イギリスの他の施設のやり方とは大きく異なっていたためであり，まずはこれを理解してもらう必要がありました。理由の2つめとして，この方式が固定時間制（時間枠の自由が利かない）であったことがあげられます。一般に，午前10時からの時間帯に人気が集中し，特に"わたしとからだ"など，特定の展示室がかなり前から予約されてしまいます。そのため多くの学校が，利用日程や時間，見学したい展示室や滞在時間を自由に選べませんでした。この方式の導入の目的は，なるべく多くの子どもたちに，適当な費用で，教育的な刺激が保証できる環境を提供することでした。導入された当初は，その規制に驚いた学校側も，後には全体的な利点を認めて受け入れるようになりました。

3．一定時間，館を団体が優先的に，あるいは貸し切りで使えるようにする。

　この方法は，教育面での利益が大きな半面，規模が極端に小さい施設以外のほとんどの施設では，たとえ短時間でも1団体に貸し切りにはできないという経営上の問題があります。この方法には，年齢や興味が異なる団体がかちあわないように管理できる利点はありますが，財政上の理由から実施が困難です。また，団体に貸し切りにする場合，それ以外の人が同様に利用できるよう，特に気を使う必要があります。ほとんどの施設では，学校がある日には家族連れや一般の来館者が少ないとはいっても，「貸し切り」にしてしまうと，同時に他の入館者が施設を利用できなくなるのです。マンハッタンこどもの博物館が午前中を団体のみの利用時間帯とし，午後は家族連れのみの時間帯としたのは，興味深い折衷案といえるでしょう。

　予約システムには運営方針が必要であり，時間通りに到着しない団体や予約

をすっぽかす団体などについての判断が求められます。筆者の経験から，たとえば希望に反して午前中の遅い時間を指定された団体が，その時間を無視して午前10時に館に着くことがあります。そのような団体に約束の時間まで外で待ってもらうのは，特に天候が悪い場合など大変につらいものです。また，時間通りに着いた団体と，やむにやまれぬ事情で遅くなった団体と，どちらを優先するかの判断は困難です。ユーリイカ！のような利用時間帯を設定していない場合は，遅れた団体をそのまま入館させると，館内を混乱させることになります。施設としての運用手順は必要ですが，現場の管理責任者はそれぞれの団体の引率者と話し合い，その時その時に応じた満足できる妥協策を探ることになるでしょう。

　予約をすっぽかす団体があると，ほかの団体に売れたはずの入場料金の分，館が損害を受けます。1つの解決法として，料金の一部か全額が支払われるまで，仮受け付けしかしないというやり方があります。金額の一部を前払いしないと予約が無効になり，その時間帯や場所が他の団体に再割り当てされるのです。このような方法は運用上非常に有効ですが，学校では保護者から事前に入館料を徴収するのが難しい場合が多いため，受け入れられにくいでしょう。

　さらに問題が大きいのは，あらかじめ利用料金を全額支払いながら，たとえば急病などで当日予定より少ない人数で来館し，欠席者分の払い戻しを要求される場合です。このような事態には，適切な対応策が必要となります。予約時の条件で払い戻しをしない方針の場合，担任教師が個人的に保護者に返金することもあり，そうなると必然的に施設への印象が悪くなります。また，欠員分の無料入場券を料金返還の代わりに渡すのは，遠方から訪れる団体にはあまりありがたく思われないようです。

　ここまでは，学期中の学校団体の予約について検討しました。これに加えて複雑なのは，団体が週末に予約を入れたいという場合や，学区によって学期の時期が異なる場合です。集客範囲が一部の地域ではなく広い範囲に及ぶ場合，所属する学区によって休日がまちまちになることがあります[6]。たとえば，あ

---

[6] イギリスでは学区によって独自の休日がある。たいていは国の休日の前後にとられているが，必ずしも日にちが一致しない。

る学区の登校日に別の学区では休日で，後者の地域からの家族連れで施設がいっぱいになります（さらには，学校団体と家族連れのどちらに対してもサービスが行き届かなくなります）。ユーリイカ！では，当初これがかなり大きな問題となりました。解決法として，ユーリイカ！まで片道90分の範囲内にあるすべての学区の休校日を調べ，前もって1年間のすべての日を次の3つに分類しました。

1. 登校日（すべての学区の登校日）
2. 一斉休校日（すべての学区の休日）
3. 週末およびその他の休日（学区独自に設定の休校日）

職員，学校団体や家族連れ対象のプログラム，団体の予約はこの分類に従って割り振られました。2の「一斉休校日」には長い列ができ，予約団体を優先することでトラブルが生じるので，団体を受け付けませんでした。このシステムは，ガールスカウトやボーイスカウトなど，学校以外の団体には不評でしたが，これらの団体には普通の週末や全体休校日以外の休日に予約をするようにお願いをしました（ただし，この場合，展示室の占有利用はなし）。

予約システム
　導入するのにふさわしい予約方式の検討が終わったら，次はそのシステムのコンピューター化についての判断が必要になります。その場合，さらに既存のソフトを購入するか，特別のプログラムを開発するかも決めなくてはなりません。コンピューターを導入せずに予約を手作業で行う場合，明らかに費用は安く上がりますが，人為ミスが生じたり，予約受け付け場所が1カ所に限定されることになります。傾向として，たいていの大きな施設では，複数の場所から予約可能で，予約状況の一覧などを作成できるようなチケット販売状況のデータ処理機能をもつコンピューターシステムを入れたがる場合が多いようです。
　ここで求められるのは次のことを可能にする予約システムでしょう。
1. 日時を入力すると，メインの施設と付帯施設（昼食をとる場所，教室，ワークショップスペース）の空き状況が一目でわかる。
2. 1件あたりの予約受け付け時間が短縮できる。予約の多くが，教師が電

話しやすい昼休みや休憩時間に集中するため（同時に複数の教師が予約しようとする可能性があり，予約受け付けスタッフの数や勤務時間，休憩時間を考慮する必要が生じるので）。
3．予約受け付けスタッフが扱いやすい設計で，操作に関する研修が短くてすむ。
4．必要に応じて料金計算ができ，自動的に伝票と予約の詳細が書かれた確認書の発行ができる。
5．将来の需要や拡張，値段の変更に対応できる。
6．予約受付番号を付けて，問い合わせにすぐ答えられる。
7．チケットの販売状況や将来の運営についてレポートを打ち出せる。

手作業と比べたときのコンピューターシステム最大の利点は，団体来館者数や予測される来館者数についてのレポートを，必要な時点ですぐに作成できることです（たとえば，ある特定の時間や居住地ごとの団体来館者数など）。予約受け付け時間の短縮に加えて，教育市場開発のために，たとえば子どもの年齢や，使われるカリキュラム，交通手段といったような実態的な情報を追加して得る機会にもなります。教育担当の責任者とマーケティング担当の責任者が，収集する情報の種類についてあらかじめ合意し，予約時に尋ねるなどして必要度が高い情報から優先的に収集する必要があります。

昼食時間の問題点

博物館や科学館などの施設を計画する際に，学校団体の昼食時間と場所の管理は最も軽視されてきた項目です。いくつかの例外（ロンドン国立自然史博物館の教育センター[7] など）は別にして，学校が利用するハンズ・オン系の博物館や科学館の設計者は，いつもこの問題を見過ごしてきました。しかし，学校

---

[7] ロンドン国立自然史博物館地階に設けられた"ディスカバリーセンター"（平日は学校利用が優先される子ども向けの展示室）の横にある教師向けの情報センター。教材の見本などがあり，利用について相談できる。ただし原著者がここで例としてあげているのはセンターそのものではなく，隣接する学校利用のための昼食スペースのことであろう。団体ごとに分けられるように，ブロック別にテーブルといすが色分けされている。なお，"ディスカバリーセンター"は2000年春に"しらべてみよう"という名称で改装オープン予定。

団体が館内に2時間以上滞在する場合，当然考慮されるべき事項です。真夏でさえ，天候によっては屋外で食事をとれなかったり，スクールバスの運転手のなかには車内での食事をきらう人もいます。1日の間に施設を利用する子どもたち全員（終日の利用者だけではなく，午前のみ，午後のみの利用者も昼食場所を要求することが多い）への昼食場所の提供は，職員の休憩なども考えると，ハンズ・オン系の博物館や科学館にとって大変大きな問題となります。

　ユーリイカ！では，2時間ずつの3つの時間帯に，それぞれ30人のクラスが10クラスずつ来館したとすると，1日あたり900人分（！）もの昼食場所が必要となります。教室などの教育設備を，昼食場所として時間いっぱい提供することはほぼ不可能で（込んでいる時間帯に，清掃の時間を入れると2時間以上の使用となるため），一方，カフェの担当者は有料で食事をする場所を学校団体に使わせるのをいやがります。ユーリイカ！，テクニクエスト，国立鉄道博物館の"マジシャンズロード[8]"では，学校団体の昼食用に電車の車両を設置しています。オプションの1つ（学校から積極的に選択されることはあまりないが）として，カフェでランチセットを購入することをすすめる場合があります。また，専属のスタッフが清掃を行う付帯設備を，有料で貸し出すという手もあります。

　現実には，昼食場所は他の目的（たとえば教室やレストラン）との併用が難しく，有料場所の利用やランチセットの購入は，学校側があまり望まない選択肢になります。

展示装置の故障

　ハンズ・オン系施設に寄せられる苦情の最大の原因は，展示装置の故障です。常識として，展示装置の5％が故障していた場合，利用者は「展示の半分が壊れていた」といい，10％が故障していると「全部壊れている！」と苦情を寄せます。ユーリイカ！では，イネイブラーと呼ばれるフロア解説スタッフが開館前にすべての展示を目でチェックし，同時に消耗品の在庫が十分かどうかも

---

[8] 国立鉄道博物館のなかにつくられた子ども向けの展示室で，鉄道に関したハンズ・オン展示が行われている。

調べていました。イネイブラーに報告された，あるいはイネイブラー自身による故障レポートが受付に集められ，それに対して適切な処置がとられました。週に1度は，すべての展示装置について機械の状態やグラフィックその他の装飾の検査を徹底的に行いました。現場管理の責任者はこの検査によって週のある時点で展示装置の何％が故障中かがわかり，故障した展示装置の状態を確実に改善することができるようになり，よく壊れる（再開発や撤去の必要がある）展示装置を特定する助けにもなりました。ユーリイカ！では，このようにして故障している展示装置の数を調べて苦情に対応できるようになり，さらに展示開発に際してどの新しい展示装置に問題が起こりそうか経験的にわかるようになりました。

　テクニクエストでも同様の運営方針を採用していますが，ここではさらに進んでいて，ある時点で故障している展示装置が受付に常時表示してあり，その日の担当職員の名前もわかるようになっています。この掲示板1枚の設置により，テクニクエストが展示装置の動作をいつも把握しているというメッセージが利用者に伝わります。

　ハンズ・オン系施設の現場運営責任者は，作動しない展示装置の原因を特定しなければなりません。これは簡単そうに思われます。実際，故障が機械的または電気的な原因による場合はそう難しくありません。事態が複雑になるのは，その機械本来の働きをしている状態でも，何をしているのかがわかりにくいため利用者が理解できていないと考えられる場合です。つまり，ある展示装置が利用者に対してどのような理由であれ適切に作動しないと，その利用者は展示装置が故障しているという印象を受けます。さらに，利用者が展示装置が何をするためのものかをすぐに理解できないと，物理的に使い方を誤ることも多くなります。2章で強調したように，どのような理由であれ展示装置が適正に作動しない場合，施設側に責任があります。これは例外なく展示開発者のミスが原因で，展示装置を複雑にしすぎたか，信頼性の低いものをつくってしまったかのどちらかです。重要なのは，展示デザイナーとフロア解説スタッフ，展示制作者が，必ず互いに協力しながら仕事をすることです。展示制作の早い段階で行う試作品の制作途中評価は，展示装置の物理的なデザインやグラフィックの受け取られ方から生じる問題を減らすためには欠かせません。

利用者が展示装置の故障を訴えるとき，実は装置そのものは故障しておらず，使う側が操作の指示に従わなかったために動かない場合があります。しかし，その事実を利用者に知らせるべきではありません。この問題は特に最新の技術を使用した場合に起こりやすく，たとえばコンピューターを用いた展示装置で目的を達成できない場合，実際には展示方法が悪いとしても，使う側はまるで自分に落ち度があるように感じます。そうすると，その技術の経験のない利用者の気分は沈み，将来同様のものに対して恐怖心を抱くかもしれません。このように，新しい技術を使うようにつくられた展示装置は，状況によって全く逆の効果を与えかねません。つまり，すべての利用者にわかりやすいものを設計するのは実際には困難ですが，この過程が展示装置が意図したように作動するかを左右する大きな要素です。そのためには展示装置についての評価が必要になります。

　どのハンズ・オン系施設でも，絶対に故障しない展示装置をつくり，それでも故障した場合には直ちに修理をしたいと考えていますが，現実にはそうはいきません。ありがちなパターンとして，それほど忙しくない日には修理担当者がすぐに作業を始めることができるので，苦情はほとんど寄せられませんが，混雑した日には来館者の数が増えるほど故障とその苦情も増えてきます。家族連れが入館するまで2時間も列に並び，やっと接した最初の展示装置のいくつかが故障していると当然ガッカリするでしょう。その館にとってシンボルのようなメインの展示装置が動かないと，状況はさらに悪くなります。その展示装置の人気が高く主要であるほど，正しく動かない場合は利用者の施設へのイメージが悪くなります。ハンズ・オン系施設の運営責任者は，どのような故障が生じると利用者の気に障り，引き続きどれくらいの時間がたつと苦情が寄せられるかを必ず知ることになります。同時に，利用者のイメージを決定するカギとなる展示装置がどれかもわかってくるでしょう。

　展示装置の故障がわかったら，すぐにそれを記録して調べる必要があります。したがって，展示運営デスクは故障の情報や苦情などが集まりやすい中央の場所（できれば案内カウンターの隣）に置くのが望ましいと考えられます。利用者から故障の報告があったときは，担当責任者はその利用者に頼んで具体的にどう動かないかを見せてもらえばよいでしょう。もし作動しない原因が故障と

いうより使い方の誤解であれば，そのときに誤解を訂正できます。あとでイネイブラーは，生じた問題の原因をほかのフロア解説スタッフに十分に説明する必要があります。そして，もし展示の機械そのものが故障しているのであれば，次のような確認を行います。

1．その展示装置は利用者にとって安全か。

　もし安全でない場合は，立ち入り禁止の柵を立てるか，展示室を閉鎖するかします。また，その展示装置の電源は切っておきます。

2．もし展示装置が安全で，しかし動かない場合，何らかの表示をする。

　「故障中」の表示を見た来館者はガッカリしますが，表示なしで故障している展示装置を使ってガッカリするより断然ましです。後者の場合，展示装置自体に問題があっても，利用者は自分が悪いように思うからです。

3．運営責任者は，どの展示から修理していくかを判断する。

　ここで判断の基準になるのは，その展示装置が主要なものかどうか，ワークショップなどの行事に必要か，修理担当者がすぐに手配できるか，といった項目です。

4．展示装置の修理は現場でできるのか。

　展示装置の多くは，展示室の床や壁に固定されており，容易に動かせない状態にあります。しかし，時には展示室を公開しながら修理はできます。展示技術者がてきぱきと故障した展示装置を修理する光景は，それだけで教育的な効果を高めることがあります（しかも費用は修理費だけで）。私は，何度となくユーリイカ！の"ともに生きること，はたらくこと"展示室にある銀行の現金支払機でお金の補充や機械の修理をしましたが，たくさんのお金を前にした子どもたちが，どんなに目を丸くして驚いていたことか。機械の裏側やそれが動く仕組みには，誰でも子どものような好奇心で引きつけられるでしょう。もちろん，安全のために，一時的に柵を立てて人が近づけないようにし，修理をするスタッフが現場から離れるときには，道具やはしごを残さないようにするなどの配慮が必要です。

5．展示装置を移動する場合，複製品か代替物はあるか。

　理想をいえば，ハンズ・オンの展示室ではすべての展示装置の複製や代替品をもつべきですが，現実にはこれは不可能です。しかし，よく修理が必要な部

品の在庫をもつことならば可能です。2章で述べたように, ハンズ・オン系施設では, できるだけ一般部品（ポンプやベアリング, モーターなど）を標準規格に合わせ, 近くで入手可能な部品のみを使うべきです。もし外国から部品を輸入しなければ展示の修理ができないとしたら, 故障の際こまります。規格部品を使用して修理をしやすくすることは, ハンズ・オン展示物のデザインにとって必要条件なのです。

苦情の対応

　人気も実績もあるハンズ・オン系施設でも, 時には苦情が寄せられます。その施設が利用者の意見を尊重して何度も来てもらいたいなら, 提案や苦情を寄せやすいように工夫し, 寄せられた意見には素早く効率よく対応しなくてはいけません。しかし, 苦情や提言をもらうシステムさえつくれば, 利用者の満足度がすべてわかると決め込むのは早計です。アメリカの消費者行動の研究によれば, 消費者全体の25％が自分の買った商品に不満足ですが, 実際に苦情を寄せるのは不満を感じた人の5％にすぎません。アメリカの消費者のデータが, そのままイギリスの集客施設にあてはまるわけではありませんが, 実際問題として, 自分たちの苦情がささいなことで, 苦情をいってもバカみたいな気持ちにさせられるか, 対応措置がとられないのではないかと, 依然多くの人が感じているのは事実です。つまり, 苦情のみでは利用者の満足度を測ることはできず, 苦情は来館者調査のデータ代わりにはならないのです。

　利用者は不満を感じると, 2度とその施設を訪れないか, 訪れる回数を減らします。再びアメリカの消費者調査の結果を見ると, 満足した客は口コミで3人によい商品について伝え, 不満足な客は11人もの人々に不満足であったことを伝えます。これを聞いた人が, さらに他の人にも同様のことを伝えるとすると, よいことも悪いことも口コミであっというまに広がっていくでしょう。さらに, 不満足な状態に対して最も気分を害するのはそれまでよい顧客だった購買客で, 苦情をいう客はその問題がうまく解決されると, 以降, 最も忠実な顧客になります。

　苦情受け付けを効果的に行うためには, 利用者にとって簡単でわかりやすい方法が必要です。たとえば, 館の中央に「ご意見募集」と明記した場所（通常

は案内デスク）を設置し，様式の決まった記入用紙を作り，意見の交流と苦情に応じる窓口や担当者を明らかにしておきます。この担当者は，苦情を受けたら素早くしっかりと対処できるように研修されるべきでしょう。調査によると，苦情への対応が速ければ速いほど，補償が大きければ大きいほど，顧客の満足度は大きくなるといわれています。

補償については，明確な方針が必要です。たとえば，入館料を返すのか，代わりに無料チケットを渡すのか（それによってカフェやショップの売り上げが伸びるかもしれない）などです。組織のどの部署で料金を返還するのか，館側の過失が確認された場合，交通費やその他の費用の補償を行うかについても方針が必要です。もしこれが学校などの団体の場合，補償の費用が支払われる入館料をはるかに上回ることになりかねません。

苦情への対処の最後の手順は，その苦情の原因となった問題点の発見と修正です。3章で強調しましたが，利用者が苦情を寄せやすくするのに加え，その満足度を知り，改善への提言をもらうために，定期的な来館者調査を行う必要があります。満足度を知るのに，「また来たいと思うか」，「友人にすすめようと思うか」といった質問は有効です。ほかには，「覆面利用者」を雇い，職員にも知らせずに来館してもらい，サービスについて通常のアンケートに答えてもらうという方法もあります。

最後に付け加えると，定期的に館内を歩き，展示装置を自分で試したり，職員や利用者に話しかけたりするのがよい管理責任者です。ユーリイカ！のオフィスの造りが展示室を通り抜けないとデスクに戻れないようになっているのは，単なる偶然ではありません。展示室でよく仕事をする管理責任者は，ただ苦情を引き起こした原因を見つけるだけではなく，職員の尊敬と自信を喚起し，結果として将来生じるかもしれない人材についての問題を修正できるようになります。

まとめ

ハンズ・オン系施設における効果的な現場運営とは，すなわち教育目的にみあう堅実で質の高いサービスを提供することです。これは，館の財源をはじめ，あらゆる物的人的資源と相まってもたらされます。来館者を引き寄せるのに口

コミ情報が大変重要な広報手段であるため，ハンズ・オン系博物館や科学館を効果的に運営するには，首尾一貫したサービス提供が極めて重要です。込み合った休日に訪れても，12月の金曜日の閉館1時間前の空いた時間帯に訪れても，すべての利用者に同じレベルの博物館体験をしてもらわなければなりません。事実，これら2つの両極端な例は，最も問題が起こりやすい状況でもあります。前者では，さまざまな条件が限界ぎりぎりで建物が人であふれ，展示装置が故障したり苦情が寄せられやすくなります。反対に，後者のように暇なときは，職員などが削られて利用者へのサービスが行き届かなくなります。どのようなサービスの提供にも"人"の存在は欠かせません。ハンズ・オンを用いた学習における「人の要素」の重要性を知り，高度な研修を受けたフロア担当スタッフがどのような問題をも解決しうることがわかると，人材管理の水準を高く保つことはハンズ・オン系博物館や科学館の効果的な運営にとって必須のことがらであるとの理解が得られるでしょう。この分野についての考察は，次の章に譲ります。

ユーリイカ！こどものための博物館
入り口での行列
込み始めるとロープで人の流れを誘導する。外には『オズの魔法使い』になぞらえた「黄色いレンガの道（利用者からの寄付でレンガが追加される）」があり，入場者が多くて混雑する日には一定の入場制限が行われ，この道まで列が続くという。
（撮影：稲庭彩和子）

ロンドン国立自然史博物館
教育センター横の昼食スペース
地下のディスカバリーセンターと教育センターの間にある昼食スペース。機能的なテーブルといすが用意され，少しでも多くの人が利用できるように設計されている。団体利用者を受け入れるには不可欠な施設である。

ユーリイカ！こどものための博物館
昼食用電車車両
本館のすぐ隣にある昼食用の場所。鉄道駅に隣接するユーリイカ！では敷地内にレールなどもあり，この車両がただ子どもの人気を当て込んでいるだけでなく，まわりの風景と違和感なくフィットしている。

7章
組織・人材管理

さまざまな館のフロアスタッフたち
上）ユーリイカ！のイネイブラー（撮影：稲庭彩和子）
下）ロンドン国立科学博物館のエクスプレイナー
右）ヨーク市にあるバーリーホールのフロア解説スタッフ。昔の衣装をつけている。

7章 組織・人材管理

　この章では、インタラクティブ系施設の人材、なかでもフロアに出て利用者に直接接する解説スタッフやボランティアの人事管理について、実践的な内容を検討します。

はじめに

　ハンズ・オン系博物館や科学館で必要な人の技能は他の集客施設と同様で、経営、現場の運営管理、人材管理、マーケティングと広告・宣伝、教育プログラムの企画、イベントの運営管理など、管理的な仕事すべてにわたります。しかし、インタラクティブな博物館体験の成功のカギとなるのが利用者と職員の間で行われる人による交流であるため、人材の募集や採用、機会の均等化、研修、能力開発などがうまく行われなければなりません。これは、ハンズ・オン系施設でよく見られるフロア担当スタッフの疲労、つまり「燃え尽き現象」を避けるためにも欠くことができません。ボランティアも、多くのハンズ・オン系施設にとって欠かせない人材で、この人たちを実効があるように活用するには綿密な計画に基づく管理が必要です。多くの博物館、特にアメリカの例では、有給職員と無給職員（ボランティアなど）両方に配慮した人材活用方針を定めており、さらには広く社会的な不平等や教育の不足などをなくす目的の革新的なプログラムを工夫して、人材の雇用と研修を行っています。この章では、人の活用をうまく行っている英米のハンズ・オン系博物館について紹介します。

ハンズ・オン系施設における"人"の重要性

　どんな集客施設においてもサービスを提供する職員は必要ですが、利用者とのやりとりでその質を一定に保つのは難しく、人による交流には常に不確実性がつきまといます。このため、いつでもどこでも一貫した高い質のサービスを

提供できるようにするための人材を確保することは、どのようなタイプの集客施設にとっても常に最重要の課題です。しかし、ハンズ・オン系博物館ではその性格上、一般の集客施設に比べてさらに次のような要素が追加されます。

(1) サービスの無形性

　ハンズ・オン系施設の利用者は自分が何を期待して訪れたかを必ずしも理解しておらず、フロア担当職員は大人と子ども両方の利用者を安心させるという重要な役割を果たす。たとえば、子どもがどのくらいまで羽目を外していいのかなども示す必要がある。

(2) 客の性質

　利用者の中心は子どもであり、展示自体も子どもを喜ばせるような手法でつくられているため、利用者（なかでも子ども）の行動は予測しがたい場合がある。フロア担当職員はどのような状況にも対応できる準備をしなくてはならない。

(3) 体験の性質

　インタラクティブ系施設には教育目的がある。フロア担当職員が親に協力を依頼し、子どもが展示との相互作用でより多く学べるように手助けしてもらうと、学習の質が高まる。

(4) 展示の性質

　インタラクティブな展示は、連続使用や誤使用にも耐えられるように高い水準でつくられなくてはならない。しかし、うまく考えられた展示装置でも壊れることがある。このような場合、同時に複数の異なったタイプの整備作業を安全かつユーモラスに、時には利用者の目前で行えるような器用な技術者が必要である。そういった技術者は、インタラクティブ系施設にとって貴重な人材である。

　ロンドン国立科学博物館の"もの"展示室[1]を対象に行った展示評価調査によれば、子どもと親、教師、エクスプレイナー（フロア解説スタッフ）などの大人が相互に作用することで展示体験の質が高まることがわかりました。調査全体を通じて、大人の働きかけがあると子どもはよく展示に集中でき、その場

---

[1] 2章58ページ脚注12参照。

にいる時間が長くなりました。学校団体の場合は，エクスプレイナーによる教育的で生き生きとした説明が，子どもの注意を引くことが確認されました。この調査では，エクスプレイナーが行う展示室でのさまざまな活動（簡単な実演やディスカバリーボックス[2] を利用しての説明など）を増やすべきである，という結論が出ました。フォークとダイアキングは『博物館体験』のなかで，体験の質を高めるための"人"の重要性を強調し，「結局，展示と利用者を結ぶ"人"の存在が，一般の人々の理解と学習を決定する最も重要な要因らしい」と述べています。さらに2人は，実際に人とのかかわりによって，博物館体験が利用者の記憶に残りやすくなるという証拠があると述べ，場合によっては，来館して何年も忘れないという事実があると例をあげています。

> 少しずつでも1人ひとりに注意を配り，自分が特別で大切な存在であると感じさせることで，その博物館体験は実際的で忘れられないものになる。……博物館職員，それもよく訓練され献身的に仕事をしている職員の存在は，教育を質の高いものにするために依然として重要な役割を果たしている。

また，トーマスが「壊れた展示よりも，ほほえむスタッフのほうがより記憶に残る」と書いているように，利用者とフロア解説スタッフによる交流の質の向上はマーケティングの面からも意味があります。

博物館の組織構造

科学技術館協会（ASTC）では，世界中の従来型の科学博物館，こどもの博物館，ハンズ・オン系科学館について定期的に調査を実施していますが，館の大きさや組織構造には「典型」がないという結果が出ています。1987年の調査では，131館から回答がありました（うち18館はアメリカ以外）。このなかで，職員の配置に関して回答してきた館について，フルタイム，パートタイム合わせた全職員をフルタイム職員に換算した場合，1館あたりの職員数は28.5人になりました。もちろん，職員数は館の規模の大きさと比例しています。1館あたりの職員数は，最小規模の館（面積1857㎡以下）では17.5人，小規模

---

[2] 2章57ページ脚注11参照。

館（1858〜6968 ㎡）では46人，中規模館（6968〜1万8580 ㎡）では118人，大規模館（1万8580 ㎡以上）では242人でした。

　グリネルの『科学学習のための新施設：科学館の開設と経営』には，館種がさまざまなので，館の組織構造もまたさまざまであるが，一般的には①本部機能・財務，②マーケティング・開発（基金調達），③プログラム立案・管理（展示部門と教育部門が別組織になっていることが多い）の3つの部門から成る，とあります。ASTCの調査結果では各館の性格や規模が異なるため，「すべての施設にあてはまるような望ましい組織構造は存在しない」とまとめています。たとえばキュレーターや資料保存担当の人材は，その施設がこれらの職種に関した博物館機能をもつ場合にのみ採用されます。またハンズ・オン系施設では，展示開発計画に教育部門と展示解説部門の責任者が欠かせないため，その担当者として上級の職員が雇用されることがよくあります。この職責は一般の博物館ではあまり見られません。

　ASTCの調査では，回答のあった館では予算の50〜70％を人件費にあてていました。この数字は，イギリスの施設で一般に年間予算の約50％を人件費にあてているという経営データ（第4章を参照）によって裏付けられます。博物館体験における人のかかわりの重要性と予算の大きな部分を実際に人件費にあてている意味を考えると，人材の採用・能力開発・管理を上手に行おうとすることは明らかに道理にかなっています。特に採用と能力開発には膨大な費用がかかるので，職員が頻繁に入れ替わると割に合いません。

フロア解説スタッフの役割

　ハンズ・オン系博物館や科学館の職員中で最も大きな比率を占めるのが，展示の解説補助のためにフロアに出て利用者にじかに接する人々です。彼らは施設によってさまざまに呼ばれており，いくつか例をあげると，パイロット（エクスプロラトリー），イネイブラー（ユーリイカ！，バーミンガム市博物館ディスカバリーセンター"科学に光をあてて"），ヘルパー（テクニクエスト，ラヴィレットのインベントリアム），エクスプレイナー（ロンドン国立科学博物館，エクスプロラトリアム），インタープリター（ボストンこどもの博物館），オグジリアリー（ロンドン国立自然史博物館），ホスト（オンタリオ科学館），

デモンストレーター（テクノロジーテストベッド），ギャラリーアシスタント（ロンドン国立科学博物館"ラウンチパッド"）などです。フロア解説スタッフの名称には施設間で統一意見がなくさまざまですが，ド・カリエが「ハンズ・オン学習の人的要素」として報告しているように，ハンズ・オン展示におけるこれらの職員の役割についての考え方は驚くほど共通しています。これはヨーロッパのハンズ・オン系施設が，この分野で特に先駆的役割を果たしたアメリカの2館，すなわちサンフランシスコにあるエクスプロラトリアムとボストンこどもの博物館を主なお手本にしているためです。

事例紹介：エクスプロラトリアム（サンフランシスコ）のエクスプレイナー

　エクスプロラトリアムでは，88年にフルタイムの職員90人，パートタイムの職員118人（うち45人がエクスプレイナー）と，その職員たちを支える常勤のボランティア25人およびイベントのボランティア75人が勤務していました。69年から86年までの間，「やる気，人種などの背景の多様性だけを基準に選ばれた」ティーンエイジャー900人がパートタイムの有給エクスプレイナーとして雇われ，これが博物館のフロア解説スタッフの先駆けとなりました。当時館長であったオッペンハイマーの哲学は，エクスプレイナーを雇うことで館側と雇われる側双方に利益をもたらしたいというものでした。つまり，学生たちは館と利用者の役に立ち，その見返りとしてただ給料を受け取るだけではなく，価値ある仕事の技術を身につけたのです。

　エクスプレイナーは，平均4カ月ごとに年3回採用されました。これは，多くの学生たちがこのプログラムに参加できるように1回の雇用期間を短くし，さらに「燃え尽き現象」の影響を最小限にするためでした。彼らの仕事は利用者に対する科学的事象の説明でしたが，科学の知識よりは好奇心の強さ，親しみやすさ，熱意や人材の多様性が雇用の条件として重視されました。エクスプレイナーの半数以上は白人ではなく，採用にあたっての必須条件は子どもと大人の利用者とすぐにうちとけられる能力でした。エクスプレイナーに選ばれるとまず週末3回で50時間の集中講習を受け，その後は館の職員から日常的な研修を受けました。

　このプログラムの成功には，展示と同じくらい社交的な環境も重要であ

る。エクスプレイナーは互いによく助け合い，結果として出身背景が全く異なる学生たちの間に，相互に頼り協力しあう気持ちが生まれてくる。そして，職員と学生たちの間にはすぐに師弟関係ができあがる（ダイヤモンドらの論文「エクスプロラトリアムのエクスプレイナー養成プログラム」）。

　エクスプレイナーの勤労意欲が高く保たれたのは，新しい展示装置やその試作品が頻繁に導入されたからです。このティーンエイジャー向けプログラムに参加した若者に与えた長期的影響を調査したところ，特に学生たちの科学学習においていい結果が生じていることがわかりました。参加学生はいずれも自信を深め，新しい学習技能を磨き，出身背景の異なる者同士がともに働くことを前向きにとらえていました。しかも彼らは，ほかの仕事に就いていたティーンエイジャーより労働に積極的になっていました。

事例紹介：ボストンこどもの博物館のインタープリター
　ボストンこどもの博物館の公式な目的の1つに，「ともに子どもたちとかかわり，博物館の仕事に創造性と専門性をもたらすような多様な人材を引きつけ支えること」とあります。ステュワートが『開かれる博物館』にまとめた館の戦略と歴史を読むと60年代の最初の頃，ボストンこどもの博物館では，館の利用者，幹部職員，一般職員すべてが白人でした。60年代の終わりの頃から博物館が推進した多文化プログラム[3]のために出身背景の異なる職員が採用され始め，91年に在籍している105人のフルタイム職員のなかには，さまざまな人種や民族的な背景の人々が組織内のどの地位にもいました。新聞に求人広告を出すよりも時間はかかりますが，この館では採用に先だち多文化社会である周辺地域社会に接触し，職員候補者がいるかどうかを努めて探していました。しかし館側は，多様な希望者からの採用を積極的に進めながらも，最適な人材

---

[3] ボストンこどもの博物館では，開館当初から多様な文化的背景をもつ子どもたちに利用してもらうことを大きな課題としていた。文中の1960年代頃から次第に取り組み始め，79年に町なかに移転したことを契機に，多様な文化民族的背景の人々を利用者のみならず職員にも受け入れる方向で動き出す。80年代後半からはアメリカ社会全体で文化の多様性が重視され始め，助成金を受けたプログラムとして，スタッフ養成から展示，組織の構造の変革まであらゆる面で全館的に取り組まれた。

を選ぶことがなによりも重要だとしています。

　ボストンこどもの博物館の博物館教育実習プログラムは，博物館でのキャリアや学校以外の教育現場に興味をもつ個人に体験の機会を与えるため世界中から応募者を受け付けています。その主要な役割は利用者との交流であり，続いて安全性の確保，清掃，展示の消耗品の補充などがあります。可能なかぎり多様な人を受け入れるため，インターン（実習生）という職の前提条件は特にありません。志願者は年3回採用され，5カ月勤務か夏季の12週間勤務となります。選考されると，館の先輩職員による10日間の入門プログラムを受けます。まず，最初の4日間で館の考え方や展示および運営に関する集中オリエンテーションを受け，次の2日間ですでにフロアに出ているインタープリターについてシャドーイング（真似をしながら仕事を習得すること）を行い，最後の4日間で実地研修をこなします。すべての展示コーナーにはそれぞれの考え方や目的を記した研修マニュアルがあり，館の職員も各人1日1時間の研修プログラムを担当します。ここでは，館の考え方に沿って，特に利用者への配慮とインタラクティブな学習についての研修に重点が置かれています。

　以上見てきたエクスプロラトリアムとボストンこどもの博物館におけるフロア解説スタッフの役割は，ヨーロッパの科学館やこどもの博物館にとってよい手本となっていますが，このほかに，たとえば雇用機会の均等化，ボランティアの起用，学生トレーニー（見習い）の活用，スタッフの研修や能力開発について手本となる実践も数多くあります。いくつか例をあげてみましょう。

事例紹介：ニューヨーク・ホールオブサイエンスの理科教育キャリアラダー

　ニューヨーク・ホールオブサイエンスでは理科教育キャリアラダー[4]という女性や黒人に科学関係の仕事に興味をもってもらうためのキャリアアッププログラムを，他に先駆けて実施しました。91年には，8つの大学から科学と教

---

[4] 青少年に科学や科学に関する職業に興味をもってもらうと同時に，館の顔でもあるエクスプレイナーを確保する目的で行われているプログラム。ニューヨーク・ホールオブサイエンスが改修ののち86年に再オープンした際，フロア解説スタッフが不足していたこともあり，エクスプロラトリアムの有給エクスプレイナーをモデルとして始まった。沿革については，シーゲルが「キュレーター」41/4（1988）で紹介している。

育を専攻する黒人の大学生60人をパートタイムのエクスプレイナーとして雇い，週に15時間，全体で10週間にわたるプログラムを実施しました（年に3回）。彼らに与えられた役割は利用者を迎えて展示にかかわるのを手伝い，実演を行うことでした。さらに研修に参加する学生が自信をもち，科学的な知識を得て，人との交流技術を磨くのを援助するのも大きな目的でした。エクスプレイナーはそれぞれ仕事の内容を記した説明資料を渡され，2日間の入門研修を受け，毎日30分ずつ講習に出席し，講習課程の中間と最後に到達度を評価されました。しかもそれは大学の専攻履修単位として認められ，さらに勤務に対して給与が，研修に対して手当が支給されました。参加者のなかには150時間の講習が終了した後も続けた学生もいました。この教育プログラム実施後の総括評価によれば，参加学生の多くが最終的に数学や理科の教員になったということでした。このほかに高校生レベルの「ジュニアエクスプレイナー」が，週末や夜間，夏季に大学生エクスプレイナーを補助する見習いとして雇用されています。何人かは有給ですが，参加によって学校の単位を取得した者もいました。ボストン科学博物館にも学生インターン制度があり地元の企業が資金を提供しています。

アメリカのハンズ・オン系博物館とボランティア

　ASTCの調査によると，回答のあった125の館でそれぞれ平均98人のパートタイムのボランティア（フルタイムでは11のポストに相当する）を受け入れており，これは教育やプログラムづくりにかかわる人材の28％を占めていました。これらのうち半数の館ではボランティアの配置などを調整するボランティアコーディネーターを有給で雇っており，7％の館ではこのコーディネーターの仕事自体がボランティアによって行われていました（これ以外の館では，ボランティアの調整機能が分散していたため，コーディネーターがいなかったと考えられる）。ボランティアの60％が18歳から59歳で，15％が17歳以下，25％が60歳以上でした。

　ボストン科学博物館では大規模なボランティア活用制度を実施しており，91年には450人が延べ6万時間仕事をしましたが，これはフルタイムの職員に換算すると25人分に相当するものでした（ボランティア1人につき月12時間ず

つ勤務)。ボランティアは年に3回採用され、最初に2日間の入門プログラムに参加した後、毎日30分の研修を受けました。ニューヨーク・ホールオブサイエンスやボストンこどもの博物館と同様に、ここでも展示装置のすべてにそれぞれの研修マニュアルがありました。すべてのボランティアが仕事の内容を明記した職務明細書をもらっており、ほとんどが書面で契約を交わしていました。

　インディアナポリスこどもの博物館(世界一の規模をもつ、こどものための博物館)でも大規模なボランティア活用制度を実施しており、90年には152人のフルタイムの職員と80人のパートタイム職員のもと、555人の大人のボランティアが2万3297時間、737人の青少年ボランティアが5万3429時間勤務しました。インディアナポリスでは青少年と大人のボランティアを大変重視しており、独自にボランティア部門をもっています。同じように、フィラデルフィアのプリーズタッチ博物館でも100人のボランティアが30人のフルタイム職員と20人のパートタイム職員を支えていました。この館のボランティアは正規の面接を経て職務明細書をもらい、日常的に研修を受けていました。ボランティア職員の仕事範囲は館の事業のすべてにわたっており、展示室と裏方の両方をこなし、場合によっては有給職員と同じ仕事をしていました。マンハッタンこどもの博物館でも同じように仕事が重なっていましたが、ボランティアは職務明細書をもらっていませんでした。一方、ブルックリンこどもの博物館では、91年に地方自治体の予算削減のためボランティアコーディネーターを雇えず、残った正規職員がボランティアの起用によって自分たちの仕事が脅かされると感じたためボランティアを使っていませんでした。

ヨーロッパのハンズ・オン系博物館

　ヨーロッパのハンズ・オン系博物館は当初、フロア解説スタッフの採用や選考、研修について、アメリカの科学館やこどもの博物館から影響を受けていました。パリのラヴィレットにあったインベントリアムでは、家族連れの大人の利用者を元気づけたり、学校団体の不安をやわらげたり、展示の内容をわかりやすくする目的でヘルパーが雇われました。彼らの仕事は、機器を点検し、簡単な維持調整作業を行い、展示の使用を管理し、子どもの学習を助ける質問をし、子どもからの質問に答え、教育的な活動の実演や運営をすることでした。

その仕事の内容はヘルパー自身と利用者双方にとってわかりやすくある必要がありましたが、それはヘルパー自身が多彩な仕事を効果的に行えるようになるためでもあり、一方でツアーガイドや制服を着た案内係に慣れた利用者にフロア解説スタッフの役割を理解させるためでもありました。インベントリアムではボランティアも働いていましたが、混乱を避けるために有給職員とは別の仕事が与えられていました。

ユーリイカ！のイネイブラーは当初、利用者が楽しめ、展示から少しでも多くのものを学べるようにする目的（イネイブラーは「できるようにしてあげる人」の意）で設置されました。さらに、団体利用者を出迎えてつきそい、週末や休日には家族向けの活動を実施し、列で待つ人々を楽しませ、警備と安全を確保する役割も担っていました。彼らは、教育と展示解説のチームの中心的な役目を果たしていました[5]。イネイブラーのうち11人が無期限契約（当初の短期契約に引き続き）のフルタイム勤務で、それ以外の多くが臨時雇用でした。臨時職員も契約職員も給与は同じで、4人のチームリーダーのもとに所属して仕事を行いました（リーダーはそれぞれ、学校との連絡調整、イベント、日常維持管理、ボランティアコーディネーターといった仕事を担当）。利用者サービスの責任者が、チームリーダーとイネイブラーたちの統括を行い、教育展示解説部長のもとにこの責任者と2人の教育官、1人のカリキュラム助成教師が所属していました[6]。

通常イネイブラーは1時間ごとに持ち場を交代しましたが、学校団体が訪れる日には、団体を入り口で出迎えてその後も同行しました。学校がある日には11人、週末には15人、休日（夏休みや祝日）など混雑する日には19人のイネイブラーが雇われました。週末と休日には特別な行事の運営や列で待つ人々を楽しませるために、イネイブラーを追加して雇いました。この人数から計算すると、学校のある通常日は展示室273㎡あたりに1人、休日などの混雑日には158㎡あたり1人のイネイブラーが担当していたことになります。クインの

---

[5] この章で取り上げられるユーリイカ！の事例は、基本的に原著者が在籍していた1992～93年の内容に基づいている。
[6] 教育官とカリキュラム助成教師というポストは、原著者がユーリイカ！の教育・展示解説部長であった1992～93年に公の助成金で雇用した臨時職である。

調べによると，他館の例としては，インベントリアムでは一般の展示場で 300 ㎡ あたり 1 人でしたが，同館のディスカバリールーム[7] では子ども 5 人に 1 人のイネイブラーがついていました。

展示室によっては，イネイブラーの仕事はただ利用者を助けたり，安心させたり，安全性を確保するだけで十分でした。しかし，工場の展示の生産ライン[8] などはイネイブラー不在では全く動かせず，結果として開館中のかなりの時間運転が停止するため，明らかに運営上満足できる状態ではありませんでした。特にロールプレイを行うような展示室では，その効果を大きく高めるためにイネイブラーの存在が重要でした。92 年に行った展示評価調査によると，イネイブラーが常駐している銀行の展示[9] ではロールプレイがうまく行われ，子どもたちはお金や両替について効果的に学べました。しかし，店の展示[10] ではイネイブラーが子どものレジ操作の手伝いにかかりきりになってロールプレイがあまり行われず，活動が混乱したという報告がありました。

ユーリイカ！の最初のイネイブラーは，館が一般公開される 2 カ月前に採用されました。地方や地域の新聞に募集広告を載せた結果 400 人もの応募があり，75 人を面接し，最終的にフルタイム，パートタイムをとりまぜて短期契約で 24 人のイネイブラーを採用しました。大学の卒業生や教職経験者，保育園の保母などからの選択的な採用も可能でしたが，その頃ユーリイカ！ではさまざまな技能や経験をもつ幅広い人々に機会を提供するという方針があったため，特定の人を対象とした採用は行いませんでした。採用されたイネイブラーの 3 つの共通点は，子どもたちと接する仕事をした経験，人から好かれる性格，そして若さでした。若者だけを雇うことについては仕事の肉体的な厳しさを理由

---

[7] 2 章 57 ページ参照。
[8] ユーリイカ！の 1 階にある工場を再現した展示コーナー。ここでは，たとえば牛乳パックができあがる機械を観察したり，スタッフの指導のもと実際に生産ラインの流れ作業に参加することで工場の仕組みを体験できる。
[9] ユーリイカ！の"ともに生きること，はたらくこと"のなかにある展示コーナーで，銀行を再現してある。実際に現金支払機をカードで操作したり金庫室に入ったり，お金や銀行の役割りや仕組みをロールプレイを通して知ることができる。
[10] ユーリイカ！の"ともに生きること，はたらくこと"のなかにあるストア。本当の店と同じく商品が並んでおり，子どもたちが店員やお客に扮してカートに品物を積み込んでレジで精算をしたりできるようになっている。こどものための博物館では定番ともいえる展示である。

にこの方針を正当化していましたが，実際は差別的であったと思われます。また，ユーリイカ！のイネイブラーにはさまざまな文化的背景をもつ人々の応募があり，職員の顔ぶれは大変多様になりましたが，一方で全般的に男性の採用は困難でした。

　最初のイネイブラーたちは，教育部の職員や管理職，さらに消防署員などから，1週間の集中的な研修を受けました。その後は，毎日仕事前に30分のチーム会議を行い，その日のプログラムについて話し合ったり，イネイブラーと責任者の間の情報交換が行われました。さらに研修の必要性についての総合調査の結果に基づき，学校がある期間の月曜日の午後に長期の研修プログラムが設定され，教育チームのメンバーや外部の専門家による指導が行われました。このように，最初の年は劇団シアターインエデュケーション[11]の専門家による指導から手話まで，幅の広い内容の研修が実施されました。

　最初の短期契約が終了したとき，多くのイネイブラーたちが引き続き無期限契約をしました。そのとき館長は，アメリカの事例から，短期契約によってイネイブラーの「燃え尽き現象」を防止できると主張しました。しかし，当時のイネイブラーが仕事の安定を希望し，採用や研修などの初期投資が大きかったため，無期限契約を行って核となる熱心なスタッフに忠誠心をもってもらうのが実際的であると考えました。結果として，最初の1年間は再び大規模な募集をする必要がなくなりました。一方，臨時職員のフロア解説スタッフは週末や休日のために大量に雇用され，そのたびに短期の入門的な研修が行われ，ボランティアや青少年のトレーニー，学生たちもこの研修を受けました。研修の1日目は，教育チームによるユーリイカ！とその展示の基盤となる運営の考え方の講義が半日，イネイブラーのチームリーダーによる避難訓練と主要な展示コーナーの研修が半日で構成されていました。2日目は，経験のあるイネイブラーを先生として1日中シャドーイングを行い，3日目には新しいイネイブラーが自分たちで仕事をしました。

　ロンドン国立科学博物館では，86年に"ラウンチパッド"に白衣を着た6

---

[11] イギリスの劇団で，学習のための教育的なメッセージを取り入れた劇を子ども向けに上演している。

人のギャラリーアシスタントが配置されました。94年には，30人のエクスプレイナーを雇いましたが，ユーリイカ！の場合と同じく，彼らはやる気のある社交的な若者たちでした。その役割はただ展示の科学的な原理を伝えるだけではなく，利用者が質問をしたり互いに学び合えるよう促すことでした。エクスプレイナーはあらかじめ用意した答えを与えるのではなく，利用者が自ら発見できるように働きかけるよう，研修を通じて訓練されました。ユーリイカ！と同様に，彼らの仕事は展示室の活動や実演を行ったり，学校から来た子どもたちを指導したり，展示装置の状態を監視したり，展示室の安全性を確保したり，人込みをさばくことでした。科学博物館の場合，フロア解説スタッフに技能と性格の両方を求めており，科学の理解力はもちろん，熱心に上手に人と交流できる能力がさらに重要だとしています。また，展示の背景にある科学的事実，学習スタイル，ナショナルカリキュラム[12]，プレゼンテーション技能，自信をもつ訓練などの研修に大きく投資しているのもユーリイカ！と同様です。

イネイブラーの「燃え尽き現象」

　イネイブラーのようなフロア解説スタッフを長期契約で雇用しているインタラクティブ系施設では必ず疲労，つまり「燃え尽き現象」といった問題が生じます。アメリカの博物館の多くは雇用期間を短くしてこの問題を防いでいますが，エクスプロラトリアムのように展示装置を新しくすることで勤労意欲の低下を防いでいる例もあります。ロンドン国立科学博物館やユーリイカ！では，技術を磨くためだけではなく「燃え尽き現象」の影響をなくす目的で雇用期間途中の研修プログラムを実施しています。頻繁に仕事の内容を変えたり仕事の成果を表彰するなどできないため，このような方法は大変重要です。熱心なイネイブラーほど，教育担当職員や展示デザイナー並みの，より責任の大きな仕事をしたいと考えます。ユーリイカ！ではイネイブラーから昇進したり，運営側の責任ある地位についたり，技術を身につけて他の施設に移っていった者もいました。インタラクティブ系施設では"人"は明らかに多くの費用のかかる資源で，できるだけ効果的な育成と活用が必要です。ユーリイカ！のイネイブ

---

[12] 5章134ページ脚注4参照。

ラーたちは，展示の改善について提言を奨励され，組織のなかのすべての部署と職種をとりまぜたチームで行事などのプログラム開発をする制度が取り入れられました。同じように，ロンドン国立科学博物館でも，エクスプレイナーからの展示のための新しい提案を奨励しました。93年には科学博物館とユーリイカ！，バーミンガム市博物館ディスカバリーセンターの"科学に光をあてて"が，それぞれのイネイブラーやエクスプレイナーなどのフロア解説スタッフの交換についてその可能性を検討しています。

ユーリイカ！と国立科学博物館ではフロア解説スタッフの疲労を軽減するために，若い人だけを雇用する方針をとっています。この方針は93年4月に行われた英国インタラクティブグループ（BIG）の「ハンズオン学習における人の要素」に関するセミナーで，ほかのハンズ・オン系博物館の人事担当者から「高齢者差別」だと厳しく非難されました。これに対して，たとえばエクスプロラトリーではパイロットを年齢制限なしに雇用し，またテクニクエストでも55人のフロア解説スタッフ（ほとんどが臨時雇用）をすべての年齢層から採用しています。テクニクエストでは高齢のフロア解説スタッフを疲労させないために，彼らの勤務時間を短く回数を少なくしています。この館ではほかにもすぐれた人材管理法を取り入れており，職員の研修目的やフロア解説スタッフの評価の基準が明確にされています。

例にあげた以外の施設では，エクスプレイナーやイネイブラーなどのフロアスタッフのあり方について全く違った方法をとっています。既設の展示室にハンズ・オン展示装置を導入しているイギリスのいくつかの博物館では，もともと警備などが主要な仕事であった係員を積極的な教育的役割をもつ博物館アシスタントに換えていこうとしています。たとえば，コルチェスターの博物館群[13]では，かつての案内係が今では団体を迎えて館内ツアーを行うようになりました。またハンプシャー州博物館サービスと南東地区博物館サービス[14]では，ハンズ・オン系施設におけるインタープリター，デモンストレーターの研修について，話を聞く，質問をする，発表するなど主要な技能を網羅したマニュアルを作成しています。

考古学リソースセンターのボランティア活用事例

　ヨーク市にある考古学リソースセンター（ARC）では「燃え尽き現象」を避けるために，フロア解説スタッフにはボランティアのみを起用しています。これは，ハンズ・オン系施設を訪れる人々に十分対応できるだけの人材を有給で雇用するのが難しいため，その解決法をボランティアの起用に求めたもので，館の責任者であるジョーンズが発案しました。ボランティアの採用と研修にお金をかけており，希望者には学生も含めて必ず1度ARCに来てもらい，その後に正式に応募してもらいます。採用されると非常時の安全確保の手順について2時間の講習を受け，研修マニュアルと研修項目のチェックリストが手渡されます。研修講師はARCの職員が担当し，受講者はどのような研修が必要か申告するよう促されます。フロア解説スタッフのために月例パーティーが催され，復習講座や非公式セミナーが定期的に行われます。ジョーンズが「ハンズ・オン系施設における無給スタッフの役割」で報告しているようにARCは不満を感じるとすぐにボランティアが辞めることを知っているので，帰属意識を高め，要望に応えるためにこのような工夫はボランティア活用において大切になります。

　ARCでボランティアをする人にはさまざまな動機があります。考古学の世界でキャリアを積む第一歩であったり，人との出会いのためであったり，仕事から離れていた人が復職するためであったりします。結果として，学生や現在仕事のない人（結婚などで離職していた人を含む），退職者たちがボランティアの中心となります。全体で約50人のボランティアを抱えており，年に200人ほどの学生（ほとんどが考古学研究者か遺物保存専攻の学生）にボランティア先の斡旋を行っています。考古学の世界ではボランティアと有給職員が一緒に仕事をする長い伝統があり，これがARCでトラブルが少ない理由でもあります。ボランティアの採用と研修に大きな投資をした結果，ARCは一般の

---

[13] エセックス州のコルチェスターにある城などの史跡を含むいくつかの博物館の集まり。コルチェスターはイギリス最古の街といわれ，多くの史跡があり，現在でも考古学の発掘などが盛んに行われている。

[14] 南東地区博物館サービスはイギリスの地域博物館協議会の1つで，イギリス南東部を担当している。博物館にかかわる国の専門機関によって運営されており，当該地域の国立以外の博物館や史跡について，修復・展示・教育・職員研修など，あらゆる活動に関する援助や助言を行っている。ハンプシャー州博物館サービスはその管轄下にあり，ハンプシャー州の施設を統括している。

人々を対象とした考古学教育という本来の目的を達成しています。常に生き生きとした面白い場所に保たれ，「燃え尽きる」解説スタッフはほとんどいません。「インタラクティブ系施設にとって，このようなお金がかかるボランティアや学生は決して安い労働力ではありません。しかし，彼らの起用によって，このハンズ・オン系施設がいつでも生き生きした状態に保たれるのです」と，ジョーンズは述べています。

ハンズ・オン系施設における人材管理の実践例

　人材管理のすぐれた方法は，基本的にどのような組織にも応用できます。人材を上手に管理するにはまず職務を分析して，組織の目的達成のために必要な仕事や組織構造上での管理職の役割を定める必要があります。ASTC の調査結果では，すべてのハンズ・オン系施設や科学館に一律に適用できる組織図は存在せず，施設の規模や性格によって異なっていました。1つの問題は，予算的に大きな割合を占めるフロア解説スタッフを，組織のどの部門に組み込むかです。現場運営責任者の管轄下に入るか，あるいはハンズ・オン系博物館の教育目的を考慮して教育担当の責任者のもとで働くか。これら2系統のどちらに属するかは常に議論の的になっています。フロア解説スタッフが教育系の仕事だとすると，教育プログラムをしているところに現場運営の雑用が割り込みます。反対に，彼らの仕事が現場運営だとすると，その教育的な役割が消えていき，従来型の博物館の係員と大差なくなってしまいます。前に引用したコルチェスターの博物館群など多くの博物館で，それまでの係員を再教育して利用者の体験に働きかけるような教育的な役割をもたせようとしています。インタラクティブな学習には人のかかわりが大変重要であるため，フロア解説スタッフの研修と能力開発に関しては少なくとも教育関係の職員が責任をもつべきでしょう。

　ハンズ・オン系施設でも他の多くの組織と同様にすべての職務（有給無給にかかわらず）について，仕事と義務・職場環境・所属する部署・求められる成果などを記した職務明細書がなくてはいけません。内容がしっかりした職務明細書には雇用された職員が報告を誰にするのか，仕事はどのように評価されるのかなどが明記してあり，このような職務明細書がない場合，職務について誤解が生じる恐れがあります。また職務明細書には仕事の内容のみが記載されて

いればよいわけではなく，どのような希望者が選考されるかを決める基準などがくわしく記されるべきです。その基準が仕事の内容を公平に測れる指標であれば，主観的な価値観によって人事が決められる可能性が少なくなります。

　募集と採用の過程では，広い範囲から応募してもらうために目標を定めて求人の広報をする必要があり，引き続いて客観的な選考を行ってよい候補者を選びます。選考方法はいろいろありますが，一般的にはまず書類審査で仕事に必要な条件を備えた候補者を選び，書面でわからない項目についてさらに面接を行います。面接を受ける全員に規格を統一した面接票を用い，そこに仕事に必要な条件とその判断基準を明記しておくと客観的な選考ができ，差別が生じません。給与の有無を問わず，利用者と接する仕事を任命された人については犯罪歴を調べ，幼児虐待などの記録がないか確認する必要もあります。

　実際は，フロア解説スタッフの選考は多分に主観的です。それは，多くの施設でその仕事をするための重要な資質として「明るい性格」や「瞬時に人とうちとける能力」をあげているためです。主観的な選考を防ぐためにも，職務明細書には，その仕事に必要な性格的な基準をも明らかにしておくべきでしょう。免許や資格，子どもと接する仕事の経験などを考慮した選考は可能ですが，エクスプロラトリアムやロンドン国立科学博物館のような大きな科学系の施設でさえ，資格などより個人的な性格のほうが重要だとしています。理由は簡単です。フロア解説スタッフは，一瞬で利用者とうちとける必要があり，「よい第一印象を与えるチャンスは一度しかない」という古くからの言い伝えは，この場合極めて重要です。したがって，採用になるべく主観的な判断を交えないようにするのは，館側にとって挑戦であるともいえます。より客観的に選考する方法として，たとえば受験者全員を実際に博物館のフロアに出して利用者と交流させ，その内容を判断するというやり方もあります。

　すべての雇い主にとって雇用機会均等化は重要な課題です。博物館業界では多くの施設が利用者の底辺を広げたいと思っています（恐らくは，受けている公的助成金の使い道の正しさを証明したいため）。なかにはニューヨーク・ホールオブサイエンスのように，社会の中の不平等に取り組むことを研修の目的として明言しているような館もあります。イギリスでは雇用機会の均等化はイギリスと欧州共同体（EC）の法律に含まれており，性別や既婚未婚，人種，

身体障害などによる差別は法律違反となります。この課題に長い間取り組んできたすぐれた実践例としてボストンこどもの博物館の例があります。この博物館では，広い範囲のさまざまな社会に対して求人広告を出し，広く募集されているかの確認を徹底して行っていますが，最終的には本当に能力のある者しか採用しないとしています。雇用機会の均等化をよりよく実践するには，可能な限り広い範囲で募集を行い，その中から必要とされる職務上の技能をもつ者を選抜する必要があります。

イギリス国内に限れば，年齢と性別による差別は特に法律に違反しませんが，機会均等に配慮する雇用主らはそういった差別に反対しています。インタラクティブ系博物館では，働く環境が高齢者には厳しいという理由で生じる高齢者差別が問題になっています。しかし一方で，イギリスとアメリカの博物館の中には，高齢者の技術と能力の活用に成功している例も多数あります。テクニクエストのように勤務時間を短くするのも1つの方法です。

募集と採用の後も，入門研修，仕事別研修，評価，継続研修や能力開発など，人材管理の仕事は続きます。入門研修のすぐれた実践例は数多くあり，なかでもボストンこどもの博物館の実習（インターンシップ）プログラムはほかの館のモデルにもなっています。しっかりした研修方針を立て，足りない項目を分析すると，組織の目的を達成するために各職員に必要な研修内容が明らかになるでしょう。職員は，任期途中の仕事の評価によって，自分たちに何が期待されているのか，組織の目的に自分たちの仕事がどうかかわっているのかを知り，それによって自分たちの仕事の成果が認められることになります。職員にチームの一員だという自覚をもたせると，やる気が低下しにくくなります。また仕事の評価は，職員側と評価する側との双方向のやりとりなので，管理職も職員側からのフィードバックを受けられるようになります。

フロア解説スタッフの「燃え尽き現象」といった潜在的に起こりうる問題を避ける方法は多数あります。多くのハンズ・オン系施設では，その対策として雇用期間を短くしていますが，この方法では労働人員の入れ替えが常に可能であるものの，最初の研修にその都度大きな投資が必要となります。エクスプロラトリアムやニューヨーク・ホールオブサイエンスのように，研修目的が社会的背景をも考慮したより大きなものである場合，募集人数や職種を増やすとそ

の目的を達成しやすくなります。多くのハンズ・オン系施設では、フロア解説スタッフを長期の契約で雇い、研修や能力開発プログラムを工夫し、「燃え尽き現象」などの問題をなくすよう努めています。

　ハンズ・オン系施設において、フロア解説スタッフは年間予算の中で大きな比率を占めており、一般に支出の50％以上にもなります。さらに増員したい場合、その方法の1つにボランティアの活用があります。ヨークの考古学リソースセンターやボストン科学博物館、インディアナポリスこどもの博物館のように、多くの施設がボランティアをフロア解説スタッフの中心に置いたり、あるいは有給職員とともに働かせるなど、その活用に成功しています。機関によっては、ボランティアと有給職員が同じような仕事をします。一般的に多いのはボランティアが有給職員を助ける形で補助的な仕事（職務明細書に基づいて）をする場合です。この方法であれば、ブルックリンこどもの博物館で見られたような、予算の削減によって有給職員が自分たちの仕事がボランティアに脅かされると感じるといった事態を避けられます。しかし、ボランティアをどのように利用するにせよ、これをただの労働力と考えてはいけません。ボランティアの場合も、有給職員の場合と同じように調整も管理も必要だからです。実際、ボランティアからの特別な要望に館の側が答えなければ、人の入れ替わりが激しくなり、結局研修などの費用が高くついてしまいます。

　最後にまとめると、募集、採用、雇用機会均等化、研修や能力開発などのすぐれた実践方法は、ほかの多くの組織でも利用可能です。ハンズ・オン系博物館や科学館での博物館体験における人による交流の重要性を考えると、組織としては給与の有無にかかわらず最良の人材管理をする必要があります。それがうまくいかない場合、利用者との交流の質が低下し、フロア解説スタッフが疲労つまり「燃え尽き現象」に苦しみ、結果として人材の定着が悪くなり、新規の補充や研修にお金が余分にかかってしまうのです。

ボストンこどもの博物館
ボストンこどもの博物館のインタープリター。展示制作と呼応して開発されたキットやプログラムを使って、展示室で活動する。その後、呼称はプログラムアシスタントなどに変えられ、組織や養成方法にも若干の変更がみられる。

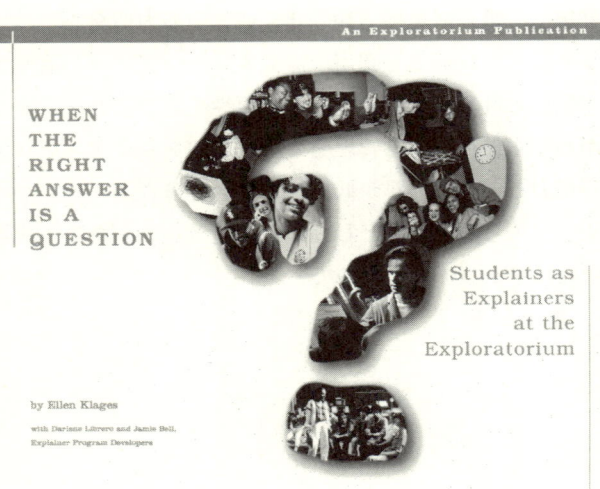

エクスプロラトリアム発行の書籍
エクスプレイナー養成プログラムの成果を記した報告書で、エクスプレイナーというプログラム自体が教育を目的として組まれていること、また科学の素人である高校生などを雇うことで、館の専門家が一般の人々にどのように科学を表現していけばよいかを学べるとしている。
Ellen Klages, *When the right answer is a quesion : students as explainers at the Exploratorium*, Exploratorium, 1995 より

7章 組織・人材管理　195

ボストンこどもの博物館
1993年初夏のインタープリター養成講座の様子。カジュアルな雰囲気で進められるが，内容は利用者への働きかけなど実践がかなり重視され，ハンズ・オンでの学びのあり方をまさにハンズ・オンで習得させる。

8章
教育プログラムと特別イベントの運営

ブルックリンこども博物館建物入り口（同館のホームページより：http://www.bchildmus.org/）
今や博物館の利用は建物を訪れるだけにはとどまらない。ブルックリンこども博物館は，ブルックリン美術館，ブルックリン公共図書館とともに"Broolyn Expedition"（www.brooklynexpedition.org）という教育用ウェブサイトも開設し（1999年），より多くの人が3施設のもつ資料や情報にアクセスできるようにしている。

全員が教育担当!?

キュレーターが展示内容や展示方法を決定し，できあがった展示を教育担当の職員がわかりやすく一般の人に解説する。これが従来の博物館での構図であり，教育担当者はキュレーターの補助的役割にすぎなかった。しかし，欧米の博物館では最近この構図が崩れつつある。博物館の教育的側面や利用者との関係への関心が高まるなか，利用者にとって意味のある博物館体験を提供しようとする教育担当者の声が博物館の内部で重要視されるようになってきたのだ。展示開発の過程に，キュレーターやデザイナーとともに教育担当者が参加するようになったのもその現れである。利用者への配慮が徹底しているこどもの博物館では，次のように述べているところすらある。「私たちの博物館には特に教育を担当する職員はいません。博物館の職員全員が教育担当だからです」。　　　　　　　　　　（井島真知）

8章 教育プログラムと特別イベントの運営

　この章では，イギリスやアメリカのハンズ・オン系博物館や科学館における，教育プログラムや特別イベント[1]，アウトリーチ活動[2]の運営を概観します。

はじめに

　ハンズ・オン系博物館や科学館では，教育[3]がすべての活動の中心です。展示にはすべて教育目的があり，博物館の職員は，来館者が展示をより効果的に利用できるように手助けするための研修を受けています。展示やプログラムの効果も特定の学習目的に照らして評価されます。インフォーマルな教育の場[4]として，ハンズ・オン系博物館の教育活動は幅広い層の人が対象ですが，多くの館は，既存の利用者が館をより有効に使えるように，または，斬新なプログラムやアウトリーチ活動によって新しい利用者を開拓するために教育戦略を展開しています。

　現在博物館を利用している人，または現在の利用者と類似した特徴をもつ人は，すでに博物館のサービスの届く範囲にいるといえるので，こうした人々に対する戦略は，今まで博物館を訪れたことがない人に対するものより費用効率がよくなります。5章で見たように，博物館を利用する人の多くは家族連れと学校団体です。彼らにもっと博物館に来てもらうためには市場浸透戦略が有効です。たとえば，キャンペーンを行ったり，料金体系を変えるという方法です。学校用カリキュラムの開発，学校や家族向けのワークショップの実施，子ども

---

[1] ASTCの報告書によれば，特別イベントとは，年に1度のイベントや記念日など，日常のプログラムとは異なるもので，資金集めや広報の目的で行われる。サイエンスフェアや写真コンテスト，オークション，日食観察イベント，その他のお祭りなどがある。
[2] 1章14ページ脚注5参照。
[3] 1章31ページ脚注1参照。
[4] 2章34ページ脚注4参照。

のクラブ活動の組織，そして宿泊会などの特別イベントの実施など，サービスを充実させることも考えられます。伝統的な博物館が既存の展示室にハンズ・オン展示を取り入れているのも，より多くの来館者を引きつけ，展示への理解を深めるためのサービス充実化の例です。

　既存の利用者により多くのサービスをより有効に利用してもらうほうが，アウトリーチ活動によって新しい利用者を開拓するよりずっと簡単です。博物館を訪れる傾向を示す人の特徴や意見，行動は比較的簡単に調べることができるので，来館者のニーズに見合った教育戦略や集客戦略を練ることができるからです。たいていの博物館では，博物館の利用傾向を示す人が利用者層の中心（つまり主な収入源）を占めるので，館のサービスを継続的に利用してもらうためには，こうした人々の関心を大切にしながら戦略を練る必要があります。他方でやっかいなのは，博物館を訪れない人々です。非利用者の特徴を明らかにしようと思っても，市場調査で彼らの関心や意見を調査すること（非利用者調査）は非常に困難なうえ，ハンズ・オン系博物館や科学館に来る習慣のない人を来館するように変えるのはとても難しいことです。非利用者に対しては，市場拡大戦略（たとえば，ある特定の非利用者層を対象とした宣伝や入場料割り引きを行って博物館の知名度を高める）のほか，新規のサービスを開発するなどの戦略の多様化が効果的でしょう。5歳未満の子ども，ティーンエイジャー，早期退職者，または老人向けの展示やプログラムの開発などが考えられます。ところが，こうしたプログラムは開発にお金がかかる一方で，その効果は予想がつかないため，財政的に安定している館だけが，少ない財源をアウトリーチ活動に向けられるのが実情です。しかし，多くのハンズ・オン系博物館と科学館は，幅広い層の人々にプログラムを提供するという目的を定めている以上，さまざまな人に効果的にプログラムを開発・提供しなければなりません。アウトリーチ活動が困難で効果が予測できないことを考えると，館の活動理念や教育方針のなかでサービスを提供しようとする来館者層を明確に定めておく必要があります。

　ハンズ・オン系博物館や科学館は，学校のカリキュラムに対応してフォーマルな教育機関を補足する側面もありますが，基本的には館自体が重要な教育機関です。第2章では，インフォーマルな教育の場で多くの人がより効果的に学

んでいるという裏付けを示しました。つまり，ハンズ・オン系博物館は単なる学校の延長ではありません。第5章で見たように，主にハンズ・オン系博物館を訪れる人は車で1時間以内の距離に住んでいる家族連れで，学校団体は家族連れに次いで2番目に多い利用者層です。イギリスの博物館来館者の33％が子どもですが，家族連れの子どもが学校団体より多くを占めています。しかし，家族連れほどではありませんが，イギリスの博物館にとって学校団体が大切な利用者層であることは確かです。館種によって，目的，提供するプログラムや教材，マーケティングなどに違いがありますが，民間非営利の博物館のいくつかでは，全来館者の10～20％が学校団体のようです。イギリスの博物館全体で見ると，教育目的でイギリスの博物館を訪れる学校団体は，館によってばらつきがあるものの，総入場者の5％以下から半分以上を占めています。学校団体はすいている平日に来館することが多く，博物館を開いておくのにかかる固定費を相殺できます。また，学校団体として来館した子どもが後に両親を連れて博物館に来るケースも多いようです。イギリスのある伝統的な博物館では，学校行事で来館した子どもの7人に2人が，2カ月以内に両親と一緒に博物館に戻ってくるといわれています。

アメリカの博物館教育

　1章でふれたように，現在のイギリスやヨーロッパのハンズ・オン系博物館や科学館ブームは，ハンズ・オン系博物館がインフォーマルな教育機関としてアメリカで成功したことに端を発しています。科学館技術館協会（ASTC）は1987年に教育活動に関する調査を実施し，123の科学系博物館とこどもの博物館，そしてハンズ・オン系博物館から回答を得ました（123館のうち97館はアメリカの施設，また約3分の1は伝統的な科学博物館や自然史博物館）。この調査によって，博物館や科学館において多彩な活動が行われていることが明らかになりました。各館とも，気ままに館を訪れた人が展示に関連した教育的体験ができるように力を注ぐ一方で，アウトリーチ活動にも徐々に力を入れ始めています。つまり，既存のサービスに新しい観客を取りこむだけでなく，地域の多面的文化施設としてサービスを多様化させ，来館した人以外のより幅広い層の人にサービスを提供するようになっています。

先の調査によると，回答を寄せた館の半数以上が，一般来館者を対象に8種類にのぼるプログラムを提供していました。実演と講演会（94％），教室やワークショップ（94％），特別イベント（88％），展示室のガイドツアー（67％），野外学習（66％），映画またはIMAXシアター（64％），学生インターン[5]（64％），プラネタリウム（52％）がその内訳です。そのほかにも，パフォーミングアーツ[6]（46％），宿泊会（44％），旅行（43％），科学クラブ（34％），講師派遣（36％），ラジオ・テレビ番組（32％）が，一般向けプログラムとしてあげられています。

　学校向けには，回答を寄せた館の半数以上が5種類の教育プログラムを実施していました。博物館での授業や実演（94％），現職教師の教育（81％），学校での授業や実演（67％），カリキュラムの提供（66％），学習キットの貸し出し（53％）がその内訳です。そのほかにも，サイエンスフェア（44％）や職業講習会（30％）[7]などがあげられています。この調査では，フロア解説スタッフ養成プログラムや出版活動は含まれていませんが，こうした活動も博物館が地域社会にアプローチするための非常に重要な教育手段でしょう。

　一般向けと学校向けを合わせると，回答を寄せた館の88％が3種類もしくはそれ以上の教育プログラムを提供していました。一般来館者向けのプログラムは幅が広く，あらゆる種類の博物館で実施されていますが，館の規模や種類によって活動に多少の違いが見られます。大規模館では，映画会やガイドツアーを実施するところが多いのに対して，小規模館では大規模館ほど宿泊会や旅行を行っていません。また，ハンズ・オン系科学館では（そのうち63％が図書館か資料室を備えている），他の博物館よりもプラネタリウムでのプログラムや科学クラブを実施している例が多く見られました。

　回答を寄せた館の64％が3種類もしくはそれ以上の学校向けプログラムを提供し，50％以上の館が年間2万5000人の生徒にサービスを提供していまし

---

[5] 高校生や大学生を対象に行うところが多い。ある一定期間，博物館の実務を経験することによって，ある特定分野の技術を習得する。学校の単位となる場合もある。7章に事例。
[6] 人形劇や寸劇，ストーリーテリングやパントマイム，音楽やダンス，劇など。
[7] 科学や数学，技術分野の専門家を招いて対話の機会を設けるなど，子どもたちが科学の分野での仕事に興味をもって，その可能性を追求することを促進する目的で行われる。

た。平均すると，博物館や科学館の年間入場者の 24％を学校団体が占めており，大規模館よりも小規模館で学校団体の占める割合が大きくなっています。本調査ではその理由について，大規模館においても受け入れる学級数には物理的制限があること，また，大規模館の多くが遠方からの来館者を引きつける主要観光施設であることをあげています。また，アメリカの博物館のほうが，他国の博物館よりも学校での授業・実演や，学習キットや資料の貸し出しを多く実施しているほか，新設の博物館では，旧来の博物館よりも学校団体の占める割合が少なく，学校団体向けの授業や教師のためのワークショップ，カリキュラムの提供も少ないことがわかりました。全体の 74％の館が教室の設備を整えているのに対し，新設の博物館で教室の設備を整えているのは 44％にすぎません。新設館は，まずは，学校団体よりも展示に関連した一般向けのプログラムを優先するのではないかと，調査報告書では推察しています。

　アメリカの大規模な科学館では，一般向けプログラムと学校向けプログラムは異なる部署の管轄になることが多くあります。ASTC の調査で報告のある 94 のアメリカの科学館では，施設の公開面積の平均 10％が学校向けプログラムにあてられていました。また，運営予算の平均 14％が学校向けプログラムに，さらに，ほぼ同額が劇場やプラネタリウムなどの一般向けプログラムにあてられており，両者を合わせた予算は，館の総運営費の 27％を占めていました。しかし，その一方で，特別イベントやプログラムへの参加費，出版物による収入は総収入の 19％に過ぎません。学校向けプログラムを担当する職員は全職員の 19％を占めていますが，その人件費は全体の 14％を占めるだけです（つまり，学校向けの教育担当職員は平均以下の賃金ということになります）。一般向けプログラム担当の職員の賃金は，総人件費のさらに 14％を占め，アメリカの科学館では，学校向けプログラムと一般向けプログラムに関わる雇用が主なものでした。また，アメリカの科学館のボランティアのおよそ 53％，中央値でいえば 1 つの博物館につき 23 人が教育部に配置されています（多数のボランティアを雇っている博物館もあるため，平均値を出すよりは中央値を示したほうが適切な数値であると考えます。たとえば，カリフォルニア科学産業博物館では教育部だけで 620 人のボランティアがいます）。

アメリカの事例

　ASTCの調査では，各館が自館の教育プログラムをどうやって評価しているかを尋ねた結果，教育プログラムに関しては展示に関するものほど評価活動がないと報告しています。アメリカの博物館では教育プログラムの参加費を来館者が支払うことが多いので，人気のある楽しいプログラムが優先され教育目的がないがしろにされる恐れがあります。調査への回答によると，成功する教育プログラムとは，威圧感のない環境でハンズ・オン活動を提供し，質のよいスタッフとプログラム内容で，「実物」の資料や科学現象にふれることができるものです。さらに，仕事と家庭の両立で忙しい親たちに対応して，デイケアを行ったり，放課後や休日，週末にプログラムを提供するなど，融通のきくものが必要とされているようです。

　私（筆者）が見るかぎり，アメリカでは学校団体や白人の家族連れ以外に利用者層を広げようとするすばらしいプログラムが実施されています。たとえば，ボストンこどもの博物館は新たな利用者層に対して博物館を開いていく方策として，多文化をテーマに地域でプログラムを提供してきた長い歴史があります。また，ブルックリンこどもの博物館はさまざまな文化が交差する治安のよくない地域に位置していますが，ここには「キッズクルー」というプログラムがあり，地域の7歳から15歳の子どもを年間1200人以上受け入れています。およそ45人の子どもが，毎日放課後に親の同伴なしで館を訪れ，無料で活動に参加します。91年当時，ブルックリンこどもの博物館は，子どもが大人の同伴がなくても行ってよいニューヨークで唯一の文化施設でした。キッズクルーのメンバーは，10歳になるとジュニアキュレーターとして研修を受けたり，展示室でフロア解説スタッフとして活動したり，プログラム運営の手伝いをしたり，またはクロークルームで働いたり，博物館のあらゆる分野でボランティア活動をするようになります。14歳になると，これらの実習生（ティーンインターン）には賃金が支払われるようになり，仕事探しや仕事に関連する技術について基本的な研修を受けながら，より責任のある活動をするようになります。ブルックリンこどもの博物館のこのユニークな取り組みはミュージアムチームと呼ばれ，職員がきめ細かい指導・研修を行って子どもを支援する点でアメリカの青少年向け文化施設の手本となっています。このほかにも，ブルックリン

こどもの博物館は夏の金曜日の夜に家族連れを対象に屋上パーティーを開きます。また，博物館に隣接する公園で行う毎夏のイベントは1万5000人の観客を集めています。虐待や犯罪から無縁な安全な場所として，ブルックリンこどもの博物館は地域社会へ貢献しています。

　同じニューヨークでも，よりにぎやかな地域にあるマンハッタンこどもの博物館も地域社会にサービスを提供しています。ここでは，学校用のプログラムと一般向けのプログラムを明確に分けており，学校向けのプログラムを午前中に行い，午後には一般向けプログラムを実施するほか，両親とも働いている子どもを対象として放課後に施設を提供しています。私が視察した幼児向けのクラスは，子どもに遊ぶ機会を提供すると同時に，親に子どもを手助けする役割を経験させることを目的としていました。フィラデルフィアのプリーズタッチ博物館も似たような役割を担っており，博物館のグラフィックパネルは，親が子育てをするのを支援する目的でつくられています。年間約15万5000人がプリーズタッチ博物館を訪れる一方で，さらに5万人が地域でのさまざまなアウトリーチ活動を利用しています。たとえば，"旅行かばん"は展示や展示を利用した活動を内容とするキットで24種類あり，地域の施設やイベントで使うことができます。また，地域の資金提供者が設立した恵まれない子どものための基金のおかげで，日曜日の朝には入館料は任意となります。91年には，通常の入館料5ドルに対して，日曜の朝に来館者が払った額は平均1ドル60セントでした。こうした任意の入館料のおかげで，博物館が広く利用される結果になっています。

　ニューヨーク・ホールオブサイエンスは「アフリカ系アメリカ人の子弟の数学や科学に対する苦手意識を克服させる」という明確な目標を掲げています。ボストンこどもの博物館が展示やプログラムを通じて多文化問題に取り組んでいるのと同じように，ニューヨーク・ホールオブサイエンスもさまざまな方法を用いてその教育目的を達成しようとしています。理科教育キャリアラダーというプログラムについては7章でも触れましたが，このプログラムでは高校生たちはまず大学生の解説員と一緒に実験室のアシスタントをしたり，特別イベントの手伝いをしたり，誕生日パーティーや宿泊会を運営します。ニューヨーク・ホールオブサイエンスの活動のなかで最も印象的なのはこうした特別イベントや一般向けプロ

グラムで，大規模な宿泊会や家族向けのワークショップ，サイエンスハロウィーンや発見ゲーム，夏の大イベントなどが行われています。また，これらのイベントがすべて自己資金で運営されていることも注目すべきことです。

　こどもの博物館や科学館は地域社会のニーズに応じて各々独自の特色をもっていますが，なかでもティーンエイジャー（一般的に学校の行事以外でほとんど博物館に来ない年齢層）を対象にしたプログラムが数多く実施されていることは注目に値します。たとえば，ブルックリンこどもの博物館はミュージアムチームを行い，ボストンこどもの博物館は思春期の子ども向けプログラムのほか，「青少年による評議会」を設けて博物館職員とティーンエイジャーが一緒にプログラムを開発・実施しています。そして特筆すべきは，インディアナポリスこどもの博物館の青少年向けプログラムです。インディアナポリスこどもの博物館には，ティーンエイジャーとともにつくったティーンエイジャーのための展示室があるほか，青少年による評議会を設けたり，地元の新聞に独自のニュース欄を毎週掲載していますが，なかでも博物館実習プログラムは特にすばらしいものです。このプログラムに参加するティーンエイジャーは，博物館の4つの主要展示室のうち，どれか1つの展示室でボランティアのフロア解説スタッフになります。各展示室でおよそ100人の子どもが働いており，学校がある時期は週に2日，学校が休暇の時は週4日活動します。90年にこのプログラムに参加した450人の子どものうち20％は非白人で，60％が女の子でした。子どもたちの採用は半年毎に行われます。まず最初に，両親とともにオープンイブニングという説明会に参加し，自分が働きたい展示室を1つ選び，丸1日の研修を受けた後，より経験を積んだ実習生の指導を受けます。長く勤めると，報酬としてバッジやティーシャツがもらえます。このプログラムはとても好評で，参加するためには順番待ちが必要です。博物館では子どもたちが展示内容について深い知識を得るように促してはいますが，最も重要視しているのは，子どもたちが日常生活で接することのないさまざまなタイプの人々と交流する社会的技術を身につけることです。ティーンエイジャーが解説を担当することによって，もしも展示解説の正確さが若干損なわれたとしても，このプログラムが社会にもたらす利益はたいへん大きいと博物館は考えています。しかし，このプログラムの大きな問題点は管理が大変なことです。各ギャラリー

につき1人の指導員がいますが，博物館側は前日までどの子どもが来る予定なのかわからず，30分ごとに予定が変わる子どもたちのためにスケジュールを調整しなくてはなりません。

イギリスの事例

　イギリスの科学館やハンズ・オン系博物館は，アメリカの事例をもとにしつつ，各地域の特色に応じた新たな目的を加えながら，学校向けや一般向けのプログラムを実施しています。アメリカと同様にイギリスの新設館も，ライフサイクルの初期の段階では家族連れや学校団体を中心に核となる利用者層の獲得に専念し，その後館が成熟期に入るとアウトリーチ活動を行って利用者層を拡大しようとする傾向にあります。開館当初のユーリイカ！の家族連れに対する戦略は，テーマを決めて週末や休日に連続イベントを実施することでした。つまり，来館することに付加価値を加え，リピーターとなるように動機付けをしたのです。学校に対しては，学校利用が可能な博物館施設について知名度を高める戦略を取り，無料でカリキュラム教材を配布したり（民間や公立の組織，公益団体の援助による），現職教師のための講座を開いたり（INSET），無料の施設開放日を設けたり，教師が無料で実地踏査ができるようにすることによって博物館の名を地域でできるだけ広めようとしています。当時，学校団体がユーリイカ！を訪れる場合には，8つの場所から1つを選んで予約することになっていました。そして，博物館見学をより意義あるものにするために，教育部職員が一連のワークショッププログラムを開発し，若干の割り増し料金で提供しました。つまり，草創期のユーリイカ！は，博物館の知名度を高め，さらに博物館での体験に付加価値を加える戦略によって，学校や家族連れを中心に核となる利用者層を確立することを目的にしていたのです。

　エクスプロラトリーが学校団体に対してとった戦略もこれに似ています。ギャッツビー財団の補助金を得て，エクスプロラトリーは93年に小学校団体向けのプログラムを開発しました。ここを訪れる学校は，ナショナルカリキュラム[8]の理科と関連したいくつかの学習テーマ（パスウェイと呼ばれる）に的を絞り

---

[8] 5章134ページ脚注4参照。

ます。これは，サンフランシスコのエクスプロラトリアムが開発した方法をもとにしました。エクスプロラトリアムでは，生徒たちは互いに関連する2～3の展示装置を集中的に見学した後で，館の残りの部分を自由に見学していましたが，同様にエクスプロラトリーでも，パスウェイのプログラムを利用する学校は，最初の45分間はクラスを二分し，各グループに2人の博物館スタッフがつき，後半の45分間はセンター内の他の場所を見学することになっています。教師向けの資料には，見学の前後に学校で行う授業案が提示されているほか，学習テーマについて子どもたちがもっている予備知識や誤解について知るためのヒントが示されていました。このプログラムの運営はすべて補助金に頼っていました。補助金が得られるまでは，エクスプロラトリーは資金不足からこのような事業の多くを先延ばしにしていたのでした。

　カリキュラムを開発し，多くの職員を使ってプログラムを実施する戦略は費用がかかりますが，ハンズ・オン系博物館や科学館が競争の激しいイギリスの教育系集客施設市場で生き残っていくためには必要不可欠なことです。教育プログラムの開発を促進する方法のひとつに，COPUS（科学普及推進委員会）や科学普及事業を支援する公益団体からの資金獲得があります。公的助成または公益団体から安定した資金援助を得ている大規模な施設のみが，多様なプログラムを開発できるという現状があるのです。しかし，小さな施設でも，科学週間（英国科学振興協会主催で科学や工学，技術について学ぶための国の行事）などの事業に参加するところも多く，成功を収めているプログラムのなかには採算がとれているものもあります。ロンドン国立科学博物館では多様な学校向けプログラムと一般向けプログラムを実施しており，ユーリイカ！やエクスプロラトリーと同様に，アメリカのやり方を広く取り入れています。たとえば93年に，博物館としてはヨーロッパで初めて宿泊会，つまり博物館内でのキャンプを実施しました。また，現在毎月実施しているサイエンスナイトにはいつも400人あまりの子どもが集まり，採算ベースに乗っています。綿密に計画された活動，実験，ストーリーテリング，たいまつをつけてまわるツアー（もちろん"月面着陸船"の下で眠る機会もある）などを見てみれば，こうしたプログラムが成功を収めているのも不思議ではありません。実際，イギリスの他の科学館もここのやり方にならっています。また，国立科学博物館では女性の

ためのサイエンスナイトも実施しています。

　テクニクエストは，現在，第3期に入り，イギリスで最も成熟した科学館ですが，その教育プログラムはアメリカの科学館のプログラムにとても似通っています。年間8万人の生徒がテクニクエストを訪れ，これは全来館者の3分の1に相当します。テクニクエストでは，小・中学生向けに，ナショナルカリキュラムの理科に対応した活動を週単位で用意しており，それを利用する児童・生徒は，まず科学劇場かプラネタリウムで約40分間の説明を受け，その後，フォーカスカードで学習テーマと関連付けながら展示装置を見て回ります。テクニクエストには"ディスカバリールーム"もあり，子どもたちが探究できるようにディスカバリーボックス[9]が用意されています（これはボストンの科学博物館のディスカバリールームと非常によく似ています）。館外で利用できるキットもあり，利用する児童・生徒数は毎年およそ2万5000人です。5つのテーマのキットがあり，各キットは5つのハンズ・オン展示装置から成っています。キットは学校へ半学期間貸し出され，貸し出し料は運搬費込みで100ポンドです。テクニクエストでは移動プラネタリウムも貸し出しています。また，芸術と科学のギャップを埋めるためのアウトリーチプログラムであるパン・テクニコンというプログラムを実施しており，二千年紀記念委員会に代わって30万ポンドの補助金（1万ポンドの補助金を30件）を科学普及活動を行うウェールズの団体に給付しています。さらに，グラモーガン大学と共同で，科学普及教育の修士課程を実施しています。つまり，新しい展示やイベントを行って学校や家族連れという既存の市場に浸透していくだけでなく，新規の利用者を開拓するための活動を開発し，より幅広い層の人が科学に対する理解を深めるように努めているのです。

　イギリスのハンズ・オン系博物館や科学館は，アメリカの科学館にならって，学校向けプログラムや一般向けプログラムの開発を急速に進めています。しかし，イギリスとアメリカでは，明らかな違いがいくつか見られます。イギリスでは人種問題にアメリカほど直接的に取り組んでいません。また，イギリスでロンドン国立科学博物館がティーンエイジャーを対象としたインタラクティブ

---

[9] 2章57ページ脚注11参照。

展示を開発しているものの，インディアナポリスこどもの博物館やブルックリンこどもの博物館，またはニューヨーク・ホールオブサイエンスのような規模での青少年向けプログラムは行われていません。

学校でのハンズ・オン展示

　イギリスの博物館は，教師が教室で博物館資料を利用できるように，学校への資料貸し出しサービスや移動博物館などのアウトリーチ活動を長年にわたって実施してきました。現在のハンズ・オン系施設もこうした伝統に従っており，車での移動展示が学校を巡回しています（テクニクエストのキットやサイエンスプロジェクト社の"スクールワークス"など）。この節では，科学や技術に関する4つのトレーラーを地域の小学校に貸し出しているノッティンガムシャーの斬新な事業を検証しながら，学校の教室で展示装置を利用する場合と，常設の科学館へ見学に行く場合と，どちらが学習環境として望ましいのか考えていこうと思います。

　常設のハンズ・オン系施設の強みは，親子が一緒になって探求し，発見し，話し合うことができること，そしてそうした親子の学習過程を手助けするように研修を受けたスタッフがいることです。こうした方法は，一般に全来館者の4分の3を占める家族連れに対して有効であるといえます。一方，こどもの博物館や科学館を学校の授業で訪れることは，もちろん楽しく知的刺激に富むものですが，そうした機会を生かすためには，教師が博物館での見学や教室に戻ってからのフォローアップの授業を非常に注意深く計画する必要があります。子どもの発見の過程を手助けする大人が十分にいなかったり，学校に帰ってからのフォローアップがないと，施設見学がかえって科学をわからなくさせてしまう危険があり，本来の目的とは正反対の結果になってしまいます。そこで，教師の目の行き届いた環境で子どもが展示について質問を発するように促すような環境をつくろうという考えが生まれました。これが移動科学館のあり方を裏付ける考えです。つまり，展示を使った活動は，教室内でさらに調査や勉強を進めるための出発点として位置づけられています。では，ハンズ・オン展示が総合的にナショナルカリキュラムに対応した教材とともに学校で利用されれば，科学館やこどもの博物館へ見学に出かけるよりも，教師は学習環境をコン

トロールしやすいのでしょうか。もしそうならば，移動科学館のほうが，常設の施設よりも教師にとって魅力的なのでしょうか。

初等科学・技術トレーラーという名の付いたプログラムは，ノッティンガムシャーの教育委員会と同市の企業協議会による興味深い共同事業です。トレーラーの運営費は学校が支払う料金によってまかなわれていますが，資本金と開発コストは双方が出資しました。この事業の目的は以下の通りです。

1. 子どもたちが科学的現象を体験し，制御できるような，興味を誘う活動を提供する。
2. 通常，学校で用いられないような科学器具を提供する。
3. 校内のナショナルカリキュラムに沿った授業の開発を支援する。

展示装置（この事業の主催者たちはアクティビティーと呼ぶほうを好むようです）を運ぶトレーラーは4つあります。それぞれのトレーラーにはテーマがあり，12～13のアクティビティーから成っています。さらに，地域の助言委員会や教師たちが作成した教師向けガイドと，カリキュラムに対応した教材が付いています。学校は週単位でトレーラーを借りることができます。地域の博物館の資料貸し出しサービス用の車がトレーラーを学校まで引っ張ってきますが，運転手はアクティビティーの積み下ろしを手伝うだけで，アクティビティーを使って子どもと交流することはありません。車が去ってしまえばアクティビティーは学校の責任下におかれます。校内でのトレーラーの使い方については多くの提案があり，たとえば以下のような使い方があげられています。

1. 単元の最初に用い，単元のテーマに対する生徒の興味を喚起する。もしくは，単元の最後に用いて生徒の理解を補強する。
2. 全校行事の科学週間の目玉にする。
3. 父兄や理事を招いた親睦会の中心にすえ，子どもが主要な役割を担う場にする。
4. 中学校との関連をつくるため，つまり，高学年の子どもが低学年の子どもと一緒に使えるようにする。

93年の11月に始まったこのプログラムに関して，私は調査をしてみました。試行期間の後，94年の1月から6月の間にプログラムを利用した最初の25校について，どのようにトレーラーを使ったのか，教師の観点からプログラムの

運営を調べてみたのです。

　トレーラーのアクティビティーがよく利用されたのは小学校では全学年，養護学校では高学年の子どものもとでした。半数以上の学校が，特別に科学週間を設けたといっていますが，それを上回る4分の3以上の学校が，全校生徒がトレーラーを使ったと報告しています。ほとんどすべての学校が，アクティビティーを1カ所（たいていは講堂や空き教室）にまとめて設置していますが，さらに学習を進めるために，個々のアクティビティーを教室へもっていった学校もいくつかありました。アクティビティーに費やした時間は，15分以下から2時間以上と非常にばらつきがありますが，平均するとおよそ1時間で，1つのアクティビティーにつき5分ということになります（ハンズ・オン系博物館や科学館で費やされる時間よりずっと長い）。4分の3以上の学校が，子どもがアクティビティーを繰り返し使う機会があった（授業中や，休み時間中，もしくは放課後に父兄と一緒に）と報告しています。移動科学館が常設の施設よりも人気を集めているのは，このように何度も訪れることができる点にあるのでしょう。

　この調査に協力してくれた教師たちは，プログラムの運営に関して驚くほど好意的でした。たとえば，故障やメンテナンスに関する不満はほとんどありませんでした（アクティビティーが全く学校の管理下に置かれることを考えると，これは驚くべきことです）。運営に関する問題点の多くは，アクティビティーを持ち運びできるのはいいが，せわしい教室内では大きくてかさばるというものでした。また，予想通りの意見として，教師は忙しくて新しく大きなプログラムの準備をする時間がないので，カリキュラムに準拠した効果的な教材が非常に重要だ，というものがありました。

　プログラムの利用料金に関しては，興味深い評価のばらつきが見られました。1週間150ポンド（94年）という値段は，当時，1週間の巡回展に学校が支払えるぎりぎりの額でした。教師の多くは，トレーラーを使ったほうが博物館に見学に行くよりも多くの子どもが資料を利用することができるので，1回きりの見学に比べてずっと価値があると述べています。しかし，トレーラーが料金に対してすばらしい価値を示す一方で，子どもにとっては博物館へ見学に行くほど魅力的でも興奮することでもないと指摘した教師もいました。学校外へ

見学に行くことが科学に対する興味を引き起こす可能性をもつ一方で，トレーラーは単に普段の学校の授業の一部とみなされるかもしれないのです。また，教室外で1日を過ごすことは子どもの社会性を助長すると，教師の多くが強調しています。都心の過密貧困地区に住む子どもにとっては，見学に行くという社会に出る体験自体が，見学中に行う学習よりも重要であるともいわれています。

　子どもを自由に探求するように促す環境で，教師が統率力を失ってしまうと感じていることは注目すべきです。自分の体は1つしかないので一度にたくさんの子どもを見てやることができず，かといって父兄や博物館解説員の助けには質の点で満足できない教師が多いのです。したがって，教室内でハンズ・オン展示を使用し自分が学習環境を統率できることを，教師たちは明らかに評価しています。見学に出かけるよりも，教室でハンズ・オン展示を使うほうが教師は効果的に準備ができるうえ，子どもにアクティビティーを繰り返し使わせることもでき，同時に，子どもの好奇心や学校外からの影響も保つことができるのです。ある教師は，「学校内のほうが，見学に出かけるよりも学習には適している。見学に出かける主な目的はお金を使うことなのだ」と述べています。

　したがって，ノッティンガムシャーの教師たちが初等科学・技術トレーラーを高く評価し，調査に対するコメントも「すばらしい事業だ」「ずっと続けてほしい」「他の分野のカリキュラムにもプログラムを広げられないか」といった肯定的なものばかりであるのも，驚くことではありません。常設のこどもの博物館や科学館は，トレーラーとは明らかに異なった役割を果たしています。つまり，経済的，地理的に施設見学が可能な子どもたちに対して，学校のカリキュラムとは違った価値を提供するのです。厳しい経済状況，また，教師が教室内の学習環境の方が授業がしやすいと感じている事実を考えると，ノッティンガムシャーのトレーラーのような斬新な事業は，一般の人々の科学に対する理解を深めることに重要な貢献をしているといえるでしょう。

イギリスの博物館教育

　イギリスには博物館教育のすぐれた伝統があり，実際，ハンズ・オン運動の

考え方の多く（たとえば資料や現象を直接体験する効果）は，この伝統から生まれています。アンダーソンは，イギリスの博物館教育に関する最近の報告書『コモンウェルス』のなかで，さまざまな規模や分野の博物館の事例が示すように，博物館は教育に対して，特にインフォーマルな学習において，他の機関にはない重要な貢献をし得ると述べています。しかし，すぐれた実践を多く報告しているにもかかわらず，伝統的な博物館における教育活動は散漫であると，この報告書は述べています。この報告書では，これまでイギリスで行われたなかで最も包括的な博物館教育に関する調査結果を示しています。96年の最初の調査では566館から回答を得ました。その後，最初の調査で設けた23カテゴリーのうち3種類もしくはそれ以上の教育サービスや活動を実施していた210施設を対象に2度目の調査を行い，88館から回答を得ています。この調査によると，回答のあった博物館のうち，3種類以上の教育活動をしているのは全体の37％だけで，なんらかの教育活動をしていると答えた博物館も51％にすぎませんでした。教育方針をもっている博物館は23％のみで，登録博物館[10]でも職員のなかに教育の専門家がいるのは24％だけでした。また教育のためのスペースを何かしらでも有する博物館は36％だけで，館で実施する教育活動の効果の評価を行っている博物館は半分以下でした。

　イギリスでは375の博物館に755の教育専門職ポストが置かれていますが，これは登録博物館の22％にすぎません。教育の専門家は，博物館における有給職員，ボランティア職員全体の3％を占めるだけです。教育担当者に学位が必要と考える博物館は25％にすぎず，教育に関する資格が必要と考える博物館は15％のみです。40％以上の博物館で，教育担当職員の賃金は同格のキュレーターよりも低く，多くがより悪い雇用条件のもとにあります。展示やイベントの企画に教育担当者が正式に参加している博物館は33％しかありません。

　回答のあった博物館の64％で，その幹部たちが教育は博物館のサービスの重要な部分であると答えているにもかかわらず，現場の運営責任者の多くは，教育よりも資料管理や展示を重要視しています。実際，28％の博物館が博物館教育を必要不可欠というよりは望ましいくらいにしか考えておらず，教育には

---

[10] 1章11ページ脚注4参照。

ほとんど、もしくは全く価値を認めていない館が2％ありました。こうした博物館の多くが教育活動に関する公益団体としての社会的地位を得ていることに照らすと、その多くが設置認可に関する法律を犯しているといえます[11]。

現在実施されている教育サービスのなかで最も一般的なものは、学校への情報提供や小学生に対するサービス、それに大人対象の講演会や出版物です。次いで、大学生や就学前の幼児を対象にしたものが多く、マイノリティーの多い地域や障害のある人々、失業者などを対象としたサービスは最も少なくなっています。障害者に対する方針を立てている博物館は15％にすぎず、多文化に関する方針をもっている博物館は7％だけです。また、たとえこうしたサービスが利用できたとしても、たいていの場合、それを利用しているのは一部の人にすぎません。

つまり、すぐれた実践も多くある一方で、多くの博物館で、教育が危機的な状況にあることをこの報告書は強調しています。博物館の種類や規模による一貫性は見られません。つまり、たとえ教育的サービスがあったとしても、そこには何の理論的根拠もなく、似たような収蔵品をもつ2つの博物館が全く異なった教育サービスを提供する例もみられます。これは、イギリスの博物館規定が法によらないことが大きな原因といえます。多くの博物館が公教育政策の手段として19世紀に設立されましたが、時がたつにつれて、博物館で一般市民が学習するという概念は薄れていきました。その一方で、博物館教育はフォーマルな教育（主に学校教育）に対する専門的サービスであるとみなされるようになり、博物館での教育は、資料収集や保存・記録といった伝統的な博物館の仕事とはほとんど関係のないものとなってしまったのです。

英米の博物館教育の比較

本章の最初に引用したASTCの調査とイギリスの調査を直接比較することはできません。ASTCの調査は9年早く行われているうえ、伝統的な博物館やア

---

[11] イギリスで公益団体として認められるためにはチャリティー法による条件を満たす必要がある。教育の普及を活動の目的とすることは、公益団体として認定されるための条件の1つであり、多くの博物館がこの条件のもとに公益団体としての認定を受けている。

メリカ以外の博物館も含みつつ，アメリカのハンズ・オン系施設を中心により少ないサンプルで行われたものだからです。しかし，2つの調査結果を見ると，イギリスの伝統的な博物館に比べて，アメリカやその他の国の科学館やハンズ・オン系博物館のほうが教育プログラムが活発で広く普及しているのは明らかです。科学館やハンズ・オン系博物館では，あらゆる意思決定に際して教育目的が最重要視されますが，イギリスの伝統的な博物館では，教育よりも資料管理が優先されることが多いので，博物館はフォーマルな教育の付け足しでしかなく，それ自体が価値のある教育機関とは考えられていません。これは，教育活動に従事する職員の数にも現れています。アメリカでは，博物館にイギリスよりもずっと多くの教育担当職員がいます。イギリスでは有給とボランティアを合わせても職員全体の3％であるのに対して，アメリカでは，有給職員の19％，そしてボランティアの53％が教育担当です。イギリスでは，博物館の支出のうち，5％以下が教育にあてられているだけですが，アメリカでは，27％が学校向けや一般向けのプログラムにあてられています。

2つの調査はいくつかの類似点も示しています。イギリスの調査によれば，教育プログラムの多くは小学生を対象としたもので，マイノリティーや障害をもつ人を対象にしたものはあまり重要視されていません。同様に，アメリカの調査でも小学生を対象としたプログラムが最も多く，続いて中学生・高校生向けが多い一方で，障害者に対するプログラムは最も報告例が少なく，マイノリティーや女性を対象にしたものが次いで少なくなっています。学校市場について見てみると，アメリカの科学系博物館を訪れる学校団体の割合（24％）は，イギリスの科学館を訪れる学校団体の割合（およそ25～40％）より若干少ないのですが，イギリスの博物館全体と比べるとずっと多くなっています[12]。『コモンウェルス』（前出）のデータにはイギリスの博物館を訪れる学校団体の割合は示されていないので正確な数字を出すことは困難ですが，博物館によって5～50％とばらつきはあるものの，平均すると来館者の15％以下と概算できます。

---

[12] イギリスでは実物資料をもたない科学館は博物館とみなされていないため，この数値も科学館と博物館を分けて算出している。

アメリカの科学系博物館は学校と一般来館者へのサービス提供の手本を示しているように思います。80年代後半には，一般の人々と学校の双方に対してアウトリーチ活動を行ったり，マイノリティーや幼児，老人にサービスを提供したり，地域の教育機関，もしくは教育以外の機関と連携したり，現代科学や技術に関する情報源としての役割を果たすなど生涯学習を支援する活動を行う傾向が見られるようになっています。

イギリスの博物館教育のこれから

『コモンウェルス』のなかでアンダーソンはイギリスの博物館教育の暗い状況を示す一方で，博物館と博物館教育の将来像も示しており，その見解はハンズ・オン系博物館や科学館の考え方に通じるものがあります。そこに示されたこれからの博物館像は，教育をその存在の基石とし，教育があらゆる活動の本質となるものです。こうした新しいタイプの博物館では，教育担当職員も展示の開発にかかわり，展示やプログラムの教育効果を評価することは，博物館で不可欠な実践となります。博物館という資料が豊富な学習環境で実物を直接体験して学ぶことは最も重要と考えますが，新しいタイプの博物館は，扱いやすく，かつ最新の技術も取り入れながら，子どもだけでなく大人にも開かれた探求的学習の場をつくりだします。教育という新たな目的をもった博物館は幅広い観客を引きつけ，文化の発展と経済振興にも大きな役割を果たすようになり，その結果，地域社会や資金提供者，メディアからも大きな支持が得られるようになるでしょう。こうした新しい博物館像は，地域社会における個人や家族，団体のインフォーマルな学習，そして自主的な学習を支援する大きな文化運動の一部といわれています。博物館はそれ自体が教育的な機関です。つまり，博物館教育そのものが博物館の存在理由であって，単に学校やその他のフォーマルな教育機関を補完する付属的サービスではないのです。

つまり，アンダーソンは，今日のハンズ・オン系博物館と同じように，伝統的な博物館でもすべての意思決定において来館者のニーズを最重要視すべきであると強調しています。もちろん，伝統的な博物館はそのコレクションに対する責任があります。しかし，これからの博物館は，来館者が自分のまわりの環境を理解できるようにするために，さまざまな手法（博物館資料，ハンズ・オ

ン展示，新しい技術，インタープリター，特別イベント）を採用していくことになるでしょう。9章では，この考え方をさらに深めたうえで，ハンズ・オン系博物館と科学館の将来像について考えてみようと思います。

8章 教育プログラムと特別イベントの運営　219

ブルックリンこどもの博物館のキッズクルー
「なんでも私に聞いてね」。カウンターで情報提供を担当するキッズクルーのメンバー。キッズクルーには年齢と経験別で学習や仕事の内容に段階があり，平日は放課後になると小さな子どもから順番に集まってきて，名前を登録するとその日の作業に入る。

ブルックリンこどもの博物館の屋上イベント
地上の建物としては入り口だけがある同館。博物館の地上部分は公園とイベント用のステージが複数ある。大きなステージでは地元住民のルーツとなる国，プエルトリコなどカリブ海の島々やアフリカなどの音楽や踊りなどのイベントが頻繁に催され，家族ぐるみ，町ぐるみで盛り上がる。

ニューヨーク・ホールオブサイエンスの高校生と大学生
「私たちがお手伝いします」。高校生と大学生たちがさまざまな疑問に答えたり，実験を見せてくれ，指導というよりは一緒になって楽しむ環境を用意してくれる。

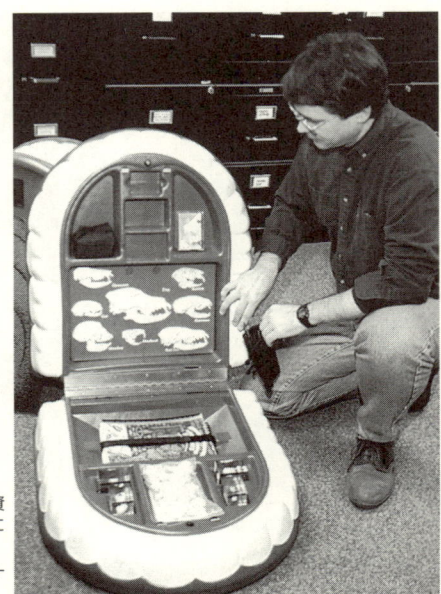

ブルックリンこどもの博物館の貸し出し用キット
歯を形づくった大きな箱には，歯について知るための資料や教材がぎっしり。学校の教室や地域の集まりなどに貸し出すためのキット。
Arthur John, *WORKING AT A MUSEUM*, L'Hommedieu Children's Press, 1998 より

8章 教育プログラムと特別イベントの運営 *221*

インディアナポリスこどもの博物館の貸し出し用キット
大きな部屋にはずらりとキットが並び,人気のものは複数のコピーが用意され,貸し出されるのを待っている。希望者に格安で配布される分厚いキットの案内書があり,教師を中心とする利用者に喜ばれている。

9章
これからの
ハンズ・オン展示

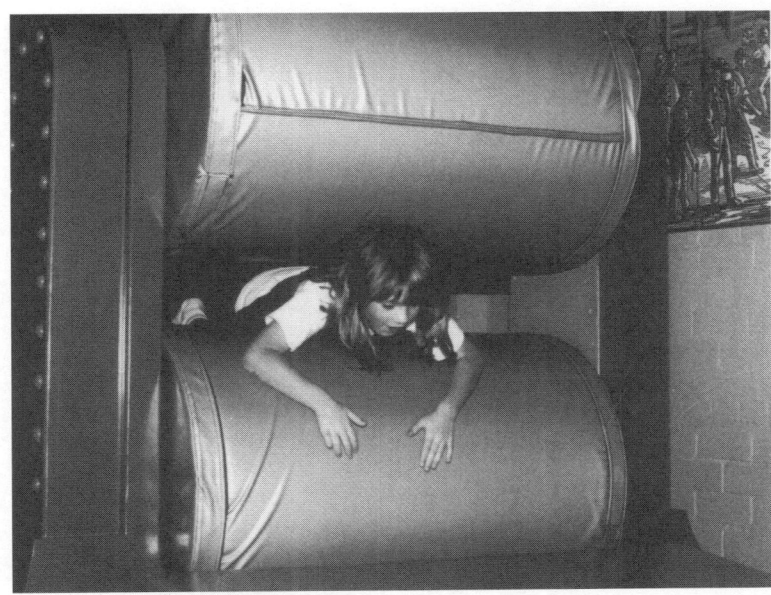

シェフィールド市ケラム島博物館の1コマ
原著の表紙を飾ったこの写真は、シェフィールド市の基幹産業である鉄をテーマにした展示室。鉄の圧延工程を鉄になって試す女の子。

宝くじが文化を支える？

宝くじがイギリスの文化をこれほどまで潤したことがかつてあっただろうか。94年に導入された国営宝くじによる収益金は，2001年までに100億ポンドになることが見込まれている。文化事業だけでなく，スポーツ，慈善事業，ミレニアム記念事業など幅広い分野がその恩恵を受けた。ロンドンにこのほどオープンしたミレニアムドームの総工費7億5800万ポンド(約1360億円) の約半分にあたる3億9900万ポンドもこの宝くじの収益金である。イギリスの新しい1000年は，化粧直しをしたさまざまな博物館や科学系施設の誕生とともに始まることになりそうだ。宝くじという大衆的な娯楽を財源にしているからには，その恩恵はできるだけ幅広い層の人々に行きわたらなければなるまい。文化活動の裾野を広げようと必死になっているイギリスの文化政策の裏には，そんな宝くじの性格が影響しているのかもしれない。

（竹内有理）

9章 これからのハンズ・オン展示

　最終章では，競争激化，公的援助の減少，さらに技術の進化といった局面におけるハンズ・オン展示の将来について考えていきます。インタラクティブ化の最も素晴らしい長所はその多様性にあるのですが，一方でハンズ・オン系博物館や科学館が，商業的な余暇施設とは一線を画し，より広範な社会的，教育的な目的を達成できるとすれば，最適最善の経営が行われなければならないという点について論じます。

　伝統的な博物館もハンズ・オン系博物館も，ますます複雑になる余暇市場の一部分をなし，その多くが全く異なる目的をもつ公立，私企業，非営利の集客施設と，利用者の時間とお金を競うことになります。文化遺産・産業遺産などの施設に限っても，その競争の徴候はあきらかです。イギリスでは近年，博物館の利用者数は増加し，集客施設の数も急激に増えました。ある調査によると，家族連れに人気があって教育と娯楽を融合させた集客施設がもっとも成功しているといいます。1960年代以降アメリカで，また1985年以降イギリスとヨーロッパで，ハンズ・オン系博物館や科学館が劇的に増加した背景にはこのような理由があるのです。

　一方で，伝統的な博物館では，ハンズ・オン系博物館や科学館の成功に対抗しようと，展示をデザインし直す動きが出てきました。それは利用者市場でシェアを増やして伝統的な博物館を維持し，かつ展示の教育的効果を改善するという2つの目的をもっていました。利用者を奪いあう激しい競争のために，多くの博物館（いくつかのハンズ・オン系博物館も含まれますが）では，公的資金からの予算削減と並行して利用者数が伸び悩んだり，または減少するという事態に直面しています。つまり，減少する公的援助と自前の営業活動の不振という二重の収入減に苦しんでいるのです。この状況は，イギリスにおいては市

場が過密状態になっていることに加えて，国営宝くじが助成する新規事業や改修事業によってさらに深刻になっています。そのうえ，最新技術をまとった第3世代の集客施設が博物館と余暇産業の両分野にいかなる影響を及ぼすのか，予測のつかない面があります。1996年のアメリカでの科学館技術館協会（ASTC）の会議では，科学館や博物館が直面している重要な課題として，最新技術ならびに経済環境の変化に焦点をあてています。

このように，余暇市場において確かな見通しをもてないでいることがハンズ・オン系博物館や科学館に相当な圧力をかけているといえます。要約すると，つぎのとおりです。

1. ハンズ・オンの手法を採り入れて対抗しようとする伝統的な博物館がますます増加する。
2. さらに多くの収益本位の集客施設が参入して利用者の時間とお金を奪い合おうとしている。
3. 技術の進化が博物館と余暇産業いずれにも新機軸を導入する機会を与えている。
4. 公的援助が減少することで，非営利団体であっても市場を認識し，経営感覚を磨かなければならない。

かつては，伝統的な博物館が独占状態を保っていました。博物館資料の維持管理が一番の重要性をもち，予算は国庫から保障されていたので，キュレーターは利用者の要求にとりたてて関心を払う必要がありませんでした。そうした第1世代の博物館は資料中心型で，公共の財源でまかなわれ，学校教育型の教育活動をしていました。対象とする利用者像が明確にされることはめったになく，「地域コミュニティーの誰でもみんな」というような漠然とした扱いでした。評価にさらされたとしても，その博物館が成功しているかどうかは批評家が与えるほめ言葉と利用者数によって決められました（ただしふつうは無料なので，利用者数はあてになりません）。一方では，全く異なる対象の市場を取り込もうと，娯楽性を追求した商業ベースのテーマパークが初めて出現したのです。そこでの体験はきわめて受動的なものですが顧客満足が商業的な成功のカギとなりました。教育と娯楽は，伝統的な博物館とテーマパークにとって互

いに全く正反対の意味をもつものであったように思われます。実際，ディズニー・エンタープライズの十戒の第9番目は「お薬はちょっぴり，お楽しみは山ほど」というものでした。つまりはどんな教育的メッセージも，まるでおいしくない薬のように水で薄められていたのです。

　第2世代の博物館，ハンズ・オン系科学館は多くの局面で，伝統的な博物館と余暇産業の両方に異を唱えてきました。そのうち，教育と娯楽が必ずしも相容れないものではない事実を明らかにした点が重要なのです。ハンズ・オン系博物館と科学館はわくわくするような，斬新で楽しく，しかも歴史的にも正確で科学的にも整合性のある展示を用意できます。展示評価によって，人々は楽しみながら学ぶことができると証明されていますが，利用者数の増加は，家族ぐるみで思い思いに学んで楽しめる安全な場所を社会が本当に望んでいることを示しています。こうした集客施設の成功は伝統的な博物館には著しい脅威となり，そのうちの多くがハンズ・オン方式を採り入れたので，文化遺産・産業遺産などの施設の市場競争はますます激化したというわけです。

　第1世代と第2世代の博物館はいずれも同じ利用者を奪い合っていますが，両者の基本的な目的は異なるわけではありません。主な違いは目的というよりは戦略の問題です。伝統的な博物館は資料を収集して保存する機能がその役割の中心となることは明らかですが，こどもの博物館の場合は資料を収集・保存することはさほどありませんし，科学館の場合はなおさらです。しかし資料を収集するにせよしないにせよ，博物館の第1世代も第2世代のいずれも，利用者が事物や現象の本質を理解するのを助けるために存在するのです。その展示手法は時代の経過とともに変化するに違いありませんが，あくまで学校とは違った教育機関としての博物館と科学館のこうした基本的な機能は変わりはありません。ハンズ・オン展示がガラスケースの陳列にとって代わったり，構成主義の考え方に立つ展示が逆に教条的な陳列に入れ替えられたとしても，私たちをとりまく世界を表象し解釈し伝達するという博物館の根本をなす目的は本質的に変わりません。最も重要なのはその基本的な目的から発せられる内容であって，伝達の手段ではないのです。

　博物館はほとんどが公立または非営利の団体が設置主体なので，その目指す

ところは利潤の追求ではなく教育ですが，第1世代と第2世代の博物館の相違点は，余暇産業とこうした博物館ほど大きくはありません。にもかかわらず，多くの博物館は外部からの収入減を埋め合わせるために商業的手法を採用するようになってきました。そのため利用者にはその施設が商業的なものなのか，教育的なものかという区別がわかりにくくなってきています。たとえば，イギリスの少なくとも2つのハンズ・オン系博物館は，経費を埋め合わせる収入源としてライドシミュレーションシアターの導入を計画しています。またアメリカの博物館と科学館のいくつかは，IMAXシアターを採り入れていますが，ある批評家が記している通り，収入の助けになるのなら，ロック音楽映画を科学映画として見せることすらありそうです。博物館や科学館はその収入をますます事業活動で稼がなければならなくなっているのです。アメリカでは公的財源からの予算の低下に伴って，多くの科学館で全収入に占める事業収入割合が80％を超えるようになってきました。激しい競争環境において収入を生み出す必要性は，教育的，社会的な目的をもった施設に重圧をかけることも起こり得るし，いくつかの科学館に本来の目的を見失わせることになる恐れもあります。実際に，フィラデルフィアのフランクリンインスティテュートはテーマパークとデイケアセンターの交ざり合ったもののようだと書かれたことさえあるのです。

　ハンズ・オン系博物館が提供している施設体験は，人手がかかり維持費もかさむので，余暇産業を脅かす商品とはなりません。テーマパークの場合でいうと，管理しやすい環境を整えて客を効率よくさばくことが優先されます。ハンズ・オン系博物館や科学館での利用者本位の学習とは全く対照的です。ハンズ・オン学習で採算がとれるなら，テーマパークの経営者はとっくにその難しい事業に手を染めていたでしょう。イギリスでは教師たちがナショナルカリキュラムの条件を満たすのに追われるようになった結果，学校は学期末のごほうび遠足を実施しにくくなりました。テーマパークにすれば，入場者が少なく維持費が高くつく閑散期に利用してもらえる学校団体は無視できない存在です。事態に対応するために，カリキュラム教材を用意するなどの教育色を高めた商品で学校への売り込みを強化しましたが，それでもハンズ・オン学習を採用して中心的な商品を変更したわけではありません。

テーマパークがインタラクティブな学習空間を提供する方向にまだ進出していないのに対して、余暇産業の他の分野では、営利目的の水族館や家族向け娯楽施設の増加を一例として、博物館施設と競合するようになってきました。アメリカでもヨーロッパでも、急成長した家族連れの市場に対応するために、ファンファクトリー、ディスカバリーゾーン、プラネットキッズ、プラネットファン、アクションステーションなどの施設が開発されたのです。こうした施設は、遊びを通じた学習が収益事業として可能なことを検証しています。安心して安全に遊べる環境を確保しながら、ふつう1時間に限定して子どもたちを短時間で入れ替える仕組みのなかにインタラクティブな遊びの要素を導入したのです。ハンズ・オン系博物館とは異なり大人がここで果たす役割はほとんどなく、アクションステーションなどで見受けられたようにカフェだとか、大人は入場料がただになることもあるコンピューターエリアに追いやられました。また誕生日パーティーや会員制プランに大変力を入れて、繰り返し訪れてもらおうとしています。遊びの教育的価値は認識していても、この種の施設では教育を第1の目的としてはいません。つまり収益事業としての成功が根本的な目的であり、子どもの遊びが利益を生まなくなったら他の集客事業に入れ替えられるに違いないのです。

　余暇施設と博物館の双方が増えてくれば、このような施設を利用しようと考えている人には紛らわしいに違いありません。それぞれが互いの長所短所を混同してきたのです。ASTCのメンバーの間では、ハンズ・オン系博物館のような非営利で利用者本位の教育機関が商業的経営との差別化を図ろうとしないならば、はたして生き残っていけるのだろうかとの深刻な懸念が示されています。ある論文は、ハンズ・オン系博物館が独自性を失い、本来の目的を達成できなくなることのないように、商業的なテーマパークとは一線を画しその根本的な違いを明確にすべきであるとしているのです。ハンズ・オン系集客施設は事業活動から収入を図る必要が増していますが、その成功の最も重要な評価基準は、利用者が教育と娯楽の2点について満足したかどうかでしょう。商業ベースの余暇施設の場合は、一部の家族向け娯楽施設や水族館は教育的な目的を主張するかもしれませんが、普通は娯楽と教育の目的は対立すると考えられるので、実際に業績を評価する唯一の基準は、オーナーや株主にもたらす利潤というこ

とになります。利用者が楽しんだかどうかは余暇産業にとっては再度の来館や友人への口コミを左右するので非常に重要ですが，社会的，教育的な目的はさほど重要な関心とはなりにくいのです。テーマパークがカリキュラムに対応した商品を開発することがあるとしても，これはその使命の根本的な変化の表れというよりは，学校団体の利用者数減少について対応したマーケティング戦略だといえます。

　ハンズ・オン系博物館や科学館の大きな強みは，本物の利用体験を与えてくれることにあります。館によって資料の収集や歴史的な立地，科学的な現象の再現などさまざまな基盤を有しているわけですが，それらはすべて「本物」なので，テーマパークのファンタジーの世界に対して競争上は有利に働くに違いありません。さらに，ハンズ・オン系博物館では，利用者は自分の意思のとおり展示テーマを選んで，しかもほぼ自分のペースを保つことができるのです。その結果，施設での体験は展示物と自分自身との相互作用によってまさに自分だけのものとなります。テーマパークではアトラクションそのものが管理されているので，スリルがあって怖いもの，また刺激的であるかもしれませんが，利用者はだれも同じような体験に終わるしかないのです。

　一言でいえば，ハンズ・オン系博物館と余暇産業との境界が非常に不明瞭になってきているなかで，ハンズ・オン系博物館が財政的に健全であるためには，その本来の目的を見失わずにいることがどうしても必要なのです。実際にその相違点が競争の上で有利に働くこともあります。ハンズ・オン系博物館は自らの使命に集中すべきなのはもちろんのこと，テーマパークや家族向け娯楽施設と同じ利用者のお金と時間を競い合うなかで，両者が提供する利用体験は全く性質の異なるものだという事実を，利用者に対してきちんと伝えていかなくてはなりません。

　最新技術を身にまとって今まさに生まれようとしている第3世代の博物館については，博物館界で多くの議論がなされてきました。アメリカのある批評家は，今後25年以内に博物館はもはや我々が今日知っているような形では認識できなくなるだろう，と予言しています。つまり，資料を収集し展示するだけの機関ではなくなって，人類と地球の過去を博物館資料という形で広範に集積

する場となるだけでなく写真やビデオ，音楽，ダンスや物語を記録していくためにマルチメディアを採り入れていくはずだというのです。そうなれば，博物館，図書館，公文書館，学校，ショッピングセンター，公園，動物園，美術館，パフォーミングアーツのための空間，さらには公共公益機関との区分すらも不明瞭になるでしょう。実際に，私たちはそうした新しい施設を訪れるために，わざわざプライバシーと快適さを犠牲にしてまで外出する必要はなくなるかもしれないのです。この異種混合のプロセスは従来の博物館にはない取り組みを行っている多くの博物館ですでに始まっており，その傾向はますます強まるはずです。同様に，アンダーソンは『コモンウェルス』のなかで，将来のビジョンとして，利用者本位の教育と自主的な学習を支える広範な文化的運動の一翼を担いながら，地域社会の発展にさらに活発な役割を演じるというような，これまでにない概念をもつ博物館像をあげています。このように，最新技術は博物館が融合し拡張する形に新たな収入の道を生み出す機会を与えるかもしれませんが，効果的な事業を展開するためには，今まで以上にその目的に集中することが求められるでしょう。

　博物館がどのように新しい技術を採り入れていくかは，確信を持って予言することはできません。現段階の技術は，すでにインターネット上やCD‐ROMの上にバーチャルな形で博物館が存在することを可能にしています。バーチャルリアリティーは，遺構そのものを傷めずにその上に建物を復原可能にしました。膨大なデータベースを使って，収蔵資料を盗まれたり傷められたりせず，恐らく家にいながらにして資料を利用してもらうことが可能になるはずです。また展示物に近寄っただけで自動的に始まる解説を聞いたりして，利用者自身の関心によって個別の博物館ガイドを組み立てることができるようになるでしょう。この種の技術革新はここ数年のうちに博物館ではどこでも見られるものになりそうです。そうした将来を左右するものといえば，展示開発者が抱える創造性と想像力の限界だけなのです。

　第1世代と第2世代の博物館は，本物の場所，事物，現象についての展示に依存する内容志向型といえます。最新技術に重きをおけば，本物であることを重視する立場からバーチャルリアリティーへと重点が移っていく危険性があります。しかし第2世代の博物館が，利用者が収蔵品や展示プロセスを理解をし

やすいようにハンズ・オン展示を導入したのと同じように，最新技術が多様な展示手法と併存して展示のプロセスに役立つとしたら悪いわけがありません。それがハンズ・オン展示においてであろうとタッチパネル式のコンピューターであろうと，最新技術は博物館の展示解説者が利用者に意思を伝達するために使う単なる道具であり，それ自身が最終の目的ではないのです。余暇産業では，商品のライフサイクルが短くても高利潤を生み出せるような最新技術の目新しさを利用した余暇商品を開発するでしょう。しかし本物の事物や現象の解明に深くかかわる博物館界は余暇産業と一線を画して，教育的，社会的な目的を達成しようとしているのですから，余暇産業と同じような方法で最新技術に惑わされてはならないはずです。

　未来の博物館は，利用者が自分を取り巻く環境を理解しやすくするために，収蔵品，ハンズ・オン展示，インタープリター，最新技術などあらゆる種類のインタラクティブな展示装置を融合した場になりそうです。それぞれの展示手段にはそれぞれ長所短所があるので，利用者が展示の対象となっている事物や場所，現象についての理解を深めるように，選択して使用されなければなりません。最新技術に惑わされた博物館はすぐに時代遅れになる恐れがあるだけでなく，現代の子どもたちがバーチャルリアリティーばかり与えられることに反発して，ガラスケース展示型の博物館スタイルへと戻っていく可能性さえあります。この見方を実際に証明する根拠はまだほとんどありませんが，ある評論家は，子どもたちはもはや特殊効果の展示に刺激されることはなく，むしろ伝統的な展示に関心を示す方向にあることを示唆しています。

　ハンズ・オン系博物館と科学館に関する本書の考察から得られる教訓は，効果的な展示をつくりだし，管理する唯一の方法はないということ，文化遺産・産業遺産などの施設と余暇施設の多様な展開なしに高い需要は生まれないということ，展示の革新的なアイデアは枯渇しない，ということです。イギリスでは近年，公益団体，国営宝くじ，ECの財源や企業からの助成が新規事業開発に資金を提供してきました。新たにハンズ・オン系集客施設を開発するにあたり資金は調達できるとしても，その事業が将来長期間にわたって経済的に存続していけるかどうかが大きな問題です。二千年紀記念委員会や文化遺産宝くじ

基金が，現在進行中の計画に高い水準を要求するのもこうした理由からなのです。

　公的助成金が減少するなか，施設が経済的に存続できるかどうかはすぐれた事業計画の立案にかかっています。それは，まず施設の中核をなす展示を，対象とする利用者層から開発の各段階ごとに展示評価を受けてしっかりつくりあげることから始まるのです。さらに，マーケティング，財政，現場運営，人材管理などあらゆる面で最適の業務を遂行すれば，利用者数と利用者の満足度は向上していきます。このようなすぐれた事業計画にもとづいて，ハンズ・オン系の博物館も余暇産業とは一線を画した社会的，教育的な目的を達成していかなくてはなりません。これからのハンズ・オン系博物館が過密状態となった余暇市場で生き残っていくためには，社会的，教育的目的に確固として焦点を定め，その目的を利用者にも資金提供者にも効果的に伝え，すぐれた経営実践を遂行しなくてはなりません。こうした積み重ねがあればこそ，多くの人に利用される展示や，事物や科学現象の本質にふれ理解を深める場をこれから先も提供していけるのです。

原著 参考文献

Anderson, D., *A Common Wealth: museums and learning in the United Kingdom*, London: Department of National Heritage, 1997.

Belcher, M., *Exhibitions in Museums*, Leicester University Press: Leicester, 1991.

Bicknell, S., 'Here to help: evaluation and effectiveness', in Hooper-Greenhill, E. (ed.), *Museum, Media, Message*, London: Routledge, 1995, pp. 281-93.

Bicknell, S. and Farmelo, G. (eds), *Museum Visitor Studies in the 90s*, London: Science Museum, 1993.

Bicknell, S. and Mann, P., 'A picture of visitors for exhibition developers', in Hooper-Greenhill, E. (ed.), *The Educational Role of the Museum*, London: Routledge, 1994, pp. 195–203.

British Interactive Group, *Handbook 1*, 1995.

Brooklyn Children's Museum, *Doing It Right: a guide to improving exhibit labels*, Washington, DC: AAM, 1989.

Cleaver, J., *Doing Children's Museums*, Charlotte, VT: Williamson, 1992.

Danilov, V, J., *Science and Technology Centers*, Cambridge, MA: MIT Press, 1982.

Davies, S., By *Popular Demand: a strategic analysis of the market potential for museums and galleries in the UK*, London: Museums and Galleries Commission, 1994.

Diamond, J., St. John, M., Cleary, B. and Librero, D. 'The Exploratoritum's Explainer Program: the long-term impacts on teenagers of teaching science to the public', *Science Education*, 71, 5, 1987, pp. 643–56.

Dierking, L. D., 'The family museum experience: implications from research', *Journal of Museum Education*, 14, 2, 1989, pp. 9–11.

Dierking, L. D. and Falk, J. H., 'Family behavior and learning in informal science settings: a review of the research', *Science Education*, 78, 1, Jan. 1994, pp. 57–72.

Durant, J. (ed.), *Museums and the Public Understanding of Science*, London: Science Museum, 1992.

Falk, J. H. and Dierking, L. D., *The Museum Experience*, Washington, DC: Whalesback Books, 1994.

Feher, E., 'Interactive exhibits as tools for learning: explorations with light', *International Journal of Science Education*, 12, 1.

Fisher, S., 'Bringing history and the arts to a new audience: qualitative research for the London Borough of Croydon', unpublished research by the Susie Fisher Group, 1990.

Freeman, R., *The Discovery Gallery: discovery learning in the museum*, Toronto: Royal Ontario Museum, 1989.

Gardner, H., *The Frames of Mind: the theory of multiple intelligence*, New York: Basic Books, 1983.

Gardner, H., *The Unschooled Mind: how children think and how schools should teach*, New York: Basic Books, 1991.

Grinell, S., *A New Place for Learning Science: starting and running a science center*, Washington, DC: ASTC, 1992.

Guichard, J., 'Designing tools to develop the conception of learners', *International Journal of Science Education*, 17, 2, 1995, pp. 243 – 53.

Hanna, M., *Sightseeing in the UK*, London: BTA/ETB Research Services, annual series.

Hein, G. E., 'The constructivist museum', *Journal of Education in Museums*, 16, 1995, pp. 21 – 3.

Hein, G. E,. 'Evaluation of programmes and exhibitions', in Hooper-Greenhill, E. (ed.), *The Educational Role of the Museum*, London: Routledge, 1994, pp. 306 – 12.

Hill, E., O'Sullivan, C. and O'Sullivan, T., *Creative Arts Marketing*, Oxford: Butterworth-Heinemann, 1995.

Hood, M., 'Getting started in audience research', *Museum News*, 64, 3, 1986, pp. 24 – 31.

Hood, M. 'Staying away: why people choose not to visit museums', *Museum News*, 61, 4, 1983, pp. 50 – 7.

Jackson, R. and Mann, K., 'Learning through the Science Museum', *Journal of Education in Museums*, 15, 1994, pp. 11 – 13.

Jones, A., 'The role of unpaid staff in hands-on centres', British Interactive Group, *Newsletter*, autumn 1993, pp. 4 – 5.

Kennedy, J., *User Friendly: hands-on exhibits that work*, Washington, DC: ASTC, 1994.

Lewin, A. W., 'Children's museums: a structure for family learning', *Marriage and Family Review*, 13, 3 – 4, 1989, pp. 51 – 73.

McCormick, S. (ed.), *The ASTC Science Center Survey: administration and finance report*, Washington, DC: ASTC, 1989.

McCormick, S. (ed.), *The ASTC Science Center Survey: education report*, Washington, DC: ASTC, 1988.

McLean, F., *Marketing the Museum*, London: Routledge, 1997.

McManus, P., 'Families in museums', in Miles, R. and Zavala, L. (eds), *Towards the Museum of the Future*, London: Routledge, 1994, pp. 81 – 97.

McManus, P., 'Towards understanding the needs of museum visitors', in Lord, B. and Lord, G. D. (eds), *Manual of Museum Planning*, London: HMSO, 1991, pp. 35 – 51.

McManus, P., 'Watch your language! People do read labels', in Serrell, B. (ed.), *What Research Says about Leaning in Science Museums*, Washington, DC: ASTC, 1990, pp. 4 – 6.

Mulberg, C. and Hinton, M., 'The Alchemy of Play: Eureka! The Museum for Children', in Pearce, S. (ed.), *Museums and the Appropriation of Culture*, London: Athlone Press, 1993, pp. 238 – 43.

Nuffield Foundation, *Sharing Science: issues in the development of the interactive science and technology centres*, London: British Association for the Advancement of Science, 1989.

Oppenheimer, F., 'Exhibit concept and design', in *Working Prototypes*, San Francisco: The Exploratorium, 1986, pp. 5 - 15.

Palmer, A., *Principles of Service Marketing*, Maidenhead: McGraw Hill, 1994.

Peirson Jones, J. (ed.), *Gallery 33: a visitor study*, Birmingham: Birmingham Museums and Art Gallery, 1993.

Pizzey, S. (ed.), *Interactive Science and Technology Centres*, London: Science Projects Publishing, 1987.

Quin, M., 'Aims, strengths and weaknesses of the European science centre movement', in Miles, R. and Zavala, L. (eds), *Towards the Museum of the Future*, London: Routledge, 1994, pp. 39 - 55.

Quin, M., 'The Interactive Science and Technology Project: the Nuffield Foundation's launchpad for a European collaborative', *International Journal of Science Education*, 13, 5, 1991, pp. 569 - 73.

Quin, M., 'The Exploratory pilot, a peer tutor? - the interpreter's role in an interactive science and technology centre', in Goodlad, S. and Hirst, B. (eds), *Explorations in Peer Tutoring*, Oxford: Blackwell, 1990, pp. 194 - 202.

Quin, M., 'What is hands-on science, and where can I find it?', *Physics Education*, 25, 1990, pp. 243 - 6.

Russell, T., 'The enquiring visitor: usable learning theory for museum contexts', *Journal of Education in Museums*, 15, 1994, pp. 19 - 21.

Screven, C. G., 'Uses of evaluation before, during and after exhibit design', *ILVS review*, 1, 2, 1990, pp. 36 - 66.

SEARCH, *Going Interactive*, Hampshire County Museums Service/South Eastern Museums Service, 1996.

Serrell, B., *What Research Says about Learning in Science Museums*, Washington, DC: ASTC, 1990.

Silberberg, E. and Lord, G. D., 'Increasing self-generated revenue: children's museums at the forefront of entrepreneurship into the next century', *Hand to Hand*, 7, 2, 1993, pp. 1 - 5.

Siegel, E., 'The Science Career Ladder at the New York Hall of Science', *Curator*, 41, 1, 1998, pp. 246 - 253.

Stephenson, J., 'The long-term impact of interactive exhibits', *International Journal of Science Education*, 13, 5, 1991, pp. 521 - 31.

Steuert, P., *Opening the Museum: history and strategies towards a more inclusive instruction*, Boston: The Children's Museum, 1993.

St. John, M. and Grinell, S., *Highlights of the 1987 ASTC Science Center Survey: an independent review of findings*, Washington, DC: ASTC, 1989.

Swift, F., 'Time to go interactive', *Museum Practice*, 4, 1997, pp. 23 - 31.

Taylor, S., *Try It! Improving exhibits through formative evaluation*, Washington, DC: ASTC, 1992.

Thomas, G., 'How Eureka! The Museum for Children responds to visitors' needs', in Durant, J. (ed.), *Museums and the Public Understanding of Science*, London: Science Museum, 1992, pp.

88 - 93.

Thomas, G., ' "Why are you playing at washing up again?"Some reasons and methods tor developing exhibitions for children', in Miles, R. and Zavala, L. (eds), *Towards the Museum of the Future*, London: Routledge, 1994, pp. 117 - 31.

Thomas, G. and Caulton, T., 'Communication strategies in interactive spaces', in Pearce, S. (ed.), New Research in Museum Studies: Vol. 6 *Exploring Science in Museums*, London: Athlone Press, 1996, pp. 107 - 22.

Thomas, G. and Caulton, T., 'Objects and interactivity: a conflict or a collaboration', *International Journal of Heritage Studies*, 1, 3, 1995, pp. 143 - 55.

Trevelyan, V. (ed.), 'Dingy places with different kinds of bits: an attitudes survey of London museums amongst non visitors', London: London Museums Service, 1991.

Wood, R., 'Museum learning: a family focus', *Journal of Education in Museums*, 11, 1990, pp. 20 - 3.

関連施設・機関一覧

　本文中に出てきた関連施設および機関を国別に50音順に列挙した。原著刊行時と多少の異同がみられるが，知りうるかぎり2000年2月現在の情報に修正し，旧名称は備考欄に付記した。本文中に出てきた展示名についても備考欄に付記した。

凡例
施設・機関名称
　　名称　　所在地
　　電話　　ファクス番号　　ホームページアドレス
　　備考

＜イギリス＞

■科学館・博物館

アットブリストル
　at-Bristol, Deanery Road, Harbourside, Bristol, BS1 5DB
　Tel: 0117 909 2000　Fax: 0117 909 9920　http://www.at-bristol.org.uk
湾岸地域再開発プロジェクトとして二千年紀記念委員会の助成を受けて建設中の科学施設。2000年春オープン予定。テクニクエストと並んでイギリスの科学館の先駆的存在だったエクスプロラトリー（Exploratory）は，この中にエクスプロア（Explore）という名前で再オープンする。

ウェールズ産業海事博物館
　Welsh Industrial and Maritime Collection, 126 Bute Street, Cardiff Bay, Cardiff, CF1 6AN
　http://www.nmgw.ac.uk/wimm/index.en.shtml/
ウェールズ国立博物館群（The National Museums & Galleries of Wales）の1つで，カーディフ市の産業と海運に関する展示を行っている。

エルスカー・ヘリテイジセンター
　Elsecar Heritage Centre, Wath Road, Elsecar, Barnsley, South Yorkshire, S74 8HJ
　Tel: 01226 740203　Fax: 01226 350239
19世紀の産業遺跡の跡地に建てられた体験型の野外施設。蒸気機関車や職人による実演など生きた歴史を体験できる。"パワーハウス"（Power House）ではハンズ・オン展示を通してエネルギーのしくみを紹介している。

グリーンズミル科学館
　Green's Mill and Centre, Windmill Lane, Sneinton, Nottingham, NG2 4QB

Tel: 0115 915 6878　http://www.innotts.co.uk/greensmill

ノッティンガム市博物館群の1つ。数学・物理学者ジョージ・グリーンが所有していた19世紀の風車や彼の業績についての展示のほか，科学に関するハンズ・オン展示がある。1985年開館。

考古学リソースセンター
Archaeological Resource Centre, St Saviourgate, York, YO1 2NN
Tel: 01904 654 324　http://www.jorvik-viking-centre.co.uk/arc.htm

発掘資料を使ったさまざまなハンズ・オン展示を通してバイキングの暮らしや考古学者の研究について学ぶ体験型学習施設。ディズニーランドのような展示手法が話題となったヨービック・バイキングセンターの姉妹施設。

国立海事博物館
National Maritime Museum, Romney Road, Greenwich, London, SE10 9NF
Tel: 020 8858 4422　Fax: 020 8312 6632　http://www.nmm.ac.uk

1934年にオープンした海事に関するコレクションでは世界最大規模の博物館。最近，新しく12の展示室がオープンした。その1つである"オールハンズ"（All Hands）展示室は，船乗りの生活や技術をテーマにしたインタラクティブ形式の展示で，学校のカリキュラムにも対応している。

国立科学博物館
Science Museum, Exhibition Road, London, SW7 2DD
Tel: 020 7942 4455　Fax: 020 7942 4302　http://www.nmsi.ac.uk/welcome.html

科学・技術に関する膨大なコレクション展示とともにハンズ・オンの要素を取り入れた展示改装を積極的に行っている。イギリスの博物館内につくられた初めての科学系ハンズ・オン展示"ラウンチパッド"（Launch Pad）や"フライトラボ"（Flight Lab），子どもを対象にした"もの"（Things）などがある。

国立自然史博物館
Natural History Museum, Cromwell Road, London, SW7 5BD
Tel: 0171 938 9123　http://www.nhm.ac.uk

大英博物館の自然史部門として1881年にオープン。イギリスの自然史系博物館では最大規模のもの。最近インタラクティブな要素を取り入れたさまざまな展示改装に積極的に取り組んでいる。7～11歳の子どもを対象にしたハンズ・オン展示室"ディスカバリーセンター"（Discovery Centre）は名称を変えて2000年に再オープン予定。

国立鉄道博物館
National Railway Museum, Leeman Road, York, YO26 4XJ
Tel: 01904 621261　Fax: 01904 611112　http://www.nmsi.ac.uk/nrm/

ロンドンの国立科学博物館の分館として1975年にオープン。鉄道に関する収蔵品の規模は世界最大級で，鉄道発祥の地イギリスならではといえる。インタラクティブ学習センターやピクニックや鉄道の試乗ができる野外施設など，学校団体や家族向けのサービスも充実している。

ジョドレルバンク科学館
Jodrell Bank Science Centre, Lower Withington, Macclesfield, Cheshire, SK11 9DL
Tel: 01477 571259　Fax: 01477 571695　http://www.jb.man.ac.uk/scicen

ジョドレルバンクはマンチェスター大学にある天文台。当館はそこに併設された科学館で天文・物理をテーマにした展示がある。

スニブストン・ディスカバリーパーク

Snibston Discovery Park, Ashby Road, Coalville, Leicester, LE67 3LN
Tel: 01530 510851　Fax: 01530 813301

レスター州が1992年に設立した産業，科学，自然をテーマにした施設。約40万㎡の広大な炭鉱跡地に展示ホール，科学体験エリアなどのさまざまな野外施設，自然観察公園などがある。

タリーハウス博物館

Tullie House Museum and Art Gallery, Castle Street, Carlisle, Cumbria, CA3 8TP
Tel: 01228 534781　Fax: 01228 810249

イギリス北部にあるカーライル市の博物館。郷土の歴史，自然，美術などを扱う。歴史展示室にはいろいろなハンズ・オン展示を取り入れている。

テクニクエスト

Techniquest, Stuart Street, Cardiff, CF1 6BW
Tel: 01222 475 475　Fax: 01222 482 517　http://www.tquest.org.uk/

1986年にオープン。単独の科学館としてはイギリスで初めてのもの。約160種類のハンズ・オン展示のほか，"ディスカバリールーム"（Discovery Room）や科学劇場もあり，家族連れや学校団体でいつもにぎわっている。

ニューキャッスル・ディスカバリー

Newcastle Discovery Museum, Blandford Square, Newcastle upon Tyne, Tyne & Wear NE1 4JA
Tel: 0191 232 6789　Fax: 0191 230 2614

タインアンドウィア州の州都，ニューキャッスルにある博物館。イギリス北東部に関連した科学，技術，歴史を扱う。タインアンドウィア博物館群の1つで1934年に設立。

バーミンガム市博物館

Birmingham Museum & Art Gallery, Chamberlain Square, Birmingham, B3 3DH
Tel: 0121 303 2834　Fax: 0121 303 1394　http://www.birmingham.gov.uk/bmag

1885年に設立された歴史の古い総合博物館。バーミンガム市科学産業博物館内にあったハンズ・オン展示"科学に光をあてて"（Light on Science）は現在，バーミンガム市博物館内に設置されているが，2001年秋にミレニアムポイント内に"ディスカバリーセンター"（Discovery Centre）として新しくオープンする。

ビーミッシュ野外博物館

Beamish, The North of England Open Air Museum, Beamish, County Durham, DH9 0RG
Tel: 01207 231811　Fax: 01207 290933　http://www.merlins.demon.co.uk/beamish/

1970年にオープンした野外博物館。イギリス北東部の郷土史料を収蔵，展示するほか，実演やインタープリターによる解説など生きた歴史を体験できる。

ポピュラー音楽センター

National Centre for Popular Music, Paternoster Row, Sheffield, South Yorkshire, S1 2QQ
Tel: 0114 249 8885　Fax: 0114 249 8886　http://www.ncpm.co.uk/

シェフィールド市が芸術宝くじ基金の助成を受けて設立。1999年にオープンした。ロックを中心としたポピュラー音楽を映像や音響装置，インタラクティブな手法を通して楽しく体感

できる。"作曲してみよう"（Making Music）という展示室では特にインタラクティブな要素が多く取り入れられている。

マンチェスター科学産業博物館
Museum of Science & Industry in Manchester, Liverpool Road, Castlefield, Manchester, M3 4FP
Tel: 0161 832 2244　Fax: 0161 833 2184　http://www.msim.org.uk

産業革命発祥の地，マンチェスター市にある科学と産業をテーマにした博物館。世界最古の鉄道駅舎を含む5つの歴史建造物で構成されている。"エクスペリメント！"（Xperiment!）ではハンズ・オン展示を通して楽しく科学を学ぶことができる。

ミレニアムポイント
Millennium Point, Curzon Street Station, 1 Curzon Street, Digbeth, Birmingham, B4 7XG
Tel: 0800 48 2000　Fax: 0121 303 4317　http://www.millenniumpoint.org.uk/

バーミンガム市が二千年紀記念委員会の助成を受けて建設中の複合文化施設。バーミンガム市科学産業博物館の収蔵資料をベースにつくられる"ディスカバリーセンター"（Discovery Centre）はこの中に設置される。

ユーリイカ！こどものための博物館
Eureka! The Museum for Children, Discovery Road, Halifax, HX1 2NE
Tel: 01422 330069　Fax: 01422 330275　http://www.eureka.org.uk

アメリカ型のハンズ・オン展示を取り入れたこどもの博物館として1992年にオープン。子どもに対象を絞った博物館としてはイギリスで最初のもの。"わたしとからだ"（Me and My Body），"ともに生きること，はたらくこと"（Living and Working Together），"発明・創造・通信"（Invent, Create, Communicate）"もの"（Things）などの展示室がある。

ヨービック・バイキングセンター
Jorvik Viking Centre, Coppergate, York, YO1 1NT
Tel: 01904 643211　Fax: 01904 627097　http://www.jorvik-viking-centre.co.uk

カーライドに乗って10世紀のバイキングの村にタイムスリップしたり，音やにおいを再現した展示などで話題となった。古都ヨークで人気の高い観光スポットにもなっている。

■関連機関

ビビアン・ダフィールド財団
The Vivien Duffield Foundation, Unit 3 Chelsea Manor Studios, Flood Street, London, SW3 5SR
Tel: 020 7351 6061

さまざまな科学プロジェクトや施設の建設に助成を行っている。ユーリイカ！の建設にも出資し，現在ダフィールド女史はユーリイカ！の理事長職に就いている。

英国インタラクティブグループ
The British Interactive Group =BIG, Roger Coleman, Membership Secretary, c/o OrangeLeaf Ltd, 'The Inventing Shed', Unit 2A Merrow Business Centre, Merrow Lane, Guildford, Surrey GU4 7WA
Tel: 01483 459090　Fax: 01483 459191　http://www.big.uk.com/

ハンズ・オンの役割と可能性について理解を深めるために，イギリス国内においてハンズ・オン教育活動に取り組む個人，団体が情報交換を行うフォーラムとして設立。関連機関の名簿の作成やニュースレターの発行を行っている。

関連施設・機関一覧　*243*

英国学術協会
British Association for the Advancement of Science, Fortress House, 23 Savile Row, London, W1X 1AB
Tel: 0171 973 3065　Fax: 0171 973 3051　http://www.britassoc.org.uk

科学の進歩・発展を目的として1831年に創立。毎年3月に行われる科学週間や9月の科学フェスティバルなどを主催している。

王立協会
Royal Society, 6 Carlton House Terrace, London SW1Y 5AG
Tel: 0171 839 5561　Fax: 0171 930 2170　http://www.royalsoc.ac.uk

自然科学の振興を目的に1660年に設立されたイギリス最古の学術団体。研究支援や科学教育普及など，イギリス国内はもとより国際的な活動を行っている。

王立研究所
Royal Institution, 21 Albemarle Street, London, W1X 4BS
Tel: 0171 409 2992　http://www.ri.ac.uk/

科学の研究と普及を目的に1799年に創立。人気の高い有名なイベントとして，1826年から続いているクリスマスレクチャーがある。

科学普及推進委員会
The Joint Committee on the Public Understanding of Science =COPUS, c/o Royal Society, 6 Carlton House Terrace, London, SW1Y 5AG
Tel: 0171 839 5561

王立協会，王立研究所，英国学術協会の合同委員会として1986年に設立。大学，学術団体，博物館などの科学関連組織と協力して科学に対する理解の促進のためにさまざまな活動や支援を行っている。

ギャツビー財団
Gatsby Charitable Foundation, 9 Red Lion Court, London, EC4A 3EB
Tel: 0171 410 0330　Fax: 0171 583 0909　http://www.tep.org.uk

セインズベリー家の信託財団の1つ。科学・技術分野の教育に対する支援を行っている。テクニクエストの建設にも多額の資金援助をした。

サイエンスプロジェクト社
Science Projects Ltd, 20 St James Street, Hammersmith, London, W6 9RW
Tel: 0181 741 2305　Fax: 0181 741 2307　http://www.science-project.org

科学の振興を目的に設立された公益法人。科学関連のハンズ・オン展示の設計，制作，移動展示の企画を行っている。"ディスカバリードーム"（Discovery Domes）は同社が企画制作した移動展示の1つ。

ナフィールド財団
Nuffield Foundation, 28 Bedford Square, London, WC1B 3EG
Tel: 0171 631 0566　Fax: 0171 323 4877　http://www.nuffield.org

1943年の創設以来，教育と社会福祉の発展のためにさまざまな斬新的な事業に対する支援や研究を行っている。ブリストル市の旧エクスプロラトリーや移動展示"ディスカバリードーム"にも資金援助を行っている。ECSITE（後述）の設立にも貢献し，当初本部は同財団内に置かれていた。

＜ベルギー＞

欧州科学系展示施設協力機関
The European Collaborative for Science, Industry and Technology Exhibitions (ECSITE), Executive Office, Bd du Triomphe 69, B-1160 Brussels, Belgium

科学・技術に対する理解の促進と科学系の展示施設間の協力を推進するために1988年，ECとイギリスのナフィールド財団の支援を受けて設立された。ヨーロッパ7カ国の代表と世界各国の会員からなる。

＜ドイツ＞

ドイツ博物館
Deutsches Museum, Museumsinsel 1, D-80538 München, GERMANY
Tel: 089 2179 1　http://www.deutsches-museum.de/e_index.htm

1925年にオープンしたドイツ博物館は科学・技術をテーマにした世界で最も古い博物館の1つに数えられる。大型実験展示や炭鉱の再現，プラネタリウムなど世界中の科学系博物館に影響を与えた。

＜フランス＞

発見博物館
Palais de la Découverte, Av. Franklin-D.-Roosvelt, 75008 Paris
Tel: 01 40 74 80 00　http://www.palais-decouverte.fr

セーヌ川沿いの古い建造物を利用した科学館。天文学，化学，数学，物理学，地質学，生命科学などをテーマにした展示がある。ここでは1日に数十本もの講義や実演（分野は上記の全てにわたる）が行われており，講義や実演用のスペースが展示室内のさまざまな場所に広くとられている。

ラヴィレット科学産業都市
Cité des Sciences et de l'Industrie, 30 avenue Corentin-Cariou, 75930 Paris cedex 19
Tel: 01 40 05 70 00　http://www.cite-sciences.fr

1986年にフランスの国家プロジェクトとして建設された世界最大規模の科学施設。開館当初ラヴィレット内にあった子ども向けの体験型施設インベントリアム（Inventorium）は，現在は拡張されて3～12歳の子どもを対象にした"こどもの国"（la Cité des Enfants）という名前の施設になっている。

＜アメリカ＞

■科学館・こどもの博物館

インディアナポリスこどもの博物館
The Children's Museum of Indianapolis, 3000 N. Meridian Street, Indianapolis, IN 46208
Tel: 317 334 3322　Fax: 317 921 4019　http://www.childrensmuseum.org

1925年にオープンした世界で4番目に古いこどもの博物館。約14万点のコレクションを有し，資料を基盤に置いたインタラクティブな展示や学習プログラムを実施。博物館実習プログラムなど，ティーンエイジャーが主体的に参加するプログラムも充実している。

エクスプロラトリアム
The Exploratorium, 3601 Lyon Street, San Francisco, CA 94123

関連施設・機関一覧　　245

　　Tel: 415 563 7337　　http://www.exploratorium.edu

物理学者で教育学者であるオッペンハイマーによって1969年に設立。ハンズ・オン方式の科学館の先駆的存在として世界中の科学館に影響を与えた。館内に工房を備え，展示はすべて自主制作されている。

カリフォルニア科学館
　　California Science Center, 700 State Drive, Exposition Park, Los Angeles, CA 90037
　　Tel: 323 724 3623　　http://www.casciencectr.org

博物館や競技場などが多く建ち並ぶエクスポジション・パーク内に位置する。宇宙や惑星，生命や地球などのテーマが，ハンズ・オン方式で展示されている。移動展示の開発も積極的に手がけている。

クリーブランドのこどもの博物館
　　Rainbow Children's Museum and TRW Early Learning Center, 10730 Euclid Avenue, Cleveland, OH 44106
　　Tel: 216 791 7114　　http://www.museum4kids.com/

1986年に開館。水の展示や，レイスウェイ，恐竜，砂などをテーマにした，ハンズ・オン展示を行っている。

シカゴ科学産業博物館
　　Museum of Science and Industry, Chicago 57th Street and Lake Shore Drive, Chicago, IL 60637
　　Tel: 773 684 1414　　http://www.msichicago.org

1933年にオープンした科学と産業を扱う博物館。2000種類以上のインタラクティブ展示をもつ大規模な博物館である。約5万点の資料を有し，ボーイング727など大型資料も多い。

シカゴこどもの博物館
　　Chicago Children's Museum, 700 East Grand Avenue at Navy Pier, Chicago, IL 60611
　　Tel: 312 527 1000　　http://www.chichildrensmuseum.org

公立小学校の補助金カットを受け，全米青年連盟が中心となってこどもの博物館建設運動が起こり，1982年に市立図書館の中に開館。現在はネイビーピアというレジャー施設の中に設置されている。資料を全くもたないハンズ・オン展示施設。

デンバーこどもの博物館
　　The Children's Museum of Denver, 2121 Children's Museum Drive, Denver, CO 80211
　　Tel: 303 433 7444　　http://www.cmdenver.org

ハンズ・オン方式の博物館の設置を願う市民と教師によって1975年にオープン。資料をもたず，遊びや体験を通して学ぶ展示やさまざまな教育プログラムやアウトリーチ活動を行う。

ニューヨーク・ホールオブサイエンス
　　New York Hall of Science, 47-01 111th Street, Flushing Meadows, Corona Park, NY 11368
　　Tel: 718 699 0005　　Fax: 718 699 1341　　http://www.nyhallsci.org

アフリカ系アメリカ人の子どもたちの数学や科学に対する苦手意識を克服することを目的に掲げている。理科教育キャリアラダーなど，高校生が大学生と一緒に実験のアシスタントをするプログラムや，宿泊会などの家族向けのイベントも行っている。

フランクリンインスティテュート
　　The Franklin Institute Science Museum, 222 North 20th Street, Philadelphia, PA 19103
　　Tel: 215 448 1200　　http://sln.fi.edu/

本体の研究所は，1824年にベンジャミン・フランクリンとその発見を讃えるために設立され

た。博物館部分は1934年に，科学の教育と普及を目的に開館。フランクリンに関する科学知識はもちろん，天文学や生命科学（心臓や脳），数学や電気などのほか，サイバーゾーンというコンピューターの展示もあり，学校との連携や独自の教育プログラムも盛んに行われている。

プリーズタッチ博物館
Please Touch Museum, 210 North 21st Street, Philadelphia, PA 19103
Tel: 215 963 0667　Fax: 215 963 0424　http://www.pleasetouchmuseum.org

子どものための文化施設の設立を願う教育者，アーティスト，親たちによって1976年につくられたこどもの博物館。7歳以下の幼児を対象に，ハンズ・オン展示や教育プログラムを実施している。"旅行かばん"（Traveling Trunks）という移動展示など，アウトリーチ活動も積極的に行っている。

ブルックリンこどもの博物館
Brooklyn Children's Museum, 145 Brooklyn Avenue, Brooklyn, NY 11213
Tel: 718 735 4400　http://www.bchildmus.org

1899年にオープンした世界で最も古いこどもの博物館。2万7000点のコレクションとハンズ・オンの手法を使った展示や学習プログラムを実施している。"ものの不思議"（The Mystery of Things）などの展示がある。アフリカ系やヒスパニック系のアメリカ人が多く居住する地域性を反映した，さまざまな多文化プログラムにも取り組んでいる。

ボストンこどもの博物館
The Children's Museum, 300 Congress Street, Boston, MA 02210
Tel: 617 426 8855　http://www.bostonkids.org

大学教授らによって1913年に設立されたアメリカで2番目に古いこどもの博物館。「こどもは体験を通して最もよく学ぶ」という考えに基づき，当時のスポック館長がハンズ・オン展示を最初に実施した館で，その展示やプログラムは各地のこどもの博物館に大きな影響を与えた。

ボストン科学博物館
Museum of Science, Science Park, Boston, MA 02114
Tel: 617 723 2500　http://www.mos.org

1830年に設立されたボストン博物学学会が母体となり，ニューイングランド自然史博物館を経た後，ボストン科学博物館としてオープン。科学・技術への関心と理解を深めることを使命に掲げる。400種類を超えるインタラクティブ展示がある。

マンハッタンこどもの博物館
Children's Museum of Manhattan, The Tisch Building, 212 W. 83rd St. New York, NY 10024
Tel: 212 721 1234　http://www.cmom.org

1973年に子どもと家族の学習を促進する目的で設立された。都会の子どものための施設として，十代の母親へのサポートや低所得者層の子ども達へのインターンプログラムなどを行っているほか，自然史博物館やブルックリン美術館などと共にニューヨーク市のミュージアムスクールの事業にも参加している。

関連施設・機関一覧　*247*

■関連機関

科学館技術館協会
Association of Science-Technology Centers Incorporated =ASTC, 1025 Vermont Avenue NW, Suite 500, Washington, DC 20005
Tel: 202 783 7200　Fax: 202 783 7207　http://www.astc.org/

科学・技術への理解の促進と，科学施設を支援することを目的に1973年に設立。科学館，動物園，水族館，プラネタリウム，こどもの博物館など，アメリカを中心とする世界の500施設が会員となっている。

青少年博物館協会
Association of Youth Museums =AYM, 1300 L St., N.W., Suite 975, Washington, DC 20005
Tel: 202 898 1080　Fax: 202 898 1086　http://www.aym.org

こどもの博物館や青少年のためのプログラムやインタラクティブな展示を行っている博物館の情報交換の場，協力の場として1962年に設立された国際組織。年次大会の実施，会員の名簿や機関誌の発行などを行っている。

米国博物館協会
American Association of Museums =AAM, 1575 Eye Street NW, Suite 400, Washington, DC 20005
Tel: 202 289 1818　Fax: 202 289 6578　http://www.aam-us.org

博物館の資質向上をサポートする機関で1906年創立。博物館関係者のための研修プログラム，お互いの情報交換，博物館の基準認定事業などを行っている。全世界に1万6000人を超える会員がいる。

＜カナダ＞

オンタリオ科学館
Ontario Science Centre, 770 Don Mills Road, North York, Ontario, M3C 1T3
Tel: 416 696 3127　http://www.osc.on.ca

エクスプロラトリアム開館の年に，オンタリオ州からの助成を受けて開館した草創期の科学館のひとつ。13の展示室に800種類以上の展示装置をもつ大型科学館である。

ロイヤルオンタリオ博物館
Royal Ontario Museum, 110 Queen's Park, Toronto, Ontario, M5S 2C6
Tel: 416 586 5549　http://www.rom.on.ca

1977年に，世界に先駆けてディスカバリールームを設置し，利用者が直接資料を手に取って学ぶ専用の展示室をつくった。この展示室は，後に利用者調査をもとに改装され，"ディスカバリーギャラリー"（Discovery Gallery）として再オープンしている。

＜ベネズエラ＞

ロスニーニョス博物館
Museo de los Niños, Parque Central, Nivel Bolivar, Caracas, 1011-1, Venezuela, Apartado 14029, Candelaria.
Tel: 58 2 573 4112
http://www.caveguias.com.ve/informativas/museos_nacionales/museo_ninos/HomeMuseoNinos.html

名称は，スペイン語で「こどもの博物館」の意。首都カラカスのセントラルパークにあるカラフルな外観のこどもの博物館。1983年に開館。物理や生物，環境などの展示コーナーをもつ。ベネズエラの自然や歴史を紹介するマルチメディア展示も行っている。

訳者あとがき

　本書は，Tim Caulton, *Hands-on exhibitions: managing interactive museums and science centres*, London: Routledge, 1998 の翻訳です。

　ハンズ・オンの考え方にたつ博物館展示は，アメリカのこどもの博物館で生まれ，一方ではすぐれた活動を展開する科学館の展示手法としてアメリカやヨーロッパで普及してきました。特にこどもの博物館ではほとんど不可欠の展示スタイルとして定着しており，著者ティム・コールトンはイギリスで最初のハンズ・オン展示によるこどもの博物館を成功に導いた人物として，先駆的な業績をあげています。

　また，欧米では一般の博物館や科学館などその他の展示施設でも，よく工夫されたハンズ・オン展示をふつうに見かけるようになりました。そうした世界的な流れを受けて，1999年度に日本の文部省でも「親しむ博物館づくり事業」を展開したことは知られているとおりです。文部省はこの事業で初めて"ハンズ・オン"ということばを使いました。学校が完全週5日制になる2002年までに，子どもたちの学びの場として博物館でハンズ・オン的な活動を推進したいと考えたのです。

　ところが，ハンズ・オン展示とは何か，という問いに的確に応えてくれる参考書はこれまでありませんでした。ハンズ・オンの本場ともいえるアメリカにおいても，博物館学の専門書や事例集はあっても，ハンズ・オンは一種の常識のように扱われているせいか，意外にも平易にまとめられた著作は見あたりません。

　そこで1998年に本書がようやく登場しました。しかも，わたしたちが待ち望んでいた仕事はアメリカ人ではなくイギリス人によるものだったのです。そして，偶然にも著者は，わたしがこどもの博物館の魅力にひきこまれた頃に，かの地で出会ったあのティム・コールトンだったのです。著者その人の案内でユーリイカ！こどものための博物館でそのハンズ・オンの魅力にもふれたわた

しが，その素晴らしい仕事をこうして日本の読者に紹介することになるなんて，当時は思いもよらないことでした。

　この本の翻訳には二重の意義があります。1つは，日本に初めて紹介されるハンズ・オン展示についての入門書だということです。著者が博物館の現場において培った豊かな経験を背景として実践的な内容を展開しているのが特徴ですが，単純にハンズ・オンの教育論だけを主張したり集客施設の経営論に終始するものでもありません。まず，ハンズ・オン展示とは何かを歴史的に検証し，楽しみながら学ぶハンズ・オンの魅力について教育的立場から迫ります。利用者が博物館で接する展示法の実際について展示開発の各段階を細かく紹介し，いかに展示評価が大切かを強調しています。経営的視点からは具体的な数字を分析し財政上の問題点を明らかにしています。マーケティング戦略を中心とした経営の実態を観察して，これからの博物館のとるべき営業手法を説くあたりは著者ならではのものです。さらに現場運営や人材管理，教育プログラムと，最後まで目配りを怠りません。こうした調和のとれた観点を終始支えているのは，おそらくクライアントセンタード，つまり資料よりも利用者を中心にした考え方であるといえるでしょう。著者がハンズ・オンに行き着くまでの過程は，利用者の博物館体験をいかにして単に与えられたものから発見に満ちた獲得に変えられるかについて日々腐心したことに始まっています。もちろん他館での先進的な取り組みから刺激を受けたでしょうが，現場で利用者に学ぼうとする出発点こそ，ハンズ・オン展示を実現させたに違いありません。

　2つめは，この本がアメリカ人によって書かれたのではないということです。ハンズ・オンがまるで常識のようになったアメリカでは，この本のようにハンズ・オン全般にわたる著作が企画されにくいのかもしれません。著者は独自に現場の経験からハンズ・オンに到達したのですが，アメリカのこどもの博物館にも多くを学んでいます。すぐれた事例からハンズ・オンを学ぼうとするわたしたちにとって，大いに興味深いことではないでしょうか。ただ導入する，真似をするというのでなく，自分の国に合うスタイルを確立するために，いかにじょうずに学ぶか，という点において貴重なお手本を示してくれたといえるで

しょう。近い将来わたしたちも，ハンズ・オン展示の開発プロセスを自分たちの手でつくりあげたいものです。

　日本におけるハンズ・オンの本格的な取り組みは始まったばかりだといえます。ハンズ・オンの真の意味をさらに学ぶために，本書が少なからず役立つことを願っています。

　この日本語版では，読者の理解を助けるために写真を掲載しましたが，そのうちの何枚かは現在イギリス留学中の稲庭彩和子さんが撮影してくださったものです。ありがとうございました。また，最新の情報をアメリカから提供してくれた太田歩さんにも感謝します。

　尾山純一さんがお力を貸してくださらなかったら，この翻訳はこうして世に送り出されることはなかったと思います。訳者はみな感謝の気持ちでいっぱいです。

　最後に，この本の翻訳出版の機会を与えてくださった東海大学出版会に心から感謝申し上げたいと思います。仕事の遅いわたしたちをつねに優しく見守ってくださった三浦義博さん，辛抱強く励ましてくださった辻浩子さんのおふたりには，意義のある仕事をやりとげることの素晴らしさを教えていただきました。

染川香澄

索引

【ア行】

アウトリーチ活動　14, 143, 199-218
アンダーソン Anderson, D.　62, 214, 217, 231
『イギリスの観光』　19, 107, 125, 135
イングリッシュパートナーシップス　113
インタラクティブ　4-6
インタラクティブ科学技術プロジェクト　16, 110
インディアナポリスこどもの博物館　9, 96, 183, 193
インベントリアム　8, 80, 81, 154, 178, 183, 185
ウェールズ産業海事博物館　12
ウェットン Wetton, N.　80, 81
営業指標　107
英国インタラクティブグループ(BIG)　19, 188
英国学術協会　110, 114
エクスプロラトリアム　7, 69-70, 178, 179-180, 187, 191, 192, 208
エクスプロラトリー　8, 15, 16, 24-25, 98-99, 103-118, 178, 188, 207-208
エバリュエーター　70
エルスカー・ヘリテイジセンター　71, 110, 112, 115
"オールハンズ"　59, 111
欧州科学系展示施設協力機関(ECSITE)　15, 110
欧州共同体(EC)　15, 191
王立協会　16, 110, 114
オッペンハイマー Oppenheimer, F.　7, 34, 69, 70, 179
オリエンテーション　41, 45, 46, 52, 53, 54, 56
"オンタリオ・サイエンスサーカス"　7
オンタリオ科学館　7, 178

【カ行】

カーディフ港湾開発公社　12, 14
ガードナー Gardner, H.　35, 36, 61
会計報告　98
開発基金　110
科学館技術館協(ASTC)　9, 15, 95, 106, 109, 177-178, 182, 190, 201-203, 204, 215, 226, 229
"科学に光をあてて"　113, 178, 188
科学普及推進委員会(COPUS)　16, 110, 208
学習
　インフォーマルな——　34, 199, 201, 214, 217
　——スタイル　35-36
　——の個人的側面　33-39
　——の社会的側面　39-43
　——の物的側面　44-56
家族連れの行動　37-43
カンパニーズハウス　98
企画段階評価　77
キッズクルー　204
基本市場　133-134
ギャツビー財団　12, 111
教育市場　133, 134-135, 143, 163
クイン Quin, M.　16
苦情の対応　168-169
『クックブック』　7, 69
「くらしと健康」　80, 81

クリーソープス・ディスカバリーセンター　41, 79
クリーブランドのこどもの博物館　139
グリーンズミル科学館　22
クロア財団　111
芸術宝くじ基金　114
研修　175-193
ゴールドスミス Goldsmith, R.　111
構成主義　60-62
考古学リソースセンター　24, 189
国営宝くじ　17, 97, 113, 116, 226
国民遺産省　129
国立海事博物館　59, 111
国立科学博物館（ロンドン）　6, 8, 19, 37, 58, 71, 88-89, 90, 111, 131, 141, 154, 176, 178, 186, 191, 208
国立自然史博物館　111, 141, 163, 178
国立鉄道博物館　164
故障（展示装置の）　164-168
こどもの博物館（定義）　9-11
コミュニケーション戦略　45, 52, 53-56, 124
『コモンウェルス』　62, 68, 214, 217, 231
雇用機会均等化　181, 191, 192
コルチェスターの博物館群　188

【サ行】

サイエンスプロジェクト社　8, 71, 210
サイエンスワールド　24, 113
シード基金　110
シェフィールド産業博物館　110
シカゴこどもの博物館　96
時間制限　153-155
社会経済的階層区分　129
収容力　151-158
職務明細書　183, 190
初等科学・技術トレーラー　211-213
人口統計的傾向　126-128
人材管理　175-193
スティーブンソン Stephenson, J.　37-38, 39
スニブストン・ディスカバリーパーク　112
スミソニアン協会　113
セインズベリー財団　8, 16, 109
制作途中評価　78
青少年による評議会　206
青少年博物館協会（AYM）　10
総括評価　78
組織構造　177-178
損益評価指標　104

【タ行】

ダイアキング Dierking, L　42, 177
ダイヤモンド　41
ダフィールド Duffield, V.　111
タリーハウス博物館　143
昼食時間　163-164
デービズ Davies, S.　125, 129
定員の設定　152
"ディスカバリーギャラリー"　57
"ディスカバリードーム"　8, 16, 71, 110
ディスカバリールーム　8, 14, 57, 185, 209
ディスカバリーボックス　57, 177
ディズニー　13, 227
テクニクエスト　8, 11-15, 24, 71, 98, 101-103, 104-109, 112, 130, 137, 139, 141, 155, 164, 165, 178, 188, 209, 210
展示開発　67-90
展示の物的側面（デザイン）　44-62, 67-90
展示評価　75-90
デンバーこどもの博物館　139
トーマス Thomas, G.　80, 177
ドイツ博物館（ミュンヘン）　6, 7
"ともに生きること、はたらくこと"　55-56, 74, 80, 82
ドロー・アンド・ライト法　81-83

【ナ行】

ナフィールド財団　8, 15, 16, 109, 110
南東地区博物館サービス　189
二次市場　135
二千年紀記念委員会　24, 97, 113, 233
ニューヨーク・ホールオブサイエンス
　181-182, 191, 205

【ハ行】

バーミンガム市博物館　113, 178, 188
パートナーシップ助成　113
『博物館体験』　32, 177
パスウェイ　207
発見博物館（パリ）　6
"発明と創造"（"発明・創造・通信"）
　55, 56, 75, 84
"パワーハウス"　71, 110, 115
ハンズ・オン展示（定義）　4-6
ハンプシャー州博物館　189
ピアジェ Piaget, J.　33, 34, 62
ビートルストーン Beetlestone, J.　12, 69
ビーミッシュ野外博物館　141
ヴィゴツキー Vygotsky, L.　33, 39
ピジー Pizzy.S　8, 16
ビビアン・ダフィールド財団　111
フィーハー Feher, E.　38
フォーカスグループ　77
フォーク Falk, J.　41, 42, 177
"フライトラボ"　37, 97
フランクリンインスティテュート　6, 40,
　228
ブリストル2000　24, 113
プリーズタッチ博物館　96, 140, 183, 205
ブルックリンこどもの博物館　9, 34, 58,
　183
フロア解説スタッフ　178-193
文化遺産宝くじ基金　114, 232
米国博物館協会（AAM）　10-11
貿易産業省　8, 16, 80, 110

ボーラン Borun, M.　40
募集（採用）　185, 191-193
ボストンこどもの博物館　9, 34, 178, 180
　-181, 192, 204, 206
ボストン科学博物館　182
ポピュラー音楽センター　78, 114, 116
ボランティア　175-193

【マ行】

マーケティングミックス　124, 138-144
マイクラリアム　23
マインズ・オン　5
マクメイナス McManus, P.　40, 42,
　79
待ち行列　155-158
マンチェスター科学産業博物館　20, 134
マンハッタンこどもの博物館　96, 160,
　183, 205
ミュージアムチーム　204, 206
ミレニアムポイント　113
「燃え尽き現象」　175, 179, 186, 187, 189,
　192
"もの"　58, 88, 176
"ものの不思議"　58

【ヤ行】

ユーリイカ！こどものための博物館　17,
　22, 48, 53-56, 73-75, 77, 79-87, 90, 98, 99
　-101, 104-109, 110, 111, 115, 116, 132-140,
　141-142, 152-157, 159-163, 165, 167, 169,
　178, 184-186, 187-188, 207
ヨービック・バイキングセンター　154
ヨーロッパ地域開発基金　14, 113
余暇時間　128-131
予約システム　158-163

【ラ行】

"ライトワークス"　16, 110
ライフサイクル　21-24, 59, 101, 103, 117,
　141, 207

"ラウンチパッド"　　8, 20, 37-38, 97, 112, 154, 186
理科教育キャリアラダー　　181, 205
リバーヒューム信託　　8, 112
料金設定　　138-140
利用者調査　　75
利用者の属性調査　　76
旅行者市場　　135-136
ロイヤルオンタリオ博物館　　57

【ワ行】

"わたしとからだ"　　54-55, 74, 80-87, 160

著者紹介

Tim Caulton（ティム・コールトン）
イギリス・シェフィールド市産業博物館を経て，1990年にハリファクス市のユーリイカ！こどものための博物館の教育普及部長。93年からはハンズ・オン運動などの実践と研究に従事。シェフィールド大学講師を勤めたあと，現在は2001年開館予定のロザラム市のインタラクティブ系施設マグナの開発部長。

訳者紹介

染川　香澄（そめかわ かすみ）
1958年生まれ　バンクストリート教育大学大学院博物館教育プログラム履修
ハンズ・オン・プランニング代表。各地の博物館の基本構想，展示企画，職員養成などに関わる。
著書：『こどものための博物館―世界の実例を見る』（岩波書店），『ハンズ・オンは楽しい―見て，さわって，遊べるこどもの博物館』（共著・工作舎），「新版博物館学講座」『第9巻博物館展示法』『第12巻博物館経営論』（共著・雄山閣出版），『イギリスを旅する35章』（共著・明石書店）他

芦谷　美奈子（あしや みなこ）
1965年生まれ　千葉大学理学部生物学科卒業
同大学院理学研究科修士課程修了後，1991年より現所属の準備室に勤務。博物館の展示や研究に取り組む。
滋賀県立琵琶湖博物館　学芸員
同館ディスカバリー・ルームには，企画段階から現在の運営まで深く関わる。

井島　真知（いしま まち）
1968年生まれ　早稲田大学第一文学部（教育学専修）卒業
バンクストリート教育大学大学院博物館教育プログラム修了
フリーランスで博物館の調査研究，展示やプログラムの企画に携わる。玉川大学非常勤講師。

竹内　有理（たけうち ゆり）
1969年生まれ　法政大学文学部史学科卒業
1993年英国レスター大学大学院博物館研究課程修士取得
国立および民間の研究機関で非常勤研究員として国内外の博物館に関する調査研究，設計などを手がける。
著書：『ミュージアム・マネージメント』（共著・東京堂出版），『私も美術館でボランティア』（共著・淡交社）

徳永　喜昭（とくなが よしあき）
1944年生まれ　早稲田大学第一文学部（心理学専修）卒業
児童書出版社勤務を経て，現在フリーランスの編集者・翻訳者
訳書：『あかがすき』『おにいちゃんかな，あかちゃんかな』（P-PRESS）
著書：『五郎8データベース構築ガイド』（共著・ジャストシステム）

ハンズ・オンとこれからの博物館
インタラクティブ系博物館・科学館に学ぶ理念と経営

2000年3月20日　第1版第1刷発行

訳　　者	染川香澄・芦谷美奈子・井島真知
	竹内有理・徳永喜昭
発 行 者	古菅　昇
発 行 所	東海大学出版会
	〒151-0063 東京都渋谷区富ヶ谷2-28-4
	TEL 03-5478-0891　振替 00100-5-46614
	URL　http://www.press.tokai.ac.jp/
組 版 所	株式会社武井制作室
印 刷 所	株式会社平河工業社
製 本 所	株式会社石津製本所

ⒸK.Somekawa, M.Ashiya, M.Ishima, Y.Takeuchi, Y.Tokunaga, 2000

ISBN4-486-01499-5

Ⓡ〈日本複写権センター委託出版物〉
本書の全部または一部を無断で複写複製（コピー）することは，著作権法上の例外を除き，禁じられています．本書から複写複製する場合は，日本複写権センターへご連絡の上，許諾を得てください．
日本複写権センター（TEL 03-3401-2382）